'12/11

JACK FINNEY

THE WOODROW WILSON DIME

MARION'S WALL

THE NIGHT PEOPLE

A Fireside Book
PUBLISHED BY SIMON & SCHUSTER, INC.
NEW YORK

THREE
BY
FINNEY

A Fireside Book
Published by Simon & Schuster, Inc.
Simon & Schuster Building
Rockefeller Center
1230 Avenue of the Americas
New York, New York 10020

FIRESIDE and colophon are registered trademarks of Simon & Schuster, Inc.

Designed by Bonni Leon

Manufactured in the United States of America

Library of Congress Cataloging-in-Publication Data
Finney, Jack.
   Three by Finney.
   "A Fireside book."
   Contents: The Woodrow Wilson dime—Marion's wall—The night people.
   I. Title.
PS3556.I52A6   1987   813'.54   86-31948
ISBN: 0-671-64048-8 Pbk.

The Woodrow Wilson Dime © 1968 by Jack Finney was originally published by Simon & Schuster, Inc. The idea for this story evolved from my short story "The Coin Collector," which was published by the *Saturday Evening Post* in 1960 under the title "The Other Wife," copyright © 1960 by the Curtis Publishing Company.

Marion's Wall © 1973 by Jack Finney was originally published by Simon & Schuster, Inc.

The Night People © 1977 by Jack Finney was originally published by Doubleday & Co., Inc. Grateful acknowledgment is made for the use of random lines of lyrics from the following copyrighted material: Maraville Music Corporation: "All the Way," words and music by Sammy Cahn and Jimmy Van Heusen. Copyright © 1957 by the Maraville Music Corporation. Reprinted by permission of Maraville Music Corporation.

CONTENTS

THE
WOODROW
WILSON
DIME

CHAPTER ONE

At 6:30 A.M. of a dishwater-gray, electric-lighted dawn, the echo of the alarm clock still in my ears, I felt my way into the bathroom with my eyes shut, thus gaining an extra six seconds' sleep. At the medicine-cabinet mirror, eyes still closed, I stood, hoping as always that when I opened them something would have happened overnight, and I'd see a change. But nothing had changed, not for the better anyway.

There was the same old unshaven, dumb-looking, twenty-nine-year-old face; the same drab, straight, brownish-red hair sticking out in all directions like a pile of rusty nails; the same bloodshot, basset hound eyes. "Mirror, mirror, on the wall," I said, "who's the biggest slob of all?"

"No change today," said the familiar, deep voice. "Still a three-way tie between an alcoholic Australian sheepherder, a Beirutian loan shark, and you. If anything, you've got the edge." A huge Hand, protruding from the wide gold-embroidered sleeve of a long white robe, descended from the ceiling and clapped me across the forehead with an enormous rubber stamp, leaving the word FAILURE in black capital letters stretching from temple to temple.

I washed it off in the lukewarm, permanently dripping bathtub shower, but back in the bedroom, dressing, I knew it was still branded deep in my soul. I knew it from the inept way I then treated Hetty; later I figured out that it was four years, three months, eleven days, and thirteen hours after we'd been married.

Still blear-eyed and stupefied, I stood buttoning my shirt, feeling guilty because I was able to wish, as I did every morning now, that we each had our own bedroom. Small as the room was, we didn't quite bump into each other. Our paths were long since taped out, crossing and recrossing but rarely colliding. We missed only fractionally though, shoulders brushing, hands reaching just past noses and eyes; and since my wattage is low first thing in the morning, the bulb of life flickering orangely, the idea of dressing alone was as irresistibly attractive as the opposite had once been, four years, three months, eleven days, and thirteen hours before.

Today I couldn't find my belt; it wasn't in the pants I'd worn yesterday, and I thought maybe I'd tossed it onto the room's one chair last night. Hetty was sitting there, smoothing a stocking up her leg, and I walked over, lifted the hem of her slip, and looked carefully at the chair, but no belt, and I stepped to the closet and found it on the floor.

Hetty stood up as I threaded my belt through the pants loops, and she walked to the dresser mirror. There's only one dresser, which we shared about 60-40, and you know who had the 40. Hetty stood there, her hands working on her back hair, elbows winged out, and I needed my wallet, keys, change, and stuff from the dresser top. I reached past her, under one upraised arm, my hand brushing her chest, got my wallet, stowed it in my hip pocket, started to reach for my keys and change, and saw Hetty's eyes in the mirror staring at me.

There was something about her expression I couldn't quite figure out that warned me of something I wasn't sure of, and I warily postponed keys and change. I walked—one step—to the closet, took a tie, stepped back to the dresser, and with knees bent, my neck barely visible in the lower left corner of the mirror so I wouldn't interfere with Hetty's view, I began tossing the long end of my tie around the short end. I kept an eye on Hetty in the mirror, and watched her place a hand on one hip. When she saw I'd noticed, she began walking back and forth in tiny mincing steps, her shoulders swaying exaggeratedly the way models walk in the movies. I stared for a moment, hands on my tie, then turned around, and Hetty clasped her hands on the back of her neck, thrust her hips toward me, did a couple of vicious bumps and grinds, and burst into tears.

My lower jaw dropped like a gallows trapdoor, I stepped toward Hetty, and she ran—half a step—and fell face down on the bed, sobbing, and I thought momentarily of all the many little-appreciated values of being dead. Squatting uncomfortably beside the bed, I began poking, stroking, patting, prodding, murmuring, soothing, and pretty soon Hetty lifted her head, saying, "So you finally saw me? I was afraid I might have to strip and paint myself blue!"

"What's the matter, honey?"

"Matter!? Ben, you're how old, twenty-nine? Or ninety-nine? Or am I so damned homely and repulsive? My god, you're alone in a bedroom with a young, nubile, half-dressed girl—"

"But I have to get to work."

"—and you can actually pick up the hem of her slip, and not even *see* her! You can brush against her in about as *intimate* a way possible, without a flicker of expression, just as though I were a *door* or something—"

"Honey—"

"Look, Ben," she said in a dry, calm, I'm-through-with-tears voice, "I don't want to sound like a comic-strip bride. But it's obviously true, something, quite simply, to be faced and accepted, that you just don't love me any more." And oh boy, there at 6:43 A.M. she began to bawl again.

I killed her. Later, pacing the Death Cell, my pants legs slit, I regretted it, but now I took her soft white throat tenderly in my hands . . . What I actually did was just what you do: I stroked her hair, occasionally patting her head and scratching behind her ears and assuring her that yes, I did too love her, a statement—have you noticed?—almost impossible to pronounce out loud.

But I did it; my tongue shoved the words out over the edge of my teeth so that they sounded aloud in the room, and after a while Hetty lifted her head and asked me to tell her *truthfully, honestly*, whether I really meant it, and I smiled tenderly and sneaked a look at my watch and knew that while I'd have to skip the book review and James Reston at breakfast, I was still going to have time for the bridge column.

We smiled at each other a lot during breakfast, teeth shining, eagerly passing things. I finished my coffee, put down the paper and said gaily, "Well, off to Saf-T Products, I guess!"

She smiled brilliantly and said, "Darling, *why* must you *always* say *Saff*-T? It's Safe-T!"

Lovingly I said, "No, dear. The *T* is pronounced *tee*, I'll grant you. But S-a-f must be pronounced as spelled: *saf*. However much my idiot boss may want it to, S-a-f cannot possibly oblige him by spelling *safe*. It spells *saf*, damn it!" Hetty smiled so widely her eyes were narrowed to slits, and I continued reasonably, "It's like *Holsum*, as I've often pointed out; you simply cannot pronounce it *wholesome*. H-o-l must rhyme with s-o-l, it's *Hol*sum bread, and if you want it pronounced *whole*sum, you've got to *spell* it that way! And take TraveLodges; as long as there is still an English language they are *not* Travel Lodges; they're *Trave* Lodges! A Ranchotel is not a Ranch Hotel, it's a Ran-*chotel*! As for Do-nut Shoppes, you canNOT buy *dough*nuts in them! The only things they can possibly sell—"

"What in the hell does it *matter*!"

"What does anything matter, for that matter! It matters as much—"

She said, "Dear, you'll be late. Better hurry," and we smiled enchantingly, quick-kissed goodbye, and I rode downstairs in the automatic elevator, wondering as always if this would finally be the time when it would stick between floors. A woman was in it, about sixty, face coated with white powder, smelling like the main floor of a large department store. I pointed to the emergency phone and said, "You suppose this is actually connected to anything?" and she glanced at the phone, looked startled, glared at me, then looked away quickly, and got off fast when we hit the street floor.

Our apartment was on Twenty-eighth Street and I worked in the Chrysler Building, so I generally walked to work. Today, as on more than one morning lately walking along the street, I tried to explain things to Hetty. I said "Look, honey," and she appeared beside me, transparent and still wearing the pink terry-cloth robe with the rip in the sleeve that she'd worn at breakfast, "it isn't that I don't *love* you. Of *course* I do! It's just that people get used to anything—to being rich, blind, in jail, or President. So it's only natural—inevitable—that eventually a man gets used to his *wife*." I chuckled affectionately, nudging her in the ribs. "So if sometimes I seem to take you just a little for granted, you can understand *that*, can't you!"

She didn't seem to, refusing to answer or look at me, staring sullenly across the street, so I switched to stern reality. "Het, you've got to realize that for a man there are basic contradictions in marriage. He has been ingeniously designed to father hundreds of children by a spectacular variety of females"—I gestured appreciatively at some of them walking along to work. "While you, however lovely, are *only one woman*. You are a five-foot-two, nicely made, though somewhat overweight," I added maliciously, "blonde. With a pretty and reasonably intelligent face. None of this is to be deprecated. Not even the extra poundage. But it *also* means—and why can't women ever understand this?—that you are *not* a tall, curvy-hipped, gracefully undulating redhead." I pointed to a tall, curvy-hipped, gracefully undulating redhead in front of us. "It means, unfortunately for both of us, that you can never possibly be a slim willowy brunette," I said, nodding at a slim willowy brunette just getting off a bus. "Or even a buxom little brown-head, a China doll, a Japanese—" I sensed that I was getting carried away and calmed down.

"So if at times, dear," I resumed, but Hetty wasn't even trying to understand; she glanced at me with veiled, questioning, inscrutable eyes, and faded away.

I appealed to the men around us, speeding past in cabs, pouring up out of subway exits, sitting at crumby little lunch counters fortifying themselves with one more cup of vile coffee for the long sick day ahead. "The honeymoon fades, and vision returns!" I yelled. "That's easy to understand, isn't it!" And all up and down the street as far as you could see they nodded in sad agreement.

Encouraged, I appealed to the young women on the sidewalk around me; waiting at the lights; sitting at the coffee counters. "Surely you can all see that, too!" I called to them, smiling encouragingly. "That after a time—" But they couldn't. On both sides of the street and for blocks ahead and behind, they leaned away from me, repulsed, staring down their shoulders at me in disgust and apprehension, and I knew they saw the truth: I was no good; I was rotten; I didn't deserve even the least among them, let alone Hetty.

At Forty-second and Vanderbilt I cut through Grand Central Station. There was a new machine standing in a little alcove; it looked like the old take-your-own-photo booth that had once been there, with a place to sit and curtains for privacy, but the sign on this one said TELL ME YOUR TROUBLES! I sat down, drew the curtains, dropped in my quarter, and behind a glass panel, tape began slowly revolving on reels to show me it was listening.

"I'm a failure," I said, "maritally, financially, socially, creatively, and employment-wise. Where is the bright promise of youth? I can't *communicate!*" From a small loudspeaker in the ceiling there came frequent gentle sounds of *"Tsk, tsk, tsk! . . . That's too bad. . . . Oh, you poor boy!"*

"I still *like* Hetty, you understand," I said. "Always glad to see her. Any wife of old Ben Bennell is a wife of mine! It's just that I don't seem to *love* her any more."

"What a shame!" the machine was saying. "I'm so *sorry! Chin up!"* And I felt a little better when I peeked through the drawn curtains, saw no one I knew passing by, and ducked out.

I intend to sturdily resist the temptation, of which I feel none whatever, to tell you all about my work and just what I do every day at the office. You may want this information for an in-depth psychological understanding of me, but I'm damned if I want you to have it. Ever think of that? I'm *ashamed* of what I do, it's so *dumb*, it's so *dull*, so routine, uncreative and underpaid. Anyway, what I do and what we all do at my office is just what they do in all the others. Charter a helicopter and fly low around New York peeking in the windows of the taller buildings, and you'll see that we've built twenty-odd bridges and several tunnels in order to fill Manhattan with people in offices passing pieces of paper around. And of course we now duplicate these papers on expensive machines, which, as a matter of fact, is kind of fun; I often stand for minutes dreamily duplicating sheet after sheet simply for the narcotic effect.

So that's what we do at my office; we fool around with paper while trying to hold insanity, raging and snapping at the edges of vision and mind, at bay with frequent cups of kidney-destroying coffee and nervous trips to the washroom. As for what Saf-T Products actually *are*, I couldn't possibly bring myself to tell you except that they're useless, foolish, and made of easily breakable and dangerous plastic.

"Well, why don't you get another job," Hetty always says, "if you hate this one so much?" In the calm reasonable way that I know infuriates her, I reply, "Doing what else? Serving humanity in what rich and rewarding way while still managing to pay the rent on this hovel?" She generally answers, "What do you *want* to do? What do you *really want to do*?" and since the answer is "I don't know. Something . . . *creative*," I shrug and change the subject, and continue reporting to Saf-T Products eleven mornings a week.

Today at my desk I drew the morning's first sheet of blank paper toward me, thinking (a little cloud appeared over my head, just the way it does in comic strips) of the picturesque Canadian lumberjacks who were even now leveling forests to bring me next month's supply. They disappeared, and the words *What is love?* appeared in their place in the cloud. The cloud disappeared, and I printed *Love* in the middle of the sheet, sat back to look at it, then drew a heart around it. I fancied up and shaded the letters, then drew an arrow piercing the heart, working carefully on the feathers. I added a realistic jagged crack plunging down the middle of the heart, and a line of drops descending from its point, and realized that I'd just defined love pictorially. All day I felt sad, depressed, guilty about Hetty, not liking the feeling at all, and wanting to do something about it.

Skip to that night: Should I buy Hetty some flowers? I wondered, stepping out of the elevator into the lobby of the Chrysler Building. No, I thought, flowers are kind of a phony thing to bring your wife; Holden Caulfield would never approve. There's a drugstore in the building with a door from the lobby, and I walked in and stood looking around. Scattered on a display table I saw a lot of fancy little pillboxes on sale for a buck. I picked one out, a tiny rectangular box of gilt metal, less than an inch wide and not much longer, the lid crusted with glass jewels. I took it over to the counter, where the girl was checking her register, and while I stood waiting noticed some candy hanging from a wire stand on the counter. It was a long thin cellophane sack of four or five chocolate-covered nougats and creams; regular candy in little brown waxed-paper dishes like the kind that comes in boxes.

I opened one of the sacks, took out a nougat, and put it in the little box. It just fitted, as I'd thought it would, though it was a shade too high I found as I closed the lid; I could feel it squash a little. The girl was watching when I looked up, and I nodded at the little box.

"Could you gift-wrap it, please?" I said, and when she just stared at me I said, "It's for a dieting midget," and her eyes narrowed evilly. "Actually, it's for my wife," I said, laughing ruefully and shyly scraping my foot on the floor. "She's mad at me, and it's either make her laugh or kill myself." The girl smiled delightedly then, all eager to join the cause, and did a fine job of gift-wrapping the tiny box in a little hunk of white paper and some narrow gold ribbon she found in a drawer behind the counter. She wasn't bad-looking, and while she worked I offered her a chocolate cream, which she took, and I ate the others myself, leaning on the counter pretending to watch her work while I looked her over.

The signs were everywhere, it occurred to me walking out of the store; even buying some lousy little gift for Hetty I was eyeing another girl, and I felt more than ever depressed and increasingly tired of myself. At the green-painted newsstand down the street I bought a paper as always, from Herman or whatever his name is. He's supposed to be a character; everybody who works around there knows him—wears enormous fuzzy earmuffs in winter, and an old-style flat straw hat with a fancy band in the summer. Sometimes he calls out funny fake headlines, about the *Titanic* sinking or something like that. A real pain, eh, Holden? Nearly every night I urged myself to find a new place to buy the evening paper but I never remembered to do it. Tonight I laid my dime down on the counter as always, he snatched up a *Post* saying, "Yes, sir!" with humorously exaggerated servility, and I smiled with delight, both our lives a little richer. Someday, I promised myself, I would heat up the dime with a cigarette lighter, and when he snatched it up he'd know from thence forward how things really stood between us.

At home I found Hetty stirring something on top of the stove, and I kissed the back of her neck, feeling nothing but hair tickling my nose, and said, "Brought you something!"

"You *did?*" She whirled around so fast a drop of gravy flew off her spoon and caught me on the forehead, her eyes lighting up with excitement, and my distaste for Benjamin Bennell, Boy Bounder, increased.

"Yep," I said, spuriously cheerful, "a box of candy!" and opened my hand to show her the little package. Her mouth actually hung open in anticipation as she stood unwrapping it, and when she came to the tiny box I'd picked up in a drugstore in one minute flat, she exclaimed with pleasure, and I could tell from the sound that she meant it and wasn't faking. She lifted the lid, saw the squashed nougat inside, and for a terrible instant I thought she was going to cry with delight at my loving whimsy, and I grinned quickly to keep things at the smile level, and condemned myself to solitary confinement in the Dry Tortugas for one hundred and forty-five years.

"A box of *candy*," she said in fond scorn, prying the nougat out. "What a perfectly darling idea! Wait'll I tell Jenny. Oh, Ben," she said, as though certain recent doubts had suddenly been resolved, "you *are* sweet." For a moment she stood staring down at the nougat in her palm, then popped it into her mouth; Hetty sometimes goes on a sort of diet which consists of frowning at anything she shouldn't eat, then eating it.

I mixed a quick pitcherful, and we had drinks in the living room, Hetty in the chair beside the end table on which she'd set her pillbox so she could smile down at it frequently. I sat on the davenport across the room—on the broken spring to punish myself. Hetty chattered about other cute things I'd done; mostly, it seemed to me, before we were married: the phone calls in a slightly disguised voice at odd times of day and night; the little notes, generally containing lewd suggestions, that I'd slip into her purse or the finger of a glove where she'd find them later; the telegram to her office that all the other girls thought was so cute. I sat nodding happily, reached up to my ear, and surreptitiously turned a tiny switch in my brain which cut off all sound. Hetty's lips continued to move in the silence, and I sipped my drink, occasionally smiling, even laughing out loud.

I saw from her expression that she'd asked a question, and I said, "What?" reaching quickly to my ear as though it itched, and turning the switch back on.

"Remember the darling way you proposed?" she repeated, for what may well have been the one-thousandth time, and I smiled and nodded. "I didn't know *what* to think," she went on, "when you brought me a box of stationery; it seemed such an odd kind of gift, even a little dull. I'd noticed right away, of course, that my name was printed on the envelopes and paper. I'd noticed my first name, that is. Then all of a sudden I saw the *Mrs.* printed in front of it, and I looked closer and just couldn't believe my eyes! I actually blinked, I remember, to make certain I was right; but sure enough, it said Mrs. Hetty H. *Bennell*, and the address was your apartment! Well, then I knew. I knew what you meant, and that I was going to say yes, and absolutely *every*one I've ever told thinks it was the most original proposal they ever heard of."

I sat smiling and apparently listening to all this, even lifting my glass once in a silent toast to our married bliss, but though I hadn't turned the switch and could still hear Hetty, the volume was way down because I wasn't listening; I was sneaking looks at Tessie.

She'd come walking into the room, transparent but perfectly visible, to me anyway, during Hetty's reminiscence about notes in purse and gloves. She sat down opposite me, crossing her splendid knees, and as Hetty finished the lewd-note story, Tessie said, "Hey, Ben, how about the notes you sent *me!*" and winked.

She hadn't changed a bit, looking as completely edible as the last time I'd seen her, long ago. There she sat, the wallpaper and davenport visible through that luxurious big body—oh *boy*, she'd been a fine big girl, I remembered. She was tall as I was; lavishly, even extravagantly built, no skimping at all. She had a bushel of dark dark red hair that hung, swaying like spun lead, to her shoulders, which, I now recalled with pleasure, were lightly peppered with golden freckles. So was her face, the skin paper-white, and her eyes were the deep red-flecked brown that goes with that kind of complexion and hair. Her figure was just great, and she was also as amiable and likable a human being—man, woman, or child— as I've ever known. She was looking at Hetty now, frowning a little; then she drew back her shoulders, expanded her chest, and turned to me. "How could you ever give *me* up for her?" she said, and all I could do was give her a sneaky little one-shoulder shrug. Sitting there looking her over, I suddenly smiled with pleasure, and Hetty smiled lovingly back.

" . . . most original proposal they ever *heard* of," she was saying, suddenly loud and clear as my inner monitor flashed a red alert. "And I've still got the stationery. Want to see it?"

She was up and turning toward the dining nook without waiting for my answer—which was a silent scream of *No-o-o-o!*, both hands cupped at my mouth. Hetty walked over to the battered old china cabinet her mother had given us, probably because the Salvation Army had indignantly refused it. Kneeling before it, she opened the lower doors, the oval panes of which were made of stained glass salvaged from the washroom windows of one of the first Pullman cars, and began poking through the bundled-up Christmas cards, flat glossy department-store boxes of place mats, and shoe boxes full of partly used candles from ancient dinner parties saved in case the lights went out in a storm. With Hetty's back turned to the living room, Tess hopped up, darted across the room, and dropped onto the davenport beside me, where she began gently blowing into my ear, and my arm came up involuntarily to lie along the back of the davenport, my hand cupping that smooth, round, entrancingly freckled shoulder.

The good old days Hetty had been talking about apparently jogged the needle of her memory into the same grooves as it had mine, because she turned to look over her shoulder at me—Tessie instantly disappear-

ing—and said casually, "What was that girl's name you were seeing just
before you met me?"

I frowned at the difficulty of remembering any girl but Hetty. "What
girl?"

"You know. You *ought* to, anyway; you were with her the night you
met *me!* Tessie or Bessie or some such unlikely name. That big cowlike
girl." She turned back to the china cabinet, and Tessie reappeared,
glaring at Hetty in complete disdain, in about the way I'd imagine Linda
Evans appraising Cyndi Lauper; then she turned back to me and began
nibbling the lobe of my ear.

I looked at the box of stationery Hetty brought me, while she stood
before me intently watching my face for an appropriate reaction. I knew
I couldn't manage ecstatic delight, so I settled for riffling the little stack
of notepaper with my thumb, fingering the envelopes reminiscently, and
finally shaking my head in rueful deprecation of my famous premarital
charm. Just behind Hetty, watching over her shoulder, Tess stood looking
with some interest at the stationery on my lap. Then she quirked a corner
of her mouth and strolled off, fingering one of the drapes as she passed
it and shrugging. I set the stationery on the coffee table—which I'd
made, not very successfully, from a flush door—stood up, put my arm
around Hetty's waist, and walked her to the kitchen, my empty glass in
hand. Just as we turned in at the kitchen door, ushering Hetty on before
me, I looked over my shoulder wistfully, but Tessie had disappeared, and
I went into the kitchen and mixed another drink: a double.

CHAPTER TWO

"Mirror, mirror," I began next morning, but before I could finish the voice replied.

"The Australian sheepherder joined AA; today it's neck and neck between you and the pimp from Beirut."

"I thought he was a loan shark!"

"He's branching out, he's ambitious. A lot more than I can say for you," and the Hand came down, smacking my forehead with another stamp. This time, I saw in the mirror, the letters were in Old English script and even larger but they still spelled FAILURE, as I proceeded to demonstrate again, this time at the office.

Today more than ever I dreaded going, and wanted company, lots of it. Walking desperately along Forty-second Street, I shouted alliteratively to the men in the buses and speeding cabs: "Avoid strokes; strike!" Sticking my head in the doorways of coffee shops, I yelled, "Do what you *really want to do*; don't show up!" But today they didn't hear me, and I turned to the girls.

Walking directly behind the choice ones, I murmured into their ears, "Come dally with me today; let's slip off, just you and I beneath the sky, wrapped in the arms of sweet romance!" But they kept right on glancing at their watches and at their own sweet faces in the store windows, hurrying to their ten thousand paper-filled offices.

In my minuscule office I sat down at my desk, pulled the first sheet of paper toward me, and the little cloud appeared over my head; in it giant logs floated down a tree-lined river, spinning under the spiked feet of tassel-capped lumberjacks singing *Alouette*. I picked up my ball-point, and stared down at the final result of their dangerous, romantic work: clean white paper, ready to receive anything I wanted to say—a sonnet, a manifesto, a ringing reaffirmation of the truths that set men free. In capital letters I printed HELP! in the center of the page.

During the next half hour I added serifs, shaded in the thick strokes, fancied up the letters into pseudo Roman. Then I walked out to our mighty new beige-plastic and chrome duplicating machine, put a finger in the Dil-A-Copy dial (pronounced *dill-a-copy*), set it for 25, and fed in the sheet. Back came the copies, faintly smudged, redolent of chemicals, slightly tanned, drifting into the receiving tray like autumn leaves—

HELP! . . . HELP! . . . HELP!—while I watched soporifically, my nerve ends unknotting.

Back at my desk, I let them slide one at a time off my hand and out the window, watching them sail in great sweeps over Manhattan. When I turned from the window, my boss, Bert Glahn—two years younger, three inches taller, thirty pounds heavier, mostly in the shoulders, making twice as much money as I did, and considerably handsomer—was standing in the doorway of my tiny office, stroking his chin with thumb and forefinger, staring at me thoughtfully. "Morning, Ben," he said, glancing at his watch.

"Oh, hi! Hi! Hi!" I said, perhaps a bit nervously. "I was just, ah . . ." I didn't know what the rest of that sentence was, so I sort of moved my hand through the air and shrugged, smiled brilliantly, then frowned deeply, but by that time he was gone. I cupped a hand at my mouth and shouted after him, silently, "I hate you, Glahn! Come back here, and I'll judo-chop you down to size!" I made a fast cut through the air with the back of my hand, and felt better but not much.

A little after ten I had coffee in the drugstore downstairs with Ralph and Eddie at a crumb-littered, strawberry-jam-smeared table, ankle-deep in lipsticked paper napkins, discarded straw-wrappers, and crumpled cigarette packages. In a flurry of time-tested whimsy we matched to see who'd pay, and Ralph lost, pantomiming chagrin, while Eddie and I joshed him humorously. "You just don't live right, Ralph!" I said; then we crept upstairs again, and I found a note from the boss's secretary on my desk. He'd been looking for me; he was in a hurry to see a copy of a report I had, and it took me forty-five minutes to find it, in a folder it had no business being in.

The red second-hands of the office clocks continued to revolve in perfect, irritating synchronization sixty times every hour, and another lost day slipped by. About four-thirty I walked down the hall, and turned into Accounting to see Miss Wilmar, high priestess of our office computers. "Hi, honey. Do me a favor."

"Sure."

"Slip off your dress and lie down." She grinned happily, shivering her shoulders. "But first," I added, "multiply 365 days by, let's say, 74 years, if I'm lucky."

She poked keys, sparks flickered across the screen, a jet of blue flame shot from a chromed orifice, smoke puffed, and the machine waited, panting. "27,010 days."

"Subtract one-third for time spent in the blessed Nirvana of sleep."

A high electronic whine rose to supersonic pitch. "18,006⅔ days."

"Drop the 6⅔ for oversleeping, and divide the single horrible day I have just spent by the eighteen thousand waking days of a brief lifetime."

Transistor relays relayed, a violet light pulsed like a hummingbird's heart and the smell of ozone twitched our nostrils. ".0000555. Why do you want to know?"

"That is the precise fraction of my life I have today given to Saff-T Products in exchange for the dubious benefit of the means to continue living it. 'Night."

"G'night, Ben. Honestly, you're a card."

At eleven minutes past five I stepped safely out of the automatic elevators for one more time, fully aware that the odds against me increased each time I used them. I walked out of the building, toward Herman's newsstand, a dime in one hand, the other gripping the butt of a Colt .45 Frontier model with a filed hair trigger, Holden beside me murmuring encouragement and all. At the counter I put down my dime, and in one blurred motion Herman snatched up a *New York Post*, simultaneously folding it and humorously slipping it under my gun arm. To raise my arm and fire meant losing my paper, so, outwitted again, I smiled weakly and walked on, letting the gun slide from my fingers and drop in the gutter as I stopped at the curb for the DON'T WALK sign. Without glancing at me or moving her lips, a lovely black-haired girl who was standing beside me murmured, "I've been following you for days; the very way you hold the paper under your arm thrills me. I have a suite just down the street at the Commodore Hotel; please come with me!"

Seeming merely to glance around, I looked at her, and—lips motionless—whispered, "I can't. Gotta get home. The wife's expecting me."

"Just for half an hour! She'll never know; tell her you had to work late. Please? Oh, I beg you: please, please, please, please, please!" The light changed to SPRINT, and, knowing her cause was almost hopeless, she hurried bravely on without a glance at me as I followed, observing the charming flash of her ankles till she turned uptown on the other side.

". . . will let me know the number of the pattern," Hetty was saying when I got home, following me down the hall toward the bedroom, "and I can knit it myself if I get the blocking done."

I think she said blocking, whatever that means. I nodded, unbuttoning my shirt as I walked, anxious to get out of my office uniform; I was thinking about a dark-green forty-two-thousand-dollar sports car I'd seen during noon hour.

"... kind of a ribbed pattern with a matching freggelheggis," Hetty seemed to be saying as I stopped at the dresser. I tossed my shirt on the bed and turned to the mirror, arching my chest and sucking my stomach in.

"... middly collar, batten-barton sleeves with sixteen rows of smeddlycup balderdashes ..." Pretty good chest and shoulders.

"... dropped hem, doppelganger waist, maroon-green, and a sort of frimble-framble daisystitch ..." Probably want ten thousand bucks down on a car like that; the payments'd be more than the rent on this whole apartment.

"So what do you think?" Hetty said. "You think they'd go well together?"

"Sure! They'd look fine." I nodded at her reflection in the mirror, and her eyes narrowed, she folded her arms, and stood leaning in the bedroom doorway, glaring at me. I walked to the closet and began looking for some wash pants, trying to figure what I'd done wrong. "What's trouble?" I said finally.

"You don't *listen* to me! You really don't! You don't hear a word I say!"

"Why, sure I do, honey. You were talking about ... knitting."

"An orange sweater, I said: *orange*. I *knew* you weren't listening, and I asked you how an orange sweater would go with—close your eyes."

"What?"

"No, don't turn around! And close your eyes." I closed them, and Hetty said, "Now, without any peeking, because I'll see you if you do, tell me what I'm wearing right now."

It was ridiculous. In the last five minutes, since I'd come home from the office, I must have glanced at Hetty maybe two or three times. I'd kissed her when I walked into the apartment, I was pretty sure. Yet standing at the closet now, eyes closed, I couldn't for the life of me say what she was wearing. I worked at it; I could actually hear the sound of her breathing just behind me and could picture her standing there, five feet two inches tall, twenty-four years old, nice complexion, honey-blond hair, and wearing ... wearing ...

"Well, am I wearing a dress, slacks, medieval armor, or standing here stark-naked?"

"A dress."

"What color?"

"Ah—dark green?"

"Am I wearing stockings?"

"Yes."

"Is my hair done up, shaved off, or in a pony-tail?"

"Done up."

"Okay, you can look now."

Of course the instant I turned around, I remembered; there she stood, eyes blazing, her bare foot angrily tapping the floor, and she was wearing sky-blue wash slacks and a white cotton blouse. As she swung away to walk out of the bedroom and down the hall, her pony tail was bobbing furiously.

Well, brother—and you, too, sister—unless the rice is still in your hair you know what came next: the hurt indignant silence. I finally found my pants, and got into them, a short-sleeved shirt, and the running shoes I walk around the house in, strolled into the living room, and there on the davenport sat Madame Defarge grimly studying the list, disguised as a magazine, of next day's guillotine victims. I knew whose name headed the list, and I walked straight on into the kitchen, mixed up some booze, and found a screwdriver in a kitchen drawer.

In the living room, coldly ignored by what had once been my radiant laughing bride, I set the drinks on the end table, walked behind the davenport, and gripped Hetty's chin between thumb and forefinger. Her magazine dropped, and I instantly inserted the tip of the screwdriver between her clenched indignant teeth, pried open her mouth, picked up a glass, and tried to pour in some booze. She started to laugh, spilling some down her front, and I grinned, handing her the glass, and picked up mine. Sitting down beside her, I saluted Hetty with my glass, then took a delightful sip, and as it hurried to my sluggish bloodstream I could feel the happy corpuscles dive in, laughing and shouting, and once again the Bennell household was about as happy as it ever got lately. But you see what I mean: these days the journey through life was like walking a greased tightrope.

We had dinner, and Hetty asked me what had happened at the office that day. I told her, and her brows rose frequently in interest, lips forming occasional moues of surprise and delight, ears hearing not a damned word. I asked about her day, turning the little volume control in my brain so that her voice, describing her adventures in the supermarket and her phone conversation with Jenny, receded to a murmur. For dessert we had more of the custard we'd had last night; it had shrunk a little so that the surface was now cracked like a drying mud flat, and the level had fractionally dropped leaving a tiny high-tide mark of darkening custard skin.

While Hetty did the dishes, I went down the hall to Nate Rockoski's apartment for about half an hour, came back, sat down before the television, and slowly, at intervals of from one to three seconds, clicked the remote past one channel after another. On the first, two cars, one chasing the other, sailed over the crest of a steep city street, soaring fourteen feet into the air, and I clicked on before the first hit the pavement. A cowboy in a 1931 black-and-white movie with funny sound, whose two-tone shirt complete with pearl buttons had been cunningly painted on his bare torso, said, "Here in Dodge—" Joan Rivers said, "Shit," getting a huge laugh followed by a standing ovation. Forty zebras stood grazing in the high grass of PBS. A pair of cars, one chasing the other, came sailing over the crest— A giant athlete took a sip of beer, then smiled adoringly at his upraised glass. A beautiful child holding her teddy bear and smiling charmingly, told me how much nicer "Mummy" was now that she'd switched hemorrhoid remedies. A plateful of something looking hot, steaming, and revolting, enlarged to fill the screen, and I clicked, and watched the world of television shrink to a blazing atom, and I wondered as always what made it do that.

Hetty said, "Ben, we've got to decide which bills to pay this month. I can't get your other suit cleaned till we pay the cleaner's, and we need a new—"

"I know, I know," I said, "but not now. Let's keep tonight gay and carefree, our troubles forgotten: Okay?"

So we did: Hetty got out her book from the rental library, reading fast and skipping a lot, because it cost twenty-five cents a day; and I lay down on the davenport to look through a magazine that had come in the mail that morning: the *Scientific American*, which I like even though I don't understand a word of it. Time passed, during which we occasionally glanced up while turning a page to smile at one another. After an interval which I could have predicted within seven seconds, Hetty said, "Anything interesting?" nodding at my magazine, showing an interest in her husband's hobbies.

I said, "Yeah," and turned back a couple pages. "They now think the universe is neither expanding nor contracting, but stretching sideways so that we're all a lot wider than we used to be. We don't notice because everything else has stretched in proportion. It's called 'The Funhouse-Mirror Theory of the Universe,' and recent observations of distant galax—"

"Fascinating." Hetty turned her book to glance at the back of the book jacket and the photo of the bearded author who was looking thoughtful, angry and intelligent all at the same time. "Anything else?"

"Scientists think homing pigeons navigate from a set of rough calculations based on a birdlike table of logarithms. They're very simple, of course, carried to only three decimal places, and that funny way they keep ducking their heads when they walk means they're counting. There's an interesting set of graphs—"

"Amazing, absolutely amazing, the way they train animals." She held up her book. "Have you read this?"

"No. There's another article says all the infinite number of other possible worlds may actually exist; the world as it would be if Napoleon had won at Waterloo exists somewhere or other right along with this one. Or if old Dad Hitler, walking along the street kicking a tin can, had turned left instead of right, he'd never have met Moms, and little Adolf wouldn't have been born. That world exists, too; an infinite number of alternate worlds, some different in enormous ways, some in only the most trivial. You exist in those just as you do in this one, except that maybe the drugstore you go to is painted green instead of brown, or—"

"Darling, since you aren't reading, could you get me a Coke?"

"Sure," I said, tossing my magazine high in the air; and smiling charmingly, I went out to the kitchen, finished off Hetty with a few fast chops, then came back to the living room with a cool refreshing drink for each of us, mine of a slightly different color.

Then it was bedtime, and the day ended as it had begun, with automation taking over, the dial set at X-3. Lift the lid of our tiny apartment, and watch us trundle along the slotted pathways into the bedroom, like windup toys. The concealed gears revolving, tiny motor humming, I hang tie in closet, turn jerkily to dresser, bring out wallet, lay it on dresser top. Hetty's tiny metal palm pats mouth as hinged lower jaw opens in yawn, other hand moving to zipper in skirt. I take soiled handkerchief from pocket, drop it without looking into wicker clothes hamper by door, little painted face expressionless. Hand takes change from pants pocket, lays it on dresser beside wallet.

Suddenly the slotted pathways disappeared and the little figures turned real. Because, poking at the coins, examining them as I did every night, I said, "Hey, look! Here's a Woodrow Wilson dime!" I picked it up for a closer look; it had a profile of Wilson, and was minted in 1958.

"*Why* must you look at *every* last coin in your pocket? *Every* single night?"

I glanced in the mirror; I knew exactly where Hetty would be in the room, and precisely what she'd be doing: sitting on the edge of the bed in bra and panties, peeling her stockings off. "Just habit," I answered, shrugging. "Started when I was a kid. There was an ad used to run in *American Boy* magazine that said, 'Coin Collecting can be FUN! Why don't *you* start, too? Tonight!' It said 1913 Liberty-head nickels were worth thousands; I used to watch for them, and I guess I'm still looking."

"Well, you never used to," Hetty said irritably. "Not when we were first married." For a moment, motionless, we looked at each other in the mirror, our eyes meeting. Then I looked away. I wondered what was going to happen to us, knowing that something had to give, and soon; that you don't reach your golden wedding anniversary on sheer will-power alone.

CHAPTER THREE

"*You!*" said the mirror the moment I closed the bathroom door next morning, which was Saturday.

"I didn't ask!" I yelled, and tried to duck, but the big Hand caught me smack on the forehead, knocking me back against a towel rack. I saw in the mirror that this time the word stamped on my forehead was a screeching fluorescent red. But it still said FAILURE, and that morning, with the help of Nate Rockoski, I proved it was as true of me creatively as I'd demonstrated maritally and businesswise.

Nate and I had met while waiting for the building elevator in the morning; we lived on the same floor. And sometimes we were on the same bus coming home at night and we talked. He was a short, dark, skinny, round-shouldered, homely, nearsighted, untidy man in his late twenties, with big round black eyes behind round black glasses. Consult your copy of *Who's Who*, and on page 1800, between Rockefeller, Nelson, and Rockwell, Norman, you will not find Rockoski, Nathan. If you did, the entry would read, or ought to: Born 1958, unwillingly and of reluctant parents, on West 41 Street, NYC. Clubs: none. Accomplishments: trivial. Outstanding characteristic: greed.

Nate and I shared this last trait, we'd discovered early in our acquaintance, along with semipoverty and a desperate feeling that there must be more to life than *this*. As Nate walked to work to save bus fare, the knots in his shoelaces cleverly hidden under the lacing-flaps of his shoes, where they pressed on his insteps, his mind was filled with stories he'd read in *Reader's Digest*, and *Popular Mechanics*. These were of men home with a cold, for example, who'd sat watching a wife hang up clothes to dry, then whittled out a new kind of clothespin, patented it, and retired at the age of thirty. Just open your eyes and look around you, these articles preached; a little effort, a little ingenuity, was all it took! And Nate had convinced himself, half convinced me, and fractionally convinced our wives—by a figure so small that eleven zeroes followed the decimal before the first actual digit—that we could do it, too.

So far, working on weekends to the encouraging jeers of our wives, we'd produced several marvels. One was what would apparently be a framed color photograph hanging on a living-room wall—Nate was an inept camera bug—and which actually moved; a pleasant view of a lake,

for example, in which waves flowed and trees stirred in the breeze, to
the amazement of guests. But since this required a super 8 projector,
concealed in the wall and plastered over, continually projecting a looped
film onto a mirror also hidden in the wall and which would right-angle
the beam onto the back of a ground-glass pane set in the living-room
wall and edged with picture-frame molding, we had certain reservations
about its practicality. As Nate put it, there were "a few bugs to work
out."

But we did produce—using thin nylon balloon-cloth, epoxy glue, and
part of the works from a rechargeable seltzer bottle—an inflatable
umbrella. It looked a lot, too much, like a lopsided mushroom; our best
customers, Hetty said, would be elves. But it compressed as planned into
a fist-sized wad of light cloth wrapped around a CO_2 cartridge in the
plastic handle; milady to carry it in a corner of her purse, all set for a
rainy day. Nate's wife Miriam carried it, ready for trial by genuine rain,
and on the first day—bright, clear and sunny—as she was being shoved
and jostled in a crowded Madison Avenue bus, the cartridge went off
and the cloth handle, inflating steadily, forced its way out of her purse
like a snake from a Hindu basket, the cartridge hissing ominously: a pale-
white snake with rigor mortis, perfectly straight and upright. A couple
women screamed, there was a considerable scramble, the bus driver set
his hand brake and sat with arms folded, and Mrs. Rockoski walked home
and didn't eat much for several days. But Nate, the fanatic gleam of
failure blazing in his eyes, carried on, dragging me with him.

Now, at nine sharp, Saturday, Nate rang our bell, and I answered it,
still chewing a piece of breakfast toast; Hetty was out doing the weekly
food-shopping. Balanced on Nate's head and held there with one arm
were two large semicircular frameworks of light wood, and under his
other arm was a box of varnished wood with brass fittings, which Nate
had found in a pawnshop and bought for six bucks. We'd worked in his
living room last night; now it was my turn; I'd already rolled back the
rug. I said, "What happened to last night's? They turn out?"

"Yeah, they're drying; I'll get them soon as we're through. My god,
they're big; I had to project them fifteen feet. Will you get these damn
things off my head?"

I stepped out into the hall and lifted the two curved wooden frames
from Nate's head. First tilting them sideways to work them through the
door, I carried them to the center of the living room and set them on
their edges. Then I pushed them together to form an open cylinder four
feet high and seven feet across. Tacked onto the upper rim of this
cylinder was a wide-gauge toy railroad track, and Nate fitted the track

joints together to complete the circle. Then he fastened two hook-and-eye door catches, which kept the two halves of the big circle from moving apart.

Working like circus roustabouts setting up Ring 2 under the Big Top for the eleven-hundredth time, I carried my swivel chair from the bedroom and set it inside the raised circle of track, while Nate took down from the hall-closet shelf a toy locomotive I'd had as a kid. This had been mailed to me by my mother, along with the track and some cars, because she thought Hetty would like to have it: a thought only a mother could have. I plugged in the transformer cord; Nate fitted the locomotive wheels to the track. Then he unhooked the hinged front of the varnished box and pulled out the red-leather accordion bellows and the brass-mounted lens of an ancient camera. Three of my toy flatcars hooked together were tightly fastened to the underside of the camera with tape that ran up and over the camera's top. On our knees, we fitted the wheels of the little cars to the track, and I hooked the head car to the locomotive; now the camera lens pointed to the center of the raised circle of track. Nate adjusted the lens, setting it as though he knew what he was doing, while I watched closely as though I did, too.

"Okay, all set," Nate said, and I climbed into the wooden enclosure and sat down in the swivel chair. As I sat, my head was exactly in line with the camera lens. Nate pushed the transformer lever, and the little train strained, trying to move, making an electric groan of protest. Nate gave it an assisting push, and it slowly began moving. He eased the control lever all the way open and began trotting around the wooden trestle, keeping pace with the train as it gathered speed, bent forward at the waist, hands ready to catch the camera if it toppled.

He made two full circuits of the track, while I turned in my chair, watching. He yelled, "Okay! Full speed! Hold your breath!" and I braked the chair to a stop, drew a deep breath, then sat motionless, absolutely rigid and unblinking. Still trotting beside the camera, Nate pushed a control and the camera began the slow buzzing of a time exposure. As it buzzed, Nate ran with it around the track, and a long rectangular metal film-holder moved slowly through the camera from left to right, while I sat motionless and staring, holding my breath.

The circuit completed, the buzzing stopped; Nate shoved the transformer lever, and the little train with its giant camera stopped dead. "Okay, now method two," Nate said. "I'd do this one myself," he added apologetically, "but we built the track for your height. Start shoving."

Pushing against the floor with one leg, I began revolving my chair. I shoved again, slightly increasing the speed, and—keeping my face and upper body rigid—I maintained the speed with regular rhythmic thrusts against the floor. After a couple revolutions, I said, "How's the speed?"

Nate was bent over the camera, fitting in a new film holder, and he looked up to watch me turn in my chair through another full revolution. "Seemed a little slow," he said. "Let me time it." I speeded up a little, and Nate, eyes moving between watch and me, timed a turn. "Still slow. Just a tiny bit faster." I pushed against the floor a little impatiently. Nate timed me through another turn, then said, "A shade too fast now. Slow it just a—"

"Damn it, Nate, I'll throw up again!"

"Well, that's close enough," he said quickly. "Maintain speed!" The little train remaining motionless this time, Nate started the camera, the buzzing began again, and I revolved before the camera, one leg surreptitiously pushing against the floor, eyes half closed, face stiff.

The buzzing stopped just about as I completed the circle, and Nate said, "Nearly perfect! Step it up just a tiny bit next shot." He began changing plates, then looked up at me. "You can stop while I'm changing film."

I kept on pushing against the floor, slowly turning, my eyes squeezed shut. "No, it gets worse if I stop."

Nate finished changing plates. "Okay!" He started the camera, the buzzing began, and I revolved, my eyes held open, wide and staring. "Fine, great," Nate said as the buzzing stopped, and I snapped my eyes shut. "Now just one more for safety."

"Nate, I can't! I get dizzy dialing a phone!"

"Okay, just sit there and rest; I'll go get yesterday's." Nate lifted off camera and train, yanked the transformer cord, unhooked the two raised half-circles of track, and carried them out and down the hall to his apartment.

I stood up, and—a hand over my eyes, looking through my fingers at the floor—took two steps toward the davenport to lie down, stood swaying for a second or two, then whirled around and made it back to my chair. I dropped onto it to sit motionless, elbows on my knees, a hand over my eyes, the other across my mouth.

I opened my eyes for a moment when Nate came back; he was carrying an enormous roll of paper, a glossy photograph as tall as he was. He hooked a curled end of the huge print around a chair, and as I closed my eyes again he was walking backward across the room, unrolling the rest of it. Then, very gently as though I were asleep or something, he called, "Ben? What do you think?" and I opened my eyes.

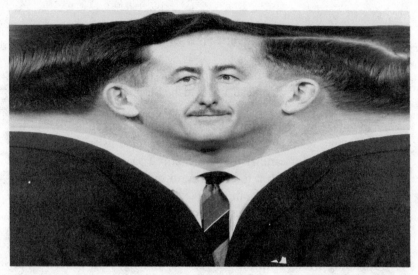

"Oh, god," I said, and closed them again, "it looks as though my whole head had been scalped!"

"I know," Nate said mournfully. "You ought to see Miriam's." He let go the edge of the big print, and the natural springy curl of the paper caused it to skid upright across the wood floor, revolving itself into a standing cylinder, and revealing behind it a second giant print of Nate's wife, stretched between his hands and the chair. Again I looked.

"Will you cut it *out*, Nate!? I'll be sick!"

He let go, and the enormous photograph revolved across the floor, curling itself into a cylinder, stopping beside the first one. I got up, and we walked over and stood looking at them. I said, "Let's quit kidding ourselves, Nate; they're terrible, and the new ones won't be any better.

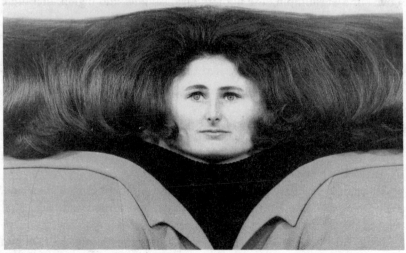

It's a lousy idea, and no advertiser is ever going to pay us a dime for it."

"I thought maybe wrapped around the pillars in Grand Central Sta—" I was shaking my head no, and he stopped. "What about the kiosks in Paris?"

"I'll give you my share of the French rights." I walked around to the back of my own giant cylindrical portrait and pulled its two edges apart. "Might sell them for sandwich-board men," I said, and stepped inside the big cylinder, allowing it to curl around me. It concealed me almost to the eyes, and I lifted it from the inside, hiding my head completely and revealing my feet and ankles. "If you cut holes for the eyes," I added, and began walking around. "How's it look?" I called out to Nate, my voice sounding kind of muffled.

"Something wrong with the way you're walking; your knees bump." He pulled the other cylinder open and got inside, then lifted it to expose his feet, his head disappearing from view; I'd lowered mine and stood watching him. Nate began walking around the room in very short, rapid steps. "It doesn't work, walking," he called then.

"I know." We stood looking at each other across the top edges of the two huge photos. "Try hopping," I said then, and we lifted the cylinders, our heads disappearing, and—our feet and ankles right together, springing from our toes—we began hopping around the room. The floor shook, and dishes rattled in the kitchen as the two giant cylindrical portraits leaped around the living room; we were both howling with laughter. We bumped into my swivel chair, into the davenport, then into each other, and Nate shrieked, "Fresh!" and we were howling so loud now, our feet thumping the floor, the leaps higher and higher, that there wasn't a chance of hearing the front door open.

It did, though, and I don't know how long Hetty stood staring, frozen in astonishment. She said, "Ben," but very faintly, and with no effect on the hopping or howling. She yelled then, *"Ben!"* and the two cylinders stopped and stood motionless.

I said, "Hetty?"

"Yes, for heaven sakes! Will you *take that damn thing*—which one *are* you!"

I lowered my cylinder to the floor and looked across the top of it at Hetty. "Hi," I said; then Nate lowered his.

He said, "Hi, Hetty," and she stood for a moment longer, then said, "Oh, my god," in a kind of hopeless voice, and turned and walked off toward the bedroom.

Nate and I got out of our cylinders. "I guess I better go," he said, and

I didn't argue. "I guess this didn't work out," he said, and I still saw nothing to dispute. He stuck the two big cylinders under his arm, picked up his camera, and walked to the door, which was still open. "There's something else I've been thinking about, though," he said, but I held up a hand.

"Save it, Nate," I said. "I'll call you. Sometime after the first of the century."

CHAPTER FOUR

After that my mirror didn't volunteer anything any more, and I didn't ask. I didn't have to; all I had to do was look, then nod in agreement. Nor was anything stamped on my forehead again; there was no need. FAILURE was permanently impressed there now, invisible to anyone else but I could sense it; I could feel it with my fingers, lips moving as I read it letter by letter like Braille. Walking to work Monday, it was blue skies and bright sun for everyone but me; I alone walked, coat collar turned up, in a little circle of rain.

In Grand Central Station I sat down in the TELL ME YOUR TROUBLES! booth, drew the curtains, dropped in my quarter, and began, and the machine listened for a while, the tape reels slowly revolving; then it said, "So what do you expect, a slob like you? Take your quarter and get the hell out of here!"

The coin rattled down into the coin-return cup, and I picked it up and looked at it. "It's Canadian," I said.

"Take the hint: go to Canada! As far north as you can."

I nodded, and left, feeling that it wasn't the worst idea I'd ever heard.

At work, I printed *You are a Failure* down the center of a page in thin, droopy-looking letters, walked out to the big shiny machine, spun the Dil-A-Copy dial to 25, and fed it the sheet. *You are a Failure.* . . . *You are a Failure.* . . . *You are a Failure*, the duplicate sheets began informing me, and I stood nodding each time one dropped into the tray. About the tenth or eleventh sheet, one came out that said, *Damn right!*, and I nodded twice.

The day passed like a life sentence. I rode downstairs in an express elevator, my eyes closed; at the main floor it slowed, leveling itself, and I held my breath. But once again the doors slid open, and I opened my eyes and stepped out into the Chrysler Building lobby, still a temporary winner at elevator roulette. As I passed the lobby door of the building drugstore, I glanced in, but doubted that Hetty wanted another pillbox, and walked on.

Out on Lex, walking south toward Herman's newsstand, I took my bankbook from my inside coat pocket and stopped at the curb to look at the balance. Then I looked up at Herman's funny straw hat. "The fine for yanking that hat down around his neck," I said thoughtfully, "would be about $150." I glanced again at my bankbook balance of $153.12.

"Leaving $3.12 of my life savings." Again I stared thoughtfully at the hat. "It would be worth it," I said. "It would even be worth a few days in jail besides. But I need a new suit, soon as there's a sale," and I put the bankbook away reluctantly, walked up to the stand, and meekly laid a dime on the counter.

Herman was waiting on another customer, grinning servilely, and I glanced down to look at my dime; it was the Woodrow Wilson I'd found a night or so before. Then Herman turned, grabbed up a paper, this time folding it *lengthwise* as he shoved it under my arm, so that it stuck out half a yard front and back, making me look like a fool. I returned Herman's smile of contempt with an appreciative grin, and turned away refolding my paper.

Stopping for the light at the corner, I watched a tiny car pull to the curb across the street; it was a new foreign make, I thought, although the headlights flowed up out of the tops of the front fenders in a way that was dimly familiar. The sign jumped to WALK, changing to RUN almost immediately, and as I hurried across the street, the door of the little car opened on the curb side and a man began heaving and hauling himself out. Cars interest me, and on the other side I stopped to look at this one: the man, yanking at the skirt of his off-white raincoat, feet braced on the curb, trying to break loose from the suction of the tiny car, glared up at me as though his troubles were my fault, and I had to say something to justify my staring. "What kind of car *is* that?" I said pleasantly.

"A Pierce-Arrow, what else?" he said with the courtliness for which New Yorkers are famous.

"A *Pierce-Arrow?*" I lifted a corner of my lip and dropped a sneer into my voice to reveal my opinion of this pitiful joke. "They haven't made Pierce-Arrows for years."

"They haven't?" He broke loose from the car, struggled to his feet, and leered with pleasure at this opportunity to demonstrate his contempt for a brother New Yorker. "Then a hell of a lot of people who've just bought new ones are going to be pretty damn surprised." Sneakily he turned and walked quickly away before I could think of a return insult. Then I saw passing in the street another little car just like this, and as it moved on I read *Pierce-Arrow* in chrome script on the trunk lid. Just behind it came a Ford sedan looking a lot like, but not quite like, any other Ford I'd ever seen; and behind the Ford a low, sleek, baby-blue Hupmobile convertible.

At the extreme out-of-focus edge of my vision far to the left, a cop was strolling toward me, and I realized how strange I must look standing

at the curb gaping at passing cars. I turned toward him smiling reassur-
ingly; he was young, thin-faced, and wore glasses, looking more like a
student than a cop. I opened my mouth to say something that would let
him know I was a respectable *Times*-reading citizen, but I never said it,
though my mouth kept on opening. Because I'd seen, first, his dark-blue
uniform pants walking toward me; then his familiar brass-buttoned cop's
coat; his pale scholarly face; and now, finally—his hat. It was a low-
crowned derby with slanting sides, and made of what looked like stiff tan
felt; there were little metal-rimmed air holes in the sides, and running
clear around it was a turned-down brim of dull black leather; his shield
was fastened to the front of the hat. Of its own accord my mouth, already
open, said, "Where did you get that *hat?*" and his face tensed for
trouble.

"Somethin' the matter, mister?" he said, stopping before me, planting
his feet well apart; they must teach things like that at cop school. "You
sober?" Then his face cleared. "Or from out of town?"

I nodded and said, "Yeah, something like that," but I couldn't stop
glancing up at his hat. "It's just that I've never seen a hat like that
before."

He shrugged tolerantly. "Must be from a long way out of town, then;
we've always worn them in New York." His eyes narrowed again.
"Mister, you sure you're all right?"

I couldn't answer. I'd been standing at the curb, half facing the street,
when—dragging my eyes from the cop's brown derby—I glanced back
across the street, and . . . the Chrysler Building was gone. It was
impossible, of course. I'd gone to work there every weekday for nearly
three years now; I'd just walked out of it! But there, where the tall,
needle-spired, gray old Chrysler Building belonged, stood a ten- or
twelve-story building of yellow brick and white stone. The blood left my
skin, and I actually cried out in fright. "Where's the Chrysler Building!"
I yelled, and grabbed the cop's upper arms, shaking him as though I
could make him put it back.

He yanked free, hand moving to his nightstick. "The what?" His eyes
searched mine, alert for anything.

All I could do was point for several seconds, and I saw that my arm
and hand were shaking. "The Chrysler Building. Isn't it . . . ? It's
supposed to be. . . . I thought it was . . . " I couldn't finish a sentence
or a thought.

The cop was slowly shaking his head, watching me carefully. "There's
no such building," he said warily. "Not in New York, anyway." He risked
turning his head for a moment to nod at the yellow-and-white soot-

marked building that stood, incredibly, on the northeast corner of Forty-second and Lex. "That's the old Doc Pepper Building, and always has been," he said, and even while he was speaking I knew what had happened.

"I'm in an alternate world," I murmured to myself, "I really am," and when the cop frowned I tried to explain. "There's an article in this month's *Scientific American*. That's a magazine that—"

"I *know* it's a magazine," he said, offended. "I subscribe, and have for years."

"Excuse me. Then maybe you read an article in the current issue, about an infinite number of alternate worlds, each differing slightly from the others, and how they may actually exist, and how—"

"Yeah, I read it. But it wasn't this last issue; must have been six months ago, at least."

"Oh. Well, in *my* world it didn't appear till this month, and—"

He grinned at me, suddenly delighted, and reached out to give me a good-fellow clap on the shoulder. "*I* see; you just stepped out of one of those alternate worlds and into this one. Is that it? Everything here a little strange and funny?"

"Well, yeah; I guess that's what happened, anyway. I was walking along, bought a paper, and—"

"And where the Doc Pepper building stands"—he nodded at it—"is what, in your world? The Cresswell Building?"

"Chrysler Building. And the cops wear different hats; caps, actually. And they don't make Pierce-Arrows any more, and—"

"Wonderful, wonderful." The cop was shaking his head with pleasure. "Boy, you advertising guys kill me. Best kidders I know, bar none. No birking, you really had me farreled for a minute there. Where you work? Kenyon and Sample?"

"Yeah, that's right," I said. "In the Doc Pepper Building. Well—" I glanced at my watch, smiling with regret that the fun was over.

"Yeah, take it easy." The cop in the derby grinned at me, then turned away, and I started to walk on. "Hey," he called, and I looked back. "Who won the pennant last year in the other alternate world? The Mets?" He slapped his knee, mouth wide with laughter.

"Well, as a matter of fact . . ." but then I just grinned, he laughed, and I walked on.

I walked briskly, purposefully, in case he turned to watch, but what I wanted to do was stagger. Just a moment before, a car slowing then stopping at the curb beside me for the traffic light, I'd seen my reflection in its side window. I looked just the same except—my hair wasn't red any more. Here in this alternate world, I realized, I wasn't quite the same. The genes I'd inherited were just a bit different here, and now, in this world, my hair was dark brown. I wanted to reel and stumble over to the curb, and sit down with my head in my hands and rock back and forth. I couldn't really think; I couldn't get hold of what seemed to have happened. Then, after half a block, I stopped and looked over one shoulder. The cop was nowhere in sight, and I walked back in the direction I'd come from, crossed at the corner again, stopped at the newsstand, and ducked my head to look in under the little projecting eave.

He was wearing an old Mickey Mouse cap with ears, but it was Herman, all right, and I nodded at him. "Yeah," I said slowly, "you're in *both* worlds, aren't you? In a few places the alternate worlds intersect; and this newsstand is one of them."

"What're you, mister, some kind of wise guy?"

"No. Don't you know me?"

He shook his head contemptuously.

"Sure you do. I buy my paper here every night."

"I know all my regulars, and you ain't one of 'em. Sumpin' you want, mister?" he said belligerently.

"Well, as a matter of fact, I'm sort of a coin collector. And the other night I found a very unusual dime. I think I must have used it to buy this paper, and I wondered if I could get it back. Exchanging another dime for it, of course."

His eyes were slitted in suspicion. "What kind of dime?"

"A Woodrow Wilson. It had a profile of Woodrow Wilson on it."

He smiled cynically. "Why, sure! Here!" He shoved a worn lidless cigar box at me. "Just pick yours out, buddy, and it's all yours!"

I looked down into the box; among the pennies, nickels, and quarters there must have been a couple hundred dimes, and every one that I could see face up bore the sharp profile of the late President Wilson. I stared, then snapped my fingers in amused rebuke at my own stupidity. "Did I say Wilson? I meant Roosevelt!"

"Who?"

I grinned; it was kind of fun baiting the humorist. "Roosevelt. A Franklin D. Roosevelt dime; you ever see one?" He shook his head, watching me intently, and I said, "I thought so. They're from another alternate world. And Woodrow Wilson dimes are from *this* one. Somehow, a Woodrow Wilson dime strayed into the other world, and I found it. When I planked it down on your counter for a *Post*, here at the intersection of two alternate worlds, it was like a ticket of admission to this world. And I stepped into it."

"Boy, you're full of it, aren't you, mister? A what kind of paper?"

"*New York Pos—*" I stopped, stared at the pile of papers on his counter, then yanked mine out from under my arm and opened it. The date was today's, all right, but at the very top of the page was a little drawing of the world, the sun shining down on it; *The New York Sun*, it said underneath it. I glanced quickly over the front page, but there was nothing unusual: a couple stabbings and a shooting; a tenement fire; a head-on collision between two stolen cars, each of them, by an amusing coincidence, driven by a nine-year-old girl drugged to the ears; the headline read PRESIDENT MONTIZAMBERT VETOES TAX CUT.

My mind had accepted it, now. There *were* other alternate worlds, and this was one in which the New York *Sun* hadn't gone out of business years ago; it was still being published. And Pierce-Arrow cars were still being made. I existed in this world, too, but things weren't quite the same; I was maybe an inch taller here; my hair was dark brown, and this other me had lived here, of course, all his life. I was beginning to vaguely remember that life now, and I realized I was one of the few people, perhaps the *only* one, who was conscious of *both* alternate worlds, and with memories of each one of them.

I looked up. Herman was staring past my shoulder, and I turned; the same young cop was crossing the street toward us, pretending to stroll but moving pretty fast, and I knew Herman had beckoned him over. Just as casually but just as fast, I strolled to a cab parked on Forty-second Street a dozen yards from the corner. It was headed west, and I got in saying, "Straight ahead, and in a hurry," and as the meter went down and the cab pulled away from the curb I looked out the back window. The cop and Herman, leaning far out over his counter, were staring after me, and I put both fingers in my mouth, stretching the sides far out, crossing my eyes, and stuck out my tongue at them.

We went barreling along the street at just about ninety-five miles an hour, the lights changed, we stopped in six feet, and I sat back, relieved that this New York wasn't basically different from the other. "You still have Central Park?" I said, and the driver looked at his mirror.

"What're you, mister, some kind of wise guy?"

"No, not at all; I'm from out of town. Haven't been here for years, is all."

"Well, we still got it; wha'd' you think?"

"My god, *look!*" I pointed; half a dozen young women had come out of an office building and were crossing in front of the cab.

"At what?"

"Their skirts! Oh, boy, I thought *mini*skirts were short, but look at *that!*"

He shrugged. "So they lowered their skirts this year; so what?"

"*Lowered!?*"

"Yeah. How far out of town you come from, New Zealand?"

"I don't know," I said happily, my head out the window to stare back at the ladies, "but believe me, it's good to be back!"

The light changed, we started up, and I sat watching the automobiles and streetcars flow past. "Hey! You've still got *street*cars!"

"Well, of course! They wanted to get rid of them, said buses were cheaper, but the public wouldn't stand for that, naturally."

"They wouldn't? Amazing."

"Amazing? Mister, I don't know where you come from, but in New York we don't believe in getting rid of everything the minute it gets a little old. People *like* to have streetcars around."

"Oh, me, too! Me, too. Tell me—does Pennsylvania Station still stand? Firm, true, and pigeon-fouled?"

"Yeah, why not?"

"And where's Madison Square Garden?"

"Right where it's always been, buddy; some things never change." He slowed, and stopped for a light.

"This Madison Avenue?"

"Yep."

I sat far forward, looking up Madison to Forty-sixth Street, and there it stood, snow-white and pretty as a wedding cake, looking just as I remembered it the day my father took me to lunch there when I was six years old, and I shook my head in happy astonishment. "The old Ritz Hotel," I murmured. "Don't tell me the Brevoort is—"

"Still there, Mac," he said, starting up across Madison, "and always will be. Can't tear them down; they been classified as municipal monuments the way they been doin' in Europe for years."

I said, "Well, friend, this is a nice place to visit, but I'd sure like to live here. *Wow*, would you look at *those* skirts!"

"Last year's, last year's; way out of style. Look, mister, I don't care myself, you understand, but you going anywhere in particular?"

I didn't answer; I was on the very edge of the seat, staring straight ahead, mouth open with astonishment. "Yeah," I said then, "let me out ahead. On the other side of Fifth. I be Billy-be-damned if I don't ride one of those," and I nodded at the fine old double-decker Fifth Avenue bus with the open seats on top, that at this moment was trundling across the intersection of Forty-second and Fifth.

On the west corner of Fifth I stood waiting for the next bus, glancing all around; this was fun. Things looked about the same, yet just a little different; the street signs, for example, fastened overhead to the lamppost beside me were white numerals and letters on a bright red background. The cars moving past were Buicks, Chevrolets, Fords, Oldsmobiles, all looking familiar—though not quite. But I also saw a Winton, a Reo, and a Braden. Although I watched carefully, I saw no Hondas, Toyotas, Subarus, none at all. I happened to glance west on Forty-second, and way up, near Broadway, I saw a big movie marquee. Squinting, I could just make out what it said: ELVIS PRESLEY in GOOD-BYE, MR. CHIPS, and I was more pleased than I'd have imagined that in this alternate world old Elvis was still around.

The bus came, I stepped on, paid my fare, and as it started up I climbed the winding stairs to the top. I got a seat near the front, and it was great, riding along up above Fifth on an open-top bus the way I'd done when I was a kid, and I wondered why the New York I knew had ever allowed them to be discarded. It occurred to me that no sensible individual among us would ever run his own life in always the cheapest possible way. As individuals, all of us keep at least some old things for the sheer love of them. Instead of invariably acting in the cheapest possible way, we permit ourselves a few luxuries at least. So why should a city, which is only the sum of us, act as no one of us, even the poorest, ever would? Why should the pleasure of riding an open-topped bus on a fine day be denied us just to save a few lousy dollars? Who saved them, I wondered for the first time, and what did they do with them, that I should have had to give up this? Why, in my New York, shouldn't these buses have been saved as San Francisco had saved at least some of its cable cars, to the joy of all but the unbleeding hearts who cared for no one and nothing but money and themselves? There were alternate worlds in more senses than one, and it occurred to me that my New York needn't have been so damned destructive of the little things that make life worth living.

The ride was fun. Most of the street looked as I'd last known it: the main Public Library was there; Lord & Taylor's; nearly all the buildings I passed were familiar to me. But here and there were some new ones, or at least new to me; one of them, just past Thirty-ninth Street, I knew I'd never seen before in my life although it was obviously at least thirty years old. At Thirty-fourth the Empire State Building stood where it belonged, on the southwest corner, and it looked the same as ever—or did it? I stared up at it, trying to decide; was it maybe half a dozen stories shorter?

At Twenty-eighth I got off, walked east, crossed Madison, and I had actually turned in a step or two toward the door of my apartment building near the middle of the block before I glanced up and saw that it wasn't there. There was an apartment building, all right; an ordinary-looking building of brick with steel-casement windows, double glass doors opening into a lobby in which I could see a bank of potted plants. And the number in gold leaf on the glass above the doors was mine— mine in the other alternate world, at least. But in this world it wasn't the same building, and I stood gaping at it. The glass doors pushed open, a uniformed doorman walked out, frowned at me, and came over. "Looking for someone?"

I nodded doubtfully. "How long has this been here?"

"The building?"

"Yeah."

He shrugged. "It was here when I came, and I've worked here six years. Who you looking for?"

"Bennell. Benjamin Bennell."

The doorman shook his head.

"You sure? I could have sworn he lived at this address."

"Sure I'm sure. I know every tenant in the building; no one here by that name."

"Then I don't know where to go," I said wonderingly, and pronouncing the words made the truth of them sweep over me. "My god, *I don't know where to go.*" For a moment or so I just looked at him blinking; then I was able to think again. "Do you have a phone book?"

He nodded, and I followed him into the building lobby. From the shelf under his little wall desk he brought out a Manhattan phone book, and—my hand trembled as I turned the pages—I looked up Bennell. There were half a dozen of them, and after *Alfred N, Andrew W, Ann,* and *Barney,* I found *Bennell Benj* 560 E 62 539-0090.

"Find him?"

I looked up at the doorman, a little dazed. "Yeah. Looks like he lives on Sixty-second Street. And you know something? I'm beginning to remember the building." I stood frowning, concentrating on this, the memory coming clearer. Slowly I said, "It's new. Only a year or so old . . . set well back from the sidewalk . . . lots of glass and aluminum . . . little spindly trees at the entrance." Then I realized. "Hell, I ought to remember it!" I said, slapping my forehead, laughing at myself. "I go there every night!"

I didn't even bother trying to explain that. I just yanked a bill from my wallet, slapped it into the doorman's hand, and was out of there running down the street toward Lexington Avenue before he could say anything; if, indeed, he had anything particular in mind. I got a cab at the corner, we tore up Lexington at just under takeoff speed, east on Sixty-second Street; then I got out at a corner, walked half a dozen steps, and there it was, all right, directly beside the East River: 560, glass-and-aluminum front, set well back from the walk, a beautifully clipped little tree on each side of enormous double glass doors.

I stood and looked at it; I lifted my head and looked up the front to the roof; then I closed my eyes, tapped my forehead gently with my fingertips, and opened my eyes again. The building was still there, and I walked on to the glass doors, pushed through, and stopped in the lobby, which I vaguely remembered.

Ahead, across the gray carpet, the elevator doors stood open and—frightened, wary—I walked over to them, hesitated, then stepped in. My hand went out to press the button; then it stopped in midair while I stood trying to think. Nothing came to mind, and I stepped out, walked back across the lobby to the bank of mailboxes, and among the other printed cards found *Benjamin Bennell*, 14A. Back in the elevator my finger touched button 14, hesitated, then jabbed, and the doors began sliding shut. At the last instant I tried to stop them, but it was too late. They closed, and the elevator rose, carrying me toward—I glanced upward because I could almost, but not quite, remember.

The door to 14A stood slightly ajar, and I stopped in the hall and looked at it. With the tip of my forefinger I pushed it open a little wider and peeked in. I saw a magnificent living room, furnished in what I thought was French Provincial, though I'm not too sure about terms like that. It seemed absolutely new and strange to me, but then, after I had peered in a moment or so, my head began to nod; it was all beginning to seem familiar. It was the feeling, upon coming into a place you know you're entering for the first time, of nevertheless having been here before, and I pushed the door open a little more and stepped in.

It was a beautiful room with a tremendous view of the river, and it was empty; I searched it quickly with my eyes, then eased the door closed behind me. Then I actually stood watching my own hands in astonishment. One of them reached across my chest, pulled the newspaper out

from under my arm, and tossed it over onto the top of a white Steinway
grand piano with the ease of old habit. The other hand reached up, took
off my hat, and scaled it expertly onto a table in the hall at the front
door. Then a woman's voice called from the kitchen. "That you, dear?"
she said.

CHAPTER FIVE

I couldn't answer; my throat closed, and I ran back to the front door. There I stopped, my hand on the knob; I didn't know what to do or say, and I turned to look back at the kitchen door. "Ben," the voice repeated, "is that *you?*" and my head nodded, my lungs inhaled, and my voice spoke.

"Yes, darling, it's me; I'm home," I heard myself say. A refrigerator door slammed in the kitchen, a spoon clattered on the enamel top of a stove, and high heels crossed linoleum toward the closed kitchen door—and me.

I stood like a hypnotized bird; I forgot to breathe. Who in the world was coming through that door? Who in *this* world? It swung open toward me; I saw fingers on its edge, a flash of green skirt, then a woman was crossing the living room toward me: a tall young woman, wide-hipped but thin, lean-faced, very, very good-looking, and with dark-red hair. "Tessie!" I yelled, and she stopped abruptly.

"Well, who in the fat hell *else* were you expecting? Or should I say *hoping* to see?"

I stood waggling a hand in protest until I was able to speak. "Believe me, there's *nobody* I'd rather see," I said then. Looking her over, head to foot then back again, enjoying the trip a little more each time, I suddenly grinned. "My god, what a preposterously good-looking female you are!" I said, and she walked up to me, stood very close, lifted her lovely freckled face to mine, and as my eyes began closing in swooning anticipation she sniffed my breath.

"No," she said, shrugging thoughtfully, "you're sober," and started to turn away.

"Hey! You didn't kiss me hello."

"Oh. Yeah. How could I possibly have forgotten that?" She gave me a dismal peck on the cheek, turning away in almost the same motion, and my arms reached out and grabbed her. Then, that long lush length of scenic womanhood in my arms, I gave her a kiss that would have been censored from a porn movie. It lasted, I estimate, an hour and forty-five minutes during the last half of which she sighed a little, squirmed a little, then responded deliriously; air tanks finally exhausted, we rose to the surface just in time to escape the bends. Tess stood blinking at me then, her hands rising to push a few pounds of hair out of her eyes, and eventually she recalled how to formulate words. "Good god almighty!" she said. "What the hell has got into you!"

"Nothing that hasn't been there since I was thirteen years old. Why? What's wrong? Guy comes home to something as fantastically assembled as you, my good, good friend, and what's he supposed to do? Sit down and read the paper or something?"

"Well, that's exactly what you've *been* doing, kiddo, every night starting a month after our honeymoon a hundred and five years ago!" Then she smiled. "But don't think I'm complaining," she murmured, stepping close, and poured herself against me from shoulder to ankle like a giant pitcherful of hot fudge.

As though by magic we found ourselves wafted effortlessly to the davenport, and there we kissed without breathing, absorbing air through vestigial gills. The legerdemain continued; having done nothing I could recall to bring this about, we found ourselves comfortably lying at full length. "Ben, darling," she said presently, her lashes sweeping her cheeks as her eyes fluttered, "I left dinner on the stove."

"Let it burn, too," I said. "Oh boy, oh boy, oh boy, oh *boy!*" My eyes blinked lazily, and I found myself staring at Tessie's entrancingly freckled shoulder off which her blouse seemed somehow to have slipped. "Hey," I said, "the Big Dipper!"

"What, darling?"

"Half a dozen of your freckles—they form the Big Dipper."

"Oh, yes. Look a little lower, and you can see Orion."

"I will, I will! Then on to other galaxies!" I studied the Big Dipper, Orion, then Gemini, Sagittarius, Leo, and was looking for the Southern Cross when my eyes blurred. Blinking to clear them, I glanced up—I was lying on the inside of the davenport as it happened—and there standing on the rug, transparent, furious, arms folded in rage, foot tapping, eyes flashing ghostly sparks, stood Hetty.

It was a figment of conscience, of course, and instantly disappeared as I jerked with a shock equivalent to six thousand volts applied to a shaved scalp and wet soles, spilling Tessie, a veritable Niagara of goodies, over the edge of the davenport. I grabbed instinctively, yanking her back before she could actually drop, and by sheer strength held her there on the knife edge of balance. She took this for passion, responding with girlish abandon by pulling me toward her, and the davenport slowly tipped up onto its front legs, then dumped us onto the floor and rolled over us like a tent. "How perfectly di*sgusting!*" it seemed to me I could hear Hetty saying. I yelled, "Something's burning!" and Tessie rolled right on out from under the overturned davenport, landing on her feet and running toward the kitchen.

She was gone, I would say, just under three seconds, during which I gestured apologetically and helplessly at the indignant, transparent Hetty. Tessie, sprinting, came back even faster than she'd left, yelling, "I turned everything off; we'll have dinner later! When it's cooler!" But in those two and six-tenths seconds I had moved even faster, heaving the davenport upright, running across the room, snatching the evening paper from the piano, then hurtling back through the air in a sitting position to land on the davenport apparently reading just as Tess skidded into sight around the corner from the kitchen.

She sat down next to me, fitting herself to my right side like spray paint. I felt the column of her breath, essence of a thousand springs, press my cheek, and Hades—not hot and sulphurous but cozy and perfumed—yawned at my feet. My fists up at ear level, I had the evening paper clutched in both hands, almost wrapped around my head. "Good god, they've torn down Brooklyn Bridge!" I babbled.

Zephyr-borne words floated erotically into my ear. "So you like coming home to me? You haven't said so in years . . . "

"Central Park invaded by giant ants! Macy's blown up!"

"Preposterously good-looking, am I? Darling, look: here's Scorpio! And Sirius!"

"Library sold to Burger King!"

I heard the click of metal on the wood surface of the end table beside us, the preliminary *snick-snick* of a pair of scissors; then a horizontal slit appeared in my newspaper, was immediately enlarged by two hooked fingers, then filled by an enormous jewellike brown eye which stared into mine, then slowly winked.

I surrendered. I plumped for the life of sin, heigh-ho, turned and gathered up that big bundle of joy, mentally screaming to Hetty for forgiveness, when all of a sudden it really dawned on me: for the first time I understood that it was *actually true in this world*, and I yelled it aloud. "Hey, we're MARRIED, aren't we?" and Tessie drew back to stare at me. "As a matter of fact," I said wonderingly, "not only are you and I *married* in this world, long since, but I've never even *met* Het—"

"Never met who?"

"Never met anyone, Taffyapple, as packed with enriched goodness as you. Imagine us *married*! Holy cow, it means this is okay! For a moment there, I almost forgot."

"Well, forget again, handsome," she murmured, closing her eyes, I closed mine, and what then transpired was so good it would require not only new words to describe, but eleven new letters in the alphabet.

We had dinner on the balcony overlooking the river. Tonight Tess had candles on the table, the living-room lights off. There was wine, it was balmy outside, and a long block away we could hear a vague murmur, the sound of the Second Avenue el, and I said, "Hear that, *ma petite?* It is the whisper of the Seine," and when she looked at me to smile, her eyes were awash with love.

"Tonight it doesn't seem that we've been married for years," Tess said. "It's like a honeymoon. Remember the darling way you proposed?"

"Good lord! Don't tell me it was . . . ?"

"And I've still got it." She stood, walked to a closet beside the front door, fumbled on the top shelf, and—I'd known she would, of course— came back opening a familiar green box: in this world I'd still been going with Tessie when I'd wandered through Macy's and seen the stationery display. "Such a charming idea," she said, sitting down and opening the lid. "My name as it would be if I married you." She sat brushing her fingertips over the engraving. "The very moment I saw it, I knew I was going to accept."

I reached over and put my hand on hers, lying on the tabletop, the way they do in the brandy ads. I said, "Terrible price to pay just to make your name match ten bucks' worth of stationery."

She turned her hand over and squeezed mine. "I'm so happy tonight I don't know what to say. Imagine feeling the way we do, four years, five months, and twenty-two days after we were married."

"Well, I can tell you truthfully," I told her truthfully, "that for me it's as though the honeymoon had just begun." From a corner of my eye I thought I saw a movement, the indignant swish of a departing skirt. But when I turned quickly no one was there, and now I remembered that in this world not only had I never met Hetty, but she might never even have been born. With my conscience lying on its back in a hammock sipping a tall cool glass of iced absinthe, I smiled at Tessie. "Tired, darling?" I asked.

"No," she said, pushing back her chair, so we went to bed.

CHAPTER   SIX

In the morning, after Tess served me a breakfast of fantastically delicious toast and coffee, I rode fearlessly downstairs in the automatic elevator, together with several other tenants: a famous Metropolitan Opera soprano; several members of the Rockefeller family; a maharajah in full costume. I bowed them out before me, then walked on across the lobby and out into an absolutely wizard spring day.

The branches of the two skinny little trees beside the doors were loaded with birds: a Great Blue Heron, a Purple Gallinule, a Bird of Paradise, a Roseate Spoonbill, a robin, a Penguin, two Marbled Godwits, a Grosbeak, a Free-flying Ferruginous Duck, and a large number of tropical macaws never before seen this far north. My own joyous whistle was instantly joined by theirs; we all stood for several seconds warbling together in tribute to the day. Then I tipped my hat, walked on out to the public sidewalk, and stopped, not knowing which way to turn.

I walked back into the building lobby, nearly bumping into Sam Donaldson on his way out. Inside I turned, walked out again, whistling even more joyously, and a number of the birds flew over to perch momentarily on my shoulders and hat. Again I walked on, this time refusing to let thought intrude, continuing to whistle mindlessly, relying entirely on habit. At the sidewalk, I noted, looking down with interest, that my feet and legs turned unhesitatingly toward Fifth Avenue, just as they did, I remembered now, every morning.

When I reached Fifth, a southbound double-decker was pulling away, and I jogged athletically across the street—I seemed to be in better condition in this world—hopped aboard, and climbed to the top, still whistling. Two men were just getting up from a front seat, and I edged forward past them and sat down. Then I rode down that wonderful sunlit old street, sniffing the delicious blue-tinted air, happy as mortal man is meant to be.

After a block or so I looked behind me and saw hardly a face: nearly everyone was reading a newspaper or turning the pages of one; the few who weren't sat staring vacantly at the passing sidewalk. I reached into my pocket, brought out a baton, stood up, and said, "All right! Attention please, everyone," rapping on the wooden back of my seat; everyone looked up. "This is much too nice a day to sit reading a newspaper. Put them away, please, take a deep breath of this glorious air, and—all together now!—join me in song!" I blew a note on a pitch pipe, stood with baton poised, then brought it down decisively, and rumbling along Fifth Avenue in that fine old bus, we sang "Oh, What a Beautiful Morning!" and before we reached the second chorus people on the sidewalks were waving at us, and a bus passing the other way joined in.

We reached Forty-second Street on the last notes of "Blue Skies," I turned the baton over to a Wall Street executive, and hopped off the bus, waving; they all waved back. The light turned green, they rolled across Forty-second Street and on down Fifth singing "Hello, Dolly," while I walked east toward Lexington, leaping into the air every now and then and clicking my heels together, a trick I'd never before been able to do.

In the lobby of the Doc Pepper Building I had to step aside for a moment out of the stream of people heading toward the elevators, and stand frowning, unable to remember my floor. Then, as I'd done earlier, I walked back to the door and came in again, whistling quietly, looking happily around, letting habit run things. I stepped confidently into an elevator, and stood watching my forefinger reach out and press the button marked 11. At the eleventh floor I got off, walked down the hall, turned and pushed through a pair of glass doors—genuine cut-glass, each marked with a large gold N—and stepped into a big lobby. There was a receptionist's desk from the Palace of Versailles before me, but no one there at the moment, and I stood looking around.

It was an expensive lobby: walls of wood panels alternating with slabs of polished green marble matching the green-and-white-patterned carpeting; a crystal chandelier. I turned and walked down a corridor into a large square area of stenographers' desks in rows, office doors around the outer edges. I walked past doors, each bearing a name and title, the girls at their desks smiling, saying, "Morning, Mr. Bennell!" As I passed them, the successive doors increased in quality, width, and even, it seemed to me, in height, until I came to one of carved teak, bearing my name in inch-high gold metal letters.

I walked in, tossing my hat expertly and out of long habit onto the head of a life-size, full-color, photo cutout—an advertising display— standing in a corner of my office. It was of a splendidly rounded girl wearing feathers in her hair, jewel-encrusted high heels, and not too much else, actually. She was smiling and stood with a forefinger pointed discreetly at her stomach. From her mouth issued a cardboard cloud, a speech balloon like the kind in comic strips, and I started to read what it said when my office door opened, and my secretary, a lovely flower, said, "They're ready with the new commercial, Mr. Bennell."

I told her to send them in, and sat down behind my free-form desk, glancing at the original Picasso on the wall. Then my door opened, and in stepped a couple of advertising types with eager, clean-cut, corrupt young faces, followed by—Bert Glahn, as I lived and forgot to breathe! Bert was my *boss* in the other alternate world, and I almost jumped to my feet, but I stopped myself because something about him was incredibly different.

Not only was he unctuously bobbing his head and nervously dry-washing his hands, but—suddenly I realized it!—he was a good six inches shorter! As Bert humbly wished me good morning, and turned to fit a reel of video tape he'd brought with him into the works of a huge viewer across the office, I stood up, leisurely, majestically, walked over to watch, and surreptitiously measured my height against his. I was an easy three inches taller, and at least as heavy; and while Bert was still handsome enough, he looked older, more haggard, and his suit didn't fit very well. Whatever gene or chromosome of Bert Glahn's had been added or left out in this happy alternate world had cut him down to the size and manner appropriate to his status here of my assistant.

"Ready if you are, Mr. Bennell, sir!" said faithful old Bert, bowing, scraping, and tugging at his forelock, while one of the young ad-agency men ran across the room to draw the expensive drapes. I allowed as how I was ready, and the other young ad man touched his control, and the screen came to life.

A close head-and-shoulders shot of a doctor appeared. You knew he was a doctor because he wore a pair of heavy glasses in his hand, and a high-necked jacket of the kind worn by doctors, barbers, and Russian politicians. He had thick, wavy gray hair, a handsome face inscribed with dignified lines, and was obviously either head of the Royal College of Physicians and Surgeons or of the world's most expensive fat clinic; he was smiling with the friendly open candor of an extreme right-wing fanatic.

Beside him was a cardboard display carton which was tilted toward the viewer. The carton was packed with a dozen small pink boxes wrapped in polyethylene, and the back of the carton rose up to form an advertising display-panel, showing a lovely young girl in a thin nightgown pointing to some words in a graceful flowing script.

From the carton the doc picked up one of the small pink boxes, opened a flap, and rolled out onto his palm a little cylindrical object in pink cellophane, which he unwrapped, then held up to the camera; it was a small plug of pink wax looking very much like a wax earplug. In a deep we-have-discovered-the-cure-for-cancer voice, he was saying,

"We in science wholeheartedly recommend to the women of America
. . . " Now he pointed to the display panel, which came up big to fill the
screen so that you could read the printed script, his voice continuing off
screen for the benefit of viewers who couldn't read: " . . . *Navel-O-No
for beauty, health, and to show that you care!*" The display panel grew
some more till the girl's printed head filled it; then the head came to life
and movement. She smiled, and in a soft lilting voice said, "Yes, ladies,
Navel-O-No, the antiseptic flesh-colored putty that helps YOU put up a
better front!" The camera moved down to her stomach, and—it was
done beautifully and with exquisite taste—you could see through her
filmy nightgown, and her stomach was absolutely smooth and rounded.
Her voice, continuing off screen as we stared at that lovely unblemished
belly, said, "Smoothes invisibly into unsightly navels! Fits any size, any
shape, to form a new, flawlessly rounded LOVELIER surface! Used by
stage, screen, and TV stars!" The doctor's off-screen voice said sternly,
"TODAY, banish lint-filled germ traps! Fill that ugly gaping crater!"
The girl's voice came in again as the camera moved up from her stomach
to her beautiful ethereal face. "Look your *smoothest*," she said, "for
HIM! Navel-O-No tonight!"

Smiling, she walked off screen left as a lovely Polynesian girl, similarly
dressed, crossed the screen from the right. "Also available," she was
saying, and she twitched her hips so that her gown opened momentarily
to reveal a marvelously unbroken expanse of dusky skin, "in Tahiti tan!"
A beautiful Chinese girl following directly behind her murmured, " . . .
in sunset yellow!" demonstrating as she walked how effective this shade
was, too. " . . . midnight black!" said a magnificent black girl as she
crossed the screen. "And in the West," said a terrific-looking Indian girl
in full tribal headdress and almost nothing else, "dawnblush red!" She
moved off in a cute little war dance, thrusting her unblemished red
stomach forward at each step. To soft harp music, the screen went black
and the film ended.

"Terrific!" I said, leaping to my feet and walking over to shake the
hand of one of the ad-agency men. "Absolutely great, Perce!" I said,
remembering his name, which was Perce Shelley. "You, too, Orville!" I
said to the other.

"Mostly your idea," one of them said.

"Sure, but you could have muffed the execution. Thanks a million."
They left, and I walked over to the cardboard cutout of the girl pointing
to her stomach, and—it was all coming back to me now; I was general
manager of this great company—I read the words printed in the cloudlike
speech balloon at the side of her head. It said, *Wilma Shakes-heare,*

Queen of the Skin Divas, says, "I *look* better, *feel* better—with Navel-O-No! And men just *love* its friendly fragrance. Ends cigar-ash nuisance, too!" Sales, I saw from a chart on the wall, were up 13 percent in the last quarter, which meant my stock options had become operative, and turning back to my desk, I knew that in this world I had found my metier.

At my free-form desk—beautiful, but with a tear-shaped hole in the middle through which I tended to occasionally knock one or more of my telephones with my elbow—I read my mail, dictated some replies to the lovely-limbed goddess who was my secretary, made a phone call to Frank Flannel in Production, and what with one thing and another it was nearly noon before I even leaned back in my chair to stretch. For a moment I sat there, glancing around my office, admiring the Jacob Epstein bust in one corner and the tremendous view of Manhattan to the south. Then I grinned, and on impulse pulled the Manhattan phone book over. I turned to the S's, ran a forefinger down the first column, and sure enough, though the address was different, there it was: Saf-T Products.

"Safety Products," the switchboard girl said when I called, and I asked for the head of the company.

When he came on I said, "This is Ben Bennell."

"Who?" said the old familiar permanently irritated voice.

"Ben Bennell. Don't you know me?"

"No! Who the hell are you!"

"I'm the world's leading expert on pronunciation, and I called to tell you that S-a-f spells *saff*, you illiterate, power-drunk boob! It does not, and never can, spell *safe*; it's *SAFF!* Now, I'm warning you, either change the spelling or the pronunciation, or get out of town within twenty-four hours."

I hung up feeling great, pulled a sheet of paper toward me, sliding it around the tear-shaped hole, and in elaborate shaded italics printed, *Wonderful (alternate) World, I love you! Benjamin B. Bennell.* I wheeled my big shiny private duplicating machine over to the window, inserted the sheet, spun the Dil-A-Copy to 5,000, opened the window, and left for lunch, the obedient machine rhythmically rolling copies out into the sunlit polluted air to swoop, glide, and dance over Manhattan like giant confetti.

The day flashed by, and at five-thirty I rode downstairs, anxious and happy to hurry home to Tess and renew our glorious acquaintance. Stepping out into the Doc Pepper lobby, I glanced into the building drugstore and on impulse turned in. It looked just about the same, it seemed to me, as the Chrysler Building drugstore. I glanced around, and yes, there it stood: the bargain counter of various doodads such as pillboxes. I began poking through the stuff and found it right away: the little gilt pillbox with the jewel-encrusted top. Walking toward the counter with it, I looked for the candy display but it wasn't there.

"Can I help you, sir?" a man's voice said from the counter; it was a familiar voice, though I couldn't place it, and I looked up at him to answer. But I didn't speak; I stopped and stood staring at the face over the tan pharmacist's jacket.

"Good lord," I said finally, "you look just like Paul Newman!"

"I *am* Paul Newman," he said, frowning, and he pointed to a framed document hanging on the wall above his head. I looked at it: it said he was a graduate pharmacist from NYU, licensed to dispense prescriptions in the State of New York. Just over a large red seal, *Paul Newman* was lettered in black gothic.

"I see," I was able to say after blinking at the certificate for a while. "Where's the candy?" He pointed to a counter; I stepped over to it and found a small box of nougats. Opening it as I walked, I took it back to the cash register, and said, "Mr. Newman, have you ever considered acting in the movies?"

"At my age? Don't be silly. Now, what can I do for you?"

I pushed the nougat into the pillbox; it was an even tighter fit than the last time I'd done this, and when I squashed the lid down, the nougat overflowed a bit, and Newman stared at it in distaste, then looked up at me with the same expression. Humbly I said, "Could you gift-wrap this, please?"

"Glenn!" he called across the store, and a young woman answered. "Could you come over here, please? And gift-wrap this—package? For the . . . gentleman?" He walked off, shaking his head, while I stared at the floor in embarrassment. I heard the young woman arrive, glanced up at her, and once again my mouth fell open.

"Saints preserve us," I said, "but aren't you Glenn Close?"

"No, I am not," she said icily. "My first name is Glenn, but my last name is Heppelwhite. What do you want wrapped?"

I nodded even more humbly at the box. She leaned forward to stare down at it as though it were a freshly killed roach, and I said, "It's a box of candy. For a dieting midget," and she looked up at me, her lip curling. "There's some gold ribbon in there," I murmured in utter abasement, and she turned, opened the drawer I had pointed to, poked through it suspiciously, then pulled out a length of gold ribbon, looking surprised. She wrapped my package very rapidly then, refusing my offer of a nougat with a curt shake of her head.

Going out the door, I glanced back. Both Paul and Glenn were staring after me, and I stepped up my pace, turning to face front just in time to avoid banging into a policeman in a brown derby: the same one I'd talked to before. "Hi, there!" I said sickly, and—fortunately the light at the corner was green—I trotted across Lexington toward Fifth before he could think of a reason to stop me.

Then, once more, I rode along Fifth Avenue through a warm spring afternoon on an open-topped bus. The sports page of the guy next to me headlined a spectacular ninth-inning home run, saving the game for the Giants: the *New York* Giants, I suddenly noticed, making a resolution to see lots of home games. I smiled serenely; I was on my way back to that vast expanse of glowing womanhood, Tessie; and all in all it was a fine world to be alive in, in spite of Paul Newman.

Tess loved the pillbox. While I stirred up a pitcherful of transfusions in the kitchen, she unwrapped it, squealed with pleasure at sight of the little gilt box, rapturously fingered the fake jewels on the lid, then opened the box and shrieked with amusement at the candy inside. She followed me into the living room, saying, "Ben, you're an absolute *darling!*"

I grinned at her as she sat down on the davenport, and poured and handed her a drink. She took a sip and shuddered happily. Her pillbox lay on a table beside her, and her glance lingered on it as she set her drink down. "Remember the sweet little obscene notes you used to hide in my gloves?" she murmured, and I nodded gleefully. "And the fake tattoo I thought was real, your initials and mine intertwined in a heart? What a place to put it!" I smiled, nodding reminiscently, and she reached out to touch the pillbox again. "And now this, just like the things you always used to do." She frowned in puzzlement and murmured almost to herself, "I don't understand it," and looked over at me again. "Ben, how come you're so sweet to me all of a sudden?"

Of course I couldn't tell her, so as a mild little joke—I have a fair enough voice and can carry a tune—I answered with the words and tune of an old song. "Because 'I've got you under my skin! I've got you deep in the heart of me. So deep in my heart you're really a part of me!'"

Her lovely brows shot up in astonishment. "Ben! What a perfectly *darling* little song! Did you just think of it?"

For a good three or four seconds I stared at her without answering. Then I said slowly, "Tell me, Tess, did you ever hear of Cole Porter?"

"Who?"

"He's a composer."

"No. *Ralph* Porter, naturally, but not Cole."

"Yeah, I just thought of it," I said. "Sitting here looking at you, pet, the words and tune came drifting into my head. Ever hear of Rodgers and Hammerstein?"

"Who are they?"

"A law firm. Listen, here's a song I worked out at the office today, just thinking about you and how we met and all. Want to hear it?"

"You know I do!"

I walked over to the piano, and sat down, Tess following to stand beside me. I struck a preliminary chord, then looked up at Tess. " 'Some enchanted evening,' " I sang slowly, looking deep into her eyes, " 'you will see a stranger . . . across a crowded room . . . ' " I never finished the song. When I reached " 'Then fly to her side . . . and make her your ownnnnn!' " Tess fainted and fell into my arms.

CHAPTER SEVEN

"Mirror, mirror, on the imported-tile wall," I said one morning after I'd been here in this alternate world a few weeks, "who's the biggest success of all?"

"In just what way?" it answered craftily.

But I was equally crafty, alert for the put-down. "Oh, I don't know," I said casually, "let's say maritally."

"Well, we're still checking," it said grudgingly, "but right now it looks as though you are. Some guy in Eagle River, Wisconsin, came pretty damn close, though! If only he didn't say things were 'yay high' and—"

"Never mind! If I edged him out, that's all that matters. Now, how about businesswise?"

"Actual or potential?"

"Potential! I know there are plenty guys who've made it a lot bigger than I have *so far*, but—"

"All right, all right! Then you are."

"Okay," I said, and snapped my fingers commandingly, "let's have it, then."

"Any other category you'd like to ask about?"

I just smiled. "Not just now," I said, and snapped my fingers again. Two Hands in gold-embroidered sleeves descended and reluctantly set a fresh-picked laurel wreath on my brow. I examined it in the mirror, then tilted it to a slightly more jaunty angle. The Hands came abruptly down again to set it straight, and I left it that way, wearing it humbly but with justifiable pride all through my shower.

Because I deserved it; that showed in a million ways. A few minutes later, for example, while dressing, I managed—even though this bedroom offered plenty of leeway for coeducational dressing—to bump into my wife as much as ever. More than ever. But here in this best of many possible worlds, it elicited not muttered curses but happy giggles.

It showed in startling contrast between me and other husbands on our floor. Opening my door one morning, I saw ffoulke-Wilkinson, in 14C, step out into the hall, checking through his alligator-hide attaché case. His wife—in hair curlers and without makeup looking like Mrs. Dorian Gray, senior—gave him a peck on the cheek which, by some complicated mental trick, he was able to ignore, continuing to look through his case as though she didn't exist, as—for him—maybe she no longer did. He snapped his case shut and walked on to the elevator without a glance at or word to her.

I heard Hildebrand, in 14B across the hall, come out one morning just before I opened my door, and if I hadn't understood English I might have been touched: from somewhere inside the apartment his wife called sweetly, "Don't hurry back, darling!" and he replied liltingly, "Drop dead, my dear!" Then the door slammed.

And now today, waiting at the elevator, I saw Yaphank and his wife appear in the doorway of 14D at the end of the hall. "Bye, darling!" each of them called as he turned toward the elevator, and he looked back, smiling. Each blew a kiss to the other, but this time as he turned away he made a horrible face, cheeks inflated, tongue protruding, eyes crossed. Behind his back, as she closed the door, she was sticking her tongue out at him and, thumb on her nose, waggling her hand.

At the door I kissed Tessie goodbye at nine o'clock sharp, and again at a quarter of ten, realizing that I was the only guy on this floor— maybe in the whole world—who was sometimes forty minutes late for work in the morning just from kissing his wife goodbye.

Leaving the building, finally, I greeted my bird friends as they fluttered round my head; like bird-lovers everywhere, I'd learned their names. "Hello, Edward," I said. "Good morning, Bernice!" On the bus, I smiled and nodded at most of the other upper-deck regulars, then sat down and read the ads on the backs of the seats: for Yucatan Gum; Maxwell House Toothpaste; "Painless Don" Regan's E-Z Terms Dentistry. Passing the end of the Park at Fifty-ninth Street, I glanced admiringly at the monument to Winnie Ruth Judd.

At work, I again proved my right to the laurel wreath, which I was still wearing invisibly. Little Bert Glahn was waiting in my office, and we took a cab over to a recording studio in the Fifties; Perce Shelley and Orville from the agency were already there. The Navel-O-No doctor-campaign had upped sales 16 percent—we were beginning to tap the preadolescent market—and now the agency was ready with the follow-up campaign.

The film was completed, and we sat in the studio watching them dub in the sound. On the screen the filmed countdown flicked past; then on cue a gong sounded, and in shivering haunted-house lettering appeared the words *Fascinating Disappearances!* At a floor microphone, a gilt-haired young man in tight pale-green slacks and a fluffy sweater, the sleeves of which were pushed up his forearms, said in a deep ominous masculine voice, "Throughout history there have been *fascinating disappearances!* Where is the *missing Bierce?* Where is the *missing Earhart?* Where is the *missing Crater?*"

The guy at the gong whacked it again, and the scene switched to a fancy boudoir. A beautiful model in a thin negligee stood smiling at us. At another floor mike, a fat lady chewing gum said in a breathy sexy voice, "Yes! Here to enhance milady's charm is the most fascinating disappearance of all! Where is the *missing crater?*" The girl on screen swung her hips, and her negligee ballooned open: she wore feathered mules, brief pants, and a brassiere, and for just an instant as the negligee opened, there was a glimpse of her stomach, smooth as an egg.

Music from a small orchestra at the end of the studio swelled up, and on the screen at the spot where the girl's navel would ordinarily have been visible, a tiny package of Navel-O-No appeared, and enlarged swiftly to fill the entire screen. Then the guy in the green pants came on with a sales pitch, the commercial ended, and they all turned to look at me.

I sat nodding thoughtfully, consideringly, feeling the thrill of power, then made my decision. "Tremendous," I said quietly, and relief filled their eyes. "Subtle, delicate, real creative craftsmanship. Perce, Orville, get a tape ready with sound for a board meeting. They'll like it, I guarantee. What do you have in mind for a follow-up?"

"A terrific variation," Perce said. "Sound of helicopter, and open with a spectacular aerial shot of Vesuvius; a real grabber!"

Lyndon said, "The guy's voice opens with 'A volcano! An *ugly frightening crater!*' Cut to the girl in the negligee as the voice says, 'Until it's extinct!' "

"The girl turns," said Perce Shelley, "her negligee flies open—"

"Yeah, yeah," I said, standing up, "I get it."

"Think they'll do a job saleswise?" Bert said anxiously.

"Yep, this series ought to open up the entire West for us."

"Even Texas?"

"Especially Texas." I turned to walk rapidly out of the studio, my hand brushing my head as though smoothing back my hair; actually, of course, I was adjusting my wreath.

It was a nice day, brisk but sunny, so I walked back to the office with Bert, refusing an offer by the ad-agency boys to carry me. Cutting through Grand Central Station, I caught a glimpse of a familiar-looking curtained booth. It looked a lot like the tell-me-your-troubles booth, but as we came closer, I saw that the sign was red and orange, not blue, and that it said LET'S HEAR YOU BRAG! YOU DESERVE IT!

I sent Bert on ahead to the office and glanced around. No one was looking, so I ducked in, pulled the curtains, dropped in a quarter, and began discussing my marital and business successes in a calm impartial way. The tape reels slowly revolved, and from the speaker in the ceiling a soft, sexy voice murmured, "You don't *mean* it! . . . Oh, god, you're wonderful . . . and so good-looking. . . . I wish I'd seen you first! . . . Kiss me!" and it was worth every penny of the $1.75 I spent before they refused to give me any more quarters at the newsstand.

And yet . . . something was lacking; it was no good trying to pretend. In this world, as in the other, I was still a man unlucky enough to have been born with an unfulfilled need. Successful executive though I was now, I sometimes envied really creative people like Orville and Perce. I was like the occasional man who carries inside him the spirit of a concert pianist but is all thumbs at the keyboard; the urge to bring into this world something that would leave it a better place still nagged at me here as much as in the world in which I knew Nate Rockoski. Now, leaving Grand Central Station and the cozy, curtained little booth to walk on toward my office across Lexington Avenue just ahead, I was reminded of this by one of the curious coincidences in which life abounds. I stopped at the curb, joining a little group waiting for the lights to change, and my eye was caught, as were all others, by a spectacular, candy-striped, stretch Rolls-Royce. It was, I estimated as it approached the corner, about thirty feet long. Then I became aware of excited voices around me saying, "It's *Nate! Nate Rockoski!*"

Sure enough: the lights changed, the Rolls stopped, and there in the back seat I saw him, looking just the same here in this world, except that now he was wearing a silk hat, a long coat with an astrakhan collar, and his chin and clasped hands rested on top of a gold-headed cane. No one crossed the street, everyone stood staring; I felt the awe and wonder of the crowd. He lifted his head to smile and nod benignly, like Queen Elizabeth, and as he moved, his unbuttoned outer coat fell open, and I saw that his obviously expensive suit was patterned with dollar signs. "He's rich, isn't he?" I said to the man next to me, who looked at me, astonished.

"Of course!" he said, and when I asked how Nate had done it, the man said, "Just the way he says he did in this month's *Reader's Digest:* a little effort, a little ingenuity, is all it takes; anyone can do it, he says."

"But what did he *do?*"

"Invented a soft drink, patented a nutty name for it, and oh boy, how the money rolled in."

"What's the drink? I'd like to try it."

I heard mechanism click in a metal box on a standard beside us, the lights about to change, and the man next to me pointed to an enormous neon-lighted billboard on the roof of a building down the block. COCA-COLA, it said, and the traffic light changed. "He used to be poor, a sort of crackpot inventor," the man said, staring lovingly at Nate as the Rolls soundlessly moved forward, "but things have gone better with Coke!"

At the intersection just ahead, a fire truck, its hooter hooting, was about to cross Lex, but the driver saw Nate's Rolls approaching and slammed on his brakes, politely gesturing Nate across first. As the Rolls passed in front of the fire truck, Nate nodded his thanks, touching the brim of his silk hat with the shining gold head of his cane. On the curb with the others, I stood staring after him, then reached to my forehead and removed the wreath. Staring at it for a moment, I saw that its leaves had turned to brown; then I dropped it into a trash can and, as the light changed again, walked on across the street with the others.

I felt better after work: who, on his way home to Tess, would not? And on Forty-second Street I stopped at one of those little places that print fake headlines while you wait. When I got home and Tess came in from the kitchen to pick up the paper I'd just tossed onto the piano, glancing at the headline as she always did, she was astonished to see a double line of large black type spelling out a particularly lurid invitation specifically directed to her; which, blushing prettily, she instantly accepted.

That evening, as I often did, I wandered to the white grand piano, and played a medley of songs I'd written just for Tess, including "Tea For Two," "The Way You Look Tonight," and "You'd Be So Nice to Come Home To." As always, Tess was astonished at how *apt* they were; how out of all the millions of people in the world they seemed to fit us alone. She was so pleased that I sat a little longer, idly fingering chords, humming experimental notes, occasionally muttering a few trial words of verse. And in no more than five or six minutes, while Tess sat on the bench beside me, her eyes shining, I'd worked out another song for her: just a simple little thing which, with equal simplicity, I called "Stardust."

Hell with Nate Rockoski, I thought happily as Tess and I walked hand in hand down the hall to our bedroom: who wants more than this? But the Human Being always wants More Than This, and as I stood in our bedroom unbuttoning my shirt, I still felt a lack in my life. Like any husband anywhere, however happy with his wife, I could and often did carry on routine domestic conversations without engaging the mind at all. Undoing my cuffs, staring absently into space, I murmured, "What'd you say, dear?"

"These stupid buttons," Tess said, and I glanced at her. She was frowning at a button in the palm of her hand; then she twisted her hip attractively to look down at the side of her skirt, from which a short thread stuck up among a row of three or four similar buttons. "They come off all the time, and spoil the line of the skirt besides." I nodded absently, making a sympathetic little murmur about putting in a zipper instead, not even listening to her reply.

And yet some diligent little cell of the brain, resolutely doing guard duty while the others were resting, must have been listening. Because incredible as it sounds, we were in bed, the lights out, my mind on the stars, when it somehow and nevertheless managed to claim my attention. *"What did you say!"* I said to Tess.

"I said, 'Stop that, you fresh thing,' but I was only fooling."

"No, no, I mean *before!*"

"When?"

"When I told you to put a zipper in your skirt, *what did you say?*"

"Why, all I said was 'What's a zipper?' *Ben!* What did you turn on the *light* for? What are you doing with the *phone* book!?"

" 'What's a zipper,' " I quoted happily, the yellow pages a blur as I flipped through them, my creative urge ecstatic. "I am looking for the name and address of the best patent lawyer in town!"

CHAPTER EIGHT

"*You* are! *You* are!" the mirror snarled next morning. "Will you shut *up* about it!" though I hadn't said a word.

"Okay," I said with quiet dignity, "where's the wreath?"

"You got one yesterday. What's the matter? You can't wear a wreath two days?"

I didn't argue; the fact was worth more than the symbol, and my cup was full. There was absolutely *nothing* now that I'd have changed in The Wonderful Alternate World of Ben Bennell. It was perfect, and of course—you've noticed this, too, haven't you?—it is precisely at such a time that Life grins nastily, spits on its hands, picks up the Big Club, and takes aim at your head.

But I'd forgotten that, and the day began blissfully. Outside it was a beautiful morning as I started for the office, and a Brazilian macaw said, "Morning, Ben, you look like ten million. After taxes!" I said, "You, too, Fred; fine feathers make fine birds," and he said, "Hey, pretty good, have to remember that."

On the upper deck of the bus I stood up front, facing the rear, and sounded a note on my pitch pipe. All the newspapers were lowered, and the mighty Hallelujah Chorus of Handel's *Messiah* burst forth. At Forty-second Street I hated to get off because Miss Poindexter, a rather plump, glasses-wearing, but very pleasant computer operator in a Thirty-fourth Street garment factory, was standing in the aisle, a hand on the seat back, the other outflung, in the middle of a marvelous soprano solo rendition of "Ave Maria."

In Grand Central Station I sat down in the booth and dropped in my quarter, but today it rattled right back into the coin-return cup. As the reels began revolving, the sexy voice murmured, "For you, and from now on, darling, it's free."

At the office I phoned and made an appointment with Cox and Box, prominent Madison Avenue patent attorneys; Box's great-great-great grandfather, his secretary informed me, had obtained Whitney's patent on the cotton gin, beating out Benjamin Franklin's lawyer by six and a half all-important minutes. That afternoon when I kept the appointment, although I didn't yet know this, didn't yet feel it, the Big Club swung down toward my head: the young attorney into whose office I was ushered at Cox and Box was Custer Huppfelt!

There was no mistaking him; we'd gone to grade school and high
school in the other alternate world, and I'd known him afterward. And
his smile now, as he stood up from his desk watching me walk into the
office, was the same weary-cynical, look-what-the-cat-dragged-in smile
he'd always had, even in fourth grade, and he lazily put out his hand as
though just barely willing to grant me that boon. *But did I know him in
this world, too!?* I wondered, panically, shaking hands. Custer answered
the question for me. "How are you, Ben?" he said, and then I remembered. Life in the two alternate worlds, as I'd already realized, was more
alike than different, and here, too, Custer and I had gone to school
together, although in this world, I recalled, he'd gone on to study law at
Harvard.

"Nice to see you, Cus," I said, smiling, looking him over. He seemed
the same: tall, thin, good-looking, skin permanently tanned. Except, I
suddenly realized, in the other world Custer was brown-eyed and black-
haired. Here he was blond and blue-eyed, probably because of a pair of
blue genes somewhere in his ancestry.

We reminisced together, then brought each other up to date. He was
new in the firm here, but *extremely* well thought of; probably be made
a partner before long. He still lived in the Village, and he was thinking
about buying a new car. He wasn't married yet, but was seeing a lot of
a girl who was absolutely nuts about him. Finally he remembered,
probably only because I was a client now, to ask how Tess was. Same old
Custer, I thought, in this or any world.

I described my invention, sketching it on the back of an envelope,
and naturally Cus didn't think the zipper would work; I had to admit to
myself that it did sound ridiculous, even to me. Cus didn't think the
name would catch on either, but he agreed to handle it for me and took
my drawing for the patent search and application. It would cost money,
he reminded me, but I didn't care; visionary though I might be, I had
faith in the zipper.

It was odd, what happened then. We'd never been friends; this was
just a guy I'd happened to go to school with, and I hadn't seen him for
quite a while in either world. But when I stood up, there in his office,
time to say goodbye, I suddenly didn't want to lose Custer. Here in this
world, of course, I remembered everything about all my previous life in
it. So did Custer, naturally. But unlike Custer, I also recalled life in
another alternate world—about which the Custer Huppfelt of this world
knew nothing. I still had my memory of that world, so this meeting with
Custer was almost like being in another country and suddenly running
into someone from your old hometown. At home you'd just nod in

passing, but in another country you have dinner together. And now I was more pleased than I'd have thought possible at running into Custer Huppfelt. He played bridge, I remembered, and so did his girl, he said when I asked, so I invited them over for a game that evening; practically insisted, in fact.

Tess was pleased when I told her. We were having dinner, and I said, "You know what we're going to do this evening?" She said, "Of course," and I said, "No; I've invited some people to play bridge."

When the doorbell rang a little after eight, she hurried in from the kitchen where she'd been fixing some refreshments for later. I was sitting at the card table, set up in the middle of the living room; I'd just finished checking the two bridge decks for missing cards and concealed jokers. Waiting, I sat practicing the shuffle in which you bend the deck like an arc in one hand so that the cards flutter up into the other. Tess opened the door, and I heard Custer's voice in the building hallway. Then they all walked into the apartment, I saw them, and the muscles of my hands lost their strength, the cards shooting toward the ceiling in a black-white-and-red spray, because the politely smiling girl standing in my living room with Custer was Hetty.

They turned at the sound and sight of the flying cards, and Custer smiled complacently; he thought I'd let them go purposely, a little joke in tribute to his girl, and he said something mildly humorous which I answered but didn't hear. No senses were working coherently, and certainly my brain wasn't. I was able to press the soles of my shoes against the carpet under the bridge table, causing my body to rise into a gorillalike posture of semi-erectness, staring at Hetty like Quasimodo as played by Lon Chaney. But there was no possible mistake.

There in a pink linen dress, with shoes, purse, and hat to match, blond as ever, small as ever, and thinner by a dozen pounds, stood my wife, and I panicked. Did she know me? Would she shriek in outrage at finding me living here with Tessie? I watched myself walk toward them, a diseased smile on my face. Custer introduced us to Hetty, and when she spoke she put out her hand, and I took it—the hand, I realized, that had stroked my cheek, smoothed my hair, mended my clothes, cooked my meals, tickled me, and once slapped my face. And as I acknowledged our introduction, speaking in tongues, I looked into Hetty's eyes and saw that she didn't know me from Calvin Coolidge.

I couldn't help it: "We've met before, haven't we?" I said.

Hetty frowned consideringly, then shook her head. "No, I don't think so. Where?"

I shrugged a shoulder, smiling, as though I couldn't remember, but I answered. My voice loud in the apartment, hearing every syllable, I said silently, *When we were married! Remember the time you hid all my clothes? And that time in the bathtub* . . . I stopped then because no one was listening.

I know I dealt cards, shuffled, wrote down scores, played hands, sat as dummy. I poured drinks in the kitchen and carried them in. I smiled, answered when spoken to, and even originated a few stupid remarks of my own. But through every instant I was tense with guilt. I could not get rid of the feeling that at any moment Hetty would suddenly look at Tess, then at me, her eyes narrowing in realization that Tess and I were living here in blatant sin, and that she'd burst into tears, violence, or hysterics, or all three. Irrational though I knew the feeling to be, it still seemed incredible that Hetty and I should be sitting here at this table, elbows nearly touching as we sat holding our cards, knees occasionally brushing as we leaned forward to play them, and that—in *this* world— she'd never even set eyes on me until tonight.

Then Tess was dummy while I played the hand, and she went out to the kitchen to bring in a tray of coffee, cups and saucers, and a plate of little frosted cakes she'd gone out and bought right after dinner. Tessie returned, set the tray on the coffee table, then came over to stand behind me, looking at my cards, watching me play the last few tricks. Unexpectedly, I won the final trick, just making the contract and giving us game and rubber. And by way of congratulation Tess leaned down, gave me a quick kiss on the back of the neck, and I leaped straight out of the chair in a convulsion of guilt.

Landing on my feet, I shot a look at Hetty. But she was merely gathering up the cards, smiling fondly at our touching display of domestic concord, and at last I was able to realize the truth: this was Hetty, all right, sitting there in her pink dress, yet she did not know. She knew nothing at all of our life in another alternate world, and I had a sudden rush of wild release. I felt like a kid who suddenly discovers he is miraculously invisible, free to commit any mischief he chooses, and I turned and in apparent response to her kiss on my neck, I grabbed Tess and gave her a big noisy parody of a kiss.

I turned back and found myself grinning at Hetty, I didn't know why; then I realized it was a grin of triumph. This was *fun*, kissing Tessie right out here in the open, knowing it would never occur to Hetty to object, and I did it again. Custer had stood up to stretch; now he grinned. He didn't know the reason for this sudden new game, but he didn't object to joining in. He leaned down, gave Hetty a vigorous kiss, then looked over at me with a smiling look of okay-now-it's-your-turn. I hooked Tessie to me with an arm around her waist, sliding my other arm under her shoulders, and bent her back so far she shrieked. Then I gave her a long, squirming, five- or six-second kiss, heaved us both upright, staggering a little, and looked over at Hetty again. She was getting up quickly from the table, trying to dodge away, but Custer caught her wrist, pulling her to him, and gave her a nine- or ten-second kiss, Hetty struggling to escape—though not trying too hard, it began to seem to me.

The seconds flowed past, and my grin congealed, my neck flushing; Custer was overdoing this, damn it! My hand almost moved out to break them up; I didn't like the way this bastard was kissing my wife! Instantly I got hold of myself, astonished at feeling like that. Then it no longer surprised me; after all, I *had* been married to Hetty, even if no one else, including Hetty, knew it. To cover my sudden movement I swung toward Tessie again, but she was ready this time, fending me off, giving me a quick peck on the cheek, ending the game.

She began serving the coffee and cake then, but as Custer sat down at the card table again he glanced at Hetty, who was saying something to Tessie and didn't see him. Custer looked at her for a moment, then with a quick lewd grin he turned and winked at me, and the message—*Wait till I get her later!*—was clear. I didn't respond; I just sat stirring my coffee into a whirlpool; some of the cream began turning to butter. Hetty passed the little cakes then. We sat eating them and sipping our coffee, while I thought about Custer getting Hetty later. I said, "Cus, remember the time in fourth grade"—he started to smile reminiscently—"when you ate the worms?"

He shook his head rapidly, frowning, dismissing the subject, saying, "Good coffee, good coffee, very good coffee!" to Tess.

"Sure you do, Cus!" I said genially. "You had a dime bet with Alf Dillon. And won it!" I said, turning proudly to Hetty. "You should have seen him; ate three great big fat angleworms one after another, rolling his eyes and saying how *good* they w—"

"Ben, for heaven sakes, *stop* that!" Tessie said, and she glanced dubiously at Custer, a faint hint of disgust in her eyes. "I don't believe it!"

I sprang to old Custer's defense. "It's true! He was the hero of the fourth grade. To the boys anyway. Some of the girls seemed to feel it was revolting—"

"That's *enough!*" Tess said, putting a hand over her mouth. "What's the *matter* with you, Ben?" Hetty was glancing at Custer in puzzled distaste, and Custer was concentrating on stirring his coffee, glowering at it, trying to think of something to say to stop me.

I nudged him in the ribs with my elbow. "Squeamish, aren't they?" I chuckled companionably. "They should have seen you the time you got in the horse-manure battle with Eddie Gottlieb!"

"Ben!"

I shrugged. "Just reminiscing," I said, and turned to smile at Hetty in fond memory of childhood's golden days. "You should have seen him," I said. "What a mess!" Custer was gulping his coffee, hot as it was, his wrist raised so he could look at his watch over the rim of his cup. Shoving his chair back, he clapped his napkin onto the table, saying it was late, that they had to rush; and despite my urgings to have some more little cakes, they were out the door, it seemed to me, in just no time at all. As I stood in the doorway calling a genuinely genial good-night, I had a pretty good idea, from the last look I'd had of her face, that Hetty would bid Custer good-night at her door with nothing more than a firm and rather quick handclasp.

That night, for the first time since our second honeymoon, Tessie was cool to me: I'd been rude to a guest, she said, and she was disappointed in me. But—women *are* intuitive—she lay well over on her side of the bed, not speaking, and I knew that wasn't all that was bothering her, whether she understood why or not. *What the hell*, I said to her silently, *there's nothing to be concerned about; it's just that, in another world, I am married to Hetty*. But that didn't help Tessie and it didn't help me; lying there in darkness, I had to wonder what it all meant, trying not to think about it.

But in the morning I knew, and my world turned to ashes. I tried to hang onto it; walking out of the building I spoke to my beloved bird friends, but today they ignored me, none of them replying but Fred, who answered with a coarsely phrased two-word command, the essential meaning of which was *Shove off*, which I did.

Boarding the bus, starting to climb the narrow little winding staircase, I was stopped by the conductor coming down. "No room!" he said, and I sat inside by myself, listening to them singing, "Yes, We Have No Bananas!" topside, and wondering who was conducting. At Forty-second Street I got off and walked along toward my office under a bright and sunny sky, the only man—as once before, far in the past—upon whom it was raining. Before I reached the office it started to snow, with a little sleet.

At my desk—it had been a long time since I'd done this—I pulled a sheet of paper toward me, working it around the hole in my desk, stared at it for a moment, then printed, in ornate Neo-Gothic, using a variety of colored felt pens, *What Is Love?* Then I stood at my XX-1190 giant duplicating machine, moodily watching the sheets slide into the receiving tray: *What Is Love? . . . WHAT Is Love? . . . What IS Love? . . . What is LOVE? . . .* Then out came a sheet, in the same Neo-Gothic, saying, *Whatever It Is, You've Still Got It For Hetty,* and I knew it was true.

It was stupid! I made faces, pounded my head with both fists, stamped my feet, and staggered around my office, bent double at the waist, clutching my stomach with both arms, violently shaking my head, saying, "No, no, no! I'm not, I'm not, I'm not! I'm in love with *Tessie!*"

I didn't *want* to be in love with Hetty! I liked it *here!* With great big marvelous old Tessie, and everything going okay! But none of that mattered. What the hell *is* love? I didn't know, but I knew I had to see Hetty again, and I ran to the desk, snatched up a phone, and dialed old Cus at his office.

They couldn't make it again for bridge that night, he said. As it happened, they couldn't make it the next night either. Or the night after that, or all of next week, and as a matter of fact, for one reason or another, they were pretty well tied up till late next fall. But then—old Cus liked bridge—when I started in on December he remembered he could break a date they had with friends this very next Friday, so we played bridge again.

Hetty wore a plain black dress that seemed to fit extremely well; Tess looked it over pretty thoroughly several times, then began looking at *me.* Hetty and Custer seemed in a good mood. Once when Hetty and I were partners and Tess was dealing, Hetty laid one hand on the table top, and Custer reached over and put his hand on hers. She smiled at him rather tenderly, and I said conversationally, "Cus, you still break out in that awful-looking rash you used to get?" He shrugged slightly and, still smiling at Hetty, said he didn't remember breaking out in any rash. When I assured him he did, and in order to help his memory described how it always appeared on his hands first, then rapidly spread everywhere, and how the gym teacher wouldn't let him use the showers, Tess cut me short, and Custer shrugged vaguely and said that in any case he didn't have rashes any more, if he ever did. He smiled at Hetty, she gave his hand a final squeeze, and they picked up their cards, Custer glancing at his watch.

Over coffee and cake I watched Hetty give Custer a taste of her cake from the tip of her fork, and I chuckled and began reminiscing fondly again, telling her how Custer, during a week-long series of recesses in fifth grade, won the school belching contest, moving up day after day with tremendous endurance and virtuoso resource through semifinals, finals, and then winning the championship itself in a thrilling face-to-face slugfest with the big fat girl in eighth grade who never bathed. But although Tess heard me out in deathly silence, I realized that Cus and Hetty hadn't even been listening. His hand on hers again, they sat smiling stupidly at each other, and when I finished, they became aware of the silence and looked up as though startled to see us. Suddenly Hetty giggled, and Custer grinned.

"Should we tell them?" he said. Hetty nodded excitedly, and they told us. They were engaged—since dinner that night at their favorite little restaurant. I jumped up and pumped Custer's hand, congratulating him delightedly, chuckling, cavorting, dancing around the room, and inside me, at the thought of Hetty married to someone else, my stomach shrank till it was the size and consistency of an olive pit.

"Engaged!" Tessie said while we were getting ready for bed. "And in our house, practically. Isn't it marvelous!"

"Yeah. Great."

"He's *awfully* nice. You must be very fond of him, the way you're always teasing him."

"Yeah, I'd give old Cus the hair shirt off my back."

"And of course Hetty's lovely, absolutely lovely, don't you think so?"

I shrugged, and made the proper answer. "Oh, I suppose so. In a way. But of course she can't compare with you." Tessie smiled, pleased, and I stood buttoning my pajamas and watching her as she stepped out of her slip and began unfastening her back garters; lord, what a good-looking woman this was! And even more than that, what a hell of a nice one. It was stupid to be in love with anyone else but this buxom lass; and later, lying in bed, Tess asleep, the words of an ancient popular song wove themselves in and out of the convolutions of my brain like the reeds of a wicker basket: *Who's your little sweetheart? Who's your turtle dove? Who's your little sweetheart, oh, who do you love?*

What, I inquired once again, *is love?* Whatever else it might be, it was a nuisance. Why should I be giving Hetty even a thought? I'd *escaped* her! And was happy with Tessie! Tessie: beautiful, intelligent, amiable, *good*; you name it, she had it. While Hetty—lying there in bed, I made myself remember, the little cloud appearing over my head, the pictures forming within it, sharp and clear: Hetty tapping her teeth with a pencil point; putting wet things in the garbage sack so that the bottom fell out when you picked it up; looking at her tongue in the mirror; wetting her finger to pick up crumbs; watching Bob Hope; looking absolutely horrible when she came out of the shower with her hair wet and stringy. But it didn't help.

I got up, wandered out to the living room, shrugged, and said aloud, trying to persuade myself, "What do *I* care if Hetty is engaged? Matter of fact, what do I care *if right this moment she and Custer . . .* " I stopped, wrapping both arms around my stomach, bending double, the olive pit cramping violently. Then, still bent double, I ran to the phone.

With trembling hands, I found Hetty's name and number, and, a finger marking the place, dialed her number, then stood listening to the phone ring once . . . twice . . . four times . . . five times . . . the cramp rate increasing in proportion. The sixth ring was cut in two as she answered.

"Hello?" she said sleepily.

Holding my nose shut, pitching my voice high, I said, "I'm sorry, beautiful. Wrong number," and hung up, feeling relieved. A moment later I slapped the heel of my hand to my forehead. "*She's* home," I said desperately, "but is *Custer!?*" The cramps coming like a fast pulse now, one arm clutching my middle, I found *Huppfelt, Custer* X in the book, and dialed. On the eighth ring he answered, sounding a little mad.

Hand pinching my nose, I said, "Hello, this is the telephone company's new service—wishing you good-night and pleasant dreams! The charge will appear on your next phone bill." Smiling happily, the cramps gone, I stood there chuckling, listening to him curse for a while, then hung up and walked back to the bedroom. Lying in bed, raised on one elbow, I looked at Tess asleep, breathing softly, looking lovely. Then I blew her a kiss, lay back, and composed myself for slumber. The cloud appeared instantly and lighted up. In radiant close-up, looking down at me, was Hetty's face; she slowly winked at me, and I groaned aloud. "What's matter?" Tessie said sleepily, and I said, "Nothing, just stomach cramps," and lay there till dawn.

CHAPTER NINE

" 'Dear Miss, Ms., or Whatever,' " I dictated to my secretary as I paced my office. " 'Although you don't know me, I feel impelled, as former probation officer for Custer Huppfelt . . . ' " I shook my head. "Cancel that: the son of a bitch would lie out of it.

" 'Dear Miss. The records of my divorce from my former husband, Custer Huppfelt, are filed' "—I paused, thinking—" 'under the alias he used at the time. And I am obliged to sign this anonymously, for even yet I fear his revenge . . . '

"Cancel that. 'Dear Friend. As retired head of the Vice Squad, most of the city's sexual degenerates are only too well known to me. I could not live out my declining years without warning you that among the very vilest and most depraved . . . '

"Never mind the letters," I said to my secretary, who got up to leave. "Hetty's so prejudiced she'd never believe them." I sat down and yanked the phone book toward me. It fell through the hole in my desk, but with the skill of much practice I shot myself far down in my chair and caught it in my lap. I looked up the place Hetty worked at, phoned her, told her I had to see her right away about something terribly important; and after a moment's hesitation she said she'd meet me right after work.

Outside her office, just after five, I sat waiting in a cab, and when Hetty got in, I asked her where she'd like to go, and she gave the driver a lower Second Avenue address.

It was a little neighborhood saloon. We walked in, I stopped short, and stood looking around at the long old-style bar and the booths along one wall. "Good lord," I said, "this is where I used to come with . . . "

"With whom?"

"A girl I used to know. Long ago"—I smiled sadly—"in another world." There were half a dozen people sitting at the bar, and I nodded at the bartender, said, "Two old-fashioneds, please; one with soda," then led Hetty to an empty booth.

"Who's the old-fashioned with soda for?"

"You."

"How did you know?"

"Just guessed." I looked around. "And I can guess why you like this place, too."

"Why?"

"Because the tables are wood, not plastic. Because the bar is old, the ceiling made of stamped tin, and there's still a gas fixture sticking out of that wall. Because the place is a little ugly, a little dirty. Because it's unfaked and it's been here a long time." Our drinks arrived.

Hetty was smiling. "You're right; how did you guess?"

"Because I like it, too. And I'll make another guess." Her brows rose questioningly. I took a swallow of my drink, then said, "Custer doesn't like the place at all."

She looked at her glass for a few seconds without answering, then looked up at me again. "No," she said, her voice carefully neutral, "he doesn't care for it." She smiled a deliberately polite and perfunctory smile, and said, "What did you want to see me about, Ben?"

"Well." I sat working up my nerve, going through the business of sliding my glass around on the table, making wet tracks, a bit of dramatic business I'd learned from movies. "I guess I better just come out with it, Hetty, and hope you won't get too mad to listen: I don't think you ought to marry Custer."

She took several moments, staring over at the bar, to decide what to do about that, then decided to hear me. "Why not?" she said coldly, the polite smile all gone.

"Because he doesn't like this bar."

She nodded, then said, "I nodded to show that I know what you mean, not because I agree that it's of any importance."

"Yes, it is, Hetty." I leaned over the table toward her. "There's nothing *wrong* with Custer; I don't mean to say that. On the other hand . . ." I sat looking at her for a moment, then sat back. "The hell I don't mean to say that. He's a self-centered, egotistical, selfish bastard, and if that sounds like I'm repeating myself, I'm not; there are shades of meaning, and I mean them all. He doesn't love you or anyone, Hetty, except old Cus himself. He's no good! He just misses being a slob! You *can't* marry him. My god, Hetty, you'd die! In ten thousand years that guy would never know anything about you!"

"You see all this, do you?" she said, smiling with exaggerated politeness. "*I* don't; I've been going out with him for nearly a year, but things that have escaped me completely in all that time are crystal-clear to you in only—"

"Het, cut it out. You *haven't* missed seeing them; you've just denied them. There's a place somewhere inside your head where you know damn well I'm right, if you'll just look at it. I've known this guy since fourth grade, when he cheated in tests and lied to get out of things. I knew him—"

She was gathering up her purse and gloves. Then, ready to slide out
of the booth, she looked at me and said, "I won't tell Custer about this,
because I have to accept, I suppose, that you meant well: the excuse
that covers so much. But you ought to be able to see that I can't sit here
and listen to you slander him. Can't, and don't want to." She slid across
the bench, about to rise.

"I love you," I said. The words weren't hard to say now; I wanted to
say them again.

Hetty was staring at me, astonished. For just an instant—at least I
thought so—there was a response in her eyes and almost imperceptibly
she leaned toward me. But even as it happened and before she realized
it herself, I think, the feeling was shut off, and she said angrily, "I hardly
know you. And you hardly know me. I think you're out of your mind."

"Hetty, I love you," I said helplessly.

"Are you telling me you want to divorce your wife and marry me?"

I knew it was angry sarcasm, no answer expected, but I thought about
it for a moment, then shook my head. That wasn't something I could
possibly do to Tess even if Hetty had been serious.

"You're insane," Hetty said coldly, "you really are," and she put her
hand on the table top, starting to rise.

"Hetty . . . " I laid my hand on hers, leaning far across the table
toward her. Nearly whispering it, I said, "He'll never notice that
you're scared of lightning and won't admit it. That you half believe the
daily horoscope. And that you count the steps when you're climbing
stairs . . . "

But now, her eyes rounding, she was frightened; she stood abruptly
and hurried out. After a moment or two I set my glass on top of a few
dollar bills to pay for our drinks; then I left, too.

I don't much want to talk about the next few weeks. Tess didn't know
what was wrong with me; she noticed I was quiet and subdued, of course,
with a tendency toward wan smiles, but I said I was working hard, under
strain, and she believed it. When the wedding invitation came from
Custer, she was all excited when I got home, eager to talk over what to
get them for a wedding present. I mixed drinks, and while I sat back on
the davenport, Tess suggested ideas. They were the usual things people
give as wedding gifts, and I sat sipping my drink, watching Custer in a
little cloud over my head as he used them.

"What about a pair of very handsome silver candlesticks?" she said.

"That'd be nice," I murmured, watching Cus just overhead as he lit
the cleverly wax-coated sticks of dynamite.

"Or an electric toaster?"

"Sounds great," I said, nodding as Custer plugged in the specially wired, 13,000-volt model.

"He still smokes. So maybe one of those big table-model cigarette lighters."

"Might be best of all," I said, and smiled as the foot-long jet of blue flame shot down Custer's throat.

But I wasn't smiling the day of the wedding. Like a condemned man who can't believe they're really going to do it, and then one day finds himself being strapped into the chair, I found myself standing in the church with Tessie, while Hetty walked up the aisle in a wedding gown to the horrible organ throbbing of you-know-what, toward the grinning face of Custer Huppfelt. And when presently the minister said, "If any man can show just cause why they may not lawfully be joined together, let him now speak . . . " my cry rang through the church. *Because she's my* WIFE! I shouted silently, but it didn't help. Incredulous as the man strapped in the chair watching the switch actually being pulled, I heard the minister say, "I now pronounce you man and wife." And as they walked down the aisle, I saw the woman next to me nudge her neighbor. "First time in my life," I heard her whisper, glancing at me, "that I ever saw a man cry at a wedding."

On the church steps I aimed pretty well with a double handful of rice, catching Custer right in the mouth as he turned to say something to Hetty, and he had to gulp and swallow hard to get rid of it. I figured he'd swallowed a good third of a cupful, and tried to believe it would swell in his stomach till it burst through that night, *early* that night, killing Custer on his honeymoon in an absolutely unique way.

It was a noon wedding, and I had to go back to the office and work, or at least go through the motions. When I got there I had a phone call from the chairman of the board. He was all excited about a new promotion idea of mine, a series of ads in show-biz publications offering to chorus girls and nightclub entertainers, for a limited time only, a free navel-size zircon with a trial box of Navel-O-No. He raised my salary and gave me a stock option.

A delegation from *The Skin Game*, trade paper of the cosmetic industry, was waiting when I hung up the phone. They were here to present me with a "Helena," a silver statue very much like the hood ornament of a Rolls-Royce, except that it was three and a half feet high, *for his contribution*, the citation read, *to the well-rounded woman, by filling a gap in her life.*

When they left, with my thanks and a check for a full-page ad, I read a phone-call memo, a call earlier that morning from Custer himself: a large safety-pin manufacturer had offered to buy the zipper for two hundred and fifty thou.

It should have been a great day, but somehow all I could think of when I left the building that night was that my wife was on her honeymoon. Turning from the lobby of the Doc Pepper Building toward the corner just ahead, I wondered how I was going to get through an evening of smiling, nodding, and talking to Tessie just as though nothing had happened. I knew I couldn't do it, and I stopped dead on the sidewalk as I realized, too, that I couldn't get through a lifetime of it, knowing all the time that Custer and Hetty . . . I shook my head rapidly, not wanting to even finish that thought.

People were bumping into me, cursing me in friendly New York fashion; a small dog bit me in the leg, and I had to move on, habit taking over. Just as though this weren't the worst night of my life, I walked on toward the newsstand, my hand bringing out some change; two or three pennies, a nickel, a couple dimes. Then once again I stopped dead, directly before the stand, people bumping into me again, Herman snarling at me to get the hell out of the way of the customers, a silvery-haired executive, trying to reach a *Wall Street Journal*, biting me on the shoulder. But I didn't move. For there on my palm lay a Woodrow Wilson dime, that sharp-cut profile staring sternly off at Kaiser Bill, I suppose . . . and beside it lay another dime that seemed to grow—to the size of a quarter, the size of a half, the size of a silver dollar—until finally it filled the entire screen of my vision.

Carried here somehow from another alternate world, there lay a Roosevelt dime, and as I stood staring down at it—a magnificently dressed society matron reaching past me for a copy of *Vogue* gave me a judo chop in the neck with the other, gloved, hand—I was struggling with the most important decision of my life: which dime to choose.

There beside the little newsstand which somehow stood at a point where two alternate worlds intersected, existing simultaneously in both of them, I hesitated. Spend a dime of *this* world at the little stand, a Woodrow Wilson dime, and you were *of* this world, receiving the paper that belonged in it. But lay down a dime belonging to the other world, a Roosevelt dime, and you were of *that* world. I stood staring at the two dimes on the palm of my hand, trying to make my decision.

Then I made it. I slapped the dime on the counter, took the folded paper that Herman humorously thrust at me like a sword to the throat, and walked a few paces off, my eyes on the walk. At the curb I opened the paper, skipping past the headline which had something to do with weapons for peace, and looked at the paper's masthead. *New York Post,* it said, and I whirled around to look back the way I'd come—and then up, up, up, and up to the needle point of the marvelous gray familiarity of the Chrysler Building. Then, dodging at the intersections around the fronts of Saabs, Nissans, Björks, and Subarus, I ran all the way to Twenty-eighth Street . . . to *home!* To Hetty! To my wife.

CHAPTER   TEN

I ran across the sleazy, bug-infested, fine old lobby of my ancient, rat-ridden, splendid old apartment building and, without breaking stride, kissed the skid-row alcoholic in threadbare uniform who posed as door-man, leaped into the deathtrap elevator, and almost punched button 4 through the wall. As the doors began sliding shut, the white-faced old lady crouched in the corner, who had just come down, seized her chance and scuttled into the lobby just before they nipped closed.

Fingers snapping in Latin rhythm, I danced all the way up, *entre-chated* out into the hallway and down to my apartment door, which stood slightly ajar, and floated in. "I'm HOME!" I shouted. "Home, home, *home!* Hetty, darling, where *are* you!?" Then I heard her dear, dear steps hurrying across the kitchen floor, and I raced for the doorway to fling my arms tight around her just as she stepped through—except that, used to Tessie's height, I missed, clasping empty air just over her head, mussing her hair with my coat sleeves, both hands clapping hard against my ears.

"BEN!" she shrieked.

"Yes! Oh, YES, darling, it's me!" I yelled, staggering from the blows on the ears. Then I located her again and, aiming a couple feet lower, tried to grab her once more. But she stepped back, swung hard, and caught me smack on the side of the head with a tremendous slap, and the ringing in my ears became a mighty carillon. "*Hetty*, what's wrong!" I yelled through the tintinnabulation of the ringing of the bells.

"Wrong? What in the hell are you *doing* here?"

"What do you *mean*, what am I do—" I stopped and clapped a hand to my forehead, memories of the life I'd been living in *this* world flooding my mind. "Oh, my god," I said, "I forgot. We've been divorced!"

"Well, if it slips your mind again"—she lifted her slapping arm—"I'll remind you!"

"And I live"—I was rapidly tapping my forehead—"oh, lord help me, in a four-by-eight airshaft room at the YMCA!"

"Who knows? Who *cares* where you live—just so you get back there. Fast."

"But, Het, baby, I *hate* that room! And I don't like the fellows. I want to come home! To you! I've realized that I love you, only *you*, in all the worlds. So let's forget this divorce nonsense, cutie: I forgive you."

She looked at me for five long seconds. "You're not drunk," she said thoughtfully. "Alcohol alone couldn't explain this. You must be simultaneously drunk, drugged, and insane. Years of neglect, long evenings of silence punctuated by fits of irascibility, nights filled with music and snores, and now *you* forgive *me*. OUT!"

"Honey, this divorce is only a lover's spat; let me help you to understand that—"

"OUT!!"

"What's the hurry? Why can't we—"

"I'm expecting company for dinner!"

"Who?"

"My fiancé!"

The doorbell rang. A voice in the hall said, "Hi, there! May I come in?" The door pushed open, and—I was already nodding; I knew it—in stepped Custer. In this world, of course, he wasn't blond. Here his hair was black, his eyes were brown, but just the same this was this world's Custer. "Hi," he said to me coldly, suspiciously; then, to Hetty, "What's he doing here?"

"He left something!" Hetty said quickly. "He just now came for it!" She opened an ornamental box on an end table, filled with half-used book matches and other similar valuables, poked through it quickly, whipped out an old Sherlock Holmes-type pipe I'd once bought, and shoved it wildly into my mouth, chipping a tooth. "Here you are, Ben! Goodbye, goodbye!"

"Thanks." I puffed on the empty pipe, shaking my head to express keen enjoyment. "Helps pass the lonely evenings," I said wistfully, looking deep into Hetty's eyes, but the gleam in her eyes, staring back into mine, was the shine of a naked blade.

I walked out, pulling the door closed, but just before the latch clicked I turned, pushed the door open, and stuck my head back in. "In fourth grade," I said to Hetty, pointing at Custer with the stem of my calabash, "he used to eat worms." Then, remembering that I was in the semifinals of the Ping-Pong contest, I headed home to the Y.

I won't say that my room at the Y was small; I merely state that it's the only room I've ever seen in which a six-foot bed was bent at a right angle in the middle, like an L, so it would fit into the room. I had either to lie down with my knees bent back in kneeling posture, or in a sort of horizontal sitting-down position. Where they got L-shaped sheets and the one thin L-shaped blanket I don't know. But it was certainly a bed that took some getting used to, and in the mornings, a little stiff, I often had to walk down the hall to the communal bathroom on my knees.

Right now, snug in my room after leaving Hetty's, I lay on my back for quite a long time, legs up the wall, careful not to scuff the rather low ceiling with my feet: I was trying to "think things out." After a time it occurred to me that one of the first things to think out was how to survive on the money I made in this world, and I opened my top dresser drawer to get a pencil and a scrap of paper.

In order to open the drawer, I had to lie on my side on the bed, legs bent back at a right angle, my back to the dresser. Then I had to reach one arm back and up to pull open the top drawer. This was because the top drawer projected over the bed when open, with about a one-foot clearance, nearly touching the wall. The lower drawer opened *under* the bed and was pretty unhandy.

Now, lying on the bed underneath the open top drawer, I reached back with one arm, then around the side of the drawer, up, and into it, something like a snake. I fumbled around till I found a pencil and an old envelope, then closed the drawer pretty quickly, drawing a deep breath or two to get rid of the claustrophobia. I rolled onto my back, legs up the wall again, wrote down the familiar figures, stared at them, then went down to the lobby to talk to Jose Mountbatten, perhaps the best budget-shaver in the Y. He claimed to have lived for six months entirely on stolen cough-drop samples, and while I didn't quite believe that, I didn't doubt a month or so, and he certainly didn't have any sign of a cough.

We sat in the Morris chairs beside the potted ferns, and Jose said, "Breakfast?"

"Nineteen cents a day," I answered proudly. "Corn flakes and powdered milk; I keep them under the bed, and mix up the milk in my toothbrush glass."

Jose shook his head. "You can't be using the giant economy-size corn flakes, or it'd be fift—"

"I tried that: the economy-size won't fit under the bed when the bottom drawer is open. I had to sleep with the box in bed with me for three weeks till I used it up. Allowing for corn flakes that spilled in bed, I don't think I saved a cent, and I didn't sleep so well either."

"Okay, okay. Lunch?"

"Two dollars and two cents a week: six apples, at sixty-nine cents a pound."

He considered that, then nodded. "Dinner?"

"Dollar ninety-nine a day, here at the cafeteria."

"You could cut—"

"I know, I know; it's just that I always seem to be pretty hungry, come dinnertime."

"Okay. Laundry?"

"Fourteen cents a week. Tide in the big bottle."

"Try bath-size Camay: three cents cheaper and your clothes smell nicer. Rent?"

"Thirteen seventy-five a week," I said sheepishly. "I know it's high, but what can you do?"

"You know damn well what you can do: move to a room without a window. I can't help if you won't economize. How much for savings?"

"Dollar eleven a week."

"Don't change that; got to have something laid up for a rainy day. Recreation?"

"Seventy-five cents a week."

"Eliminate that. After all, a Saturday-night game of pinball goes by pretty fast; you'll never miss it. That'll help, but look: here's my analysis." He nodded at the figures on my envelope. "You got a take-home pay of $619 a month," he said shrewdly, "and that's good; that's fine. But I think this is the item that's lousing things up." He pointed to the $250 a month alimony.

The cafeteria doors opened then, and we raced for the door, walking, not running, which wasn't allowed. Jose won, being three feet closer, and I followed him along the line, thanking him for his help, watching him hide three olives in his mashed potatoes.

After dinner I sat around the lobby talking to the fellows, most of whom were in their thirties and forties and looked like Ernest Borgnine in *Marty*. Some of the other fellows were discussing the eternal question of how well Jack Dempsey would have done in his prime against "Gentleman Jim" Corbett, and I listened till it was time for the Ping-Pong tournament. I lost to a pretty active bald-headed Hawaiian fellow of around sixty. Then I watched one of the other matches, and it was exciting, reaching 20-up, but was never finished because our ball cracked and there was a big argument about who ought to pay forty-five cents for a new one. I went upstairs then, said my prayers kneeling beside my bed, and hopped in without changing position.

In the morning I hitchhiked to work, and as soon as I got there, the receptionist said the boss wanted to see me, and I tiptoed into Bert's office, slowly easing the door shut behind me so that the sound of the latch click wouldn't startle him. He was standing at the window, his back to me, and for a moment it was odd to see how tall he was again. "Sit down, Ben," he said, in a voice so friendly I knew it was bad news. I sat down very slowly so that the creak of the leather upholstery wouldn't frighten him. "Ben," he said, still staring out the window, "I'll lay it on the line." Then he turned to face me, and I wet my lips and sat still farther forward. "I don't have to tell you that you've been fouling up lately." I told him yes, sir, I was sorry, sir, but that I'd had things on my mind. "Be that as it may," he began, and in my mind I sprang from the chair and killed him with a lightninglike series of judo chops, "I'm afraid office discipline would suffer if I didn't lower your salary. Actually, it's for your own good in the long run, though you may not see it that way now." I brought out my lunch apple, breathed on it, rubbed it briskly with my tie, and set it shyly on his desk. " 'Fraid that won't help, Bennell, though I like your attitude. Your salary's been reduced to $576.35 a month. That's retroactive to the first, so you owe us $6.33. Bring it in any time, and forget the thirty-three cents, for crysake." He reached across his desk to shake hands. "Now, buckle down, Bennell, and do your level best; I still think you've got good stuff in you!"

I thanked him, and walked out to my office. Saf-T Products, I knew, had subtle ways of letting a man know where and how he stood in the organization, and I wasn't surprised to see that the partition around my office had been cut down to only four-and-a-half feet, the sawdust still on the floor, and my name on the glass had been scraped off, repainted, and misspelled *Benel*.

Inside my office—I had to walk with my knees bent so my head wouldn't show outside—my desk was the same, but my swivel chair was gone and a canvas camp chair substituted. I still had a phone, but no longer on my desk; now it was fastened to the wall, and was a pay phone. Things looked black.

Yet somehow, for so it is with the human spirit, I felt a little better back at the Y after work. Coming in, I checked the coin-return cup in the lobby phone booth as always, and this time found a quarter, which I blew on dessert at dinner, then went up to the room to wash out my other socks.

Around eight I went down to the phone booth and tried the coin-return again, but no luck. I dropped in a quarter and dialed Operator. My quarter came back and the Operator came on. I told her I'd dialed Hetty's number and got no ring, and she dialed it for me free.

"Hello?"

"Hi, this is Ben."

"Ben who?" Hetty said coldly.

"Ben so lonesome and blue since I last seen you!"

She hung up.

Half an hour later I called again; no answer. Then, until ten-thirty, I tried every half hour, reading a 1951 copy of *Life* in between. At ten-thirty, desperate, I began calling every fifteen minutes, recklessly using my own quarter, and at eleven forty-five she answered. "ThisisBen! NowHettyyou'vegototalktom—" Dial tone.

Perhaps I went a little mad. I yanked out my wallet and stared into it. As I'd known perfectly well, there were eleven dollars: my food, clothing, rent, insurance, savings, transportation, recreation, miscellaneous, and charities allowance for the next week. But I didn't care; I walked out and turned toward Lexington Avenue, running the last two blocks.

There wasn't actually too much choice: the florists were all closed, so were the jewelers, a candy store, and a pet shop. Finally I found an All-Nite Sport Shoppe and looked around inside. Hetty wasn't really too much of an athlete, so I settled on a gift certificate good for a half-hour private jai alai lesson, figuring it was the thought that counts.

At my—I mean Hetty's—apartment, I tipped the doorman fifteen cents; by that time of night he wasn't sure but what I still lived there and was just going out. Then I stood outside, coat collar forlornly turned up, staring at my old bedroom window to make sure he made the delivery.

The bedroom light came on; there was an interval long enough for Hetty to walk to and return from the door. Then—she probably guessed I was down here—her hand came out under the open window sash, and a stream of torn paper fluttered prettily off in the moonlight, and her light snapped off.

Back at the Y, I walked across the lobby, which was tiled with those octagonal white tiles about the size of a quarter that you see in old-fashioned bathrooms. Spelled out in blue tiles, just in front of the desk, it said: GIVE ME OUR YOUNG PEOPLE'S BODIES, AND I'LL LET WHO WILL WRITE THE NATION'S SONGS! ISAAC PEABODY—whoever he was. Most of the lights were out; the desk clerk was asleep, the lobby deserted except for our two "night people" who were playing cribbage.

Up at my room I unlocked my door. Actually it was a half door, which isn't as quaint as it may sound because it was a half door *lengthwise* so that I had to walk in sideways. It was practical, though, because it gave wall space for the dresser, the bottom drawer of which I now opened. Reaching down behind my bed into the drawer, I fumbled around till I found my bankbook, then lay back on the L-shaped bed, feet comfortably flat on the ceiling, and studied the figures. This didn't take long, and I changed position, knees under chin, and considered my plight.

I thought about life in the other alternate world. There I had everything a man could ask to be happy. Yet I felt no regrets. Because all I wanted, and now finally I knew it, was Hetty, and I suddenly felt strangely exhilarated.

I hopped up, and—I can't say I *paced*, exactly. But by keeping one foot at the precise center of the floor and pivoting on it—the step used in the army in *To-the-rear-march!*—I managed an approximation. I was remembering my courtship of Hetty: the delight in her face, eyes, and voice at my barrage of jokes, funny phone calls and telegrams. "I won her before," I said excitedly, "and I can do it again!" and I began pacing more rapidly till I was twirling as in a fast waltz. I knew it wasn't going to be so easy winning Hetty this time, when she wouldn't see or speak to me. But Love, I also knew, would find a way; at least I was pretty sure it would; it was what I'd always heard. Still whirl-pacing, I glanced at my bankbook again; after years of serfdom my entire life savings were something less than two months' pay, even at the new reduced salary, but I didn't hesitate. "Darling," I pledged aloud, "I'll spend it all to win you back!" Then dizzy, nauseated, and full of hope, I dropped onto my bed, feet on the ceiling, and fell asleep.

I was up at five-thirty, and after a little initial difficulty managed to straighten up and stand erect. By six I was at the office, strangely empty and silent except for my steps across the brown vinyl tiles. I unplugged the giant duplicating machine, rolled it across to Bert Glahn's office, and inside. I put it in the center of the room facing the doorway, plugged it in, then sat down at Bert's desk, drew a sheet of paper toward me, and in mod-style lettering printed *You are a Neanderthal jackanapes and I quit*, and signed my name. I inserted it into the behemoth, set the dial at 5,000 copies, turned it on, and removed the receiving tray so that the duplicates floated, gliding and swooping, out into the room.

For a moment or so I stood watching; it was pleasant, very much like a snowstorm with extra-large flakes. Then I started to leave, remembered something, and walked over to Glahn's desk. In his lower desk drawer I found it—my apple—and walked out through the storm eating it for breakfast, a clear saving of thirty-four cents.

As soon as they opened, at eight o'clock, I bought a pocket-size Japanese tape recorder at a discount house for $19.95 and took it to my room. With my transistor radio facing the microphone on the dresser top, I recorded a WNEW station announcement, then shut off the tape and sat listening for an hour or so to one commercial after another, switching from station to station to hear as many as I could, sort of getting the tone. I wrote briefly on the back of an envelope, switched on the tape, and read into the microphone in a fine, sonorous voice.

Skipping occasionally, I walked over to Twenty-eighth Street and, just down the street from my old apartment, phoned Hetty from the corner. No answer, so I walked on down and, evading the doorman, took the elevator to my old apartment and let myself in with my key.

Hetty's clock radio was where it always was, on the lower shelf of the end table at her side of the bed, the radio dial set for WNEW, the alarm set for seven. Leaving the alarm alone, I turned off the radio, connected my tape recorder, and set it on the floor out of sight under the end table. Testing, I turned the hands of the clock; when they touched seven, the tiny reels began to revolve, and a voice said clearly, "WNEW, sunny and clear out, in case you're wondering whether to get up. Hang on now: time for the commercial touch." Then my own recorded voice, sounding very much the same as his, said, "Today, *try* the new improved *Ben Bennell!* With the new miracle ingredient! Pick up your phone right now, call the Y, and a *free sample* will be delivered to the pillow beside you! He's amazing! Brighter, smoother, lighter, whiter, longer-lasting, too! Tests PROVE the new Ben Bennell is forty-seven times better, smoother, bigger, less irritating by far than Brand C, AND . . . he is guaranteed for a lifetime. You'll LOVE the new, improved Ben Bennell! And, believe me, baby . . . he'll love you. This offer limited to Hetty Bennell." Wishing, for a variety of reasons, that I could be here tomorrow morning to see it, I pictured Hetty's face as she listened: the initial astonishment and bewilderment, followed by simple delight, then wide-eyed tenderness as she reached for the telephone. I rewound the tape, reset the alarm, and left.

Next morning my recorder was delivered to me at the Y in a paper sack, but I couldn't take it back for a refund, smashed as it was. Reminding myself that, after all, we'd been divorced and that I could hardly expect to win a battle with the opening gun, I returned to Hetty's apartment to reconnoiter. I didn't find much: just my own photograph with mustache, glasses, and crossed eyes added, and the head redrawn to a point; and a W-2 form with the name and address of the place Hetty now worked at, which I copied.

I was there at five o'clock, loitering in a doorway just down the street; Hetty came out a few minutes later, but unfortunately with Custer, who must have been waiting in the lobby. I followed them to a restaurant and, walking slowly past the window, my coat collar turned up, saw them greeted as old friends by the proprietor, and ushered to what was obviously their favorite booth. Gnashing my teeth, I walked slowly back past the window again, a handkerchief at my face, and watched Custer give an order, the proprietor bowing gleefully and scurrying away. They didn't have menus, so I knew they'd ordered drinks; I also knew that unless Hetty had changed enormously, the drinks would arrive and she'd taste hers, smile, stand up, and go to the ladies' room to fix her face.

I scooted into the drugstore next door, dialed the restaurant, and asked if Mr. Huppfelt was there yet. They knew him, called him, and when he came on, I pinched my nose and raised my voice. "Meester Custair Hawpfeelt? Long-deestance, Ambidexter calling from Mehico; hol' on pleese!" I set the phone down, walked quickly into the restaurant, face averted from the phone booth at the back and the frowning Custer inside it, walked past their empty booth, picking up one of Hetty's gloves in passing, and sat down in the next booth just long enough to shove a small folded note into the forefinger of the glove. No one had noticed me yet, and I stood immediately and walked quickly out, dropping Hetty's glove back on the table in passing.

Three drinks and a long dinner including dessert and two cups of coffee later—I counted them all, occasionally walking past the window at various heights, and in various disguises, such as hat brim up all the way around, turned down all the way around, and up on one side only— they came out, Custer stifling a burp, Hetty pulling on her gloves.

She felt the note and stiffened. Chattering gaily, she surreptitiously pulled off the glove, allowing it to turn inside out, and unfolded the note at her side with one hand. At a street corner, when Custer turned away to check oncoming traffic, Hetty glanced quickly at the note, crumpled and dropped it, and stood waiting for the light to change, blushing very much the same shade of red. The light changed, and as they started to cross, Hetty tossed a quick look behind her. I was waiting, expecting it, and stuck my head out from behind the lamppost. In the instant before she turned away, I blew her a kiss and she stuck out her tongue. Then I turned the other way, resisting an impulse to walk duckfooted like Charlie Chaplin, the forlorn little tramp moving off into the sunset jauntily whirling his cane.

Later it occurred to me that Hetty might have stuck out her tongue affectionately; there were two ways to interpret it. So I phoned her around ten-thirty. "Darling? This is B—" Dial tone.

Next morning I dropped in at the studio of a commercial artist friend of mine, with a photograph of myself. He drew on a George Washington wig, added a fancy border, two twenty-two cents in little circles in each lower corner, and in a curved ribbon under the photo lettered,

GEORGE WASHINGTON *loved Martha like Ben loves Hetty.* I took this to one of the Times Square places that duplicate your photograph on a gummed, perforated sheet while you wait, each little picture the size of a stamp, and ordered a sheet. They looked good; exactly like stamps, till you looked close. Then I took a bus to Twenty-eighth Street and stood on a street corner a dozen yards from the entrance to Hetty's apartment building, pretending to read a newspaper.

I had it spread open wide, held up before my face, with the uneasy feeling that I'd never in my life actually seen anyone standing on a street corner reading a paper like this; that it was something you read about but never actually saw. Several times middle-aged women passing by looked at me suspiciously, trying to see my face around the edge of the paper. Once one of them ducked down in front of me to look up under the paper, but I drew it to my chest and brought my hands closer to my ears, practically wrapping my head in newsprint. "I only wanted to see what Reagan says!" she said irritatedly.

"He says he can explain."

"That's what he said yesterday."

"This is yesterday's paper."

"It is not; I can see the date on the front page here, and it's today's."

"Well, what Reagan says is *on* the front page, isn't it?"

There was a pause, then reluctantly she said, "Yes."

"What's he say?"

"He says he can explain."

"That's what he said yesterday."

"I'm leaving! You're so unfriendly! Why don't you show your face?"

"It looks like Lon Chaney's in *Phantom of the Opera.* Remember?"

"Yeah, I saw it on TV; I liked *The Unholy Three* better."

"That was good, too."

"Well, I have to go now. Bye!"

I heard her footsteps, but the sound didn't decrease in volume and I knew she was just standing there marching up and down in place.

She stopped, there was a moment's silence, then I said, "You're still there, aren't you?" There was no answer, and I said, "I know you're out there; I can hear you breathing."

She said, "I hate you! You're just like my husband." This time, listening to her steps, I knew she was really walking away.

I took the newspaper down and saw what I'd been waiting for: the mailman. I walked toward him, and just before he turned in toward Hetty's building, I said, "Morning! Anything for me?"

"Morning, Mr. Bennell. Yep." He shuffled through the stuff, then handed me a little stack of mail.

Around the corner at the counter of a little coffee place, I looked them over. There was a letter from Hetty's mother, several bills, some junk mail with unsealed envelope flaps, and the new *Reader's Digest*. I slid the wrapper down and read the paper flap pasted to the front of the magazine. It said, *Science Reveals: Give Up Smoking, Feel Better* 15 *Ways!* With a felt-tip pen, I inked out *Smoking*, lettered in *Custer*, and pushed the magazine back into its wrapper.

The circular in one of the junk letters said, "Accept this amazing offer! Try *Time* for a month, and see if your evenings aren't more rewarding!" and I replaced *Time* with *Ben*. The other ad was a soap coupon, "Good for one bar of Dove"; I replaced *bar* with *night*, and *Dove* with *Love*, and added my name at the bottom. I pasted one of my own stamps over each real stamp on all the envelopes, walked around to the apartment building, and dropped the mail into Hetty's box. That night, around six, I phoned. I said, "This is Ben, sweetie," and she replied with a short string of words I didn't think she knew and hung up before I could reply. Still, I told myself, she'd at least answered me, and that was progress.

Two nights later Hetty and Custer were back at the little restaurant; I felt sure Custer called it "our place." But old Cus wasn't liking it so well a minute or so later when Hetty picked up a cigarette and Custer took a book of restaurant matches from the slot in the glass ashtray to light it for her. Because she puffed, lighting the cigarette, then her eyes widened and she made a sudden squeaking sound, pointing at the matchbook in Custer's hand with my face instead of the proprietor's printed on the cover and smiling up at her. Still holding the lighted match, old Cus turned the matchbook to look, bringing the tip of the flame to the matches—which flared up like a torch, burning Custer's hand. He threw them aside in panic and they landed across the aisle on another table, the man leaping up to beat at the flame with his napkin, while the woman with him snatched her glass and threw the water at the flame, almost but not quite hitting it, landing on the man's pants instead.

It was a delightful tableau, and the instant Custer jumped to his feet apologizing and dabbing at the man's pants with his napkin, Hetty raised her eyes to the restaurant window, knowing full well who she would see. She knew I couldn't hear her through the window, so with careful exaggeration she slowly mouthed her three-syllable message.

I wasn't quite sure what she'd said, so in the drugstore next door I stood on the weighing machine looking into the mirror: "I . . . love . . . you,"

I said slowly, very carefully forming each syllable just as Hetty had done. Then I smiled happily; the lip movements, it seemed to me, were the same as hers. "I . . . loathe . . . you," I said then, and frowned, because this, too, looked exactly the same. Even more slowly and distinctly I again said, "I love you!" and smiled, almost sure that was it. Then "I loathe you," I said, and now it seemed to me that maybe the odds favored the latter. The guy behind the prescription counter and a couple customers were staring at me, so I dropped a dime in the slot and left. I weighed 158, and the other side of the card said YOU WERE BORN TO HANG.

An hour and thirty-seven minutes later Hetty and Custer came out of the restaurant, Custer touching his mouth with his fingertips, cheeks puffing in a revolting belch. Then, with the tip of his tongue, he began working on something caught in his teeth, while I skulked along in the street beside a line of parked cars, following them to J'Ambon, a small *intime* nightclub not far away.

The doorman, dressed like a short, stout Marshal of France in what appeared to be a cut-down uniform of de Gaulle's, greeted them—"Bon joor, mess aimees!"—and they went inside. I came out from behind a raked Rolls, stepped up onto the curb, and studied the entertainment poster: it was a mother, father, and nine children, called The Jukes Family, who sang folk songs. Then for half an hour I sat in the back of the Rolls, the fur lap robe over my knees, occasionally mixing up a drink from the portable bar and writing on the other side of my budget envelope with a pencil stub, frequently altering and correcting.

In the alley back of the nightclub, I walked in through the fire door, and found the Jukes family sitting morosely in the tiny dressing room, most of the younger kids on the older kids' laps, the youngest of all lying under his mother's chair, thumb in his mouth, clutching a copy of *Variety* like a security blanket. They were all in sort of Robin Hood costumes. Dad Jukes accepted my proposal, fifty bucks, and envelope, in that order, and I left as he sounded a "mi, mi, mi," for a quick half-hour rehearsal before show time.

When the show began, I was sitting in the gloaming at the bar, staring through enormous dark glasses over the heads of the people at the tables, including Hetty's and Custer's, at the tiny stage. The Jukeses were first on the bill, and they straggled in, each carrying a stool, and sat down in a line of descending order of height, beginning with Dad on the right. He wore a guitar on a sling, gave it a plonk, and to the tune of "Blue-tail fly" they all sang—rather nicely, I thought:

Custer eats worms; he don't care!
Custer eats worms, medium-rare!

Custer eats worms, the kind with hair!
Hetty, marry Ben today!

Then, to the same tune, but rapidly double-timing the
words, they jumped into the second verse:

Custer-HAS-the-social-graces-of-a-cretin-and-a-boor!
And-a-GLIMPSE-of-Custer's-mind-is-like-a-journey-
through-a-sewer!
Oh-CUSTER-lost-a-battle-that-was-fought-with-horse-
manure!
Hetty-marry-Ben-Bennell-shout-hip-hooray!

Old Cus was on his feet in gorilla posture, knees bent, fingers clawed,
looking around the room for my throat; Hetty threw a quick glance at
the bar, our eyes met, and I blew her another kiss. She drew her
forefinger across her throat, and since Custer was turning toward the
bar—I had prudently paid my bar bill when the Jukeses first appeared—
I left, a shade puzzled over Hetty's gesture until it occurred to me that
she'd probably meant to blow me a kiss but that her hand had missed
her mouth.

Next morning I was up early, as on every morning; I didn't sleep too
well at the Y. I did my exercises, not as with so many people by touching
my toes, but the opposite, gradually easing into an upright position. At
breakfast, by which I mean I was walking down Lexington Avenue
eating an apple, I stopped for a morning paper. Hunting through the
wire basket for the one in best condition, I suddenly stood frozen—it's
always astonishing to see a newspaper photo of someone you know.
Smiling up at me from the trash basket were Hetty and Custer in black-
and-white newsprint, the caption over the photo rather horribly reading,
COMING NUPTIALS ANNOUNCED.

Hypnotized, I read on, ignoring the cigarette stubs, apple cores,
orange peels, and wads of gum dropped onto the page by inconsiderate
passersby. They were to be married, the paper said incredibly, in EIGHT
DAYS—at St. Charley's, a small informal church—and I turned and ran
for a phone booth half a block ahead.

In the booth I dialed, finger trembling, then glanced at my watch;
Hetty would just be having breakfast. The phone rang a couple times;
then the recorded voice came in: The - number - you - have - reached -
is - no - longer - in - service. The - new - number - is - unlisted.

I hung up and walked out, so stunned I forgot to retrieve my quarter and had to go back for it. Again I looked at my watch, then hailed a cab; there might just be time to get to Hetty's before she left for work.

There wasn't, though. She didn't answer my ring at her door, and when I tried my old key, it wouldn't go into the lock. I stooped to examine the lock and saw that it was new. Standing there staring at her closed and silent apartment, then turning slowly away, I wondered if perhaps she was trying to avoid me.

It wasn't easy to smile as I walked out of the building, greeting the doorman and replying that yes, I had been away on a trip, and yes, it was good to be back. "Your wife getting married, Mr. Bennell?" he said, swaying slightly. "Lotsa wedding presents arriving!" I said that yes, she was; he said, "Congratulations!" and I thanked him and gave him a half-dollar, still smiling, still trying to see the bright side of things.

But *was* my courtship really working, I had to ask myself, out on the sidewalk; working slowly, perhaps, but with a cumulative effect not visible to the eye, like water dripping on granite? Maybe, but the trouble, I'd begun to realize, was that before Hetty realized this, too, she might be married. I had to see her, I knew, *had* to; a few minutes alone with her, I told myself, and this little tiff would soon be forgotten.

The big box I got free of charge: an empty color-TV carton on the sidewalk in front of a store. But eleven yards of white tissue paper, a huge white ribbon, and a pair of paper wedding bells cost me $14.90 at Dennison's. It was worth it, though: that night when Hetty came home from work, there before her door stood the huge white-wrapped box, obviously a wedding present, and—crouched in a ball inside it—I heard her gasp of excitement and felt happy to be bringing her such pleasure.

I'd allowed for the fact that with my weight inside it, Hetty couldn't drag the box into her apartment, and I'd cut the bottom out of the carton. As Hetty picked up the box by the white cord, I pulled down from the inside a little to give the illusion of weight, and we walked into the apartment together side by side just like old times, except that I was crouched to a height of two and a half feet and was momentarily invisible.

Exclaiming in anticipation, wondering aloud what in the *world* this *was*, Hetty had a little trouble deciding where to set the box down, and I worked up a bit of a sweat, scurrying around underneath the carton, rapidly changing directions, even scooting backwards for a couple yards, and if you think that's easy, squatting in the dark under a box, give it a whirl sometime. Fortunately the living room was carpeted, and she didn't hear my steps; and while she untied the ribbon, carefully saving the bow and paper bells, I had time to catch my breath.

Finally, the paper off, Hetty pulled open the flaps, and I popped up in the box, on my knees and flinging my arms out, like Al Jolson, and yelling, "Surprise!" I got one: a hard open-palmed right to the cheek, another with the left. Then Hetty burst into tears, clapped her hands over her ears as I tried to speak, and began stamping her feet frantically up and down, violently shaking her head, refusing to listen, eyes squeezed shut, and shrieking, "Get out, get out, get out, get out, get out—GO!"

Well, a house doesn't have to fall on me. I left, wandering out into the city, feeling I didn't understand women and wondering what to do about this momentary infatuation of Hetty's. I turned onto Fifth Avenue, the only idle-paced wanderer in the rush-hour crowd, and it occurred to me that there might damn well be *nothing* to do; that once again Hetty and Custer were going to be married. I was glad I wouldn't be getting an invitation this time; I didn't think I could go through it again.

I was, I suppose, at the lowest ebb of my life, almost beaten. Then I remembered King Bruce in the peasant's hut watching the spider patch up the broken threads of his web—once, twice, thrice, and finally succeeding! "By George," I said aloud, "I'm not beat yet!" and a surge of determination, an actual outpouring of adrenalin, science tells us, moved through my veins. Suddenly I began excitedly walking in little circles on the pavement, people ducking around me, because I could feel it, I could feel *something coming*. Then it came! A little cloud formed just over my head, and inside it an enormous light bulb with a short brass chain. The chain pulled, and the bulb came on: brilliantly, people squinting in annoyance, averting their faces. It disappeared, the cloud breaking up quickly and blowing away, and I stood on the sidewalk grinning with excitement. A middle-aged clubwoman bumped into me and began beating me angrily about the head with a rolled-up newspaper, but I just went into defensive position, arms around my head, ducking away, walking rapidly down the street, still grinning, a man with a destiny and a destination.

I was nervous: this was make or break, a spectacular idea and a splendid gamble, but a gamble I knew I could lose. If so, I also knew, it meant I'd never had a chance to win.

Custer was home, in his East Fifty-first Street "digs": living room, bedroom, kitchenette, and bath. He answered his doorbell in shirtsleeves, tie pulled down, his face astonished when he saw it was me. After I pried his hands from my throat and got my voice back, I suggested that he listen, just *listen*, for crysake; he could kill me afterward if he still felt like it.

We sat down in the living room, and I said, "Custer, how would you like me to give you two hundred and fifty thousand dollars in cash?"

He laughed. "*You?* You haven't a dime. Hetty told me; she felt sorry for you, you're such a pathetic little grub. She wanted to cancel the alimony till I argued her out of it!"

"Thanks; you always were a generous bastard with other people's money. But Hetty is wrong. Look me in the eye while I say it, and you'll see that it's actually true: I can give you two hundred and fifty thousand dollars, Custer, in cash; and I will."

There's something about the truth that's recognizable: a sound of the voice, a look in the eye, that hardly anyone can fake. Custer stared at me and knew that somehow it was actually true. He laughed again, trying to bluster. "And just what do I have to do?"

"You know what you have to do: give up Hetty."

"So *you* can marry her? Well, I'll tell you something, stupid: you haven't got a chance."

"I know that. I did once; she loved me once. A lot more than she could ever love you. But I kicked it all away. Forever. I know that, finally. But I still love Hetty! And one thing I'm sure of is that the worst thing that could happen to her is to marry a son of a bitch like you." He started to get up. "Hold it! If I'm wrong you can prove it right now. And I'll apologize. Tell me, Cus: what would you do? If somebody gave you two hundred and fifty thousand bucks." I was watching his eyes, hardly daring to breathe, not at all sure I was right about Custer. Then, way down deep in his eyes, far below the surface, something moved. Something stirred and shifted down there, and hope roared through me.

Custer shrugged, "humoring" me. "Well, if you must play games," he said casually, "it just happens I could buy out my boss for that: the stupid bastard has got himself in a money bind. It's almost a million-dollar business," Custer said, a note of excitement creeping into his voice. "And it'll be a lot more than that in just a few years. Right at this particular moment I could get it for a quarter million—cash." He pretended to laugh as though he knew we were only talking. "You trying to tell me you're serious?"

I nodded slowly. "Yes. I am. And you know it. I can, and I will, hand you that quarter million. Break off with Hetty, and it's yours."

"Just for laughs, how do I know you can do it?"

"Give me till the wedding. If I don't produce, we have no deal. That's simple enough."

He grinned at me nastily. "You manage to sound pretty holy about this, but are you really thinking about Hetty? Or is it just dog-in-the-manger? You think it's right to break up her wedding plans?"

"You'll decide that, Custer, not me. If you *really love Hetty*, you'll turn me down. You'll actually refuse the one chance you'll ever have"— I leaned toward him, lowering my voice—"to own the business that you'll only *work* for otherwise." I sat back again. "In that case I'm wrong about you, and Hetty *ought* to marry you. And will. So there's no harm done. But I think I know you, Cus, old friend. From way back. I don't think Hetty or anyone else is worth two hundred and fifty thousand dollars—not to you. In that case, hell, yes, I'm right to do this! Because I'll be saving Hetty from another lousy marriage. To a miserable fink like you."

I stood up. "You know I mean it, Cus: I'll give you a quarter million in cash, to let Hetty go. To give her the chance to find happiness, finally . . . with someone . . . somewhere." He sat staring up at me, hypnotized. My voice very soft, I leaned toward him, and said, "Cus, take the money. You know damn well you're a bum. Do something decent for once in your life: break off with a girl you'll only make miserable. Do something decent and get *paid* for it! You'll be rich in five years." I waited, motionless; I'd shot my bolt.

After a few moments Custer came out of his trance. "She's a nice girl," he said casually. "You were nuts to lose her." He smiled at me amiably. "But there are other nice ones, too, aren't there? And I don't know if there'll ever be another chance to grab this business. I'll take the money, you bastard!" His arm shot out, pointing at me like Uncle Sam in the poster. "But I'm telling you: you don't show up with the dough, I'm going to marry Hetty, and to hell with you! Now maybe you better just run along out of here before I decide that killing you is worth more than two hundred and fifty grand."

"Okay." I nodded, walked to the door, and opened it. In the doorway I turned to face him again, a hand on the knob. "Just think, Cus," I said, "when you're rich, all the worms you can eat!" Just before he got to it, I yanked the door shut behind me, and had the pleasure of hearing him plow into it, cursing, as I clattered down the stairs whistling "Blue-tail Fly."

It was only nine blocks, and I walked, leading an invisible band playing a hymn of triumph—"Pomp and Circumstance" with some pretty nifty triangle and timpani work—to Forty-second and Lex. But there I stopped, the music fading, staring out at the passing traffic, trying to get things straight in my mind. Was I doing this selfishly, in a last desperate and probably hopeless attempt to get Hetty for myself? Or was I doing it for the reason I'd said I was: for Hetty's sake, not mine, simply because I loved her? Well, I said finally, maybe a little of each, and I crossed Forty-second Street simulating nonchalance, flipping and catching a coin like George Raft in an old black-and-white.

The coin was a dime, the other of the two dimes I'd found in my hand the last time I approached Herman's newsstand at the intersection of two alternate worlds. This was the Woodrow Wilson dime, and now I reached across the stacks of *New York Posts* and slapped the dime on the counter, opening my mouth to ask for a paper. Before I could speak, Herman had snatched one up, double-folding it in the same motion and sticking it sideways into my mouth, my teeth automatically closing down on it. "Home, Rover," he said humorously, and I grinned, turning away with the paper still in my mouth and, to Herman's contempt, pretending to wag my tail.

But I didn't care; from a corner of my eyes I could read part of the masthead of the folded paper: *World-Sun*, it said. Just across Forty-second Street stood the fine old yellow-brick Doc Pepper Building, and as I started to cross toward it I was almost hit by a Hupmobile.

CHAPTER ELEVEN

It's true I loved Hetty, but I certainly wasn't mad at Tessie, and if you think she wasn't a hell of a welcome change from the Y, we just aren't communicating. She was pleased with the sudden change in me. I'd been a little indifferent lately, she said: taking her too much for granted again. But tonight I was my old self once more . . . Gemini, Virgo, Betelgeuse, Andromeda; it sure beat Ping-Pong with the fellows!

In the morning though, very conscious of where I was going now and why, I felt guilty about Tess as I kissed her goodbye. She smiled happily, still tired and half asleep because the odd L-shaped way I'd slept last night hadn't given her much room. I reminded myself that I was concerned with another world now, a world in which I didn't even know where Tessie was. I had to do what I had to do, and did it: downstairs I took a cab to Custer's office.

It was hard not to laugh when I walked in and saw him look up from his desk and smile, then stand, shoving out his hand to shake mine; except for his blond hair and blue eyes, he looked exactly the same as the Custer Huppfelt of another world, who would liked to have killed me.

We went through the preliminaries. Forcing my lips to move, I asked how Hetty was; she was away for the next week or so visiting her mother, he said, and hope rose momentarily. Trouble? Divorce ahead? But it was too soon, and I knew it. Cus asked after Tessie, I inquired about his health, he asked after mine, and we made a joke about bridge. "Well," he said then, "what can I do for you, Ben?"

"Something pretty unbusinesslike, Cus; you'll hate it. I know I could get rich developing my invention myself, but riches don't matter; I want to sell it. To the safety-pin company that offered to buy it last week. No bargaining, no haggling: I'll take the two hundred and fifty thousand bucks they offered just as fast as you can wrap up the deal."

Cus sat frowning as though he couldn't understand, and I thought I knew what he was going to say, that he'd urge me not to be hasty, but I was wrong. He said, "What invention?"

Even as I tolerantly smiled at his lapse, I knew what you know; I knew what everybody knows; I knew what I should never have forgotten: a Custer Huppfelt is always a Custer Huppfelt, in any world at all. "The zipper, of course," I said, still smiling, but my blood was congealing into an icy slush because I knew what he was going to say.

He sat shaking his head as though baffled, but way back in those snakelike eyes there gleamed a needle point of pure malice. "The zipper?" he said. "Ben, I don't understand you. That isn't your invention; it's mine."

It wasn't the past that flashed instantaneously through my mind; it was the future. Even as I opened my mouth to reply, I foresaw all the shouts, the rage, the threats of suit and murder, the bland denials, and the complete futility of everything that was about to happen. I went through it all; I couldn't help it. I yelled at Custer, pounded his desk, raged and stormed around his office, threatened to kill him and would have, except that in this world, too, he was a lot bigger, heavier, and stronger than I was. But all the while I knew how useless it was; I hadn't even a scrap of proof that I'd invented the zipper. Laughing at me deep in his eyes, Custer acted solicitous, worried about me, suggesting that I was working too hard. He was actually taunting me, of course, and he let me know that *he* was accepting the offer next Friday when his patent papers had come through—getting his kicks out of robbing me, and driving me into a wilder and wilder rage.

Suddenly I had to turn and run out of the office, knowing that something would burst in my head if I didn't. This unspeakable—any word or phrase I'd ever known was far too mild—this *Custer*, this *Huppfelt*, had stolen Hetty in this world, and now he'd just stolen the only way I had of keeping him from stealing her in another. Outside on the walk, I wanted to lift my head to the sky and howl like a dog; I wanted to roll in the gutter, tearing my clothes and hair.

I walked, block after block, I didn't know where and still don't. Then, by what I can only feel was a miracle, the traffic lights changed just ahead of me, I stopped at the curb as traffic rolled by, and a lavender Rolls-Royce floated past my glittering eyes. In it, chin and folded hands resting on the golfball-size cut diamond which formed the head of his cane, sat the brooding, mysterious, silk-hatted figure of Nate Rockoski. Once again I caught a glimpse of an incredibly expensive suit—this one a pattern of enlarged stock-market quotations woven into a yellow-gold background of shark's-tooth cloth—and I could feel the cold slush in my veins melting; then it turned to steam.

This skinny little plutocrat was an inspiration to America's youth, as the very symbol of persistence. As I knew, and as the entire world now knew, from the foreign-language editions of *Reader's Digest*, this was the man who had persisted through the bitter years of the scenic living picture, the inflatable umbrella, the cylindrical portrait, until finally he had invented Coca-Cola. Inspired by him, touched by the flame of his genius and greed, I reminded myself that I *had* invented the zipper, even if no one else in the world was ever to know it. And I was inspired again. Eyes calm once more, and smiling, albeit a little grimly, I knew what I had to do, and I turned in my tracks and walked back toward the office.

Passing through Grand Central Station, steps brisk and purposeful, I glanced out of habit over to where the familiar little curtained booth had stood, but it was gone. In its place stood a chrome-and-enamel waist-high machine, about the size and general shape of a cigarette machine. It was a pleasant forest-green, and across its front in large white capital letters it said, TRY ME! I walked over, and in the lower right corner a neat white arrow pointed to a slot; the green words in the arrow read ONLY 50¢

Intrigued, I dropped in a half, and a little glass button began flashing red, on and off rapidly like a pulse, and a buzzing began. Then the button flashed green, there was an inner clunk of mechanism, and a card dropped into a cup below the coin slot, as the light went out and the machine was silent. I picked up the card, and read it. It said *Thanks, and god bless you, sir! Your Friendly Automated Panhandler*, and I walked on toward the office with that warm inner glow that I knew Custer had never known, which comes only from offering a helping hand to those less fortunate than ourselves.

In my office I pressed a button on my desk, then walked over to stand staring out a window. Behind me I heard the office door open quietly, close almost soundlessly, then the faint squeak of cheap shoes. The sound stopped, and, almost whispering it, little Bert Glahn said, "Yes, sir?"

Without turning, I said, "Bert, I'll lay it on the line," and heard him gulp. Then I turned to glare at him. "I don't have to tell you that you've been fouling up lately."

"Yes, sir, I'm sorry, sir, but I've had things on my mind."

I stood looking at him, but I couldn't bring myself to lower the poor devil's salary. "Things in your life even more important than Navel-O-No?" I said in soft rebuke. "Come to attention!" He snapped erect, heels coming together, thumb along trouser seams, eyes straight ahead. I walked around him, inspecting, but found nothing wrong. "I'm going to give you a chance to redeem yourself."

"Thank you, sir!"

"If you care to volunteer," I added softly.

He went a little pale, but said, "Yes, sir."

"For the next week or so, Glahn, I'm leaving you in charge. As a test! It's make or break. Every now and then I'll check in, and if you absolutely have to, you can phone me at home. But I want to see what you can do on your own. So buckle down! Do your level best! I still think you've got good stuff in you." I threw him a salute, dismissing him.

He snapped one back. "Yes, sir!" he said, eyes shining. "I'll make good! Just you wait and see!" He about-faced, marched out, and I picked up my phone, called Perce Shelley at the agency, told him I wanted him to arrange a couple of important appointments for me the first of next week, using the agency's influence, then I left the office.

Back at my apartment building, using two hundred-dollar bills, I arranged with the building super to use the furnace room and the nondescript collection of tools he had there, for the weekend, while he took the time off. He told me what to do about the furnace, garbage, and complaints from the tenants; for these last I was just to answer the wall phone, listen, say, "Be up first chance I get," and forget it. It left plenty of time for work, and I started Saturday morning, explaining to Tess that it was a new hobby.

I had problems, of course; the only wheels I could find Saturday were a pair of thin, wooden-spoke affairs with metal rims: an old pair of buggy wheels, actually, somewhat larger than I wanted, that I found at an antique shop. Metal tubing, on the other hand, I found and bought with no trouble, and I rented a welding outfit easily. Welding isn't as easy as it looks, though, I discovered, and I never did get the hang of making a neat seam. But I was in a fantastic hurry and assured myself it was the *idea* that counted; refinements could come later.

Late Sunday afternoon, working in the super's coveralls, I finished. The wall phone was ringing, and I answered in a fake Polish accent; it was some sort of complaint, about a bathroom flooding, and I said I'd be up first thing Monday. Then I set right to work again, using a rechargeable seltzer bottle and five pounds of sugar I'd brought downstairs. Mixing up bottle after bottle, I finally got pretty much the taste I was after. Then I sat sketching; first in pencil, discarding; then refining; and finally, around midnight, finishing up pretty carefully in colored inks.

Monday at ten I kept my first appointment, on Long Island, with half a dozen officials of the American headquarters of Mitsuhashi, meeting them on the office parking lot where a space had been cleared for my demonstration. They stood watching, smiling politely though skeptically, as I climbed on. They say you never forget how, and I didn't. But of course I was used to rubber-tired wheels a lot closer to the ground, and

I started out wobbling badly. That loosened a weld: not instantaneously but through four or five slow and terrible seconds, the front and back wheels drawing farther and farther apart as I sank toward the ground. Then I was sitting on the asphalt, still holding the crude plumber's-pipe handlebars, watching both wheels of this world's first and last bicycle rolling straight toward, and scattering, my board of review.

Not too many people, actually, have imaginative ability, and certainly this bunch didn't; but . . . They were polite, commiserating, urging me to try again and come back; but it was plain that they didn't believe and never had believed in anything as absurd as a vehicle with only two wheels. And when I tried describing a refinement that would, I assured them perhaps a little too excitedly, sweep the world—simply adding a motor, that is, and calling it a Honda—they nodded and smiled even more, bunching together for protection.

There was no time for self-pity. At two o'clock—Perce Shelley had done his work well—I sat in the office of the president of a large and important company. He listened to me, nodding politely; then I took the glass from the carafe set on his desk, and filled it from the stoppered bottle I'd brought along. "Looks like water," he said doubtfully, holding it to the light; then he tasted it, and shrugged. "And what would you call it?" he said.

This was the big moment, and I was ready; I had my large color sketch mounted on cardboard, with a heavy paper flap the way the ad agencies do. I held it up and then slowly and a little dramatically, I'll admit, lifted the flap to reveal the label I'd sketched. He stared at it for several seconds, then turned to me. "*Seven-Up?*" he said. "What the hell kind of name is that?"

I tried to tell him it was a *good* name, that I guaranteed it would succeed, but he didn't even let me finish. "What does it *mean*, what does it *mean?*" he kept saying, and when I told him it didn't mean *any*thing, he just looked at me, then at his watch, and I knew I was finished, and gathered up my stuff.

Just before I walked out the door I turned, and said bitingly, "What the hell does *Coca-Cola* mean!" but of course—no imagination again—it didn't help a bit.

Four days left till the wedding: sitting in front of the furnace that afternoon, working feverishly—an eyelid had begun to twitch—I cut sheet after sheet of cellophane into half-inch strips. Then I scraped the sticky surface from a dozen sheets of flypaper.

Next morning, for the first time, there in the offices of the Minnesota Mining Company, I met real enthusiasm! Tearing off an inch or so from the crude roll I'd made, I stuck a piece of paper to the wall, and the president stared at it. "Scotch tape!" I said, and he grinned and began nodding eagerly. He walked quickly toward the wall, his hand reaching out for the paper as I mentally upped my price to three hundred thousand, and—*damn* that flypaper!—it slid slowly down the wall to the carpet, and when I looked up at prexy again: fish eyes.

All that night I typed, down in the furnace room; my fingers were literally bleeding when I stoked up the furnace at dawn. But I delivered my stuff at nine sharp, then walked the streets, sat in parks, and drank a dozen cups of coffee in a dozen places till my four o'clock appointment, when I was back. "We don't usually read quite this fast, you know," my man said reprovingly, "but since Manny put it on the basis of a personal favor . . . " He shrugged, and leaned back in his swivel chair; he was a guy around forty, I thought, who looked twenty-six, wearing a gray tweed coat and a pipe. "Anyway, I've read your first chapters and outlines. This first one"—he riffled the pages with his thumb—"what's it called again?"

" 'Huckleberry Finn.' "

"Well, believe me," he said, chuckling, "that's a name you'd have to change! Surely you can see that it's much too—well, *cute*, I'm afraid I must say. I gather from your outline that the book is entirely about a boy floating down a river on a raft?"

"Pretty much."

He didn't say anything for a moment; just stared at me. Then he slowly shook his head. "What in the world ever made you think . . . Well, never mind. No sex in the book, Mr. Bennell? I don't find any in the outline."

" 'Fraid not."

"None whatsoever?"

I shook my head.

"Quite frankly, I think you'd better add some! It's about your only hope. Suppose, and I'm only thinking out loud, suppose Aunt Polly and the Widder Brown—'Widder' Brown, Mr. Bennell, really!—were both a lot younger, Huck a bit older, and—"

I was shaking my head.

He shrugged. "Then I'm terribly afraid it's not for us. Frankly, I doubt if even a vanity press would touch it. As for the other, what's your title?"

" 'Gone With the Wind.' "

"Try shortening it. And eliminate a good half of the characters. Rhett Butler, for one; he's incredible. Meanwhile"—he stood up—"don't give up your job in—what is it, advertising?" He handed my material across the desk. "Nice of you, I suppose, to let us see these."

Two days till the wedding—I still think that with only a little more time . . . But I had none to spare; at the union office I had to hire practically the first three men I talked to, and there was no time to really work on the outfits. Yet we looked pretty good, I thought, and after only half a day's practice we were working together surprisingly well.

I had real hope when we kept the appointment, although there was some trouble getting into the studio. Once inside, though, the guy who was to see us—Fred Something—looked at us for a while, not saying anything. Then he shrugged, and said, "Okay; you're here, so go ahead."

I glanced around at my group, nodded, and we jumped smack-bang-boom into a fast, pounding, hard rock, electric guitars whanging away, drums pounding, our long-haired wigs swaying in rhythm, dark-lensed glasses actually bouncing. Then, in the correct high-pitched howl, I began singing the "words," using a combination Oklahoma whine and Deep South mushmouth, as is proper.

We finished with a final flesh-atomizing twang, the sudden silence painful to the ears, and Fred looked at us. He studied my gold pants and wide belt, glanced at the tambourinist's bare feet, stared at the wide-brimmed shapeless felt hat of the drummer, looked deep into the one eye visible behind the guitarist's bangs; then he said quietly, "And what was that called?"

" 'Love is a Sandwich,' " I said.

"Sweet," he murmured. "Really lovely. Haunting."

"Glad you like it!" I said, and he started to reply, but we were into 'Yowl,' banging, whanging, and twanging away, but just as I began the vocal, Fred yanked a fuse-box lever, and the amplification drained right out of our instruments, a strange and, on the whole, unlovely effect.

In the new silence Fred said gently, "And what do you call your-selves?"

" 'The Grateful Dead.' "

He nodded. "Very apt," he said quietly; then he snarled. "Because you're *dead*, all right, abso*lutely* dead! And believe me, I'm grateful! Out!" He jerked his thumb at the door.

In the street outside, a group of musicians were unloading their instruments from the side luggage compartment of a bus, surrounded by a knot of squealing teen-agers. GUY LOMBARDO, JR., I read on the side of the bus, AND HIS ROYAL CANADIANS, and I snatched off my wig, and walked on.

Instruments and wigs returned to the rental agencies, the musicians paid off—one of them said he sort of liked the new music, and wanted to know if he could keep his hat—I came out on Forty-second Street and walked along it, without destination. *One day left:* tomorrow night at this time Hetty would be getting into her wedding dress, and now I knew there was no longer anything I could do about it. *Kleenex?* I thought hopelessly. *Dial-A-Prayer? Bloody Marys?* But I shook my head, all faith in inventing gone.

At Bryant Park, the little square of oxygen-starved greenery back of the main Public Library, I turned in and dropped tiredly onto a bench. I was about to lose Hetty in *both* worlds, and if I couldn't quite face that fact yet, I at least squinted at it sideways. I sat under a tree whose leaves hung like limp tongues, realizing that like Leonardo da Vinci staring at his fourteenth-century carburetor, I was ahead of my time.

You are going to lose Hetty! I repeated to myself; then, forcing my mind into logical thought, I said, *Why?* The answer was clear: *For want of a quarter million dollars that Custer stole from me.* And then, for such is the power of logical thought, the solution shyly presented itself: *Steal the quarter million back from Custer . . .*

I liked it! I began to smile because I'd always wanted to commit a Master Crime: detailed maps . . . flawless planning . . . watches synchronized . . . split-second timing . . . impeccably executed . . . "Okay, now let's go over it once more" . . . "Geez, boss, how many times—" . . . "Till you can do it in your sleep!"

I brought out a little notebook I carried, and at the top of a page I carefully printed PLAN: To STEAL $250,000 FROM C----R H------T. Underneath this I printed 1. *Difficulties:* (a) MORAL. Below that, Roman numeral I: WRONG TO STEAL? Capital (A): NO. MORALLY SPEAKING, MONEY YOURS IN FIRST PLACE. (B): ANYWAY, YOU GOING TO GIVE MONEY BACK TO C. (b): PHYSICAL DIFFICULTIES. I: C BIGGER THAN YOU. II: MURDER HIM? EXCELLENT! BUT RISKY. I wasn't sure whether the next item should be Roman numeral III or (d), and I tried to recall, from Miss Wunderlich's sixth-grade English class. But I couldn't remember then, and I couldn't remember now. Mentally tossing a coin, I wrote (d): MODUS OPERANDI: TRICKERY AND STEALTH.

So far, so good, I thought, sitting back on the bench and admiring the PLAN. The *Modus Operandi* quickly outlined itself then, although I had a little trouble with Roman numeral nineteen. Was it an X, a V, and four I's? Or an I and two X's, meaning subtract I from XX? I doubted if even the Romans were sure, and just wrote a plain 19, and to hell with Miss Wunderlich, who always favored the girls anyway.

Briefly, the *Problem*, or *P.*, which the *Modus Operandi*, or *M.O.*, was designed to solve—I wrote *Modus Operandi: Problem*, or *MOP*— was this: Custer would undoubtedly be paid by check, but a check made out to Custer was no use to me; also, it would be presented at his office or theirs, alive with strangers and dangers; and if Custer recognized me, I'd go to jail.

I was elated. I *wanted* this difficult; I wished I had to lower myself into a building by rope, the way they did in that movie—remember?— where they stole the emerald from the turban in the glass museum case. I knew I had to work fast—tomorrow was Friday (*F*)— and I swung my legs over the stone railing, dropped down onto the Forty-second Street sidewalk, and moved instantly into *Phase One*. Crossing the street to a phone booth, I chewed and swallowed the PLAN, which I'd memorized. Surprisingly, the page had a rather pleasant minty flavor, and I ate another.

In the booth I executed *Step One: Drop in Quarter*, and presently reached Mr. Swanson of the E-Z Pin Co. I have an excellent ear and am a very good mimic; you should hear my Edward G. Robinson. Sounding just like old Cus, I said, "Custer Huppfelt here; how are *you*, Mr. Swanson!"

He told me: he'd had a little cold, and stayed home from the office a couple days, but he was back now; he still felt a little stuffy, but was definitely better. What could he do for me? I said I had a very important favor to ask. I would like him, if he would, to pay me in cash *tomorrow*. In comparatively small bills; say hundreds. And I'd appreciate it if the transaction could take place with just the two of us present; in my home, perhaps. I lowered my voice conspiratorially: it was a matter of taxes, I said; I knew he'd understand. He replied, with the businessman's chuckle, that he certainly did, would be glad to oblige, and I gave him my address, suggesting six-thirty tomorrow evening.

Phase Two: I walked half a block to another phone booth, so that my calls couldn't be traced. I wasn't sure who would be tracing them or how, but felt it best not to take unnecessary chances. I'd listened carefully to Swanson's voice, and when Custer came on, I said, "Ed Swanson, Mr. Huppfelt," and knew I sounded just like him. He asked how my cold was, and I said it was better, though I was still a little stuffy; I'd stayed home a couple days, because I'd noticed that if you went right to bed with a cold, you saved time in the long run. He asked what he could do for me, and I said I had a very important favor to ask. I preferred to pay him in cash tomorrow; in comparatively small bills, say hundreds. And I'd appreciate it if the transaction would take place with only the two of us present; I thought his home might be best; say six-thirty tomorrow? Lowering my voice, I said it was a tax matter, and that I knew he'd understand. I doubt if there's a businessman with soul so dead that he'd admit he didn't, and Custer chuckled, businessmanlike, and said he certainly did; it was fine with him, and at his house; he had a wall safe in his study. Stepping out of the phone booth, I hardly cared for the moment whether crime paid or not; this was fun!

From fairly extensive rental-library reading, I knew the next step: Follow Subject. I was practically certain Custer would go right home from work. He hadn't been married quite long enough to start the sordid philandering which I instinctively knew was inherent in his nature. Of course I knew where he lived, but somehow it didn't seem right to just go on out there and wait for him. I noted all times in my notebook, the way you're supposed to.

5:11, *and—oh, about 25 seconds:* Subject walked out of office-building lobby; took cab. I foresightedly had cab waiting just down street, me inside. Avoiding cliché, did not say, "Follow that cab!" Said, "Just trail along after that guy." Cabbie said, "What?" Said, "Just string along behind the fellow in the Yellow." Cabbie said, "How do you mean, Mac?" Said, *"Follow that cab!"*

5:43, *aboard ferry to Jersey:* Subject reading paper. I skulk in shadows, hat brim down, coat collar up. Can't see. Turn collar down, brim up. Much better.

5:43, *watch stopped.* Anyway, Cus went home, taking a bus for the five or six miles to Whipley, New Jersey, then walking three blocks from the bus stop. I envied him a little, "shadowing" him, as we say; this was a nice old-fashioned-looking town, with quiet streets and a lot of trees. Like others we passed, Custer's house occupied what must have been nearly an eighth of a city block. It was on a corner lot surrounded by a shoulder-high wall of fine old brick; along the top of the wall ran a foot-high fence of ironwork. Two tall arch-topped wrought-iron gates opened onto a brick path leading up to the house, which was set far back from the street. The house was a fine steep-roofed Victorian with gables, dormer windows, and trim around the eaves; there was a round tower at one corner with a skyrocket-shaped roof, a great wide front porch, everything nicely painted in maroon and white.

I was a good block or more behind Custer, and when I reached the house I just glanced in at it and walked on past, on the other side of the street, giving Custer time to settle down inside before I reconnoitered. Presently I walked back, this time on Custer's side of the street; all around me the street and walks were empty, this being the cocktail hour.

Stooping a little so that only my hat would be visible from the house, I walked slowly along beside the wall, again glancing in through the wrought-iron gates as I passed; no one in sight, in the yard or at any of the windows. I turned back; stopped; looked in at the long wide expanse of lawn up to the porch steps, noting the many trees and bushes. What was Subject doing; what were his Habits? I looked up and down the sidewalk—no one in sight—pushed open the gates, stepped quickly in, and closed them soundlessly behind me.

Darting from tree to bush to shrub, I zigzagged my way toward the house. Alertly, I noticed a St. Bernard dog the size of a Shetland pony come ambling around from the back of the house. Peeking between the branches of a small Christmas-tree pine, behind which I had been lurking when he appeared and which I prudently continued to keep between us, I watched him stroll down the brisk walk to a patch of late sunlight and lie down precisely between me and the gates. I watched his gigantic head rise, black-rubber nose twitching as he suspiciously sniffed the air; fitted with horns, he could have fought a bull. Then he yawned, looking as though he could swallow a bowling ball without blinking, put his head on the walk, and lay staring at the closed gates, apparently forever.

I couldn't possibly climb the tree; it was hardly higher than I was. So I stood, crouched, motionless, trying by will power to exude no scent of interest to a St. Bernard. I put in fifteen minutes there, thinking up and discarding as somehow implausible many ingenious explanations to Custer of what I was doing here. A boy walked by the gates; he was wearing a canvas sack full of folded copies of *The Whipley Whig*, and he yanked one out, tossed it over the gates in passing, and was gone before it hit the bricks. It landed, sliding, the dog snatched it up, and, tail erect and swaying proudly, he trotted up the walk and scratched at the door. Several moments later Custer let him in, closed the door, and I scurried to the side of the house in a Groucho Marx crouch and peeked in.

Living room: empty. Den: Custer, in shirtsleeves, came walking in, drink in one hand, paper in the other, dog at his heels. Cus dropped onto a lounge chair, set the drink on a table beside him, and unfolded the paper. He glanced up expectantly, and the dog was waiting before him, slippers in his mouth. Cus took the slippers, saying something to the dog, whose tail wagged in response like the mast of a sailboat in a wallowing sea. As Custer put on the slippers, the canine behemoth lay down beside the chair in a wicker dog bed larger than mine. Then, for a dozen minutes, Custer sat reading his paper and sipping his drink, one dangling arm scratching the dog's ears and neck.

Then Cus got up and walked out of the room; standing clear over at one side of the window, I could just see him, out in a hall and cut in half by the doorframe, turn onto a flight of stairs. Doggy stayed where he was and so did I; in five minutes Custer came down in faded blue swimming trunks, a towel slung over his shoulder.

The only place a pool could be was back of the house and at the other side; I took a chance on the dog's staying inside, though I kept mighty close to the walls, ready to leap. I worked my way around to the back of the house and saw the pool in the opposite corner of the lot. Custer tossed down his towel, walked out onto the diving board, and went in; a little awkwardly, I was pleased to note. He did a fast dozen lengths—I could have done a lot more, with a little training—climbed up the ladder in the corner by the board, and walked back to the house, drying his unpleasantly lean tanned body.

Dressed again, this time in one of those ridiculous one-piece nylon jumpsuits, Custer moved to the kitchen where he stood frying some hamburger, the dog present as an observer. It was getting dark, I couldn't see to write in my notebook, and I was tired and hungry: I left, walked back to the bus stop, and after only a forty-five-minute wait caught a bus back to the ferry, which left half an hour later.

Twelve hours left: In the morning I set out to look for an unethical druggist and found one immediately: in the first three stores I tried, as a matter of fact. Actually, they still had some ethics left; that is, they wanted from ten to twenty-five bucks to forget them. So I went on to a fourth store, with cut-rate ethics, and got what I wanted for only ten bucks extra, asking for it by generic term instead of brand name, as recommended by Consumers' Report.

Handcuffs I found in an ethical pawnshop; he wasn't supposed to sell them to me, he said; it was sort of illegal. But I explained they were just to play a joke on a friend, and he took the extra fifteen bucks and said that in that case it was okay.

A couple of other and perfectly legal stops, at a sporting-goods shop and a butcher's and it was time for an early lunch, at a stand-up lunch counter. I felt like a relaxed meal, having a busy time ahead, and paid the extra seventy-five-cent cover charge, entitling me to an overhead strap to hang onto, and had a pastrami on toasted Wheat Thins. Then I set out on a tour of the costume shops, which took most of the afternoon.

It was worth the search, though, because I found exactly what I was looking for, in a shop one flight up, the owner in one of the Bela Lugosi costumes he was closing out at $19.95. He was lying in a coffin when I walked in, reading the *World-Sun*. "Drrrink your blut!" he said in greeting, not looking up; he finished the item he was reading, then stood up, spreading his cape like bat wings. "Blood-stain-resistant! It's Cravenetted!" he said, but I said no, explained what I wanted, and he produced just the thing, an absolute marvel. At 5:03—less than three hours left!—I was on an early ferry to Jersey.

CHAPTER TWELVE

In Whipley I rented a car. Then, parked a dozen yards from Custer's gates, I unwrapped my pound and a half of choice hamburger and my bottle from the drugstore.

I glanced around; a man was on the other side of the street walking toward the corner, and I waited till he was gone. Then I got out and walked to the wrought-iron gates. Rover was there, lying on the sun-warmed bricks, and he rose up and lumbered toward me, like a fur-covered bulldozer. "Nice doggy," I said, reached quickly in through the gates, and plopped the big wad of meat down on the walk, withdrawing my hand instantly in case he was nearsighted. This was it! It was strange standing here and realizing that my entire future depended on whether a dog liked hamburger.

He sniffed it, then looked up at me, staring deep into my eyes trying to see whether I was trustworthy, and I smiled with a frank and boyish openness, like a movie actor running for president. It worked on the dog, too; he believed me, nodded his thanks, then gulped down the hamburger in one enormous bite, taking a small portion of one brick along with it. He wiped his mouth, using his tongue as a napkin, and turned, tail swaying in stately gratitude, and lay down again.

I waited twenty minutes in my car, then took off my suit coat, tie, and shoes, came back to the gates, bundle under my arm, and my friend was still lying on the brick walk, eyes closed. I whistled softly, but he didn't move. I opened the gate a foot, ready to yank it closed; he still didn't move. I stepped in, prepared to step right out again, waited, then whistled once more. He lifted one eyelid one millimeter, looked at me without interest, then closed it again, sighing, and I knew that the hamburger-encased sleeping pills had done their kindly work.

Dragging a four-hundred-pound—my lowest estimate—St. Bernard twenty yards across a lawn, forearms under his armpits, hands clasped on his furry chest, his hind feet dragging, giant head and tongue lolling as he gently snored—it's an experience! I laid him comfortably behind a bank of shrubbery, and waited. Fifteen minutes later Custer and Swanson walked in through the gates, chatting; Swanson, carrying a locked attaché case, was a tall, cave-chested but wide-shouldered guy in his fifties, kind of powerful-looking; if anything went wrong I knew I'd collect some bruises, and maybe a busted skull.

The instant they stepped into the house, I unwrapped my bundle and got into my rented suit. Then, remembering how I'd looked in the costume-shop mirror, I studied the sleeping dog at my feet. Possibly his tail was a little handsomer than mine, I had to concede, but all things considered it was a remarkably good match. Seventy-five bucks a day was the rental fee for this outfit, and worth it; this was real fur, I was certain, and inside the expertly molded papier-mâché St. Bernard dog head, my eyes were pressed tight against the foam-rubber-padded viewers, staring out at the yard through the big transparent brown glass eyes. All was quiet, and I drew my head back from the viewers.

The tiny light was on in here, just over the miniature control panel, which was level with my mouth. Like a pilot at flight time, I began testing my controls. *Tail-wag*, read the tiny plate under the first switch; I flipped the switch with my tongue, felt the spring-operated tail begin wagging at the rear of the suit, and turned it off to conserve power; you had to wind the tail motor like a clock, and it was good for only about forty wags. I was about to test *Mouth Op.—Cls.* when I heard a plop, and jammed my eyes tight against the padded viewers like a submarine commander scanning the horizon; a folded paper was sliding to a stop on the brick walk; my adventure had begun.

Thoughts crowded my mind: ahead lay what? Happiness? Disaster? I shook my head to clear it for action, my chin bumped the end switch, and the tiny reels of the transistorized tape recorder in the huge concave chest of my suit revolved, and a deep bark sounded through the yard. Turning hastily toward it, I stuck out my tongue too soon, accidentally flipping on *Tail-Wag* and *Mouth Op.—Cls.*

Huge mouth slowly opening and closing, tail wagging majestically, another bark sounded; panicked now, I lunged for *Bark*, tongue way out, striking *Sigh* and *Ears Up* simultaneously. Barking, sighing, wagging, mouth slowly opening and closing, ears lifting alertly, I forced an iron-willed concentration—the submarine commander undergoing a depth-charge attack—and rapidly flipped off switches one after another just as the front door opened and Custer looked out. He whistled, but I stayed behind my bushes, sweating, trembling, hoping. After a few long moments Custer went inside again.

I wished I could postpone everything for several days, but knew I couldn't. Trying to "think dog"—that was all-important, the man at the costume shop had said—I started toward the paper, doing my best to simulate an eager canine trot. I felt I was succeeding, and flipped *Ears Up*, then realized I'd forgotten to drop to all fours. Thinking fast, I raised my forearms, wrists limp, paws dangling, suggesting a dog who was practicing walking on his hind legs; at the same time I turned and trotted back to my bushes.

A moment later I peeked out cautiously, looking both ways: no one in sight, no one had seen. I ambled out on all fours, leaned over the paper, flipped *Mouth Op.—Cls.*, shoved down my muzzle, it closed over the paper, and I felt better. Walking up to the porch, trying to keep my rear end down, I was glad no one could see me; I could sense that I hadn't quite yet got the hang of the coordinated four-footed walk.

"Think dog," I told myself, negotiating the steps, and I did pretty well, falling down only once. "*Master . . . wants . . . paper. Him good. Ughh!*" I said to myself, then realized this wasn't dog but Indian. I was on the porch now, rear end sitting down. Ducking my head, I looked underneath my hind legs and saw my tail lying properly outspread behind me on the porch; I was as ready as I'd ever be, and, paper in my mouth, I scratched at the door.

No one appeared. I scratched again, and waited. But still no Custer, and I knew that, involved in conversation with Swanson, he hadn't heard. I had to get in, and quickly; that was vital. Desperate situations call for desperate remedies, so I stood up and rang the doorbell.

Quickly squatting again, I checked my tail once more, then sat looking adoringly upward, paper clenched in my jaws. Custer opened the door, looking straight out, and saw no one; then he glanced down and said, "Oh, it's you. Come on," and he held the door open. As I ambled in I saw him frown, and glance from the doorbell to me and back again. But his mind was on two hundred and fifty thousand dollars, not minor mysteries or dogs, and he closed the door and hurried on down the hall. The less he saw me walking the better, and I prudently waited till Custer hurried past, then trotted along at his heels.

Into the den we turned, Swanson glancing up from a typed sheet in his hand. I was still directly behind Custer, hidden as much as possible by his legs, and I squatted before Custer's chair as fast as I could; instinctively I'd realized that this was my most canine pose. Swanson was sitting in a low leather-upholstered easy chair, a small table between him and Custer's lounge chair, and he smiled as he saw the newspaper in my mouth. I felt pleased, and flipped *Ears Up*, cocking my head intelligently, and Swanson smiled a little more at that. "Pretty cute," he said to Custer, who'd dropped onto the chaise lounge.

Custer nodded, pleased at the compliment. Showing off his dog a little more, he said, "Here, boy," reaching for the paper, and before I could flip *Mouth Op.—Cls.*, he took hold of it. But my mouth was gripping it like a vise, and Custer tugged, then frowned, glancing at

Swanson. My tongue shot out, and—I wished I'd had time to *practice!*—it flipped on *Bark*. The sound was pretty loud in the small study, and somewhat odd since my mouth stayed closed. Swanson jumped, and Custer looked mad. This time I successfully flicked on *Mouth Op.— Cls.*, the huge jaws slowly opened, Custer reaching for the paper again, and just before his hand touched it—I'd forgotten to turn off *Bark*, damn it!—another tremendous *wuff* sounded, he snatched his hand away, and the paper dropped to the floor. I got *Bark* turned off, and *Tail Wag* on; Custer glared at me, then picked up the paper, sat frowning at me, and finally said, "Well!?"

I didn't know what he meant. I'd used up seventeen tail wags already, according to a little dial on the control panel, and was getting worried, but didn't dare turn it off yet. I flipped *Ears Up* several times, causing my ears to rise and fall alertly, and cocked my head intelligently till it almost fell off. "My *slippers*, you idiot!" Custer said, and I nodded rapidly. Trotting to the corner of the room, I flicked off *Tail Wag*.

Muzzle directly over the slippers, I carefully turned on *Mouth Op.— Cls.*, and shoved down my muzzle. The big jaws closed, but slid right off the polished leather. Again I flicked the switch, and again the huge jaws opened, then closed, sort of nuzzling the slippers, moving them, but not getting hold of them. "Some of these big dogs aren't really too well coordinated, actually," Swanson said kindly, and I gave *Tail Wag* a flick, then turned it off to concentrate. This time when the jaws opened, I shoved my muzzle down hard, directly against the carpet on either side of the goddamned slippers, and they closed down tight, nearly biting them in half.

I turned toward Custer's chair so fast I stumbled, and fell sprawling in front of him, but got up quickly, snapped on *Mouth Op.—Cls.*, and the slippers dropped to the floor just as Custer reached for them. Glaring at me, he picked them up, and I quickly got into the big basket beside his chair. Cus sat back then, smiling fixedly at Swanson, and—I was at the side of the lounge chair away from Swanson—Cus reached down and, pretending to pat me, gave me a hard judo cut behind the ears. I flipped *Growl* on and off, and lay flat, chin on the bottom of my basket, which smelled.

They didn't take long to transact their business. Swanson gave Custer the typed page; it was a release, he said, and Custer read it quickly, then signed it. Swanson tucked it carefully into a long black-leather wallet he carried in his inside suitcoat pocket, then rubbed his hands together, grinning. "And now for the piece dee resistance," he said, and I considered biting him. The attaché case was lying on the table, and Swanson unlocked it and lifted the lid.

I couldn't help it; I stood up to look, too, remembering to cock my head to one side, ears rising alertly; I was "thinking dog" pretty good now. They didn't notice; they were staring at the money, too, and the fact was, I saw, that two hundred and fifty thousand dollars in hundreds wasn't too impressive a display. The money occupied only half the case, the rest being newspapers; there were only twenty-five packets of a hundred bills each, and Custer counted them quickly. Then he stood, money in hand, walked to a picture on the wall, and removed it, revealing the round door and combination lock of a small wall safe.

This was the moment on which everything depended: the moment I'd planned and worked for. I had guessed correctly that Swanson would occupy the chair he did, and not Custer's lounge chair. The safe was on the wall at Swanson's right, and knowing Custer's innate suspiciousness, I had also figured correctly that he would stand facing the safe at a slight angle to keep his back between Swanson and the dial. That would put my basket on a direct-line view as Custer worked the combination, shielding it from Swanson.

I was ready. Slowly, soundlessly, I withdrew one arm from the front leg of my dog suit as Custer walked to the safe. Then, drawing my head back from the viewers, I took from my shirt pocket the small, three-inch, 9-power telescope I'd bought this morning, and fitted one end to my eye, then brought the other end to the viewer; there was just barely room inside the big head.

Something was wrong! I saw Custer, all right, focused sharp and clear, but he seemed only an inch high and miles away! Quickly I reversed the telescope, and Custer's head and shoulders sprang into close-up, the safe big as a dinner plate, every number and line of the dial etched sharp and achingly clear as Custer began turning it; I was tempted to flip on *Tail Wag*.

But then—I never seemed to learn!—a Custer Huppfelt is *always* a Custer Huppfelt! This one, suspicious to the rotted depths of his wizened soul, *didn't even trust his own dog!* As he began twisting the dial, he stepped very close to the safe, the dial directly under his nose now, completely hiding it not only from Swanson but from me. All I could see was his back, and I wanted to run over and bite him! I wanted to run over to his pants leg and—but there was no switch for that. The little round safe door slammed shut. Custer twirled the combination knob and turned to face Swanson, rubbing his palms together, grinning happily, drooling slightly.

With perfunctory politeness he invited Swanson to stay for a drink and join him for a swim, but Swanson was already standing, reaching for his hat and attaché case, speaking polite refusals as he glanced at his watch. Cus walked him to the door then, while I lay back in my basket, heartsick and desperate, growling occasionally, and—by flipping *Mouth Op.*—*Cls.* up and down very fast, I found I could speed up the action—snapping.

What could I do? What could I DO!? Overpower Custer? *Force* him to give me the combination to the safe? It was my only hope, and was no hope at all; I simply wasn't big enough, for one thing, and he'd recognize me anyway. I heard the front door close, heard Custer's returning steps, saw him turn onto the staircase. Suddenly, in desperate inspiration, I knew what I had to try!

My paws were thin fur-covered nylon with sponge-rubber pads, quite flexible, and I stood up on my hind legs and snatched a ball-point pen from Custer's desk. Near it lay a clipboard with a blank sheet attached, and I thrust it under my right front leg and ran out the back door, careful not to let the screen door slam, then ran across the grass to the pool. Momentarily safe behind the fence that partially hid the pool from the house, I stood looking frantically around for something that would work; a garden hose would do! There was no hose, but I saw a pool skimmer: a thin flat net stretched on a wire hoop attached to the end of a ten-foot aluminum pole long enough to reach more than halfway across the pool.

I grabbed up the net, yanked hard, the net loop pulled out of the aluminum handle, and I tossed it into some bushes. The other end was covered with a yellow plastic cap, which twisted right off, and now I had a ten-foot hollow aluminum tube, slightly curved at the end where the net had been. It was the work of a moment to firmly tie the straight end of the pole to the inside of a rubber inner tube floating near the pool ladder; the other end hung straight down into the water. Holding my breath, carrying my things, I climbed down the ladder to the bottom. It was deep, here at the diving-board end of the pool, and when I stood on the bottom, finally, I was glad to take the curving end of the hollow pole into my mouth and draw a breath.

I waited no more than a minute or two, I suppose; then the water's surface far overhead was shadowed momentarily, I heard the sudden jounce of the diving board, heard the tremendous splash, then Custer appeared, head down, arms outthrust, skimming along the bottom of the pool in a wild trail of bubbles and turbulent water, gliding rapidly toward the foot of the ladder, beside which I stood motionless in the shadows. Custer's groping hands found and gripped the ladder, he set a foot on the first rung, and—*click!*—I snapped one ring of the handcuffs around his naked ankle, the other ring being already fastened to the ladder. The bubbles of his downward splash ascending, the water steadying and clearing, Custer stood, one foot on the bottom of the pool, the other held to the rung of the ladder, and now he saw me for the first time.

There are a handful of pictures of the mind that I will always treasure: a mother I once saw gazing at the face of her newborn child; a little girl staring at her first Christmas tree; a small boy walking slowly toward his brand-new bicycle. But above them all I will forever treasure the sight of Custer's face as he stood clipped to the bottom of his pool, wild-eyed, staring at, and realizing that, it was his own dog who had done it.

There I stood, shaggy ears outspread and swaying in the last of the upward stream of bubbles, aluminum tube in my muzzle, clipboard in hand, rapidly writing, *I want . . . $250,000 to let you go.*

I have to give Custer credit: he had grit! He had the courage of his lack of convictions! Though he was inexplicably held prisoner by his dog sixteen feet under water and was holding what might well be his last breath, Custer's nature didn't change. He gestured rapidly for clipboard and pen, I passed them to him carefully, keeping well out of his reach, and Custer frantically wrote, *No, but all the bones you can eat—for life!*

I shook my head, took the clipboard, and wrote, *I'll buy my own— with the $250,000.*

Custer snatched pen and board, and scribbled, *$100,000—that's my top offer!*

Taking back clipboard and pen, I momentarily considered offering to split the difference, except that I had to have two hundred and fifty thousand, and it didn't seem to me that Custer was really in any position to bargain. *$250,000 or nothing!* I wrote.

I believe he actually considered both alternatives. Finally he took pen and board, and wrote, quite fast, *All right. Is a check okay?*

Don't be absurd. I want the combination to your safe.

It was hard to believe even as I saw it, but Custer actually turned pale, there under the water. He thought for a moment, releasing a few more bubbles of air, then snatched the clipboard and rapidly printed, *53 left, clear around to right, stop at 14, left to 36. Now unlock these cuffs!*

I'm not that dumb! You stay here till I try the combination.

Cus grabbed the clipboard, and changed the 53 to 71. I passed him the air tube then, which he accepted gratefully, and I dog-paddled to the surface.

The safe opened at the first try; I was so excited I'd forgotten to take off my suit, and dripped on Custer's rug, and had trouble manipulating the dial. But I got it open, scooped up the two hundred and fifty thousand, and trotted out with it clutched in my forepaws.

On the lawn, behind the bushes, I unzipped the dog suit; it was a good suit, almost waterproof, and I was only slightly damp. The real St. Bernard was yawning, beginning to blink lazily. Carrying the money wrapped in the suit, I walked out to my car thinking of Custer. He'd be sitting down now on a rung of the ladder at the bottom of the pool, thinking who knows what bitter thoughts on the true nature of man's best friend.

Just before time for the ferry to leave, I phoned the Whipley police from a booth on the pier. I gave them Custer's name and address, and said Cus was attempting suicide by handcuffing himself to the bottom of his pool; that he was insane and dangerous. I figured that by the time they got out to Custer's place, the real St. Bernard would be up and dogging their footsteps. So when they asked who I was, I barked several times and hung up. I hated to do it—he was a nice old dog—but I felt certain he'd eventually be able to prove his innocence, and by that time I'd be in the clear.

CHAPTER THIRTEEN

A dozen yards from the southeast corner of Forty-second and Lex, I piled out of the cab, slapped several dollars into the cabbie's hand, and began running toward Herman's newsstand, glancing at my watch. Just short of the stand, I stopped dead, rammed my hand into my pocket, and brought out a nickel, a penny, and two dimes, and came as close as I've ever been since I was twelve years old to bursting into tears—they were both Woodrow Wilson, of course.

I didn't know what to do. I took a fast step in one direction, turned and walked rapidly in the other for a couple steps, stopped, and stood looking helplessly around me. Then I whirled, hurried to the corner ahead, and the instant the light flashed WALK, I ran, dodging between pedestrians, across to the drugstore in the Doc Pepper Building. With a snarl of hatred, Paul Newman gave me ten dimes for a dollar, and I stepped to one side, flicked through them with a flying forefinger, then tossed them over my shoulder and walked out.

This time I didn't wait for the light, or even walk to the crosswalk. I ran through traffic, while horns blasted in rage, to Grand Central Station just across the street, got ten more dimes and a muttered malediction at a newsstand, fingered through them, then handed them to a small boy walking through the station with his mother. "Throw them away this *instant!*" she said to the boy. "There must be something *wrong* with them!" and he flung dimes down among the cigarette stubs in a sand-filled urn as though they were hot, cleverly palming half of them, I noticed. Passersby watching me suspiciously, I walked quickly around a corner, blushing with guilt.

There was a row of a couple dozen phone booths here, and I moved quickly from one empty booth to another, feeling the coin-return slots, with no luck. An elderly woman stood watching me as I came out of the last booth. "You that hungry, son?" she said sadly. "Here." And she gave me a Woodrow Wilson dime.

It was an idea: I hurried outside, stood against the station wall, turned mouth corners down and coat collar up, sucked in my cheeks to look hungry, and held out a cupped hand. I got three W.W. dimes, a Canadian nickel, and a wadded-up gum wrapper before I saw a cop coming toward me and ducked back into the station.

A porter leaned a two-wheeled hand truck against a wall, walked away,

and three seconds later I was wheeling it in the opposite direction along
the marble floor of the station, looking blank-faced and casual as though
I had every right; no one even glanced at me. A minute later, the cart
loaded now, I was down on the far less crowded lower level, in among
several aisles of coin lockers, not another soul in sight. We never know
to what depths necessity may take us; never in my life had I dreamed I
could lower myself to robbing the poor. Yet I didn't hesitate now—I
blame society. Using the knife-sharp lifting bar of my handcart as a pry,
I jimmied open the locked coin box at the rear of the friendly automated
panhandler, and filled both coat pockets with dimes. In a washroom
booth three minutes and several hundred dimes later, I found it: a thin,
worn, absolutely marvelous-looking Roosevelt dime. Hurrying up the
ramp toward the upper level again, I saw the kid and his mother, gave
him a double handful of dimes in passing, and his mother swung at me
with her handbag.

Across the station floor, running, across Lexington Avenue, while
drivers leaned on their horns in insane fury, I made my way to Herman's
stand and slapped FDR face up on the counter. With only a glance,
then, at the Chrysler Building just across the street, and at the masthead
of the *New York Post* which Herman had amusingly thrust down into
the front of my pants, I sprang into a cab at the curb and began waving
a fifty-dollar bill under the driver's nose, which twitched appreciatively.
It was his, I said, if he got me to Fifty-first and Third in under five
minutes, and I was flung back into the seat as we shot forward. In a
rubber-burning stop, we were at Custer's building in four minutes, the
driver turning to yank the bill from my hand, and I was out and racing
for the building lobby.

He was home. My thumb jammed against his bell, and Cus yanked
open the door; he was wearing a white shirt, dark tie, dark-blue suit,
white carnation in lapel—wedding-bound. He stared, then began shaking his dark-haired head. "Too late, too late, too late!" he kept saying,
but I shoved past him and walked to a desk across his living room.

I didn't say a word; from my inside coat pocket I took a stack of bills,
set it on the desk top, and stepped back. His mouth slowly opening,
Custer stared at the lovely green back of the uppermost bill, and at the
marvelous little figures in each corner reading 100. Money talks, and this
said, *Touch me, Custer.* He reached out a forefinger hypnotically, and,
his other hand pressing down on the stack, began flipping through the
bill ends of the top packet, counting; there were a hundred. His brown
eyes glazing, Custer's counting forefinger moved down the side of the
little stack, reverently touching the brown-paper bands which

enclosed each of the packets; there were twenty-five. A neat little stack, only a few inches high, but Custer murmured in a choked voice, "My god . . . it's a quarter million bucks." Then he whirled to face me. "Where *were* you!" he yelled in anguish. "You're too *late*, too *late!*"

I was nodding slowly, suddenly stunned. "I know . . . I should have *realized* . . . I didn't think! The wedding's in an hour—*less* than an hour. It wouldn't be right, not *now*"—I reached for the money—"to do this to Hetty!"

"Hetty, hell!"—He slapped my hands away. "I'm talking about my boss!" He grabbed the phone, dialed at top speed, then stood wild-eyed. "*Al!* My god, I thought you'd left! I've *got* it, Al, the money! Is there still time to . . . ?" He stood listening, actually holding his breath; then his eyes flamed with an unholy light. "Thank god! Don't move! Wait for me! I'm coming!" He snatched up the stack of bills and raced for the door, cramming them into every pocket.

I should have felt triumph, wild exultation. Instead, walking slowly out, and then down to the street, I was scared. Had I done right? *Yes!* I kept telling myself. Whatever temporary shock Hetty would feel tonight was infinitely better than marrying a man who would actually sell her out for money. I'd done right, I knew it, but slowly walking the streets, I couldn't stop thinking of how she must feel. And presently—I'd told myself I was wandering aimlessly, but all the time I knew where I was going—I stood outside my old apartment, the tiny apartment where, if only I'd known it, I could have found happiness with Hetty. Maybe she needs me, I told myself, and went in.

"Your wife's out, Mr. Bennell," said the doorman. "Gone to get married. Probably be back soon. Any message?"

"Nothing special; just tell her her husband called." She'd left for the church—what if she heard the news there! I ran out, raced to Lexington, shouted at passing cabs for ten minutes, and when I got one the driver didn't know where St. Charley's was. We found a phone booth after a while, found it listed way downtown, we got there, the church was lighted, doors closed, I tiptoed in, and—recurring nightmare!

Once again, a crowded church, a robed and smiling minister. Once again, Hetty standing facing him, though this time her dress was different. And once again—oh, sure, *you* knew it all the time, but *I* didn't; I never learn!—there stood Custer, dark-haired and brown-eyed this time, but still the same, always the same! Once again, in this world and every world, probably, he'd stolen my money, and now he was stealing my wife!

And once again now, with awful finality, the terrible words began: "If any man can show just cause . . . " Once more, nightmarishly, my mouth opened to cry out, and once more I was unable to speak. "If any man can show just cause why they may not lawfully be joined together, let him now speak," the minister concluded, and for a dizzy, spinning, insane moment I thought my voice had replied.

"Reckon maybe I can," drawled a voice from the other end of the aisle, obviously that of a tall lean Ranger. Like everyone else, I turned and saw, walking up the aisle toward the front of the church, a short, stout, bald man in a gray double-breasted business suit, apparently a TV fan. He looked calm, but the man with him, much the same type, in a dark suit, looked furious. "Shore am sorry, ma'am," the first little man said, stopping before Hetty; then he turned to Custer, opening his coat to reveal a small gold-and-blue-enamel badge pinned to his shirt. "You're under arrest," he said.

"Why?" "*Why?*" "Why!" "WHY!?" said Custer, Hetty, the minister, flower girl, organist, janitor, and a hundred others, and it was the second little man who answered, actually shaking with rage, flickering a fist under Custer's nose.

"Because you're a crook! A fraud! A cheat!" he said, and I nodded my head each time. "*You* gave me these! Two hundred and fifty thousand bucks' worth!" He was holding a greenback stretched between his hands up to Custer's eyes, Cus drawing back, trying to see it.

"And what's wrong with *that!*" Cus was saying. He'd turned, trying to get away from the enraged little man, and now he was actually being backed down the aisle, the man following right after him still shoving the tautly stretched bill at Custer's face. Standing on tiptoes like everyone else, I could see it now: the dark face of a hundred-dollar bill, the numerals in the upper corners, the familiar oval engraving of a President's face in the center.

"Wrong!?" the little man said, nearly choking. "Wrong!?" He was still shoving the bill at Custer's white face as they moved down the aisle, and now I had a much closer look at the bill I had brought from an alternate world, and suddenly saw what Custer was staring at, and what the little man meant. "Just tell me," yelled the man, "*tell* me: WHO IS 'PRESIDENT GEORGE C. COOPERNAGEL'!" And once again handcuffs clicked for Custer, this time around his wrists.

Let me skip over the next ten days and bleak nights at the Y; the Saturday-night chop-suey special at the cafeteria, bread-pudding-with-hard-sauce dessert included, being the only bright spot of all those long days. Skip to the knock at my door as I lay in my L-shaped bed hopelessly trying to sleep, and to Jose's voice saying, "Phone call."

"Ben," said the forlorn tiny voice in the lobby phone-booth receiver, "it's Hetty. Could you come over? I'm lonely!" she said, and began to cry.

I was there, still in pajamas, before she hung up, I believe, and when I saw on the davenport, where she'd been looking at it, the box of stationery, the famous box of stationery with which I'd proposed, I gulped. "Remember?" said Hetty, and I nodded, unable to speak. Then I was able to speak—"Be a shame to waste that good paper," I began—and was unable to stop.

Yes, of course we're married again, but do not think—life is real!—that living with Hetty has somehow become a permanent idyll. Just exactly as before, I've regressed to ignoring her—life is earnest!—to not seeing her, not listening, hardly speaking. And then the tears, recriminations, and sometimes, lord help us, even reminiscences of gallant and courtly Custer begin. But things are not what they seem, and these periods don't last long now. They're soon followed by smiles, adoration, compliments on how loving I've been lately. It's as though, Hetty generally remarks, I'd been away, and my old self come back. I smile at her then, just standing there looking at my darling Hetty with renewed love and appreciation, idly flipping and catching the good-luck piece—a thin dime—that I always carry with me nowadays. Wherever I go.

You come across them, you know, every once in a while, if you just keep your eyes open: Ulysses Grant quarters, Coopernagel nickels, Woodrow Wilson dimes. They're worth finding because it's just as the ad said when I was a kid: Coin Collecting can be FUN! And all I can say in farewell is: Why don't *you* start, too? Tonight!

MARION'S
WALL

CHAPTER ONE

Dear Son: Just a quick note to say that if you and Jan feel sure you want an old Victorian, so called, I think you could do a lot worse: they've got a charm today's penny-pinching architecture completely lacks. I lived in one during my own San Francisco days, and I write mostly to say that if in the course of your house-hunting you should find yourselves near a place called Buena Vista Hill, I wish you'd see if it's still there, and let me know. It was in the last block at the southernmost end of Divisadero Street, Number 114, and was a fine old two-story frame building—I had the bottom apartment—with a gable roof, bay window, and a view of the city and Bay that would knock your eye out. I have fond memories of the place, and if you found one like it am sure you and Jan would be happy in it—happiness is often just a matter of making up your mind to be. Nuff sed!

Not much news from here. Usual lousy Chicago February, though not too cold lately. Last Saturday . . .

I was standing near the top of a six-foot ladder, my hair almost brushing the high ceiling, flexing my hands to work out the stiffness. My fingers made a soft popping sound against my palms, and I raised my hands to my ears, listening. Then I lifted each foot in turn and revolved it at the ankle. Jan was kneeling at the foot of my ladder lifting handfuls of wet shredded wallpaper into a cardboard Tide box and at the sound of my fingers she looked up. I said, "I'm doing a dance. Of joy. Because this is such fun. What the hell time is it?"

"Eleven-ten." She was wearing blue denims and a black turtle-neck sweater. Jan has long dark hair—today it was tied back with a ribbon—she's pale-skinned, and now without any make-up, in the hard daylight from the tall unshaded windows of the empty living room, she looked pale.

"Eleven-ten, and we started at eight-thirty; nearly three hours so far. Goody. Hot dog. Son of a bitch. We'll be at this all day right up till time to drive to the airport. All next weekend, too, probably."

"I thought it would just peel off with that thing." She nodded at the wallpaper "remover" lying on top of my ladder, a shallow foot-square metal thing with a handle, a fog of wet-looking steam rising from its perforated faceplate. It was connected by a thin plastic hose to a chromed tank on the floor plugged to an electric outlet.

"If you thought that, your vision of life has been corrupted. Outside of television commercials things never just peel right off." I picked up the steamer, pressed it to the wall just under the ceiling, and began sliding it back and forth as though I were ironing the wallpaper. It was kind of fun, watching the paper darken from the moisture, but hard on the arms. I could feel flecks of wallpaper drying on my face and knew there were more lying on my hair, which is combed straight back but kind of springy, worn a little long like everyone else's. My name is Nick Cheyney, incidentally, and I'm thirty; Jan's twenty-seven. I'm fairly tall, skinny, my face has been described as "amiable," and I wear metal-rimmed glasses. Today I was accoutered in dirty tan wash pants, a worn-out striped shirt frayed at the collar and torn at one shoulder, and sneakers of really record-breaking filth and raggedness over bare feet.

Jan stood up and walked out to the kitchen with the filled carton on one hip. She came back with the empty carton and two mugs of coffee held by their handles in one hand. Of necessity she left the hall door open and our dog, Al, a tri-colored basset—which means brown-white-and-black, not red-white-and-blue—walked in. As Jan crossed the room toward the window seat, eyes on the coffee mugs, Al sat down on some wet curls of wallpaper to watch the activity, and I didn't betray him. I winked, and he opened his mouth to smile, tongue lolling. I was working with the scraper now, wet paper wrinkling into pennant-shaped strips to hang limply or drop to the floor. Jan sat down on the bay window seat, setting the mugs on the sill, turned and saw Al, who smiled in friendly fashion. "Out!" Jan pointed. "You know better than that! You'll have wallpaper all over the house!" He looked at her closely, wondering if she meant for sure. "Out! In the kitchen! Or go on out and play; it's a nice day." Al stood up, looking to me for help.

"He says you're violating his civil rights."

"He hasn't got any today. Go on now!"

Al left reluctantly, Jan following to close the door. "Take it up with ACLU, Al!" I called. "I'll testify." Using both hands now, I worked the scraper up and down rapidly till the entire dampened area was clear. "There you are. First preview of layer number three." The newly exposed paper was a pattern of brown latticework entwined with dark-green ivy. I climbed down, walked to the window seat, and picked up my mug. "Well? Where do you place it? Early Horrible? Late Atrocious?" We stood tasting our coffee, staring up at the wall.

"I don't know exactly: the Thirties?"

"Oh God. Is that all? If we have to work our way layer by layer back to 1882 or whenever, this place'll be a foot larger all the way around, time we're finished. And we'll be in our sunset years."

"I know, but it's interesting. To see what other people lived with. Most of them long dead, I suppose. You know something? Now, don't bother teasing me about it, because I know it's obvious, but—"

"If these wallpapers could only talk?"

"Yes."

"Probably bore the hell out of us. Mumbling away about the good old days. If I know these walls, and believe me I do, they'd never shut up."

"With you around they wouldn't get a word in. Oh, I wish I knew who'd lived here, Nick! What woman picked out that ivy pattern? It's not bad, you know. What did she look like, and who lay on a couch in this room staring up at the paper, counting how often the design was repeated. I wish there were some way to know." She sipped her coffee.

"There is, for a certain sensitive few of us." I closed my eyes. "It was a big fat lady. With mean piglike eyes. Stark naked, her obscene tattoos writhing in the gaslight, she killed her husband in this very room."

"She may have started a tradition. Let's see what the next layer looks like."

"No, that's cheating. You have to take one layer off completely, all around the room, before you can look at the next. Same principle— honored by all men, ignored by all women—as a box of candy. You have to finish the top layer before—"

"Oh, come on; say yes to life." She set her mug on the sill.

"Okay." I had a couple more gulps of coffee, then climbed the ladder and began soaking the new ivy-patterned strip I'd just uncovered, slowly sliding the metal steam box back and forth till the white portions of the pattern were nearly indistinguishable from the green of the leaves. A corner of the paper dropped loose and peeled down an inch of its own soggy weight. I set the steamer down, took the corner, and with a steady gentle pull drew it down, slowly exposing a pink-and-green pattern of roses and leaves on a white background. "Okay, what's this? Colonial? Elizabethan? Chaucerian?"

"I don't know, Nick, I'm really no expert. I've only read about it a little. Maybe it's from the Twenties. I'd say the Twent—"

She stopped because, still carefully drawing the dampened paper downward, I'd suddenly exposed three small arcs several inches apart. Each was an inch or so high, and of a red much brighter than anything in the pattern itself. I peeled on down to the bottom of the dampened area, the paper tore off in my hands, and I dropped it to the floor, then rubbed my thumb across the tops of the small red arcs. The red smudged, and I looked at my thumb, then at Jan. "Lipstick."

"Well, peel off some more, see what it is!"

Directly below the layer I'd just exposed, I soaked through another foot-high strip, the height of the steamer plate. Here the ivy-patterned paper was still covered by the layer before it, but I worked till I'd soaked both layers through. I began tugging them loose, carefully working with the scraper blade between wall and wet paper, and was able to loosen and peel both together. "Two layers at once; the gods are sleeping." Jan didn't answer; she stood motionless, watching as there was gradually exposed a foot-high letter *M* scrawled gracefully across the rose-patterned wallpaper in bright lipstick. "M for murder? Mopery? *Merde?*"

"Nick, keep *going!*"

Leaning out to the right from the side of the ladder, supporting the weight of the steamer with both hands, I soaked a double layer of paper beside the big *M* as far as I could reach. Again with help from the scraper blade both layers peeled, and the red *M* was the initial letter of a yard-long *Marion* lipsticked across the wall under the high old ceiling.

Neither of us spoke now. As I scrambled down the ladder we glanced at each other, grinning with excitement. Jan helping, I dragged the ladder to the right, its legs shuddering across the bare wood floor, and trotted up again. And when I'd peeled down the next few feet of the adjoining wallpaper, Jan and I read *Marion Marsh* in a six-foot length of slanted red foot-high script. Just beyond the *h* of *Marsh* the fireplace chimney jutted from the wall, the paper ending at the bricks, and I climbed down to pull the ladder back to the left. "It's a will! Written on the wall! And we're the heirs. The first people to discover it. She's left a million—"

"Nick, shut up and hurry up. Or I'll die."

Working fast, peeling the wallpaper down in yard-long, foot-high strips, I exposed a second line of script centered under the first: *lived here*, it said. The line below that was near the middle of the wall, within Jan's reach, and as I moved the steamer she worked the scraper, eyes snapping with excitement. *June*, it said, followed by *14*, and as my steamer grated against the projecting brick of the chimney Jan was working off the wet paper to reveal a *1*, then a *9*, then the entire date, *1926*. The line below that, Jan's hands following my steamer so closely its mist curled over her fingers, said, *Read it*. And the final line, just above the baseboard—we knelt side by side, fingers flying to uncover it—said, *and weep!*

Sitting back on our heels, we stared up. From ceiling to floor the immense red script covered half a wall nearly eleven feet high and some twelve feet horizontally, and now Jan read it aloud in entirety: "Marion Marsh lived here, June 14, 1926. Read it and weep!" She clutched my arm. "I *will* weep if we don't find out who she was! Nick, I have to know, I absolutely have *got to know*."

"Yeah." I nodded, and stood, still staring at that enormous scrawl of writing. "I'd give something to know, all right. Maybe Dad knows; we'll ask him tonight. *Look* at that. Must have taken a couple tubes of lipstick."

"At least." Jan stood. "It's a very distinctive handwriting. You get the feeling of an interesting person."

"I'll bet she was that, all right. Well, what do we do about it before I peel it off? Take a picture, maybe? I've got film in the camera."

"Oh, no, let's leave it! For the housewarming, at least. It'll make a marvelous conversation piece."

" 'Conversation piece.' " I began dragging the ladder around the fireplace. "Sometimes I wonder what the conversation is really like when folks gather 'round the conversation pieces. 'Hey, is that ice bucket really your mother-in-law's skull?' 'Yep, made it myself. Just before she passed on.' 'Well, I'll be damned.' End of conversation. 'Don't tell me that life-size panorama of Lincoln's War Cabinet is entirely made out of feathers?' 'Sure as hell is. Took three nuthatches for Stanton's eyebrows alone.' 'You don't say!' End of conversation. And there'll be even less talk about this, Kiddo. What's there to say? The odds are that no one in the world knows who Marion Marsh was any more; that writing is probably all that's left of her. And we'll never find out any more than this."

But we did. For the rest of the day except for a fifteen-minute sandwich lunch in the kitchen—Al, tidy soul that he is, kindly disposing of my crusts—we peeled wallpaper, watching for more writing to appear. None did, and by four-thirty the room was stripped to the rose-patterned paper on all four walls and in the window-seat bay. Once more, then, we stood looking at the wall to the left of the fireplace: *Marion Marsh lived here, June 14, 1926. Read it and weep!* we read again. Then I changed clothes to drive to the airport.

This was early March but it had been a warm sun-filled day after nearly a week of rain, and all I wore over an open-necked sport shirt was a light sleeveless sweater. The car was parked at the curb down in front of the house, wheels toed in; we're on a hill. The car is the best thing I own: a forty-six-year-old Packard roadster I'd bought half restored before I was married, finishing the job myself; gray body and wheels with navy-blue striping. It ran beautifully, and we used it regularly, our only car.

Today the black canvas top was down, the finish dirt-slashed after the rains, and I stepped up on the running board, slid over the door top, higher than the roofs of some of today's so-called cars, and dropped onto the black-leather seat, glancing up at our windows.

Jan was at the window seat, and she lifted an arm to wave, a little limply, shoulders drooping. She was tired, of course, and had the living room to sweep, dinner to get, and—biggest job of all—get dressed for company. Jan is a shy girl, not so good at meetings with anyone but old and trusted friends. And while she'd met and liked my dad, it had been nearly four years. It helped her poise when she managed to feel she looked her best, so I knew she'd fuss and worry about what to wear.

Driving down the Divisadero hill I felt pretty good: still excited about the writing on the wall; pleased with the day's work; looking forward to seeing my dad. Things were looking up in general, I thought. Jan and I had been married six years, and while we were happy, we had our problems sometimes; what couple doesn't after a while? But we had our new apartment now, the best we'd ever had. There was plenty of work to be done on it yet, including installing some new bathroom fixtures, which the landlord would pay for if I'd put them in. But I liked doing things like that, even removing wallpaper, and so did Jan. We felt busy and full of plans these days, a good feeling. Sometimes I think most everyone needs a new start every once in a while.

The airport is always crowded but it wasn't bad this time of day and year, and the plane was on time. We were home by six-thirty, talking all the way back to the city catching up on the news. There wasn't much: we keep in fairly close touch with a letter every couple of weeks or so and an evening phone call once in a while. We get along pretty well, my dad and I; my mother is dead.

When we turned into our block it was dusk at ground level but still plenty of daylight in the sky. We could see the white-and-pastel city spread out below our hill, every building sharp in the rain-washed air. A beginning fog was moving onto the Bay and the orange lights of the Bay Bridge were on. It was a nice time to arrive.

My dad got out, hatless, his tie still over one shoulder from the top-down drive, and stood in the street staring up at the house, as I got his bag from the trunk. Our living-room windows were dark but I thought I could see the blur of Jan's face. It always interested her how much alike my father and I were, and she'd be comparing us again: same height, and he just as skinny as I am. He's bald, and his face is thirty-odd years older than mine, but it's the same face, and I'm Nick junior. He's intelligent, and has the look in the eye of a humorous man. When I glanced at him now, closing the car trunk, picking up his bag, he nodded at the house. "Good to see it again." Then he shook his head. "And strange."

The house, like all the others on that side of the street, sits high on a ridge with a long flight of concrete stairs before you even reach the wooden stairs to the porch. Halfway up them, our middle window rattled, Jan leaned out to call down to us, and Dad grinned and waved. On the porch I was glad to set his bag down for a moment, and we stood looking out over the city at the Bay, fogging over very fast now. "Last time I stood here," my dad said, "you could still see a few sailing ships anchored out there." He turned to look at the lower-apartment windows beside us, but they were curtained, people living there, and he couldn't peek in at his old apartment.

Looking good in an orange dress, Jan stood waiting at the top of the inside stairs with Al, who began barking as soon as the lower door opened. I shushed him, threatening to hand him over to the vivisection-ists, and he looked down at me alertly, ears coming up, wondering whether "vivisection" was something to eat. Dad spoke to him, and Al recognized a friend, and said so with his tail; all he'd wanted was to show whose house this was in case the arriving stranger had any doubts. When we were halfway up, Jan came hurrying impulsively down to meet Dad, feeling shy—I saw her face flush—but her eyes were excited. Dad puts people at ease; I've seen it all my life. He slid an arm around Jan's waist, kissing her, greeted her, and walked her on up the stairs; I reached up and pinched her. He likes Jan, genuinely, and I was sure she felt fine, now. "I simply can't *wait* to ask you!" I heard her saying. "Do you know—" She turned on the landing to see me waggling a hand—*Don't say it!*—and cut herself short.

"Know what?" He stood smiling at her, then reached down to pat Al.

"Whether the building looks the same. How does it seem to be back in it?"

"Looks as though I'd just left it last month. It may seem foolish to fly out here for only one evening just to see it again. But it's worth it, believe me. Especially with you two in it now. Amazing that you should be here."

I'd set my father's bag down under the hall hatrack, and now I sidled past them and into the living room. Jan was saying, "Well, we looked it up and fell in love with it on sight. And when we learned the top apartment was empty . . . " She shrugged, smiling.

"Come on in here," I called. "Get the view before I turn on the lights." They came in and walked to the bay windows. The street lamps had come on, faintly illuminating the room, and we could see the city, lighted too now, spread out before us from the uneven mountaintop horizon far ahead down to the shores of the Bay. Nick senior and Jan stood at the windows; I was just behind them. "Furniture's stored in the basement till we finish the room," I said conversationally, and Jan flicked a glance at me, detecting the false casualness of a planned-in-advance remark. "We're still peeling the old wallpaper off; hell of a job." Staring out at the enormous view, comparing it, I suppose, with the way it had been once, my dad didn't answer, and I walked back to the wall switch beside the hall doorway. For a moment I hesitated, looking at his back, wondering if I should do this. Then I flipped on the overhead chandelier, and Dad and Jan turned, squinting in the new glare. "And look what we uncovered this morning," I said casually, and his head turned to follow my gesture.

"Oh, my God," he said softly, staring at the enormous red script on the wall.

When I spoke my voice was suddenly tight; for an instant I was a boy again, afraid he'd gone too far with his father. "Did you know her, Dad?"

A second or so passed, then he turned abruptly to the window, standing with his back to us. "Did I know her," he repeated flatly. "Did I know Marion Marsh. Oh, yes. Oh, yes, indeed." He turned back into the room to stare at the writing on the wall again. Then he walked toward it, his hand coming up as though he were going to touch it, but he didn't. He stopped before it, stood for a moment, then without turning to look at us he said, "When she wrote that I was here in the room with her." His head shook wonderingly. "I was twenty years old." For a moment longer he stood staring. "You know how she reached the top lines?" He turned to look at us, smiling now. "Walking along the back of the davenport. In high heels. She knew I was afraid she'd fall. I stood ready to catch her if she did, and she all but turned somersaults up there. Three-quarters drunk probably, though maybe not; it was never easy to tell. You'd think she was, and she wasn't. Then you'd think she was sober, and she'd be blind." He turned to look at the wall again, his head slowly shaking in awe and astonishment. "And it's still there. *Still there*: I can't believe it."

Jan said, "I have to go out to the kitchen; there are things cooking. Come on along, will you? Both of you. I don't want to miss a word."

The kitchen was large enough to hold a big round wooden table, covered now with a linen cloth checked in a pastel-blue-and-white pattern, and set for three with the good china and blue tumblers. Around it stood four old-style wooden chairs, each of which Jan had enameled in a different color, the four slats in the back being all four colors. There was an old black gas stove with a white-enamel oven door labeled WEDGEWOOD in blue letters. The sink was old, with a splintering wooden drainboard; I'd have to do something about that. The refrigerator was new, and so were two Formica-covered work counters with cupboards underneath, and there was a big walk-in pantry. Jan stood at the stove, a large wooden spoon in one hand, an old-fashioned in the other, her apron longer than her skirt—she has good, good legs, which still interest me enormously. I'd put Al out in the back yard with his dinner, and Dad and I were at the table lounging back in our tipped-up chairs, sipping our drinks.

"Why did she write it?" he was saying to Jan. "I don't know; impulse. The way she did everything. She'd suddenly decided to move to Hollywood; she'd been in two, three pictures down there. The first as part of a crowd scene that didn't even survive the cutting room. But after the second and third she thought she had a career in pictures." He shrugged. "As she damn well may have; she was an actress. This was a good theater town then, and I saw her a number of times. At the old Alcazar." He nodded once or twice. "She was good all right." He took a swallow of his drink.

"Maybe I shouldn't ask this," Jan said, and stopped, her face flushing.

He smiled. "And maybe I shouldn't answer it." He lifted his glass to the light. "But what with two stiff drinks, the pleasure of being here, and the shock of seeing Marion's writing still on that wall—I will. The answer is that I thought I was. In love with her. That's what you meant, isn't it?" Jan nodded, her face flushing a little more, and she pushed her hair nervously back off one shoulder. "Well, I thought I was, and she thought she was. We'd been talking about getting married, in fact." He turned to grin at me. "If we had, you wouldn't be here, would you? Serve you right, too, for springing that stunt in the living room."

"Oh, I'd still be here," I said. "You couldn't have kept me out. But I suppose I'd look a little more like Jean Harlow than I do now; that's how I picture Marion Marsh, anyway." Like a lot of people, I'm interested in old movies; I collect films, in a small way. So this fascinated me.

"No, she wasn't even particularly good-looking. Pretty enough, I suppose; I don't know really. You just didn't think about that when she was around. She was a year older than I was, you know." Jan had begun to spoon things into serving dishes, and he and I got up to help her bring them to the table.

We began dinner. Jan told me to plug in the coffee maker, which stood at one edge of the table, and I did. Then I poured wine; Dad sipped it and smiled at me, nodding appreciatively, then tasted his food and complimented Jan on her cooking. And when these things had been done, Jan leaned across the table edge toward him and with the bluntness of a shy person who's momentarily overcome it, said, "Why? Why didn't you? Marry her, I mean."

"I wouldn't just throw up everything, pack, and move down to Hollywood with her." His face flushed suddenly, the old quarrel momentarily alive again. "What would *I* have done there? The movies weren't after me, and I didn't expect them to be! It made no sense. Then or now." He was frowning, and he glanced uneasily at me, picked up his wine-glass, and drank. "And of course I'm glad. *Very* glad," he said to me sternly, as though I might be thinking of denying it, "or I'd never have met your mother." He began cutting his meat, eyes on his plate. "We argued about it. I could see her point, though I didn't want her to go. She had a small part in her second picture that brought her some attention. Before the picture was even released, it got her a pretty good part in still a third. She'd kept working up here, see; it's where the money was, and her real career. She'd go to Hollywood for a couple days' work, maybe, then home again. But this was a bigger, longer part, she had to stay down there, and she suddenly decided that pictures was her career, and came up one weekend to get me. But I wouldn't go. After a while she cried. Then she began cursing me, and you can believe she knew how to do *that*. Then she jumped up suddenly, ran to the front windows"—he looked up, grinning—"and yanked the middle one up. I was supposed to be scared she was going to jump out. But I knew better. She was the last person in the world to do *that*. I just sat there, grinning at her. So she knelt on the window seat, leaned out, and looked over the city as though that's what she'd meant to do all the time. It was a fine, cool, sunny San Francisco day, I remember; the kind we ought to import to Chicago. And she said she loved the view. Loved San Francisco. Loved this apartment. And loved me. But she was blankety-blank well going to Hollywood! I didn't say anything, and she pulled her head in, turned around, and looked at me for a minute. 'Some day you'll brag that you knew me, you bastard,' she said. And she was right about that, wasn't she? Then she yelled, 'And this'll be known as the house I lived in!'—all excited in a fraction of a second, the way she could be. She jumped up off the window seat, ran across the room, and climbed right up on the back of the davenport. Still trying to punish me by threatening herself, you see. And demonstrating to herself, I suppose, that I still cared for her. Well, I did. And this time I jumped up and ran over to the davenport, because she could easily have fallen. Then she walked along the back, writing on the wall with her lipstick. Wearing a short skirt, knowing I was standing there watching her." Dad was smiling, looking past us off across the kitchen, fork motionless in his hand. " 'Marion Marsh lived here,' she wrote, and looked back over her shoulder at me. Then—she was a crazy girl, all right—she said, just murmuring it, really, 'Catch, Nick,' and without any other warning she let herself fall straight back."

He looked at Jan, then at me, still smiling. "Well, I caught her. Damn near broke my back, but you can be sure I caught her. I'm sixty-seven years old now, and this may sound strange to your young ears, but I can still remember exactly and precisely how that nutty girl felt, there in my arms. Meaning no disrespect whatever, son, to the memory of your mother. She smiled at me, all sweetness and light, lifted her head to kiss me, then hopped down to the floor, saying, 'Pull that blanking davenport out from the wall, you blank,' only she didn't say 'blank' and she didn't say 'blanking.' Then she wrote the rest of what you saw in there."

I was staring across the table at him wonderingly. This was a new look at a father ten years younger than I was now. "If she'd stayed in San Francisco," I said, "you'd have married her, wouldn't you." It was hardly a question.

"I don't know. How can I say. I hadn't met your mother then. I don't want to discuss it." He was silent for a moment, then he added, "But I will say that most women would have had mighty tough competition against Marion Marsh."

Jan said, "I'm delighted, fascinated, that she lived here. Right here in our house. Oh, I'm so glad you told us!" She shoved her chair back, jumping up. "I've just got to look at her wall again!" Carrying her coffee, Jan walked to the living room, and my father and I followed with ours.

In the living room we stood sipping our coffee under the hardness of the overhead bulbs, staring again at the huge lipsticked message from across the years. My voice hollow in the empty room, I said, "I've never heard her name before. She ever make it in Hollywood?"

"She never got back." He took a sip of his coffee, then looked at us. "In nearly every book or movie about the Twenties there's an obligatory scene: a bunch of people tearing down a country road in an open car, bottles waving, singing, yelling, having a fine drunken time. Well, it did happen. I've done it myself. And that's what Marion did the night before she was to go back to Hollywood. I wasn't along; she was mad at me, and I wasn't invited. The car turned over, injuring several of them and killing her." Jan winced, making an involuntary sound of protest in her throat, and I was frowning. "That was over in Marin County. On a back road near Ross. They had to refilm a couple parts of the picture she was working in. With another actress unknown then, but who turned out to be Joan Crawford. Marion never even saw the one complete picture she did appear in. It was released a month after she died."

After a moment Jan said gently, "But you saw it, didn't you?"

"Of course. It was called *Flaming Flappers*." He smiled at her. "I'm sorry, but that's what it was called. I saw it more than once, I can promise you, and felt as bad as I've ever felt, almost. Because when I saw it I knew Marion had been right. I was certain then that she'd had a career ahead of her, maybe even a great one. She wasn't especially good-looking, but she had more vitality and . . . sheer animal magnetism, I guess you'd call it, than anyone else I ever knew. When she was in a room, anywhere at all, you knew it. Not just me, everyone felt it. And when she left a room you felt it, too, almost as though the light had dimmed. Well, that came through in the picture. Except for a last little glimpse of her at the very end, so short it didn't count, she was in only one scene. A party scene: you saw her talking to a group of admiring men. That's all; it only lasted half a minute, maybe less. But it got her a real part in the next picture, the part Joan Crawford ended up having and which began her career. I've often thought that that should have been Marion's career. Because she had that same direct personal appeal and power over you that only a handful of the really great stars ever have; the ones you never forget, like Garbo; Crawford; Bette Davis. She had a career coming to her, all right." Taking a sip of his coffee, he looked back at the wall. " 'Read it and weep!' " he murmured, and nodded. "She was right about everything that day, wasn't she?"

CHAPTER TWO

A couple weeks later we had the apartment looking pretty good; we'd painted nights and weekends till it was done. We had a housewarming then, and Marion's wall was the life of the party. There were nineteen guests, a lot of them friends from college days at the University of California at Berkeley, which is where Jan and I met. There were others from my office at the Crown Zellerbach company, on Market Street. And the couple from downstairs, the Platts; Jan had gotten acquainted with Myrtle Platt in meetings at the porch mailboxes. She was a cheerful overweight housewife, and when they arrived and had the wall explained— the first thing every guest had to know, naturally—she went back downstairs and came up again with a big, shiny coffee-table book, an illustrated history of the movies, which I knew about but couldn't afford. Everyone gathered around it, spread open on the cloth-covered table Jan had arranged against one wall on which liquor and drink-making stuff was spread. And Myrtle turned the pages hunting for a still from *Flaming Flappers*. But there wasn't any; the picture wasn't even mentioned.

Ellis Pascoe said, "There never was such a picture." He was a former instructor of mine at the University, a thin, bearded man who used to tell me he wished he were a don at Oxford. "Don't you recognize Nick's disguised handwriting, Jan? Lord knows I do from all the semiliterate papers of his I had to read. He's putting you on; he wrote that so he wouldn't have to peel off the rest of the wallpaper."

Drinks in hand, staring at Marion's wall again, the group rang changes on what might appear on further layers of the Cheyneys' wallpaper: a huge X covering the largest wall, which would be King Kong's autograph; Walt Disney's denunciation of Mickey Mouse's sexual extravagances. But the actuality of the great red scrawl couldn't be joked away, it retained its mystery, and there wasn't one of us, including Jan and me, who at some moment of the evening didn't find himself standing and staring at Marion's wall. After the party, doing the dishes, letting Al in for a little midnight snack before throwing him out again to his backyard dog-house, we decided there was no question now of removing Marion's message; it had become the showpiece of the house.

Spring arrived; we had our last skiing weekend of the season at Sugar Bowl in March, and the next weekend a college friend of Jan's invited us to her parents' place on Tahoe, and we went water-skiing. There's a marvelous old-time-jazz nightclub in San Francisco called Earthquake McGoon's, and a couple times a year they run a film festival in a tiny California town, Volcano. They invite friends and customers, including us, and short of a hundred-and-five fever I wouldn't miss it: great old films from Dr. James Causey's collection, of which I wish I owned even the discards. We went to that; and we saw some new movies, read some books, went to an A.C.T. play. We visited friends and were visited by them. Six of us went bike riding in Golden Gate Park one weekend. And on my birthday in May, Jan gave me a full-length feature on 8-millimeter film, Doug Fairbanks' *The Mark of Zorro*. That costs $55.98 from Blackhawk Films, a lot more money than she was supposed to spend on my birthday present, but I was glad to have it.

Summer arrived, and we began talking about what to do on my three weeks of vacation in July, but couldn't really think of anything that would be a hell of a lot of fun while costing practically nothing. We'd gone to Tahoe for ten days of my vacation last summer, and New York the one before that, so we didn't mind not doing anything much this time. A couple weekends we went sailing on the Bay with friends and talked about buying a boat of our own, knowing we couldn't. I finished some painting and put a new muffler on the Packard. And in between all this gaiety I went to work nine to five-fifteen, five days a week, Lincoln's and Washington's birthdays off.

One night in the middle of June, coming home from work, I got off the bus as usual two blocks from home. The walk from there is nearly all uphill, and it had been fairly warm all day, in the high seventies, a great day, and I took off my suit coat; the temperature was only just now beginning to go down as the first fog slid onto the Bay. As I climbed Buena Vista hill, coat over my shoulder, my view of the city gradually expanded, and looking out over it I was pleased as on nearly every evening with its white-and-pastel look. And with the marvel of the Bay, the hills and mountains around it, and how much of an older San Francisco remained. The money-makers were destroying the city as fast as they could go, blocking off the old views with higher and higher buildings—praised by the Mayor, approved by the Supervisors—and the destruction of the Bay itself with fill and pollution continued. But there was still an awful lot of beauty to destroy before they finally Manhattanized or Milwaukeeized San Francisco, a lot still left that was good to look at meanwhile. As a Midwesterner, a flatlander, I appreciated this place, and had been here long enough to feel a part of it.

On my front porch, winded a little from the climb from street level,

I thought as always that I ought to start jogging. And I stopped to look out over the city once more, expecting a renewal of the way I'd been feeling. But, perversely now, without any reason I understood, a stab of depression killed the feeling. It had happened before, and I was used to it, and to the almost automatic sequence of thoughts that came with it. The very thought of these thoughts bored and depressed me in advance, and I skipped right past the big ones, the big national and international problems that you're tired of too. Next in line came the thought that it would soon be five years that I'd worked at a job meant only to be a stopgap between college and whatever it was, when I discovered it, that I really wanted to do. But all I'd discovered so far was that I didn't have anything I really wanted to do. And the unnerving idea had begun occurring to me that this job—which was pleasant enough, and at which I was fairly successful, but which had no relation to anything important in my personality—might be permanent. Someday, incredibly, I might be pensioned, having spent my entire working life at Crown Zellerbach. Next came the nagging feeling that it was time Jan and I had children. We wanted to, genuinely; I like kids, so does Jan, and we're going to have them, but like a lot of people we'd decided to have a few carefree years first, and I didn't quite seem to be ready to say I'd already had them. There were other equally dreary commonplace thoughts; the entire sequence had become mechanical, and I was just standing there, my mind barely ticking over, staring off across the city—hundreds of windows were a blank glittering orange from the lowering sun—when I heard a bay window open above the porch roof, rattling in its frame.

"Nick?"

"No, he's working late. I'm your neighborhood mugger, Rupert the Raper. Open up, lady; you're next."

"What are you *doing* down there?"

"Balancing on one leg. Setting a world's rec—"

"Well, come *up* here, Nick! I've got something to show you!"

"Okay." I turned toward the door, getting out my key, but before I could get it unlocked I heard Jan clattering down the inside stairs. She opened the door and stood grinning at me all excited; she was wearing the gray sweater and slacks she'd bought with the I. Magnin gift certificate her mother had given her at Christmas. In her hand was a small magazine, *TV Guide*, I saw, and her finger was holding a place. She didn't speak, just opened the magazine and pointed, eyes bright.

Thursday Evening, June 14, I read at the top of the page, and saw that Jan's lacquered nail was touching the little TV-screen-shaped spot on which a 9 was superimposed in white. This was today's date; Channel 9 was the Bay Area Public Television station. I took the magazine and, walking upstairs behind Jan, read the listing: 9:30 *p.m.*, *THE TOY THAT GREW UP.* "*Flaming Flappers,*" *silent film of the Twenties starring Richard Abel and Blanche Purvell: hip flasks, flaming youth, fast cars, and fast parties. Piano accompaniment following original cue sheets by Mabel Ordway.*

I was grinning when we hit the top of the stairs and said, "Kiddo, you don't know it, but you probably just saved my life." I kissed Jan, genuinely, so that she actually flushed. "Now how in the hell am I going to wait till nine-thirty?"

At nine-twenty-eight I switched on the set in the living room, turned to 9, and stood waiting for sound and picture; across the room Jan sat on the chesterfield watching, and Al lay on the rug before it, more or less knocked out as he generally is after his dinner. The sound came on, music over a man's voice, the music rising in volume as the voice receded. Then the picture popped on, swelling to fill the screen, rolling slowly; I tuned it to sharpness as the rolling slowed and stopped. Two men in molded-plastic chairs sat facing each other, one listening and slowly nodding, the lips of the other moving soundlessly as the music overrode his voice completely. They began contracting into the distance as the camera drew away, the men continuing to talk, one of them throwing his head back to laugh, as though they were so caught up they were unaware the program was ending.

I sat down on the chesterfield, and we watched the station's call letters, KQED, appear on the screen. For some time then, maybe twenty seconds or more, the letters remained there silently, the set humming. I said, "Shows class, you see; no commercials." I slouched down comfortably, extending my legs, and put my feet—I was wearing soft slippers—on Al; he was in exactly the right place. His head lifted to stare at my feet, then at me. You could read his mind; he was wondering which was the least disagreeable course: to actually make the effort of getting up and moving out of range or to lie back and put up with it. He thought about it, then lay back again, sighing. I said, "This is part of the job of 'being the dog,' Al. It's not all carefree barking. You've got to earn that daily seventy-nine-cent can of dog food; nothing's free." Making a supreme effort, he thumped his tail twice against the floor, and I took my feet off. The call letters disappeared and THE TOY THAT GREW UP appeared superimposed across a still figure of Charlie Chaplin, the sudden background music a thumping nickelodeon piano. A neat young man in suit and bow tie came on, standing before a painted backdrop representing a movie box office. He spoke pleasantly with seeming authority about films of the Twenties, the usual stuff. I said, "See the faintly amused smile? That shows he knows the old films are a little ridiculous. But get the careful voice, the scholarly note; you can't claim he's patronizing them."

"What's the matter with you tonight?"

"I'm Samuel Johnson, my mind a scalpel; I see through pretense everywhere. The truth is that ridiculous as it sounds, I'm all excited."

"Me too."

The screen faded to black, and—Jan's shoulders actually hunched up in glee at this—the title of the picture appeared in white letters on a black that seemed faded and less than black. *"Flaming Flappers,"* it read incredibly, in a thin graceful italic of the period, *"A Paramount Picture."* The piano accompaniment, no longer nickelodeon, thank God, receded in volume to become an almost unnoticeable background sound, but it made all the difference; we were in another time long before sound came to the movies. Cast and credits came fast, and not very many of them. The screen went momentarily dark, then lightened rapidly to show an enormous chauffeured car entering a circular white-graveled driveway between high wrought-iron gates, and Jan gripped my forearm. "I can't *believe* it. I can't *stand* it. We're actually going to see Marion Marsh!"

The car on the screen slowed, then stopped before the wide shallow stone steps of a great country house. I sat forward, peering, then identified the radiator ornament. "Pierce Arrow." A subtitle appeared: *"A Wealthy Long Island Estate."* The chauffeur opened a back door of the sedan and began helping an elderly woman out; she carried a lorgnette, wore a long dress and a round, straight-sided hat with a slightly curved top. I said, "Looks like she's wearing a cake."

The scene cut to a huge room—tapestries and crossed spears on its walls—whose open French doors led out to a stone veranda with a heavy stone balustrade; beyond the veranda an enormous lawn stretched into the distance. I couldn't tell if it was real or a backdrop. The elderly woman with the lorgnette was entering the room, and walking toward her from the veranda entrance was a young woman, Blanche Purvell, I recognized, the star of the picture. In contrast to the older woman's dress, hers was knee-length and sleeveless. "Nice legs," I said, and smiled as Jan glanced at me.

The story developed fast: Blanche Purvell was rich, an heiress, in love with a poor man in the nearby town, even though her mother, the woman with the lorgnette, objected. The young man appeared to deliver groceries, wearing a cloth cap with a long curved peak, a white shirt, tie, and a sweater. With the help of a middle-aged woman in servant's uniform, he unloaded them from a wicker basket onto a wooden-topped table in a strangely old-fashioned kitchen, and the girl happened in. They smiled lovingly at each other when the servant wasn't looking, then walked out the back door and across a grassy expanse, passing a pair of tennis courts on which young people were playing. I wondered where it had been filmed, and what stood there now: a freeway on-ramp, I supposed; or a shopping center with a five-acre parking lot. The couple walked on toward a delivery truck, a black Model T Ford with a long, curved roof extending from windshield to tailgate, its sides open. It stood parked on a dirt road.

As they crossed the grass toward it the girl looked around her, glanced at the house, then she and the boy held hands for the rest of the walk to the truck. "He's after her money," Jan said.

"Of course. He wears that nutty cap because he's bald as a bowling ball, and she doesn't know it."

"What a surprise when he takes it off on their honeymoon."

"If he does."

A roadster with wooden-spoke wheels appeared, top folded back, and braked to a fast skidding stop, its wheels seeming to revolve backward slowly. A cloud of dust enveloped the boy and girl and Jan murmured, "Goody." A young man in tennis flannels, a white knit sweater tied by its arms to hang down his back, slid over the closed door of the open car, a pair of rackets in one hand. He glanced superciliously at the truck, then imperiously beckoned the girl to follow as he walked on toward the tennis courts. "I adore him!" Jan said.

"You're a snob." On the screen the girl turned to follow the young man in flannels, then looked longingly back at the boy left behind at the truck. She spoke and as her lips moved I said, "I love you, Ralph, but Frank smells better." On the screen a subtitle said, "*I'd rather stay with you!*"

We lost interest: the story developed too fast and too obviously, and the world, if any, to which it referred was remote to the point of incomprehensibility. The film was a copy of a copy, probably, the faces washed out, very white, and Jan murmured, "They're all eyes, lips and eyebrows, like old snapshots."

"Yeah. You know something? This film was made by light reflected into a lens. From the faces of real people. Who were once really there in exactly that scene, doing just what you see. I know that but I don't believe it: that's always been an old film, and they've never existed outside it."

The tink-tinkle of the piano never stopped, the blacks, grays and whites continuing to shift on the little screen, and we watched apathetically. Occasionally, one of us on guard, the other left to get something to eat, something to drink, to go to the bathroom, to wander the house. We'd watched for over forty minutes, and I was in the kitchen sitting at the table reading the green sport section of the morning *Chronicle*, eating potato chips. The sound and smell of these had miraculously brought Al out of his coma, and he was sitting on the floor looking up at me like a clumsy basset imitation of the terrier in front of the phonograph in the old ads, head cocked, ears up, as high as he could get them at least, and I tossed him the occasional potato chip. I've tried to teach him to catch, but his hound eyes don't see well enough, and each chip simply landed on his nose, bounced off, and he'd have to hunt for it. Then he'd gobble it down and sit and yearn up at me for more.

I like old Al, as I guess I've made clear, and his eyes fascinate me. They're so huge and brown, so human and *innocent*. It's as though a completely trusting four-year-old was staring up into your eyes out of a furry brown-and-white dog face. He sat doing this now, and I leaned down from the table to stare back into his eyes and ask him an old and familiar question in this situation. "Listen, who *are* you in there? Really? You're not fooling me, you know, with that crazy dog suit." I flipped up one of his incredibly long brown ears. "No dog has ridiculous ears like that; there's where you made your big mistake!" I suddenly dropped to my knees beside him, grabbing him under the arms, and lowered him swiftly to his back. Holding him on the floor with one hand, I began rummaging rapidly through his white chest fur. "Where's the zipper! I'm going to pull off this nutty dog suit right now! Exposing you for the impostor you are!" It was an old game, the kind of roughhouse he loves, and he struggled and fought with his hind legs and careful teeth. After a minute I let him up, quieting him down with a little ear-scratching. "Okay, you've won again." I gave him a potato chip. "You're clever, all right; we know that. But that zipper's in there and someday I'll find it."

"Nick, here it is, I think!" Jan called, and I slid the last chips out of the bowl onto the floor for Al and hurried back.

The scene was a party in the big room of the picture's beginning, now filled with people. Playing a grand piano, his shoulders bouncing rapidly to the rhythm, sat a young man with a hairline mustache and straight black hair slicked glossily back from his forehead. Beside him on the piano bench a short-skirted girl sat holding a drink from which she took frequent rapid sips, her free hand waggling at shoulder height, apparently in time to the piano. Another girl lay sprawled across the top of the piano, chin propped on elbow, and holding a cocktail glass. Rugs were rolled back and couples were dancing rapidly. On a great curved staircase people sat kissing; several others lay on a large chesterfield pantomiming drunkenness. Nearly everyone held a cocktail glass, drinking frequently, heads tossing far back.

It was entirely unreal; there had never been such people nor such a party. These ancient photographs silently cavorting to the music of a steadily tinkling piano were absurd. Slowly the camera's eye moved around the edges of the party to reveal: a couple sitting under a table exaggeratedly drunk; an expressionless butler entering the room with a tray of filled glasses and an opened bottle that someone immediately snatched; a fast-moving dice game on the floor, everyone in it on his or her knees, fingers snapping; a little cluster of men, including the arrogant tennis player, now wearing a tuxedo, surrounding a girl, nearly hiding her.

Then two of the men moved casually apart, revealing the girl, and we sat staring: this, we knew from what my father had told us, was Marion Marsh. In short flapper dress like all the other women, her hair bobbed like theirs, a strand of hair lying on each cheek curved into a J, her face equally white, she stood listening to one of the men. Then she smiled and replied, and I could feel my attention gripped, I can't quite say why. In a way past defining, with the simple magic of an occasional rare personality, this girl seemed real while the others did not. She was a small grainy figure in a corner of the glass screen but somehow she was truly speaking; I actually caught myself inching forward on the chesterfield as though I might hear her if I got closer, and I *wanted* to hear. Her hand came up, her forefinger shook in playful rebuke to one of the men, then she smiled, and Jan and I smiled with her. Now, in burlesqued entreaty, one of the men put his palms prayerfully together, then took her elbow, trying to lead her away from the others; and at the gentle sympathetic shake of her head and the rueful twist of her lips in refusal I felt a yearning for her as a woman. For no reason I really understood then or now, and unlike every other figure in the absurd scene, this one tiny gray-and-white figure was alive.

She glanced away from the men around her to look across the room. And the flick of boredom that touched her face in that moment and was instantly gone as she turned back to them was genuine. Watching as she resumed her banter with the group, it seemed to me I understood the real feelings of the woman she was playing; afterward I remembered the whole scene as though I had heard her voice. And right now it even seemed believable that the caricatures around her, almost hopping in the exaggerated emphasis of their attention to her, felt what they were pantomiming. The camera was moving on, her image diminishing in size as the scene receded into the background, and I sat straining to see the last of her. And when the edge of the screen cut her from view, I sat, still in the spell of her presence, feeling that she was still smiling and speaking somewhere just out of view.

For a long moment, the never-ending piano and the moving photographs continuing without any more meaning for me, that feeling lasted. Then I came out of it and turned to Jan. "Oh, *boy*," I said softly. "She had it. She really did."

"*Yes*—oh, I could cry! Nick, she'd have been a *star!* We'd have known her name like—"

"I know; Norma Talmadge or Clara Bow. There really isn't any doubt about it."

"Well, it's a shame! Think how your father must have felt, watching that."

"He's gotten over it long since, I'm sure."

We sat watching the picture for a few moments longer, then Jan said, "I don't think I can take another half hour of this, Nick; it's nearly ten-thirty, and I'm tired. But I'm so glad I saw it." She turned to look up at the writing on Marion's wall behind us.

"She comes on again, you know; right at the end."

"Only for a second or so your father said, and I'm too tired; I cleaned the house today. You watch, if you want. I'm going to bed and just lie there thinking about it till I fall asleep."

"Okay. Cookie the old man out first, will you?" I don't remember how this got started but instead of just pulling rank and ordering Al out at the end of an evening, we'd rub a cookie across his nose. His tongue would come out automatically and swipe across his nose, he'd taste the cookie crumbs, his eyes would pop open, and he'd leap to his feet and actually trot out to the kitchen and the hinged dog-door I'd put into the bottom of the back door. He'd hop out, the cookie would be handed to him, and his door latched for the night. Quick, simple, no arguments, and everyone happy, at least till the cookie was gone.

Jan kissed my cheek, cookied Al out, and I stayed for the end of the picture, about another thirty minutes, slumped on the chesterfield, staring at the screen, half awake. In the last moments of *Flaming Flappers* a bride, Blanche Purvell, tossed her bouquet to a cluster of bridesmaids at the foot of the staircase, and there was a final glimpse of Marion Marsh. Her actions were identical with those of the other bridesmaids, actually, and you saw her for no more than four seconds before her face was hidden by an upflung arm. But she had me; she'd made a fan. And I told myself, nodding my head, that even in that tiny scene she stood out from the rest. *"The End"* said the screen subtitle abruptly, the piano accompaniment rising to conclusion as I got to my feet and walked over to switch off the set before the guy in the bow tie could come back and tell us what we'd seen. "Well, Marion," I said, murmuring into the new silence, "you were great. Absolutely great."

"Yes."

The light in the picture tube shrinking to a diamond point, I stood motionless, feeling the blood withdraw from the surface of my skin. I made my mind work, trying to consider alternatives. But there weren't any. The unmistakable difference between what you imagine and what is real couldn't be denied; I knew I'd really heard the word quietly spoken, with normal clarity, in a pleasantly husky feminine voice that was not Jan's. I didn't quite like to move, but I did, turning my head to search the entire room in the faint illumination from the front windows. A roof beam cracked, contracting after the warmth of the day, but I knew what it was, I was used to it, and I continued searching the room with my eyes.

It wasn't dark enough for anyone to be hiding, and there was no one to be seen. I'd known there wouldn't be—I knew more than I'd let myself admit—and the hair on my neck and forearms was erect and prickling.

"Nick, it's me."

"Who?"

"Marion," the voice said impatiently.

"Marion"—it was hard to make myself say it—"Marsh?"

"Of course! I just *had* to see my picture. Oh, *God*, wasn't I good!"

I nodded, then it occurred to me that maybe I couldn't be seen, and I said, "Yes," but my voice croaked. I cleared my throat, tried again, and it came out too loud: "Yes, you were!" I said. "Are you a"—and again it was hard to say the word, it sounded so ridiculous—"ghost?"

There was a long silence, and I thought I wasn't going to hear any more. Then, startled and faintly amused, the voice said wonderingly, as though this were a new thought, "I suppose I am." She laughed. "Imagine! But yes, I expect that's what a ghost must *be*. We can come back to where we once lived, you know, though not many ever do. It takes so much . . . what would you call it?"

"Psychic energy?" I was so fascinated I'd forgotten to be afraid. I was wildly elated, in fact, my mind racing ahead to picture myself telling Jan about this, telling people at work, at parties.

"Yes, something like that, I suppose; you really have to want to return. Which I did, believe you me! My own picture, and I never saw it before! Finally shown right here in my own house! What *is* that thing?"

"A television set."

"For showing movies?"

"Mostly."

"It's not very good, is it? So tiny. But what's the diff, I've seen my picture at last! I was cut off—remember?—at only twenty."

"Twenty-one, wasn't it?" I hadn't moved; it didn't occur to me.

"Oh, who cares? Why is that so important! You always did like to rub it in that you were a teeny bit younger than me."

I couldn't see any point in correcting her. I said, "Tell me, what's it like? On the"—I hate phrases like this but couldn't think of a substitute—"other side?"

"Oh . . . " The voice paused. "Something like being drunk: you feel pretty good, and don't think very much. What's it like being alive? I've actually sort of forgotten."

"Just about the opposite. Marion, listen, could you possibly appear? As you really were? Are. Were."

"Oh, Nickie, it's fantastically hard. Even for just a second or so. It must be why ghosts disappear so quickly, don't you think? The only way you can stay around for any time at all is by possession."

"What's that?"

"Inhabiting someone; you'd only do it for some terribly important reason."

"But you *can* appear for a few seconds. Would you? Please?" It occurred to me finally that I could sit down, and I did, on the edge of the chesterfield.

The voice was soft. "You want to see me once again, don't you, Nickie? You're sweet. If only we hadn't quarreled! How different things might have been. All right; watch in that corner by the hall, away from the windows."

I sat staring, watching a gathering up, an *assembling*, of light from the rest of the room. At the edges of my vision I saw the corners and the overhead whiteness of the ceiling perceptibly dim; then they faded into complete darkness. The light drained to the floor. Then it moved rapidly along the baseboards in a foglike flow, gathered and began rising in the dark corner across the room—mist-gray at first, then shimmering a little, iridescent. Suddenly it sparkled with deepening color, the colors shifting, separating, rapidly coalescing, steadying into definiteness and shape. And then she stood there, smiling.

The figure was transparent. The wall was clearly visible behind her. But she nevertheless stood sharp and clear in a green-and-blue dress, its hemline at the knees of—I was stunned at myself for realizing—a pair of marvelous legs. Her complexion was a lovely pink and white, and surprisingly, because it hadn't shown blond in the movie, her hair was yellow. She stood regarding me, her blue eyes occasionally blinking; not beautiful, though pretty, and with the astonishing feeling of vitality she'd shown in the picture. Her voice very much fainter now, she said, "You haven't changed, Nick; not really. A little older; you're older than me now! And you're married, aren't you? That was your wife. Both of you here in my old apartment."

My mouth was opening to reply, to tell her who I really was. But her last words had faded very nearly to inaudibility, and the colors and the vision itself were losing strength fast. She was suddenly very nearly gone, just barely within vision, when I saw her head lift slightly. For the first time she seemed to have noticed the writing covering the wall behind the chesterfield, and the fading away stopped. Form and color seemed to strengthen slightly, then they held firm as though by an act of will. I saw her hand move to her chest, saw her eyes widen and her face twist. Very faintly I heard her cry, "To have been *alive!*" The vestiges of color and form dwindled to nothing, and once again I could see the room corners, and the dim whiteness of the ceiling returned. I whispered, "Marion?" But I didn't expect an answer and didn't get one.

At the front windows, I stood looking out at the city and the long string of orange lights that was all I could see of the Bay Bridge. I'd thought I'd stand here thinking about what had just happened, but my mind was empty, refusing to think; it was too much just now. After a few moments, glancing at Marion's wall as I passed through the room again, I went down the hall to bed.

In bed Jan was facing me, and I touched her lips in a habitual good-night kiss, lightly so as not to awaken her. But she was awake or partly so; she moved closer, and I put my arms around her, letting my eyes close, feeling exhausted, glad for sleep. But Jan's arms tightened, drawing me closer, and I smiled, surprised; once asleep Jan was ordinarily as unlikely as a child to awaken again before daylight. I'd thought I was exhausted but Jan astonished me, and I discovered I wasn't exhausted at all. But when we lay side by side again, my arm snugly around Jan's waist, I could feel myself sliding into sleep like rushing down a toboggan slide, and was glad: what had happened in the living room needed a lot more thought than I was ready to begin tonight. I felt happy, too, more than in a long time. Things hadn't been going as well as they ought to between Jan and me for a while, I really didn't know why. It was nothing serious but we couldn't seem to stop it, and of course that sort of problem moves into bed with you. But tonight it had been gone, that's all; really gone. I felt happy and, sleepy though I was, almost exuberant. It had been one hell of an evening, I thought, grinning in the dark, then wham—I was asleep.

CHAPTER THREE

My office is just an office, not tiny but a long way from big. I have a carpet in a nice shade of forest-green, a decent-looking desk and chair, another chair for visitors, a table to put things on. And I have a couple of my own pictures on the wall. One is a Brueghel print called *The Tower of Babel*, which I like to look at because it's crammed with little people doing all sorts of things to build an enormous tower that is shown actually reaching the clouds. It reminds me of covers on *Boys' Life* magazine when I was a kid—filled with boys swimming, hiking, playing ball, climbing trees, a thousand things. You could study one of those covers time and again, thinking at last you'd seen everything in it, but usually you'd find something you'd missed before. Well, I think the Brueghel is every bit as good as the old *Boys' Life* covers, and when I got bored I'd get up and stand in front of it hunting for something new. The other picture was a still of Fay Wray in jungle costume that I liked a lot.

The day after I'd seen Marion's ghost I was sitting in my office, pencil in hand, the sharp end pointed down, apparently looking at the papers spread out on my desk. I work in Sales Promotion: dealing with my counterparts in the advertising agency; getting to go to a few West Coast conventions and sales meetings now and then, a dubious benefit, but at least a change; and I do a fair variety of things connected with selling our stuff, which is paper products of more different kinds than a sane man could imagine. A lot of the stuff we make is actually useful, and none of it is downright harmful, so at least I'm not ashamed of what I do.

But I wasn't doing it now; I had more on my mind than Zee paper towels. All morning, beginning as soon as my eyes opened, I'd done my best to think sensibly about whatever it was that had happened last night. At noon I grabbed a quick lunch alone so that I'd have time to walk—first to the Ferry Building at the head of Market Street, then along past the covered docks and the glimpses of Bay between them—and think some more, trying to reach some conclusion.

But there didn't seem to be much of any to reach. Mostly all I did was live over the experience in my mind again and again. I experimented with trying to persuade myself that I'd only imagined or vividly dreamed what had happened, but everyone knows the difference between dreaming or imagining and reality: this had happened. Sitting at my desk now, the only conclusion I could reach was that on rare occasions ghosts actually did in truth appear.

I hadn't told anyone, of course, and except for Jan no longer intended to. The moment I stepped out of the elevator into the fluorescent-lighted, electric-typewriter, air-conditioned busyness of Crown Zellerbach I knew I wasn't going to try to convince anyone of what had happened last night in the dark of our old house. And at breakfast I didn't tell Jan; it would take repeating, take talking over, and there wasn't time. I'd tell her tonight, and—it was a hell of a story—I smiled at the thought, looking forward to it. And looking forward, it occurred to me, to seeing Jan. Remembering last night after the movie, I felt very warm and tender about Jan today, appreciating her good qualities, feeling fond of the bad ones.

My phone rang, and because I'd been thinking about her it was Jan; things work that way, and everyone knows it. After the hellos, she said, "Don't forget the party with the Hursts tonight."

"I know, I remembered. I'm sort of looking forward to it."

"Me, too. It's been a while since we've gone out and had some fun."

I smiled and pulled out a lower drawer to put my feet on. "I don't think it's in to look forward to a cocktail party."

"I know; especially a no-host fund raiser. Nickie, I called because I. Magnin's is advertising a dress sale. It's a real sale, and I do need a new party dress. Something simple. Plain black, I expect, that I'll use forever, but—"

"Get it, then."

"Well, I wasn't sure we could really afford—"

"We can't really afford food. So get the dress. I want to experience that glow of pride a man feels when his wife's ass is pinched by every man at the party."

"Fine, you can have first pinch. See you tonight."

Walking home from the bus after work, looking out over the city as I climbed Buena Vista hill, I was fond of the world and of this moment, in which a boy of four or five squatting on a single roller skate came wobbling toward me unseeingly, concentrating on balance. I stepped aside, pleased with the boy and the evening ahead; I like parties of any kind, at least in anticipation.

On the porch I stopped for breath as usual, but only for a moment or so, and I climbed the inside stairs two at a time; I had to change clothes, then we had to drive across Golden Gate Bridge and on up into Marin County. At the top of the stairs I yelled, "I'm here!"

"Well, I'm in here!" Jan's voice answered from the bathroom. She paused, then said, "I'm afraid to come out."

"What's that mean?" I said to the bathroom door as I passed it; I turned into our bedroom, loosening my tie.

"You'll kill me."

"Well, come on out and get it over with then. I'll give you a choice of methods." Unbuttoning my shirt, I stood watching the bathroom door just across the hall. It was slowly opening, into the bathroom, Jan out of sight behind it. It opened nearly all the way and she suddenly stepped around it and out into the hall to stand both smiling and frowning appealingly as I stared at her. I was astonished; her new dress was wild, the pattern a really dizzying whirl of color, the material dyed to look as though paint in primary colors had been flung onto it in handfuls, and it was shorter by inches than any she'd ever before owned. Actually, I realized, staring at it, the dress was cleverly done, the blobs of color artfully arranged and proportioned. But it was an eyeful, and I said, "What the *hell?*" I didn't want her to think I disapproved of the party dress that, after all, she'd have to wear tonight, and I quickly added, "It looks great." And it *did*, I realized then. "It really does," I said, and she smiled at the sincerity in my voice. "I like it fine; legs like yours *ought* to be shown off." For an incredible fraction of a second I caught myself comparing her legs with Marion Marsh's, and pushed the idiotic thought away. "You really look marvelous; I may have to rescue you from sexual attack all evening long. Incidentally, if we had time—"

"We don't."

"Too bad. What happened to the plain black dress?"

"I don't *know*," she said in a mock wail, and walked on into the bedroom and stood looking down at her dress. "That's what I went in to get, then I saw this, tried it on just for fun, and"—she looked up to smile and shrug—"I don't know what got into me but I bought it. Do you really like it? You don't at all."

"Yeah, really." I was pulling on a clean shirt. "But every other woman there will be invisible; they'll lynch you. You feed Al?"

"Yes; he insisted."

On the drive through the city toward the bridge, the top down, I told Jan what had happened last night, factually but including every detail, really trying to convey it. She listened, then we talked about it; she had questions, and I answered them. And she said she wished she'd been there. She believed me, I saw, in that she knew I wasn't lying; that I thought what I'd told her was true. But whether it really had happened, whether it wasn't an illusion . . . how can anyone else ever tell?

The town of Ross is old, by California standards, and it's rich. It has enough people with enough money to give them enough power to keep it old. There are still streets too narrow for modern traffic, some of them only dirt lanes unchanged since horses drew buggies along them, and they are kept so. There are very few parking meters, not many street signs or even street lamps, a considerable absence of house numbers, and in the very heart of the town are acres of tree-covered land owned by the local Art and Garden Club that could very profitably be filled with apartment buildings and are not. Along some of the dirt lanes are enormous sprawling houses fifty, sixty, seventy, eighty, or more years old. They're well preserved and kept painted; they're spaced far apart and set well back from the roads behind high hedges or rows of trees on shrubbery- and tree-filled acreage; they and their surroundings look as they always have for decades past. I'd live in one of those houses if I could, and the party was in one of them, I was pleased to see.

It was covered with beautifully weather-grayed wood shingles, was two stories high but so large it seemed low, and lay far back from the road at the end of a long dirt driveway lined by trees. Cars were parked on both sides of the drive, and I added the Packard to one of the lines, and we walked on up the driveway toward the house. I could hear music from the house, very faint, and felt excited. I said, "What's this party in aid of? As our British cousins have probably quit saying."

"Some sort of day-care center. For preschool kids of working mothers. Interracial; Hazel's on the committee."

"Fine; means the drunker you get, the more you're improving race relations. Which frees up the conscience considerably. Anything short of a roaring hangover and you're a goddamned bigot."

Approaching the wide wooden steps of a screen-enclosed old-fashioned porch that ran clear across the front of the house and around both sides, I could hear the music clearly now, piano cocktail music. We climbed the steps and walked around to one of the side porches—we could see a pair of big double doors standing open there—and began to hear the sustained conversational hum of a lot of people. Then we walked into an entrance hall paved with brick-red clay tiles and stood for a moment looking into the room into which the hall led, and I understood why the party was here.

It was an immense room, fifty or more feet in each horizontal direction, the ceiling two stories high and with skylights that could be opened by cog-and-chain apparatuses fastened to the walls. The room must have been built as a ballroom because a permanent raised platform

stood directly across from the entrance we stood in. It was large enough
to hold a small orchestra, though there was only a piano up there now,
a grand piano in full view of the entire room played by a plump gray-
haired man in a tuxedo jacket of gray cloth with a silver pattern. Eyes
half closed, he sat swaying to his own slow, rippling music, holding a
professional smile; just now he was tinkling out "The Way You Look
To-night." There were a hundred or more people in the room, standing
in chattering smiling groups or moving slowly through the crowd or
sitting along the walls on countless chairs and large old-fashioned
chesterfields upholstered in faded blue or maroon velvet. Then we saw
the Hursts, Hazel and Frank, making their way toward us, smiling, and
we walked out into the big room to meet them.

We were introduced to a group of the Hursts' friends and stood with
them in a circle for a few minutes, and I watched the women storing
complete details of Jan's dress in the memory banks. One of the women
told us about the day-care center till my eyes began glazing. Then two
more couples, apparently knowing most of the others, joined the circle,
and in the rush of greetings and jokes I touched Jan's arm. "Let's go hit
the sauce for the working mothers."

I'd seen the bar at one end of the room, several cloth-covered trestle
tables pushed together end to end. Behind them, against the wall, a
duplicate set of tables was the back bar. When we got there, three red-
jacketed bartenders were serving six or eight people, and at one end of
the bar a smiling, distinguished-looking gray-haired woman sat on a
wooden folding chair, a roll of tickets and a black metal cashbox on the
cloth before her. I paid for two tickets, each good, the lady told me in a
cultured voice, "for any sort of drink from white wine to martini," and
I thanked her, hearing my own voice trying to sound cultured, too, then
I turned to Jan to ask what she wanted.

I was puzzled by her expression: she stood staring at the back bar, her
mouth hanging open slightly. The back tables were covered with bottles,
a really lot of them, both opened and full. There was whiskey of every
type and many brands; dozens of bottles of gin and vodka; there was
wine and sherry; rows of Cokes, 7-Up, ginger ale, soda, and the like; on
the floor under the tables stood stacked-up cases of still more liquor and
mixes. It was an impressive display, but still—Once in a while out of
excitement and exuberance Jan took it into her head, as shy people
sometimes do, to clown at what I usually thought was an inappropriate
moment. I thought this was one of them, and started to nudge her to
cut it out, but it was too late. A bartender stood waiting, brows raised

inquiringly, and Jan smiled brightly and said, "Wow! Would you look at all that hooch! Is it good stuff?"

"Come on now, Jan," I muttered, "what do you want?"

"Well, just to start things rolling I'll have a Bronx cocktail."

The bartender frowned; a man down the bar was staring at us.

I muttered again. "I don't think they serve fancy cocktails at a thing like this. Takes too much time."

"Okay, we aim to please. I'll have a gin buck." Jan stared at the bartender, then shook her head in amazement. "You don't know what *that* is? Where have you been! It's just gin, ginger ale, and lime juice. Put in plenty of gin, and you can forget the lime; it's the booze that counts!"

"Oh, for God's sake," I said through my teeth, and turned to stare down the people near us. The bartender brought Jan's drink, face almost expressionless, though he let me see a little sneer way back in his eyes. I said, "Bourbon and soda," and put down my two tickets. I stood watching the bartender, who mixed my drink fast enough, and I took it, glad to turn away. Jan was halfway down the floor, making her way back to the Hursts. Then I saw her stop in the midst of a crowd and, throwing her head way back, toss down her drink like a thirsty longshoreman. She turned and walked back to me.

"Do it again, Big Boy," she said, handing me her empty glass. "That's real stuff; right off the boat!"

"Baby, you're a laff-riot, believe me," I said. "I know we haven't been out much lately, but let's try to get it out of our system, eh? Before we rejoin the Hursts and their friends? I'll meet you there, and bring back your drink." I made myself smile at her and turned back to the bar; goddamn, I'd looked forward to tonight!

There was a bar at each end of the room, I discovered. Walking back toward the Hursts once again, I saw Jan and Frank Hurst turn from the circle toward the other end of the room, then I saw the other bar. When I'd worked my way through the crowd, carefully carrying Jan's full glass and my own drink, she and Frank were on their way back, Jan sipping from her new drink as she walked. She rejoined the circle, eyes sparkling, face flushed, finishing her drink, then handed me her empty glass, took the new one I'd brought, and drank off half of it. A couple of women were watching her, still eying her dress, and Jan looked at them insolently till they glanced away. She suddenly flicked a hip sideways and began snapping the fingers of her free hand. "This party's dead on its feet," she said. "Let's get things moving!" She tossed off her drink and, without looking at me, held out her glass. I had to take it—I was holding three glasses now—and Jan turned from the group again.

I was as mad at Jan as I've ever been, I guess, and I made myself hang onto my smile and stand there, the two empty glasses down at my side inconspicuously, or so I hoped. I stood listening attentively to what one of the women was saying about the day-care center's need for more room and equipment, refusing to turn and see where Jan was going; I knew she didn't have any money.

The woman finished, someone replied, and I took a swallow or two from my glass, casually shifting my position a little as I did so to sneak a look after Jan. I was absolutely astounded: she was standing at the bar smiling and accepting a drink from a man, a complete stranger to her, I knew. He was bowing slightly, waggling a hand in response to her thanks. Jan raised her glass in toast to him, drank off a third of it, then turned into the crowd—not back toward our group as I'd thought for a moment, but angling off toward the other side of the room. For a few steps I could follow her dress, then it was lost in the crowd.

I didn't know what to do. I just didn't know. I couldn't bring myself to embarrass either of us by obviously going into the crowd looking for her, though I wanted to. I made myself stand there, and finished my drink. Then I smiled at Hazel Hurst beside me and, gesturing with my own empty glass, said, "Can I bring you one, Hazel?" She drank very little, I knew, and when she said no, I smiled again, turned and walked toward the bar, slowly and casually, looking brightly around me, trying to suggest a man enjoying himself. I thought if I took my time about this, I might catch Jan returning to the bar and somehow get her the hell out of here.

Halfway to the bar I heard the piano abruptly stop in mid-tune during a medley of songs from musicals, heard a slight rise in the level of conversational hum, saw heads turning toward the platform. I turned, too, not knowing what I'd see, but the instant I did, it seemed to me that I'd known all my life. Up on the raised platform the pianist sat smiling politely, head bowed over the keys, listening to a woman whose head was ducked level with his as she spoke into his ear. The bulk of the piano stood between her and me, and her head was partly concealed by the pianist's. I couldn't actually see her, but I knew. Then, smiling broadly, Jan stood erect up there on the platform, her dress the most vivid object in the room, and as the pianist began what I knew must have been her request, she hopped up onto the piano top, legs swinging, and began to sing along with him, "Bye Bye Blackbird," singing the words when she knew them, and *da-da, DA-da* when she didn't.

She carried the tune well enough, her voice true though thin. And as I worked through the crowd toward her, the song—the pianist cutting it a little short—ended, and people immediately around the platform applauded, but the hands came together limply, lazily, the applause sardonic; someone mockingly called "Yay!" Jan had slid from piano to floor, her head ducking down beside the pianist's again. He nodded, his smile rigid, and began playing "Sweet Sue" with a pronounced rapid beat.

Incredibly, Jan began to dance: knees together, feet and elbows flying, her dress a blaze of flying color. And she was *good*; she did it beautifully, feet flashing in perfect easy rhythm, fingers snapping, face lifted to ceiling, eyes half closed in ecstasy. It was her shoulders and arms that moved, and her legs, but from the knees down mostly. Except for the sway of her hips, her body moved very little, and she stayed in one spot. You could hear her feet shuffling, leather on wood, and it was a wild exciting dance, primitive and with a kind of innocent sexuality, and when I'd pushed my way to the edge of the platform, all I could do was stand and stare up at Jan—angry, really furious, and at the same time with a ridiculous feeling of pride in this astonishing accomplishment.

With a flutter of notes and a chord, the pianist finished, and now most of the room applauded, this time genuinely, a dozen or more voices calling out *"More!"* and meaning it. Jan was bowing almost professionally; left, then right, slowly revolving to face all her audience. Turning, she saw me staring up at her, and she walked to the platform's edge, directly before me. "Catch, Nick!" she said, revolving as she spoke to let herself fall backward off the platform into my arms, my three empty glasses exploding on the floor.

I wouldn't let myself even think about the meaning of this, not now. My smile fixed, forever it seemed, I set Jan on her feet, slid an arm around her waist, and gripped her left wrist with my left hand. I took her right wrist in my other hand, and, keeping our hands low and out of sight, I led her—forced her, really—through the grinning still-applauding people around the platform, who stepped aside reluctantly to let us through. I'd seen a glass-paned door beside the bar at this end of the room that led onto one of the side porches and a short flight of steps to a lawn, and we moved toward it fast. We'd nearly reached it, walking along beside the bar toward it, when Jan stopped so suddenly her left wrist was yanked loose. I turned to face her, still holding the other arm, and she stuck her hand out at me, palm up. "Give me twenty dollars."

"Outside," I said softly, nodding eagerly, placating her. Come on outside and I'll—"

"No." She waggled her hand impatiently. "Here. And right now. Or I don't move a step."

People watching, I yanked out my wallet, found a twenty, and pushed it at her. Jan took it and—I had had to let go of her—she walked around the end of the bar past the staring gray-haired woman to the back bar. She picked up an unopened bottle of Gordon's gin, turned and slapped the twenty down on the cloth before the woman, and—me following—walked on toward the exit smiling and blowing farewell kisses to the grinning, murmuring, incredulous room.

In the Packard I was so confused I had trouble getting the key in the ignition, and when I got the car started and backed out onto the driveway, I almost nicked a fender of the car behind us. I swung out onto the dirt road then and drove half a block leaning toward the windshield trying to see by moonlight before I remembered to turn on the headlights. I was driving away from the freeway toward open country and a place to pull over and talk; just now I couldn't speak.

But the top was down, a smooth flow of air cooling my cheeks, and pretty soon I felt I'd be able to make my voice speak calmly. I said, "Jan," but she ignored me, frowning and picking at the seal of clear plastic around the neck of the bottle in her lap. Impatiently, she began to twist the cap off without removing the seal. My control was thin, and I yelled, "*Jan!* Goddamn it!" We'd reached more or less open country, nothing behind us, and I swung onto the narrow shoulder and stopped, braking hard. "Jan, answer me, or so help me I'll—"

She smiled pleasantly. "Call me by name, and I will."

I sat looking at her, but once again I knew, and had known, it seemed to me, for a long time. I knew who, this afternoon, had bought the screaming dress with a hem eight inches above her knees, who knew most of the words to "Bye Bye, Blackbird," and who could dance the Charleston as though she'd invented it. "Marion?"

"I'll tell the cockeyed world. Open this goddamn bottle, Nickie; you need a little drinkie!"

She was right. I grabbed the bottle and began peeling the plastic seal loose, the driver of a passing Volkswagen turning to stare back at us. And three drinks and four miles farther on down the winding dirt road— we were beyond the town limits and the last of the houses, out into open farm country—I needed another. I took it, steering with one hand, straight gin gurgling out of the bottle mouth down my throat.

"Pass it here." I did, she swigged, then grinned. "That's no bathtub gin, Baby; that's real prewar stuff!"

"We have *got* to talk." A short driveway just ahead led to the gate of a field, and I slowed to pull off.

"Sure, but not now; this is fun! *Drive!*" She put her foot onto mine and jammed the accelerator flat. The car bucked, leaped forward, and I yanked the wheel away from the driveway and the ditch just beyond it. "Step on it! Let's take a spin!" she yelled and turned to climb up on the leather seat and sit on the folded canvas top. *"Whoopee!"* she screamed, and some fragment of my mind was able to note that I was grinning and that my foot on the acclerator stayed flat on the floor.

This was dangerous, the curves unbanked, the rear end of the big car fishtailing around them. But without slackening speed I leaned forward and with one hand loosened the big nickel-plated wing nuts of the windshield and lowered it to lie flat on the hood.

The rush of night air, cool and fragrant with country smells, whipped my hair, pressed my glasses to my brows and cheekbones, and narrowed my eyes. We took another curve, sliding sideways for a yard this time before the wheels bit in again, my heart soared in my chest from excitement, and I yelled, "Whoopeeeeee!" Upon the folded top, Marion sat waving the bottle of gin in the air, a look in her eyes, half closed against the rush of air, of utter pleasure in the moment, her lips molded in a little smile of pure, unthinking, animal joy.

"To hell with the speed cops!" she yelled, and took a long swig of gin, her taut throat white in the moonlight, then shoved the bottle down at me. I snatched it and drained the last of the gin without lifting my foot from the accelerator. A tree was rushing toward us, and I half stood behind the big wheel and with all my might threw the bottle at it. It hit squarely, smashing magnificently, splinters of glass flying like ice, and we both howled with delight, wild and free, more than I'd been since I was a child, more than I'd remembered it was possible to be.

But a quarter mile farther on I slowed, pumping the brakes, then jounced off onto a two-rut dirt road leading toward a farmhouse whose lights showed in the distance. There were horses in a field, and trees extending over the shoulder of the road. I pulled off under them, set the hand brake, and turned off the ignition and lights; we had to talk.

Marion was sliding down onto the seat beside me, her skirt pushing back, turning toward me, lifting her arms. "Oh, Nickie, Nickie," she said, "it's so *good to be back.*"

"Hold it." I put a hand up. "Listen, do you think I'm my father?"

"Of course not. I did last night. When we saw my movie. I was still confused then: you lose track of time. Because it doesn't matter."

"These aren't the Twenties, either, you know."

"Ain't it the truth! Some party. Everybody standing around talking about nursery schools! What the hell kind of party was that? Nobody getting any kicks. What was that big red bridge we came over?"

"Golden Gate Bridge."

"What happened to the ferries?"

"They got rid of them."

"Good night! How stupid! They were fun."

"Well, we kept the cable cars. A few of them."

"That's nice. Oh, listen! Did Dempsey beat Tunney?"

"No. Tunney won. Twice. They had a rematch."

"Darn. Dempsey's *so* attractive, much cuter than the Prince of Wales. What year *is* this?"

"Nineteen eighty-five."

"*What?* Why, that's . . . fifty-seven years."

"Fifty-nine."

"I hate arithmetic. That means I'm . . ."

"Eighty."

Her mouth dropped open, then she smiled. "No, I'm not. And you know it."

Something stirred in the back of my mind. It had been there for some time, now it moved forward, demanding recognition. "Marion. . . . Last night. After the movie. Was that . . . *you?*"

She leaned back against her door to face me, her shoulders trembling with silent laughter. Then she nodded.

I swung away, staring across my door top at the tree beside us. I heard Marion slide across the seat toward me, then she poked me in the ribs. "Hey," she said softly, "what's so interesting over there? Hey, Nickie, look at me!" I shook my head. "Why not?"

"No, goddamm it!" I swung around to stare at her, then shook my head in disbelief. "Lord, I'm sitting here looking at my wife's face and body, talking to *you* about how I was unfaithful to *her!* It's like incest! Only worse!" I set my elbows on the lower rim of the big wooden steering wheel and put my face in my hands. "Jesus! I must be the only man in fifty thousand years to discover a new kind of sin."

"And wasn't it nice?" I didn't answer or move. "Come on," she said softly, coaxingly, "it won't hurt you to say it was nice. Because it was. And you know it."

"The hell it was."

"Oh, yes, it was. A lot better than what's-her-name, Dishwater Janice, knows anything about." She was quiet for a moment. "*Look* at me, damn it! I don't really look like your wife at all!"

I turned, then narrowed my eyes. This was Jan's face, her dark hair, her arms, hands and body, but . . . there was a recklessness in the eyes, a fullness to the smiling lips, a tension and excitement in every line of that familiar body, that I'd never seen before. There was a resemblance to Jan but, incredibly, nothing more. This was another woman, this was Marion Marsh and no one else, leaning toward me now, moist lips smiling, offering herself. "Kiss me, Nickie."

I shook my head and turned away fast.

"Why not?"

"For an absolutely ridiculous reason: I don't want to be unfaithful to my wife!" I was staring almost blindly at the trees beside me fighting back a temptation—oh, Lord, I wished I hadn't drunk that gin—so intense it caught my breath, *wanting* so much I couldn't believe it. I squeezed my eyes shut and began taking slow deep breaths, thinking cool thoughts, knowing that this girl was right beside me waiting, offering . . . and I won. Opening my eyes, finally, I felt actually weak.

I took a few more slow calming breaths, then turned to Marion to make her understand that she had to get out of our lives. Still turned toward me, smiling, she didn't move, and said nothing, just waited as I hunted for words. She looked—but how *could* she, how was this possible?—voluptuous, the most sensual absolute *female* I've ever seen. It shone from her eyes, exuded from that familiar, utterly strange body, filled the air. "Nickie," she said softly, "do you realize that under these clothes there's a naked girl?" and the intensity of the sudden disappointment I felt, the cold shock of knowing I had won and was going to successfully resist, was more than I could stand, and I grabbed her. I grabbed her, she grabbed me, and there, staring horses and all, parked on a country road like a high-school kid, my wife's body in my arms, I was wildly unfaithful to her all over again; oh, Jesus.

We passed the house where, incredibly, the party was still going on and reached the highway before I felt I could talk. I heard myself then, voice solemn and actually trembling a little with the seriousness of what I had to say. "Marion. Listen to me. You can't ever, *ever* do this again." But she didn't answer, and in the greenish light of a highway lamp I saw that she was asleep.

All the way across the Bridge and San Francisco she slept, but at the sound of the ratchet as I set the hand brake, she opened her eyes, glanced up at the house, then at me. "Hi," she said.

Blinking against the gin I'd had, forcing my vision, I studied her face;

we were almost directly under the street light before the house. "Hi, Jan."

"Hi." Her hand came up to her mouth, ladylike, to stifle a belch. Then she pressed the back of her hand to her forehead. "Nickie . . . I don't feel so good."

CHAPTER FOUR

A little before noon I stood in the kitchen in pajamas and slippers waiting for the toast to pop up, trying not to listen to the loud plopping pulselike gurgle of the percolator. I had a full-blown hangover, and it helped to stand absolutely still while I waited, arms hanging at my sides, eyes closed; when the toaster popped it made me wince. I had to make my way to the other side of the kitchen then, but by walking without lifting the soles of my slippers from the linoleum I managed. Getting the plates out wasn't too bad, but the trays are propped in the narrow space between stove and refrigerator, resting on the floor on their edges, and I had to stoop. I made it by bending very slowly, at the knees only, eyes straight ahead, locating a tray by feel.

Al scratched at the back door; it was past time for him to be let in, and he knew it. I called to him, eyes closed; I told him we'd decided to get rid of him and had bought a plant instead. Maybe he believed me, because as I walked to the refrigerator I heard him pattering back down the stairs.

I was looking for, praying for, tomato juice, pushing milk cartons aside; vodka and tomato juice, I'd remembered, was supposed to be the remedy for this kind of pain. There wasn't any, though; we seldom drank it. But there was a big chilled bottle of California champagne Jan had bought at a local liquor-store sale and was saving for our anniversary. This was an emergency, and I got it out, peeled off the imitation lead foil, and worked out the plastic cork, careful about noise.

The tray vibrated in my hands all the way down the hall, the liquids slopping over. Jan's face, as I turned into the bedroom, was bone-white above her pink nightgown and the dark knitted shawl over her shoulders; she'd had more gin than I'd had. She was sitting up against her pillow, and she said, "Oh, thank God. I couldn't possibly have gotten up myself, I'd have starved right here. Thanks, Nickie, darling," she added so nicely, so lovingly, that my conscience began to ache more than my head.

"I made it entirely by touch; didn't dare open my eyes." I set the tray at the center of the bed and climbed back in again. Then, slowly, slowly, chewing by an act of will, swallowing carefully, we got the dry toast down with careful sips of ice-cold, incredibly delicious champagne; washed down aspirin; swallowed coffee. When we sat holding our second cups, I said, "How you feeling?"

Jan considered, cup cradled in both hands. "Better," she said, voice a little surprised. "My headache's not too bad now; I guess the aspirin's taking hold. And I feel a bit less horrible in general; the coffee and toast, I suppose."

"With a big assist from the champagne. You aren't supposed to do this, you know, or you're on the road to alcoholism."

"Well, it helps." She sipped a little more champagne, a little more coffee, then sighed, put down the cup, and sat back, closing her eyes, and dozed.

I sat looking at her, pale and vulnerable: this was *Jan*, this was my *wife*. Last night and the night before that I had . . . It didn't matter that it was her body; it was another woman, absolutely no question about that. Once in a while I'd daydreamed a little about other women, but still the answer to whatever problems we had was never actually someone else; I wanted to work things out with *Jan*. I sat looking at her—there was a little color returning to her cheeks—remembering times before we were married, remembering our honeymoon, that kind of thing, feeling very tender toward her and almost fiercely protective. Then I slipped off into sleep, too.

"Nick?"

"Yeah?" I opened my eyes and ran a quick check over my system. I was definitely healing.

"What *happened* last night? I can't remem . . ." Her voice trailed off, and she sat frowning at the foot of the bed. Then she focused her eyes on me again. "Nick! Last night. Did I—*dance?* I did, didn't I?"

"Well. Yeah. A little."

"By myself?"

I nodded, watching her.

"It's funny, I can barely remember. It's like catching a little glimpse of myself for a moment, then it's gone." Her eyes widened. "I *sang*, too, didn't I? Up there on the platform!"

I nodded again.

"Oh, Nick, how *awful!*" She covered her face with her hands. "Why didn't you *stop* me! What'll I ever say to the Hursts!" She lowered her hands and sat staring at me wonderingly. "And afterward . . . I'm not sure I really remember this; it's like a dream you can barely recall. But . . . didn't we drive around? *Speeding?* Skidding on the curves? And didn't you—you *did*, Nick! You threw a bottle at a tree!"

I nodded again.

"I don't understand it. We're not people who get drunk!" She sat staring at me.

I didn't know what to tell her or whether to say anything. I shrugged and said, "Well. It happens sometimes. Sneaks up on you." There was beginning color in her cheeks but dark smudges under her eyes. She looked delicate, fragile, and a wave of guilty tenderness moved through me. "I'm glad you're feeling better."

She smiled at the truth in my voice. "I know you are. You're better, too, aren't you?" I nodded. "I'm glad."

I leaned toward her and kissed her lightly. Then I leaned far across the tray, took her shoulders in my hands, and kissed her again, much longer and harder. I wanted to make things up to her, and it seemed to me this was how. "Well!" Jan pretended to catch her breath. "What's this all about? And with a hangover at that."

I grinned. "Especially with a hangover. That's how it works with me, I don't know why; always has."

"Always? Does that mean—"

"Never mind the ancient history. This is what matters." I leaned across the tray again, reaching for her.

"Well, maybe we should get rid of this, for heaven sakes." She lifted the tray and set it on the floor. Then she turned back to me as I moved closer, and we kissed, long but gently. Presently we slid down to lie heads comfortable on her pillow. We both smiled, appreciating each other, appreciating in anticipation the leisurely, almost languorous, hangovers-still-persisting quality of the domestic lovemaking just ahead.

Again we kissed, snuggling closer, making ourselves comfortable. Jan searched for and found the handkerchief she keeps under her pillow and wiped at her nose. I pulled the blanket up over our shoulders and punched up my pillow; a pulse had begun at the base of my neck, a headache deciding whether to come back or not. But I didn't care. I had a burden of guilt to make up to Jan, and the nice thing was that I was enjoying doing it. I was kissing her now with a slow passion, she was responding, I felt the beginning blur of my senses, and grinned with relief because I was enjoying this every bit as much as, even *more* than, last night. Jan's hands met behind my neck, clasped, and she drew me tightly toward her, kissing me harder and again and again very rapidly, and my arms tightened around her till she gasped. "Jan?"

"Yes? . . ."

I was overwhelmingly tempted to kid myself into thinking I'd been fooled. I wanted to. Lord, how I wanted to. But I knew this was the moment of truth, the test I must not fail, and I shoved her away so violently her clasped hands were torn apart and she cried out. But I kept

on shoving, brutally, frantically, using both hands. "No, goddamn it, no!"
I was yelling. "It's you, and I know it!"

"Oh, what's the diff!" Marion said angrily.

"All the difference in the world!" I'd thrust my leg straight out,
holding her off, the sole of my foot flat against her stomach.

"Yes, there *is*, isn't there? All the difference in the world." She lay
smiling at me, Jan's face but Marion's hot and mischievous eyes.

I'm a silent-movie buff, a term I don't much like but I haven't a better
one. And I've watched many an old Keaton, Laurel and Hardy, Chaplin,
Mack Sennett. So I know that the best of the old slapstick routines are
far from slapdash. Granted the beginning premise, some of those fine
old sequences—like Keaton and the mortar on the flatcar in *The
General*—are marvelously logical, each event deriving inevitably from
the one preceding. In a weird way they're true to life; they could have
happened. So it doesn't surprise me that what occurred now, right in my
own bedroom, turned into something the Keystone Kops would have
understood.

She tried to move toward me, but my foot was still pressed to her
stomach, holding her off, and she said, "Nickie, you want to and you
know it!"

I knew it. "No, I don't. Now, *cut it out*."

She ran her hand suddenly up the back of my leg under my pajama
pants, her fingers scrabbling, and my leg yanked away reflexively.
Instantly she was scrambling toward me, and I backed right off my edge
of the bed onto one foot, and stood up stumbling. She flung herself
toward me, shrieking with laughter, and a hand shot out to grab an end
of my pajama cord. It yanked, dissolving the knot, and my pants
instantaneously dropped to the floor in a white puddle of ankle-deep
cloth. I stooped quickly, reaching for them with both hands, but she was
at the edge of the bed grabbing for me, and I swung away, one foot
coming loose from the pants, which trailed after me from the other ankle
as I ran. Marion was rolling off the bed in a whirl of pink cloth and
flying legs, and—feeling naked and exposed, tugging the front of my
pajama coat down—I ran across the room, yanking my other leg free
from the trailing pants. There's a big closet running clear across the end
of the room, the door nearest me open, and I stepped in. It's a sliding
door, and I rolled it closed.

Instantly it was rolled open again, and Marion stood there grinning
with excitement. She stepped toward me, and I whirled away, shoving at
the clothes hanging beside me. "Marion, for *god sakes!* This is absurd!"

"But fun! Fun in a closet, hey, Nick! I'll say!"

I was at Jan's end of the long closet, moving off into it, frantically sliding armloads of her clothes back along the rod toward Marion, who was struggling after me, flinging the hangered clothes behind her almost as fast: it was as though we were swimming through clothes. "Nickie," she called happily, her voice muffled, "isn't this exciting!"

Weirdly, it was. If she so much as laid a finger on me I knew what would instantly happen, right here, and using both arms together in a kind of side stroke, I began shoving still greater swaths of hanging clothes back past me as I fought toward the other end of the closet.

I stopped suddenly and stood motionless: light had just appeared ahead, the door at that end of the closet soundlessly rolled open. I stood silent, listening, hearing nothing, breathing as shallowly as I could. The silence continued, and I knew she was standing somewhere outside the closet, gleeful, waiting to hear me commit myself to one direction or the other. I stood halfway between the two open doors in an empty little no man's land between my end of the long closet just ahead and Jan's behind me. Reaching silently out toward my end, my fingertips brushed nylon and I recognized my ski jacket. Very slowly I reached under the jacket, touched softer material, and closed my hand on it.

Then I heard her, empty hangers suddenly jangling, shoving her way toward me through Jan's clothes, probably hoping to catch me coming toward her. Under my own hanging shirts, suits and folded pants was an empty space a yard high. I squatted quickly, then waddled rapidly along under my clothes, and walked silently out into the empty bedroom like a duck, my sky-blue ski pants in my hand. I stood and, balancing on one leg, quickly thrust the other into a pant leg. But I'd moved too quickly, lost my balance, and had to hop, my bare foot thumping the floor like a hammer.

Instantly I heard her switch directions inside the closet, and she appeared in the doorway at Jan's end. She stood looking at me, then slowly raised both hands to shoulder height, her fingers curving into claws, and distorted her face into an idiot parody of lecherousness, her hunched-over shoulders shaking with silent laughter. She began walking slowly toward me.

There's a kind of mindless panic in being chased, and without thought I simply dropped to the floor of the bedroom onto my hands and stomach, shoving hard with both legs against the closet wall, and slid right across the polished floor and under the foot of the bed.

Revolving frantically on my stomach, I turned to face the room, then lay there under the bed watching her bare feet and pink hem as she staggered around the room gasping through peal after peal of helpless laughter. I had one leg in the ski pants, and in the foot-high space under the bed I tried to slide the other leg into them but couldn't find the opening, couldn't maneuver or see behind me; I was sweating horribly. Then my toes found the opening, and—enraged—I shoved my leg violently down the pants by sheer force.

She was stooped over, watching me, her hair hanging almost straight down, her excited upside-down eyes looking into mine. For a moment, both motionless, we stared at each other. Then a hand appeared beside her inverted face, the hooked forefinger slowly and lasciviously beckoning, and I began to curse.

She stood, then the bed was rolling swiftly forward on its casters, about to expose me. I reacted before thought and, like an infantryman crawling under fire, began scrambling to keep up with the bed. Then at last my mind worked. I'd banged my head hard on the underside of the bedsprings; I'd hurt my wrists in the fall to the floor; I was hot, dusty, angry; right now I could resist any woman in the world. I stopped moving and let the bed roll forward till it cleared me.

With difficulty I pulled myself up by the headboard, the bed out in the middle of the room now, and stood erect, looking something like a merman, I suppose, both legs bound tight together by the stretch cloth of one leg of my ski pants. Marion couldn't talk; her outstretched arm pointing at my sky-blue-wrapped legs looking like one thick, strangely contorted leg with two feet emerging from a single stretched cuff, she whooped with laughter, eyes enormous with astonished delight. I was damned if I'd hop, I told myself, and just stood there, holding onto the bedpost, then I had to grin, too. Marion collapsed helplessly onto the bed, rolling and shouting with laughter, and I watched her, grinning sheepishly, until I had to laugh, too.

She stopped presently and lay there, tears running down her cheeks, gasping for air, shaking her head in disbelief. I looked at her lying there, and fought. Fought harder. Fought furiously. And lost. I couldn't walk, so I simply leaped—dived through the air, a streak of white tapering off into sky-blue—landed beside her, and grabbed her on the first bounce.

When presently I sat up, it was very slowly. I reached for the blanket, dragged it up, and wrapped it around my shoulders, a corner of it lying on top of my head, and sat there, knees drawn up, huddled. "Oh, damn," I said. "Oh, goddamn, damn, damn."

"You get my goat!" Marion was punching up a pillow, then she lay back, drawing the sheet up over her. "That was some pajama party! And you know it!" She smiled. "Oh, it's so good to be back! To love *again*."

"Then possess someone *else*, goddamn it!"

"It can't be just anyone! This is my house, it's where I belong, so it has to be Jean, Jane, June, whatever the hell her name is. You don't suppose *I* like it?" She held a strand of hair out before her eyes. "Look at this scraggly hair. What a punk color." She let the hair drop. "And thick eyebrows! Skinny arms!" She brought one leg out from under the sheet, and lifted it high, extending it gracefully. "Not bad legs, I must say. Though mine were better." Smiling wantonly, she held the pose till I looked away, then brought the leg swinging closer to me, toes straightening to show off the graceful arch.

"Cut it out."

She drew the leg back under the sheet and began making smacking sounds. "The inside of her mouth feels funny. Not quite big enough, or something. But fine for kissing, eh, Nickie?" Suddenly she flung her arms out, arching her body under the sheet till it was supported only at the shoulders and heels. "Oh, it's so wonderful, Nick! Everything is! It's wonderful just to *stretch!* I'd forgotten!" Lying back, she saw the tray on the floor beside her. "Hey! Been a long time since I tasted champagne!" She leaned over the side of the bed, filled two glasses and sat up again, handing one over to me. I sipped mine gloomily, she tasted hers, then drank it down. "Oh, boy! This is *swell!* Where'd you get hooch like this?"

"Liquor store near Haight Street."

"The bootlegger has a *store?*"

"No. Prohibition's over, Marion. Since long before I was born."

"Well, that saves a lot of trouble." She picked up the bottle, filled her glass, held the bottle impatiently till I'd finished mine, then filled it, too.

"Marion. You've got to go. And leave us alone. *Got* to."

"While there's still some champagne left? You don't know Marion Marsh."

"I'm beginning to."

We finished the bottle; there was less than half a glass left for each of us. Marion emptied her glass, head tilted far back, draining the last drops, then set it down on the table beside her, smacking her lips. "We need some more of this good, good booze, Nickie."

"Not a chance. You've got to *go,* damn it!"

She threw back the sheet, and stood up, naked and beautiful, walked to Jan's end of the closet, standing open, and pushed one foot and then the other into Jan's oldest and only pair of high-heeled shoes. She took Jan's purse from the dresser, turned toward the bedroom door, and as she walked out, her arm reached into the closet to drag Jan's street coat from its hanger.

In record time I got pants and shirt on right over my pajama top, and a pair of loafers on my bare feet, shoving in shirttails as I ran down the stairs. But when I hit the sidewalk she was far down the street, almost at the corner. I slid into the Packard over the door top, then rolled down the hill after her, accelerating as much as I dared. Before I reached the corner she turned it to the right.

I swung around after her, directly into a parking space at the end of the block. Marion was fifty yards ahead of me, just passing the delicatessen and the beauty parlor and wig salon heading toward the liquor store whose sign hung out over the walk at the end of the block. Almost directly under the sign a stout woman stood facing the direction Marion was walking from. Her mouth was moving, and when I turned off the ignition I realized that she was feebly calling "Help." She repeated it, not so much yelling as just saying it: "Help"; then, "Police." She was staring not at Marion but at the back of a man who was walking away from her. He wasn't old, as I'd thought at first glance, but shabby, wearing an excessively long dirty overcoat to the tops of his broken unlaced shoes and a knitted cap pulled down over his ears and forehead. He was eying Marion walking toward him, I realized suddenly, and in that instant—not ten yards from Marion now, and walking slowly toward her—the man suddenly opened his coat wide. I cursed and began scrambling out of the car. Because except for his shoes, the man was completely naked under the coat, an exhibitionist, the sides of his coat held stiffly out before him, his eyes riveted to Marion's.

Marion didn't screech, look away, break stride, or even hesitate. Instantly, she flung her own coat open wide, and for another step or so the two of them, naked as eggs under their coats, walked steadily toward each other, the sides of their coats held straight out before them.

The man's jaw dropped in shock. He stopped, stared, horrified, then flung both arms tight around himself, wrapping himself in his coat, hugging it to him, turned and ran.

The stout woman he was now suddenly running back toward, screeched, turned, and began to run, too. Both of them then—the woman lumbering in panic, the man shuffling to avoid losing his shoes—ran down the street in weird slow motion while Marion, coat snugly around her again, swept grandly into the liquor store.

I was laughing too hard, silently, shoulders trembling, to even protest when I followed her into the store, and she bought three quarts and a pint of champagne, spending all but nineteen cents of the money in Jan's purse.

I remember some of what happened then with a shining clarity, and the rest not at all. I remember Marion and me running down the steps from my apartment, bottles in hand, Marion in Jan's red-velvet gold-trimmed robe and matching slippers. On the front porch we pounded on the Platts' door with our fists, choking with laughter. And I remember their faces when they came running to the door, yanked it open, and saw us standing there; they'd been having lunch. I remember inviting them up for champagne, though I don't remember them coming up.

And I remember Marion and me in the kitchen opening a champagne bottle; I held it while she twisted the cork. Al scratched at his little door, and I unlatched it with my foot, he nosed it open, walked in, and stopped dead. Motionless, frozen in the moment of taking a step, he stared at Marion. Obviously he saw nothing of Jan; this was a stranger, and he studied her warily. Then Marion got her cork out, bent down, snapped her fingers gently, and Al came cautiously over. A little neck-scratching and they were friends.

The Platts must have come up because they were there: Frank on the window seat, glass in hand, grinning at everything that happened or was said; Myrtle rushing downstairs, then back up again with a stack of old phonograph records that she set on the coffee table. Marion shuffled through them, said, "Hot diggety dog, Eddie Cantor!" and handed me three or four of them. I got them onto the spindle of the record player after a stab or two, turned the thing on, and the sound came out at Donald Duck speed, and we all howled, Marion delighted since it was the first time she'd heard it. I set the dial at 78 then and restarted it.

I clearly remember lying on the chesterfield, scratching Al's ears, Myrtle and Frank side by side on the window seat grinning, as Marion sang the words to "Ida! Sweet As Apple Cider!," fingers snapping, along with the round lush voice of Eddie Cantor. And I remember Marion teaching us "how Eddie Cantor dances." Each of us standing separately, she had us spread the fingers of both hands, then bring our hands rapidly together and apart in a soundless clapping motion, only the fingertips touching. When we mastered that with the help of more champagne, she coached us in holding our eyes exaggeratedly wide while rolling them frequently. Then, eyes rolling, fingertips clapping, knees rising high, we pranced around the room, Al barking, to "Makin' Whoopee!"

If this was how Eddie Cantor danced, we liked it, and we all seemed to more or less know the words to "Makin' Whoopee!"—including Al, who howled them, head aimed at the ceiling. Together with Eddie Cantor's own voice, the volume turned on full, we screamed and howled out the song as we pranced around the house through every room the way Eddie Cantor dances, floors and window glass vibrating, till a picture fell off the living-room wall.

But it never seemed to me that I was drunk; or if I was, it was a different, *lighter* kind of thing with champagne; we just seemed to float through the afternoon. Marion asked what time it was, over and again it seemed to me, though it never annoyed me. I'd just smile and say, "Quarter to five" ... "Six-fifteen" ... "A little after seven" ... I don't remember us beginning to dance, but I remember us dancing dreamily, cheek to cheek, hardly moving, to "The Sheik of Araby," sung by Rudy Vallee, Myrtle sitting on the chesterfield beaming at us, Frank asleep in a chair. I remember with a hard, sharp embarrassment how foolishly flattered I felt that Marion should think I was worth all this trouble, and murmuring something to her about it. She said, "You think you're the only reason I'm back? Don't kid yourself, Sheik. There's a lot more reason than that, I'll say! What time is it?" We danced past Myrtle and she said how wonderful it was to see how Jan and I still felt about each other, and my conscience screamed at me. What else can I *do*, I said silently; sit in a corner and sulk till she leaves?

I remember slamming the door of the Packard and letting my head drop back onto the leather seat back, hearing the other door slam, hearing the whir of the starter motor.

Marion was driving when I woke, but while there was champagne left in my veins and mind, I still didn't seem drunk. My head on the leather seat back as I opened my eyes, I saw the low skyline of a building sliding along beside us and knew I'd seen it before. We were slowing at the curb: that's what had awakened me. And yes; I knew these tiled roof surfaces, beige stucco walls, the arched doorways of this vaguely mission-style building. What was it?

I sat up, staring at it as we stopped, Marion pulling up the hand brake, turning off engine and lights; it was a handsome building still, but old now, feebly lighted by too few bulbs, not another car at this long empty stretch of red-painted curbing before it. "Nick, hurry! Get rid of the car somewhere, park it in a garage, we'll be late!" I turned; in Jan's street coat Marion was sliding out on her side, then she slammed the door, ran around the front of the car and across the sidewalk, and in through one of the long row of double doors stretching across the building's front.

I didn't know what she was talking about, but I knew where we were now; this was the SP depot. After a moment or so, I got out, walked inside, then stopped. Across the tiled floor Marion stood at a ticket window, her back to me. Except for the man behind the window there was only one other person in all of the waiting room, an old man waiting on one of the long, varnished wood benches, a brown-paper shopping bag, its entire surface wrinkled and creased many times over, between his feet.

Marion turned from the ticket window, walked to the center of the empty floor, and stopped. I walked toward her but she didn't see me immediately; she was looking slowly around at the old depot, even glancing up at the ceiling. Her eyes, I saw, walking toward her, were bewildered. She heard my steps then and turned. "Nick, he says there isn't a *Lark* any more!" She turned to glance back at the man behind the one open window; a boy, actually, of no more than nineteen, a Mexican, with a wisp of mustache, sitting in shirt sleeves, elbows on the counter, cheekbones on fists, reading a magazine lying open on the counter before him. "He says there's no night train to Los Angeles at all!" Her words were a wail; I was afraid she might cry.

"I know." I reached out to take her elbow. Gently I said, "Marion, people don't ride trains any more. There are hardly any left."

She didn't answer or move. She looked slowly around at the worn empty benches; at the long row of ticket windows nearly all permanently boarded over with raw plywood; at the dusty-windowed restaurant in a corner of the waiting room, the big handles of its entrance doors chained together and padlocked; at the great overhead blackboard labeled ARRIVALS—DEPARTURES, its green-ruled spaces empty; at the dismantled lunch counter, its row of metal stool supports still bolted to the floor, the stool tops gone. She said, "I came down here one night. I was in a play at the Alcazar. I was in the first and third acts but not in the second, and there was time to rush down here and back before my last entrance. Doug Fairbanks and Mary Pickford were leaving for Hollywood.

"They were going home to Pickfair; they'd been here for three days. They saw the play the second night, from the fifth row; I spotted them. And they were going back to Hollywood. On the *Lark*, of course. I got here in time to see them get out of a big dark-green touring car with a tan canvas top folded back; it was a nice night. It was right out there." She nodded toward the street and began walking toward the open door. I walked along, still holding her elbow. "Doug was waving and grinning, you know that wonderful, wonderful grin, as he helped Mary out of the car. And she was smiling that beautiful smile." We stopped on the walk, Marion staring out at the dark empty street. "She was carrying a tremendous armful of yellow roses. And their car was stopped just where yours is; they'd held the space open for it. I couldn't get anywhere near it, though. There must have been a thousand people here on the walk and out in the street calling 'Doug! Mary!,' the people nearest trying to touch them. Doug was still grinning, and he had an arm around Mary, working their way across the walk. Right here, right where we're standing! People who were arriving to take the *Lark*—there were hundreds every night, Nick!—had to get out of their cabs and cars in the middle of the street at the edge of the crowd. And people were standing on running boards, and jumping up in the air, trying to see Doug and Mary over the heads of the crowd. Then everyone followed them into the station, every doorway jammed, and we all went on through to see them off. When the *Lark* pulled out, right on time, Doug and Mary were on the observation platform standing just above the big, round lighted circle that said '*Lark*.' Doug was waving back at the crowd, and Mary stood throwing her roses out to the people one at a time; some men ran along the platform beside the train for the last of them. Doug stood waving and Mary blew kisses for as long as we could see them down the track, and we waved back till there were only two red lights and the big round lighted *Lark* sign." Marion turned to look up at the faded station front, then turned abruptly away, and we crossed the empty walk to the car.

I drove, watching Marion. She'd look out at the city moving past us, look away to stare down at the floor of the car, out at the city again, then back to the floor. Presently, eyes on the floor, she said, "Drive to O'Farrell Street, will you, Nick? Between Mason and Powell," and I nodded.

We crossed Market Street, drove to O'Farrell, waited for a light at Mason, then drove slowly on toward Powell; near the middle of the block I slowed. "Here?"

"A little farther, I think . . . No, we're too far now. Or are we? Wait."

I pulled to the curb. The top was still down, and Marion looked back over the rear of the car, then turned to lean forward, staring through the windshield. She studied a building just ahead, on the other side. "Moatle? What's *that* mean?" She was pointing at an enormous sign of yellow-red-and-white plastic hanging out from the front of the building.

"Motel," I said. "It's a . . . well, it's something like a hotel. But without any lobby or anything. Just rooms and a place to park your car . . . " My voice trailed off; she was shaking her head to shut out my words, eyes squeezing closed as she turned from the motel.

Then they popped open, and she stared up at it again. "*Look* at that thing!" she said angrily. "Jesus, it's ugly! Get us *out* of here, Nick. That's where the Alcazar once stood."

A block farther on I said, "Anything else?"

"Nothing."

"Then maybe you ought to tell me what this is all about."

Listlessly she said, "We were going to Hollywood."

"To Hollywood." I nodded. "What for?"

"What *for*? You saw *Flaming Flappers*! I was great," she said simply. "I was already at work on another picture. And in that one I was greater still. We were going to Hollywood, Nickie—the way we should have once before! So that I could resume my career."

I nodded several times, then said very gently, "Well, now you know. It's a different world, Marion. The Alcazar's gone. So is the *Lark*. So will the SP station before long. And the world is filling up with motels. *Flaming Flappers* was long, long ago. And I'm not my father."

She nodded, then dropped her head to the back of the seat, and I glanced at her. Her eyes were closed; tears were sliding down her cheeks. "Goddamn it. I had a career coming to me!"

In front of the house I set the hand brake, and Marion opened her eyes and lifted her head to look up at the house. For some seconds she sat staring up at it, then she turned to me. "Good-bye, Nickie." She shook her head slowly. "I'm tired, so *tired*." Then she smiled and reached out to put a hand on my arm. "But it was nice, wasn't it." I didn't answer; to say yes seemed disloyal to Jan, and I felt guilty enough as it was. "Come on, Nickie," she said reproachfully, disappointed in me, "say it was nice. That won't hurt you!"

I sat looking at her for a moment or so. "You're really going? Forever?"

She nodded, and swallowed. "Yes."

"All right," I said. "Why not, then? I'll admit it was nice because it was; I can't help that." I thought about it, then smiled at her. "So, yeah; it was *very* nice, Marion. In fact, it was wonderful, and I'll never forget it."

"I'll say." She smiled and laid her head back.

I was feeling enormously better just being able to say these things out loud, to speak the truth. "You're a terrific girl, Marion. Different than any other I ever knew. In more ways than one."

"You tell 'em," she murmured, eyes closed, "I stutter."

"Don't ask me to make comparisons between you and Jan, because I won't do that." I sat staring through the windshield at the deserted street. "But hell, yes, I'll admit it was nice. It was wonderful, Marion. Absolutely marvelous."

"What in the world are you talking about?" She sat up.

"Jan . . . ?"

"Jan? Well of course it's Jan." She glanced around her, then said,

"Oh, my God," and put her hand to her forehead, squeezing her eyes shut. "Nickie . . . I don't feel so good. *Again!*" she added, and her eyes popped open. "Nickie, we've been *drinking* again, haven't we? I have those same . . . fragmentary memories. Little glimpses now and then. What's *happening* to us! Drinking this way two nights in a row like . . . a throwback to the Twenties or something!"

"Champagne for a hangover; that was our big mistake." I reached over and opened her door, trying to end this conversation, and she slid out.

But upstairs every light in the house was on, the living-room furniture was shoved out of place, there were spilled potato chips all over the rug, an empty champagne bottle lying on a chair, and—final triumph of anarchy—Al lay asleep on the chesterfield. Jan looked, then just shook her head, and we walked on down the hall toward the bedroom. In the doorway she stopped short. "What in the world is the bed doing clear out there in the middle of the room?"

"Well. You. Said. You. Wanted to rearrange the furniture."

She wasn't listening. Walking on into the room she pointed at the floor. "And what are your pajama pants doing over *there?*"

"Well." I tried to grin lewdly. "You threw them."

"I don't remember doing that." She frowned. "Why would I throw your pajama pants. In fact, I don't even remember when we . . . Or do I? I remember *starting* . . . " It seemed to me that the thing to do was get us to bed and the lights out, and I began unbuttoning my shirt. But Jan was pointing upward now, to the top of the open closet door, her mouth open in astonishment. "What are your *ski* pants doing up there!"

"Well. You. Wanted to mend them. That was to remind you. One of the cuffs is torn. See?"

"*Mend* them? Your *ski* pants? Why should I be worrying about them at a time like . . . " She had turned, unbuttoning her street coat, and stared at me. "You've got your pajama tops on!"

"Oh, Christ." I had run out of things to answer, but Jan didn't notice. She stood thinking, then walked slowly to her closet, taking off her coat, hung it up, turned, then noticed the dress she was wearing, very short, its pattern looking as though it had been designed by throwing globs of thick paint in primary colors. "I said I'd never wear this again . . . I hate this dress!"

She walked to the bed and sat down, staring thoughtfully across the room. I walked slowly and unobtrusively over to my pajama pants, making as little sound as possible, hooked them up with my foot, slipped out of my slacks, and got them on. I was hanging up the slacks when I heard Jan murmur, "*Now* I remember us," and I turned quickly to look at her. But she was smiling, nodding slowly. "Sort of," she added. "It was *wild*; my God . . . " She looked over at me, suddenly happy. "And you said it was wonderful. You said it was absolutely marvelous. Oh, Nickie, it's been a long time since you've said anything like that." I tried to smile, holding my breath.

Her hands folded in her lap, Jan's face went thoughtful. "But it's as though . . . it *wasn't* me. It was, of course, but . . . " She shook her head. "But it *wasn't*. I don't even know what I mean by that, but . . . " She shook her head again. "I *remember* us. Sort of. In little bits." She sat staring, then repeated firmly, stubbornly, "But it *wasn't me*." I just stood there across the room in my pajamas, waiting. Jan suddenly swung around to look at me, her eyes widening. "And it wasn't me *last* night! Dancing! Singing! Up there on the platform making a fool of myself! I'd never do that!" I thought about yelling, slumping to the floor, hopping around on one leg as though the other had a cramp, but I just stood hypnotized. Jan turned to face the wall again. Very slowly she said, "It wasn't me the night before that, either. Here. In bed. After Marion's movie." Moving as though in a trance, Jan stood up. Barely breathing the word, she whispered, "Marion . . . What you said downstairs in the car was, 'It was absolutely marvelous . . . *Marion*.' " She yelled it. "You said 'MARION'! My God . . . " Abruptly she sat down. "She's been . . . taking me over. Hasn't she! And you knew it. You *knew* it! Oh, Nickie," she wailed, "I never *dreamed* you'd be unfaithful to me!"

I lied. I ran to the bed, sat down beside her, an arm around her shaking shoulders, and listening to myself I sounded convincing because I began with the truth. "I didn't *know*, Jan! I came to bed after Marion's movie. You woke up, and . . . I thought it was you! My God, why wouldn't I!" Under my arm the trembling stopped, she looked up, and I saw in her face the realization that that had to be true. Then the lie began. "Same thing the next night. After the party with the Hursts. I thought it was y—"

"Out in the *open!*? Parked in a *car!*? You thought that was *me!*?"

"Well, it sure as hell *looked* like you! And don't forget—we were drunk."

She thought, then shook her head, shrugging her shoulders out from under my arm. "But this morning you knew. Because downstairs in the car tonight you said, 'It was wonderful, *Marion*'! You're having an affair with her!"

"Oh, for cr—"

"Do you want a divorce?"

"Jan, for crysake! What for? *To marry Marion?*" Soothingly I said, "Baby, Baby, listen to me. Today I knew; yeah. But I didn't find out until . . . *during.*"

"Well!?"

"Well, what?"

"When you knew it wasn't me, *why didn't you stop!*"

"*STOP!?* My God . . . what an inspiration. That idea is typical, absolutely *typical* of a hell of a lot that's wrong around here!"

She jumped to her feet, gripped the hem of Marion's dress with both fists, yanked, ripped it straight up the front, slipped it off, and—bursting into tears—began ripping it to shreds, and the lurking headache I'd had since morning roared up like a skyrocket.

CHAPTER FIVE

Sunday morning when I came out to the kitchen, breakfast was cooking, and I smiled and said, "Morning," to Jan. But she only nodded, and didn't speak, didn't smile. During breakfast I let Al in to liven things up a bit, tossing him the occasional toast crust. As always with anything thrown to him, they fell to the floor or bounced off his nose, and he had to track them down, sniffing the floor like a bloodhound. Jan sat absolutely engrossed in the front page of the Sunday paper, and I began talking to her through Al: "Would you tell Jan to pass the sugar, Al? Thank you. . . . Ask Jan if she'd like some more of this absolutely delicious coffee; and help yourself, too, of course."

Pretty soon she smiled a little, and said to Al, "Tell him he can just help me clean the house today; it needs it!"

We got through the day then, with great politeness toward each other, a thorough reading of every last section of the Sunday paper, and in the afternoon, after the house was cleaned, Jan took a nap while I took a walk with Al.

But Monday night when I got home, she had drinks and a bowl of potato chips waiting on the living-room coffee table, and we sat down to them, on the chesterfield, our backs to Marion's wall. Jan said she'd been thinking things over, she understood that I'd been tricked, and that it wasn't fair to blame me. That's what she said, but her eyes didn't; not quite; not yet.

But at least we'd made up, officially, anyway, and Jan sat back with her drink, and in a parody voice and smile to match said, "Well, dear? And how was your day at the office?"

"Break a leg," I said amiably, then Al came wandering in to greet me and accept a few potato chips. "And how was your day, Al?" I said.

Jan said, "Busy; both the garbage man and gas man to bark at, all in one full rich day."

"Well, that's his job. Isn't it?" I said to Al. "Goes with the position of 'Dog.' He takes care of all the barking. Singlehanded. No one else ever helps or even offers, but he never complains." I'd leaned forward toward him, and though I'm pretty skilled at ducking, this time he got me right on the cheek with his tongue. Wiping my face with one of the little paper napkins Jan had set out, I said, "I hesitate to mention this, but where did you dogs ever get the idea that it's some kind of treat to be swiped over the face by a wet dog tongue? Five thousand years of domestication and you still haven't learned that it's no big deal. You don't see the *cats* doing that." His ears went up at "cats." "They're smart." I picked up a chip, and he sat staring at it. I gave it to him and said, "You know what I'm going to do with you, Buddy-boy? I'm shipping you to Denmark." He wiped his mouth daintily with his tongue and sat watching the potato-chip bowl. "They have an operation that will turn you into a *cat*." The ears rose, head cocking. "Yep. They'll trim those big, long, dingly-dangly, dopey-looking ears into the kind of nice, pointy, *beautiful* little ears that *cats* have." I tossed him another chip. "Teach you to walk fences—they use training wheels, at first, then it's up to you. And there's a crash course in meowing. Oh, you'll *love* being a *cat!*" I took one of his ears and slapped him softly in the face with it. "A duel, m'sieu?" and he exposed his teeth in a lazy token threat, tail going. I picked up a last potato chip and pointed to some crumbs he'd left on the floor. "Any more of that and I'm putting out a contract on you for a hit; understand?" I tossed the chip, it bounced off his nose, and he walked around sniffing, tracking it down—it was about a yard away—and Jan and I smiled at each other.

We talked. My vacation began next week, and for lack of anything special to do we'd decided to stay home; visit the museums, see a play that was supposed to be pretty good, try a couple restaurants we'd been told about. And there was still the spare bedroom to be painted. We had another drink, and Jan told me what Myrtle Platt had had to say that morning when they met at the mailboxes on the porch.

All in all we were pretty relaxed, yet at the same time we were tense and on guard, and we stayed that way all evening. Was Marion really gone? It looked like it, but still—in bed we didn't make up in the way that counts. Jan was afraid, she said, and I couldn't blame her. Talking in the darkness, we decided that on my vacation I'd also peel off Marion's wall.

Tuesday I got home a little late—some solemn foolishness at the office that could just as well have waited till morning or 2001. Jan was in the kitchen fixing dinner; I heard the sounds and walked straight back. First thing I said, passing through the doorway, was "Well?" and she knew what I meant. She shook her head, smiling, and held up a hand, fingers crossed: Marion hadn't returned. I kissed her hello, hugging her, working a free hand up under her skirt till I found something elastic to snap. Then I changed clothes, fixed drinks on the wooden drainboard, and we had them, Jan at the stove mostly, me leaning back against the sink.

I said, "Jan, how did you feel? About being . . . taken over?" I thought we could talk about it now.

"Horrible." She had the oven door open and was poking with a fork at something that sizzled. "It was terrible, Nick," she said, still poking, then closed the door and stood up. "I was appalled." I nodded. Jan stood absently sipping her drink, staring down at Al, who sat fascinated by her stoveside activities. Then she shook her head and set her glass on the work counter next to the stove. "No," she said. "That *isn't* how I feel. It's how it seems to me I ought to feel, but I don't. It *was* sort of frightening." She stood thinking. "Sort of . . . ghostly." She smiled at the word. "I only had glimpses of what she was doing, you know. Very dim, mostly. Like looking through a dozen layers of glass. And for only a moment now and then—when she got tired, I think, and had to let go for an instant."

"What were they like? Those occasional moments."

She thought about it, then smiled in surprise at her answer. "*Interesting*. Life can be a little dull at times, of course; anyone's can. And I have to admit, it was *interesting* to be—what would you say?— spliced right into someone else's mind and feelings. Someone all excited and pleased with practically everything she saw. It's fascinating to know, *really know*, Nick, how things seem through someone else's mind." She stood sipping from her glass, and looking—was I right about this? I wasn't sure—a little sad, and I had the sudden odd feeling that maybe something had gone out of her life. Absently sipping her drink, she stood staring at nothing, then her eyes focused on me, glaring angrily. "And she thought *you* were the bee's knees!" She swung away, stooping to yank open the oven door and jab at whatever was in there.

After a little of that she stood up, said she was sorry, and I smiled, said that was okay, and—well, we got through Tuesday.

Every other Wednesday Jan played bridge downstairs with Myrtle Platt and a couple of Myrtle's friends, and Al and I always helped with the dishes so she could get away early: Al by getting rid of scraps I tossed him while scraping plates for Jan to wash. She changed clothes then, went on downstairs, and I wandered the house a little, looking for something to read. A Blackhawk film catalog had come that day, and I sat down on the window seat—there was still some daylight—and marked a couple things I'd like sometime; for Christmas, maybe: the 1920 *Dr. Jekyll and Mr. Hyde*, with Nita Naldi, my second-favorite-sounding silent-movie name—Lya de Putti being first—and maybe *The Social Secretary*, with Norma Talmadge and Erich von Stroheim.

I put the catalog down and for a few moments sat looking at Marion's wall. *Marion Marsh lived here*, I read once more, *June 14, 1926*, the back of the chesterfield cutting off the rest. Then I stood up, walked out to the kitchen and the phone, and dialed my dad's area code and number; it was about eight o'clock here, ten in Chicago. He answered right away, and we talked; every once in a while one or the other of us phoned, particularly when a letter was a bit overdue. He'd run into an old friend of mine in the Loop, Eddie Krueger, who'd been at our house a lot when I was in high school and when I'd come home during vacations from college, my mother still alive. "And," he said, "the weather's been lousy, but that's to be expected."

"Yeah. Something I wanted to ask you, Dad. Just idle curiosity, but I've been wondering about it."

"Shoot."

"Well. The Twenties. I've been wondering—"

"The what?"

"The Twenties; the Nineteen-Twenties."

"Oh, yeah; what about them?"

"Were they really as great as we're always reading? Were they actually all that different from now? Were the *people* different?"

There was a long pause. I was opening my mouth to speak again, not sure we were still connected, when my father answered. "Well, I've given that some thought myself. You have to make allowances for the fact that at least part of the Twenties were my twenties, too. I was young, carefree, and you tend to look back at your own youth through rose-colored glasses. And in general, we tend to remember what was good in the past and forget what was bad. We're propagandized about the Twenties, too; they've been glamorized. Allowing for all that, Nick, really considering those things and allowing for them—the answer is hell, yes. Ah, Nick, they were great. Such a *different* time, everything was different then. It was just a grand and glorious time to be alive and young in."

"Well, *why? How?*"

Again there was a pause. "I won't really be able to tell you that; things were so damn different. The times, the look of things, the country itself; hell, in the very way drugstores used to smell. And my God, yes, the people were different. We were dumber. Not nearly as smart as you. It never entered my head at twenty-one years of age to question the way things were. Any more than you'd question whether the sun should rise, or whether it ought to snow in winter. But it seems to me we were nicer. More tolerant; I don't remember the hatred there is now. We were more easygoing, more *interested* in things—we were livelier, damn it! We knew how to have fun! I think we knew what life was for. I can't really explain it, Nick. It was just a better time. I feel I was lucky to have been young in the Twenties. And I feel sorry for young people today. It's all so goddamn grim."

We talked a little more; I wondered what he'd say if I told him about Marion, but of course I didn't. When Jan came upstairs I was asleep; they'd played an extra rubber, she said at breakfast, and it turned out to be a long one.

Around ten o'clock Thursday evening, I put down a magazine and looked over at Jan, who was knitting something that was eventually supposed to turn into a sweater for me. I sat watching her, knowing factually that what she was doing would, in fact, result in a sweater. But emotionally it's always impossible for me to believe that twitching a pair of pointed sticks at a ball of continuous yarn will somehow turn it into a usable garment; what holds it *together?*

Jan knew I was looking at her, and pretended she didn't. She was wearing a plain white blouse and a black skirt, rather severe but she looked nice, very pretty. I said, "Jan," and she looked up, smiling brightly, needles poised. "If you'll excuse the saying, 'We can't go on like this.' "

"I know"—she looked quickly down at her knitting.

"Well, then, if I may offer a suggestion to a lady, why don't we skip merrily down to the bedroom, hand in hand, and fuck?"

She blushed freight-car red.

Jan and I must be the tag ends of the very last generation brought up as kids really believing there were "bad words." A lot of our friends are only a little younger, just a couple of years or so, but it seems to have been the dividing line, and they're able to say these words with ease. And while they're polite, well-bred people who wouldn't have mentioned it if we'd never said them, still it would have been noticed. I've managed all right; I was in the Army, and as a child I was a boy. But Jan had a hell of a time. I learned—she confessed this—that she'd practiced at home. Washing the breakfast dishes, for example, alone in the house, she'd stand there, hands in the soapy water, working up her nerve, then take a deep breath and say, "Fuck!" She could tell it sounded all wrong at first, tense and strained, just not good enough for polite society. But she persevered, working it and the several other *de rigueur* words into casual sentences, practicing the way you would to perfect a French accent, until at last she could drop them into sentences with butter-smooth casualness, no hint of either emphasis or de-emphasis. Finally she tried it in what my father would call "mixed company" and it came out beautifully. She sounded to the manner born, the only trouble being that she turned brick-red and stayed that way for thirty minutes.

She was blushing now, but she nodded gamely. "Let me just finish this row."

When she came into the bedroom I was buttoning my pajama coat, scratching Al's ribs with my toes; he was lying on our furry bedside rug in his after-dinner coma. "Better cookie him out," Jan said.

I squatted beside him and tapped him on the shoulder. A brown eye opened slightly, and I made the umpire's *out* gesture, thumb jerking over shoulder, and the eye closed. "He says he doesn't care to go out."

"Well, he has to. Nickie . . . I'm scared."

"Yeah. Me, too." I tapped Al's shoulder again; this time he didn't open an eye. "He claims he has as much right in here as anyone else. Says he's a human being, too."

"Well, tell him that people with hair on their eyelids aren't people at all. Are you really scared?"

"Yeah; I don't want her back either. But still—"

"I know. I know."

"You're not a human being at all. You're a dog! You think we can't tell?" I picked up Al's limp tail—"What about *this?*" I flipped up a long basset ear—"How do you explain *that!*" I tapped his black-rubber nose. "And *this!*" I picked up a paw. "And *this:* there are all *kinds* of clues; you can't fool us!" I looked up at Jan, who was unzipping the side of her skirt. "But if you'd really rather not."

"Oh, no! No. We can't. Just go on. Forever. Without."

Al was feebly wagging his tail, and I pointed. "That movement is final conclusive proof: *you're a dog.* Come on, get your cookie." He stood, yawning, stretching, smiled up at Jan, and followed me out and down the hall. When I came back Jan was in bed, sitting up, wearing the rigid smile of a determinedly happy corpse.

These weren't really ideal conditions for love-making, but we went at it—slowly; tentatively; bravely. It began to go a little better, then quite a lot better, then I gave Jan an extra-special kiss, and she returned a real post-office, special-delivery, registered-letter-with-return-receipt, and things were going fine. I said, "You're a filthy nasty girl, and I'm going to tell your mother."

"Go ahead; she'll never believe you."

I kissed her long and hard, Jan returning it. Then I rose up on one elbow and snapped on the light. Jan lay staring up at me, astonished. "Jan?"

"*Yes,* for heaven sakes!"

I snapped off the light, then snapped it right back on again. "Where
were you born?"

"*What?*"

"Where were you—"

"Kankakee, Illinois! My God!"

I reached for the light, then paused. "What was your mother's
name?"

"*Sellers!*"

I snapped off the light, Jan reaching for me in the darkness. My lips
at her ear, I murmured, "What's your social-security number?"

Softly she said, "481-03-2660."

"*Darling*," I said, and Jan and I finally made up for real.

Friday at the office came and finally went, three long weeks of
vacation stretching ahead. We weren't doing anything much with it, but
it was still a vacation, and I came home ready to celebrate: we were
going out to dinner with Fritz and Anita Kahler.

I got home, and Anita had phoned that afternoon: she was coming
down with flu; we'd have to postpone going out. I didn't want to accept
it, I didn't want to stay in for another evening, I wanted to do *something*
to celebrate, I didn't know what. And finally we went to a movie.

There was nothing worth seeing; I read through every movie listing
in the pink section, the entertainment section of the Sunday *Chronicle*,
which we save to see what's doing in the week ahead, and not a movie
in the entire city or suburbs was worth looking at, but we went anyway.
To a Western I'd never heard of, which is rare for me, at the Metro on
Union Street, and it was an enormous mistake.

I bought popcorn, really celebrating, but Jan didn't want any, and we
sat watching the damn thing, a big wide-screen Technicolor job. I tried
to interest myself in the scenery, at least, which was pretty spectacular.
The accompanying music soared to frequent crescendos and sank to
dramatic silences. Wind whistled through canyons, shots barked and
pinged in dusty streets, hoofs pounded, wagon wheels creaked, and
people of the Eighteen-Seventies, cleverly anticipating the idiom of
today, said such things as, "Would you believe two hundred Indians?"

I sat recalling the names of minor actors and in what other pictures
I'd seen them; no movie is entirely a waste of time for me. But when I
glanced at Jan in the middle of the thing she was actually asleep, dozing
chin on chest. I knew I shouldn't have dragged her to this, and if she'd
been awake I'd have suggested leaving. But I now had a feeble interest
in how the picture turned out, and she was sleeping peacefully, so we

stayed. Later when I saw she was awake, I turned to ask if she wanted to go, but she seemed to be enjoying it now, smiling faintly, mouth slightly open to listen, so we stayed till the end.

The lights came up then, the sparse, scattered audience rising, and she turned to me. "How wonderful!" she said, and I smiled at the sarcasm.

"Yeah, great." I sat waiting for her to stand but she was staring at the empty white screen.

"That scenery!" she said, and I realized there was a note of excitement in her voice; the people moving slowly up the aisle beside us turned to stare. "The costumes!" she said, still looking at the screen. "And the *color!*" She swung to look at me. "Nickie, you bastard, why didn't you *tell* me movies were in color! And that the screen was so *big!*" She leaned toward me, eyes enormous, people in the aisles openly smiling, and her voice dropped to an awed whisper. "And that they *talked.* Oh, Nickie, I came back for one last look at the world, and it's lucky I did." Her voice rose again, excited and exuberant. "*Imagine!* You can actually *hear what they say!* Oh, boy. Oh, *boy,* oh, *boy,* oh, BOY!"

She blinked and glanced up at the empty screen. "Oh! Is the picture over?" She stood quickly, turning for her coat. "I'm sorry; I was asleep, I guess." Pushing an arm into her coat sleeve as we side-stepped toward the aisle, Jan said quietly, "Terrible, wasn't it? But you know something?" She took my arm as we turned toward the exit. "I have that same kind of glow you get sometimes when you've just seen a marvelous movie."

CHAPTER SIX

It was doubly a sleep-late morning—not only Saturday, but the first day of vacation besides—and I did my best. Eyes still closed, I lay telling myself I was drowsy and would go right back to sleep, but behind the eyeballs, I was wide awake. Because I knew.

There was no sound in the bedroom, I realized then; no movement, no presence beside me, and my eyes snapped open, head turning to look at Jan's empty side of the bed, the covers tossed back. Then I sat up fast, looking beyond the bed at the floor. Everywhere I looked fragments of cloth lay on the floor, their edges fuzzed with unraveled thread: Jan's good black dress torn into dozens of fragments.

Dressing as fast as I could go, I said, "*Damn*. Goddamn!" but I heard the false vehemence in my voice, and for a moment stood motionless. Then I nodded, finally admitting it to myself: I'd missed Marion. I'd missed her all week long; it wasn't anything I could control.

I'll say this for myself. Grabbing the first shirt I could find, a white one, buttoning only every other button; snatching a pair of tan wash pants; stepping barefoot into a pair of moccasin loafers—I had the grace not to try and blame Jan. It just took someone else, apparently, someone as wild and exuberant as Marion, to bring out what was undoubtedly not the real me at all but someone else who had a hell of a lot better time. I didn't like it, didn't like the implication, didn't want to think about it; it made me sad; that was how I wanted to feel about Jan.

The house was silent in the way a house never is if anyone else is in it. But as I stood buckling my belt, I heard the lower door open, heard her footsteps coming up, and I walked out into the hall to the head of the stairs.

A blond Valkyrie was coming up them, wearing Jan's black slacks and turtle-neck sweater. She looked up at me, smiled, and patted her hair. "Fake. And cheap. But at least it's not mouse color. Bought it at the salon on Haight Street; Jan has a charge. Hope you don't mind." She stepped up beside me. "Welcome me back, Nickie." She kissed me on the forehead, brushed past, and walked on into the living room.

"You weren't coming back!" I followed her. "You said you weren't coming back!"

She swung around, her face going hard. "Can that! All bets are off. They're in *color* now! On a big wide screen. And they t—" She cut herself off, then grinned. "Hey, they aren't *movies*, any more, are they? They don't just move, they. . . . Hey, Nick! They're *talkies!*" She turned to look at the wall over the chesterfield, then walked toward it, reading aloud. " 'Marion Marsh lived here, June 14, 1926.' " She looked over her shoulder at me to nod. "That's the day I should have gone to Hollywood. With Nick Cheyney." She looked back at the wall, blond head nodding in agreement with what she was saying. "I'd have had a career. A great one. As big as Joan Crawford's." Absorbed in her own vision, she turned away. "That's how it was *meant to be,*" she said vehemently, nodding again. Then more quietly, "And that's how it's going to be." She looked up at me. *"I'm going to have my career."* Suddenly she grinned. "In color and sound."

I walked toward the window seat, pointing at the chesterfield, and after a moment she sat down. On the window seat I leaned forward, forearms on knees, and clasped my hands. "Listen. All your life you acted on impulse, and what happened? It finally got you killed. Well, nothing's changed. Your old picture shows up on television over half a century later, you come back to see it, and on pure impulse make a grab for me just because I look like your old flame. But all that does is cause trouble, and you find out that everything's changed since your day anyway. You *see* that it has! You *know* it's no use! But you get a glimpse of a lousy movie in sound and bad color, and whammo—you're back once more to pick up your old career, not a thought in your head about how. Do you ever *think,* goddamn it!"

I'd reached her; I could see it. She didn't have an answer, and for a moment or two, face sullen, she was silent. Then all she could think of was "Sez you."

"Tell me how then."

Again she had to hunt for a reply; then defiantly she said, "I had friends in Hollywood."

"In 1926, Marion! They're gone now. Dead."

"Baloney! The people I knew weren't stars, they were kids! Like me." She thought for a moment. "Like the prop boy on *Flaming Flappers,* Hugo Dahl! He was only seventeen, third assistant prop boy or something." She jumped up and walked quickly toward the bookshelves. I keep a few out-of-town directories I've stolen from hotels on the living-room shelves: a two-year-old Manhattan directory, one from Portland, Oregon, the three main Los Angeles books, another from Reno. Marion took down the one with BEVERLY HILLS on the spine, and standing at the shelves she hunted through the D's, pages flying. Her finger moved down a column, backtracked, stopped, then she looked up at me triumphantly. "And he's still there. He'll help me," she said complacently, clapping the book shut, putting it back. "He had a crush on me."

"Jesus, Marion, he's not seventeen now, he's in his *seventies!*" I said pleadingly. "Probably retired, and long since out of pictures."

"Maybe. And maybe not."

"Okay, it doesn't matter, because look: the longest you've ever possessed Jan is a few hours. It takes something, doesn't it? Psychic energy or whatever you want to call it." She didn't answer, just looked sullen again. "And you run out of it, don't you. Then you've got to let go, and Jan is back: right?"

"Maybe."

"Maybe, hell. You wouldn't even *get* to Hollywood before Jan would take over again and come right back home. And if you *did* get there, she could do ten thousand things to wreck any comeback before it ever got started."

For a good dozen seconds she sat glowering at the floor, then looked up. "She ought to *let* me go!" she burst out.

"*Let* you? Just hand over a . . . chunk of her *life?* To you? Why the hell would she!"

Marion muttered something, refusing to look at me.

"What?"

"I said I didn't mean for*ever!*"

"Oh? Just how long did you have in mind?"

"I don't know. Exactly." She looked at me, head cocking shrewdly, like someone testing out an offer. "A few years maybe?"

I laughed, and she blew up.

"All right, *one* year, for crysake!" She jumped up from the chesterfield, arms folding tensely across her stomach, hands clasping elbows as though she were cold. And in her blond wig, artificial though it looked, in the black slacks and sweater Jan hardly ever wore, and in the fierce expression of her face as she began walking up and down the living room, she didn't look like Jan at all. "*I* don't know how long it'll take!" she said. "What the hell does it matter anyway! What does she *do* with her punk little life? Nothing! *Good night*; she even plays bridge!"

I just shook my head. "Jesus. . . . You're completely ruthless, aren't you? Completely."

"You don't know your onions!" She flicked me a contemptuous glance. "I'm no more ruthless than anyone else would be. Who felt the way I do." She walked over to stand facing me, leaning belligerently forward. "*That's* what you don't understand: *the way I feel.* You've thought about Jan. Thought about yourself. Think about me!" She stared at me for a moment longer, then turned away again, walking the room. "I lost everything," she murmured, to herself as much as to me. "The most anyone could lose. Most of a life that would have been wonderful." She turned to me again, pleading now. "I'm asking for a gift. Of just a little of it back. *Make her do it, Nickie!*"

After a moment—what else could I do?—I just shook my head helplessly, and she turned abruptly away. I sat watching her walk slowly around the room: absently touching a lampshade, feeling the material between thumb and forefinger; picking up an ashtray, glancing at the inscription on the bottom, setting it down; stopping to look at a picture; walking on. "Punk taste," she muttered once. "Everything dull. Afraid of colors."

She walked out to the hall and back. To the front windows, where she looked past me down at the street, then turned away again. "Pacing restlessly," I said to myself, then realized that was only a phrase, and wasn't true; she was calm enough. I've watched a zoo tiger glide endlessly around and around the limits of his cage, eyes no longer even seeing the curious changing crowd outside it. And realized that he's not restless but everlastingly patient. He doesn't know what he's waiting for. But when and if it finally happens he'll recognize it: the latch left unfastened one day; the grating gradually weakened by unnoticed rust.

Marion was simply wandering the house waiting for whatever might happen next; we'd said all there was to say. I watched her; my wife's face under the absurd blond wig, but not her. Not Jan but Marion Marsh, who might have become a star of the silents. She'd been *down* there! Actually been in Hollywood in the far-off, almost mythical days of the silents. I said "Marion, did you ever see any of the stars?"

She nodded. "Lon Chaney; once."

"No kidding? Where?"

"On a studio street. At lunchtime. I was on my way to buy a box lunch at the canteen, and I cut through an alley between buildings." She stopped before me, and I crossed my legs, looking up at her, listening. "And there he came around the corner walking right toward me. They were making a picture; he was in full make-up and looked absolutely horrible. He had a scar down across his left eyebrow, and his eye was dead white."

"Singapore Joe! He was in his Singapore Joe make-up for *Road to Mandalay!*"

"Did you see it?"

"No, I'd sell my soul for a print; I've only read about it. His eye was covered with the skin from an egg."

"How do you know?"

"I collect old films, not that I have much: *The Mark of Zorro, Broken Blossoms*. A couple serial chapters. Some early newsreel footage. But I know a lot about them, and they say that egg skin permanently injured Chaney's sight."

"Well, it looked just awful, Nickie." She sat down beside me. "He saw I was a little scared, just the two of us alone in that narrow alley. And as he came close, he deliberately closed his *other* eye so there was only that one white eye just staring at me! I let out a little shriek, and he grinned, closed the white eye, and just as we passed he winked at me with the good one. He was really a very nice man, you know; everyone said so. Actually kind of good-looking, in a tough kind of way."

"Lord; to have actually seen Lon Chaney. In his makeup for *Road to Mandalay*." I was smiling, shaking my head. "Who else did you see?"

"Oh . . . Laura La Plante."

"You *did?*"

"Yeah. She was filming on the set next to ours. And when they didn't need me on our set I'd go next door and watch."

I nodded; in silent-film days, noise didn't matter, and they often filmed pictures side by side on adjoining sets. "What was the picture?"

"I don't remember."

"You don't remember!"

"No." She glanced at me curiously.

"Well, what were some of the scenes? I might recognize it from that."

"Oh, Nickie, what's the diff! She was in a kitchen fixing dinner or something. It was Laura La *Plante* I wanted to see."

"Well, how was she?"

She shrugged. "Okay. But I was better." She saw me smile, and smiled, too. "I know. It sounds conceited. And is. But it's also true: I was far better. Still am. And still will be."

"You ever know any stars?"

"Yes. Well, not really, not very well. But I did get to know Valentino a little; he was on a set next to mine once, too, and we talked a little, two, three times."

"My God: Valentino. What did you talk about?"

"Oh . . . " She frowned, looking down at the floor. Then she looked up. "About how proud the people of his village were of him, some Italian village. I think he was really a very simple man. And a very nice one. To me, anyway."

I sat shaking my head. "You actually *knew* Valentino. I can't get over it. There's a picture of his playing now at the Olympic. *The Four Horsemen*. I've seen it twice."

"You really *are* a movie nut, aren't you. I knew a man at Paramount who collected films, too. Stole them, actually."

"What?"

"Yeah. He worked in whatever you'd call it—the distribution department. He was just a shipping clerk, actually; he'd pack prints of the new films and ship them to distributors. A dozen to New York maybe, half a dozen to Chicago, a couple to Milwaukee, and so on. It was a punk job, and didn't pay much, but he was a movie nut, too. So was I. So were most of us. We were all crazy about movies; being *in* them, being *connected* with them. One time—"

"Wait a second: what about this guy who collected films?"

"I told you. He was crazy about movies, but he knew he couldn't ever be in them; he had a snub nose, turned way up. I didn't really like looking at him, though he was nice, and liked me a lot. Pictures he liked, he'd keep, that's all; just order an extra print and take it home with him."

I was slowly standing, turning to face her. I could feel the excitement welling up and tried to stop it: it seemed to me I had to be very careful somehow, or everything I was hearing would break up and fade away like a dream you can't recall any more. "Marion. Listen. What kind of films did he like?"

She shrugged, then turned away, thinking. "Oh . . . " She looked at me again. "Griffith's, for one. You know; the director? D. W. Gr—"

"Yes! I know."

"Well, he had all his films, I remember; all the features."

"All?" I said softly. I felt my knees go momentarily weak and fluid. "All of D. W. Griffith's features? Oh, Jesus. Do you know that several of them are *gone* now? Lost! Not a copy known to exist anywhere in the world! And he had them . . . all?"

"Yes." She sat looking up at me wonderingly.

"What else? Marion, what else did he have?"

"Nickie, *I* don't know. Lots of pictures. He traded prints with friends in the same job at other studios."

"Oh, my God." I sat down beside her, then stood right up again. "Where, for example?"

"Well, he had a buddy at Universal he traded w—"

"*Universal!* NO! Listen, there was a fire at Universal! After your time. Hundreds of absolutely priceless films lost! Fabulous films! *Mythical* films now!" I stood blank-faced for a moment, staring down at her. "And he *had* some of them. To think he once had them. Listen, when was this?"

"Nineteen-twenty-six."

"And how old was he then?"

"Oh . . . thirty."

I did the arithmetic, then shook my head. "Be dead by now. Maybe not, though; maybe not. *What was his name?*" I swung around, ran to the bookshelves, grabbed up the three Los Angeles books, and hurried back to the window seat. "What was his *name*, Marion? He just *might* be alive, just might be in here!" I sat down, the three books in my lap, BEVERLY HILLS on top.

"You know, when I was down there, there was only one phone book, and it wasn't any bigger—"

"*Marion!*" She shut up. "What . . . was . . . his . . . *name?*"

"I can't remember."

"YOU CAN, TOO, REMEMBER!"

"Well, *wait* a second! Good night, Nurse! It was an unusual last name. And a short first name. Dick? No, not Dick—he was that tall electrician—but something like that." She sat frowning. "Norman? No, that was that dark young carpenter. And Ned Berman was a cameraman . . ."

"Didn't you know any women, for crysake!"

"I don't remember them as well. I'll think of this in a minute; quit interrupting."

I sat trying to wait, but I was so excited I had to jump up and go to the bathroom, but I hurried back. She was still frowning, staring at the floor, lower lip between her teeth. "Did you think of it?" I stopped before her.

"No, not yet. What's all the *excitement*, Nick? I know you're interested in movies, but so am I, and I don't get all—"

" '*Interested*'?" I had to laugh at the word. "Oh, boy. If you'd ever collected anything—You never did, did you?"

"Just men." She was smiling up at me, pleased as always at any excitement. "Why?"

I couldn't stand still. Hands jamming into my back pockets, I began walking up and down before her, fast. "Listen, if you're a collector, you always have your—what?—your Holy Grail. A manuscript collector probably pictures himself in the back of some run-down, out-of-the-way secondhand bookstore. Finding a bundle of old papers at the back of a bottom shelf in a dark corner behind some books, where it's been for years. He unties it and looks through old paper after useless old paper.

And then—down in the middle of the bundle—*there it is*. His hands start shaking because there under his eyes at last is the tiny handwriting he has so often studied in reproductions of the man's signature. Just his *signature*, the only specimen of that handwriting ever before found. Kept under glass and permanent guard in the British Museum. Worth a million dollars, they think, if it were ever sold. Yet now"—I was listening to myself, enjoying my own eloquence, and Marion sat grinning—"now here is page after page of that tiny, rusty-inked handwriting. With notes in the margins! And then, *then* . . . far into this long handwritten script, he finds a speech. The first words have been crossed out, but he can read them. And they say"—I stood thinking—"they say 'To exist or die is my dilemma,' and there's a pen stroke through them. And just above them in even smaller letters is written for the first time in the world, in the author's own handwriting . . . 'To be or not to be: that is—' ''

She burst out laughing, and I grinned. "All right. Okay. I went too far, it's ridiculous. Only not quite, Marion. Just barely not quite. The unknown Rembrandt hanging on the wall of a Goodwill Thrift Shop marked four and a half bucks has been *found*. So was a secondhand metal teapot marked seventy-five cents, and also marked on the bottom in lettering so small and tarnished that everyone else missed it . . . *P. Revere, Silversmith*. A little book was picked up out of a ten-cent sidewalk bin. Printed in Boston in 1827, according to the title page, which also read, *Tamerlane and Other Poems, by Edgar A. Poe.*' The almost impossible dream is why you collect. And you want to know what mine is?"

She nodded, smiling.

"All the reels . . . all forty-two incredible reels of Erich von Stroheim's lost masterpiece . . . *Greed*."

"He had them."

"You don't know what you're talking about!"

"I do too! I remember that picture; everyone in San Francisco was talking about it! They filmed it here, and I watched some of it! Finally Von Stroheim finished it, and it was dozens and dozens of reels long; and they cut it way down. That was at . . . M-G-M!"

I nodded, barely breathing the word—"Yes. They cut it to only ten reels. And even some of those are lost now. Marion"—I squatted down before her, looking up at her face, almost whispering—"are you sure you remember? That he had *all forty-two reels?*"

"Of course; he talked about it. He'd had to trade three Paramount features to get them all. But he got them."

I got up, sat down beside her, and took her hand between mine, looking into her eyes. "Then, Marion," I said gently, "do you understand now? Do you understand why you have *got* to remember his name?"

She nodded. "Yes. I understand. How *you* feel." She yanked her hand away and jumped up. "Why don't *you* understand how *I* feel!" She stood glaring down at me, then her expression changed. "Listen, the theater, whatever it is, where they're showing *The Four Horsemen . . .* "

"The Olympic; it's an old movie house."

"Do they have matinees?"

"Today; Saturday? Yeah, every weekend."

"Take me to see it." I started to say something, and she almost screamed at me. "Nickie, don't *argue!* I'm sick of it! Just *do* it!"

"I was going to say yes."

I gave Al a couple of bone-shaped dog biscuits, the kind he doesn't much like to eat but loves to bury, and gave his tail a little yank. Then I drove Marion to the Olympic.

It's a fine old theater. I think it must date from the Twenties itself, and they run a complete old-time program, including organ accompaniment. They get good sharp prints, and the pictures are taken seriously. We bought popcorn, which they sell in old-fashioned candy-striped bags, and sat down. There was a pretty good house for a matinee, but we found two together at the side.

The lights went down, the organ began, the old red-velvet curtains parted and rolled squeakily back, and a Pathé News came on, a rooster crowing soundlessly before the trade-mark. To appropriate organ music, we watched a forgotten horse race. We saw an equally forgotten senator from Oklahoma waving from the back of a train; a caption told us that he'd just come out foursquare and courageously against repeal of the Volstead Act. And we watched a chimp on a bicycle.

A sing-along next, the words of "Rose Marie" sliding up from the bottom of the screen line by line, the organ playing the tune as a moving white ball touched each word or syllable as it was to be sung. Not many people joined in, but Marion did, loud and clear, and of course I had to join her, sliding down in my seat a little. But then eight or ten others came in, and some more after that. And after a half dozen lines of *"Rose-ma Reeee, yiii luh vue . . . Rose-ma Reeee, mide ear,"* it turned into fun, both of us belting out those fine poetic lyrics, and I was a little sorry when it ended.

Title and credits for *The Four Horsemen of the Apocalypse* came on, and we settled down to watch it. I was a little bored at first—I'd seen it twice before—but pretty soon it caught me, and I was enjoying it again. *The Four Horsemen* is the Valentino with the famous tango sequence, a big scene and a fine one. At tables surrounding the dance floor of an Argentinian cafe, dozens of spectators sit watching Rudolph Valentino, in gaucho costume as Julio, dance with Helena Domingues in a Spanish outfit, including a long-fringed shawl.

Valentino holds her romantically close, bending her far back, leaning over her to gaze deep into her eyes, and you can watch it for laughs or you can enjoy it. I sat enjoying it; I get bored with the idiots at silent-film showings who demonstrate their deep sophistication to the rest of the audience with constant guffaws. The old acting conventions and the stories can be foolish, but look past them and you can often see a lot worth watching.

This was worth watching. It's a great dance scene—Valentino was a professional before he got into pictures—and the organist was really fine, as he generally is at the Olympic, his tango perfectly synched with their movements, as good as sound-on-film.

It seems strange to me yet that I instantly recognized what began happening to me then, though it wasn't really strange: more than once I'd sat listening to Jan hunting for words to describe it. This was almost a physical sensation as though—if you can possibly imagine a sensation like this—someone had sat down in the same seat with me, pushing steadily toward me yet somehow without crowding. So that suddenly we were *occupying the same space*. All in one swift, smooth gliding motion I was taken over: literally "possessed."

My own self immobilized then—helpless and dwindling—I was some-how put aside, pushed off into a remote corner of my own being. I still knew what impulses were coming through my senses. For a few moments longer I knew what messages my eyes and ears were receiving—but remotely and from a great and increasing distance, like a child drifting rapidly to sleep. Within two seconds, three at most, I was very nearly completely gone, huddled up somewhere far inside myself, as Rudolph Valentino took over almost completely.

At intervals then—sensed like a very sleepy child, or a child in fever—the hold over my being would relax for a moment or half moment. Almost instantly the grip would tighten down again with fresh strength, but in that instant I'd have a fragmentary glimpse of what he was seeing, hearing, and feeling, and the memory of those moments can shake me yet.

Because what he was seeing, not only in but beyond the shifting blacks, whites and grays of that square old screen up on the dusty stage of the Olympic—and what he felt—were more than anyone else ever could. Sitting bolt upright, far forward in the seat, hands clenched to chest, chin lifted, he saw not only the visible flickering screen. Beyond its edges in his memory a narrow-eyed director in cloth cap and holding a short megaphone stood watching. The eye of a camera on its wooden tripod followed his movement, the man behind it standing bent-kneed, eye pressed hard against the viewfinder; he wore knickers, a white shirt and tie, and his right fist revolved in a rigidly steady motion as he cranked the film the Olympic audience sat watching now. Behind the camera, a knot of bystanders and studio technicians, two of them in overalls, one holding a hammer. And at a piano, playing the tango to which they danced, a man in a vest and, oddly, a wide-brimmed felt hat. Sitting motionless staring up at the screen, he saw all these things in memory. And above all, he felt still another memory: the skyrocketing surge of triumph at the beautiful knowledge, even as he danced, that this scene was going to be great.

Sudden nothingness then. Pure nothingness; not even emptiness. Then another drugged, half-glimpsed moment: the magnificent tango up on the screen was ending. Cut to another scene, other characters, and in the instant of that cut, a rush of feeling. It was a wave of despair so bleak that I would not convey it in all its strength if I could. It was total: an unbearable horror of longing, the very worst of all—the hopeless yearning for what might have been.

In the eyes of the face still lifted to the screen, tears began to well. They brimmed, dashed down my cheeks, and Marion's hand reached out to lie on my arm. "I'm sorry, Rudy," she whispered, "so very sorry. But he had to know. Thanks."

My head nodded, my hand reached over to lie on hers for an instant, then Valentino was gone, and I sat staring blindly up at the screen knowing what I didn't want to know: the enormity of the loss when a life, talent and career are cut short. Human ego is staggeringly immense, and with the exception, of course, of national politicians, greater self-love hath no man than an actor. For Rudolph Valentino, only thirty-one years old, decades of world-wide fame and adulation stretched far, far ahead. Suddenly and senselessly all of it is lost. Cut off! *Gone!* It simply wasn't bearable.

"Now do you understand?" Marion was watching me, and I blinked, managed to nod, then swiped the back of my hand across my eyes.

"Yes. Oh, Jesus. Let's get out." I was standing, pushing out to the aisle past six knees, two beards, and a pair of metal-rimmed glasses reflecting the screen, Marion following.

Driving home, I had the top down, letting the foggy late-afternoon San Francisco air cool my face. I didn't say anything till we sat stopped for a light a couple of blocks from home. "That poor son of a bitch," I said softly then. "The poor cheated bastard. All he yearned for was his lost career. I don't think he gave even one thought to The Woman in Black."

"Who?"

"The veiled mystery woman all dressed in black who visited his grave every year. Some years there were four or five of them."

She wasn't listening. The light changed, I started up, and she murmured, "Sooner or later everyone loses his life, and it's not too bad, really. Once it happens most people don't seem to mind very much. But for the few of us who had something tremendous *cut short* . . . " She just shook her head. "I really had to show you, Nickie. And even now you don't really know. Because Rudy doesn't feel the way *I* do; *he's* never had the will to do what *I'm* doing! He's accepted it."

I turned onto Divisadero, then slowed at the curb before my house, stopped, turned off the ignition, pulled the hand brake up tight, and Marion put a hand on my arm. "Help me, Nickie. *You've got to.*"

"But *how*, Marion, *how?*"

"Make Jan see that she *ought to!* Just for a year. Or six months. Even for just one more picture! It's a better use of a little part of her life than she's making of it: make her see that, Nickie. Please. Please."

I leaned forward and sat with my arms crossed on the big old steering wheel, staring through the windshield at the motionless street. It seemed true; it did seem true that Marion actually needed a small part of Jan's life more than Jan did. But . . . I looked at Marion and shook my head. "It's not right, Marion. To talk Jan or anyone into giving up a part of her life."

"Just talk to her! Just tell her what *happened* today. Tell her how you felt. And let her decide. You can *talk* to her, at least!"

After a moment or so I nodded and shrugged. "Yeah, I can do that. But then it's up to her."

"All right. You talk to her." Marion leaned back to rest her head on the leather seat back, staring up at the wispy fog moving across the darkening sky. "By the way," she said lazily, "I remembered that name."

My head jerked around and I stared at her, but she didn't move. Still staring dreamily up at the sky, she said absently, "Hours ago, in fact. Up in the apartment. I looked it up in the L.A. phone book while you were in the bathroom." She rolled her head to look sideways at me, face and eyes innocent. "It's there, Nickie, darling. The man with the films is still alive. And I'm absolutely certain he'd still have them." She looked up at the sky again. "So come on down to Hollywood with me and you and

I can go see him. I'll tell you his name"—she turned to smile at me again, sweetly, lovingly—"after we're down there. After you've talked to Jan."

She closed her eyes, took a slow deep breath, then another, and her eyes opened. "Oh, God—*again*." Jan sat looking around at where she was, and I spoke fast.

"Listen, all we did was go to the *movies!*"

She nodded and pressed a finger to her forehead. "I know; I always get this little pressure headache from movies in the daytime. Besides, that's so ridiculous I know it's true." She frowned; her hand on her forehead had felt something. The hand moved up, touched, then gripped the blond wig. She yanked it off and sat staring at it. "What the hell is *this?*"

"Come on upstairs"—I leaned over to open her door—"I've got a lot to tell you."

CHAPTER   SEVEN

• •

We took Al for a walk, Jan changing clothes first; she didn't like the black slacks and sweater outfit. Walking into the bedroom, she stopped short, looked around at the torn fragments of black cloth lying all over the floor, and surprised me. "Maybe she's right," she murmured, and changed to her orange dress, the brightest she owned.

We walked Al to the schoolyard three blocks away; he likes that because there are usually kids who flatter him, play with him, and occasionally feed him candy. Not a soul there today, though, so Al made the best of it, counting the swings, teeter-totters, and the one lone tree. Sitting on the wide edge of the big kindergarten sandbox while Al roamed around, I talked to Jan.

Very factually, I told her what Marion wanted and what had happened to me at the Olympic. She sat listening so intently she hardly moved. Then for a good half minute she was silent. "Would *you* do it?" she burst out suddenly, almost angrily. "Would you give up part of your *life* for—say, Valentino?"

"Well . . . I don't know about Valentino. Maybe for Cary Grant."

"He doesn't need it, for heaven sakes! Nick, I know how Marion feels; in the same way you found out, little glimpses now and then. I never dreamed anyone could want something so badly, and yet—you know something? I almost envy her sometimes: I wish *I* wanted something that much. You know what I mean?"

"Yeah. When my father was a young guy just out of school, he wanted a job. You know why? So he could 'make good.' He got one here in San Francisco with a wholesale food distributor. Working long hours in a warehouse loading delivery trucks. Really hard work, and for damn little money. But it suited him. Because it gave him a chance to 'show what he was made of.' Well, I know better than that. Who believes such stuff today? Nobody, and we're right; they were only exploiting him. But the thing is that I almost envy the way people once felt about things, falsely or not. Because I don't have anything to take its place. And neither do you. So yeah, I know what you mean."

"Tell me what to do, Nick! And I'll do it. If you say I ought to, I will! Maybe my dumb little life isn't important, doesn't matt—"

"Hey, don't say that!" I put an arm around her shoulders and squeezed her knee. "What do you mean, a 'dumb little life'? It's no such—"

"Oh, yes, it is," she said quietly. "It's a little nothing life. I think I've really done something if I try a new recipe and you like it. Or decorate a room the way some magazine tells me. Or even read all the way through a hard book."

I talked and argued, trying to comfort her, and she nodded and pretended that she was. We called Al then, snapped on his leash, and started home. It was still day, but the late-afternoon fog had whitened the sky, and it was suddenly chilly.

"Tell me what to do, Nick," she said again, walking home, but I shook my head.

"Nope. You have to decide that."

A few more steps, and she said, "All right. But tell me what *you'd* do. You can tell me that much."

It seemed to me I was thinking honestly. And I believed that if it were me, I would do it. So I nodded presently and said, "Yeah. I think I would."

"Then I will. I'll give her"—she hesitated, then finished almost angrily—"a couple of weeks, that's all. To get started. Then we'll see how long after that. Nick, is that fair?"

"It sure as hell is. Look, give her a full two weeks, and if nothing's happened, that's it; we'll drive home then, during the third week of my vacation. Take our time."

"Oh. You're going, too?"

I felt my face flush; it hadn't occurred to me that I wouldn't. "Well, yeah. You don't think I'd . . . leave you there alone? You'll be there part of the time, you know. By yourself, if I'm not along."

"All right. But you know, I can force her out sometimes; I've learned how, and I've done it. It's like a little struggle, and sometimes I've been able to . . . just push her out. She knows it. So you tell her that I'm to be there every evening, from the moment she gets back to the hotel! And all night, *every* night. Or I just might show up in the middle of her comeback and cut it off at the knees."

"Good idea, damn good."

At home we fed Al, then went out to dinner; neither of us felt like dinner at home. I was depressed, I wasn't sure why, and I thought maybe Jan was, too. We walked down toward Haight and a little restaurant I find charming because it's so cheap; "our neighborhood Up-Chuck Wagon," as I've been forbidden to call it. And as we walked, a true story I'd once read rose up in my mind.

A man was murdered, for no apparent reason, in his apartment. Left in it were money, jewelry, various valuables, including a stamp collection. But nothing seemed to be missing; a mystery. One of the detectives, it happened, was a stamp collector. He leafed through the murdered man's albums and found a page of rare stamps, the early Hawaiian issues, every one except the two cent. He knew what the other cops didn't; that stamp was the rarest of all the Hawaiians. He checked through the dead man's friends till he found another stamp collector. Then he made the man's acquaintance. Presently they became friends. And finally, one night, the man showed the detective his pride and joy, a collection of the early Hawaiian stamps, complete. Where had he found the two-cent stamp? He wouldn't say. He was arrested, charged with murder, and still wouldn't explain; couldn't. He was tried, convicted, and then he confessed; his friend had refused to sell him that stamp, the one stamp he needed to make his collection complete. So he murdered him and stole it, murdered his friend for a canceled two-cent stamp.

Walking along with Jan toward Haight Street, I told myself that a jury of that man's peers—twelve other collectors—would have acquitted him, but it didn't help. Why hadn't I told Jan about the man in Hollywood who just might have a stunning collection of incredibly rare old films? Why not? Had I really been honest in nudging her down the path of letting Marion have her chance . . . in order that I could go along? Was I selling my wife—down south!—for the bare chance of somehow getting my hands on a mess of footage? *"My God,"* I thought, *"I'm living the script of an old silent: the film I want . . . is* Greed!"

So at dinner I told her about it; showed her how doubtful my motives really were. And Jan said, "I'm so relieved, Nick. I was afraid you wanted to go down there just to be with Marion!" And all of a sudden I felt great, and expansively ordered a carafe of the mysterious muddy red liquid that the Up-Chuck Wagon calls wine. Raising our glasses in salute, we drank, mouths shriveling, eyes wincing shut, and I found myself wondering if going down to Hollywood with Marion *wasn't* my real reason, my *real* real reason. To hell with it, I said, and bravely refilled our glasses. Later, for the first time in my life, I worked up the nerve to ask for a "doggy bag" so that old Al could join the festivities.

In the morning, packing, Jan was a little grim, but if she felt like changing her mind, and I think she was tempted, she didn't, and we were ready by eight. She wore a pink washable dress, her cloth coat, and a scarf for her hair in case we drove with the top down. I had on tan wash pants, loafers, sport shirt, and a sleeveless sweater.

Last thing I did was carry a carton of dog food down to the Platts' back porch; they'd said they'd take care of Al. And when Al came trotting up onto their porch to investigate, I explained what was going on. I'm not at all sure they don't get something from an explanation, whether they understand every word or not.

Squatting beside him, I rubbed his ears, occasionally pulling up the great wad of loose skin around his shoulders and neck; bassets seem to come equipped with twice the skin they need. I said, "Listen. It's not true that you've been fired from the position of Dog; you have tenure. And it's not true that you're adopted either; you're our real son. Now, we *are* going away for a while, but we'll be back. And the Platts will minister to your physical if not your spiritual needs. So don't worry; okay?" He wagged his tail and, I'm inclined to think, nodded. I pulled up an enormous handful of skin from around his shoulders. "I don't know where you got this crummy dog suit, by the way, but it's sure a lousy fit." He tried for my ear with his tongue, but I took evasive action. "And when I get back I'd like to see you in something newer and smarter; nobody wears long ears any more." He looked interested. "Next time why not try a poodle suit? They're pretty smart. The kind with rings around the ankles and tail? Have them shorten the legs, though." I stood up. "Now, remember, we'll be back, *we'll be back.* Meanwhile, play your cards right and you can con the Platts out of all sorts of forbidden delicacies." I leaned down and punched him on the shoulder, which is stronger and more massive than mine, and went up to take our bags to the car.

We didn't know when Marion would show up, but she arrived when we were leaving. I was coming down the stairs with our bags, Jan behind me with her keys out to lock up after me, when I heard her turn and go back up as though she'd forgotten something. When I looked up from the canvas-covered trunk on the rear bumper where I was stowing the bags, she was coming down the steps, both arms raised, elbows winged out, adjusting the blond wig. And it suddenly struck me that I was actually about to drive down to Hollywood with the ghost of a 1926 movie actress. I must have stood staring at her then because she walked around the front of the car, opened her door, then stopped to look back at me. "Come on, Nickie; step on it! We're forty-seven years late."

Only a couple of things of any note happened on the drive down: it's a long haul for one day, the old Packard isn't actually the easiest car to drive for any distance, and I didn't talk a lot. I asked Marion right away if she agreed to Jan's terms and she said yes. Then I asked her the name of the man with the films, the astounding collection of old silent films— if he still had it; if they still existed.

"Bollinghurst," she said. "His name is Ted Bollinghurst." It was just a name, but my stomach tensed; I could feel the excitement rising again, and I knew that name was etched in my mind forever. "He lives at 1101 Keever Street in Beverly Hills, according to your phone book. And that's all I know, Nick. I don't know whether he still has his films or anything else about him."

Marion chattered a lot from then on, pointing out changes. There were plenty of them since 1926, and I mostly just nodded and listened. For lunch we pulled into a drive-in, and Marion loved it, insisting on leaning over to my side to give our order through the standing microphone: milk shakes for both of us, cheeseburger for me, hamburger for her, with everything. She sat back, then frowned, and leaned across me again. "Hold the onions on the hamburger!" she said into the microphone, then smiled at me wanly. "Hi, Nick," she said, and I patted her knee quickly, while she was still there; Jan gets indigestion from onions.

The only other thing that happened is that I found myself struggling with the big wooden steering wheel, the speedometer at 65, which is very, very fast for the Packard, the tires howling on a curve.

I was able to hold it to the road, decelerating cautiously, till we hit the straightaway again; Marion's scarf was around my neck, streaming romantically back over the rear of the car. "What *happened?*"

"Rudy was driving," she said apologetically. "Said he'd spell you for a while."

"Well, he's one lousy driver!"

"I know. He said it was handling a lot harder than his Isotta-Fraschini and that he'd better let you take over again."

"On a *curve!?*"

"I know; he's coo-coo."

Around ten-forty that night Jan and I had dinner in the coffee shop of the Beverly Hills Hotel. Sitting in a booth waiting for it, we were so tired we just sat and stared at each other stupidly. "I get left with her headaches, hangovers, and now her exhaustion," Jan said, massaging her forehead. Her hand brushed her hairline, and she reached up, felt the blond wig, and dragged it off, shrugging. We skipped the delicious-looking bread-pudding dessert and were in bed and asleep by eleven-ten, the blond wig on a bedpost.

I woke up once and knew Jan was awake, too.

"Nick?"

"Yeah."

"I'm not so sure I want to go through with this. What do you think?"

"Decide in the morning." I was asleep again.

It was daylight the next time I woke, and Marion, in wig and Jan's orange dress, sat on the edge of the bed, an open phone book beside her, eyes on the little traveling clock. "Is six-forty-five too early to phone, Nickie?"

"Yeah." I went back to sleep.

I woke up again to the sound of dialing and looked at the clock; it was 8:01. "It's not too early!" Marion said defensively, and then into the phone, "Hello? Mr. Dahl, please. Mr. Hugo Dahl?" She listened. "I see. I wonder if I could reach him there?" She listened, then nodded. "On North Gower Street; thank you very much." She put the phone aside slowly and looked over at me, her face suddenly frightened. "He's on his way to the studio—he's still in pictures. Oh, Nickie, I'm scared! He's my only hope, really; I've been hunting through the phone books, and of all the people I knew there's no one else could possibly still be in pictures. What if he doesn't remember me?" I didn't see how he could, but didn't say anything, and she jumped up to run over and sit on the edge of my bed. "Nickie, you're coming with me today, aren't you? I can't go to the studios alone! I'm scared, I really am!"

"All right."

She looked relieved and glanced over at the clock. "It's too early to go now; he's not there yet. Why don't we just—"

"Nope."

"We could at least *neck* a little. For luck."

"Bad luck." I rolled to the other side of the bed, sat up, dragged the phone book across the bed, found the B's, and found "Bollinghurst, Theo N, 1101 Keever Street." I looked up at Marion and grinned. "HOO-ray for HOLLywood!" I began singing, and jumped up and took a shower, still singing.

Downstairs in the cab, I sat back to look out the window as we headed east on Wilshire Boulevard. I didn't know much about this town and was curious. But every block we drove through, stopping often for lights, seemed just about like the last one—the buildings generally white, new or looking new, and of a general height, so that they merged into sameness. Yet I noticed that their individual designs were often striking, sometimes unique or even bizarre. Any one of a lot of the buildings we were passing would have been memorable anywhere else, a town monument. But here there were so many of them trying for distinctiveness that the total effect was blandness. They were of stone, but it was hard to believe anyone really meant them to last. And in the queer washed-out Los Angeles sunlight that comes filtering down through the haze of perpetual smog, these featureless blocks after block seemed insubstantial, ownerless, and without significance. There are nonbooks and noncelebrities; people whose only fame is that somehow their names are known. It seemed to me that we were in a nonplace, and I said so to Marion.

"It used to be, though. It was a wonderful place once; a town, and a real one." She looked out the window, then shook her head and sat back as though withdrawing from the scene around us. "But I don't like this, I could never like it. I don't see how anyone could." Suddenly she leaned forward to speak to the driver. "Take us back to the hotel!"

"Okay." The cabby shrugged, and checking his rear-view mirror for cops, he slowed, waiting for a break in the approaching traffic. Then he swung his wheel in a quick, illegal U-turn.

I sat waiting for an explanation, and after a moment or so she reached up with both hands and lifted off her wig.

"Jan?"

She nodded defiantly. "I don't know that I want to go through with this, Nick, now that we're here. I don't like this place! What are we *doing* here!" She blinked suddenly, jumping slightly, then leaned forward. "Take us to Gower Street!" she said, and pulled the wig back on.

"Oh, God." I slumped far down in my seat, turning to the window, disassociating myself from whoever the hell was beside me now.

"Lady, I don't mind." The driver turned to smile with forced calm. "Do this all day if you want, round and round, long as you pay the meter. But if I get grabbed for this turn, you pay the fine!" Directly in front of the hotel again, he swung in a tight U-turn and we headed back east on Wilshire.

"Back to the hotel!" She snatched off the wig.

"No!" Braking hard, he swung in to the curb and stopped. "I won't *do* it! Nothing could *make* me! Get another ca—"

"Hold it," I said placatingly. "Wait a second; we'll make up for it with the tip." Murmuring quietly, I talked to Jan, reminding her that she'd promised, urging her to hold off and see what happened, and finally she agreed. "Go ahead," I said to the cabby. "North Gower Street, and this time we won't change our mind."

I was disappointed, really let down, by the outside of the studio. I don't know what I'd expected, except that I thought it would be at least a little glamorous. But this was just a high, block-long, almost blank stucco wall directly beside the public sidewalk across from a mangy, broken-asphalted public parking lot with a broken-down white fence, and strewn with papers no one was ever going to pick up. Mounted on the studio walls were a few billboards advertising motion pictures, otherwise this could have been a warehouse. And the door, apparently the main entrance to a world-famous studio, was an ordinary street-level door, the varnish worn off around the handles, the glass a little dirty. If I'd found a cut-rate dentist's office inside I wouldn't have been surprised.

What we did find was a cubicle just about large enough for us and the small desk we stood facing, which looked as though a Goodwill Thrift Shop had thrown it out. On the plywood walls hung a few large tinted photographs of two or three movie actors and television stars, and behind the desk a pleasant-faced, middle-aged man in a vaguely coplike uniform looked up from a copy of *The Hollywood Reporter.* "Can I help you?"

If I'd been worried about Marion's reception here, I stopped when her smile came on; I saw from the man's eyes that he appreciated it. "If you would, please," she said, looking at him with what seemed to be genuine interest, and clearly wishing she could spend an hour or so talking with him. "I'd like to see Mr. Hugo Dahl."

"Do you have an appointment?" He began nodding unconsciously, trying to will an appointment into being for her.

"No, but I'm an old friend. If you could let him know Marion Marsh is here, I think he might see me."

The man consulted a printed, much marked over phone list taped to his desk top with yellowing Scotch tape, then he dialed. "Reception: Miss Marion Marsh to see Mr. Dahl." He listened, then waited, smiling up at Marion. "Just a second," he said into the phone, then to Marion, "You did say Marion Marsh?" She nodded, giving him another great smile, and he returned it. "Yep," he said firmly into the phone, then hung up. "He'll be right down."

I didn't say anything. Had Marion actually forgotten that Hugo Dahl was going to see Jan's face? We waited, taking the few paces the little room allowed, looking at the big grainy photographic enlargements. Pretty soon I heard elevator doors open somewhere down the hall to the left of the entrance, footsteps approaching, then a tall, still thin but now paunchy man of maybe seventy wearing a dark-blue suit and turtle-neck sweater walked in. He was bald, his longish hair fringe and sideburns gray, his face lined and sagging, permanently tired. But his eyes were alert and wary. "You're—Marion Marsh?"

Staring at the late-middle-aged or early-elderly man, she didn't answer for a moment. Then, dazzlingly, she smiled, and his mouth opened in incredulous surprise. "I'm the granddaughter of the Marion Marsh you knew. But maybe you don't remember her?"

He was smiling back at her, the lines of his face momentarily lifted, and now you could see what he'd looked like when he was younger. "Nobody ever forgot Marion Marsh. I remember her ten times better than the people I had lunch with yesterday. You're her *grand*daughter?" he said incredulously, and Marion nodded, still smiling. "You don't look like her, except for your smile; the smile is hers, exactly. How come your name's Marsh?"

"I was named Marion after her. And I admired her so much—she was *so* talented—that I took Marsh as my stage name." Shyly she added, "Movie name, I should say. Or at least I hope so."

He smiled, knowingly but nicely. "And that's why you're here. She mentioned me, did she? Is she . . . still alive? Seems to me I heard—"

"Oh, yes! Very much! She *was* badly hurt. Years ago. But she recovered. And she's mentioned you often." She hesitated convincingly. "Maybe I shouldn't say this, but . . . I've always had the feeling she liked you. Something in her voice whenever she mentioned your name."

He laughed. "If that's not true—and it's not—I don't want to hear it. Well, I'm running auditions this morning, and if Marion Marsh's granddaughter wants in, she's in. Come on along." He started to turn, remembered me, and said, "You coming, too?"

"Oh, I'm sorry!" Marion said. "I'm terribly nervous. This is my friend who's . . . he's an actor, too! Giving me moral support. I'm scared to death."

"Well, come on, both of you, and we'll get you outfitted, Marion." We walked out of the little reception room to the right, Marion turning to smile back at the reception cop, then down a corridor lined with flush doors and white-on-black plastic name plates. We stepped out onto a narrow asphalted street or alley—very narrow—and walked past an old-fashioned, one-story wooden building of clapboarded sides painted gray, white double-sash window frames, and a peaked shingle roof. Behind several of the windows women sat typing under brilliant fluorescent light.

Far ahead down the narrow street a row of grimy brick buildings extended, each four or five stories high; there were very few windows in any of them and the few there were seemed scattered randomly, so you couldn't count stories. Fire escapes cluttered their sides, people lounging on most of them. For at least a city block we walked along past them, building after building, and I was proud of Marion—and a little surprised, I'll admit—because she remembered me. "There's someone else I'm supposed to look up," she said to Dahl. "Ted Bollinghurst; did you ever know him?"

"Oh, yeah, sure, we were all at the same studio. He moved on then. To United Artists, I think. But I'd run into him every once in a while all through the Twenties and into the Thirties. Hollywood was a lot smaller then. Then I heard he'd left the picture business and gone into real estate, and after that I didn't hear of him for years. If you're not in pictures, you know, you don't exist. But years later I read about him, and he was rich. Like a lot of people who got into Hollywood real estate at the right time. Jesus, when I think of the land I could have bought. In the summer of 1928 I bought a secondhand Dodge roadster for exactly the price of six acres of useless land that is now downtown Beverly Hills. If I'd bought that instead and hung onto it, I'd be rich today and wouldn't have to—ah, to hell with it. Bollinghurst and lots of others did, and I didn't. Last I heard of him, some time in the Fifties, he'd bought Graustark."

"Bought what?" I said.

"Graustark, the old Vilma Banky mansion; you never heard of it?" I shook my head. "It was like Pickfair, the Doug Fairbanks-Mary Pickford place. At one time everyone in the civilized world knew about Pickfair and Graustark. Fabulous places. Built on eight or ten acres, a million rooms. Swimming pools. Tennis courts. Stables. Garages full of Daimlers, Duesenbergs and Hispano-Suizas. Well, Ted bought Graustark. Because it had been Vilma Banky's, I'm sure; he was a real movie nut. It was run-down, gone to seed, empty for years; a white elephant. Even the real estate wasn't particularly valuable for Hollywood. But he bought it and restored it, even the grounds. And moved in. For a while you'd hear about parties he gave; the place had its own ballroom. I never went, but I heard. But I haven't heard of any parties for years now. He was a lot older than the rest of us, and I doubt if he's alive any more. Or whether Graustark's still there; probably a parking lot now."

I said, "Where was it?"

He thought for a moment. "Keever Street. Out on Keever Street somewhere."

"Eleven-hundred block?"

"Be about it. Why?"

"Just wondered."

Up ahead a pair of gray-painted steel doors stood ajar, and a thin black-haired woman of forty walked out and turned up the street ahead of us. "Marie," Dahl called, and the woman turned and stood waiting. "I've got one more for you," he said as we came up, and he nodded toward Marion. "Could you outfit her? Quick? We'll take care of the paper work later." The woman measured Marion with her eyes, then nodded. "Sure." She gestured with her chin at Marion. "Come on."

They walked off ahead, and Dahl motioned me toward the open gray-painted doors of the same brick warehouse-like building, and we walked in. I had nothing better to do and was curious. The interior was enormous, the building all floor space, the ceiling lost in darkness. I couldn't see much. Except for a few scattered light bulbs that illuminated very little, and the red glow of exit signs, most of the building was dark except for a corner far ahead. Off in the gloom I could see vague bulky objects and a great wooden scaffolding of some kind.

We were walking ahead, toward the one lighted area of the huge warehouse-like space. This was a brick-walled corner starkly lit by a pair of powerful work lights mounted on portable standards. Under their light a dozen people, mostly men, two or three women, stood talking idly, most of them holding plastic coffee cups. One of them spotted us, a youngish partly bald man in blue slacks and jacket, and came walking toward us, carrying a clipboard. "Fred," said Dahl as he stopped before us, "here's another prospect. Talk to him," he said, his interest in me fading fast. "Find out his specialty if any. If you can work him in, do it." To me he said, "Fred's head of the exterior unit," whatever that meant, and he walked on toward the group around the work lights.

"Name?" Fred said, pencil poised over his clipboard. We were at the very outer edge of the circle of light, but I could see eight or ten names penciled on the mimeographed form in Fred's clipboard. I was about to reply to tell him there'd been a mistake, when I was horrified; I seemed about to faint. The man before me and the building we stood in had begun to disappear. I'd once fainted in college from economizing by not eating breakfasts; it had begun like this, and now I wondered if I'd hit my head when I fell. But I didn't fall. Dim as things were becoming— sounds growing fainter too—I heard my faraway voice reply, and its tone was calm, assured, and several notes deeper.

"Rod. Rod Guglielmi."

"Rod for Rodney?"

"No. Rodolpho."

"Any specialty?"

"Anything you want." The scene was shrinking fast, the sound fading with it.

"Well, we need a stunt man, that's about all."

A moment's hesitation, then my mouth spoke the words: "I can do it."

"Do what?"

"Whatever you want. Race-car driving. Wing-walking. Plane-to-train transfers. Parachu—" Nothingness, then; not even blackness, only pure colorless nothingness.

Just as you can tell awakening from sleep about how much time has passed, I knew that it was no more than an hour later. But this was like awakening from an unnatural fevered sleep for only a moment or so of superclarity. I was in a closetlike space, a dressing room with a mirrored table, a chair, and wall hooks on which my clothes hung. I was standing, I realized, one foot on the floor, the other on the chair, staring down at myself. My upper body, I saw, wore a white nylon shirt open at the collar and cut very full in the chest and sleeves. My pants were whipcord jodhpurs. I was wearing blunt-toed shoes laced up over the ankles, and the leg on the floor was wrapped in a leather puttee fastened with two brass buckles. The other puttee was in my hands; apparently I was about to fit it around the other leg. Then the faintness, the rushing diminishing of everything I saw into nothingness.

Again, I knew that more time—an hour and a half, maybe two—had passed. I simply opened my eyes as though from a dreamless sleep and saw—I didn't *know* what I was seeing. It was a floor, an enormous endless floor, but not in a room. I was staring down at it through an evenly distributed haze, puzzling over a random pattern of gray-white lines, sometimes straight, sometimes curving, and a succession of fingernail-sized green and red squares in parallel rows. Far, far away, near the edge of the floor, lay a thicker, irregular lead-gray curve, and then I saw a momentary glint of light on its surface and realized that I was seeing an actual river. And that the gray-white lines were roads, the red and green squares were rooftops, and that this enormous floor stretched out before me just past the edge of a fabric-covered surface on which my laced shoes were standing side by side.

There was a sound, too, I realized, a hammering roar, and a sensation: I was chilled by a steady pressure of air against my ribs and chest. And now I could hear and feel the loose-cut cloth of my shirt fluttering audibly, tugging at my skin. My eyes moved slightly and I saw a taut varnished surface just over my head and caught a glimpse of angled guy wire.

I held off the knowledge as long as I could: that I was not dreaming but actually stood crouched on the lower wing of an ancient biplane thousands of feet above Los Angeles. My head turned a little more; I saw my own white-knuckled left fist wrapped around a stanchion, and— to my left and behind me—the leather-helmeted, goggled head of the pilot, and my throat went dry, my intestines shriveled, my eyes widened in shock. For a moment longer I stared out at the misty, infinitely distant horizon miles ahead and miles below me, then the dimming sensation roared up through my senses, and this time I understood that I was truly and genuinely about to fall unconscious.

Just before it happened I felt once again the sense of someone pushing toward me, pushing against me yet without crowding, until suddenly we were occupying the same space, and Rodolpho Guglielmi was back. Curiosity is the strongest emotion, of course, and I was able to wonder where I had heard or read this vaguely familiar name, then I remembered. This was Rudolph Valentino up here with me on this cloth-covered wing, signed up under his actual name as a stunt man, if that's what he had to do for a comeback.

But he wouldn't take over completely. We stood there, far up in the sky, standing on a piece of varnished cloth . . . and then I understood that *he was as scared as I was!*

He deserted me! Took a look at the horror stretched out before and below us, and left me once again! My arm was going dead, I was squeezing the stanchion so hard. I looked past it: at the long, long old-fashioned hood of the plane; at the rusty exhaust pipe stretched along its side; at the paint peeling off its vents; at the shivering, filmily transparent circle of the propeller. And my knees went fluid, shoulders sagging, about to pitch limply forward into space.

Let me say to the eternal credit and glory of Rudolph Valentino—that he came back! He came back; we stood together, took a deep, deep breath, then he turned to the pilot and he made himself smile. It was a heroic act. He was a real man. He'd got us up here, and he'd get us back. With infinite relief I let nothingness overwhelm me.

Only minutes passed I understood this time, as—abruptly, no warning—I once again saw the vast misty plain that was most of the Los Angeles area horizon to horizon, this time from an even greater height.

But the wing was gone! I heard the steady, hammering, old-fashioned drone of the single engine close by, yet the plane had disappeared! I was looking straight up—Up? Yes, *up!*—at the tiny lines that were roads and dots that were rooftops. The backs of my knees hurt—why?—and the blood was congested in my face and neck. Then I understood: I was upside down, my head tilted far back to stare straight down through nothingness at the slightly tilted, slowly revolving earth far below. I looked away fast, looked down—up?—saw my wildly fluttering white shirt from mid-chest to wide leather belt, my jodhpurred legs to the knees, and—that's all. No puttees, no shoes, only the fabric-covered wing of the plane. I heard a strangled sound in my own throat because—*oh, God*—I was hanging upside down by my knees from the metal loop of the skid at the tip of the wing.

My head swung away in terror and I saw the helmeted, goggled head watching me. His lips grinned, he lifted a gloved hand to wave at me, and the blackout began, and I was glad, truly preferring to slide into unconsciousness and die than continue for even one more second to see and understand the horror of where I was.

More time had passed, much more, when I felt thought and consciousness returning again, and this time I felt it return all the way, felt how terribly tired I was in my body and mind both, and I knew that Valentino was fully gone. I couldn't, would not open my eyes, afraid to look. But I heard, and the drone of the airplane motor was gone. I realized that I was hearing the murmur of scattered voices in casual talk, and I opened my eyes.

I was indoors, in a room—no, it was a movie theater, though a strange one. The blank white screen up front, the first thing I saw, was miniature, two-thirds size at most. And there were only half a dozen rows of perhaps a dozen seats each. People sat here and there, maybe a dozen of them. Two rows ahead and off to my left, Hugo Dahl sat with two other men, including Fred of the exterior unit. A girl with a clipboard on her lap sat just behind Dahl; she held a metal pencil with a tiny light near its tip, and she flicked it on and off a couple of times. Here and there sat other men and women—actors maybe. I felt a nudge, turned, and Marion— I knew it was Marion from the expression—sat beside me. She'd been back to the hotel, apparently, because she wore a green dress, one Jan had never liked and seldom wore, though it looked good on Marion. I looked down at myself; I'd been back to the hotel, too; I was wearing another suit, shirt, and tie. Marion said, "I think they're going to start, Rudy. I'm so nervous."

I whispered, "It's not Rudy; it's Nick."

"Well, believe me, I'm glad! He's impossible! I never realized but with him it's nothing but I, I, I, I. I couldn't get a word in all through dinner!"

"Marion, what's *happening?* What time is it, did you take your test? Where are—"

"Oh, yes; this morning. They developed prints late this afternoon. We're going to see them now; Hugo invited us."

"Well, what are they *for?* What's the picture?"

"I don't know; no one has said. But I think—"

Hugo Dahl had turned in his seat to look around the theater. "Everyone here?" he called now and, without waiting for an answer, glanced up at the projection booth. "Okay, Jerry. Let 'em roll."

The houselights went out immediately, and a rectangle of light appeared on the screen, slightly flickering. It turned milk-white, and a scribbled number 4 in reverse flashed by, then some felt-penned letters, also in reverse, a scrap of old film used as a leader. Abruptly and out of focus, a man appeared on the screen, facing the camera and holding something: the focus instantly sharpened into a long-haired young man with a drooping mustache and wearing a fringed leather jacket. He was holding up a slate on which HUNTLEY was roughly printed in white chalk, and below it, TAKE 1, KAY MEISSNER. In his other hand he held the lower jaw of a black-and-white clap board attached to the bottom of the slate, and he immediately slapped it shut and walked off the scene.

The scene—he'd hidden most of it—was a four-man band in close-up, wearing red-and-white-striped coats and straw hats. Hands poised, the pianist sat looking at the others, then brought his hands down to the keys; the trombonist lifted his instrument and the right hands of the other two, banjoists seated on high stools, began to move so rapidly they blurred. The sudden burst of music was marvelous old-time jazz, the beat fast and pronounced.

Immediately the camera drew rapidly back to reveal a scrap of footlighted stage with a white-velvet backdrop, a girl walking out from the wings. She wore a knee-length fringed red dress and a headband across her forehead and around her short hair. Smiling professionally out at us, she began to dance. It was fast and in exact time, an approximation of the Charleston, I realized. But there was a learned, mechanical quality about her movements, and I had a sudden hunch that this girl had bluffed, saying she knew the dance when she didn't, maybe having a quick coaching session the night before the test. The dance lasted maybe twenty seconds; then, winking broadly at a supposed audience whose sound-track applause burst out, she walked quickly off the stage as a final note sounded from the banjos. From the strained quality of her wink I felt that she knew she'd failed.

There was no response from the real audience. Marion leaned toward me to murmur, "That's about as close to a Charleston as a polka," and with no pause after the final note, the young man in the fringed jacket walked on screen, holding up his slate. The bottom two lines had been rubbed out, and now chalked in new letters under HUNTLEY I read TAKE 2, JUNE VAN CLEE.

The stick clapped, he walked off, revealing the band again, the pianist's hands once more poised over the keyboard. The camera drew back as his hands came down, and the same tune began again—wild, and with a great disciplined beat; I wished I could hear hours of it. A second girl, taller and thinner than, but dressed like, the first, walked on from the wings.

She was much better, very skilled. But all she was doing up there on the tiny stage was performing an accurately done chore for money. In spite of her smile, it was joyless and uninspired. So was her departing wink—and so were the girls in takes three, four, and five.

Again with no break of the film, the slate was held up—TAKE 6, MARION MARSH—the black-and-white sticks were clapped together, and the pianist's hands dropped to the keys. The driving blare of sound began again, and now Marion walked out onto the tiny stage in a short tomato-red dress, red headband, and—this was different from all the others—a string of beads that hung to her waist. As she walked out, she, too, smiled at the imaginary audience across the footlights, but this was a smile easy with the confidence of what she knew she could do superbly. Her smile said she was pleased with herself and that she was happy, that she liked the audience that was about to have the pleasure of enjoying her. For a moment I remembered the tiny black-and-white figure I'd seen on the screen of my television set—long, long ago, it seemed—in *Flaming Flappers*. This was that girl—larger than life now, in full brilliant color and blaring sound—but with that same magic *presence*. I was smiling, responding to her happy arrogance, and I knew with an actual physical thrill moving up my spine how good she was going to be.

Her body slipped effortlessly from walk into dance without pause or transition, her rhythm free and easy. She wasn't listening to the music and carefully coordinating her movements with it: her body simply flowed into, joining and becoming part of that wild, happy jazz. Feet and elbows flashed so effortlessly that the beat seemed slower than it had in other takes. And then—just once and simultaneously—the fingers of each hand snapped, abandon shot through her body, and the dance took fire. Her legs flew in a controlled ecstatic frenzy, her chin slowly lifting, her eyes closing in sensual pleasure. She loved what she was doing— you could see that and feel it—every atom of her excited body thrilled by it. It was wild, and then on an abrupt final note it stopped, her eyes opened, and when she smiled and winked out at us, it was so lecherous a man yelped, and we broke into real applause.

On the screen the man with the slate for Take Seven was walking forward to hold it to the camera, but Hugo Dahl was on his feet saying, "I knew it! I knew it! I *said* so! Jerry, did you splice a lead-in and lead-out to a print of that? I asked you to!"

"Yeah! It's set up on the second projector," a muffled voice called from the projection booth.

"Then show it for crysake! That's it! That's the one!" On the screen the band had begun once more, but the screen abruptly went black, the sound cutting off. The little audience murmured, and in the darkness Dahl called out, "Marion, Baby, grandma never did better! You got a future in this lousy business, that I can promise you!"

Marion's hand had gripped my forearm, lying on the arm of the seat, squeezing so hard I could feel each separate finger. The screen lighted up, a numbered countdown began flashing past, and in its light I looked at Marion. Her one hand gripping my arm, the other lay spread on her chest as she stared up at the screen, her mouth slightly open in stunned, incredulous, glorious *relief*. 7, 6, 5, 4, 3—I thought we'd see Marion again, but a giant squatly shaped bottle suddenly filled the screen, and its label, though plainly visible, was read aloud by a man's deep voice: "Huntley's Old-fashioned Tomato Catsup!" The wide bottle top revolved itself loose, flew off the screen, and the bottle tilted forward, the voice continuing, "In the smart new bottle with the *great big mouth!*" On the word "mouth" a comic-strip speech balloon appeared over the bottle's mouth, and as the words popped into being inside the balloon, a high, nasal comic voice—the voice of the catsup bottle—spoke the same words: "But I've still got all my *old-fashioned flavor* . . . with all its Huntley old-time *zing!*" And now Take Six, Marion's dance, began on the screen once more, but this time as the pianist's hands dropped to the keyboard the high funny voice was saying, "Yessir! All the fine old-fashioned flavor . . . "—the blaring jazz began simultaneously with "flavor," and smiling out at us again, Marion was walking on stage in her tomato-red dress—" . . . with all its Huntley old-time *zing!*" the voice continued as she walked, and precisely on "zing" she began to dance.

During the twenty seconds of that spectacular dance, the funny voice was saying, "Yep! *Still* that fine *old-fashioned flavor* . . . that famous *Huntley* old-style taste." And again, the dance ending, the voice was saying, "With all its old-time Huntley"—precisely as Marion winked— "*zing!*"

Marion off stage, the final banjo-string fillip dying, the giant bottle again filled the screen, tilting forward to reveal its open mouth, another speech balloon appearing above it. Simultaneously the printed word and comic voice both said "*Wow!*" and the screen went white.

"Great! Oh, *great!* Hugo Dahl was shouting. "That's *it*, that's it! That's all we need to see. Marion, love, have your agent phone me in the morning. Fred, your stuff ready?"

In the moment before the projection beam cut off, I saw Marion's face. It was pale; it was stunned and astonished, as though someone she loved had slapped her. Then in the darkness I felt the breath of her voice on my cheek as she whispered, "Nick, what *is* that? What *is* it?"

Up ahead Fred was talking, and I leaned toward Marion and whispered miserably, "A commercial."

"A what?"

"It's . . . like an ad. An advertisement. It's . . . not for the movies, Marion. It's for television."

"That . . . thing we saw my movie on? That's what *this* was for? Not a movie, but—That's all my dance was for, to advertise *catsup?*" I nodded in the darkness, and reached over to take her hand.

Fred was saying, "We tried a pool-table sequence with a professional; trick shots. And the guy was great. Interesting but no excitement, no zing; I eliminated it. We tried some comic stuff; villain tying the girl to railroad track; you know. It doesn't work, Hugo. But we filmed one thing that did; a damn good day's work. We spliced on a lead-in and lead-out; wait'll you see it. Jerry, you ready? Roll it."

I knew. As the giant catsup bottle tilted forward, the comic voice booming "In the smart new bottle with the **great big mouth!**," I knew what was going to appear on the screen, and closed my eyes. But when the catsup stuff stopped, and the drone of an ancient biplane motor abruptly filled the tiny theater, I clapped a hand over my eyes just as they popped open. Then I spread my fingers and sat helplessly watching.

Incredibly, there I stood in flowing white shirt, jodhpurs, and leather puttees on the lower wing of an antique biplane against a pale-blue sky. The view was from the side and back at a little distance from the plane; I hadn't noticed the camera plane or heard its engine over the drone of our own. The view was taken from just slightly below. My stomach contracting, I knew that Los Angeles lay a mile under my feet on that cloth-covered wing on the screen, but the camera showed only the man on the wing and the sky above; it might have been only twenty feet above the ground.

Again, and almost physically, just as it had happened in the Olympic theater in San Francisco, I felt the merging, felt my body *occupied*—felt the almost irritable attempt to push me aside down into some remote corner of my own being. But this time I resisted angrily. This time I held on, and—up on the screen the scene changed, and, our interest caught—we watched it together.

An old-fashioned touring car, its black canvas top down, was speeding along a dirt road, weaving erratically from side to side; the view had obviously been taken from a helicopter flying just above and behind it and well to one side. The bareheaded driver of the old car, one hand on the steering wheel, was holding a struggling girl beside him. She wore a long white dress, her hands tied behind her back, and was gagged. "Yep!" the comic voice was saying. "All that great *old-fashioned flavor* . . . " and now the ancient biplane edged onto the upper corner of the screen from the other side of the speeding car, my own upside-down body, white shirt fluttering, hanging by its jodhpurred knees from the wing skid. Directly over the back seat of the car—I actually let out a muffled cry in the theater—the figure dropped from the plane, revolving in mid-air in a neat somersault to land on its feet in the back seat. Cut to a close-up: standing in the back seat of the racing car, I held the driver around the neck with one arm, reaching past him with the other to turn off the ignition and grab the steering wheel. Cut to another shot: the car stopped beside the road, the driver tied and gagged, the girl in my arms looking over my shoulder at the audience. "With all the old-time *zing!*" said the funny voice, and precisely on "zing" the girl in my arms winked, and I felt the sudden disengagement from my muscles, nerves, senses and mind.

Up front, filling the screen, the great catsup bottle tilted forward, the funny voice speaking. But I had turned in my seat to stare toward the rear of the theater, and I saw him. Walking slowly across the back cross aisle just under the white beam of the projector light, clear but transparent, the wall of the theater visible behind him, I saw the eagle profile, narrowed brown eyes, and slicked-down black hair—utterly familiar to me from a hundred old-movie books and a dozen pictures—of Rudolph Valentino. He was wearing what may have been the costume he had chosen for eternity: long, dark baggy pants almost to the ankles; boots; a ten-inch-wide studded leather belt; a coarse striped shawl thrown over one shoulder of his shirt. But now the once proud shoulders under that shirt and shawl were slumped. And upside down in his hand, he carried the rest of that costume by its chin strap: the broad-brimmed, flat-topped hat of a gaucho, dangling in rejection and defeat. His face averted from the screen, cringing from the voice of the Huntley catsup bottle, he walked toward but never visibly reached the exit. As the funny voice from the screen said "*Wow!*" Rodolpho Guglielmi disappeared like a light snapped off.

We left, Marion and I, slipping into the aisle and hurrying up it just before the lights came on. Outside we walked along the narrow asphalt street, badly lighted by widely separated old-style lampposts, possibly left over, I thought, from a forgotten picture. There was a high moon, almost full, the street bright and luminous in the soft wash of light. The old wood and brick buildings we passed stood unlighted and silent, their windows ink-black or shiny yellow from the light of the moon. At the corner we turned toward a studio gate and the lighted hut of the guard inside it reading a newspaper. There Marion put a hand on my arm and we stopped.

She looked back down the length of that empty moon-bright street, motionless as a ghost town. She stared up at the dark still building beside us. Then she turned to me. "Put your arms around me, Nickie." I did, and she leaned back to study my face. "You look just like him, almost. Almost exactly, but . . . you're not. You're not. Kiss me, though, Nickie, kiss me good-bye! Because I'll never be back."

I drew her close and kissed her gently and lovingly. I touched her face then, my fingers brushing her cheek, smoothing her hair back from her temples, and, pale in the moonlight, she smiled at me. Then I kissed her again, and after a moment or so she stepped back. "Well. Was that for me or for Marion?"

"For Marion. That was for Marion. I wanted her to know that someone gave a damn. And would remember." I reached for Jan. "But this is for you."

We found a cab to head back to the hotel for an early start home in the morning. I was never going to see whatever lay inside 1101 Keever Street, I understood, but I had to see it, and I asked the cabby to drive past it on the way.

When we turned onto Keever Street and I read the street sign, I glanced around, not sure whether this was Beverly Hills or not: it didn't look like my idea of Beverly Hills. There were small businesses on both sides of the street: an enormous brilliantly lighted drugstore, the people in it actually pushing shopping carts; a discount record place; a dry cleaner; gas stations; three take-out food places in a row, all busy—it was only nine o'clock. And scattered among them, alone and in twos and threes, were the asbestos-shingle-covered remains of the residential area this had once been. They were no longer one-family residences—you could see eight or ten mail slots on every porch—but rooming houses, with no future now but demolition. The area wasn't shabby, I don't think that's allowed, but it was the Los Angeles equivalent.

We drove slowly through the seven-hundred block, the eight-, the nine-, the ten-, and they were all alike. And so was the eleven-hundred block, on our side of the street. But not on the other.

Motor idling, our cab stood at the curb across from what had to be 1101 because there was no other house, and we stared. Behind us the sidewalk was bright from the lights and signs of a bicycle shop and a liquor store, both open; and a quarter block away on a corner, the brighter-than-day white lighting of a giant Standard station lit up the walks to beyond the curbs. But across the street a vast dark area lighted only by the moon stood silent and motionless in another time.

Under the high white moon lay a great city block surrounded by a chest-high stone wall that was the base for a ten-foot fence of closely spaced pointed iron pickets. The wall was interrupted in only one place, directly across from us, by a pair of twenty-foot magnificent wrought-iron gates across the entrance to a graveled driveway. Behind those gates and the wall extending far down the street in both directions lay acres— black masses washed with pale light—of huge trees, their tips outlined against the luminous sky; great clumps of high shrubbery; silvered stretches of sloping lawn; white paths and glimpses of statuary; and the wide driveway leading back through the black masses of trees and bushes to the house itself, an enormous, four-story Spanish-style mansion.

Not a window of the part we could see was lighted. The great house stood, far off and more hidden than visible, looking as though it had never been lighted and would never be. I had to get out and cross the street to those gates. And there at the curb I looked up at them. In the center of each, suspended in the wrought-iron tracery, hung a great convex metal oval framed in a wreath. On the one at the left stood a raised, ornate art-nouveau V and on the other a B. I gripped the bars and stared in at blackness. All I could hear was the sound of branches in the small nighttime wind, and the fragile sound of a leaf scraping along the graveled driveway. On impulse I tried to shake the bars in my fists but they were as immovable as though set in concrete. I stared in through them for a moment or so longer, then turned away.

Across the street, standing at the cab for a moment before getting in again, I looked back. Somewhere in there— But I shook my head irritably, trying not to think of what might be somewhere inside that distant house far back in that moon-touched blackness, and got into the cab.

Back at the hotel, I told Jan about the day and about Rodolpho Guglielmi, and she listened, shaking her head, looking at me to smile incredulously and shake her head again. And we talked about Marion, saying what little there was to say. On our way through the lobby I'd bought a Los Angeles *Times*, and we sat in bed looking through it, but it seemed hard to follow and without any real news, the way an out-of-town paper generally does. I got up and standing at the desk turned through the pages of the little magazine telling what there was to do in town, almost none of it outside this hotel, apparently. There were some postcards in a drawer, already stamped by the management, I discovered, a thoughtful "touch." And since I knew I was paying for it, I picked one—a view of the pool—and sat down and wrote a card. "Dear Al: Well, here we are in glamorous, exciting Hollywood, 'seeing the stars'! Tomorrow, Forest Lawn, to visit the world-famed mausoleum of Felix the *Cat.* Love, yr. friend, Nick." There was no one in the hall, and leaving the room door open, I darted out in pajamas, dropped the card in the chute next to the elevator, and got back safe and sound. Around eleven, or a couple minutes past, we turned out the lights, and almost instantly the phone rang.

Jan was nearest, found the phone, and picked it up. "Hello?" I fumbled for and found the bedside-lamp switch and turned it on. Jan sat wincing at the loudness of the voice in her ear, then moved the phone away from her head, and I slid over to listen. "What the hell *happened* to you!" a man's voice was yelling. "Where were you? I had to—"

"Who *is* this?"

"Hugo Dahl, goddamn it! I been phoning all night every half hour! Now, listen: you saw the guy with me in the projection room? Young; bald; brown suit? Well, that's Jerry Houk! A producer here. Movies, not television; he's a big man here, and he likes you. They're making a picture, finishing it up. But there's a part in it. Very small. One quick scene. Which they've already filmed. But they're still on the same set; tomorrow's the last day. Be there at one and they'll try to get in a couple of takes of you in the part before they wrap up. If they like it, they'll use it. Okay? Jesus, I been trying to reach you for an hour and a half!"

Jan sat staring at the phone. She looked up at me, and actually made a motion to give me the phone, then drew it back.

"Well!?" said the voice in the phone. "What *about* it? Do you— Listen, *is* this Marion Marsh?"

For an instant longer Jan hesitated. Then, voice firm, she replied. "Yes. Yes, this is Marion Marsh. And I'll be there. Tomorrow at one. I was stunned for a moment, Mr. Dahl, and couldn't talk. But I'll be there. And I can't tell you how much I appreciate it."

"Don't mention it, I always was a pushover for Marion Marsh. Good luck, kid, and say hello for me to—my God!—your *grand*mother."

Jan put the phone on its cradle and sat holding it, staring across the foot of the bed. I said, "How—"

But Jan just shook her head.

"She'll know," she said. "She'll know. And she'll be there."

CHAPTER EIGHT

• •

The same reception cop—after the same exchange of mutually admiring smiles and glances—found Marion's name on a list of expected visitors. Mine wasn't on it, but Marion just told him that that was all right, and he explained how to find Stage 2. Then we walked back down the same little studio street, bright with sunlight and busy with people now, that we'd walked up last night in silence and moonlight.

Through a pair of gray-painted steel doors onto Stage 2, another enormous barnlike building; far across the gloom of the vast concrete floor we saw a brilliantly lighted set filled with people. The sound of a hammer on wood echoed—actually did echo—through the great enclosed space, and a man in white carpenter's overalls walked in after us and hurried by carrying a two-by-four.

Approaching, we saw that the set represented three sides of a great room almost fantastically modern in its furnishings. Huge unframed paintings—smears and swirls of color—hung on the walls; statuaries on pedestals and in wall niches were intricate assemblages of metal, plastic, wood; the rugs and furniture were white; but everything else, including the actors' clothes, was aggressively colorful.

They weren't working, we saw as we walked—more and more slowly and timidly—toward the set. They stood or sat talking, drinking coffee from plastic-foam cups, as three workmen in white overalls worked to shift the angle of a small metal track spiked onto plywood sheets. The track led to the set, projecting a yard or so onto it. And at the track's far end stood a wheeled camera, low to the ground and so big there was a seat mounted behind it on which a thin nervous-faced man peering through a viewfinder sat as though mounted on a small tractor.

We stopped at the edge of the set, a few people glancing at us. Across the set from us two men, not in party clothes, stood talking earnestly; they looked to be in their middle twenties, both with sideburns and fairly long hair. They wore sweaters and wash pants; working clothes. Glancing at us, they continued talking, then one of them, a clipboard under his arm, walked across the set toward us. As he approached he lifted his brows questioningly, and Marion smiled at him. "I'm Marion Marsh."

He consulted his clipboard. "Right." He smiled back then, pleasantly enough. "Well. Mr. Hiller hopes to get to you, Miss March."

"Marsh, Marion Marsh."

"Marsh; sorry. He hopes to get to you; meanwhile . . . " He glanced around, then pointed to a big gray wooden box stenciled with the studio name. It stood beside the set a yard from where the white-carpeted floor began. "Would you sit there, please? At all times. Don't move." He smiled again and walked back to the man he'd been talking with; Mr. Hiller, I assumed.

The overalled men got their track shifted. A pair of men in dark-green work shirts and pants pulled the camera slowly along it and just onto the set, then dragged it back again, testing the track and angle as the operator sat behind the rolling camera watching through his viewer. Then the operator nodded at Hiller, who yelled, "Okay, places everyone!" and the actors began handing their coffee cups to one of the green-uniformed men who walked around with a tray collecting them. They positioned themselves on the set in pairs and groups, a few sitting down, most of them standing. A woman with a tray of partly filled liquor glasses began moving among them; some took glasses and stood or sat holding them; some lighted cigarettes. A girl with what looked to be a tray of make-up walked around inspecting the actors, dabbing powder onto some of their faces.

For three hours then, we sat on the gray box, the camera track being shifted once more, and the scene was filmed three times, with long, long waits in between; I never knew why. After two hours one of the men in green work uniform brought us two Cokes in paper cups. "From Mr. Hiller."

The actors, men and women, were young or youngish and very modishly dressed, their costumes extreme and exaggeratedly colorful. Marion sat eying them. And in each take they stood or sat, holding their drinks and cigarettes, talking, laughing. And that was all for maybe twenty seconds. Then one of the guests, a chunky bearded man talking to a girl, burst into very loud laughter, everyone turning to look at him, and the scene cut.

At a little after four o'clock the scene ended for the third time, and the director called, "All right, that'll do it." He sighed, blinked a few times, took a clipboard from the other man, and looked at it. Then he looked over at us, handing back the clipboard, and came over.

"We'll do you now, Miss Marsh," he said, stopping before us. "Sorry to be so late. You'll have to be dressed and made up, and we'll save time if I talk to you while they're doing it." Gesturing for her to come along, he walked around a corner of the set toward the wall of the building and a large trailer-like structure mounted on wooden sawhorses. There were

half a dozen doors in its side, unpainted wooden steps leading up to a
platform before them; dressing rooms, I guessed. A middle-aged woman
joined them, and they all walked in through one of the doors and pulled
it closed behind them.

The young guy with the clipboard yelled "Quiet! Quiet, please!" and
when the talk simmered down, he said, "All right, we've got a retake
now. Of . . . " he looked at his clipboard—"eighty-one. Check scripts if
you have to; this is the one with the girl in the robe." Nothing happened.
The chatter and coffee and Coke drinking continued, and the man with
the clipboard dropped into a chair and sat staring absently at the floor.

The director and Marion came out, Marion wearing make-up and a
long pale-blue gown belted with a darker-blue tasseled cord. As they
walked toward the set I saw that her feet were bare. "Places, everyone,"
the director called, and again the actors positioned themselves. Their
places were different now; same party but another scene. Again glasses
were passed out, make-up retouched.

The director walked Marion through the scene, the actors in position
but silent, watching them. Murmuring instructions, he walked her onto
the set and positioned her. An actor walked over to her, smiled, and said,
"Blah, blah, blah, blah," and Marion smiled and said something. She
was walked to a second position, the young man going with her, and
now two men turned from a painting they were discussing and walked
toward Marion.

They went through the motions of the entire scene, the director
pointing finally to a place on the floor with his toe, and I watched Marion
nod. He glanced at his watch, then called, "Okay, we'll do it now, and
we're going to film."

The actors took their original positions, lights brightened, then music
burst from somewhere, hard and raucous but not overly loud. Someone
called, "Quiet on the set!"; lights brightened still more; another voice
yelled, "Roll 'em!" A man with a slate was on the set walking toward
the camera, which had come down its track to the edge of the set. He
held up the slate, and I read 81; *Marion Marsh*; *Take One*. He clapped
the striped sticks, stepping quickly out of camera range, the party chatter
began, and I sat fascinated, excited, and tense with anxiety for Marion.

She stood just off the set, beside the director, and the people on the
set talked, laughed, moved casually apart, came together in new group-
ings. The pair of men stood looking at the canvas on the wall, seeming
to discuss it. Then the director nodded at Marion, and she walked onto
the set and stopped in the place he had positioned her first. She stood
looking the party over with a faintly amused, faintly bored air—and I

felt a sudden little thrill of anticipation. She seemed so at ease and in charge; in a way I didn't and never will comprehend, she had made me understand from the manner in which she walked, looked, and now stood that a person of importance to it had arrived at this party.

The actor who had come over to her in the brief rehearsal to say, "Blah, blah, blah," came over again now and said something that was inaudible over the music. And when Marion replied, and smiled, I saw his chin rise a little, and his smile of response wasn't acted but genuinely interested. The two men at the painting stood looking at it, one shrugged and said something, and the other laughed, turning from the wall. He noticed Marion then, and he and the other man walked over to her. She saw them, smiled with pleasure, holding out a hand in welcome, and the one nearer took a little skip step to hurry to her and take it, greeting her by name, which was Essie. The four of them stood talking, smiling, and then the room—by ones, pairs, and by groups—became aware almost at the same time that Essie was here. People would turn, see her, stare silently, then begin talking eagerly to whoever was nearest. So that there was a ragged moment of growing silence, reaching almost silence, the room staring, then an excited rise in the conversational hum. And although conversations resumed, people sneaked little glances at Essie, not really listening to one another. But what was also happening was— that it had all become real.

I don't know that anyone has ever actually explained it but there are an occasional few people born into the world who are different from the rest of us. They are able to turn on something that is as real, invisible, and as actual in effect as electricity. And Marion was doing it. Standing in the center of that party, she held it in her hand. They *were* intensely aware, not just acting it. They *were* interested and were held by Marion's each word, gesture, and smile. The party was real now—I forgot it was being filmed—because a magnetism was at work. There must have been a moment like this, I realized, when Garbo first stood before a turning camera.

Marion turned from the people she was talking to and walked on: to her final position, the place on the floor the director had touched with his shoe. For a moment she stood lazily smiling, aware of but ignoring the attention she was drawing. Then as though she hardly realized she was doing it, her shoulders, arms and hips moved slightly, idly, and a little insolently in a suggestion—she couldn't possibly have learned this, she'd intuited it—of modern dancing. She *was* about to dance; the room knew it now, all conversation dying, everyone staring in a fascination that was real. For an instant Marion stood motionless, hesitating, and the director—calling "Cut! Cut!"—was walking onto the set toward her.

But he was smiling. "Good," he called as he walked toward her. "Jesus Christ, it was great! *Listen*," he said, voice astonished as he stopped before her, "you've *got* something, you know that? It's"—he shrugged— "I don't know; *presence*, I guess. Can you do it again?" He was suddenly worried that she couldn't—"Listen, can you do it again? Exactly the same! Don't change a thing. *Except* . . . " He smiled, holding up a hand to show it was no rebuke, anxious not to upset her in any least way. "Except no hesitation," he said gently. "Okay? Essie wouldn't hesitate. Can you do that?" Marion nodded. "Okay!" he called, but the man with the clipboard was tapping his upper arm for attention. They murmured together for a couple of moments, the director glancing at his watch. "Okay, *let* it be overtime," he said. "We got to have this. Okay, places everyone!"

Again the make-up girl made her rounds, the camera operator did something to his lens, the man with the slate appeared, clapped his boards—and it happened once more. Not quite the same, though. This time—I wouldn't have thought it possible, but this time it was better. Better because now everyone on the set knew from the first moment that something important was happening today, and the air was alive with the excitement of that. They did it again, and the scene was a marvel. Who *was* this, the scene said as Marion walked forward to her final position, who was this incredible Essie, and what was she going to *do?*

Moving away from the three men, walking to the last position, she reached it, and stood there again, lazily, insolently, serene and proud. Again she moved her body to the music, just a little, but it caught the breath in my throat with the strength of its sensual promise. And without any hesitation this time, her hand moved to the dark-blue cord around her waist and pulled the single knot loose. Stepping forward as she did so, and already dancing with her shoulders, she shrugged loose from her gown, letting it fall to the floor behind her, and stood smiling at the party, completely naked. On the curve of her stomach a heart had been drawn in red lipstick; a blue-inked feathered arrow pierced the heart as though arrow tip and half the shaft had entered at her navel. And the heart and arrow turned her nudity into something salacious.

She stood smiling at the audience in the instant before her dance began; and then she frowned. She looked down at herself, then up again but staring past her audience now. And then this girl of 1926—wild though she could be but a girl of 1926 all the same—said, "No." She said it loudly enough but to herself. "Why, no, goddamn it. This isn't the movies." She looked around at them, her glance sweeping across their faces. "You bastards," she said. Then she turned around to look back at the director and, her voice rich with contempt, she said, "You bastard: this isn't the MOVIES at all!"

He came to. "Cut! Cut!"—he was striding toward her. "Listen, you! If you want to make this goddamned test, if you ever want to even *work* again—" He stopped and, like the others, stood watching.

Marion had stooped and picked up her robe, and—not bothering to put it on, not troubling to hide her nakedness—she flung it contemptuously over one shoulder, and head erect, walked off the set to the dressing room.

They were suddenly busy, everyone finding something to do, ignoring me as though I were invisible. The director especially was never still: walking angrily about; ordering the set irrevocably struck as fast as it could be got to; releasing his actors; ordering lights off and removed, equipment taken away. And when Marion came out dressed, everyone on and around the set was pointedly unnoticing as she walked down the stairs toward the set and me, her head up, ready to look at anyone. I walked forward to meet her, took her arm under mine, and as we walked across a corner of the set toward the distant exit, I had my head up, too, in challenge, trying to find someone who would meet our eyes. And some did. Some of the actors and some of the technical people met our eyes and—a little mockingly maybe, but still—they smiled in approval. But off in the gloom on the long walk toward the big metal doors and the studio street outside them, Marion cried a little, then she stopped.

I thought she'd leave. And standing outside the studio on the street flagging a cab parked at the hack stand a dozen yards down, I said, "Jan?"

"No, it's Marion, Nickie. I'm a selfish bitch, and I know it. But not all the time, not quite all of it." The cab stopped before us; she leaned toward the open front window to speak to the driver and said, "1101 Keever Street."

She wouldn't talk in the cab. When I tried, she just reached over to put her hand on mine for a moment, quieting me and letting me know she understood that I'd comfort her if I could; then she turned away to stare out her window.

We got out at the Standard station a quarter block from the great wrought-iron entrance gates. There was a phone booth at the edge of the lot, and Marion called the number listed beside Bollinghurst, Theo N. "You reach him?" I said when she folded the door back.

"No, but I sent word—that Marion Marsh was waiting. Outside the gates."

Angling across the street toward the wall and high iron fence stretching off into the distance of both directions, she said, "I've been here before. When this was new. I saw it from a sight-seeing bus." We walked along beside the wall, then stopped at the great ornate gates across the driveway, and Marion pointed at the oval plaques in their centers, one bearing a V, the other a B. "They were polished then, and shined like gold." In the daylight I could see that the plaques weren't iron like the gates themselves; they were bronze, green with verdigris. Set into the keystone of the arch that curved over the gate tops, a bronze scroll surmounted by a knight's plumed helmet read GRAUSTARK. But it, too, had turned green, and I saw that paint was flaking from some of the pickets, rusting patches showing through. On the stone wall just to our right The Word had been crudely spray-painted long ago, the paint fading.

We heard a sound, a rattle, and a man on a bicycle was riding bumpily down the driveway toward us: youngish, bald, and wearing a kind of butler's uniform, though without a coat—black pants with a narrow white stripe down the sides, black-and-white horizontally striped vest, wing collar, bow tie. Swinging off the ancient loose-fendered bike, he rode the last few yards standing on a pedal. He nodded pleasantly, and with a big brass key unlocked a small gate within one of the large ones, its design blending with the whole so that I hadn't realized it was there. He gestured us in, we stepped through, and he locked it. Then, walking his bike, he led us back up the long curved drive toward the house.

"The lawns were marvelous when I saw them," Marion murmured. "The bus stopped at the gates so we could all look in, the sprinklers were on, and every one made a rainbow, and the grass was just perfect." It wasn't now. The lawns had been freshly mowed, but here up close they were disfigured by great islands of cropped-off dandelion tops and crab grass. "The gravel was whitewashed and freshly raked." But if the thin scatter of stones left on the driveway now had ever known whitewash, it was long gone, and not enough was left to rake. Mostly the driveway was two dirt ruts through a weedy stubble half-covered with browning leaves.

Yet the grounds weren't uncared for; the banks and clumps of shrubbery and small trees we were passing needed trimming, clipping back, but they weren't running wild. The place was looked after but in a slovenly way, as though, I thought, no one any longer checked to see how well it was done.

The driveway gradually curving, the house growing larger and larger as we walked toward it, expanding in both directions, I saw that it was truly enormous: a great two-story, flat-roofed mansion in, I suppose, a Spanish style, of rough-finished beige-colored stucco. Wide shallow stone steps led from driveway to stone-flagged portico and the massive double entrance doors of carved wood.

Up the two or three stairs, across the portico, and into the entrance hall, large though not enormous, paved in great black and white stone blocks, checkerboard style. A two-story ceiling, and hanging from it by a velvet-covered chain, the largest crystal chandelier I've ever seen in a private house. And there we waited for twenty-five minutes, sitting across from each other in velvet-upholstered straight-backed chairs.

I sat facing two sliding oak doors closed across a great arched entrance flanked by standing suits of armor each holding a ten-foot lance. To my right, an angled flight of carpeted stairs and the closed arch-top door to what I supposed was a hallway. Marion sat facing me and an eight-foot window just behind my chair, which overlooked a sweep of lawn and a great empty fountain, the bottom of its bowl black with sodden leaves.

We waited, here in the luxury and grandeur, both impressive and pathetic, of another time and taste, occasionally hearing distant household sounds from behind far-off closed doors. Then the corner of my eye caught a movement, I turned my head, and there—up at an angle of the stairway, slowly rounding it to face us—there he came, wearing what I took to be an old-style tuxedo with a stiff wing collar.

No mistake, this was an old, old man. And no mistake, this was Ted Bollinghurst. If he was approaching forty in 1926, he was well into his nineties now, and that is what I'd have guessed him to be—wrinkles upon wrinkles and not to be mistaken for the seventies, but into the wispy fragility of the nineties or more. We stood up to face him; he was smiling down at us, but peering, too, not quite certain he saw us, and before we spoke I had time to study him.

It was the nose that said Ted Bollinghurst: Marion had described it as snubbed, but I wasn't prepared for a nose so turned up, the nostrils long black holes, that it was very nearly a deformity. He wasn't bald and he wasn't not bald; on an unusually high domed skull grew not much hair but so evenly thinned that there were no actual bald spots. It was strangely dark, like a Presidential candidate's, and he wore it carefully parted in the center as, no doubt, he always had. But now it hung limp and lifeless straight down on each side to the tops of his big crinkled old ears.

He was closer now, halfway down the stairs, and I saw that of course his hair was dyed, and that there was a faint touch of red just under each prominent cheekbone, and I knew why we'd waited twenty-five minutes. He'd been carefully preparing himself, making up his ancient face a little, and dressing in—not a tuxedo, I saw, but a "smoking jacket" of deep maroon with silk-faced roll lapels. To meet Marion Marsh this old, old man had wanted to look his best.

Slowly, slowly, advancing always with the right foot, one careful step at a time like a child, hand never leaving the banister, he saw us for sure now, the smile suddenly turned real, and in that instant I liked him, liked even his strange face. "Marion?"

"Yes. Yes, it is . . . Ted." She'd slowly stood up, staring, openmouthed. But now as she spoke she smiled at him, beautifully, and walked quickly toward the foot of the stairs. He moved down onto the final step and reached a hand out to her, still smiling but near to crying, too, I thought.

"Marion, Marion, *Marion*," he said. He'd once been taller, I supposed, but now, even standing on the bottom step, he was no taller than she. "How good to see you; oh, my dear, how good, how *good*." He had released the banister and was holding her hand in both of his, peering into her face; and Marion stood, smiling still but blinking, close to crying, too.

She replied, genuinely pleased and touched to see him, then she introduced me to him, and the old man welcomed me. His voice was quite firm, surprisingly deep, and if he spoke a little slower than a younger person, it wasn't much. He seemed ancient but vigorous, seemed still in complete easy possession of his mind and faculties. But I realized it wasn't true; if not actually senile he was into the kind of uncritical vagueness that precedes it. Because it seemed not to occur to him that the Marion Marsh he had known would be a woman of eighty now. Obviously Marion was simply Marion to him, and that was a young woman, just as in memory she always had been. Yet he remembered this: "You've changed the color of your hair, haven't you?" He shook a finger like a dry stick at her, smiling, and stepped down to begin moving slowly across the big checkerboard toward the sliding doors. "It was blond! And bobbed," he said, winking at me, shaking his head, as though to say, *These women!* "But you haven't changed otherwise. Not a bit; I'd have known that smile anywhere."

"And neither have you, really. I recog—"

"You recognized this nose!" He chuckled phlegmily, then suppressed a cough. "That doesn't change!"

"I think it's cute!"

"But the rest of me has changed, I'll tell the world; oh, boy, oh, boy, oh, boy." He stopped at the big doors, setting his fingertips into the grip plates. "You haven't been here before, have you?" he said uncertainly. "Were you at any of the parties we used to have?"

"No."

"And you, sir? Nick. Is this your first visit to Graustark?"

"Yes, sir."

"Well, good. People thought I was bugs to buy it, but I like to show it off." He began sliding the door open, I stepped forward to help, then he gestured us past him into a room that quite literally wasn't much smaller than the high-school gym I'd played intramural basketball in.

Like the hall, it was two stories high; the drapes drawn, every lamp softly lighted. It was more like a fashionable hotel lobby of the Twenties than a living room; obviously this had been meant for enormous parties. Standing just inside the doorway we were staring off into a room of as many as twelve or fourteen big chesterfields and I just don't know how many dozens of chairs, all fatly upholstered in a bygone style, and still it was spacious and uncrowded. There were deep-pile rugs, three grand pianos—*three*—each draped with a fringed Spanish shawl, their tops crowded with framed photographs. And tables, lamps, huge vases, ornaments, statuary, paintings. There were standing lamps five or six feet high, the kind my mother called "bridge lamps," one entirely of wicker, even the shade, the light shining through it, and most of them were draped with still more fringed, embroidered shawls. Halfway up the wall a railed balcony of closed doors ran around the room on all sides but the one we'd come in at. More Spanish shawls hung draped on these railings, one embroidered with a cactus, the others with roses.

I saw all this, an impression only, in a slow sweeping glance, then my head stopped and I stood staring at the staircase at the opposite end of this great room, realizing in the moment I saw it that this entire vast space was really a setting for it.

From the railed balcony, stairs led down along the wall opposite us, beautifully railed and banistered. Then, at no more than a yard above the floor level of the room, they ended in a landing of white marble as large as a small stage. Only three shallow but immensely wide steps from it to the floor, each a little wider than the last, the final step, its ends gracefully rounded, a good eighteen feet long. The landing *was* a stage, planned for the dramatic entrance from above, and the final pause at the center of attention, before stepping down into and joining the room.

But then I understood that even this landing was only the setting within a setting for something else. Hung on the wall of the landing, to face the length of the entire room and the great entranceway we stood in, was a full-length—and at the very least, life-sized—portrait of a woman so magnificent that a little physical chill moved up my spine as I stared at it. I knew the face: this was Vilma Banky, standing in a knee-length, loosely hanging evening gown of the Twenties, a Spanish shawl draped over one shoulder. Her head was turned, chin slightly lifted, to show her marvelous profile. In the center of her forehead a curl spiraled round and round to a final point, but if that sounds funny it wasn't: this was a beautiful, beautiful woman and nothing could make her absurd. Concealed lighting illuminated the painting without shine and from all sides, its gilt frame ten feet high if it was an inch. And it was hung just exactly high enough so that no matter who, short of King Kong, came down the stairs to pause on the stagelike landing before it, she'd be upstaged by Vilma Banky.

Ted stood waiting till we'd looked our fill, as no doubt he'd always done the first times he took people into this room. Finally we turned to him, murmuring our compliments, and he nodded, smiling, and accepted them on her behalf. "Yes. Thank you. This is Vilma's room. It's her house still, very nearly as she left it. I had a staff of researchers working full time for something over a year, while the house itself was being renovated. They consulted old newspaper and magazine photographs and accounts. Interviewed or corresponded with people who'd been here often. Of whom there were a great many. And many of whom loaned us photographs they'd taken. They consulted diaries and letters of Vilma's time here. Read her household accounts. And fortunately we had the auction catalog, illustrated and with full descriptions of virtually every-thing this house once contained. So we were able to track down many of the things that had been sold. Including the painting. Especially the painting. In most instances we were able to buy them back. Much of the furniture has been rebuilt, restored to just as it was, even to the reweaving of certain materials. Some of the furniture is duplicated. So that now—well, she'd be at home here, if only she could walk back into it. But there are a few things I've added."

He walked slowly forward to what I'd thought was a delicate, thin-legged, oval-topped table, but as we moved closer I saw first that the top was glass, and then that a small shaded light inside it illuminated the interior of what wasn't a table but a shallow display case lined with pale-blue watered silk. We stopped before it, looking down into it—and I didn't understand what I was seeing, lying there in the center of the case just above a printed card.

It was a shapeless lump about the size of a dime, its surface wrinkled and shriveled, grayish pink in color. It lay squashed down onto the center of a raggedly cut, roughly circular piece of heavily varnished canvas about the size of a man's hand. Before I could read the card, Ted explained, voice lowering respectfully. "The wad of gum Spencer Tracy stuck on the back of Clark Gable's plane in *Test Pilot*." Marion's head lifted slightly to look across his bent back at me, frowning, and I read her expression: Who is Spencer Tracy? Who's Clark Gable?

"And this . . . " Ted Bollinghurst was turning to move on, and now I saw that half the tables in the room weren't tables but duplicate glass-topped display cases. We stopped at the next, lined with identical watered silk except that it was canary yellow, and bent over it. "Ramon Navarro's whip. From *Ben Hur*." And now Marion, nose almost touching the glass, was smiling: satisfied; pleased; impressed.

We walked slowly around a piano, and among the dozens of photographs on its closed top, all inscribed to Ted and often misspelling his name, I recognized Clive Brook, Leatrice Joy, Aileen Pringle, Larry Semon, Rod La Rocque, Clara Kimball Young. Marion and I looked up from them at the same time, our eyes meeting, and we smiled in recognition of what seemed like a mutual bond. It wasn't, though; we'd each seen all these people in the same pictures, every last movement on the screen identical for each of us, but of course we'd each seen something different. For her they'd been young and beautiful people, still very much alive, the pictures new and with more to come. But for me they'd been resurrections, the miracle that movies finally made possible, of long-gone mythical people. But we smiled and nodded, each with his own pleasure, and walked on with Ted to another case like the others except that this was lined in pink.

All these watered-silk linings matched in weave and texture, differing only in color, and all were applied at the sides in tucks and flounces, but stretched tautly over smooth padding on the bottoms. On the softly lighted pink of this case lay—What was this? Hair: it was hair, jet-black, and I saw that although it lay crumpled, it retained a shape. If there'd been a way to apply it, this might have been a false beard; the Vandyke chin beard, sideburns, and joining mustache were clearly discernible. The printed card read RUDOLPH VALENTINO'S BEARD, SHAVED OFF IN THE SUMMER OF 1924 AT THE REQUEST OF THE NATIONAL BARBERS ASSOCIATION. Marion was nodding. "Yes, I remember: it was in all the papers."

"Charley Morrison bought it. Right from the barber; it's the real thing, all right. For only ten smackers, the lucky stiff. He'd never sell it to me, but when he died, in 1950, I bought it from his widow; made the deal at his funeral. Had to; I'd heard The Woman in Black was after it."

On the pale apple-green lining of the next case lay a typed sheet much amended in the margins and between the lines in several handwritings. "A real prize," Ted said. "This is the fourth and next-to-final draft of Shirley Temple's annual letter to Santa Claus, published nation-wide every December. This was written when she was fourteen, one of the last; some of the marginal corrections are in L. B. Mayer's own hand-writing." We stared in awe, bent over the delicate little cabinet, and I read the sheet down to "and plese, *plese* dear Sandy, don't ferget all the poor childern . . . " Then I stopped.

We saw Lon Chaney's hump from *The Hunchback of Notre Dame*, a marvelous thing of plaster of Paris attached to a leather harness that I wouldn't have minded owning myself and wearing around the house now and then.

We moved on to a blackened, shriveled something I thought was a meteorite lying on white silk, and I had to give Ted credit: he scrupu-lously explained that he wasn't entirely certain of the authenticity of this. He *thought*, he had reason to *believe*, that this was probably the actual grapefruit half James Cagney had shoved into Mae Clarke's face in *The Public Enemy*. He'd paid twenty dollars for it to a stagehand on the set who swore it was the real thing, but Ted wasn't quite convinced that this particular rind hadn't actually been one used only in rehearsal.

We saw, lying on silk the color of orange sherbet, three shattered ornaments shot off a Christmas tree with a popgun by William Powell in *The Thin Man*. And on deep-blue silk—this *was* authentic, because Ted had stolen it himself from Marlene Dietrich's dressing room right after the last day's shooting on *Morocco*—a bottle of leg depilatory.

On silver cloth: four crescent-shaped objects of gold. Bent over the case, I saw that their inner edges were sharp, worn to ragged paper thinness, and looking like miniature scimitars punctured with small holes. RUBY KEELER'S TAPS: WORN OUT ON THE SET OF "42ND STREET."

"*Gold?*" I said to Ted.

"I had them plated."

We saw the artificial butterfly Lew Ayres had been reaching for from his trench just as he was shot in the final scene of *All Quiet on the Western Front*; and a half dollar tossed by George Raft. And in one of the last cases, a small object about an inch and a half long, lying on scarlet silk. In shape it was a vague, elongated figure eight wrapped in cloudy cellophane, cinched at the middle by a paper band. There was no explanatory card, and Ted glanced uneasily at Marion, then leaned toward me. "From an Andy Hardy picture," he whispered. "That's the actual contraceptive Lewis Stone found in the watch pocket of Andy's pants the morning after the junior prom. It didn't actually show in the film, of course. Judge Hardy held it cupped in his hand when he showed it to Andy, and he didn't say what it was; but you knew. The Judge handed me that himself."

We'd reached the staircase landing and stopped for a moment; the wall beside it was bookshelves from floor to eye level, filled with leather-bound volumes stamped in gold on the spines. Each volume was a year's copies of *Photoplay*, *Silver Screen*, or one of the other old movie mags, each bound in its own distinctive color. The entire lower shelf was packed with leather-bound scripts, beginning with *The Great Train Robbery*.

Looking at them, I was remembering an article I'd read by a psychiatrist who said it was probably lucky that not many obsessed people were rich. He gave an example of one who was: a man ridden by fear of germs. He'd begun like people we've all encountered, who open doors with their hand in a coat pocket to avoid germs on the knobs. But he was rich, and able to let his obsession grow unchecked. Presently he was living in a Paris hotel suite into which no one else but a single servant was ever admitted. Next he rented and kept vacant the rooms on each side, then the rooms above and below him. Isolated in space, finally, he still had to eat. And eventually reduced himself to subsisting only on overcooked meat; enormous roasts brought to the door by the hotel cook, left there for him to take in when the cook had gone. And then in the room, with his own knife, he would cut out a cube from deep in the very heart of the roast, a chunk of cooked meat that no other hand could possibly have touched before.

Ted Bollinghurst, too, was simply a man with a common obsession—a movie fan, an old-film buff, of which there are a lot of us—but with the money to take it just as far as he wanted to go. And I knew that here but for a few million dollars or so stood I. At the foot of Vilma Banky's staircase, ready and anxious to see where they led.

I'd dreaded the question for fear of the answer, and when Marion asked it now, flicking a glance at me, I literally held my breath. "Ted, you used to collect prints of films you liked," she began.

"Yes. Stole them, you mean." He chuckled, and had to cough.

"Do you . . . still have them?" I wanted to put my hands to my ears, but stood openmouthed, straining for the answer.

"Well, of course. Would you like to see them?"

I exhaled so audibly that he glanced at me, and when Marion answered yes, all I could do was nod.

We turned to the stairs, and Ted led the way up them slowly but very steadily, right foot always advancing first, dry old hand sliding up the banister rail. He said, "D. W. Griffith climbed these stairs; we know that for sure. So did Mary Pickford, Dolores del Rio, Dustin Farnum, Milton Sills, Ernst Lubitsch, Alma Rubens, and many, many more. Several, in fact, have fallen down them. And I have nine authenticated instances of stars, of both sexes—several of whom would astound you—who were chased up them."

We turned left at the top to walk along the railed balcony looking down into the immense room below us, its dainty display cases pastel ovals of color from here. On our right, closed doors each labeled with a small brass plate: TURKISH BATH . . . BILLIARD ROOM . . . RADIO LOUNGE . . . two doors side by side, one labeled SHEIKS, the other SHEBAS . . . and at the end, labeled SODA FOUNTAIN, a door that Ted pushed open invitingly. The room was just that: there was a marble soda fountain with chromed spigots and a back mirror; round tables with chairs whose legs and back were made of heavy twisted wire. "Like a soda? It's all equipped; a couple dozen flavors." We said no thanks, and he nodded, letting the door swing shut, walking on. "Sometimes I go in there and fix one myself."

We'd reached the end of the balcony, turning right to face a pair of leather-padded swinging doors, and I pushed through, holding one open for Marion and Ted. We were in a corridor, and as I turned and we began our slow walk along it, I had my first look at it.

It was very wide, surely a dozen feet or more. And so long you could actually see the diminishing perspective, the four lines of its floor and ceiling angles slanting in to the corners of the distant square that was the corridor's far end—so distant I couldn't make out what was down there; something, I couldn't quite see what. The ceiling was high, and the floor white marble, white because the wall at our left was an outside wall into which four high, arch-topped windows of stained glass were set at long intervals, the first of them a dozen yards ahead. Natural light from outside these windows, augmented now by spotlights—it must have been dusk out—illuminated the corridor, patterning the white marble floor and the walls with colored light, a fine effect.

As we said so to Ted, who looked pleased, we were slowly approaching a door on the inside wall at our right. Fastened to the wall beside the door at eye level hung a shaped wooden plaque of what I took to be polished walnut. Carved into its surface, the letters picked out in gilt, was a listing of some kind. As we moved slowly nearer, I was able to read it: ALLA NAZIMOVA, ANTONIO MORENO, HOPE HAMPTON, EDMUND LOWE, DOLORES COSTELLO, RICHARD DIX, TOM MIX. "All of them stayed in that bedroom at one time or another," Ted said. "Some at the same time." I heard Marion inhale sharply and turned.

We were approaching the first of the great stained-glass windows, and I hurried several steps closer, then stopped to stare. So brilliantly illuminated that it seemed to hang in space, it was made of hundreds of pieces of glass, some as small as a thumbnail, some big as a man's arm. Marvelously cut and leaded together, they formed a vertical scene of every conceivable color and shade, but predominately green in a dozen or more shades and gradations of shades, and each piece was afire with light.

It was a picture, made of glowing flat jewels of glass. From the crest of a tree-dotted hill rose a great gray battlement, the edge of a lush forest far in the background. Before it, a blue-filled moat and a raised drawbridge. And high on that battlement—in green tights, jerkin, and peaked hat; a quiver of arrows slung on his back; a fist on one hip, bow raised high in the other hand; feet arrogantly wide apart, and grinning so widely that the dazzle of his teeth made me blink—stood—Yes, of course, and I said it aloud, "Douglas Fairbanks."

"In *Robin Hood*," Marion breathed.

Ted nodded. "These are my additions. They took the artist four and a half years." After a long minute or more, we walked on.

NITA NALDI headed the list on the next bedroom-door plaque: REGINALD DENNY, POLA NEGRI, HERMAN MANKIEWICZ, LEATRICE JOY, MARY MILES MINTER, CONRAD NAGEL . . . but I stopped reading: we'd reached the second great picture of shimmering glass.

Filling the entire lower left corner, behind the blur of its propeller, hung the engine and cockpit of an airplane headed straight at us. The plane was dramatically tilted, its double wings on one side slanting sharply toward the upper right corner. At lower right, far below the slanted wings, a shell-cratered battlefield. Above it, rising clear to the top of the window and a background for everything else, a cloud-dotted blue sky. And at upper center of the sky, a small and distant plane heading straight down and trailing black smoke, on each upper-wing tip a black Maltese cross. The pilot of the first plane, the big one filling the lower left corner of the huge window, was grinning, a hand lifted in the act of peeling off his leather helmet and goggles. I knew the grin, knew the face: Buddy Rogers, of course, in *Wings*, and I meant it when I told Ted Bollinghurst I thought this window was great.

On past the next bedroom door: CONSTANCE BINNEY, THOMAS MEIGHAN, MAE MURRAY, CLAIRE WINDSOR, RICHARD BARTHELMESS, NATACHA RAMBOVA . . . And on the window across the hall, a blue-coated, whitekepied soldier, wearing white-canvas puttees, and ankle deep in sand, looked back over his shoulder, face anguished, at the struggling column of men he was leading toward a distant fort, high in the upper left corner, the tricolor limp on its staff at the near corner of the battlements. *"Beau Geste,"* Marion said softly, "Ronald Colman. Oh, I love him!" and I nodded and said, "So do I."

LILA LEE, BARBARA LA MARR, JACK HOLT, MABEL NORMAND, WALLACE REID, CONSTANCE COLLIER, BULL MONTANA . . .

The rose in her hand a spectacular glowing red, Renee Adoree ran through the village street that slanted across and up the last great window, trying vainly to catch the olive-drab army truck from which John Gilbert, behind the raised tailgate, yearned after her, rifle in one hand, the other arm straining for the rose, in *The Big Parade.*

EVELYN BRENT, SESSUE HAYAKAWA, OLGA BACLANOVA, BUCK JONES, BILLIE DOVE, GEORGE ARLISS, MADGE BELLAMY, LYA DE PUTTI . . . "Oh, my *God,*" I said, "if I could have *been* here! If only I could have been here then." And Ted and Marion nodded.

Two carved wooden doors inlaid with gilt and flanked by gold pillars studded with lapis lazuli filled the end of the corridor just ahead; a shadowed projection jutted out over them into the hall. Ted flicked up a wall switch, and the filaments of dozens of half-size bulbs—of clear glass and with spiked ends—came to life, outlining the rectangular shape of a miniature marquee. Across its front tiny colored bulbs spelled VILMA's VISTA. They were of every color, bright and gay, flashing on and off enticingly, welcoming us, offering the old magic of "going to the movies." Ted pulled open a door, lights coming on inside, and Marion and I walked in, grinning with excitement. "Vilma's projection room," Ted said, letting the door swing silently closed behind us, "almost exactly as she had it."

It was a marvel, a pure joy; my heart leaped in envy. We stood at the back of a miniature movie palace of the Twenties: painted and gilded pillars and plaster ornamentations; burnished mahogany side walls, an elaborate tiny Spanish balcony halfway up each of them; a vaulted ceiling inset with softly lighted giant jewels. Up front, a square screen, maybe half size. And lined up before it in three rows, not seats but low softly upholstered chesterfields and chairs, enough to seat maybe twenty people, aisles at the sides only.

We stood at the rear of this little beauty, the fronts of our thighs touching the back edge of a long worktable extending nearly all the way across the rear of the theater. Fastened to the table were film-viewing and editing equipment, including a pair of hand-cranked reel holders for rewinding film. Off to the left, directly beside that end of the worktable, stood the great black bulk of an old-style arc-light projector.

I turned to Ted to say, "I'd give my arm, I really would; the left one anyway."

"It's beautiful," Marion breathed. "Oh, Ted, it is!"

"Yes." He nodded, not smiling. "It's like a chapel to me. I come in here often. Just to meditate. Then I run off an old favorite, accompanying it myself." He pointed, ahead and to the left, and I saw something I'd missed. A shell-like alcove curved into the left wall, just off the aisle and halfway up it. In it stood a miniature gilt pipe organ. "I learned to play it. To accompany the older pictures. They should never be run in silence, of course." He turned to finger the drapery that hung in loose folds across the entire back wall except for the doors, and extending up the side aisles a little. "But I had to install these for sound film," he said apologetically. "There was an echo."

We stood looking around. It was pleasantly cool, I could feel a steady flow of air rising up past us from the floor, and I turned and found the continuous vent across the back of the theater set into the wood walls just under the ceiling and above the tops of the draping. Directly behind us, the doors we'd entered by bore a red exit sign, and I thought they were the only doors. But Ted had walked across the back of the theater behind the worktable, to the right. Now he parted the drapes on the mahogany side wall to reveal another door, and when I saw it I felt the excitement close my throat.

There'd been a question I hadn't even wanted to admit existed: How could Ted Bollinghurst possibly have kept old nitrate film stock of the Twenties from disintegrating over the years? This was why so many old films had been lost; they'd slowly moldered away in the vaults of uncaring studios.

But the door Ted had exposed was white, enameled, and angled across its upper left corner a chromed script read WESTINGHOUSE. He was opening the door now; it had not a knob but a long chromed locking handle. Reaching inside, he flicked on the ceiling lights and we saw the overhead piping white with frost. It was a vast walk-in refrigerator, the kind built for meat wholesalers. "The only practical way I know of to preserve the old film," Ted said, standing half turned toward us in the doorway. He smiled. "I used ice in the earliest days; kept my film in secondhand wooden iceboxes. I didn't always eat lunch, but I always found money for ice. Later I used old Frigidaires, and now this. Every inch of film I have is in perfect condition. Every print flawless, diamond clear. Not a scratched frame in this entire vault." Suddenly he grinned. "Come on in!"

My knees were trembling minutely as I walked, my breathing shallow, and passing through the vault door I bumped Marion's shoulder. I'd forgotten she was there, forgotten everything but the lighted rectangle of that doorway, Ted standing just inside it beckoning.

It was cold, but I didn't care. Both sides of the vault were lined with stainless-steel drawers. Each had a heavy vertical handle, and above each handle a metal frame held a card. When I saw what some of them said, I had to turn and stare down at the floor for a moment because I actually felt dizzy.

Then I lifted my eyes again. I stood facing three drawers labeled WM. DE MILLE, and typed below this on each label a list of titles. I pulled a handle, the drawer rolled out on bearings, and I stared down at the double row of film cans, a dozen deep the length of the drawer. There they were. There they really were, films directed by *William* de Mille, with the small *de*, not brother Cecil, with the big *De*, most of whose films have unfortunately been saved. Here were the films of the brother who made the good ones, and I lifted out a film can, the metal chill on my palms and fingers, and read the label aloud: *"World's Applause."* I looked slowly up at Ted. "This must be the only print in the world."

He bobbed his head eagerly, eyes bright. "I'm sure of it. Want to see it! I'll run it off!"

"Wait." I held up a hand and put the can back. I'd seen drawers labeled GARBO, and I rolled the de Mille drawer shut and began reading Garbo labels. It wasn't on the first or second. Behind me Marion exclaimed, "I remember this: *Shoulder Arms!* I saw it when I was a girl during the war." On the third label, I found it: *The Divine Woman*, with Garbo and, I remembered, Polly Moran, John Mack Brown . . . *a lost Garbo*. Was this the film I wanted Ted to run off? I began to feel a little frantic; we could hardly see more than one picture, yet—I stood looking around—the vault was filled with film I had to see!

I began reading labels, yanking open drawers, staring for a moment, rolling them shut, opening another. Here lay the films of Edward Sloman, maybe a greater director than Griffith himself, but . . . The National Film Archive has Sloman's *Ghost of Rosie Taylor*, made in 1918; the Museum of Modern Art in New York has a few reels of *Shattered Idols*; but nearly all the rest of his work is *gone*. Possibly one of our finest directors, if we could only see his work, and here it *was*, certainly most of it. Did I want to see one of these? Or maybe a reel from each of several. Yes, *yes*, but . . .

"Mary Pickford," Marion murmured, rolling open a bin.

Ted stood alternately lifting one foot, then the other, in a slow little dance of excitement. "Pick one out, Marion! I'll show it! I've got *Tess of the Storm Country!*" That was another lost film, and I almost called yes, but Marion was pushing the drawer closed.

"I've seen it."

I stepped over beside her to read the Pickford labels, and found it— *Fanchon and the Cricket*—near the top of the first list of titles, and was tempted. It was made in 1915, starring Mary Pickford, and featuring a very, very young Fred Astaire and his sister, Adele.

Then I saw them, two drawers there in the row just above the Pickford bins, and they were labeled GREED. I couldn't talk, only point, but when Ted stepped closer to read the labels, I managed to say, "All? All forty-two reels?"

Eyes sparkling, he nodded. "All of them. A complete and absolutely perfect print made by their three best technicians working all night right up until dawn of the morning the studio had the negative destroyed."

I just stood there: I didn't know what to do. To see all forty-two reels of *Greed* would take ten hours. "That it?" Ted was demanding. "That what you want to see? All of it? Part of it? I'll show anything you want!" He was beside himself.

I said, "Ted. One reel was tinted—"

"I've got it, I've got it!" He yanked open a bin, ran his eyes along the cans, then plucked one out. "This is it! Right at the beginning of the reel. Want to see it? I'll thread it up!" He ducked out into the tiny theater, and, plumping the can onto the worktable, pulled off the lid.

I walked over and tapped his arm; I knew what I wanted now. "No need to run it off, Ted. Just let me *hold* it."

He'd unreeled the couple yards or so of leader and a half a dozen feet of the start of the reel; now he turned to stare at me. Then he nodded slowly and smiled. "I understand; yes, I do." Suddenly anxious, he said, "You know how to handle film?"

"Believe me, yes; by the edges only. I've never left a finger mark on a strip of film in my life."

He handed me the leader, I raised it high, then took the first of the film between thumb and middle finger, its edges lightly pressing into them. "Thread it on the viewer, if you like," Ted said, but I shook my head. I'd raised the film to the ceiling light, and that was enough: there was the famous scene, Zasu Pitts, but a very young and lovely Zasu Pitts, lying naked on a bed she'd scattered with gold coins. In the tiny progressions of each frame, I could see that she was literally rolling in gold, feeling the coins press into her body, the very epitome of greed. And this scene, *this* was the scene Von Stroheim had actually ordered to be tinted by hand: on the strip I held high to the light, every tiny coin had been tinted gold by the tip of a brush, and my hands shook at the thought of what I was holding.

I put it down finally and started to rewind it into the can, but Ted was jouncing with excitement. "I'll do that! Leave it!" I don't suppose he'd ever left film like that in his life before, but he was too excited to take time now. "Come in here; find whatever you want to see; *find it!*"

I couldn't. And neither could Marion. "Lost films" meant nothing to her; she'd seen most of them when they were new. It was pictures she'd missed that she exclaimed over: a Charlie Chaplin, a Dolores Costello, some of which you can buy from Blackhawk. Once I heard her say to Ted, "Look; I saw this being filmed."

I found *The Patriot*, a lost Ernst Lubitsch, and took it to the table to pull out just enough film to have the pleasure of reading the cast and credits. But this wasn't the one, *the* one, and Ted almost literally dragged me back to the vault to find it.

I looked through the unbelievable collection of all D. W. Griffith's features, trying to pick. I chose *The Greatest Thing in Life*, finally, because Lillian Gish always claimed it was the master's greatest. "I think I'd like to see some of this," I said, handing the first reel to Ted, and he nodded quickly, and we walked out to the worktable. But when he opened the can, I suddenly said, "No, wait! That's not the best choice," and almost ran back into the vault.

Put a hungry child in a candy store, tell him he can have whatever he wants but one choice only and nothing more . . . that was me. I could not make up my mind because, always, there might be something even better I hadn't yet seen.

I found *The Miracle Man*, directed in 1919 by the mysterious George Loane Tucker, lost for decades. And *Peg o' My Heart*, with Laurette Taylor. Films starring Marie Doro, Marguerite Clark, and Elsie Ferguson, *all* of whose films have been lost.

And then I found it. Walking past the second drawer labeled ERNST LUBITSCH, a corner of my eye caught a title on the label, and from that bin I brought out the picture I knew I had to see, the long-lost silent version of *The Great Gatsby*. At least I thought it must be, and I took the first reel out to the table to check the credits. The worktable was crowded with the film we'd opened, which bothered me; I'm sure it wasn't customary with this collection. But although it looked helter-skelter, winding lengths of film curling out of the open cans, it wasn't.

No film tangled with any other; each can lay in a little space of its own. I had to make room for *The Great Gatsby* but I moved the other film carefully, clearing a little space for this. Then I uncoiled the leader from the outer edge of the big fat disk of wound film, found the cast listing, and held it to the light.

And there in tiny white letters on the black background of each of the frames stretched between my two hands was the incredible cast: Rudolph Valentino as Gatsby himself . . . Gloria Swanson as Daisy Buchanan . . . Greta Garbo as Jordan Baker . . . John Gilbert as Carraway . . . Mae West as Myrtle, her only silent role, I was almost sure . . . George O'Brien as Tom Buchanan . . . Harry Langdon, in his only serious role, that I did know, as Myrtle's husband . . .

Ted was standing beside me peering up at my film, and I said, "Isn't this the one with the party sequence at Gatsby's estate?"

"Yes, with Gilda Gray, Chaplin, and F. Scott Fitzgerald himself as part of the crowd."

I lowered the film and stood staring up at the empty screen for a moment. Not only had this incredible picture been lost for decades, it had never even been *shown*; suppressed by Gloria Swanson, supposedly, because Lubitsch had given too much footage to Garbo and West. I turned to Ted. "This is the one," I said. "This is the one I want to see." Then, from inside the vault, Marion gave a little scream.

She was standing at a closed bin, pointing at the label. As we stopped beside her she read it aloud: "*Daughters of Jazz* . . . Oh, *damn* it, Ted, why did you keep this! I want to *see* it, and I *don't want to look at it!*" She turned to me. "That's the one, Nickie. They replaced me with Crawford . . . *I'd* have been the discovery, not her, if only—" She shook her head. "No, goddamn it! I don't want to see it!"

But Ted had opened the bin; only two film cans lay inside. "Marion . . . she's not in this."

"Yes, she—What do you mean?"

"I saved your outtakes." His chin lifted suddenly, and he stared at her, his old eyes blinking in puzzlement. "We thought you'd been killed! Yes . . . we thought that. And I had prints made of your outtakes before they discarded the negatives. When the picture was finished, with Crawford in your part, I took her bits out of my print. And spliced in yours."

He was standing at the open bin, hand still on the edge of the metal drawer. After a moment Marion reached out to put her hand on his. "Ted, why?"

He looked away. "You know why. Don't you?"

"Yes . . . I think I do."

"Because I loved you. I always did."

Watching, listening, I finally knew, really knew, why the old, old movies had once been so incredibly popular. Why out of a population only half the size of ours, sixty million people went to the movies every week of the Twenties. We laugh at their pictures and the stories they took seriously. But they were in tune with their movies, and their movies with them; that's the way people *were*, or at least how they thought they wanted to be. Now Ted and Marion acted as their movies had, and sounded like their subtitles. Ted slowly withdrew his hand from under Marion's: if I'd been filming it, their hands would have filled a close-up. His big, veined, wrinkled hand patted hers gently. Then hers turned, the two palms clasped, and parted. "But I knew it wasn't to be," Ted said. "I was older. So much older." He grinned. "And a funny-looking gink besides!"

"No, you weren't." She brought up a fist slowly and touched the side of his jaw in a pantomimed punch. "You big lug . . ."

"Come *on!*" Ted grabbed up the two film cans. "*This* is what we want to see! It's the first third only, just your part of the picture. *Your picture, Marion!*" Fade-out.

It *was* what we wanted to see. Marion did, and out of everything in that astounding vault, so did I. The old man at work bringing the massive old projector to life, I flicked off the vault lights, and let Marion lead the way, down the side aisle to the front row, then across to a low upholstered settee for two.

There we sat, Marion staring up at the empty screen, waiting like a child. Half-turned in my seat, I watched Ted thread up. He worked surprisingly fast, winding the leader through its gate, onto the sprockets, fastening the end onto the big take-up reel. He slammed the little metal door shut on the film, opened another behind the projection mechanism, adjusted the carbons, slammed the door shut, struck the arc, and ran a few feet of leader, houselights still on. He yanked open a metal door, and peered in at the reeled film, started it again, slammed the door shut, flicked off the houselights, and actually ran across the back of the theater and down the side aisle.

I didn't understand the hurry until up on the screen the last of the white leader flicked past and, superimposed on a line drawing of a saxophone, the title appeared: JESSE L. LASKY PRESENTS "DAUGHTERS OF JAZZ," A HOWARD BERMAN PRODUCTION, FROM THE NOVEL BY WALTER BRADEN. And in just that moment the first chord of Ted's accompaniment began; he'd reached the organ in time.

Rapidly, not nearly so many screen credits as now, the titles appeared, and then the cast, in white letters on black. But I never read it as I generally always do, and I don't think Marion did. Because opposite the very last listing, ADELE, something else appeared instead of the JOAN CRAWFORD that should have been there. It was a badly flickering rectangle of white, and I knew what had happened. On every last frame of that listing, Ted had carefully scraped off a narrow rectangle of emulsion and Joan Crawford's name along with it. In its place we now read—the letters jiggling and vibrating—the name he had inked in to replace it, MARION MARSH.

The picture started then, continued, and it was nothing; neither Ted nor anyone else would have preserved it for itself. I'd heard of it once, I recalled now; a film collector I'd met had seen it run off. He was a Crawford fan, collecting her pictures, and had seen this simply because it was her first, the only reason it had been preserved. She'd been good, he said. It was why she'd been noticed, how she'd got her start.

It was a comedy of sorts. The star was Alicia Conway, who'd made a few pictures in the Twenties. In this she was a show girl out to marry a millionaire. Instead she falls helplessly in love with his handsome young valet, and marries him for pure love. After a lot of nonsense, it turns out that *he* is the millionaire posing as his own valet because he's tired of women chasing him for his money.

We watched for quite a while, the organ unobtrusive, its mood skillfully shifting with the action on the screen. Once I turned to watch him, and Ted sat swaying gently on the organ bench, fingers drifting over the keyboard; happy.

I felt a nudge and turned. On the screen, a swimming pool, rectangular, old-fashioned, the scene filmed outdoors in a little too much sun. And yes, there among a group standing beside the pool—the girls in dark, short-skirted, knit bathing suits, and rubber caps; the men in dark trunks and white tops—stood the girl I'd seen on my television screen and, that same night, in transparent but vivid and colorful reality. The screen was black-and-white but in the sunlight her blondness was plain, as one by one the girls—show girls at the millionaire's pool—walked onto the diving board, posed at its end, glancing around at the spectators, then dived.

I couldn't make out how it happened. The others were simply actresses miming the part, waggling their hips and shoulders as they walked out on the board, batting their eyes as they posed, diving in. But now again, and as always, Marion Marsh made you lean forward. She walked out onto the board, not waggling, very simply and directly, but I was aware of her figure, her body, her movements, and her*self*—the person. And, genuinely unconscious, I think, of a change in their actions, so were the men beside the pool. For each of the four girls who'd preceded Marion, they'd grinned, worked their eyebrows up and down, made side-of-mouth comments. But for Marion they just stood and watched, motionless, not remembering to talk, and it made her the only moving figure on the screen. When she stood on the end of the board, ankles together, looking around with the Marion Marsh arrogance I'd come to know, even the girls dog-paddling in the pool stared up at her. Abruptly she dived in, knifing into the water out of sight, the next girl wriggling toward the board, and the scene went lifeless again.

"What did you *do?*" I whispered. "What were you *thinking*; did you actually feel that part?"

"The part? Hell, no. All I was thinking was that I was damn well going to *make them look at me.* The camera was what I thought about."

On the screen, a street scene, and beside an enormous interurban trolley car, I caught a glimpse of an ancient electric automobile, the tall old kind that ran on batteries and steered with a tiller bar.

A little later, a chase: a touring car racing along a narrow asphalt road beside a railroad track trying to catch a speeding train. On the observation platform, Alicia Conway, arm outstretched, waited for a man crouched on the car's running board to get close enough to toss her a weighted envelope containing her marriage license, the car wavering from side to side of the road.

Cut to a front view facing the car. We see the driver and three or four people in both front and back seats, men and women. They're excited, the driver hunched over his wheel, twisting it back and forth, eyes wide, demonstrating great speed. The girls shriek, grimace, sway from side to side, and it occurs to me that they don't *trust* this medium to actually record on film and, months later, make an audience believe. Except Marion.

You didn't even notice her at first. But after the first dozen seconds of that swaying, gesticulating chase, you spotted a girl in the back seat almost hidden by the others. You became aware of her, I realized, because she wasn't doing anything. She just sat, chin lifted a little, eyes nearly closed, and faintly smiling—but you sensed the rush of air she must be feeling on her face, detected her quiet exhilaration. Just as the bit ended, your eyes on her, she suddenly flung both hands up and outward, half rising in her seat, and you saw the word she spoke as though you'd heard it: *Faster* . . .

The scene was hers, locked up and stolen from everyone else while they weren't even noticing her, and when I turned to look at Marion in the darkness, she was grinning. Eyes still on the screen, she murmured, "That was my idea, the last bit. I didn't say anything for fear they'd stop me; just did it. And I'll bet Crawford stole it."

The reel ended, and Ted hurried back, turned on the houselights, pulled the reel out, set it down, and fitted in the second. Again he threaded up fast, checked both reels, slammed the little metal door closed, started the projector, flipped off the houselights. As the leader flickered by, he was hurrying down the aisle, and once again the first soft organ chord and the first frame of the reel came into being together.

"My last scene," Marion murmured. "I think it comes early."

It did, within a minute or two. A beloved old man, producer of a Broadway musical, had just collapsed backstage. Now the chorus, a dozen girls, had to go on, smiling out at the audience, snapping their jazz-age fingers while inwardly their hearts were anguished.

Eleven girls did it by baring their teeth in rigid smiles, as though the camera wouldn't record a smile unless the teeth were exposed, while blinking rapidly to show they were fighting back tears. Marion did it with a strained lips-closed smile, the lower lip just barely trembling now and then, while she stared out and beyond the audience, not seeing it, so that she made you wonder what she was thinking. But you knew what she was thinking—the picture had told you—so you believed that you saw her feeling it. The others pantomimed grief but Marion showed it to you—or let you perceive it yourself. Apparently they'd had two cameras going, one for close-ups. Because now cuts began from full-stage views to a close-up of one or the other of the girls' faces. But more and more these cuts returned to Marion's face. Beside me, she was murmuring excitedly to herself, "I *thought* they would, but I wasn't sure! They're using my close-ups, *mine*."

Again a cut to a close-up of Marion, her smile remaining, shoulders swaying, lifted fingers snapping, but now actual tears were running down her face. The camera backed off just enough to show her dancing full figure, smiling for the audience, crying in her own inner grief, and I was thrilled, wanting to shout or cry out or do something, and I knew Joan Crawford had not, could not possibly have, been better than what I was staring up at now.

The room lightened, whitening the screen, dimming the picture, and I felt annoyed the way you do when someone opens a door at a movie, and turned to see who'd done it now. But no door was open, and even in the moment it took my head to turn, the light had subsided. Only a swarm of yellowish-white moths of light, strangely, was fluttering and zigzagging over the surface of the big worktable back there. Very fast they moved, sparking a little, like fuses.

They *were* fuses, I understood then, a dozen or so twisting lengths of film burning with frantic speed back toward the cans they'd come out of, and even while I was trying to push up out of the low-slung lounge, I knew what had happened. I knew because I'd glimpsed the achingly brilliant light of the arc inside the projector, and I shouldn't have been able to see it. That meant the protective metal door Ted had slammed shut in his hurry to reach the organ had simply bounced open again, a little way at least. All it had taken then, presently, was one of the occasional sparks from the glowing carbon sticks to flare out through that narrow door-ajar opening onto a length of film. A moment when a ragged-edged hole had expanded across a single frame—of *Greed? The Great Gatsby?* A lost Griffith?—then a puff of fire lightening the screen for a moment, and now dozens of fuses were lighted and racing.

On my feet, running across the front of the little theater toward the side aisle, I saw the first can of film and an instant later all of them flare up into yellowy fire, sudden thick, black, greasy smoke swelling and expanding like a dozen evil genies, merging at their tops, then sucked like a steadily rising black curtain into the ceiling-high air vent across the back of the room. Before I even reached the side aisle the drapes directly beside the burning film at the end of the table went up suddenly— brightly and softly crackling.

Halfway up the aisle I caught a sickening whiff of the stink and stopped dead. It's a gas, the smoke produced by burning film, intensely poisonous. It'll kill you quick, and now I knew what was going to happen. Old film is almost literally dynamite, chemically allied to nitroglycerin, I believe; it was going to explode, and no one was going to be able to go into that gas to stop it.

Standing halfway up the aisle, staring at the back of the room and the open cans of film, like flat smudge pots of poisonous yellow fire, the black smoke rising like a wall from table to vents, I could already feel a pressure of heat moving down the aisle. Old nitrate film ignites at only 300 degrees. In moments now—not only the drapes but now the varnished wood paneling under them was crackling brightly—the tem-perature in the bins we'd left open just inside the vault would softly explode into flame, lids flying off. After that, the heat continuing to build, the closed bins would explode.

I yelled, "Ted!" He sat on the organ bench, stricken, frozen, staring back at the fire. Running back down the aisle for Marion, I shrieked, "*Out*, Ted, *out!* Put a handkerchief over your face and *get out!*" Turning to race across the front of the theater toward Marion, I saw her—incredibly—turn her face from the blaze to look up at the screen again. The projector, on the other side of the room from the blazing drapes and film, was still turning, Marion's movie flickering steadily up on the screen.

I gripped her wrist but she yanked it instantly and violently, shaking her head without ever taking her eyes from the screen. "No! You go, Nickie! *I've got to see my picture!*"

I tried again but she gripped the big upholstered arm and jammed her feet far under the lounge, tugging hard at the wrist I held . . . and the film rolled steadily on, sixteen frames a second, the fire behind us slowly whitening the screen. But the image was still clear: Marion in her own living body of half a century ago, fingers soundlessly snapping, smiling bravely as she danced, staring ahead almost as though at the fire, the tears sliding down her cheeks. And here, hungry-eyed before that screen sat—not really Marion, *this was my wife's body*, and I took the entire rounded back of her head into the grip of my spread left hand, drawing my right fist carefully back to hit her with just precisely the right force if I could do it to knock her unconscious without breaking her jaw. She saw me, eyes flicking momentarily from the screen to my fist. And in the instant before I struck she went limp with a little sigh, eyes closing.

Partly running, partly staggering, I carried Jan's unconscious body across to the side aisle and part way up it. There I got ready for the run around the table's end, through the wall of poisonous smoke toward the vague, smudged red of the exit sign on its other side. My right arm under her limp knees, my left arm supporting her upper body, I worked my left hand up over her face—ready to clamp down across her mouth, thumb and forefinger gripping her nostrils closed while I ran, holding my breath.

Ted sat watching me from across the theater. Then he turned on the organ seat to look up front, and involuntarily I did, too. Transparent but perfectly clear, Marion sat in the front row, the blondness of her hair apparent in the beam of the projector, face lifted to the screen on which she danced. Ted turned, both old hands dropped to the keyboard, and a mighty chord burst from the organ. He played, then, thrillingly, all stops open, and up front the dancing ghost on the screen like the ghost seated before it steadily lightened and whitened as they both moved toward final disappearance.

Then Marion turned to stare back at Jan and me. She smiled: mockingly, affectionately. And touching her forehead in a kind of casual Joan Blondell salute, she turned back to the screen.

I ran then, looking over at Ted once more as, still playing, he looked back over his shoulder at me. And what I saw then, I knew I had seen before. The human mind works strangely, at the strangest times, and even as I ran through the wall of acrid smoke with a hand over Jan's face, to crash through the doors out into the clear air of the long corridor beyond them—I was trying to remember where I had seen that face before.

Jan stirred, murmured, and opened her eyes. I set her on her feet, we raced down that long hall, and as we ran I understood what I'd seen when Ted's high-domed, sparse-haired head had turned to show his eyes, round and staring, and those strange flaring nostril holes, black in the flicker of that growing fire. It was the scene, almost precisely, far down in the cavern below the opera house, in which the Phantom of the Opera turns from the organ to stare—horribly, pathetically—across the room.

Out on the great dark lawn we stood with the dozen servants and the beginning crowd—growing fast, people pouring in through the great iron gates—staring up at Graustark, hearing the distant approaching hoot of the fire trucks' sirens. Inside, the electricity had gone off suddenly, and now the great house against the night sky was a silhouette except for three reddening windows; I didn't know where they were. Then the roof—over the film vault and projection room, the servants said— exploded in a great roaring gush of flame, thick sparks, and black flying objects, the sky turning pink.

And now the fire was free and we watched it begin its race down the long hall of bedrooms in which once had slept Vilma Banky herself . . . Nazimova . . . Tom Mix . . . Constance Binney . . . Milton Sills . . . *Lya de Putti!* Then the first of the great arched windows lighted—for the last time and more brilliantly than ever before—searingly lighted from within. In Renee Adoree's outstretched hand the rose brightened . . . brightened. And in the furious turbulence of roaring flame she seemed actually to move, straining toward the doughboy in the truck just beyond her reach. Then the great glass picture sagged, broke, and hundreds of bright fragments of *The Big Parade* fell outward and down, some actually flaming in colors.

The fire smashed through the hall roof, the light of it widening outward on the lawn, turning the people before us into rosy-edged silhouettes; and now, my arm around Jan's minutely trembling shoulders, we could feel the heat. Up on the distant fortress of the next great window the tricolor of France glowed impossibly bright. For a moment it shivered, and seemed to flutter. Ronald Colman and his weary column swayed as though about to drop to the desert sand, and then did, sagging into nothingness as the entire center of the window touched melting point.

Down the long hall the fire raced and roared, then Buddy Rogers' Allied plane, like the distant plane it had just shot down, took fire, or seemed to, flames licking its wings. Near the wing tip a pane popped out, black smoke instantly pouring through as though trailing from the wing edge. Then, still smiling, the upraised hand peeling off his helmet, touching his forehead as though in final salute, Buddy disappeared behind a bursting-out black-and-red smear of flame.

A moment later, no longer, Doug Fairbanks' costume brightened into a beautiful, achingly brilliant emerald-green, and his indomitable white-toothed grin became visible, I'm certain, over half of Hollywood in that last instant before *Robin Hood* burst outward and was gone. Then Jan and I turned, and in the flickering wash of pink light, the long shadows of Graustark's great trees wavering before us, we walked toward the gateway as the first fire truck turned through it, gravel and dead leaves spitting under its wheels.

People change with experience, we're told, or ought to, and maybe Marion Marsh changed us; maybe she did. Certainly she was an experience we're not ever going to forget. And much, much later that night in our bedroom at the Beverly Hills Hotel, I thought for a moment as I walked out of the bathroom that Marion had returned once more—smiling wantonly as she waited in bed, wearing the filmiest negligee I'd ever given Jan. But it wasn't, it was Jan, wanting to make me think, I'm almost sure, that maybe it *was* Marion. Trying at least, and not altogether failing, either, to be a little more like her, a little more wild and free. But we don't really change much. We remain ourselves, and mostly this was Jan, and that was fine with me. After all, and I knew it, I'm not Rodolpho Guglielmi myself.

We *were* a little reckless: we didn't go straight home. We spent a couple days at Disneyland and really did visit Forest Lawn cemetery, though I didn't find Felix the Cat's marble mausoleum. Then we drove home, because we were running out of money, and I had the new bathroom to finish.

Some ten days later a batch of papers arrived from Hollywood, and we filled them out and returned them, signed with our real names, with a note explaining that Marsh and Guglielmi were pseudonyms. So for a while, as long as those damned Huntley Tomato Catsup commercials ran, we got checks for something called residual payments. I bought *The*

Narrow Trail, starring William S. Hart; *Nomads of the North*, with Betty Blythe; and *Captain January*, with Baby Peggy. Al got a new plaid wool coat for winter, which he didn't like and resisted, even though, as I pointed out to him, it had a cute little pocket big enough for a dog-bone biscuit. And Jan bought a couple new pieces of furniture and had the living room redecorated.

Except for the one wall, of course. That hasn't changed, and never will as long as we're in this house. *Marion Marsh lived here*, it still says in that enormous, free-swinging scrawl of lipsticked letters across it, *Read it and weep*.

...
THE
NIGHT
PEOPLE
...

The great bridge, arched across the blackness of San Francisco Bay, seemed like a stage set now. Empty of cars in the middle of the night, its narrow, orange-lighted length hung wrapped in darkness, motionless and artificial. At its center, where the enormous support cables dipped down into the light to almost touch the bridge, two men stood at the railing staring out at the black Pacific, preparing themselves for what they had come here to do. They wore denims, sneakers, dark nylon jackets, knit caps, and each wore a daypack. Because this had been his idea, Lew Joliffe, the smaller of the two, felt he had to go first, and now he gripped the red-painted bridge railing and swung a leg over, trying not to think of what came next. He drew his other leg over, sat balanced on the rail momentarily, then pushed himself off, out and away from the bridge.

His feet stepped onto the bottom two rungs, his hands seizing the railings of the small steel ladder that is mounted at midpoint of the ocean side of Golden Gate Bridge. Its dozen rungs angle outward away from the side of the bridge to lead up to a small railed platform level with the top of the great support cable. Ladder and platform are open, a spiderwork of thin metal, and Lew's eyes looked out between the rungs at a black void he knew stretched on to China. Focusing his mind on the need to hurry, willing himself never to look down, he climbed, feeling through his rubber soles the terrible thinness of the steel-rod rungs suspended over what, on this side of the bridge, was the open sea, two hundred feet directly below. He moved with tense care; if he stumbled even slightly he was afraid he would be unable to continue with this.

Behind him he heard the small sounds of Harry following him over the bridge rail, then he stepped up onto the little railed platform, turning away from the black emptiness, and felt a rush of relief at sight of the warmly lighted roadway some fifteen feet below him. It looked wonderfully inviting; he longed to be on it. But Harry sat on the bridge railing, a foot moving out toward the ladder, and now, finally, nothing more stood between Lew and what he had to do.

Waist-high handholds run the lengths of the support cables of Golden Gate Bridge. They are of thin wire cable stretched tautly between support stanchions mounted at intervals along the big cables. Lew bent cautiously forward, reaching with his left hand, and gripped the nearer

of these handholds. It felt cold in his palm and damp, and he wondered
if they should have worn gloves. He extended his right foot, and set it
carefully down on the huge swell of the cable, gratefully feeling his
rubber sole grip. Ducking head and shoulders under the handhold wire
in his left hand, he eased his torso and center of balance forward onto
the big cable, and stood upright between the waist-high wires, facing
north toward Marin County.

Standing on the cable, Lew looked ahead along its incredible length
stretching off orange-red and almost level, it seemed; then curving up
and up, leaving the bridge lighting and turning black; and beyond that,
thinning to a thread, then fading from sight high in the night-time sky.
Under his feet he felt the awful roundness of the cable, slightly and
uncomfortably bowing his ankles, and the thought of a foot slipping off
it clenched his stomach. On the platform Harry stood in the yellow light
from the bridge, waiting: a big man, inches taller than Lew and many
pounds heavier.

Lew had to move, and he took the first step forward, then another,
and—hands gripping and regripping the taut wire handholds in unison
with his moving feet—he was walking the enormous cable; slowly, hardly
daring to lift his feet from the great round surface; then more rapidly,
beginning to stride, chin lifting. *And then they were doing it!* The talk
finally over, he and Harry were climbing up through the night toward
the distant winking red beacons at the top of the long, long arc of the
great ocean-side support cable of Golden Gate Bridge.

His motions were fluid, the steady stride of an athlete, it seemed to
Lew, and suddenly he felt exuberantly alive. The air from the ocean
pressed his left cheek coolly, and he tried to imagine how they must look
from below. The evenly spaced vertical suspension cables, touched by
the yellow-orange lights of the bridge, would stand like graph lines
against the ocean-side blackness. The heavier line of the main cable
curving smoothly across their tops would chart their steady rise; and
plodding upward along it, their two tiny figures must seem like symbols
in a newspaper cartoon. He liked this image and thought about telling
Harry, but didn't quite want to turn his head, and he walked on.

Two minutes passed, and three; they moved swiftly, mechanically,
hardly thinking. Then Harry said, "God damn," and Lew stopped,
gripping the handrails, firmly setting his feet. Slowly he turned his head,
and saw Harry staring back over his right shoulder and down, then Lew
saw it, too. Reduced in size, a model of the van that had brought them
to the bridge, he saw it standing on what had turned into a concrete
ribbon, saw the doll-like heads of the two women in the roof opening,

their orange-tinted faces staring up. "Move, Jo, *move*," Harry was muttering. "You'll have the god-damn highway patrol on our ass!" As though hearing him, a head ducked down into the van, then the other, and a moment later the van rolled on.

Lew turned to resume his climb but did not; all was changed. The thick roundness under his feet—he'd hardly noticed in the easy rhythm of the climb—was no longer lighted: now the bridge lamps stood far below, their light shaded toward the roadway. And because the upward climb had been so gradual, only now steepening and beginning to be felt in his calves, they'd climbed higher than he'd understood until he looked back and down onto the diminished roof of the van. They were up now, really *up*: What if one of the handhold wires ahead had broken? He saw his hand sliding off it before he saw the break, feet stumbling, body plunging. . . . He stopped this thought, switched it off, then made a mistake.

The temptation had always been there, nagging at him: now unthinkingly he glanced down past his left side and in the blackness saw a fleck of grayed whiteness appear, expand shapelessly, then fracture and vanish. For an instant he didn't understand, then did: that fleck, silently expanding to thumbnail size, had been a breaking whitecap, and he said, "Jesus," then, "Oh, *Jesus*," and could not move. Eyes squeezing shut, he clung motionless and frozen to the handholds; and high in the darkness four hundred feet above the black ocean he stood wondering in bewildered panic at the impossible remoteness of this moment from the evening the Night People began.

• • •

CHAPTER   ONE

• • •

On the evening the Night People began, Lew was in Jo's apartment;
she had to work. He lay on the chesterfield in Levi's and a green-checked
shirt, leafing through *The New Yorker*, looking at the cartoons, and she
sat at her draftsman's table, ruling in shapes on a sheet of bristol board.

Lew turned the last page, then closed the magazine on his chest, and
lay watching Jo: her brown hair hung before her face like a curtain,
brushing the white cardboard, her hands moving deftly in the circle of
hard white light from the cantilevered lamp head. Lew tossed the
magazine into the air, pages fluttering, and Jo looked up, swinging her
hair aside. His arms straight overhead, one hand behind the other, he
began rhythmically pumping them up and down, fingers opening and
closing. Jo said, "Okay, I'll ask: What are you doing?"

"Hypnotizing God."

"I'll inquire still further: Why?"

"It's worth a try." He lowered his arms, hands clasping on his chest.
"It could solve all my problems."

"What problems, you don't have any problems." She resumed her
rapid, precise drawing. "Your work's going all right. At least you said."

"Sure. It is. Splendidly, nay, brilliantly." Eyes lazy, he watched her
hand slide a needle-pointed pencil along the metal edge of her ruler. His
hair was black, his brown eyes almost black, and he wore a mustache
and trimmed sideburns to just above his ear lobes. Glancing up again as
she spoke, Jo liked the way he looked in just this moment.

She said, "And we're okay. I think." A folded architectural drawing
hung tacked to a corner of her board, and Jo read a measurement from
it, scaling it down in her mind on a mental blackboard. She murmured,
"Don't say, 'Yes, we're fine, Jo.' Lightning would strike."

"We're fine, except for a few of your sickening habits such as
constantly picking your nose."

"Well, okay, then let God alone."

"Right-oh!" Lew snapped his fingers at the ceiling. "Sir! Come out
of it now!" He rolled off the chesterfield onto his feet, and stood looking
around the room. A yard-wide strip along this wall contained Jo's one-
dimensional living room, her "espaliered living room," Lew said. In this
strip stood an upholstered chair, a standing lamp, the chesterfield and a
glass-topped table beside it, the rest of the room being work space. On

the opposite wall her olive-drab supply cabinet stood pushed against the fireplace; her long paste-up table stood in the center of the room; the tilt-top table at which she now sat stood directly beside the glass doors to the outside balcony.

Lew walked to the supply cabinet. Lined up in three rows on its top stood some fifteen or so miniature buildings, each no larger than the palm of a hand: some awninged stores and turn-of-the-century small-town houses, a collapsing shed and old barn, a bridge of weathered wood, a stone-fronted brick-sided little bank building. These were the beginnings of what in time was to become "Jo's Town," new buildings added at long intervals. Lew stood touching the perfect little cardboard structures, cautiously admiring them with his fingertips. Each took hours of work, and Jo wasn't sure she'd ever finish the town. What purpose it was eventually to have or where it could be laid out complete with streets, back alleys, a stream, and outskirts, she didn't know; it was to have as many as a hundred buildings.

Lew turned to the built-in book shelves beside the balcony doors. Jo's cassette player and recorder stood on the bottom shelf, cassettes lying tumbled in a green shoe box beside it, and he squatted to poke through them, glancing at titles.

But he picked up none of the cassettes, and stood again to sidle through the partly opened balcony doors out onto the narrow wooden balcony. This overlooked a strip of planted earth and, beyond that, a winding two-lane road greenly lighted at long intervals by street lamps. Forearms on the railing, hands clasping, he stared out at the empty street, and after a moment said, "Well, there it is: Strawberry Drive. Silent. Motionless. And of no interest whatsoever." A pause. "Of no interest to *us*, that is. Those of us who live here now. In 1976." This was the bottom floor of a two-story gabled redwood building of four apartments in suburban Marin County just across the Bay from San Francisco; several similar buildings lay on each side. Ahead, beyond the far curb, stood an irregular row of tall eucalyptus trees. In the darkness beyond these, and down a slope, lay the tennis courts and swimming pool which were one reason they lived here. Beyond them, the blackness of the Bay.

"But to someone of the future, a sociologist a hundred years from now, what a stunning, nay, priceless moment. To actually *be* here! Back in 1976! To look out at this long-vanished, forgotten street and see"— the headlights of a car appeared at a bend to Lew's right—"yes, here comes one now, a *car!*" Head turning, he followed its approach. "Something of which he has only read, seen only in old photographs, remote as a Roman chariot. But now here it *is*, in solid actuality, rolling along the street . . . passing under the quaint street lamps of the period . . . following the curious markings down the center of the 'road.' What was that painted line for, do you suppose?"

"Lew, what are you *doing?*"

He turned to face Jo, leaning back against the rail. "Opening up my senses. Responding to my environment. The way us modern folk is s'posed to do. I am the eye of the future." He pushed forward from the railing, side-stepped through the narrow opening, and turned to Jo's cassette player again. "Where's your microphone?"

"There somewhere."

He found it behind the shoe box and plugged it in. "You got a cassette you don't want?"

"Any of them behind the recorder."

He took one, snapped it in, pressed the rewind button, and watched the tape whir back to its beginning. He pressed the recording buttons and, microphone at his lips, stood thinking for a moment. "To you of the distant future," he said, then, "greetings! From us of the remote lost past. I speak to you from a time, a date, whose very sound will be antique to your ears: August the twenty-sixth . . . 1976! As I speak these words, you are unborn. But as you hear them, I am long dead. Who am I? Lewis Joliffe is my handle, pardner, and I am . . . nobody. Buried. Long gone. Forgotten."

"Jesus," Jo murmured.

"And with me in this distant time is the lovely Josephine Dunne: sloe-eyed, lustrous-haired, soft of skin. As I speak, that is. Back in 1976. But as you listen, she, too, is dust. Long since passed into wrinkle-skinned, trembling old age. Then buried deep. And now even the granite that once marked her final resting place is cracked, fallen, and crumbling into nothingness."

"Hey, cut it out!"

"That was her very own voice! From a century ago! We are still gloriously alive now, vibrant with youth. I am a—well, not so tall, maybe, but a spectacularly handsome fellow of twenty-nine: charming, witty, incredibly attractive to women, and master of foil and épée. Jo is magnificent, the eyes of a blue-eyed fawn, fine brown hair, big-titted and high-assed, a good-looking kid. Claims to be several years younger than I am, though she doesn't look it. Also claims to be half an inch taller, which is a lie, a tricky optical illusion achieved by deceit, about which I expect to make a public announcement soon, perhaps a major address. I am a lawyer, an attorney, and if you don't know what that is, congratulations two-thousand-and-seventy-six, and I hope your tricentennial is

better than our bi-. Jo is a free-lance architectural-model maker; makes terrific little models of our quaint old buildings, and if one has survived to your time, as paper so often survives frail flesh, it may be in your attic right now. If her signature is on the bottom, you're rich!

"But what of you? Who *are* you, and what are you like? Do you really wear those funny-looking pajamas they have in 'Star Trek'? Alas, we can never know. And so from a century ago we say . . . farewell!" He held the microphone at arm's length, and repeated softly as though from a great distance, "Farewell . . . " Then he thrust the microphone at Jo. "Say good-by to the folks in the twenty-first century."

She leaned across her table. "So long. Hope things improve in the next hundred years."

Leaving the tape winding, steadily erasing whatever else had been on it, Lew pulled the microphone cord, and stepped out onto the balcony to walk quickly along it to his own apartment next door. At Jo's insistence—she had to have a workroom, she said—they had rented these side-by-side apartments, although Lew had argued: in San Francisco they'd shared the top-floor apartment of a large Victorian. But there she'd had an entirely separate workroom. Here, she said, they couldn't both live in the small space left over. Besides, it might be a good idea, she thought, for each to have a place whenever one of them wanted, needed, or ought to be alone.

Lew was back, dropping onto the chesterfield, a wide-mouthed metal thermos bottle under one arm. He sat thumbing quickly through a packet of white-paper squares, then said, "Yeah, this one," holding it up.

It was a color photograph: Jo and Lew in tennis clothes, standing at the net holding their rackets high. She said, "Yes, I've seen it; Harry took it. It's good of us both. But what—"

She stopped: Lew had lifted off the wide screw top of the thermos, and dropped the photo into the jug. "Time capsule. Stainless steel; it'll last forever."

"Are you *serious?*"

He hopped up, walked to the recorder with the thermos, and stood watching the winding tape. "Why not? We made the tape, why waste it? Soon as it's ready I'll bury it outside somewhere, with the photo; they'll want to know what we looked like." He smiled. "God knows who'll find it, or when. It could *be* a hundred years; really. Two hundred. What a find. Imagine the excitement. You'll be immortal, kiddo." The machine clicked, the reels stopped, and Lew punched the STOP key, and lifted out the cassette. "Anything on the other side?" Jo shook her head, and Lew held the cassette between thumb and forefinger over the mouth of the jug. "Anything you want to add? Your justly famous rendition of 'Ave Maria'? Your recitation of 'Gunga Din'?" She shook her head, and he let the cassette fall, clinking, into the jug. "Now you belong to the ages." He began screwing on the cap. "One of the tiny handful of names remembered down the long corridors of time: Shakespeare, Einstein ... Washington and Lincoln ... Agnew and Nixon ... Joliffe and Dunne. I hope you're grateful." He tightened the lid, twisting hard.

"Where you going to bury it?"

"I don't know, where do you think? By the tennis courts?"

She shook her head. "They'll be building more apartments there eventually, you know they will."

"How about next to the road by the curb? No, they'll be widening the road, too: damn it, I don't want the thing dug up in the next fifteen minutes. Where's a good place?" He stood frowning, then looked up at Jo. "You know something? There isn't a single place—not the beaches, not a cemetery, not out in what's left of the country, and not home plate in Candlestick Park—that you can really be certain won't be all screwed up in the next few years, let alone a hundred. We ain't gonna be immortal at all."

"I always suspected it." Jo resumed her work.

Lew shook the cassette out of the thermos and put it back on the shelf. "Well, I'll go on back to my place—you're working, and I don't want to disturb you." He smiled at that, and so did Jo, without looking up. "Hope I sleep tonight."

"Why shouldn't you?"

"I don't know." He turned to the balcony doors and stood sideways in the opening. "I've been waking up every once in a while. For no reason. Mostly when I'm at my place. Middle of the night, and my eyes pop open. Then I lie there."

"Why don't you come over?"

"No, this is like two or three o'clock; you don't wake up so good then."

"Get up anyway." With an X-acto knife she began cutting out one of the shapes she had drawn. "My father says that if you can't sleep you should hop right up and read or something. Till you get chilled."

"He also says, 'Another day, another dollar.'"

"That's right." This was an old routine. "And, 'If it were a snake, it would bite you.'"

"A wise man. I've noticed that many of his pithy observations have been widely copied. Well, if this happens again, may what's-his-name forbid, I'll try it."

It happened again six hours later, in the way Lew was almost used to lately. At one moment he lay quietly asleep; in the next, his eyelids opened. For several seconds he lay blinking, looking across the room at the night shape of his bedroom window, the glass yellowed by the moon. Then he got up.

Barefoot and in pajamas, he sat at the living-room television, waiting. A bar of white light shot across the screen, and he watched it expand, his mustached face pale and black-stubbled in the livid light. But no sound began, no picture appeared. Through click after click of the dial the screen remained white, the set humming, all stations off the air for the night.

Lew turned off the set, and sat watching the little diamond of light shrink down. When it was nearly gone, a silver speck, he did it again; turned the set on, then off, to watch the needle point of light slide away. He reached out, turned on his desk lamp, and looked at the several piles of paperback books stacked on the shelves helter-skelter, just as he'd lifted them from the mover's carton months before. But he didn't want to read at this time of night, and he got up, rolled back the glass doors to the balcony, and stepped out.

The air slightly chilly, he stood, forearms on the railing, hands clasped, looking out at the silent street. This was the same street, the same scene, he'd stood here looking at six hours earlier, yet now it seemed different. A high waxing moon shone almost straight down, the shadows of the eucalyptus branches across the road motionless on the pavement. The moon-washed asphalt looked white, and he could see pebbles and their shadows. A mist of green light from the street lamp tinted the branches beside it a stagy green.

Nothing stirred, there was no sound, and something in him responded to this dead-of-night stillness. This was his own familiar street, winding along the shoreline of the Bay in the suburban area of Mill Valley called Strawberry. In the months he and Jo had lived here he'd have driven this road hundreds of times, seen every hour of its twenty-four. But always in a car, insulated from it. Now, greenly lit, motionless and silent, the road seemed a new place, mysterious and strange, and the impulse flared up in him to go out onto it and see what it was like in the deserted middle of the night.

In his bedroom he pulled denims and a blue windbreaker over his pajamas, sneakers onto bare feet, picked up a red ski cap. At his outer door, hand on knob, he turned back into the living room; and at his desk he printed a note in heavy black felt-tip letters on a sheet from the lined legal pad he kept there: *Jo—Couldn't sleep, went for walk, back soon.*

Amos Quackenbush. Leaving the desk lamp on, he taped the note to the balcony door, seeing his own reflection in the glass. The tasseled cap lay jauntily on the back of his head, exposing a heavy wing of black hair across his forehead, and he thought, *Pierre, ze Canadian lumberjack.* The rolled-up cap front could be pulled down as a wind mask; he did this, and in the shiny black glass saw himself turn into a sinister figure. The expressionless parody of a face patterned with streaks of yellow at cheeks and forehead suggested an African mask, and he rolled it up again.

Out on the curb facing the street, Lew stood for a moment. Across the road the great trees seemed bigger than in daytime, hugely silhouetted against the lighter sky, and the silence was absolute. He stepped out, turning left, hearing the faint scuff of his rubber soles on the asphalt. Along the horizon across the Bay, towering banks of clouds hung white in the moonlight, a gigantic background for the winking lights of a silent plane, and a rush of exhilaration at being out here shot through him.

Passing the first of the houses beyond the row of apartment buildings, Lew looked up at their dark windows, and glanced at a row of curbside mailboxes, silvery in the moonlight. Reading the name lettered along the side of the first of them, he raised hand to mouth, and in a mock shout called, "Hey, Walter Braden! Come on out, and play!" He felt excited, gleeful, and began to jog, shadow-boxing, swiping thumb to nose. From somewhere far behind him he became aware of a sound, an infinitely remote whine barely touching the air, and he stopped to listen.

For the space of a breath he thought it was a far-off siren, then recognized it: a diesel truck tooling along the distant freeway a mile behind him beyond the intervening hills. Lonely as a train whistle, the high, insectlike drone grew, deepening, as Lew stood motionless. It held . . . receded . . . was gone . . . returned momentarily, even more remote . . . then vanished utterly, and he walked on, smiling.

On around a long bend past the dark silent houses, then the lower branches of a tree across the street suddenly brightened, he heard the approaching car, and without thought or hesitation stepped up onto the lawn beside him. The engine-mutter growing, the pavement lightening, Lew sat down quickly in the black shadow of a large pine, drawing up his knees, leaning into its trunk, his hand on the lawn coming to rest against the waxy hardness of a baseball-sized pine cone. Headlight beams abruptly rounded the curve, lean pebble shadows streaking forward, immediately shortening and vanishing, and Lew yanked down the mask front of his cap.

Following its own long beams around the curve of the quiet street, a black-and-white police car appeared. Motionless in the deep shadow of the pine, Lew read the block letters through his eye slits, MILL VALLEY POLICE, as the white door panel slid past. The hatless driver, elbow on window ledge, never glanced his way. Rounding the curve, the car's headlight beams sliced off, tail lights appearing, and Lew stood, pine cone in hand, pulled the pin with his teeth, and hurled the grenade after the car in stiff-armed World War I fashion, lofting it high. Flipping up his mask, he stepped down onto the street again, grinning.

A mile, walking, jogging, past the dark houses, then the road tipped sharply downhill, and Lew saw the great community-recreation field slide into view, lying spread out and level down on the flats—a great, grassy rectangle, city-block size, livid in the moonlight. At the near end: the big swimming pool, gable-roofed dressing rooms, a small parking lot. Most of the rest: two full-sized baseball diamonds back to back, the wire cages of their home plates in opposite corners black-etched by the moon.

Lew walked across the asphalt of the parking lot to the mesh fence surrounding the pool area, and stood looking in at the mirrorlike rectangle, thin patches of mist lying motionless on its surface. Squatting, he found a walnut-sized rock in the dirt beside the fence. He stood, and drew his arm back and far down to behind his right knee. Arcing the rock high, he threw as hard as he could, and stood waiting. A satisfying *plunk*, and he walked on.

He sat down in the stands facing the nearer, Little League field, looking around at the benches bleached white by the moon. Here on the flat he sat almost surrounded by hills, the blank windows of the many houses on their slopes staring down at him. Leaning back, elbows on the bench behind him, he looked out at the long length of the field, and in one of the distant houses high on the hills beyond it, a light came on. Watching, wondering at someone else awake now, Lew lifted an arm to wave slowly. "Hey, come on down," he called softly. "And bring your mitt!"

On impulse he stood, walked down the steep aisle to the field, and onto it. For a moment he stood wondering what to do. Then, in the far-off house ahead, the light went out, and he was alone in the night again. He walked to home plate, stopped beside it, and looked around him. No light had come on anywhere else, nothing stirred, and he gripped an imaginary bat, and tapped it against imaginary spikes, each foot in turn. Stepping into batting position, he rapped the plate with the bat, his motion easy, confident, fluidly athletic. He pawed the dirt, shuffling and rearranging it with the sides of his shoes. Then he dug in, twisting hard on the balls of his feet. Bat raised high and slightly behind him, he held it motionless except for the slight menacing circling of its tip, and stood facing the pitcher who studied him, then began his windup.

A brushoff, which he'd expected, and he leaned back fast, glancing at the umpire. But the umpire, Lew's lips nearly motionless, said only, "Ball one." In a glassed-in booth high over the field an announcer, his voice reproduced by a dozen radios audible from the stands, said, "Bases full, one and oh."

Lew stepped out of the box, lifted each foot once, stepped back, and dug in, bending lower this time, bat high and almost vertical. His head whirled to the catcher to stare down at the ball nested in his glove, awed at the impossibly fast pitch. "Strike!"

In batting position again, waiting for the pitch. As fast as he could hurl himself, he fell back, grimacing with fear and anger at the pitch to his ear that would have torn his head off. His mouth dropped open in astonishment at the umpire's call, and he repeated it aloud: *Strike?* He sprang forward to protest, but instead clamped his mouth shut, and faced the pitcher again. "Three and two count," said the announcer: Could that be right? "Five to two score, Giants behind, nineteen fifty-one—two?—World Series, deciding game." Then he added, "Last of the ninth."

Lew lowered his bat and stepped backward out of the box, turning to face the manager who was walking slowly toward him from the dugout. He wasn't sure this was allowed, but the manager did it anyway. He stopped before Lew and, Lew's lips hardly moving, said, "Son, you're a brand-new rookie just up from the minors, and I know that. All the same, it's up to you now." Lew nodded, swallowing. "Do my best, sir." The elderly manager stood considering him from under the famous shaggy brows, then nodded doubtfully, turning away. "All you *can* do, boy."

Lew gulped, and shook his head hard, clearing his vision. Again he faced the pitcher, tapped the plate. Suddenly he grinned, lifted his chin, all fear gone, and in the gesture that would be remembered forever, extended his bat to point far out toward right field and beyond, and the radios and stands went silent.

The pitch came, and in exaggerated slow-motion, Lew swung the bat in a shoulder-high curve, lining it straight out from the wrists and lifting it up and far past his left shoulder in a full follow-through, ankles crossing as his body revolved. He let the bat drop, grinning as he watched the obviously home-run ball rise in the remote distance. Nodding back at the stands as he began, he made the leisurely home-run trot of the bases, tipping his hat to the fans as he jogged.

Leaving third base, he began accepting the congratulatory handshakes of the entire team, coaching staff, Shirley, Jo, and several other vague, excited young women lined up beside the base path. Stepping squarely onto home plate, he lifted his arms in the prizefighter's handshake. Then he stood, cap off, hand on heart, bowing humbly—stumbling backward in pleased astonishment as the fans overwhelmed him.

Lew turned suddenly and searched the houses around the field. Nothing moved; silence everywhere. Smiling then, hands in pockets, he began walking the length of the field toward its far end, the grass whispering against his canvas sneakers: something about the small risk he had taken of being seen playing the fool pleased him. He wondered if anyone in all the many houses looking down on this field stood watching him now from a darkened room, a small figure moving down the length of the great moonlit rectangle.

At the far end of the long field, and the sidewalk there, he turned left onto the street that wound along the base of the high ridge bisecting Strawberry. The street lay still as a photograph; just ahead the leaves of a small curbside tree hung motionless under a street lamp, and no least sound came from the distant freeway. Silent on rubber soles, Lew walked on, glancing curiously up at each of the dark houses he passed.

Just ahead he saw a ground-level concrete porch with a wrought-iron railing; a swing hung over its floor, the traditional porch swing of wooden slats suspended by chains from the ceiling. Lew stopped: the porch ran across the front of the house, a door and a large rectangular window facing onto it. Swing and door were at one end of the porch and, inset in the door, a small window overlooked the swing. Lew glanced across the street; looked back toward the rec field; looked ahead as far as he could see. Nothing moved anywhere.

He hesitated, suddenly wanting to walk cravenly on. Then he took a deep slow breath, hearing it sigh through his nostrils, his heart suddenly pounding, and turned to walk up the slight curve of concrete walk to the porch. Just short of the porch he stopped, eying the big window and drapes along its sides, then the square little window in the front door; no one stood in the darkness of the house watching him, and he stepped silently onto the porch.

The trespass made, Lew stood frozen. Then he walked to the swing, turned his back, and eased himself onto the seat, a slow squeak sounding as slats and chains accepted his weight. Silence as he listened, staring up at the small square eye of the door beside him. The pane was black; he could see no blur of white face. He sat conscious that he could still stand up and walk silently away. But that was no longer true; he'd taken the dare.

Feet tucked far back under the swing, his rubber soles pressed against the concrete floor of the porch, Lew tensed his thigh muscles, gripping the chains, and slowly and not quite silently pushed the swing back as far as it could go, feeling the slatted seat tilt almost vertical. For one last moment, heart thumping, he waited in silence; then he lifted his feet and swept forward, the chains groaning, ceiling hooks squealing like an animal. It was *loud, loud*; audible, he knew, even across the street. A fractional instant of silence at the top of the forward arc, then the swing shot back, groaning and squealing again.

It could easily be heard inside the house: Was it waking someone now, covers flying, feet swinging to the floor? If so—if the white globe on the porch ceiling flashed alight in the next second, lock bolt cracking on the door beside him—what could he do? Run? Or stay and say—what?

No explanation could make sense, and he deliberately refused to think: he had to stay here for six full swings, six screeching swoops forward and back, and he sat, feet tucked up under the bench as he swung forward the second time, scared now. What the *hell* would happen if he were caught? An angry man who was big enough might beat him up, an excitable man could shoot him, a frightened man might already have phoned the cops; and if a cruising patrol car were nearby, radio crackling into life right now with a prowler call. . . . Back he swung, then an instant of almost motionlessness at the top of the arc, Lew staring up at the blank square of glass waiting for the sudden white movement of face; the sweat sprang out under his cap. Forward again, the piglike squeal unbelievably loud.

Three more long squealing swoops forward and back. Then he was free—to jam his feet down, dragging across the porch floor, stopping. Just short of a run he hurried down the walk, turning on the sidewalk to look over his shoulder, and in that instant the white globe flashed on, the porch suddenly bright as a stage, the gliding black shadow of the still-moving swing suddenly appearing on the painted floor.

A small hedge separated this front lawn from the next, and without having thought what to do, Lew instantly did it. He took one giant step to the far side of this hedge, and threw himself like a man under gunfire lengthwise beside it.

Flat on the grass, cheek pressing into its night-time dampness, Lew lay looking through the lower branches of the hedge, eyes almost at ground level. His heart pounded, so hard and fast it piled blood behind his eyes; he had to blink to see. A door bolt had clunked, the door swung inward, and now a man stepped cautiously out onto the porch. He was in pajamas, about forty; not taller but wider, heavier, bigger than Lew. Directly under the white globe his scalp showed through mussed brown hair. He stood motionless, arms hanging, fingers open and ready, looking wary, angry, mean. Only his head moving, he searched slowly through a half circle for whoever had been on his porch, knowing he was out there somewhere.

Suddenly bolder, the man stepped to the edge of his porch, and looked straight toward Lew, staring either directly at the hedge or off across it, Lew couldn't tell. Breathing shallowly through his mouth, Lew lay motionless. Could the man make out the telltale thickening along the base of the hedge?

Seconds passed, and still he stood staring. In quick panic Lew realized that he didn't know what he would do if in the next instant the man came striding down off his porch across the lawn toward him, and he began to laugh, feeling his shoulders shake, listening to whether any sound of it escaped. No: his stomach muscles tensing, he was laughing helplessly, but in silence. Another moment, then the man's head turned slowly away to search the darkness across the street.

Abruptly he turned, and walked back inside, pulling the door closed. A *chunk* as the bolt shot, then the porch light went dark. Lew didn't move: if he were the man on the other side of that door, what would he be doing now? He would be standing at the window back out of sight waiting for whoever was out there—making himself thin behind a tree or crouched beside a neighbor's porch or lying beside this hedge—to step out or stand up. Unmoving, Lew lay trying to watch the street through the eyes of the man in the house, to think his thoughts.

Half a minute passed, perhaps longer . . . then Lew felt the moment pass beyond which the man inside the house could no longer hope to see anything move out here. In his mind Lew saw him turn away into the darkness of his living room murmuring a single obscenity, and walk back through the house. He'd explain to his wife, if she'd awakened, then lie listening, ready to move fast if the porch swing sounded again.

It popped up in Lew's mind, the idea of going back to the swing again, and he laughed aloud. But he didn't dare; this time he wouldn't get away with it, and there'd be trouble. A quick pushup, feet gathering, and he stood, turning swiftly to walk on, ready to run. *What if the man had phoned the cops!*—Lew's head swung around for the fast-moving car coming up from behind, but there was nothing.

He walked home through the quiet streets; and, back in his living room, peeled the note from the glass door, started to crumple it, then stopped. In the light from the desk lamp he stood looking down at it; after a moment he folded the note carefully across, aligning the edges, and tucked it away among the books on his shelves.

CHAPTER   TWO

• • •

Jo said, "What'd you do last night? Watch the movie?" In a pink robe over yellow pajamas, her hair brushed back and tied, she stood waiting at the stove as Lew lifted hot, dripping bacon from pan to absorbent paper towels spread on the stove top.

"No movie," he murmured, eyes intent on the fork; he wore a kitchen towel tied under his arms to protect his shirt and tie from spattering grease. "It was too late, nothing on." As Jo took over to serve, he untied the towel, tossed it to the counter, and walked out of the little kitchen area to sit down at Jo's paste-up table. "How'd you know I was up?" He realized he'd added this to forestall more inquiry; he didn't want to say what he'd done last night.

"I woke up, and you were out on the balcony; I heard you clear your throat."

Lew nodded, pulling the news section of the *Chronicle* toward him. He felt good; a little short of sleep but not tired. Jo set their plates on the table, poured coffee, and sat down across from Lew, pulling out the third section of the paper. Lew sat eating, turning pages often. Jo read Herb Caen's column, an elbow on each side of the page, cup in hands; she liked half a cup of coffee before eating breakfast. Lew turned a page, glancing up, and saw that Jo's wide sleeves had dropped, lying in pink puddles of cloth at her elbows, exposing her forearms. *Good-looking forearms*, he thought; then: *What is a good-looking forearm?* He smiled at this, Jo looked up, saw him, and said, "What?"

He shook his head. "Too embarrassing to say. Something obscene. Involving your forearms."

"What?" She looked down at her arms.

He nodded. "You'd be shocked. I know you see the books and magazine articles, you watch the TV discussions. You try to be liberated, and on a written exam you'd get A. But you've never really made it, actually, and you'd be horrified. Too bad; it might have been fun."

"I'll bet. So what did you do last night? Read?"

"No. Stood out on the balcony. Clearing my throat."

"Lew, why are you waking up like this? What's bothering you?"

"Nothing. Nothing that isn't bothering everybody. The national debt. Corruption in high and low places. Decline in moral values. Blatant sexuality. In high and low places."

"You're pretty blatant yourself today."

"So watch out."

"You watch out; I don't have to punch a time clock."

He looked at his watch, then shook his head. "It's Friday; meeting day. I can't be late."

"Pity," she said in pseudo-British accent, and Lew smiled, and got up to walk to his apartment for his suit coat.

He backed his VW, a maroon squareback, from its space in the asphalted parking area behind the row of nearly identical low frame buildings and swung around into the driveway between his and the building next door. He tapped his horn, and almost immediately the door of the lower apartment there opened, and Harry Levy stepped out: hatless, carrying a zippered briefcase. Lew watched, but today there was no sign of Shirley in the doorway behind him. On some mornings when Lew tapped his horn, she would appear in her robe, standing in the doorway to smile and wave good-by as they drove off; cupping her elbows on chilly mornings and shivering her shoulders dramatically. Watching Harry walk over to the car, it occurred to Lew that he was seldom late. Harry said, "Unhh," as he opened the door, and Lew replied, "Yeah," in ritualized morning exchange.

Lew waited, hand on the shift lever, as Harry fitted his big body into the little car, knees wedging high, black hair almost touching the ceiling. He must be twenty pounds overweight, Lew thought, obviously well over two hundred. But he didn't seem fat, Lew acknowledged, and was probably in good shape. Waiting for Harry to pull the door closed, Lew watched the big head, jaw, and cheek in profile: thick hair cut somewhat shorter than the norm, heavy black beard shaved close, sideburns sliced unmodishly short. As Harry slammed the door his eyes narrowed slightly in a concentration that resembled belligerence: when he wasn't smiling, Harry was a formidable-looking man, and as Lew drove on down the driveway, he was remembering the temperance cards.

Walking in the sun one noon hour last spring, he and Harry had gone into an antique shop, a junk shop, just outside the financial district. Harry found and bought for a dollar a packet of unused nineteenth-century temperance pledges: postcard-size with a printed pledge, blanks for date and signature, a tiny, forktailed white ribbon glued beside the pledge. For several weeks he carried these in his inside suit-coat pocket, and he got eleven signatures: twice Lew had been with him. One of the men was a salesman for a law-book publisher, sitting in Harry's small office when Lew had walked in with some papers he wanted Harry to see. The other man was a junior partner of another law firm, meeting with

Harry and Lew in the firm's conference room to discuss a case in which both firms had an interest.

Each time, presently, Harry had taken out his cards, exhibited the signatures he had, and begun talking impassively of the modern need for "teetotalism." Each time the other man had begun to smile anticipatorily, but Harry's face remained expressionless, and as he talked on with a low-voiced almost angry intensity, deep voice rumbling, Lew watched the other man's smile waver, become fixed, then fade. Finally Harry brought out a pen, pressing the other man to sign, insistently and with latent threat. And presently, each time, eyes bewildered, the man had reluctantly taken Harry's pen and signed, glancing away in embarrassment. Harry had examined the signature, nodded solemnly as he tucked the card away with the others, soberly congratulated the man with a handshake, and resumed the interrupted discussion.

The man from the other law firm had complained by phone to Tom Thurber, a senior partner of their firm, and Harry had been called into the office, and formally rebuked. He'd listened, offering no explanation, then pulled out his cards and asked Tom to sign, too, and Thurber had laughed.

Lew followed the shoreline road of this northern arm of the Bay; then slowed for the Ricardo Road stop sign, and turned toward the service road and freeway just ahead. Harry had taken a long-paged legal typescript from his briefcase, laid the briefcase along his slanted thighs, arranged his papers on it, and as they rode he followed the text line by line with the tip of a yellow wooden pencil. As Lew turned toward the freeway entrance, Harry glanced up, then resumed his reading, murmuring, "God-damned legal gobbledy-gook."

"Bring it up at the meeting this morning," Lew said. "Propose that we be first in pioneering plain English," and Harry said, "Yeah."

On the crowded freeway, Harry working, they rode in silence, a part of the sluggish river of cars, moving up the long Waldo Grade, then into the Waldo tunnel which bored through a particularly high range of Marin County hills. Watching the narrow arched opening of daylight ahead, Lew waited for the moment just beyond it. It came: as they passed through the opening, there it all was—the great red towers of Golden Gate Bridge ahead, and beyond them across the blue Bay the clean white city spread out on its hills. It was a moment Lew waited for, this first, suddenly expanding look at the city, and as always he felt a little surge of anticipation at knowing he was going down into it, followed by the little anticlimax of knowing exactly where he had to go. He said, "Harry, could you give up law?"

"Give it up?"

"Yeah. And go into something else."

"Like what?"

"I don't know: I just mean is it okay with you if this turns out to be all you ever do?"

Harry turned away to look ahead through the windshield. "Well. I get something out of it. In court, anyway; sometimes you can feel your argument taking hold." He glanced at Lew. "Something about the way a judge starts to listen, and you know you're winning if you just don't blow it: I like that. Not this shit"—he rapped his knuckles on the briefcase. "But sometimes in a courtroom. . . . It's a *fight*; you know? You can feel you're really a lawyer." Harry sat watching the great rust-red towers enlarge. "But I could give it up. Get into something else, and not even miss it a week later. Sometimes I see myself doing something outdoors. What about you?"

"Well, yeah; there's some fun in it. I like working up a brief; for appeal. Working it over, becoming persuasive; you can feel it when it starts getting some bite. But still; sometimes it bothers me that this could be more or less it from now on."

Ahead, traffic from the Sausalito entrance seeped onto the freeway. Well ahead, halfway across the bridge, brake lights flickered, everything before them slowing to a stop because of the toll plaza up ahead at the San Francisco end. Harry sat watching the stopped traffic, then said, "Hey, it's Friday: what're you guys doing tonight?"

"Nothing I know of."

"Come over for supper: we'll lay in some hamburger and junk, and do something. Or nothing. We could play some bridge, damn it, if Shirley'd settle down and finish learning the game. Come early, and we'll drink it up a little."

Friday or Thursday night generally meant food-shopping, and for that Jo waited for Lew. She owned a sun-faded blue Chevy van. She'd bought it for its floor space, using it to deliver her finished models; but it was third- or fourth-hand, the shocks nearly gone, and so cumbersome—heavy wooden bumpers projecting a foot or more front and back—that it was hard to park. So she waited for Lew and his VW.

At the Safeway, Jo inside, Lew waited in the car, angle-parked at the curb before the huge store: he wore tan wash pants and a red plaid shirt buttoned at the sleeves. The air was warm, his window open, the sun still well above the hills across the freeway behind him, Daylight Savings still on. The low, red-tiled roofs of the great shopping center extended out to the curb line, roofing the sidewalks before the store fronts; from speakers tucked up under the roof, music sounded softly. People passed steadily along the walk before Lew's bumper, and he sat watching them, studying their faces.

When Jo appeared with her loaded shopping cart—in the peach-colored cotton dress and white sandals she would wear to the Levys'—Lew got out, and helped her unload into the car. They got in, but he didn't immediately start the engine. He sat staring at the windshield for a moment, then turned to her. "You know something?" he said puzzledly. "I never see anyone I know down here. We *live* here. In Strawberry. But all I ever see here is strangers."

"Well, it's probably the biggest shopping center in the county. And right beside the freeway. So the people you see here come from everywhere."

"Yeah, I guess." He started the engine.

Driving home along the road he had walked last night, it seemed to Lew that now it was a different place. Cars passed; people moved about their yards in the late daylight; the chug of a power motor sounded somewhere. Looking out her window, Jo smiled in content, and said, "Strawberry's a pleasant area, isn't it. So green and peaceful."

They'd said this to each other before, and Lew nodded automatically. "I guess," he said, then surprised himself. "But . . . "

She looked at him. "But what?"

"But it's always the *same*, damn it. All you ever see is people out mowing their lawns, trimming their hedges, painting their houses."

"Well, what *should* they be doing?"

"I don't know." Then he laughed, shrugging. "I don't know what the hell I'm talking about."

They had supper out on the Levys' balcony, a dozen feet from Lew's, across the intervening driveway. In canvas-and-wood chairs they sat in the building's shade, but across the road and down the lightly wooded slope beyond it the pool and two of the tennis courts still lay in the last of the sunlight. Occasionally commenting, they watched a young woman in one-piece white tennis costume sweating with effort as she batted back lobs served up by a practice machine, the court littered with the yellow balls. Beyond the courts and pool, the Bay lay blue and sparkling, eight or ten sails visible.

For a considerable time, talking lazily, often silent, they sat sipping red wine, passing a gallon jug around. Then, the sun down, the Levys went into the apartment, and presently Shirley brought out hamburgers and potato chips on paper plates, trailed by Rafe, their elderly terrier, sniffing the air, tongue anticipating. Harry followed with two filled glasses and two cans of beer. "Iced tea," he said, handing Jo her glass. "Cheap beer"—he gave Lew a can, then set Shirley's glass on the floor beside her empty chair: "Hemlock." He wore frayed tan shorts, dirty, unlaced sneakers over bare feet, and a white T-shirt speckled with holes.

Shirley handed Harry his plate, and he sat down and began wolfing the fat, dripping hamburger in enormous bites, leaning forward so the squeezed-out catsup would drip down between his knees to the plate he'd set on the floor; occasional fragments of meat falling to plate or floor were snatched by Rafe. Lew sat at one end of the narrow balcony, chair tipped back against the side railing, paper plate held up under his chin, eating and watching Harry. He had noticed before that on weekends Harry liked to dress and eat as sloppily as he could; exaggeratedly so. Under the thin white material of Harry's T-shirt and curling over the neckband lay a matting of black hair so dense and springy it held the light cloth away from his skin, and the hair lay black and thick across his big forearms, and curled on his immense legs. He had, not a belly, Lew said to himself, you couldn't say that, but a general thickening around the middle; he looked effortlessly strong, and Lew was conscious of envying Harry his physical strength. He was strong, too, for his size, more than people often realized, and he enjoyed chances to surprise them with the power of his arms or legs. But still he envied the size and strength of really big men.

Hamburgers distributed, Shirley was sitting, too, plate balanced on her bare knees. Now she lifted her glass from the floor, and sipped, staring absently out over the rail. As though his eyes had simply been attracted by the movement, Lew allowed himself to casually turn and look at her; he tried to be careful not to look too often or too long at Shirley.

Tonight she wore a short-sleeved light blue middy blouse with a white sailor collar, and tailored white gabardine shorts with a blue stripe up the sides. They were very short; she liked to show off her fine legs, and once more Lew noticed how without blemish they and her arms were, no least suggestion of tiny broken vein, red mark, or unevenness of texture; probably the same all over, he thought. Her hair was black, eyes dark, skin very white; she avoided the sun. Just looking at Shirley was a pleasure, and Lew made himself turn away for fear of looking too long, retaining the last visual impression of her face, relaxed and absent. It was a pretty face, intelligent, shrewd, but not aggressive; she was ready to like people, accepting them as they seemed, had liked Lew and Jo on sight.

Lew looked past her at Jo, comparing, and she smiled and winked, and he grinned. Tonight when they got home, they'd undress, turn back a bed, and lie down together for the best kind of sex, prolonged and amiable: the mutual knowledge lay in the air between them, and Lew felt consciously happy. He liked looking at Jo, knowing what was going to happen later, and he felt proud of the way she looked in her short, peach-colored dress.

Harry scooped up his can, swigged beer audibly, the can nearly vertical, then set it down, wiping his mouth with the back of his other hand. He said, "Well? Anyone want to talk about rent control, recession, or venality and incompetence in government? If so, feel free, but don't mind if I leave: this is the weekend, and I am in unholy retreat."

Lew said, "Don't we have to at least cover pollution, racism, and the rise in violence? And who wants to be first to say 'lifestyle'? You're right," he said. "I get tired of the talk, talk, talk. Anyone says 'environment,' 'media,' or 'Women's Lib,' and I'll kill them."

"Aren't they things that *ought* to be talked about?" Shirley said.

"Sure. But after a while not unless you've got something new to add. And I haven't. And haven't met anyone lately who has."

Harry said, "What we need are some new problems."

"Well, I've got one," Lew said, and complained that no one in Strawberry was ever seen to do anything out of the ordinary, "including me."

"Well, what should they do?" Shirley said.

"Well, I'm all for lawn cutting, hedge trimming, washing the car, and other fundamentals. But just once I'd like to drive by somebody's house, and see him out painting an enormous mythical landscape on his garage door. Most of them around here are big—two-car garages with one big door painted white, like a couple hundred big, empty canvases crying out for creativity. And there are quite a few flagpoles around. Always with the American flag, if any. Well, I'd like to see a guy run up his own personal flag. Divided into quarters each bearing some symbol of his personality. Or hell with creativity, how about a guy out in his yard just having fun. Out on the lawn carrying his wife around piggyback, laughing and squealing."

"Hey, yeah," Shirley said. "Why don't we do that, Harry? Right now. You carry me around piggyback. Down there by the curb."

"I will if you'll make up the flag I design, no questions asked. We'll drape it over the rail here. Or, hey; this is better. We all strip, powder ourselves white, and pose. On Lew's balcony. After dark; I'll rig up a spotlight. Absolutely motionless in classical pose, the way they used to do in the circus. Living statuary. How about driving by and seeing something like that in Strawberry, Lew?"

Jo said, "We could do that famous statue of the couple, 'The Kiss.'"

Harry said, "Or a couple in even more classical pose called 'The—'"

"Never mind," Shirley said.

"You're absolutely right," Harry said. "Be hard to hold the pose motionless."

"You know what I meant."

"Yeah, but nobody's supposed to object to that word any more. Not since about nineteen sixty-three."

"Well, I don't care."

"Not, 'I don't care': What you mean is, you don't give a fuck."

"I mean I don't like casual, pointless dirty talk. And there *is* such a thing as dirty talk. It's so show-offy, this oh-so-casual dropping the words into ordinary conversation."

"Lew, how often do you punch Jo right smack in the mouth?"

"Once a week; that's my allowance. We talked it out. Reasonably, rationally, trying to understand each other's real feelings and basic needs. And that's what we agreed on; it was Jo's suggestion."

"Doesn't sound like nearly enough."

"Just try it, buddy-boy," Shirley said scornfully. "I watched the karate lessons on KQED, you know."

"Lew, is there much wife-swapping in Strawberry? I mean permanent swaps."

Shirley and Jo went to the kitchen and brought out second hamburgers, and Harry offered more beer or wine. They stayed out till the street lamps came on, then the air turned chilly, and they went inside. Shirley wouldn't play bridge, but got out a Monopoly board, and they sat at the all-purpose card table beside the kitchen, and played till nearly one o'clock.

In Jo's apartment then, Lew lay waiting in bed and, Jo calling from the bathroom, they talked, as people do when they've had a quiet good time with good friends, about how long they'd all known each other. Lew and Harry had gone to the same suburban-Chicago high school hardly aware of each other, the school a big one and Harry a class behind Lew. A dozen years later, finding themselves working in the same San Francisco law firm, the men had become friends. But the real friendship began, Lew and Jo agreed now, when the four of them met.

Lew was thinking of moving from the city, he'd told Harry one

morning, and Harry nodded, standing in Lew's little office. "Well, it's
not a bad commute from where I live," he said. "You might take a look."
This said casually; a friendship was developing, but Harry was cautious
about seeming premature.

Lew said, "I was thinking of a house." He sat tilted back in his desk
chair looking up at Harry.

"Buying one?"

"Hell, no; renting."

Harry shrugged. "Well, you might find one, but it's not easy, and
they're expensive; I tried. I like a house, I grew up in a house."

"Me, too."

"I like the extra room, and walking around my own place any way I
want, indoors or out, belching and scratching my ass."

"Yeah, we had a big yard; attic; full basement. My dad still had a sled
he owned as a kid in the attic, a Flexible Flyer. And I had a twenty-two
rifle range in the basement."

"I had a darkroom. We even had two spare bedrooms upstairs just for
company. My father didn't make a lot of money either, but you could
have a house then; everybody did. Well, maybe you'll be lucky. You got
your own furniture?" Lew shook his head. "People don't generally rent
their houses furnished any more, Lew; they get wrecked. But see what
you can do, and then if you want, drop in and look over the apartments
where we are. Meet Shirley, and we'll show you around."

"Can I bring a friend?"

"Sure, of course." Harry nodded, and turned to the door, careful to
show no curiosity.

Talking of that time—Jo moving about the room putting small things
away, shutting drawers, closing the closet—they agreed that the move to
Marin had worked out well. The two women had liked each other on
sight, though Harry took a little getting used to, she said. Lew and Harry,
and often the four of them, played tennis on the apartment courts. Sierra
skiing was only three hours away; they had all driven up half a dozen
times this last winter. In good weather they went to the county beaches
a lot, Stinson especially. The men had done some skin-diving with rented
equipment; tried surfing and abandoned it, neither having started young
enough to be good. Harry had gotten Lew into climbing, and they had
twice scaled high, almost sheer faces, and descended. Now the two
couples were talking with some seriousness of buying a small sailboat
together. They borrowed each other's books, ate and drank and went to
movies together. But more than what they did, Jo said—she was in bed
now, and they lay with the bedside lamp on, talking—was the way each

of the four enjoyed the others. "It's more than the usual two-couple friendship, where it's mostly the men or mostly the women who are friends: all four of us are friends. I wouldn't know what to do without them."

"Sure. It's a good life," Lew said, turning on his side to face Jo. "Especially right now," and Jo nodded, smiled, and said, "Yes."

• • •

CHAPTER THREE

• • •

A good life, but four nights later Lew again awakened from what seemed
to him like a sound sleep: for no reason he understood his eyes opened
and immediately he lay fully awake. This time he was with Jo. He could
just hear her slow breathing, and lying quietly, not to disturb her, it
occurred to him to wonder: How long would they stay together?
Months? Years? Immediately he was curious, and lay trying to think
about it clearly. Was this quiet, modest, likable woman someone he could
live with indefinitely? On and on? For the rest of his life? Did he want
to? He couldn't say, and tried to force an answer. He liked Jo very much;
more than anyone else he knew; didn't entirely know why, just did. He
would miss her; he'd do a lot for her, and gladly. He admired her, and
was proud of her. Was all that enough? It didn't sound like it. He tried
another direction: What if she left him? Well, he didn't like that, but
would survi—

What the *hell* was wrong with him? He liked his job—liked it all right,
that is, but could give it up. Liked where they lived, but could leave.
Could give up anything, it seemed. Really? Jo too?

It had to stop, he'd be awake for hours; and he got up very quietly,
almost stealthily. For a moment he stood looking down at Jo, her quiet
breathing still undisturbed. Then he turned away to walk to the balcony
and along it, the wooden floor chill and slightly damp to his bare feet, to
his own apartment. Just before he reached his doors, he glanced over
the railing out at the silent lamplighted mystery of the night beyond it,
and excitement rushed through his body with an intensity—relief and
release—that surprised him. Quickly he got dressed, as before; found his
note, stuck it onto the balcony door, and was free.

Conscious of the silence of the world asleep all around him, he walked
down the driveway. For several seconds he stood at the curb of the
motionless, green-lighted street, looking around him at the night, savor-
ing the moment. Then once again he stepped out.

This time, after a mile past the blank-windowed houses he climbed
up to, and walked the spine of, the great two-hundred-foot-high ridge
dividing Strawberry—looking down at the motionless, miniaturized street
paralleling it, half-dollar-size circles of green light lying on the pavement
under tiny street lamps. Then, at the highest point of the long ridge, he

stopped on impulse, and turned to look back at the freeway, far behind and below him.

He could see a two-mile, almost straight stretch of it; distant pale ribbons visible in the lights from the huge green-and-white direction signs cantilevered over them. Behind the long beams of their headlights two finger-length cars moved swiftly to the north, no sound of their motion reaching him here. A slower cluster of several cars followed, then the long twin stretches of concrete stood empty for a moment. A second cluster appeared and moved across the long length; then, incredibly, for perhaps three or even four minutes the great freeway stood utterly empty from high up the winding of Waldo Grade clear on to the crest of Corte Madera hill. Lew stood staring in astonishment. *"Empty,"* he murmured aloud to himself after a few moments. "My god, look at it. The *freeway*—absolutely *empty.*"

Twice each weekday, from behind his own or Harry Levy's windshield, Lew saw this road filled with commuter traffic, every lane solid with cars. And he had never seen it less than busy. Now it was a delight and a wonder to see the great lighted roadway standing as motionless as though the world had been abandoned. A final half minute passed, Lew grinning with pleasure at the strange, incredible sight. Then tiny headlights appeared up on Waldo, and an instant later two more pairs, one right behind the other on the nearly empty road, popped up over the Corte Madera crest, and Lew turned to walk on, glancing at the familiar shape of Tamalpais Mountain filling the night-time sky to the north and west.

He stopped to look down onto the rooftops of the shopping center, its huge parking lot deserted, its hash-mark parking lines like game-board markings of some sort, under the stars and a high half-moon. Here a tiny breeze pressed his face, and he could just detect the faint sound of the quiet music that flowed all day from speakers up under the roofs of the covered walkways. "Hey," he said, "who forgot to turn off the tape? You're fired! I'm sorry, I know you only had twenty minutes to go before your pension began, but rules are rules. Thank you: I knew you'd understand." Turning an ear toward the wavering distant sound, he tried to make out the tune—"As Time Goes By," he thought but wasn't sure.

Walking on, conscious of the pleasurable bite of the cool night-time air in his lungs, he enjoyed the feeling of superiority of the person awake when all others are asleep. At this thought he stopped and, turning in place, made the full circle, looking out across miles of rooftops, dim in the faint light; out at the lighted freeway and beyond it to lesser lamplit roads; at the dark, empty Marin hills and at huge Mount Tam; across the shining black surface of the Bay to the great new San Francisco towers glittering electrically beyond it. Was it possible that in all this vast area no one but he was awake? No, of course not; the police were awake, and there had to be others—yet it seemed like it. They seemed so helpless, all these thousands unconscious under the pale moonlit rooftops, and Lew stepped to the edge of the slope, facing south, and pulled down his mask-flap.

Arm straight out before him, swinging it back and forth in a slow, wide arc he said, "I . . . am the Avenger! Each night from among you I select one for sacrifice to the ancient gods of Tamalpais! Eeney, meeney, miney"—pointing here and there at random—"mo!" His arm stopped, finger pointing. "Tough luck, Harry." He pulled up his mask and, smiling at himself, walked on, descending now, toward the road and home.

Again, waking in the morning, he felt good, felt rested. Looking over at the inch-wide vertical strip of daylight between Jo's drapes—a coresample of the day, its lower half the sunwashed green of a pine, its upper half a strong blue California sky—he felt suddenly elated, felt *lucky*. Beside him Jo moved, and he turned; she lay facing him, blinking, just awakened. He smiled, she smiled back, and—there wasn't time, but— he slipped an arm under her shoulders and, Jo still drowsy, they moved wordlessly together, a good start for a lucky day.

Lew believed, as everyone does, in lucky streaks, and he watched this one continue at the toll plaza. Harry braked, slowing toward the end of a long line, then glanced quickly at the adjoining line, inexplicably only three cars long. Harry owned a used '67 Alfa Romeo, the best and fastest sport car he could afford, and he yanked the wheel, accelerating, and shot over to the shorter line. Each of the three cars ahead had exact change ready, rolling on past the booth without quite stopping, as did Harry—in the clear within seconds. Harry yelled, "That's the way to screw the common people!" and both smiled at the small triumph.

As always, they left the car at the cheapest parking lot they knew, down at the Embarcadero, a long walk from the office. But today Lew liked it, the sun-warmed air full of promise. Which was kept: an approaching young woman looked boldly and arrogantly from one to the other of their faces; then, in passing, she smiled at Lew alone. He grinned maliciously at Harry, who said, "Near-sighted bitch. Not entirely sane."

Lew began watching the sidewalk with what he felt was the certain knowledge of finding money. Half a block later a car pulled from a parking space beside them, and he stepped down from the curb to pick up a quarter that had been lying under it. "Jesus, you can't lose," Harry said. "Take the day off, and go out to the track; I'll give you my paycheck."

Lew knew these were omens pointing toward some more solid piece of good fortune ahead, which came at ten-thirty. Walking along the wide, green-carpeted corridor hung with Rowaldson prints which led past Partners' Row, he heard, "Oh, Lew, got a second?" It was Willard Briggs, smiling out at him from his desk, and Lew replied silently, *I do indeed have a second*, and turned in. Approaching the small, delicate desk, a valuable antique inlaid at front and sides with porcelain ovals depicting eighteenth-century hunting scenes, he understood that Briggs had been waiting for him inevitably to pass: ordinarily this office door was kept closed. He said, "Morning, Will"—the firm was carefully informal—and sat down at Brigg's gesture.

"Friday I had lunch with Frank Teller," Briggs said immediately. "He told me you worked out a compromise for their problems with the FDA, and that he's had reliable word the FDA is going to accept it after a little noodling around about details. So he's happy, and thinks maybe you earn your money around here."

"That's good to hear." Teller was one of the important vice-presidents of the large pharmaceutical company which was among the firm's best clients, and praise from him was valuable.

Briggs slouched down in his chair, hands clasping behind his neck, the posture flattering, suggesting plenty of time for Lew Joliffe. He was tall and thin, hair parted at the side, graying in front, and he had it all. He wore gray or blue suits and generally, as today, a bow tie. He looked like an eastern-law-school graduate of the forties, although he had always lived in California, and his degree was from Stanford. He was about fifteen years older than Lew. They liked each other, a little tentatively and warily yet, mostly because each occasionally made a small, wry joke the other appreciated. He said, "What about councilman, Lew? You had time to think about it?"

"Well, I checked with City Hall, Will. Found out how you get on the ballot. Nothing to it; you get a few signatures, and pay a twenty-five-buck fee; anyone can run. So I did it." He raised a palm, warding off premature congratulations. "But only because I can always withdraw, Will, by just forfeiting the fee." He frowned, reaching forward to move a finger across the smoothness of one of the porcelain panels. "I'm still not sure. I . . . " He paused, shrugging. "It's just that I'd want to be sure before I began kissing all those germ-laden little babies."

Will nodded. "Well, you've got time to think. How many vacancies coming up on the council?"

"Three."

"Okay"—he sat up decisively. "I've lived in Mill Valley all my life. So has my family, since the town was called Eastland. And between me and some friends we can give you some pretty good help. I think you might just pick up one of those seats your first time out." Hands folded on his desk top, he sat staring at Lew, apparently appraising him. Lew had seen him do this in a courtroom with a witness for as long as a minute; it could be intimidating. "I was a Mill Valley councilman myself," he said then. "As I've told you. Sixteen years ago. Two terms, and they led directly to my running for and being elected to the state assembly. Also for two terms. I didn't do a hell of a lot there, frankly, but . . . " He paused, spreading his hands, palms up. "It got me known. To some of the people who run things, to put it plainly. I hope that wasn't the only reason I got my partnership, but it sure helped. I might not have got it otherwise; I just might have missed out."

He sat forward, letting the weight of his arms sprawl loosely on the desk top, shoulders slumping so that his coat collar rose a little in back. This posture said that while there was still no hurry, that he still had plenty of time yet for Lew if Lew had something to say, the meeting was otherwise ending. "You know what I'm telling you, Lew. If it's what you want, and you work it right, I think eventually you can be something around here. You're twenty-nine, aren't you?"

"Yes, sir." It was time for a *sir* now.

"Well, that's young. If you're on the move. Not so young if you aren't. So think by all means. But think hard, and think soon."

Sitting on the balcony over drinks before dinner, Lew told Jo about the conversation, watching her eyes begin to blink with excitement, seeing her smile with pleasure. Lew *had* to run for councilman, she said then, *had to*, and when he didn't reply but just smiled, she said, "Well, *don't* you?"

"I guess so; looks like it. I was just trying to think what campaigning would mean. My god!—I'd have to have bumper strips, wouldn't I."

"Of course!" She clapped her hands in excitement, and stood up to lean back against the rail, facing him. She wore an old denim skirt and a worn white blouse spotted with india ink. "Saying what? 'Jolly Lew Joliffe . . . ' "

" 'Jolly Lew Joliffe, Your Jolly New Pol'?"

"Too long."

"Use two cars." He stood, taking her empty glass from the rail. "How

about, 'Jolly Lew Joliffe: He serves the People Right.'" He walked in
with the two glasses.

After dinner Jo worked, and Lew, changed into Levi's and sport shirt,
walked over to the Levys' to see what Harry was doing. Their apartment
was identical with his and with Jo's; the furniture rented, like theirs;
chosen in minutes from a glossy printed catalog supplied by the apartments' rental office. This was page after page of color photographs of
modern furniture to be ordered by groups with names such as Studio,
Design Contemporary, Nob Hill, Domani, Capri, Budget. Lew's and
Jo's had arrived by truck the next day, new or seeming to be, and had
been set up in both apartments in under thirty minutes. Its rental they
paid monthly, part of the same check as the rents. Jo had picked Budget,
also renting dishes and cooking equipment; Lew took Design Contemporary and a television set; the Levys' was Heritage.

Lew and Harry sat out on the balcony talking desultorily. Behind
them, at the all-purpose card table, Shirley sat writing a letter to Harry's
parents. Rafe had come out to lie between Lew's and Harry's chairs and,
his arm dangling, Lew scratched his ears.

Again Harry spoke of the four of them buying a sailboat, and Lew
nodded and said yeah, it might be fun. "If I could just sell the stupid
camper," Harry said. "Worst buy I ever made; half worn out, and
underpowered to begin with. Useless for the mountains, and where else
would I use it. Two hundred bucks and it's yours, Lew."

"Well, I might trade you some skin-diving equipment. Or camping
stuff. Or a pair of cross-country skis or some climbing equipment. Harry,
we buy this stuff, we buy the stupid equipment, get all buzzed up about
it, then our interest fades. You're stuck with a no-good camper. The
skin-diving's through; we know it. We still talk about climbing some
more, but don't seem to get around to it. And now it's a sailboat. What
are we *doing?*"

"Looking for a little excitement, I suppose. It's a pretty tame life all in
all, and there's a little risk, not a lot but some, in diving, climbing, even
skiing. And we'd probably find some in sailing; get outside the Gate in
a small boat and it can get a little lively, I've heard. Trouble is, Lew, you
have to expand. Dive, and pretty soon you want to start going deeper.
Maybe get into treasure hunting. Climb, and at first it's fun just learning.
Then fun getting pretty good. But after you've gone up the local cliffs
and rappelled down a few times, and then the High Sierras and maybe
Yosemite Valley, why, I guess it's the Himalayas next or forget it. That's
how it works with me anyway. You were in on the protest stuff at

Berkeley, weren't you?" Lew nodded. "Well, I was still at Illinois, and there wasn't too much doing. How'd you like it?"

"I liked it. Might have kept on, if there'd been anywhere to go with it."

"Well, some did go on; the so-called revolutionaries. But do you think they really believe the country is on the edge of revolt? Just waiting for them to push it over? With a few well-timed explosions? They know better—Lew, they're playing, too! They hide out, sneak around in disguises, plant bombs, send tapes to radio stations, have safe houses—because it's *fun*. A way to hold off the god-damn boredom of just slogging away at a job. And what we do is acquire a closet full of sports equipment. But don't let it get you; so do plenty of other people. It's why sports are so big. Everywhere in the world. Anyway, it's only money, and what good will that be in another ten years or so? So think about the boat, Lew; we'll watch the ads, and maybe pick one up cheap this winter."

Lew stayed with Jo again that night, and as he lay back against the headboard, wearing the gray pajamas in which he'd walked along the balcony from his apartment, she moved about the room in a yellow nightgown, tidying. In all she did Jo was neat: working, her tools lay arranged in order in a wide semicircle, her board kept clear of scraps. Now she folded those of her clothes which were to be washed; set her shoes onto the built-in closet rack; closed the closet door till the latch clicked; crossed to the built-in dressing table and screwed the lid onto a jar of cream. Lew sat staring ahead, and presently Jo glanced at him, and said, "What are you thinking?"

"Oh"—he turned to look at her. "Nothing. Just remembering a trip I took when I was a kid. With my folks. On a train."

After a moment she said, "Where to?"

"I don't know; I don't remember. But we spent a night in a Pullman. In a compartment or whatever it's called; three berths, and they gave me the lower so I could look out the window. In the middle of the night, maybe two or three in the morning, I woke up, and of course I raised the blind. I couldn't see much, just blackness. Then we tore through a little town—fast, racing through, the train making time at night. I had a quick flash of a little street, a row of wooden houses and big trees in the light from street lamps; and just a glimpse down a little empty main street. And heard the crossing bell: you know the sound: DING, *ding*, ding, ding, ding, fading away fast.

"Then suddenly I saw something. We zipped into and out of that little town; I don't even know what state it was in: Illinois, Iowa. And right away the houses became more and more scattered, the street lights gone, just a bare bulb hanging high over the cross roads, the corn fields beginning again. And at the very edge of town or maybe just past it, we suddenly passed the back of a house and a little yard right beside the tracks. And there up on a wire was an impossible sight. Two spotlights were angled up from the ground to the wire, and they made a little blaze of light up there in the sky, everything around it solid black night. And in that circle of light a man in white tights sat riding a bicycle across the wire. He had a long pole balanced across the handlebars, and a woman in white tights with long blond hair stood on his shoulders, balancing with a parasol.

"They saw me: watching the train flash by below them, they caught a glimpse of me staring up at them from my berth, lying on my stomach, face at the window, and they smiled, and were gone in the blink of an eye. Vanished; nothing but blackness outside my window, and I could hardly believe I'd seen what I had."

Lew turned to look at her. Jo lay in bed now, facing him, listening. "Who were they?"

"Circus people, I suppose: they had to live somewhere. And that's where these two lived. They were practicing."

"In the middle of the night?"

"Probably didn't want spectators."

"What did your parents say?"

"I didn't tell them. I was afraid they'd say I'd been dreaming. And would convince me I had been."

Jo pulled the light blanket up over her bare shoulder. "It isn't true, is it, Lew."

"No." He smiled at her. For a long time she'd recognized this trait: of occasionally spinning out a fantasy to her or others, making it as believable as he could. If it were accepted he'd let it stand, but would answer truthfully if questioned. She didn't understand why he did this, and sometimes it amused her, sometimes worried her, but she had come to associate it with some uneasiness he was feeling, perhaps now at the prospect of running for city council.

• • •

CHAPTER FOUR

• • •

The night of his third walk Lew slept in his own apartment. When his eyes opened at two twenty, by the green hands of his alarm, he knew that this time he'd actually been waiting for it in his sleep. Flipping the coverings aside, knowing what he was about to do, an excitement shot through him sharp as a touch of flame. Dressing, staring at his face in the mirrorlike window pane, it occurred to him, troubling him a little, that the intensity of his pleasure at again going out into the compelling mystery that drew him there was greater than at anything else that had happened to him all that week.

This time, stepping out onto the asphalt from the driveway, he turned right. Tonight a small breeze pressed his face, the leaves rattling overhead, and as he walked he consciously inhaled, pulling the cool air, medicinally touched with eucalyptus, in through his flared nostrils, feeling it as clean. Possibly the air *was* very nearly pure just now, the air moving in from the ocean, with no traffic. Arms swinging, legs striding easily, Lew looked up into the unending blackness of the sky, the stars a hard, electric blue, and was happy again. Passing each of the other apartment buildings, he glanced at their blank dark windows, listening to the steady scuff of his rubber soles, and felt himself alive and alone in this silent new world.

Following the Bay shore, he walked to the freeway, hearing the occasional air-rush of a fast car as he approached, usually followed by silence, the traffic at low ebb. Then, crossing the empty frontage road, stepping up onto the curb, stopping at the seven-foot wire fence, he reached it, U.S. 101. In the faint starlight, fingers hooked onto the diamonds of the fence mesh, he stood staring out at the concrete slab. Far to the north the tail lights of a car moved up the Corte Madera hill, then winked out over its crest, and now the long road stood empty; he could see possibly two miles of it from the Corte Madera crest north to the Richardson Bay bridge south.

The freeway lay there enormously, just before him, in semi-darkness except for large brightly lighted patches under the great direction signs. In the pale even light from the stars he could see separate oil spots at the edges of the dark streaks down the centers of the lanes. In the utterly black no-man's land between the two roadways, the wooden posts and metal scrape-rails stood up sharp against the paleness of the lanes beyond them.

Lew stood fascinated at the motionlessness of the great freeway. Seconds passed, yet these two miles of concrete emptiness continued to stand without motion or sound. It seemed impossible; like staring at a frozen Niagara. Or as though, coming from another world, he stood watching a motionless, mysteriously lighted expanse whose purpose was beyond understanding.

Something moved. He heard it, and his head swung to stare north. Silence, then again the stillness broken by a small sound, a gravelly scraping. Lew searched for and found the movement: a formless, solid-black small bulk crossing the slightly lesser blackness of the shoulder fifty yards to the north—an animal of some sort. Waddling, it moved onto the pale concrete, a skunk or small raccoon, too slow for a dog or cat. Lew jammed his toe into the fence mesh, and pulled himself up onto the fence to stare over its top.

Without hurry the swaying bulk moved across the three lanes of concrete, disappeared into the blackness of the median strip. A small sound, dull and metallic; the creature squeezing under the wide band of the scrape-rail. Silence; Lew felt his heart beat in his eardrums. Then the animal reappeared on the other roadway. Leisurely it crossed the lanes there, was absorbed into the darkness, and again the night-time world stood motionless and still.

Clinging to the fence, Lew stared after the vanished animal, astonished at the thought which had just occurred to him: that, incredibly, it was possible for him to go out there too. For a moment he hesitated, then heaved himself higher, arms straightening, elbows locking, to support his weight. Swinging a leg over, he straddled for an instant, then swung the other leg over and pushed off, landing crouched on the shoulder. There he hesitated—as though a whistle might blow or a voice shout. Then he stood erect, walked forward, and as his foot touched the concrete, he grinned.

Looking both ways, he walked cautiously to the center lane: except for road workers in fluorescent vests he had never seen anyone walk out onto a freeway, not a busy commute-route. Yet here he stood, grinning. He turned to face south, the direction of oncoming traffic if there had been any, pulled down his face mask, and thumped his chest: "Come on, you bastards, it's Superman," he said softly, the sound of his voice out here startling.

Still grinning, he walked in a great, irregular circle from edge to edge of the pavement, feeling the eerie experience of tramping this forbidden territory. He stopped, glanced around, then did it again, stamping his feet, making a loud, slapping sound. But in no matter what direction he walked, making the circle, his head slowly turned to keep his eyes to the direction of oncoming traffic: being out here was a little frightening.

Still no car appeared, the long lull continuing, and he sat down in the center lane, wrapped his arms around his knees, and sat staring down the freeway through the eyeholes of his mask; a foreshortened, strangely close view, the surface of the concrete rougher than he'd supposed. He sat back, arms behind him, palms on the pavement, supporting his weight. For what he thought must be a full minute he sat watching, ready to scramble to his feet: something *had* to come along. But nothing did. Slowly, working up his nerve, he lay back—watching ahead, straining for the first far-off intimation of an approaching car—till his shoulder blades touched the concrete behind him. But he couldn't bring himself to lower his head. Chin pressing chest, head upright, he lay on his back staring at the darkness for the first flash of headlights. Then he forced himself to lie back completely, ears intent, till the back of his cap touched the pavement. For an instant he lay staring straight up at the immense scatter of stars, then his head jerked up again.

But he knew that in this utter silence he would hear a car long before it could reach this spot, and he made himself lie back once more, clasping his hands under the back of his cap, lifting ankle to knee top in a deliberate posture of relaxation. Ears hyperalert, he stared into the infinite distance searching for the Big Dipper, and in his mind he saw himself from above, a tiny figure lying on a great paved expanse. Aloud, imitating a cop's voice, he said, *"Hey, you!* What the hell you think you're doing!" In his own voice, slightly muffled by the cap, he replied in mild surprise at the obviousness of the question: "Why . . . I'm lying on the freeway, Officer."

"What for! What's amatter with you! You some kinda creep!?"

"Why . . . I'm doing it for fun. To break the awful monotony of life; surely you understand? Why the fuck don't you climb down out of that pig van, and try it yourself?"

"You're under arrest!"

"What for, pork chop, what's the charge? Freeway-lying? *Malicious* freeway-lying? Crossing state lines with intent to lounge on the surface of an interstate free—" A sound cut his voice off, a scrape against the metal fencing beside the road, and Lew sat up fast.

A woman stood watching him from the other side of the fence; she had a small dog on a leash, his front paws up on the meshing, staring at Lew. After a moment Lew said, "Hi." She didn't answer, just stood staring, and he knew she was frightened. *And why not?* he thought. He felt certain that if he stood up she'd turn and run screaming, and he slowly drew up his knees, and put his arms around them, one hand loosely clasping the other wrist in the most relaxed unthreatening posture he could find. Then he sat waiting for her to find her voice, and after another moment or two of motionless staring she did.

Voice tight with the strain of trying to sound calm, she said, "May I ask what you're doing out there?" The dog had lost interest, dropping to the ground to sniff the dirt.

"Oh," Lew said slowly, and shrugged, "I couldn't sleep, I got bored." Would this make any least sense? "And decided to take a w—"

"Lew? Lew, is that *you?*"

"Yes—*Shirley?*" He yanked up his face mask.

"Oh, for godsake. *Yes*, it's me! What in the *world* are you doing?"

He stood up quickly, and walked toward her. "Well, as any fool can see, I'm freeway-lying. Malicious freeway-lying with intent to amaze and astound." Grinning, he stopped at the fence: Shirley smiling at him through the mesh, her head slowly shaking in disbelief. She wore a red scarf tied under her chin, a belted raincoat faded almost white, and plaid wool pants. "Lew, what in heaven's name *are* you doing?"

"I don't know, Shirl." He stood, still grinning at her, pleased with the encounter. "Looking the world over, I guess, in the one time when it's a little different. *Look* at that." He flung out his arm, gesturing at the freeway.

"I know: welcome to the club. Every once in a while I've come wandering down here on a white night. But it never occurred to me to wear a mask or lie on the freeway. Do you do it often?"

"First time. I've been out a couple other times, but this is my first on the freeway. Come on and try it." He grinned. "It's fun; tie Rafe to the fence."

"You serious?"

"Sure."

"All right." Stooping, she thrust the leash end through a bottom loop of the fencing, tied it, and the dog lay down, muzzle on forepaws. Shirley seized the fence, pushing a toe into the mesh, and sprang up, arms straightening, as agilely as Lew had. But she hadn't scaled fences like this as a child and didn't know how to get over. Cautiously, she tried to lie along the fence top, an arm and a leg on each side. Lew reached up quickly, got one hand on her shoulder, the other on her hip, and held her in place. She switched both hands to the mesh on his side, and tried to lower herself with Lew's help, but a button and her belt buckle snagged on top.

Lew said, "I've got you good; you won't fall. Let go with your hands, and untangle yourself." She did; then slowly rolled off the fence top into Lew's arms. He liked it; there was a moment when she lay smiling up at him which he wanted to prolong, but he set her on her feet, and as they touched the ground the electric dots of a pair of headlights appeared on Richardson Bay bridge to the south. Her ankle twisted on a small rock and, Lew trying to support her, they both half fell, half sat down, tangled together and laughing. "Stay down." Lew nodded at the approaching car. It was coming fast, its lights now touching the roadway before them, strangely close at this level. Lew yanked down his mask, then turned up the collar of Shirley's coat. "Sit close; make one silhouette." They huddled together quickly, the car no more than a hundred yards away. "Don't move." Their eyes following the car, they sat motionless, and it flashed past in the inner fast lane, the driver never glancing their way. An instant later the wind of its passing touched their faces, and as Lew turned to grin at Shirley, yanking his face mask up, she swung to face him, eyes gleeful.

"Yow!" She jumped up, ran out to the inner lane, put a fist on one hip and, raising the other high, wrist bent, did a nimble, defiant little jig behind the diminishing red lights of the car. "I don't *believe* it," she yelled. "This is wild!" She sat down on the inner lane, facing south.

Lew walking out to her, she started to lie back as he had done. Instead, scrambling on the pavement, she changed her position to lie, not lengthwise, but across the width of the lane, head toward the center of the road, feet near the dirt of the median strip. She lay back on the concrete then, but her face was turned south: "I've simply *got* to see if a car's coming."

"Right." He lay down across the center lane, feet toward the mesh fence, in upside-down relation to Shirley, only their heads side by side. She turned to look back at him over her shoulder, saw his inverted face, and giggled. Lew said, "Hey, you're on watch! They come fast this time of night," and she turned quickly to face south again.

Lew rolled to his back, clasping his hands under his head, and stared up at the stars. "Well?" Shirley said. "How's your lane? Comfy?"

"Great. Yours?"

"Just dandy." She planted an elbow on the concrete, propped her head on her palm, and lay on her side, watching. Lew turned to look through the triangle formed by her bent arm, head, and neck: nothing was coming, the smudged white of the road fading into darkness far ahead to the south. Again he lay back to stare straight up, and at the movement Shirley glanced over her shoulder at him, then turned swiftly onto her stomach, smiling down at him. On impulse, glancing first to the south, she bent down and kissed him, then lifted her head again. "First time I ever kissed anyone upside down—it's weird. But nice."

Lew reached up, drew her face down, and they kissed again, this time longer, a strange and suddenly exciting experience to Lew. She drew away, and turned to her side once more, propping her head on her hand to watch the road again, her back to him. "Me, too," Lew said. "I know you won't believe this, but it's the very first time I ever kissed a girl upside down while lying on a freeway."

"You've led a sheltered life. There are all sorts of firsts we could establish if we could be sure a car wouldn't come. Imagine: right here on the freeway!"

"Be marvelous. On the freeway or anywhere else with you." In a parody voice he said, "There! I've said it at last."

"Oh, you've said it before; this is just the first time out loud." She glanced back at him, smiling. "Think of the accident report if we were run over!"

"I don't think my Blue Cross covers it." He sat up, swinging around to sit beside her, forearms lying on his upraised knees, hands dangling. Shirley pulled herself up, and they sat side by side, staring down the road.

She said, "I used to sit on the floor like this with my brother watching television when we were kids. 'The Mickey Mouse Club.'"

"So did I. M-i-c . . ."

"K-e-y . . ."

Then, both joining in the familiar slow, sad tune, they sang, "M-o-u-s-e, Mickey Mouse . . . Mickey Mouse . . ." Faces solemn, staring ahead, they let the last note die, then Lew yelled, "*Hey, kids!* It's 'Howdy Doody' time!" Shouting, they sang, "It's Howdy DOO-dy time! It's Howdy DOO-dy time! It's time to watch the show! Come on, let's—" Lew gripped Shirley's forearm; a far-off, high, mechanical whine had touched the air, and they turned toward the other side of the freeway to look north. Just over the crest of the Corte Madera hill far behind them, they saw the slow-moving headlights and yellow toplight pattern of a trailer truck, and Lew stood, reaching a hand down to help Shirley up. "Road's getting busy as hell. We better get off while we can."

The truck whine slowly growing, they walked hand in hand to the shoulder, and Lew glanced south: a pair of headlights had appeared there, too. Facing the road, they stood watching them grow, the car moving fast in the inner lane. When it was two hundred yards off, Lew stepped out into the slow lane, and Shirley followed.

He pulled down his mask, and Shirley turned up her coat collar, yanked her scarf off, and with clawed fingers combed her hair down over her face. Hunching her shoulders, she drew her neck and chin down below the buttoned-up top of her coat. The approaching car was less than the length of a football field away, the pavement before them brightening. Suddenly it slowed as the driver spotted them, brakes squealing slightly.

The car still slowing, the driver leaning across the seat to stare, Lew and Shirley stood utterly motionless. Then Lew swung to face the oncoming car, rising high on his toes, arms shooting straight up, hands dangling, in classical Dracula pose. Only a hair-covered knob rising above Shirley's coat collar, she extended both arms out at her sides, elbows loose, forearms and hands hanging limp, and began stumping about in a small circle, bent-kneed, as though blind. A dozen yards off now, the face of the staring driver a white blur behind his windshield, the car accelerated, its front end rising, and shot past them.

Shirley screamed, a wild, cackling, banshee laugh, and Lew slowly revolved on the balls of his feet to continue facing the car, arms high. He held the pose, Shirley continuing her mindless stumping—and safely up ahead now the car's brake lights glowed, the car slowing, then it stopped. Through its rear window they saw the white shape of the driver's face looking back at them. Lew ran down the freeway toward the car as hard as he could go, arms still raised, angling over to the fast lane, rubber soles slapping the pavement. The brake lights went out, the car bucked forward, and sped on, and Lew turned to walk back to Shirley, laughing, pulling his face mask up.

He helped Shirley up onto the fence, her foot in his linked hands. When she got part way up, a toe in the mesh, his hands gripped her waist to lift her higher. Directly across the freeway behind him he heard the truck's diesel, and as he shifted one hand from Shirley's waist to her rump, boosting her to the top, he glanced over his shoulder. Leaning far out of his cab, the driver was watching them, and he reached forward, grabbed his air-horn rope, and blasted it twice. Balanced on top of the fence, Shirley turned her head, saw him, and waved. The driver waved back wildly, then reached forward again to give them a final toot.

They walked home, Rafe off his leash, sometimes following, sometimes ahead; sniffing, wetting the bushes. Following the shoreline, passing between the two- and three-story wooden apartment buildings on each side of the road here, Lew said, "Do you realize we're surrounded by dozens of unconscious bodies? Except for a few thin walls we could see them—lying motionless, some of them twenty feet up in the air, eyes closed, slowly breathing, not five yards away on either side of the road."

"That's spooky."

"I know."

Sighing, she said, "Oh, Lord, this has been silly. And fun; such fun."

For a time they walked on in silence, around the bend beside the black Bay. Then Shirley said, "Lew, what else have you done? On your walks." He told her; she listened, occasionally nodding as though in agreement; and when presently the curved line of their own apartment buildings came into view, she stopped and gripped his forearm. "Lew, let's *all* of us do this! Harry'd love it. I know he would! The Night People! So would Jo. Let's! Okay?"

He felt a sudden pang of loss, deepening as he stood searching for something to reply that would restore it. Then he knew it was too late, the solitariness of his night-time walks already gone. "Sure," he said slowly. "I guess so."

"Great." They walked on. "Maybe a few nights from now: okay? We'll get together, and figure it out."

At the driveway between their two buildings Shirley snapped her fingers for Rafe, and they turned to walk up it. "I'll never sleep," she murmured quietly, then smiled. "I'm going to wake Harry up, and tell him! All about this! I can't possibly wait till morning."

Lew grinned. "Be sure to—wake him up right away. Shake him if you have to. And tell him I said to. G'night, Shirl."

"'Night, Lew. Such fun. So much fun. Come on, Rafe."

CHAPTER FIVE

• • •

Jo listened at breakfast as Lew told her about his night-time walks; of meeting Shirley last night; and of what Shirley had proposed—listened, eyes and hands busy, buttering toast, rearranging dishes and plates. "Well," she said when he'd finished, not looking at him, hands still busy, "that's fascinating. Secret walks. In the dead of night. And I didn't even know!" she said brightly, finally looking up at him.

He made his voice mild. "They weren't exactly secret, Jo; I'd have told you soon enough. And if you'd ever happened to wake up, and come over to my place, you'd have seen the note on my door."

"Of course. More coffee?" Without waiting for an answer she began to pour. Eyes on the hot black stream, she said, "But I *could* wish I'd known before Shirley."

"Running into Shirley was an accident."

"Yes, I know." Holding his eyes, she leaned toward him over the table. "Listen: any time you get bored with me, in or out of bed, you mustn't be bashful. Just mention it, and with a quick handshake and a twisted little smile I'll be out of your life before you can say 'Jo, it's been great.' "

"I will, I'll do that. But that's hard to imagine. Not quite possible, in fact."

She looked down instantly, finding a crumb that needed flicking. "You're what my father calls a 'bullshit artist.' "

"I'll just bet he does. What a phrasemaker."

"The only time you'd miss me is maybe at breakfast." She handed him a piece of toast. "When you had to butter your own toast."

"You're crazy: I worship you."

She nodded.

"That cynical quirk of the mouth isn't justified. The fact is—you know those big religious paintings? Where the saints all wear—not halos: those big golden discs around their heads."

"Nimbuses. Nimbi."

"Thank you. Well, when I imagine you naked, as I often do—sitting around at work or right now, for example—I see you wearing not one but several golden nimbuses. Not around your head—"

"All right."

"Three of them. Gold, and beautifully polished."

"And you?"

"Just one for me. And only silver. Sterling, though. And hallmarked."

"Sounds pretty cumbersome."

"Not at all. Be like cymbals. Clashing musically while a choir of angels sings 'The Hallelujah Chorus.' "

"Is that what they mean by making beautiful—"

"Exactly, as I'll be glad to demonstrate. Right now."

"No, you won't, bullshit artist. And maybe never again, either. I'd hate to scratch my nimbi."

They finished breakfast, Lew reading the news section of the *Chronicle* while Jo read Herb Caen. As Lew walked toward the balcony doors to return to his apartment for his suit coat, Jo called to him, and he turned. She said, "They *were* secret, weren't they? The walks."

He puffed out his cheeks with a breath, held it a moment, then released a little sighing pop of air. "I guess so. Yeah, I guess so, Jo, I don't know. But I'd have told you eventually."

"I know. But meanwhile I'm curious: why so secret?"

"Well." He began walking back toward the table. "I've always liked the notion of some secret way to walk off into another world: I was a natural for *Lost Horizon*. I've got a paperback copy, and every once in a while I reread the Shangri La parts." He stood looking down at her. "And when I was a kid I ate up the Oz books, though I can't say I enjoyed them: I didn't like it that there really wasn't any such place. But I couldn't stop reading them. I think the closest I ever actually came to whatever the hell I thought I wanted, was in Illinois when it would snow at night. You'd wake up and you'd know the moment you opened your eyes, because the ceiling was different: the light reflected up onto it from the new snow outside. And it moved; shimmered like water reflections. The sounds from the street would be changed, too, and you'd get up and look out, and for once it was true: the world *had* changed. Into something different and better, or it seemed like it."

"Were you unhappy?"

"No! Hell, no; I had a good time as a kid. I miss snow. I like California all right, but I still feel a little alien out here. Probably always would. There aren't any falls or springs, and even winter isn't much different from summer except that it rains. A few years ago I got so hungry for snow—real snow, not Sierra snow—it was during the Christmas *holidays*, for godsake, yet it was warm and sunny—that I flew back to Chicago. Just bought a ticket, and went. It was great. It was snowing when I got off the plane. Few hours later it turned colder, and I wasn't really dressed for it, and the slush froze, but it was still good to see things covered with white. I got a cab, and went out to my parents' house; I thought I'd ask whoever lived in it if I could come in, and look around, but I didn't; just sat in the cab across the street, and looked."

"Why didn't you go in?"

"It was the wrong color." He smiled. "It was a frame house, and we always painted it brown, but now it was peach. And the yard was different. They'd put in some ornamental fencing, iron pipes with low chains slung between them; and there was a new concrete walk around the side, and a new front door. It wasn't our house any more. Anyway, I was satisfied. I'd seen snow, and I flew back next morning. I met you not long after." He looked at his watch. "Jo, some people are just never satisfied with the way things are, that's all. They're a boring bunch; they talk about snow a lot." He shrugged. "You just keep hoping for the big *difference* some day. And that's about as close as I can come to what I liked about the walks at night."

"When I was a girl I always liked the idea of a summerhouse. I'd seen pictures: the little lath and scrollwork places you'd go off to by yourself on a long 1890 kind of summer afternoon. I'd still like one. Maybe I'll make one when I get time. For The Town." She stood up, kissed him quickly, a little peck, and said, "You'll be late for work."

Harry Levy sat waiting at the wheel of his Alfa as Lew settled himself into the bucket seat beside him. Lew slammed the door, Harry turned onto the driveway, onto the road, then he glanced at Lew, face expressionless. "I hear you've been fooling around with my wife. In the middle of the night. In the middle of the freeway."

"That's right." Lew kept his face equally expressionless, not wanting to anticipate a joke Harry might not be making. "I didn't think you'd mind." He looked at Harry, intentionally meeting his eyes, then looked past him at Richardson Bay: they were moving along its edge.

"Oh, I don't. It was *hearing* about it in the middle of the night that I objected to. I'm told you were all for breaking the news to me at 3 A.M." He smiled, and Lew did, too, relieved.

"Right. Usually the husband is the last to know, but I wanted you to be first."

"Damn white of you. Lew, what *is* this? Shirl says you run around Strawberry night after night in some kind of clown suit, and that we're all supposed to join in the fun. That right?"

"More or less."

Harry nodded. "Well, okay. Try anything once."

Sitting on Jo's balcony Saturday afternoon drinking lemonade after tennis, they agreed to go out on Monday night: too many people were out late on weekends, Lew said—the women nodding, Harry listening skeptically—and the essence of this was the deserted quality of the night. "Play hell with sleep on a work night," Harry said, but shrugged and agreed.

Their alarms having rung in the darkness of their bedrooms some minutes before, the two couples met on the driveway between their buildings at two thirty. Glancing doubtfully around in the dim light from the stars and a partial moon, they exchanged semiwhispered greetings. Then Harry, Jo, and even Shirley stood waiting apathetically, shoulders hunched against the lingering pull of interrupted sleep. Jo wore her white Irish knit sweater and tasseled cap, Lew's red daypack containing a thermos of coffee strapped to her back; Shirley again in bleached raincoat, and pants, though without a scarf tonight; Lew in the clothes he'd worn on other nights; Harry wore a black baseball cap and green nylon jacket, fists tucked up into the slanted breast pockets of his jacket. Their interest, Lew saw, was minimal now, and he felt resentful: these walks at night had been his alone, he hadn't asked them to join him. "Well, let's go," he muttered, and walked down the driveway. Turning right, toward the shoreline road, he led them straggling down the silent street past the dark apartments.

It wasn't the same: Lew knew it the moment his foot touched the street. The blank-windowed buildings beside them offered no suggestion now of the mystery he had felt out here alone, but looked only as they ought to, the people inside them sensibly and enviably asleep. Plodding along, heads down, the others didn't even glance up at them, and Lew felt tired, wishing he were home, and thought irritably of stopping right here to call it all off.

But Jo tucked her arm under his, and he smiled at her. And after a mile, climbing and descending the hilly shoreline road winding along beside Richardson Bay, they warmed up, awakened, and when Lew abruptly turned off the road onto a level stretch of empty ground at the left, Shirley said, "What? Hey, where we going?" and he felt the interest in her voice.

"You'll see."

As they crossed the leveled stretch, there loomed up ahead the tree-covered dark bulk of Silva Island, facing a cove of this far north end of Richardson Bay. Harry said, "Hey, nice work, fuehrer; I've never been over there." They stopped. At their feet between them and the island shore lay an eight-foot ditch shaded by the overhanging branches of a large tree on the island shore. Through this ditch a shallow tide-water pond, a bird sanctuary just to the north at their right, drained and refilled; four storklike white birds stood in its shallows, stick-legged, heads tucked under their wings. "What now?" said Shirley. "Wait for the ferry?" But Harry stood leaning forward over the ditch, reaching. Then his hand found the rope suspended over the water from a tree limb; used, as he and Lew had often seen driving home from work, by boys of the neighborhood.

Rope in hand, Harry walked back a dozen feet, then turned and tugged on it hard, leaning far back, testing his weight against it. He stood erect, regripped the rope as far up as he could, then leaped high, drawing his legs up, and swung forward toward them, past them, and out over the ditch. He landed running, paying the rope out, braking with his feet. He shoved the rope back, and Lew caught it.

The women swung across, Jo as agile and skilled as Shirley, Lew was pleased to see. He followed, lifting his legs almost straight overhead to cross hanging upside down, landing with the short run and graceful bowing stop of a circus acrobat, and Shirley said, "Toss him a fish."

"All set?" Lew murmured. They stood under the tree, deep in its shadows, trespassers now, the island privately owned by the four or five families who lived on it, the uninvited not welcome. A few feet ahead, dim in the starlight, lay the narrow road which ran the length of the whalebacked little island. They walked to its edge, and stood listening. As Lew was about to step out, Harry stepped out first, and they followed, feet carefully noiseless, looking curiously at the few widely scattered old houses. The island thick with old trees, the ground under them lay sparsely grown, heavily leaf-covered. The old houses, individually oriented, stood at various ground levels, and with outbuildings. It was a country landscape in miniature, remote and rural seeming although the freeway lay only a few hundred yards ahead. "Love to live here," Jo whispered over Shirley's shoulder, and Shirley turned eagerly: "Oh, yes!"

Ascending the whaleback, they watched apprehensively but no dog came racing toward them, no light flashed on, no shout sounded. Silva was no longer truly an island: when the old highway had been expanded into the present multiple-lane freeway, the strip of bay water between island and shore had been filled in to expand the roadway. Now, a hundred yards ahead, at the end of the island road, lay the service road beside the freeway, and having seen Silva undetected, they were free to walk off it. Instead, hardly knowing in advance that he was going to, Lew turned abruptly to his left, down toward the houses. "Hey!" one of the women called in a whisper, but he walked on, downhill toward the shore. Behind him, feet scuffling the fallen leaves, he heard the others follow.

Passing between two of the houses in straggling single file, they reached the shore, stepping out onto a tiny beach. Far ahead across the long reach of black water lay night-time Sausalito, a few scattered lights on the dark slope of its hills. "What're we *doing* here?" Jo whispered urgently, and Lew turned, smiling in the faint light, and reaching to the pack on her back. "Exploring a newly discovered island. Sit down."

Embedded on the rocky little beach, a bleached log lay half exposed, and as Lew passed out Styrofoam cups and unscrewed the thermos lid, they sat alternately looking out at the view, and glancing behind them. But no sound or movement came from the dark houses up the slope to the rear, the nearest of them fifty yards off; and presently, sipping coffee, they sat in a row looking far ahead across the shining dark water. A new view for them, they identified the black shape of Alcatraz beyond Sausalito, and beyond it the shoreline lights of San Francisco's Embarcadero. Shooting out ruler-straight from the Embarcadero, the glowing yellow beads of the Bay Bridge lay across the blackness, red pinpricks blinking above them. "This is fun," Jo said, and Shirley nodded above the white of her cup: they sat side by side between the men. "I know. But a little scary." She glanced behind her.

Harry pointed ahead and, voice low, said, "Those are the drydocks, right?"

Lew followed Harry's point; far out on the Bay he saw the tiny, slightly blacker rectangle near the Sausalito shore. "Yeah." They all knew the drydocks, standing in four identical open-ended sections stranded in the shallow water before the town: they'd been a part of the scene for years, a landmark of southern Marin. Small though they looked from here, the docks were enormous; four pairs of towering wooden walls rising up out of the Bay from their rotted-out bottoms sunk in the mud.

"Quiet night like this you could row out there easy," Harry murmured. "Wouldn't be far from Sausalito." Lew nodded. In his mind he saw the scene movie-style, externally and from above the rowboat looking down at its pointed silhouette on the night-time water, two dim figures pulling at the oars. "Climb up the damn things," Harry said, and in Lew's mind the scene cut, and he watched himself climbing the wooden slats he knew were nailed to the sides of the docks. "Get a hell of a view from the top," Harry went on, and again the picture in Lew's mind abruptly cut, and now he saw himself high on the top of the great wooden wall, sharply defined against the lights of San Francisco. His arms moved alternately, rapidly: he seemed to be hauling up a weight from the boat by a rope, then it came into view, and he set it by his feet. It was a cluster of explosives, vaguely defined; he didn't know what they ought to look like.

Lew blinked, startled at himself. "Damnedest thing," he said, leaning forward to look past the women at Harry on the other end of the log. "I wasn't even thinking about it, and all of a sudden I start imagining rowing out to the drydocks. At night." Voice wondering, he said, "To blow them up . . ."

"Be something, wouldn't it." Harry nodded. "*Whammo.*"

"Blow things up," Shirley murmured. "You guys are in tune with the times, all right."

"You couldn't do it, though," Harry said, staring out at the tiny distant blackness on the Bay. "Take tons of stuff to send those things up. And you'd have to plant it under the bottoms somehow; they're *built*. I was out on them once."

"When?" Shirley said.

"That time with Floyd Weatherill. In his FJ. We tied up to one of them. The bottoms are rotted out, but the inner floors were still above water, just barely. We walked around in one, and they're immense." He turned to Lew, grinning, his face dim in the wan starlight. "What you want to do, Lew, is burn them. Forget explosives: use gasoline; that you can get. Take plenty of gas, and really soak them down. All four sections. Then row off a few feet, and heave up a torch or something."

"Flares," Lew murmured. "Half a dozen road flares." He sat staring out at the distant drydocks, seeing the film again—the sudden smoky red light flaring up. "Light one, then hold it under the others and light them all at once. Stand up. Crouched low so you don't tip the boat. All the flares bunched in one hand. Heave them up hard—"

"Sidearm; sidearm would be best."

Jo murmured, "Honestly . . ."

"Yeah. Sidearm and arched high. So they'd clear the top with room to spare. On the way down they'd separate a little before they hit bottom. But road flares wouldn't go out."

"Take a while to catch, though. For a while you wouldn't see anything."

"Give you time to row away," Lew said. "Fast as hell."

"Yeah. Then a little way from shore—rowing, you'd be facing the things—you'd see just a tip of flame, maybe. Sort of flickering up over the side for a second."

"Yeah. You'd reach shore, tie up, get back out of sight somewhere, and—"

"*Whoosh!* All of a sudden up she goes. Then all four of them catch. Jesus: you'd see the god-damn things all over the Bay."

"Sure would." Lew nodded. "Four pair of those walls; high and completely surrounded by air; and there'd probably be a breeze, they'd get all the oxygen they could use. They been soaking out there in the sun for years; the wood's bone dry. Loaded with tar. And then soaked with gas—my god, the flames'd shoot up two hundred feet. And against the darkness, on a night like this, the fire reflected in the water . . . " He sat staring.

"Well?" Harry leaned forward to grin at him. "When do we do it? Tonight?"

"Not tonight or any other," said Shirley.

Harry shrugged. "Wouldn't do any harm. They're well out in the Bay, nothing else anywhere near them. And they're no fucking good; the county's been after the owner for years to get rid of them. They're abandoned, actually. We'd be doing the world a favor. Right, Lew?"

"Absolutely. Let's ditch this pair of deadheads, and go find us a siphon."

They finished their coffee. Jo took their cups and put them into her pack, then they walked silently back to the road, and turned toward the freeway just beyond its other end.

The freeway pulled at Lew: he wanted the others to see the eerie sight of the great lighted road lying empty and motionless in the middle of the night. But they reached the service road, lying dark and empty, turned onto it, and almost immediately a car passed on the freeway beside them. As they walked, they watched its tail lights shrink, but just before they winked out over the Corte Madera rise, the blazing eyes of another pair of headlights popped up over the crest. They grew fast, lengthening into beams, then the car shot past on the southbound side of the freeway. Shirley's head turned, following it, and as she looked back over her shoulder, her eyes met Lew's, they read each other's mind, and both smiled at the memory of the night last week when they'd lain together out there on the empty concrete.

Exasperatingly, the road would not clear. Reaching the concrete overpass, they turned by common impulse onto the corkscrew ramp, then walked along the overpass, and always, at least one car and occasionally a clump of two, three, or four moved along the two-mile stretch below them.

By tacit agreement, they stopped over the southbound lanes to lean, chins on wrists, on the concrete rail and stare out over the long reach of concrete, dim and livid in the even starlight. Headlights approached from the north, and they watched them rapidly grow into brilliance, the car behind them indistinct. Fifty yards off, the windshield was a blank black sheet of reflected sky, then suddenly it cleared as the car shot toward and under them, and they saw the driver's startled face staring up at them, open-mouthed.

Smiling, they walked on, and after a dozen steps Lew realized that now once again the world lay silent all around them. He checked both ways: as far off as he could see nothing moved, no headlights appeared. As they turned onto the downward ramp Harry realized it, too. "Hey, look"—he gestured at it—"look at that *road!* My god, it's empty! It's *empty;* look at it!" He began running around and around the corkscrew ramp, the others breaking into a trot to follow, and at the bottom he ran directly onto the freeway-entrance curve, the one he and Lew took every weekday morning, and out onto the freeway itself.

The others followed, then they all stood in the center lane, heads turning, looking one way, then the other. The lull held; nothing appeared, and Harry looked at Lew, grinning. "This freaks me out, old buddy, it really does," he said, and Jo nodded happily. "I can't believe this," she murmured. "It's wonderful." And Lew felt himself nodding modestly, as though he'd made a big promise he'd managed to keep.

Harry snatched off his cap, wadding it up, tucking the bill in, compacting it. "Yours, Lew!" he yelled, running backward, arm upraised, the quarterback hunting a receiver. He threw it hard in a pass, Jo leaping to intercept, Lew running for it, but the light cloth fell too quickly to catch. Yelling, "Fumble!" he scooped it up anyway, and ran toward the women, folded cap under one arm, the other out in an old-fashioned straight-arm. They shrieked, partly real, partly faking, and separated, Lew running between them, and Harry grabbed him around the waist in a mock tackle. *"Car!"* Lew yelled, pointing; they all whirled, saw the headlights far to the north, and trotted off the road, Lew tossing Harry his cap in a short pass.

Off the road and behind the mesh fence they lay in a row on their stomachs facing the freeway; waiting, grinning. As the car approached they lay motionless, heads low, watching, and saw first the red-white-and-blue lighting strip across the roof; then, as it moved past at moderate speed in the far lane, the lettering across the white door: MILL VALLEY POLICE. The hatless driver never glanced their way, and they watched the two broad tail-light strips move slowly up and then dip over the crest of the Richardson Bay bridge to the south.

They walked back across the overpass, and at the Standard station along the service road on the other side turned in and walked past the pump islands of the dark locked-up blue-and-white little building to the drinking fountain beside the washroom doors at the side: Shirley was thirsty. Each in turn drank, then as Lew bent over the fountain, reaching for the handle, he froze, they all did, at a small sound from the front of the station, the slight but unmistakable scrape of a bumper-guard on concrete. A faint brake squeal, a muttering engine abruptly switched off, then silence.

Lew and Harry crept toward the front corner, and stopped short of it. Through two windows, across a corner of the dark office, they saw the length of the car stopped beside the nearest pump island, MILL VALLEY POLICE, across the front-door panel. Its lights were off, and behind his windshield the cop sat facing their direction but looking away, off across the freeway, watching.

He *had* seen them; running about the freeway, probably, and seen them run off. Keeping his eyes straight ahead then, giving no sign—knowing they could run off into the darkness before he could stop, get out, and reach them—he'd driven slowly past, aware of them watching him undoubtedly, on the other side of the fence.

On over the bridge, and then—out of their sight just beyond the bridge's other end—he'd have driven across the freeway through the bus-lane gap in the divider fence, and full speed back on the other side. Lights out, probably, as he came over the bridge, he'd swung immediately onto the off-ramp at the bridge's foot, and down into the station. Now, screened by the pumps, he sat waiting for them to reveal themselves somewhere.

Well, here we are, old buddy. Right beside you, Lew said in his mind, aware of a thrill of—what? Excitement: sudden, intense and deeply pleasurable. He turned to grin at Jo and Shirley behind him; but their eyes on his were apprehensive and questioning. Possibly a minute passed, then another, the cop waiting, watching across the freeway, occasionally looking slowly all around him; behind the windshield, his face was indistinct. Then he leaned forward, started his engine, and an amplified metallic click sounded from the car roof as the speaker there came to life.

Lew thought he'd drive off; instead his door opened, and they edged back out of sight. Footsteps sounded, leather on concrete. Almost immediately they stopped. A pause, then the locked front door of the station rattled in its casement. Startlingly loud, a woman's bored and distant voice squawked three unintelligible words from the speaker on the car roof. Silence, then distantly from the other side of the building, the rattling chain of a rising garage door.

They ran swiftly back to the rear of the station, then Lew and Harry walked to the opposite corner. Slowly Lew moved an eye around it, Harry beside him. White fluorescent light filled the roof-high square of the garage entrance, spilling out onto the concrete. From inside they heard the distinctive dead clunk and then the small clatter of a coin rattling down a slot. A metallic click, a soft pop, a gurgle. Slow approaching footsteps, and they drew back their heads. A light switch clicked, the garage door rolled down. The tiny metallic clickings of a key finding its lock. Slow footsteps again, receding now, and they looked around the corner. His blue-shirted back toward them, feet shuffling, the cop moved slowly back toward his car holding a steaming Styrofoam cup out to the side, apparently full almost to sloshing over.

Again they watched at the front corner: the car door stood open and the cop sat sideways on the seat facing the station, heels hooked to the narrow sill, the cooling cup in his hands. Through his door window they could see his face in three-quarter view: narrow, wedge-shaped; hair dead black, straight, and cropped short; wide, close-trimmed pistol-grip sideburns to below his ear lobes. Back in his car with no further need to activate the roof speaker, he'd turned off the engine—they could hear the small pings and cracklings of cooling metal—and he sat staring absently at nothing, waiting for his coffee to cool.

For minutes then, behind the station, they waited; sitting on the asphalt leaning back against the wall. Just beyond the little asphalted area lay the wide expanse of the bird sanctuary, no exit that way. Presently Lew said, "Well, Go'father, what do we do? Shoot our way out?"

Harry smiled but he said, "You know what annoys me? No reason we shouldn't just walk out of here. Instead we sit here because we know he'd stop us: What were we *doing* back here? What're we out for this time of night?"

Jo said, "Well, it *is* kind of suspicious, don't you think? Four people lurking around the back of a gas station. It's only reasonable to stop us. Especially if he saw us on the freeway earlier."

"Maybe. But I don't like the choice! Either go out, and we're stopped: answer questions; produce *identification*, for crysake. All that shit—I hate it. You don't *have* to produce identification, you know. All you have to do is identify yourself orally. But the dumb cops never know that. So you either do it or make a fucking court case out of it. Or sit back here hiding."

Another minute passed, then Harry got up suddenly, and walked restlessly to the back edge of the asphalted area. A fifty-gallon open-topped oil drum stood there, discarded grease rags draped over its rim, empty cartons and a discolored fluorescent tube protruding from the debris heaped inside it. Harry walked over to it, stared into it, then reached in, moving something aside, metal clinking on glass, and Shirley called, "Shhh!"

Harry brought out his hand, something in it, and shook it vigorously. He tipped it toward the open drum, they heard a soft hiss, and saw a whitish glob piling up on one of the rags. He turned quickly to walk back, holding up the tall can. Standing, leaning close as Harry stopped before them, Lew could read the larger label type: ACEWAYS METAL CLEANER/ SPRAY ON, WIPE OFF!/ DISSOLVES GREASE INSTANTLY! He looked at Harry who grinned and said, "There's some left."

Lew didn't know what to reply. "Well, good: you can clean my nail clip."

Harry shook his head, still grinning. "If I could sneak out there, back of the cop car, I could write something on it. Spray it on the back."

"Like what?"

"I don't know. 'Greetings!' 'Hello, there!' 'Fuck you!' Anything— just so he'd drive off with a mysterious little souvenir. What do you think?"

Shirley said, "I think you've lost your mind."

He didn't look at her, just stood waiting, smiling, eyes on Lew's.

Lew said, "I don't think so, Harry. Not a sound out there, nothing stirring, he'd be bound to see some movement or hear any little sound. And he's facing the station: how would you walk past him?"

"Clear out at the side, a long way from the car. Then I could—"

Lew said, "Listen! Say I *walk* out. Just come walking out by myself! I don't know he's there, see, and I walk out, see the car, and do some kind of surprised take. He calls me over: What am I doing here, all that. I just shrug: I'm walking around, couldn't sleep. I often do this, and so on, and so on. Was I on the other side of the road earlier? No, I came from another direction. His eyes are on me standing there by his door blabbing away. And you're in back of the car spraying away!"

"What'll I write?"

"Harry, I won't *have* it," Shirley said. "That's not why we came out tonight!"

A car door slammed. Almost running, Harry and Lew walked swiftly to the front corner again, but as they reached it, looking through the windows of the office, the car's headlights were swinging away, sweeping through a quarter-circle as the car turned down toward the driveway. It bounced onto the service road, straightening, accelerating, heading north, then they watched it swing up into the driveway of the car wash next door. There the cop tested the office door, then shaded his eyes to peer inside as he shone a flashlight. He drove on to the next in line, McDonald's, and Lew said, "Well, boss, we scared him off."

"Yeah." Harry idly streaked the concrete with a long spatter of white, then tossed the can into the small open drum between the pumps.

Walking home, back around the shoreline, they were quiet, and Lew felt with a host's chagrin that the outing had failed. But passing the little bird sanctuary, Jo murmured, "Look," pointing, and they stopped to stare out at the four motionless sleeping white birds, each standing on one astonishingly thin, sticklike leg, head under wing. "Isn't that wonderful," she said softly, then looked slowly around at the silent darkness, and up at the remoteness of the stars. "There's something about being out here like this that's—I don't know—magical. I'll think about it all day while I'm working tomorrow."

"I knew you'd love it," Shirley said complacently, and Lew smiled. They walked on: Harry and Shirley, Lew and Jo. "Next week, then?" Shirley said, turning to look back at Lew. He shrugged, and she said, "Harry?"

"Well. It's weird. You're a real freak, Lew. But I think maybe you're onto something. Sure. Next Monday again?"

"If you want," Lew said. "But why don't you lead, Harry? I've about shot my wad."

Before he could answer Jo said, "Let me!" And—surprised—the others nodded and agreed.

CHAPTER   SIX

• • •

It was Lew's week to drive, and in the morning the two men drove around the shoreline they had walked last night, then onto the service road: passing McDonald's, where a boy stood beside a steaming bucket, squeejeeing the windows; past the car wash, a blue Volvo just emerging, front bumper dripping; past the Standard station, four cars at the pumps; past the pedestrian overpass, three men crossing toward the bus stop. They stared curiously at each of these places, then turned to glance at each other and smile.

As they entered the freeway, sliding into an empty space in the slow lane, Harry shook his head in disbelief that they could ever have run and cavorted on this traffic-clogged road. He said, "I'll admit it, Lew: there *is* something to nutsing around like that in the middle of the night. But what?"

"Well"—Lew nodded toward the windshield—"take a look at this frigging freeway; you can hardly see the concrete. And look at us, sitting here breathing this stuff; you can smell it today. I hate the freeways, but who doesn't, and what can you do? We're on it again, we'll be back on it tonight, tomorrow morning, and for the rest of our lives—you know it." He smiled. "But last night, at least, we defied it. Played on it, pranced around on it, thumbed our noses at it."

"Yeah, maybe." Harry waited as Lew, checking his rear-view, sped up slightly to slide over into the center lane, braking immediately. Then he said, "Something like that, anyway, but . . . "

"But what?" Lew said after a moment.

"But we didn't defy anything, did we, Lew? We just sneaked onto it when it was safe. Looking both ways first. We were like kids making faces at Daddy when he's taking a nap. The time to do it would be now." He smiled, interested at the thought. "Seven-thirty in the morning. You and I climb the fence, and just bulldoze our way out into the middle of the god-damn road, cars hitting their brakes. We face the traffic, straddling the markers, and block all three lanes. The cars behind us move on, the road clears, and we turn around and start running all over the fucking freeway. Bring a real ball, and pass it, kick it, run with it, tackle. Cars backed up to San Rafael, every horn blasting, guys leaning out yelling blue murder."

"Be something," Lew murmured, eyes on the rear-view, waiting for a chance to move into the next lane, and Harry nodded, then slumped down to try and nap.

The week passed. On Wednesday night Lew and Jo saw a double-bill Hitchcock at the Surf, in San Francisco, one of them being *The Lady Vanishes*, which they'd never seen. In the ticket line just ahead of them stood a college friend, Leonard Beekey, whom Lew hadn't seen since Berkeley, and the two couples sat together, and had coffee in the little place next door.

During the last half of the week he worked hard and well, finding citations for a memorandum, in the company library and on two afternoons in the law library at Hastings. He added an invented citation, *City of San Francisco* vs. *Josephine Dunne*, as explicitly described as the real ones; but before handing it over for typing, he crossed it out.

Thursday evening, with Jo's help, he worked on devising a bumper strip for when it should be time to begin campaigning: JOLIFFE FOR CITY COUNCIL, they decided it should read, and in smaller letters underneath, TO KEEP MILL VALLEY MILL VALLEY. On Friday they bowled with the Levys. On Saturday evening, in Lew's apartment, they watched "The Mary Tyler Moore Show," lying on the chesterfield together; presently, the television still on, they made love, then watched it some more till they fell asleep. It rained Sunday, the Levys were away visiting Shirley's parents on the Peninsula, and they spent the day in one apartment or the other with the Sunday paper, books, magazines, television, and Jo's worry because she'd thought of nothing interesting to do for tomorrow's Night People Walk. "Don't worry about it," Lew said. "Just improvise as you go; I'll help you." But Jo said, "That's your nature, not mine. Oh, I hope it rains tomorrow!"

It did. When the alarm rang at two fifteen, Lew shut it off, snapped on the little bedside lamp, then swung his feet to the floor to sit on the edge of the bed, holding his eyes open. Jo had gotten up instantly, and now the kitchen light came on, then the small sounds of Jo starting the coffee maker, which she'd left filled and ready to plug in. The phone rang, he picked it up from the little table, and as he put it to his ear he heard Jo's voice on the kitchen extension: "Hello . . . ?"

"Jo!" Shirley's voice wailed. "It's *raining!*" Lew lay the phone on his pillow, walked to the windows, and parted the drapes: the glass was streaked and, stooping to look up at the white mist of the sky, he could see the slant of a soundless fine rain.

"Lew!" He heard Jo's actual voice from the kitchen duplicated in the phone on his pillow. "Shirley says it's raining, and we're to come over! To their place. For coffee, a drink, *anything*, she says."

"No!" He was going back to bed and to sleep, but he tried to temper the blunt refusal. "Tell them to come over here! And don't take yes for an answer!" He sat down on the bed, yawned enormously, then got under the covers again. From the kitchen Jo called, "Harry's on the extension: wants to know why we won't come over!"

Lew got comfortable, lying on his back, then picked up the phone, and spoke into it quietly. "Because it is raining. And I not only know enough to come in out of it, I know better than to go out into it in the first place. But apparently Harry doesn't. So cut out the argument, Harry, and get your ass over here. Shirley's, too. Shirley's especially."

"Love to, Lew, love to," Harry's voice in the phone said. "Except that it would not only mean getting out of this comfy bed and getting dressed. It would also mean getting soaked to the skin on the way over: we don't own umbrellas or raincoats."

"Teddibly unfortunate; hard cheese," Lew said. "I believe you, of course. And we'd be on our way over there this very moment, me trudging through the torrential downpour on my crutches, with Jo's kindly assistance. My old wound, you know; acts up whenever it rains."

In the phone Shirley's voice said, "Listen. I am *not* just going back to bed; I'd never get to sleep. My alarm rang, I woke up all set for the Walk, and I am now stark wide awake and ready to do *some*thing. I don't mean all night, for heaven sakes. Just a drink, a cup of coffee, tea, or a tall glass of water. It would actually help us to get back to sleep that much faster. So let's! Here or at your place, I don't care."

Lew said, "Damn it, Harry, I was just sinking back into the blessed Nirvana of sleep, when your crack-brained wife brings up this fantastic notion of venturing out into a typhoon. So the only honorable thing for you to do—"

"Listen, it was Jo, panicked by the thought that you might seize this moment of idle wakefulness to wreak your sordid will upon her, who instantly accepted that fantastic notion instead of squelching it. So if you have an ounce of decency—"

"I agree with Shirley," Jo said firmly. "To just go right back to bed would be—"

"Anticlimactic," said Shirley.

"Right. So one of you is going to have to make the supreme sacrifice of getting a few clothes on, and walking twenty yards. It'll only be for half an hour!"

Lew said, "Listen, ladies." Under the covers he crossed an ankle over his upraised knee. "As I understand the problem, you two, feeling an understandable sense of letdown, would like a brief get-together. At which Harry and I dispel your ennui with swift repartee and inimitable antics. Right?"

"Well, I'd never have thought of putting it quite that way: would you, Jo? But, sure."

"Well, fine," Lew said reasonably. "Because that happens to be exactly what Harry and I would like, too: we just think pneumonia is a little too high a price to pay. But the problem is already solved: through the miracle of science, if we will but realize it, we are *already* gathered together. What are we doing right now but happily chattering, gaily laughing, each with his own phone in hand, in the blessed comfort of our own homes? And beds. No one has to stick a foot out in the goddamned rain, and I can talk to Harry without seeing his face, a definite plus."

"Wonderful!" Harry yelled into his phone. "Lying in bed seems to have immeasurably sharpened your wits. That's as brilliant—"

"No," said Shirley. "You two aren't going to talk us—"

"Get into the mood, Shirl!" Lew said. "The party's already started! Yippee! You dressed for a party, Harry?"

"Yep. Something told me to put on dinner clothes when I went to bed tonight."

"I'm in mufti myself: white gloves and matching tennis shoes. But I'm sorry to report that Jo is still in her Dr. Dentons. What're you wearing, Shirl?"

"My old drum majorette's outfit. The one I wore to the State Finals. Listen, we can't tie up the phones like this."

"Why not?" said Harry. "Who's going to call at 2:30 A.M. with a better idea? Yippee, to quote Lew, we're having a party! What're we serving, Lew?"

"Beer, I guess. Haven't got any wine, have we, Jo?"

"Just for cooking."

"Okay," Harry said, "I'll put away this pre-Restoration chartreuse, and switch to beer for the sake of the party. Lew, take that lampshade off your head!"

Smiling, Lew put down the phone, got up, and walked to the kitchen. Jo stood in her nightgown, phone at her ear, leaning back against the little sink, nodding as she listened. She said, "I know; but at least you can reason with children." Lew opened the refrigerator, brought out two cans of Schlitz, yanked off the tabs, handed Jo a can, and started out the door. Then he turned back. Just below the formica-covered work space beside the sink was a drawer filled with old string, a broken flashlight, nails, screws, a souvenir ash tray: junk of all sorts. Stooped before it, Lew poked through this mass for something he remembered seeing, and found it, a small cellophane package imprinted with ringing bells and HAPPY NEW YEAR. From it he pulled two folded paper hats. Opening a blue one, he walked over to Jo, and pulled it onto her head. Working a red one onto his own head with one hand, he walked to the door, then turned on the threshold to look back at Jo. "Yippee," he said, saluting her with his beer, and walked on back to the bedroom.

He took a swallow of beer, sitting on the edge of the bed, then got under the covers, and picked up the phone. "—ever remember drinking beer this time of night before," Shirley's voice was saying.

Lew said, "Harry, you got your beer?"

"Yeah. All set."

"Shirley?"

"Yes. It tastes pretty good; I was surprised."

Jo said, "Shirley, is Harry in bed?"

"Of course. While I have the living-room phone. Sitting in that straight-backed chair at the desk. With the heat off."

"No suggestion that *you* take the more comfortable place? For this alleged party?"

"Certainly not. And I gather that you—"

"Well, here's to the party!" Lew said quickly, and clicked his beer can on the mouthpiece of his phone. He heard the others do the same, and he took a swallow of beer. It *was* good, very cold, just what he'd wanted.

A silence of several seconds, then Shirley said, "Some party. Beats having fun, doesn't it, Jo?"

"Well, wait a second," Lew said. "This is the early quiet stage that all parties go through at first: later on we get wild. But now it's just quiet, sophisticated conversation. Harry, toss off an epigram."

"What *is* an epigram, exactly?" Shirley said.

"One of those things that begins, 'A woman is like . . . ' *You* tell her, Harry."

"Well, let's see: A woman is like . . . " They heard him take a swallow of beer, then silence.

After a moment Lew said, "Wrong pose, Harry: you can't think of epigrams lying down. Stand up by your dresser. Can you reach it?"

A pause, then Harry said, "Yeah."

Shirley said, "Incredible: you made him stand."

"Now drape one arm negligently along the top of the dresser as though it were a fireplace mantel. Lucky you're wearing evening clothes."

"There's no top to this dresser; it's built-in flush to the wall."

"Well, just hold your arm out, then."

A momentary silence, and Shirley said, "Jo, no fooling; I think he's *doing* it."

"You bet I am. All set, Lew. My eyes are heavy-lidded with *Weltschmerz.*"

"Good. Your drink in hand?"

"No, how would I hold the phone? A yard from my ear at the end of this negligently draped arm?"

"Wedge the phone between your shoulder and ear. Like a senior partner in a big-time law firm. And hold your drink sort of high up against your chest. Too bad it's not a martini. Or chilled white chablis. I believe they're the natural drink of the sophisticate; beer and epigrams seem a little unlikely. But try. All set?"

"Yeah, but my neck hurts."

"Honestly," Jo murmured.

"Pitiful, isn't it?" said Shirley.

"A woman is like the winning horse of a race," said Harry. "Impossible to ever predict with certainty . . . forever just beyond the reach of logic and reason . . . "

"He's not just a male chauvinist pig, he's a whole herd," said Shirley. "Is it herd?"

" . . . and yet," Harry continued, "with a seeming inevitableness of result once it has occurred."

"Splendid!" Lew yelled. "Capital!"

"It doesn't even make sense," said Jo.

"Naturally," Lew said. "That's the test of your true epigram. The best ones, anyway: they *sound* as though they mean something, only you're just not quite clever enough to figure out what. And you're afraid to ask for fear of revealing your total lack of sophistication."

"I'm not afraid. Are you, Shirley?"

"Not in this league."

"A woman," Lew began, then interrupted himself. "I am standing with one elbow on a portable mantel I had in the closet, staring moodily down into my glass, absently swirling its contents. Now, then: A woman is like a pretzel, smooth and glossy on the outside . . . brittle underneath . . . creating and sustaining an unquenchable thirst for ever more . . . and holding within her preordained form the eternal symbols of Yang and Ying."

"Hot dog!" Harry shouted. "Man, that's cool!"

"Thank you, Noel." Lew clicked his beer can against the mouthpiece.

"Women's Lib, *wait for me*," said Jo.

"A man is like a bad television comic and straight man combined," said Shirley. "Roaring at his own jokes. Grinning like an ape. And puffed up . . . " She stopped.

"Like a popover," said Jo, "and just as full of hot air."

"That's right, and hollow underneath!" Shirley said, and snickered.

"That's not an epigram," said Harry.

"More like minestrone soup."

"Shirley, can't you just see them? Lying flat on their backs grinning like happy idiots. Alternate straight men and comics just like you said."

"Right. Their own best friends and kindest critics."

"Noel," said Lew, "we seem to have blundered into the wrong drawing room."

"Afraid so, George Bernard."

"All right, wise guys," Shirley said. "You're so good, what're you going to do to entertain us, this is supposed to be a party?"

"Enter*tain* you?" said Harry.

"That's right, Noel. This scintillating company has us tingling with anticipation. Right, Jo?"

"Tingling or numb."

"Lew, now is the time for all good men to come to the aid of the party."

"What about a little bridge? I'll phone Mr. Loeffler in the next building, get him to shuffle a deck, and deal out four hands. Each of us phones him, one by one, and he reads off your hand. Write it down, then get a deck, and pick out your hand. All get back on the phone, and we call out our cards as we play them. Finish a hand, wake up Mr. Loeffler—"

"Come on now, George Bernard," Jo said.

Harry said, "Lew: time out for a conference. Jo and Shirley off the phone for a minute." They heard the sounds of Shirley's phone placed on the desk top, and Jo's on the kitchen counter. Harry said, "Lew?"

"Yeah."

"Listen." He lowered his voice, and spoke quietly.

"Okay, fine," Lew said. "*Jo!* You can pick up."

Shirley picked up her phone and Harry said, "Ready?"

"Yeah," said Lew.

Harry tapped three times on the mouthpiece of his phone, then to the tune of "On, Wisconsin," Harry and Lew sang:

"On Proviso, on Proviso,
Fling your colors high!
Our whole school is backing you,
Let's pass all others by!"

"Their high school song," Shirley murmured. "Can you tie that?"

"On Proviso, on Proviso,
Ever loyal beee . . . !"

"God help us," said Jo.

"FIGHT! For Proviso High,
and *Vic! Tor! Reeee!*"

"I've reconsidered that offer of cards," said Jo. "Right now a round of
old maid would sound pretty good."

"Or slapjack," said Shirley. "Jo, I'll phone you in the morning during
my coffee break."

"Wait!" Lew yelled. "The fun's just starting! Jo: Shirley and Harry
will hang up for a minute. Then you dial the all-night drugstore in the
St. Francis Hotel. When they answer, you say, 'Have you got Prince
Albert in a can?'"

"I don't *believe* this," said Shirley.

"And when they say yes, you say, 'Well, let him out!'" Both men
howled with laughter.

"Fifth grade," Jo murmured. "That was the peak of wit in the fifth
grade: remember?"

"You must be wrong; it couldn't have been higher than third."

Harry said, "Lew, is your father a mailman?"

"Nope."

"What is he then"—Harry could hardly finish for laughing—"a
female man?" The men roared, vibrating the ear pieces of the women's
phones.

"Okay, phone me in the morning, Shirl. When the fun's died down."

"Well, too bad," Harry said. "Always a shame to end a great party."

"Best party I've ever been to," Lew said. "Lying flat on my back in
bed."

"Well, that's life, G.B.: at every party there's a party killer. And in this
case two. See you in the morning." Harry hung up.

The women talked for a minute or so longer, then Jo turned off the
kitchen light, and returned to the bedroom. In the light from the little

bedside lamp Lew lay nearly asleep, but he smiled slightly and made a small gesture without opening his eyes. His paper hat lay on his pillow, and Jo removed it. She reached up to find her own still on, and took it off. The light out, she lay for half a minute listening to the rain, heavier now, then slipped into sleep.

As often in this particular Bay Area fall, the slight rain soon subsided, and seemed to go away forever. For the rest of the week summer returned as though for good. On Monday after dinner, Lew at the sink washing dishes, Jo still at the long paste-up table finishing her coffee, she said, "Tonight's the Night People, and I'm still leader. I don't like this just waiting to see what'll happen. Maybe nothing will, maybe I won't be able to think of anything."

"Jo, so what? Maybe in that case we've had the Night People Walks. There's only so much you can do, wandering around at night, and maybe we've done it."

"Wouldn't you miss them?"

He nodded, smiling, and began rinsing dishes under the faucet. "Yeah. I count on them now. It's weird."

"We all do: we're hooked; Shirley and I have talked about it." She stood up with her empty cup, gave it to Lew, then stood looking around the tiny kitchen area, her thumb and forefinger rising to her chin, and Lew smiled inwardly, knowing what was coming. Jo liked to organize her next day aloud, and now he heard her murmur. "Eggs yesterday. And bacon Friday." She kept track of the cholesterol in their diet. "Should have cereal tomorrow. With fruit." She glanced at the aluminum bowl on top of the refrigerator, and Lew looked, too: it was like being able to read someone's mind. There were two bananas in it, and he watched her open a cupboard, take out a box of Special-K, and rattle it. There seemed to be plenty, and she put it back. "Milk," she said, and turned back to the refrigerator. She opened it, peered in, then stooped and began shoving things aside. "Damn." She turned to Lew: "I have to go down to the shopping center. For milk."

"Want me to?"

"No, you're busy." To herself she murmured, "Better go now or they'll be closed."

An angled parking space stood empty directly before the Safeway, and Jo turned the VW into it, feeling pleased; there was seldom an empty space this close. She walked briskly toward the big store to the beat of "Tea for Two" tinkling from the little overhead speakers spaced along the underside of the walkway roof: as always the store just ahead was whitely and shadowlessly lighted. She stepped onto the green rubber mat with the big Safeway emblem, heard the clunk of the automatic door-opening mechanism and barely stopped herself from walking into the glass of the locked door which had moved only a fraction of an inch. Angrily she stood looking into the vast interior, aisle after aisle in an area as big as two basketball courts, all of it now empty of people except for a man in green uniform shirt and pants shoving an enormous dry mop. She glanced up at the clock on the back wall, and saw that the store had been closed for six minutes.

At the 7-Eleven half a mile back down the service road at the foot of Ricardo, Jo walked to the refrigerator to get her milk, irritated at herself for having to shop here and pay fifteen cents more than she'd have paid at Safeway for the same quart of milk. At the counter the clerk reluctantly put aside the TV *Guide* he'd been reading to punch out the price on the register while Jo stood finding her wallet in her purse. Beside her stood a cardboard display basket filled with green bottles, their necks wrapped in gold plastic foil. MISSION CHAMPAGNE, SPECIAL $2.29 QT., a printed sign read, and Jo picked up a bottle, and stood staring down at the label as though reading it. Actually, her eyes half closed in concentration, she was calculating in the only way she was able to without a pencil. On an imaginary blackboard she printed $2.30 in white chalk, rounding off the price. Under the zero she wrote 6, and drew a line under that. Compulsively she said it to herself as she'd been taught in grade school: *Six times zero is zero*; and drew a zero below the line. *Six times three is eighteen, write the eight and carry the one. Six times two is twelve, and one are* (not *is*) *thirteen.* She wrote the thirteen, drew the dollar sign, and read the result from the blackboard. Six bottles of even cheap California champagne, with sales tax, would cost more than fourteen dollars. But the idea that had come into her mind was too good to pass up. Accepting her change from the milk, she checked her wallet to be sure she had enough money, then began lifting bottles from display basket to counter. At home, the kitchen empty, Lew in his own apartment at the moment, Jo walked to the refrigerator, and laid the six tall green bottles on their sides in the vegetable compartment.

Seven hours later, at two thirty in the morning, Lew and Jo walked toward the driveway, each carrying a Styrofoam cup of coffee steaming in the chill air: instant coffee because Jo had forgotten to prepare the percolator. She wore red plaid slacks, her Irish sweater and tasseled cap; Lew his usual dark blue nylon jacket, blue denims and sneakers, red cap. His other hand gripped the straps of a canvas shopping bag filled to the top with newspaper-wrapped packages which Jo had irritatingly refused to identify, the load heavy enough to pull his arm straight. At the driveway, seeing Harry and Shirley sitting out front on the curb, they turned down it.

Huddled together just outside the light from a street lamp, they looked up as Lew and Jo stopped before them: Harry in his black baseball cap and green nylon jacket, Shirley in a denim suit, no hat or scarf. "Jesus, it's early," Harry said. "And cold. Is that coffee? Or cyanide? I would gratefully accept a sip of either."

"Take it all, I've had enough." Jo handed him the cup. "Hi, Shirl."

Shirley made her voice and body shiver. "Hiii. What's on tonight, Jo? If you still haven't got an idea, I have." She gestured with her chin at the dark buildings behind them. "Let's all go in, get into one bed, and turn the blanket on high. Harry, save me a swallow."

Lew handed Shirley his cup. "Here, take mine. Two things you can always count on with instant coffee in Styrofoam cups: it's always lousy and always too hot."

Sipping carefully, Harry slowly stood up. "This is good," he said to Shirley. "It's called coffee. We ought to get some."

Quickly, brightly, the anxious hostess, Jo said, "You'll all feel better soon: that's a promise! Come on, now." She extended a hand to help Shirley up, who groaned and said, "Careful; I'll break."

The winding road silent except for the scuff of their sneakers and shoes, dark except for the greenish patches under the widely spaced street lamps, they moved, straggling, along the shoreline. It had been warm during the day, but at sunset the thick white fog had rolled in, the temperature dropping swiftly, and now the air was sharp, and Lew wished he'd brought his sweater. He felt hollow, metabolism barely ticking over. It was one thing to be up because you're restless and can't sleep, he thought, but something very different to be yanked out of sleep by an alarm. The loaded sack was heavier now, and with each step it brushed his leg annoyingly. Yet, looking out across the dark still water beside them, and up at the black, star-flecked sky, he was content and happy.

"What's in the bag?" Harry said presently.

"A big surprise, Jo won't say what. But it's heavy; heft this damn thing." He held the bag out to Harry beside him, who took it, hefted it, then nodded and offered it to Lew again. But Lew's fists were shoved into the side pockets of his jacket now, and he was grinning. "Your turn, sport."

"Anyone can dupe me at two forty-five on a raw, bitter morning.

What are we *doing* out here? Jo," he called to the women ahead, "this better be good."

At the foot of Ricardo Road they passed the 7-Eleven, dark now except for the night light, and turned onto the service road, heading north. Beside them the great lighted freeway stood virtually empty again, only an occasional car flashing past as they walked beside it. Half a mile ahead the large, unlighted, shell-shaped sign of a gas station stood outlined against the lavender-tinged lighting of the shopping-center parking lot.

They reached the lot, empty now except for a huddle, near the center, of four or five cars and the delivery van of the TV-repair shop. Jo turned in, and, their faces strange in the violet mist of light from the parking-lot lights high overhead, they straggled across the white-lined asphalt, their multishadows branching out from their feet, wheeling as they walked.

The shopping center was three huge, low buildings of varied shapes, covering acres; under its low red-tiled roofs some eighty-odd store fronts faced a maze of concrete walkways. The roofs continued on down across these walks, covering them; and at intervals along the outer edges of the walks, great square pillars of aged wood supported the roof at the eaves. These massive pillars were entwined with ivy, and Jo thought, approaching it, that this was actually a handsome place, the low roofs and covered walkways reminiscent of early California missions. As they walked across the wide lot toward it, the daytime blatancy of the shop windows now lost in darkness, the place seemed mysterious, inviting, and she felt a surge of hope that her impulsive plan for this night had been a good one. But to Lew, this place, before always busy with movement but shadowed and still now, the low roofline ahead black against a dark sky, seemed forbidding and almost menacing as though aware of their approach.

Then the silence was gently broken, their heads tilting as the first hint of sound touched their ears. Each step across the asphalt brought it clearer though it remained subdued: a quiet orchestral background to a softly tinkling piano. Her voice pleased with the coincidence, Jo said, " 'Tea for Two.' It was playing when I came down for milk tonight, and now the tape's come around again."

Harry said, "Music. Playing here all by itself. In the god-forsaken middle of the night. Some sort of symbolism here, Lew, if I was awake enough to figure it out."

"It's the way the world will end, Harry. Recorded cocktail music nuclear-powered to play on for centuries after all life has been destroyed.

Selections from *No, No, Nanette,* throughout eternity. That do you for 2:55 A.M.?"

"I want to go *home,*" Shirley said, but smiling.

They stepped up onto the covered walkway, Jo stopping beside a backless wooden bench, turning for her shopping bag as Harry set it down before her. The others stood waiting beside her, facing the bench and parking lot, faces ghastly in the lavender light. They saw a brown-paper sack lying on top of whatever else the canvas bag contained, and Jo opened it and brought out a newspaper-wrapped something, which she handed to Shirley. As Shirley unwrapped hers, Jo handed out others to Harry and Lew, taking the last one herself, crumpling the paper sack, thrusting it down into the side of the shopping bag. Her hand trembled slightly; this whole idea suddenly seemed to her embarrassingly absurd.

"A *glass?*" Shirley said wonderingly: she raised it to her face, holding it to the light from the parking lot, twirling it by the stem.

Jo nodded shortly. She stood unrolling a foot-long newspaper-wrapped cylinder she'd taken from the canvas sack; then they saw it was a bottle. "Open it." She thrust it abruptly at Lew.

"Champagne," Harry murmured. "It is. It really is."

Lew peeled off the imitation foil, then squeaked out the plastic cork with his thumbs: a soft pop, and a sliver of lavender smoke curled from the bottle-neck.

"Marvelous," Shirley said. "Champagne right now may kill me, but I don't care: I think it's marvelous. Gimmee." She held out her glass.

Lew poured, filling their glasses and his own. Then, standing at the little bench in the strange light just under the eaves of this great dark place, they waited, glasses in hand, looking to Jo for a cue. "Well, *drink* it," she said, embarrassed, and lifted her glass in an awkward little toasting motion. She tasted hers, then they all sipped: tentatively, glancing at each other to smile, conscious of the oddity of what they were doing. Then Lew drank again: it was very good, very cold, and he realized he'd been thirsty. "Good," he murmured, and grinned at Jo. "Damned good after that walk."

Harry stood sipping thoughtfully, testing both the taste and the idea of champagne out here at three in the morning. Then he nodded abruptly, and drained his glass. Holding it out to Lew for more, he said, "First prize, Jo. Permanent possession of the silver trophy for leadership," and Jo looked suddenly relieved and pleased. Lew filled Harry's glass, he tasted it, nodded again, then glanced up and down the long length of the covered walkway stretching off into darkness at either end.

"But . . . is this the idea for tonight, Jo? Drinking champagne at the shopping center?"

"No, of course not," she said firmly, sure of herself now. "You'll see. Lew"—she was hostess—"Shirley's ready for more."

All had second glasses, emptying the bottle, which Lew shoved into the shopping bag, neck down. He unwrapped another, the others watching, grinning. This time he pushed the cork loose quickly, deliberately making it pop. It struck the ceiling, bouncing out of sight, the champagne frothing from the neck, and he poured quickly, topping off their glasses.

Pleased with the novelty, they stood glancing around them; down the long walkway into the darkness; up at the invisible loudspeaker now softly playing, "Willow Weep for Me" in a guitar arrangement; smiling at each other because they were sipping champagne here at this place at this moment in the deep of the night.

Once again Lew refilled their glasses, then Shirley and Jo sat down on the bench, two lavender-edged silhouettes against the parking lot. Lew lifted a foot to an end of the bench, and Harry turned to sit down on the walk, leaning back against the store front of The Record Shop. "Well?" Jo said. "How's everyone feel?"

"Idiotic," said Shirley. "Wonderfully idiotic. I'll never be able to walk by here in the daytime again without giggling."

They couldn't see Harry's face, but the glass in his hand held a wavering glint as he spoke. "Twenty-odd minutes ago sitting out on the curb I felt like a burned-out dry cell. But sitting here with my third snort of this stuff"—the glass lifted, saluting Jo—"well, here's to the Night People!"

They all drank, and Lew said, "Amazing. The first glass was obviously dollar-seventy-nine-cent imitation champagne. Number two was fair; about like Korbell's." He raised his glass to twirl it by its stem. "But this is Piper-Heidsieck."

"And a vintage year," said Harry. "It's a"—he tried to give it a French pronunciation—"*formidable* little wine."

"A *charmant*, laughing little wine," Lew said.

"A snickering, giggling, grab-ass little wine."

"Well, then," Jo said, the hostess still, and she nodded at Shirley beside her, "I think Shirley wants to dance, Lew. Because that's what this is: a dance. We're having a party! Complete with music."

"My god, of course." Lew was delighted. "That's what it is—a party!" He bowed at Shirley. "Ma'am?" Grinning, she stood up; they both set their glasses on the bench and began to dance. This was shopping-center, doctor's-office music, "classics" from the forties and fifties and earlier, and they danced appropriately, old style, cheek-to-cheek.

For a dozen seconds, moving within a space of only a square yard or so, they danced slowly. Then as "Willow Weep for Me" gave way to a big-orchestra "Begin the Beguine," they moved faster, and after a moment or so began to twirl, feet shuffling swiftly, and Harry had to draw in his legs. Down the walkway they whirled for a dozen yards; here a transverse passageway between two store fronts led to the other side of the building and the shops there. Now it was a black tunnel, its other end a lighted square of roadway. They danced to the opening, glancing in, then Lew led them back toward the others. Jo sat watching, smiling, one leg crossed over the other, a foot keeping time. Lew began to feel dizzy, and he stopped the twirling, dancing them back toward the tunnel again, and this time, slightly pressuring Shirley's back, he led them into it; he'd wanted to the first time, and now he did. Shirley felt good in his arms, he was acutely aware of the light pressure of her cheek against his, and he wanted to kiss her; to move through the dance holding her close, his lips hard on hers. Then, deep into the darkness, well out of sight, and the opportunity at hand, he felt that to do this just here and now would be a small betrayal of why the four of them were all here together. Leading them out to the walkway again, he felt his face flush; he was certain Shirley knew why he'd brought them in.

They emerged, Harry's face toward them, and Harry turned to set his glass on the narrow window ledge of the store front behind him. He stood, and made the suggestion of an invitational bow to Jo. "Lovely party," he said formally.

"So glad you could come." Jo stood up from the bench, lifting her arms, and they began to dance sedately. Then Harry stepped back, and began a slow jitterbug. Surprised, Lew saw that he was very very good, his movements slightly exaggerated, parodying it. Dancing in place, Lew and Shirley watched. Jo began jitterbugging too, a little cautiously but doing pretty well, Lew thought. Harry began singing fragments of the verse, pausing during forgotten phrases or for breath. "Begin the Beguine, . . . tropical splendor! . . . Begin the *Beguine*, terrific mind-bender . . . Oh, let them beginnnn . . . the Beguine!" Then in normal speaking voice, "Yeah, quit horsing around, you guys, and let 'em begin!" Feet shuff-shuffling, jitterbugging in slow, expert rhythm, he sang words and phrases when he knew them, invented others, murmured to and amused Jo whenever he approached her. Shirley and Lew began to jitterbug, but neither really could, and Lew moved them to the bench, and stopped to pick up their glasses, handing hers to Shirley. They drained them, then resumed their old-style dancing.

The music stopped, and in the short pause they stood grinning at each other, Harry's and Jo's breathing audible. Then softly, softly, in the very gentlest of transitions from silence to sound, the music resumed with a slow, orchestral "All the Way." In the moment before they could resume, Jo said, "Change partners," turning to Lew, her arms lifting, and Shirley turned away toward Harry.

To this all danced old style, feet hardly moving. Drifting past the bench, Harry stooped to fill three glasses, swaying in place, and handed them around. Bottle in hand, he danced on with Shirley to the store-front ledge, and filled his own. Then, each couple moving in hardly more than a square foot of space, they swayed to the soft, sweet music, glasses held at partners' backs, occasionally lifting them to sip over the other's shoulder.

Quietly Shirley began to sing the words: " *'When somebody loves you, it's no good unless he loves you, all-l . . . the way.'* " Jo and Lew began to hum, and Harry whistled softly. " *'Happy to be near you,'* " Shirley continued, her voice true and slightly husky, " *'when you need someone to cheer you . . . all the way.'* " Her voice, the humming, and Harry's soft whistle joined, they moved to the quiet music in what seemed like a single moment held and prolonged. " *'Taller . . . than the tallest tree is,'* " Shirley sang, " *'that's how it's got to be. Deeper . . . than the deep blue sea is, that's how deep it goes if it's real.'* " And now at the chorus— glasses in hand, bodies swaying, violet-tinged faces bemused, the pro-longed moment magical—they joined in the words. " *'when somebody needs you, it's no good unless she needs you, all-l . . . the w—'* "

The moment was shockingly destroyed, ripped apart like an explosion by a voice: "What the *hell* you think you're doin'!"—it was harsh with ill-will. An achingly bright layer of new white light clung to Shirley's face like another skin: blinking, squinting, backing away, she tried to swing her astonished, frightened face out of it, but it followed mali-ciously. As Harry swung around to face the voice behind the glare, the beam swept off Shirley's face onto his, but he didn't move to step out of it. Staring into it without blinking, his voice suddenly gone hoarse and deep, Harry said, "Take that god-damned light out of my face or I'll *knock* it out," but it continued to hang waveringly to his face and shoulders, and Harry turned to set his glass on the store-front ledge. As he swung back, his face set, the light dropped to his chest, the voice behind it simultaneous: "All right, I said what'dyou think you're doin' here!"

Harry's hands moved to his hips, fingers splaying, elbows belligerently out-thrust. "I *know* what I'm doing. What do *you* think we're doing!?"

The flashlight reflecting from the dark store window behind Harry, Lew could see that this was a cop in insigniaed blue cap and silver-badged, short-sleeved uniform shirt. A black-and-white plastic name plate pinned to his shirt read FLOYD PEARLEY. He was tall, extremely thin, his forearms skinny but muscularly corded. His uniform pants were too large, cinched in with a belt, and strangely short, a good several inches of bony ankles in white socks showing. Under the shiny peak of his uniform cap his face—and now Lew recognized the coffee-drinking cop at the Standard station two weeks earlier—was hostile, thin and wedge-shaped, black pistol-grip sideburns to below his ears. The flashlight flicked nervously from one to another of them but, Lew noted, at waist level now: the man had lost some nerve.

For a moment of mutual assessment they stood, the cop's eyes darting angrily from one face to another as they stared back at him. It was too chill to be out on foot in a short-sleeved shirt: he'd been trying store doors, Lew decided, in nightly routine, his patrol car somewhere. And— Lew was conscious of a reluctant attempt to be fair—he had turned a corner to come upon something so strange and out-of-routine he'd had no prepared reaction. Without it he was blustering, and before Harry could continue Lew came in as peacemaker.

"No harm intended, Officer." He smiled, waggling a palm placatingly, but no response appeared in the black hostile eyes. The beam of the flashlight swung to the bench, played along it, froze on the shopping bag with the upended bottle protruding greenly, then swung to Lew's chest, a question in itself, and Lew tried to answer it. "We just had this . . . idea, is all," he began, voice carefully slow and easy; for a moment it seemed possible to explain. "You know: with the music playing, no one else around, we thought . . . " His voice trailed off. What they had been doing here could not be explained to this mind: the man stood in narrow-eyed impatience listening without comprehension. No words of Lew's would bring a sudden smile of understanding to this face, but out of sheer momentum Lew continued, "Didn't realize you were here, but all we were doing—"

The cop cut him off, and Lew understood that to this man a conciliatory tone meant weakness, had restored his feeling of having the upper hand. "I don't give a good god-damn *what* you were doin'; this ain't no playground! Now, you just haul ass out of here"—his light brushed the bench—"and take this here crap with you!"

Harry said, "I'm afraid I don't allow men I don't know to say 'ass' in front of my wife. I can say it. So can my friends. So can she: say, 'ass,' Shirley. But you can't, Floyd." His face dead serious still, he was clowning now, amusing himself and the others, the Western gunslinger facing down the sheriff. In deliberate parody, Harry hooked his thumbs into the top of his pants, fingers tensely splayed, knees bent in a slight crouch—ready to go for the nonexistent gun on his hip. Slowly, menacingly, he began walking toward the cop.

"You want trouble!?" The man's skinny rear shot backward as he bent forward and began to retreat, hand flying to the butt of his holstered revolver, the beam of his light hard on Harry's chest.

"Harry, for godsake," Shirley murmured, but Harry continued to walk slowly after him, and in the man's face Lew could see the effort to make himself stand still. But his feet wouldn't obey. For each slow step forward of Harry's, the other could not prevent a synchronized backward step. "That what you want! You want trouble! Because you'll get it! I'm tellin' you, mister, and that's the Pure-D truth!"

Lew wanted to grin but did not: this was an angry, worried man and a cop, his hand on a gun he was licensed to use. Lew reached out, and took Harry's elbow, saying, "All right," trying to give his voice a touch of authority and quiet common sense, "there's no need for the gun: we're going, we're going." He demonstrated this immediately, turning to the bench, deliberately presenting his defenseless back, taking their glasses from the women's hands, thrusting them into the canvas bag. Stooped over the bench, face hidden from the cop, he released his bottled-up smile; from the corner of his eye he saw Jo watching him, and winked.

But then, bag in hand, turning to cross the walk to the store front for Harry's glass, Lew's smile faded and he felt the heat swiftly rising in his face. He took Harry's glass from the window ledge, ready to shove it into the bag, but suddenly there wasn't even time for that, and he swung around from the store front to face the cop. "But some time, old buddy, when you're contemplating your shriveled-up little soul, ask yourself what harm we were doing. And why you couldn't have just asked your questions, smiled, and walked on. Or stopped for a drink with us; you'd have been welcome. Because if we were here to rob the place, this isn't quite the way we'd go about it!" He swung angrily back to the store front before he could say too much, and snatched up the empty bottle from the walk where Harry had left it. Still he wasn't quite finished, had to turn back. "Or if you *had* to run us off, what exactly would have happened if you'd made it an ordinary, decent request? Would they kick you off the force for unauthorized courtesy? Is there some rule that when you put on that uniform you have to act like a shit?"

"Watch your mouth! Don't talk to *me* like that or I'll put you under arrest! The whole damn lot of you!"

Lew turned angrily to the curb. "Come on," he said to the others, "let's get the hell out of here."

They walked off, angling across the big lot toward the cluster of parked cars and the service road beyond them, Lew half a step behind Jo, then Shirley, with Harry last. Eight or ten steps, no other sound but the scuffle of their shoes, the soft sweet music fading behind them: it astonished Lew; it was still "All the Way." A step or two more, then he had to glance back, and as he turned, so did Harry. Continuing to walk on, they stared back over their shoulders. The cop stood just under the eaves of the walkway, watching them, his flashlight gone now, stuck in a back pocket probably. They began angling between the cluster of parked cars out in the middle, and Lew turned away, the episode over, when he heard Harry call softly, and turned. His hand on a fender, Harry stood facing the walkway: "Hey, stupid," he called pleasantly, "your pants are too short," and did it.

"You're under arrest!" His hand flew to his gun butt. "*All* of you!"

Lew felt his face drain white. "Go *fuck* yourself," he yelled, voice shaking, and he walked on after Jo between the cars.

The gun yanked out. "Stop! Right there! *Freeze or I'll shoot! You're under arrest!*"

But Harry had shoved Shirley hard, on between the cars, instantly ducking low and hurrying in after her. Then they stopped beside Lew and Jo, turning to face the walkway, the metal bulks of several cars between them and the angry violent man with the gun.

Through the glass of the cars they watched him step out onto the asphalt of the parking lot, gun pointing. "Come out of there, I'm warning you, god damn it! *You're under arrest!*"

Lew called, "No. We're not. What's the charge? What do you think has *happened* to be arrested? You can't arrest for personal spite! We're not *taking* an arrest. Now, put that gun away: I'm a lawyer, and I—"

"*Fuck you, lawyer!* I'll put *nothin'* away! Come on out of there, or I'm comin' in after you!"

"You do that," Harry called. "Come on in here, Floyd; that's a personal invitation. And I'll take that fucking gun and shove it up your ass."

The man stood in classic TV pose, feet wide apart, bent slightly forward, pistol in hand at waist level, his other hand behind him and out to the side as though to maintain a delicate balance: Lew wondered if he'd ever before drawn a pistol in threat. Several seconds passed; no one moved. "Come out of there! I'm warning you!" But the voice had lost authority; he had to decide now that he would walk into the narrow dark aisles between the cars, Lew thought, but he didn't know what would happen if he did. They waited motionless, protected by the car bodies, and Lew wondered if the absurd situation seemed as unreal to Floyd Pearley as it did to him. Four or five more seconds, then the man whirled, and ran hard along the covered walkway, holstering his gun; they could hear the leathery scuff of his shoes on the concrete. They stared puzzledly out at him, then Lew said, "He's going for the phone! Let's move!" They turned and ran hard toward the service road, leaped the foot-high hedge onto the road, and ran straight down it into the darkness, the women first, Harry jogging beside Lew. In Lew's sack the glassware jingled musically, and he thought momentarily of abandoning it—the sack brushed his leg at every step—but was angrily unwilling to.

"Lawsy, lawsy, ah heahs de bloodhounds!" Shirley said.

Over her shoulder Jo said, "I planned all this, you know; I do hope you're enjoying it."

They were at the Shell station, running past it, their breathing audible. Stretching ahead into the dark lay a half-mile of straight road lying between the freeway fence beside them and, at their left after a ten-yard width of weed-grown flatness, the abrupt rise of the ridge paralleling the road. It occurred to Lew that they were running into a long, narrow trap, if headlights should suddenly appear ahead or behind them. "Harry! He could have help here in two minutes; let's get off the god-damn road." Lew took Jo's elbow, and veered sharply off to the left.

Harry following with Shirley, they ran through the high weeds beside the dark station. The building stood between them and the Safeway pay phones; the cop couldn't see them.

Harry said, "Son-of-a-bitch, I hate to run from that shit. He hasn't got a charge he can make stick: we didn't *do* anything, damn it!"

"He'd lie," Lew said. "Say we spit on the flag."

Shirley said sweetly, "If the sheriff comes, Harry, just take his gun away."

Reaching the abrupt rise of the slope, they began clambering up it, women first, then the men, and as they climbed laughed semihelplessly, hilarious with the excitement of what they found themselves so unexpectedly doing. The slope was rocky and steep; almost immediately they had to climb on all fours, finding footholds, grasping handfuls of weeds to pull themselves higher. These sometimes ripped loose and someone would slide back, cursing or snickering. Each time Lew managed a step upward he had to find a place overhead to set his bag.

Here on the slanted face of the ridge it was almost but not quite completely dark; they were still just within range of the freeway lighting. From the service road Lew knew they'd be moving shadows on the slope, and he glanced back over his shoulder to scan the road. "*Freeze*," he called softly.

Instantly motionless, they lay sprawled on the rocky face: Lew had seen headlight beams begin to lighten the road. Staring back over their shoulders, they watched the asphalt brighten waveringly as a fast-moving car rocked toward them. It flashed past, then brake lights flared, tires squealing, and the headlights jounced as the car shot up the shopping-center driveway. Staring across the low roof of the Shell station, they watched it, accelerating, flash across the angled white lines, the unlighted dome light winking red as it passed under the overhead lights. A side of the car momentarily illuminated, they recognized the green body and white door of a Marin County deputy sheriff car. Its brake lights flashed, the front end dipping as it abruptly stopped: from around a far corner of the long row of store fronts a Mill Valley patrol car had appeared. It drove over to the sheriff's car, swung in beside it, and stopped, the drivers' doors side by side.

Jo said, "I'd love to know what they're saying."

Shirley said, "That we resisted arrest—"

"Hell he will," said Harry. "The last thing he'll ever tell another cop is that he couldn't arrest us. He'll say he saw us at a distance or something, and that we ran off into the shadows and he lost us. Probably sorry now that he called for help, the dumb son-of-a-bitch."

A sudden tire squeal: off to their left and now well below them, the Mill Valley police car shot forward toward the service road, the sheriff's swinging in a tight, rubber-screeching half circle toward a side entrance of the big lot, headlights whitening the store fronts as it turned. Onto the service road, fishtailing dramatically, headlights jouncing, came the first car; instantly it slowed, and a spotlight shot out. Slowly the car moved toward them, the hard narrow beam of intense white light steadily crisscrossing, searching both sides of the road. "Don't move, don't move," Lew murmured.

"Hide your faces," said Harry, "he could take a notion to flash it up here."

But he did not. Harry, Shirley, and Jo lay pressed to the slope, faces on their folded arms, but Lew pulled down his face mask, and lay watching, fascinated by the searching swath of hard-edged light. Engine barely audible, the car rolled by, then the others lifted their heads to stare after it.

Her voice awed, pleased, Shirley said, "Just think, he's looking for *us* . . ."

The car merged with the darkness ahead, only its headlight beams visible, then these were cut off by the little motel half a mile down at the foot of Ricardo Road.

They resumed their climbing, the men occasionally reaching up to give the women a boost, and once Shirley said, "Harry, god damn it!"

"Only helping."

"At least I trust it was you."

"But hoping what?"

They reached the top, Harry moving past the women to turn and give them a hand up onto the path that wound along the ridge, then he took Lew's sack, and Lew scrambled up. His mask still down, Lew turned to face the direction of the vanished car and, slowly thumping his chest with a fist, called in a pseudo-shout, "Hey, Floyd! Come and get us!"

Harry said, "Che, I've got a machine gun buried up here. And a cache of rice; we can hold out for days. Shirl, Jo: now's the time to leave, if you want to rat out. It's no surrender once the action starts."

Shirley said, "Did Bonnie leave Clyde? I'm staying right here. With my foot on the bumper and a cigar in my mouth."

Lew said, "Remember, Short Pants Pearley is mine."

"What if a cop comes up here?" Jo said. "When they don't find us along the roads."

"No," Lew said. "The sheriff isn't going to come climbing around up here in the dark; it's not a big enough thing. And you know Short Pants won't."

"Anyway," Harry said, "they'll think we had a car somewhere—who walks? The sheriff will cruise around for a while, then let it go; probably get another call. And Short Pants will have to pick up on checking doors again. We'll just keep off the roads for a while; work our way back along the ridges as far as we can." He picked up the canvas sack. "Probably break our ass in the dark."

"I don't allow anyone to say 'ass' in front of Jo," Lew said, and they laughed quietly, and began following Harry along the ridge.

A mile and twenty minutes later, when finally they had to descend to the roads, it again became possible that headlights might suddenly pick them up; or that, rounding a bend, they could come upon a police car parked in the dark waiting for them. But in fact they encountered no one. And when presently they turned into their own driveway to stand indecisively between the two buildings, Lew understood that to simply say good night now would be anticlimactic. The adrenaline still flowed, and when Harry lifted the canvas sack to rattle the glass, saying, "Well, come on, there's some champagne left," turning toward his building, the others followed. "We're not letting the fucking cops spoil Jo's party."

In the Levys' living room, a newly opened bottle on the table beside Harry on the chesterfield, they sat in semi-darkness, each holding a filled glass. Harry had circled the room, pouring, then turned out the lights, drawn back the drapes, and slid open the glass doors to the balcony. Now, sipping, they sat watching the motionless green-lighted street just outside, curious to see whether or not a slowly cruising police car would prowl by. Voices low but still tinged with the exhilaration of their encounter and flight, they talked about what had happened, laughing at the cop and at themselves, quietly hilarious.

Then—it was very late now, the street outside utterly still—they fell silent. On the chesterfield beside Harry, Shirley sat watching her glass, slowly revolving it to and fro by the stem. "Damn cop," she murmured. "I was having the most marvelous, nutty kind of time."

"I know," Jo said. "And then he spoiled it. He's spoiled them all."

"What do you mean 'all'?" said Harry.

"Well, we can't go out again after tonight." She smiled. "Be a long time before they forget four people dancing and drinking champagne at the shopping center. At three in the morning."

"Of course," said Shirley. "From now on any cop cruising Strawberry at night will have an eye out for that foursome. And would see us sooner or later."

"So?" Harry demanded.

"Well, it spoils it, Harry, that's all."

"Why?" he insisted, wriggling forward to sit at the very edge of the chesterfield, glaring at the others. "If the cop is Short Pants we deny it was us; must have been four other people. He'll know better, but let him try to prove it weeks later. And if it's some other cop, we're just out taking a walk; so what?"

"At like 3 A.M.?" said Shirley.

"Why the hell *not* if we feel like it! It's what we've *been* doing, isn't it? No law against it! Jesus Christ, we've gotten to believe the police are all-powerful!" He snatched the bottle from the table beside him, jumping up to refill their glasses. Then he strode over to the balcony doors, and closed them: "The cops aren't coming, screw the cops." He turned on the nearest lamp, yanked the drapes closed, then turned to grin at them,

lifting the nearly emptied bottle to his mouth, and draining it. *"Pah!"*—
he popped his lips in a long, satisfied exhalation, rubbing his stomach.
"Stuff's beginning to work its familiar magic once more. Right, Jo?"

She nodded, smiling. "Most ridiculous night I ever spent," she said,
and surprised herself by giggling.

"Lew?" said Harry, and Lew said, "This may be the answer to
everything. Unlimited champagne, day and night. Piped into every
house."

"Shirley?" Harry said. "Report, please."

"Oh, sure," she said, shrugging, "I'm feeling fine again: Why not?
Pour enough of this into me, and I'll go back to the shopping center,
and dance with the cop."

"Right." Harry returned to the chesterfield, and began peeling the
foil from another bottle. "You know," he said conversationally, "coming
back tonight I was almost a little sorry that ducking the cops was quite
that easy. Lew, the first few times, when you were out alone, you kind
of liked a little excitement, didn't you; that little feeling of risk?"

"Well, yeah, except there really wasn't any risk, Harry. I kind of
instinctively ducked one night when a patrol car went by. It was sort of
fun—memories of Halloween—sitting in the shadows watching him."
He grinned. "And I did sit on a guy's porch swing one night. Deliberately. Creaking it a little. Courting a little trouble, I guess. The guy came
out, and I had to duck behind a hedge."

"You never told me that." Jo looked at him, startled.

"I forgot." He sipped at his drink.

"Why'd you do that? What *for?*" She was frowning.

"For the hell of it. Playing the fool, acting the kid, just out of boredom.
For whatever risk, as Harry says, that it amounted to. Which wasn't
much." He laughed, shaking his head. "I don't know what I could have
said or done if he'd come busting down to where I was, wanting to know
what I thought I was doing. Plead insanity, I guess."

"Yeah." Harry sat smiling, twisting the stem of the little wire basket
enclosing the cork. "So here's what I'd like to say, as self-appointed
chairman of this little gathering here in the deep of the night under the
great majestic wheel of the eternal stars. The young ladies say things are
spoiled. But I'm not so sure. What I think would have spoiled things,
actually, is if we'd kept *on* at the shopping center. No interruptions, I
mean, no cops. Till we were ready to go home. Would have been a
great outing. Best we've ever had; all hail to Jo!" He popped the green
plastic cork, letting it fly, to bounce off the ceiling. "But it would
probably have been the end of the Walks." He stood, and began refilling

glasses. "Because damned if I know what we could ever have done to top it. Or even compare. There isn't anything much *left* to do, actually. In the old way," he added. He sat down again, setting the half emptied bottle on the table, glancing down into the sack. "Only one more. Too bad; party's going good again: right?"

"Right," said Jo; she sat well down in her chair, holding her glass in her lap, smiling lazily—and just a little drunkenly, it occurred to Lew, amused.

"Beats sleeping," said Shirley.

They were companionably silent then, Lew conscious of how very comfortable he felt, slouched in the big upholstered chair. Was he drunk, too? No: they'd only had . . . how much? Over a quart of champagne apiece. But was that a lot, was champagne strong? He had never had enough to know but doubted that he was drunk. He felt only very content, smiling at Harry and Shirley across the room on the chesterfield, and at Jo opposite in her low, deep chair. Content, and conscious of an enormous good will toward these three people, so loving and complete that he knew it was exaggerated. But he was happy to be here, drinking champagne in the deep middle of the night and grinning at his friends, and he understood that he *was* drunk, a little, anyway. But in a completely clear-headed way, it seemed, strangely.

He hadn't seen him get up, but Harry was crossing the room toward him, palm extended. He stopped, and Lew saw two cigarettes, home-rolled, fat and puffy. "No, thanks, Harry."

"Come on!"

"Harry, it's work tomorrow. Work, work, work! I don't want to get completely messed up."

Harry shrugged, and turned away. "Jo?" She shook her head, and Harry sat down on the chesterfield again. He and Shirley lit up. They inhaled, held it, then Harry let his breath whoosh out, and grinned at Lew. "Hey, man," he said in a parody voice, "join the scene." He hopped up, crossed to Lew, offered the cigarette, and Lew took it. He inhaled, and tried to return the cigarette to Harry, but Harry turned away. "Keep it. You and Jo. Shirley and I'll have the other." Lew nodded, and still holding the lungful of smoke, he reached forward, and handed the cigarette to Jo.

They smoked, sipping champagne, talking and laughing steadily now; presently Harry brought out two more cigarettes. Things got funnier. When Shirley merely shook her head at a remark of Harry's, everyone else laughed in delight at the funny way she did it. Lew felt too warm and unzipped his jacket, but that didn't help, and he sat forward to pull it off. He had trouble doing it, and when he got it off both sleeves were inside out. He wadded up the jacket, tossed it toward the bookshelves, but the lightweight nylon fluttered to the floor, falling short; he made a kicking motion at it, and the others laughed happily. They, too, peeled off jackets and sweaters, and Harry wadded his up, and threw it at Lew. Both were still wearing caps, and when Lew snatched his off to throw at Harry, Harry yanked off his, they threw at the same time, the caps struck each other in midair, dropping to the rug, and the men roared.

Harry pulled off his sneakers without untying them, pretended to throw one at Lew, then tossed it, twirling, high into the air. It thumped the ceiling, leaving a smudge, and they all laughed. Shirley was pulling her sneakers off, and Harry stood up, yanked open his belt, unsnapped the top of his pants, and pulled them open, forcing the zipper down. He let them drop, and began kicking them loose from his ankles.

Grinning, watching Harry, Lew's eyes were caught by a movement: he turned his head and his heart jumped: Shirley was standing, body turned at the waist, fingers flickering at her side. Was she . . . ? *Yes:* she shot the zipper, and swiftly, one knee rising, then the other, stepped out of her denims.

Lew sat hypnotized, staring at the long length of her bare legs. *Lovely, lovely,* he kept saying to himself, and didn't know till it hit him in the face that she'd pulled off her blouse and thrown it at him. It dropped to his lap, and he looked up to see her grinning at him from across the room, in snug white pants and brassiere, and he grinned back lazily. "Take it all off," he said.

"Yeah. You, too, Jo," said Harry, voice muffled, and Lew turned. Face hidden, Harry stood pulling off his underwear T-shirt, exposing the mattress of black hair that covered his stomach, chest, and shoulders.

Lew knew Jo would not take off her clothes, and looked at her, curious to hear how she'd refuse. But without losing a flicker of her contented smile, she stood and began unbuttoning her blouse. Harry dropped his T-shirt to the floor, stooped, and picked up his baseball cap, slapped it across his thigh, put it on, then yanked his elastic-banded shorts down, and kicked them off. "Ahhh, that's better," he said, smiling around at the others. Naked except for his cap, he sat down on the chesterfield, and picked up his glass.

Jo's blouse was off, hung across the back of the rocking chair, and she sat bent forward to the floor unlacing her shoes. Shirley stood, chin ducked to chest, elbows winged out, hands busy behind her back, and— *Jesus!* Lew cried out to himself—the brassiere sagged loosely forward.

Then she did it: plucked off the brassiere, and Lew saw her breasts, so beautiful, so *actual*, that he heard his teeth grind.

Then, realizing, he shouted silently, *No, I'm too skinny, I won't do it!* He picked up his glass from the floor, and held it at his chest as though it were a defense. Then he drained it angrily, thinking, *What's the sense of this, what's the point!* But he knew he was angry because he had to do it, and he set his empty glass on the rug, forcing his face to smile, and sat slowly unbuttoning his shirt. *Damn Jo:* if she'd refused, as she should have, he'd have been able to say no too. He got up, and stood watching his fingers slowly unbuttoning his cuffs, afraid of what his face would show if he looked up at Shirley. But he couldn't help it: he lifted his head, their eyes met, and she grinned mischievously, standing there in her snug white pants, her breasts full, solid, round as bowls, incredibly exposed to his eyes. With both hands she pushed her pants down off her hips, lifted one leg and ankle to step out of them, let them fall to the floor around the other ankle, and stepped gracefully sideways out of them, and Lew stood stunned.

Harry shouted, a single bark of laughter, his arm rising to point across the room at the front of Lew's pants, and Lew blushed, and quickly sat down again, glancing at Jo. She stood watching him, still smiling as though in a dream, unfastening the side buttons of her plaid slacks: he didn't know what she was thinking or what she understood. She stepped forward out of her unlaced shoes, daintily drew down her slacks, and Lew looked away, his mind a roar of confusion. For a moment he sat staring at his knees, then looked up: Shirley smiled at him, shrugged a shoulder, and then it was all right. *To hell with it, hell with it all:* he could stand now, and did, and quickly took off his clothes.

It was okay. It felt strange, the air cool on his skin, all his skin everywhere, but he assured himself that it felt good and—glancing down at his naked body—that while he was skinny, you couldn't say scrawny.

Lew sat down, able to look casually around the room, careful to look at Shirley no longer than at the others. She sat on the chesterfield now, leaning across Harry to take her glass from the table, her back momentarily turned. Facing front again, raising her glass, she drank, chin and breasts lifting, and Lew looked away to watch Harry who had stood and was walking out of the room into the short hall. *Too heavy,* Lew thought smugly—the roll of fat at Harry's waist extended around to his back— *I'd rather be skinny.*

He turned to Jo beside him, but she wasn't watching. Frowning in concentration, eyes intent on what she was doing, she stooped to the red-plaid wad of her slacks on the floor; picked up and shook them, then laid them across the chair seat. Then she hung her brassiere across the back of the chair on top of her blouse. This was the way, he suddenly realized, and felt a rush of tenderness, that she got undressed at home in her own bedroom. As he continued to watch, Jo's face and thoughts focused on her own actions, she stepped carefully out of her pants, white with a flowered pattern, laid them on her slacks, turned, and stood there in the room naked with the rest of them.

As though only in this moment realizing what she had done, she quickly sat down on the floor, drawing her legs to her chest, hugging her knees, trying to smile. She flicked a glance up at Lew, he saw her eyes, and saw that she was hiding herself from *him*. She glanced away, then immediately back, and the look in her eyes had become an appeal. Lew smiled uncertainly, thinking that maybe he'd sensed something of what she was feeling, he wasn't sure. Then he made his smile confident and reassuring, nodding at her, and she smiled back at him, eyes relieved. What they had communicated he didn't know, possibly nothing, but his smile and nod seemed to have made what was happening all right for Jo.

What the hell are we doing! he thought in sudden irritation. *We're not a bunch of suburban wife-swappers!* Then Harry came walking out of the little hall back into the room so ludicrously naked in his baseball cap that Lew had to smile. Harry had a tan leather and chrome camera in his hands and, still walking toward them, he aimed it at Shirley, it flashed, he stopped to open the back of the camera, and Lew understood that it was a Polaroid.

Harry peeled off the picture, looked at it, nodded approvingly, then walked on to hand it to Jo. "Free souvenirs for the ladies." Jo reached up for it, and Harry gripped her wrist and drew her to her feet. "Okay! Everyone up for the class photograph!" He gestured toward the hearth, and Lew watched himself and the others obey, wondering why. He didn't know how to object, that was why: On what grounds? Their clothes actually off, the possibility of refusing anything lesser didn't seem to exist. He knew—the champagne, the marijuana—that he wasn't thinking well, that his thoughts and reactions were sluggish, trailing events by too long to affect them. On the brick hearth they stood accepting Harry's positioning; he pushed the women apart, indicating that Lew was to stand between them, and Lew obeyed, feeling the fixed quality of his smile. "Okay . . . " Camera at his eye, Harry retreated, bringing them all into frame, then he lowered it. "Let's see a little life, for crysake! You look like a stand-up morgue. Put your arms around them, Lew! Like you were actually pleased you're standing between a couple naked ladies. Just keep your hands off my wife's tits, is all." Lew carefully put an arm across their shoulders, smiling rigidly. He made his mind blank, simply refusing to think about Shirley's naked shoulder unfamiliarly in his cupped hand; he drew Jo close, for comfort and to get through the moment. "Okay"—Harry demonstrated a little sideways step-and-kick— "dance step!" Obediently the women began it, a step and kick to each side alternately; Lew had to join or be shoved off balance. *Flash!* The flare struck his eyeballs and, still trying to dance, bumping into Jo, Lew watched the great blind circles float up and to one side. He was interested: they dimmed, turned maroon, strengthened again, then Harry was pushing the camera into his hands, showing him where to press to take a picture. Lew walked to where Harry had stood, raised the camera, and for a moment watched the three of them, small in the viewfinder like a tiny television, the smiling women graceful, Harry heavy-legged and leering out from under the peak of his cap. Lew pressed the stud, the unreal little scene whitened, then he handed the camera to Harry and in that instant felt the focus of his attention move out of the room, and knew the party was over.

Harry insisted on one more of the four of them, and using the camera's built-in timer, took it: the four dancing, and this time thumbing their noses at the camera. Now he could get dressed, Lew thought, and turned to cross the room toward his clothes. But at the join of the heavy drapes across the front windows he stopped, and drew them apart an inch. The street and the sky had turned gray, and a light showed in an apartment up at a bend of the road. The others looked, too, murmuring in surprise. Then Lew and Jo dressed, Shirley bringing out robes for Harry and herself. For a few further moments they talked quietly, looking at Harry's photographs to smile again, but the strange, glossily colored little scenes seemed already to have receded into the past.

Outside as Lew and Jo walked through the parking area, two more lights had come on, in the next building, and a Toyota sedan passed the end of the driveway, the driver young, wearing suit and tie. "A stockbroker, I'll bet," Lew said. "I think the New York Exchange opens in half an hour."

Jo nodded without interest, turning in at their place. "How do you feel?" she said.

"All right. Kind of fuzzy. Muzzy. Buzzy. But not as bad as I thought."

"Me too." They stopped at her door, and as she found her key in her sweater pocket, Jo said, not looking at him, "I didn't really like that, Lew."

"No. I didn't either, especially. No real point to it."

She opened the door, they stepped in, and now she looked at him. "Then why didn't you stop me?"

His mouth opened for the quick, angry retort, but before he could phrase it, he changed his mind: she was right. "I should have, god damn it. Why didn't I?"

Instantly she put her hand on his arm. "I could have said something myself; I wasn't gagged." Then: "I'm glad I didn't. I'm too prim, it's incredible. I'm actually prudish."

"No, you aren't. Not when it counts."

She smiled. "Shirley's lovely, isn't she?"

He studied her face for an instant, but her expression was serene. "I guess so. So are you."

"You, too."

"Of course. But not Harry."

"No."

Lew walked on to the balcony doors, and as he rolled one open, they heard from far off, across the distance between them and the invisible freeway, the faint diesel whine of a truck. Jo walked forward, and both stepped out onto the balcony, their eyes moving across the graying landscape. She said, "When you think about it, it *was* an adventure tonight. The cops. Sneaking home over the hills. Even just now at the Levys'."

"Yeah." Lew nodded, wondering which would make him feel worse, to stay up now or sleep for only an hour and a half.

"It'll be fun thinking about it tomorrow—today. After I've had some sleep. Till like noon. Lew, I hope the Walks don't stop!"

"Well, we'll see." He yawned suddenly, blinking. "Maybe Harry'll come up with something."

• • •

CHAPTER SEVEN

• • •

They didn't see the Levys for several days. Harry began a trial on Tuesday, going directly to court each morning, so the men drove separately. Shirley and Jo spoke on the phone during Shirley's lunch hour: the Levys would be gone next weekend, visiting Shirley's parents down the Peninsula. In the early evening, Lew and Jo drove in to the Mill Valley library for a new supply of books; and each in his own apartment were reading in bed by eight-thirty, asleep before nine-thirty. At Lew's office on Wednesday a typist unaccountably lost the last two pages of the memorandum she was typing for him; it had to be finished next morning, and Lew worked Wednesday evening at the office reconstructing them from his notes.

On Thursday afternoon the two couples played tennis, in the way they sometimes arranged. Mostly young people occupied these apartments, no children allowed, and in good weather there was often a late-afternoon scramble for courts as people came home from work. Lew and Harry left the office early enough to beat the worst of the commute traffic, quickly changed clothes, then trotted across the street, rackets in hand, to join the women, who were already occupying a court.

Lew and Jo against Harry and Shirley, the most evenly matched foursome, they'd learned, they played one long set, the Levys finally winning. Then, still in tennis outfits—the women in white singlets, the men in T-shirts and shorts—they sat on Lew's and Jo's balcony sipping cold white wine: behind them Jo had her big recorder playing, the volume way down. She'd prepared a casserole that morning, and put it into the oven just before leaving for the courts. Presently they'd have dinner out here, staying out as long as the fog didn't come in.

Though the sun had set, daylight still held strong. Harry sat tilted back against the wall in a webbed aluminum chair, legs extended to the railing, ankles crossed, his heavy legs very dark against the white socks. His glass comfortably balanced on the roll of his stomach, he said, "Well, if no one else is going to say it, I'll have to: this is the life."

"You stole that from Jo's father," Lew said, and the others smiled. Lew sat on the railings at the corner.

Beside him in an aluminum chair Jo said, "It *is* nice. I feel very contented."

"Me too," Shirley murmured. Legs crossed, glass in hand, she sat beside Harry.

After a moment Harry turned to look at Lew quizzically. "Well? You want to make it unanimous?"

He smiled. "Sure, why not. Be ungrateful not to. I was just thinking—sitting here all relaxed, glass of wine in hand, music, feeling good—we're probably all of us part of the one-tenth of one percent of the world's population both present and past, who may just have the easiest, most comfortable lives anyone ever lived. In spite of all the problems, with new ones coming up, that everyone talks about. So who am I not to love it?"

"You don't, though," Jo murmured.

"Oh . . . " He grinned at her. "I probably belong in the Middle Ages. In a Walt Disney hovel with a half-door opening onto the street: look in as you walk by, and there I sit in my Robin Hood suit and Chico Marx hat, cobbling shoes. Because that's what my father did, and his father before him. Never entered their heads or mine that I'd do anything else, so it suits me fine. Couple days a week I work on the cathedral, like everyone else in town. The way we've all been doing for four or five hundred years. No hurry; just string enough lives together, and it'll get done. I'm just one of an endless series of drops dripping on the grinding wheel of life or something. And I never question it because that's my lot, what God ordained. So I'm happy."

"But now?" Jo said.

"Well, the cards are punched differently now: nobody's willing to be ordinary any more: it's how we're programmed. The guys still in their jeans and leather hats, getting on to forty, the long hair thinning, but still cranking out the talentless paintings, crappy jewelry, blobby candles and piss-poor leatherwork instead of driving a truck, pumping gas, or cobbling shoes as nature clearly intended. Because we're all *unique* now, everybody talented, all 'creative.' They even have *classes* in creativity, for godsake. For the backward geniuses who haven't quite got the hang of it, I guess." Lew sipped at his wine, then shrugged. "And I'm not one damn bit different than the leather-belt makers in the Munchkin hats. At best I'm an okay lawyer; about what anyone could be who's able to hang on through law school and get through the bar exams. Not special, it turns out. Not talented or creative. But with the feeling I *ought* to be—you know? Punched in. And that keeps you a little restless and dissatisfied, is all."

He looked over at Harry. "What about you? Are you unique? Like everyone else?"

Harry sat looking at him, blinking slowly, consideringly. "Well, god damn you," he said then, "I wasn't quite ready to say this. In the back of my mind I still thought—maybe justice of an appellate court. Not quite nobody. A little *bit* special. But shit, I guess not even that. I haven't really believed it for quite a while now. But I wasn't quite ready to say it out loud. So okay, you've brought me down. Now what?"

"Drink." Lew leaned down to pick up the jug from the floor. "What else?"

Jo sat steadily shaking her head. "I don't believe that. We're not all programmed to think we're so special."

"Oh no?" Lew said. "Look: none of us owns much, we're pared down long since, we travel light. We own very little of our own pasts; there's no room. But one thing you've got and hang onto—is the album; the photo album and scrapbook your folks kept. Pictures and souvenirs of everybody, but especially you. Starting out black and white, from literally the day you were born, then on through the birthdays, changing to color, dozens and dozens of pictures. Plus old report cards, clippings. You *were* special; programmed from the start to believe it. And we've all got something like it, I'll bet."

Shirley said, "Could I see your album, Jo? I'd love to."

"Sure. I'll check the casserole, and bring it out."

Harry said, "You know, you're right. Jeez, the stuff my parents kept: they sent me a cartonful of crap when they moved to Florida. Too bad I'll never make President; history will lose the best-documented life of all time. There must be ten pounds of photographs, newspaper clippings, a high school year book, stuff I made in first *grade*. All my Boy Scout merit badges!"

Lew smiled. "I've got a box full of scout stuff my mother saved; it was with some things of hers. It even included my hat badge. I made Star Scout, incidentally."

Jo walked out with a large tan-leather gilt-ornamented book. She handed it to Shirley, who nodded and said, "My folks have one something like this. Of me and my sister; I'll bring it up." She opened the cover, said, "Oh, these are darling!" and bent close to a page of black-and-white baby pictures.

"*Star?*" Harry was saying contemptuously. "That's nothin'! I made . . . my god, I forget. What is it? I got the badge at home; it's heart-shaped. *Life*, I think! I made Life Scout. My father was going to kill himself because I didn't make Eagle."

Lew said, "Can you still tie a sheepshank?"

They drank more wine, and—no fog rolling in over the hills—had supper on the balcony. As they ate, it grew dark, the street gradually taking on its night-time look, and when the street lights came on, Harry stared out over the railing, nodding, chewing. He'd been working on something, he said, for Monday's Night People. But, smiling and shaking his head no, he wouldn't say what. It was a good evening, and after eleven when the Levys left.

In the kitchen, Lew washing dishes, Jo drying, Jo said, "Shirley doesn't really look forward to going down the Peninsula."

"Oh? Why?"

"Her parents always have questions. Very casual and subtle. But what they all mean is: when is Harry going to be a partner?"

"Well, he could be. If he wants."

Jo nodded absently, putting dishes away in the small cupboard as she dried them. "You know, you may be right. I had to finish college; my parents insisted. And now I make models for a living, something I could do in high school. That's fine, they say, as long as I like it. But it isn't what they expected."

"I know. You really screwed up; they even have to smile about me." He lifted the plug, then moved the swing faucet in an arc, trying to rinse away the artificial suds. He turned from the sink, wiping his hands on the front of his shirt, "Well. Speaking of your father, it's another day, another dollar. And time to hit the hay. Right?"

"Right."

So the week passed. On Friday, Harry's trial recessed, he and Lew had lunch, and as they sometimes did in good weather, had a quick sandwich, then walked idly around in the sun. Today they looked at display windows; stopping at Brentano's, at a stamp and coin shop, at Brooks Cameras. Here Harry inspected everything in both windows, and Lew said, "Harry, the deal is you can have one thing here, anything in the windows. What is it?"

Harry shook his head. "No: I want it all. One of everything they got in the entire store, doesn't matter if I can use it or not. I want that enlarger, both the sixteen-millimeter movie cameras, and all the telescopic lenses. I even want the used theater projector; it's a bargain."

"Two hundred and fifty bucks?" Lew looked at the foot-high crackle-finish metal box, from which a lens projected.

"Sure, the thing's got a twelve-hundred-watt light, and that's a tremendous lens; it'll project stills for a mile. I want the stereo camera too; you ever see what they do?" Lew shook his head. "Incredible 3-D pictures; color transparencies in three dimensions; they look alive. Terrific effect."

"Harry, why don't you *be* a photographer? It's the one thing you get excited about."

"I might. I just might some day." He looked at his watch, and they turned back toward the office.

On Saturday morning, accepting a standing offer from a couple in a neighboring building to lend their bikes, Lew and Jo cycled to Tiburon along the shoreline bike path, watching the sparkling Bay beside them speckled with weekend sails. At Sabella's, sitting out on the deck with the weekend crowd, they had a gin fizz, then biked home.

After dinner Lew got out a yellow legal pad and, Jo reading on the chesterfield, worked at his desk on a talk he'd been invited to give next month, along with the other council candidates, by the League of Women Voters. After half an hour he put down his pencil to stretch, and Jo looked up. "How's it go?"

He shrugged. "I'd sell my soul for a new idea." Lew raised a hand to his mouth, and leaned toward the floor. "How about it?" he called. "One slightly used soul for a really new, fresh political talk! That a deal?" He waited, hand at ear, then shook his head. "No dice, I guess. For where is the fearful pink smoke, the dread odor of brimstone?" He sniffed the air. "You smell anything?"

"Lew, cut it out," Jo murmured quietly, and he looked over at her, amused and surprised.

"That bother you?" She didn't reply, and he said, "Hey, it *does*, doesn't it! You're actually a bit worried: a little primitive fear that there just *might* be a sudden puff of smoke, an awful stench." He leaned toward the floor again. "Price not right? Well, how about just one new phony political promise, then? For this used-up, retreaded old soul!"

"Lew."

"Okay," he shouted to the floor, "I'll throw in Jo's!" He waited, hand at ear, then sat up, shaking his head. "Doesn't look like you've got a thing to worry about. But it worries me: look at guys who sell their souls to be President, and I can't even make city council. What a miserable, shriveled-up little soul I must have."

He worked for another ten minutes, then folded the dozen long yellow sheets and tucked them away on the bookshelves.

On Sunday evening, a few minutes past ten, Shirley phoned Jo. They'd just got home, she'd just walked in the door: Harry had asked her to phone while he emptied the car. On the way home he'd decided he ought to give them an advance briefing on tomorrow's Night People: could they come over to Jo's after supper tomorrow?

They arrived a little past nine, Monday, the doorbell ringing several times exuberantly. Jo, in a yellow jumpsuit, stood closing cupboard doors in the kitchen, giving various surfaces a final wipe with a wrung-out cloth. Lew, who had rinsed and dried the dishes, then wandered out onto the balcony, came trotting in to answer the bell, knowing who it was, glad to see them, shadow-boxing on the way: he wore after-work tan wash pants and a long-sleeved lemon-yellow shirt, knowing his tanned skin, black hair, and mustache showed off well in this outfit.

Harry stood filling the doorway, grinning so broadly it pulled his mouth slightly open. He wore ragged denim shorts, sandals, a gray sweat shirt; all Lew could see of Shirley in the corridor behind him was a strip of one leg of red velvet pants and the sleeve of a blue denim coat. "Hi, come on in"—he stepped aside—"welcome home." Harry walked past him, grinning euphorically, and Lew lifted his eyebrows questioningly at Shirley, who shrugged. "He's out of his mind with whatever he's planned for tonight: chuckling, shaking, twitching all through dinner. Hi, Jo." She walked into the kitchen area, and Lew led Harry out to the balcony.

"Sit down." He nodded at a chair. "And quit grinning, for godsake; makes my face hurt just looking at you." Under his arm Harry held a large gray manila envelope, their firm's name printed in a corner, and he sat down, leaning over the chair arm to prop the envelope against the railing beside him. "Jo's still got coffee hot from dinner, or you want a beer?"

"Beer," Harry said, still grinning, and Lew walked to the refrigerator, and opened two cans; Jo stood folding a kitchen towel, Shirley at the little white table filling two coffee cups.

For a few minutes the four sat on the balcony idly talking about the Levys' weekend. Then Harry set his beer on the rail, and picked up the manila envelope. Glancing around at the others, pleased with the drama he was creating, he bent up the metal clasps and opened the flap. Lifting the envelope to peer into it, he reached in, simultaneously turning the envelope over, so that as he slid out whatever it was, it emerged blank side up: it appeared to be a sheet of thin, flexible white cardboard.

Lew sat facing Harry, both directly beside the railing of the narrow balcony. Jo sat near Lew, her back to an end wall; Shirley in the open doorway just inside the living room, on Jo's wheeled work chair. Leaning toward Lew, Harry extended the letter-size sheet, blank side uppermost, but as Lew reached for it he could see that the bottom side was a glossy color photograph, and he understood what this was: Harry owned an enlarger Shirley had given him for a birthday present.

Taking the sheet, Lew turned it over, and yes: it was the nude shot, rephotographed and enlarged, that Harry had taken of Lew, Jo, and Shirley. Before rephotographing the original print, Harry had apparently pasted narrow black strips over the girls' faces, because the strips appeared in the enlargement as part of the print. They made Jo and Shirley only a pair of anonymous bodies, but Lew's vapidly grinning face showed clear and sharp.

He sat staring at the enlarged photograph in his hands: Jo and Shirley had gotten up to lean over the back of his chair, looking over his shoulders; he could feel the faint warm breath of one of them on the right side of his neck. Lew shook his head slowly, reluctant to look up: he felt embarrassed, not so much at his photographed nakedness as at this irrefutable evidence that he had once really been this foolish, even semi-drunk.

Squatting down beside him at his right, Shirley said, "That's a brave, brave smile, Lew," and nodded at the photograph.

"I know. And your hair was lovely." Leaning forward, he offered the photograph to Harry, who gestured it away.

"Keep it. I printed up three or four of them."

"Oh, thanks," Lew said sarcastically. "We can all sign it. 'Fifi Levy, Cuddles Dunne, and Lew, the Stud: in memory of a great gang and a great evening!' I'll frame it. How come you blacked out the faces? I'd know them anywhere."

Harry smiled mysteriously. "Well, it makes the picture even more salacious, don't you think?"

Lew looked. It was true: the black strips across the women's eyes reminded him of photographs he'd seen outside topless night spots on San Francisco's Broadway, before they'd stopped troubling to use black strips. "I guess so." He passed the photo over his shoulder to Jo. "But so what? Why bother?" Lew smiled to conceal his annoyance.

"I just thought it would be more effective." Harry sat back, hands clasping behind his big head. "For the poster," he added, watching Lew's face.

"Harry, for crysake! You sound like Abbott and Costello! What poster?"

"Your campaign poster, Lew. It's not a bit too early to get started." Harry picked up the gray envelope from his lap, and began poking through it, saying, "Get the jump on your competition." Again he slid something out of the envelope face down, and again Lew could more or less see what it was; another copy of the same 8 × 10 print, this one pasted onto a larger sheet of white paper. The top and bottom of the larger sheet were folded over onto the photo, partly covering it.

Lew took it impatiently, flipped open the two paper flaps, and, the women leaning over the back of his chair again, they all looked at it. It was the same print but on the paper to which it was pasted, in careful felt-pen lettering just over the photograph, was printed, GET YOUR JOLLIES WITH "JOLLY LEW" JOLIFFE! Then came the photograph, Lew stupidly cavorting between two naked girls with blacked-out faces. And below the photo in smaller lettering: A *vote for "Jolly Lew" is a vote for Sexual Freedom! Your future Mill Valley Councilman, Lew Joliffe, between four of his consTITuents!*

The crude poster in his hands was so absurd that when Lew looked up at Harry he was smiling genuinely. Shirley said, "Harry, for godsake, that's just plain *dumb*. It's not worthy of you! That's high school humor!"

"Right!" Harry nodded vigorously. "You've got the idea: that's exactly who it's for."

"*Who?*" Lew shouted. "Who's on second! No, who's on first, *what's* on second!"

Voice patient, Harry said, "I was in the Mill Valley library one night last week." The women sat down again. "And the reference section was crammed with teen-agers, a fairly startling sight. When I checked out my books I asked the woman at the desk how come this burning thirst for knowledge? She said it was term-paper time. At Tamalpais high school. Happens twice a year. Term papers are due this week, so every night last week the reference section was packed with kids, because you can't take reference books out. Well, the climax is today and tomorrow; all day long from the time the library opens in the morning till it closes at night. Because most of the papers are due Wednesday and Thursday; all of them by Friday."

He paused, and Lew nodded. "Well, thanks, Harry, that clears up everything. Who's not on first, he's at the library."

"I was at the library again tonight," Harry said. "And just before it closed at nine o'clock, I waited till the last of the kids got out of the reference section. Then I left one of these splendid posters behind. A duplicate of the one you've got there, but even more carefully lettered. I tucked it into one of the reference books left on the table." Harry sat back, thumbs hooking into the band of his shorts, grinning around at the others. "I'd say that the odds that it won't be found tomorrow are minuscule. It's just about impossible, in fact, that one of the crowd of kids in that reference section tomorrow won't open up that particular book. And discover an absolute sensation: Jolly Lew Joliffe, Mill Valley's very own centerfold! Naturally he or she will show it around to absolutely every other kid in the library. And then—well, god knows where in Mill Valley they'll stick it up, but you can bet your ass they will. Somewhere. Prominently. Maybe Xerox a batch of them on the library machine, and plaster them all over town."

Bewildered, Lew sat staring at Harry with a weak, one-sided smile. He didn't understand, didn't know how to react or what to say. The women sat unbelieving, looking from Harry to Lew. Finally Lew said, "You're kidding, of course."

"No," Harry said judiciously, hands dangling from his hooked thumbs. "No, I'm not, Lew. I really did it."

Her voice stunned, Shirley said, "Lew, he *did*. We stopped at the library just before we came here; he said he had to reserve a book. I waited in the car. He had that envelope in his hand when he went in."

"Right." Harry nodded. "They were just starting to turn off the main lights when I tucked a magnificent specimen of your poster into one of the books in the reference section. So it's there right now. Just waiting for the kids who'll descend on that section like knowledge-devouring locusts when the doors swing open in the morning."

"*Why? Why*, for crysake!" Lew lunged forward in his chair toward Harry, eyes fierce and demanding.

"To give you a chance to get it out, Lew. *Tonight*. Before those doors open tomorrow!" Harry sat forward suddenly, leaning eagerly toward Lew, their faces hardly a foot apart. "It's tonight's *project*, Lew! You and Jo go in after it! Shirley and I out front in the getaway car!"

Shirley said, "You've finally done it, Harry. You're out of your mind."

Her voice tight, Jo said, "Harry, you can't *do* this. You've got to go back there! To the library! First thing tomorrow! And get that thing back the very minute it opens."

Harry didn't answer or even glance at the women; just sat leaning toward Lew, grinning, waiting, watching Lew's face.

The things he ought to be saying were rising up in Lew's mind: that Harry's insane poster shown around town could kill any chance he might have in local politics, or later on in state; any chance at a partnership in the firm, perhaps any real career in law at all, he wasn't sure; at the very least it would cripple his prospects at work, might even lose him his job. Yet he found himself unable to hold back a smile, and what he was, voice thoughtful, "You mean sneak back in there tonight. And get that thing back."

"Lew, *no!*" Jo said sharply.

"Harry, cut it out," said Shirley. "This isn't what the Night People is about at all."

"You're wrong"—he swung toward the women. "It's the essence of it! Did you think it was sitting on the shore on Silva gazing over at the city? Or dancing under the stars at the shopping center? That was nice, and I liked it, but when did the real fun begin?" He leaned closer to them over the arm of his chair. "It was when the *risk* began. The little touch of trouble. The chance of actually getting arrested. Lew sensed it from the start; when he stepped up on the curb, and watched the cop cruise by. When he sat on the guy's porch swing deliberately making it creak. Hell"—he threw himself back, glancing around at them all— "what do you think got us all so god-damned *high* last time that we didn't come down till dawn! Stripped off our clothes. Damn near had a gang bang! It wasn't a little booze or marijuana. What sent us up was the run-in with the cops! Which we won!" For a moment or two Harry sat glancing from one face to another, then he resumed quietly. "I don't know what life was like in times past. Back in Lew's Middle Ages. But these days it's mostly a lot of shit. Well, we stumbled onto something that puts a little boost into things: The Night People. And tonight I'm leader and that's tonight's project. Your turn next week, Lew, and you can tell *me* what to do." He grinned, "If you aren't in jail."

After a moment Lew said, "What book is it in?" but Harry shook his head, still grinning. "Harry, make sense!" Lew said. "There must be two thousand books in that section! Or more!"

"That's why you can't just wait till the library opens in the morning, and then walk in and get it. While you were hunting through thousands of books, one of the kids would stumble onto it first."

Jo leaned forward, but Lew heard the squeak of her chair, and turned to waggle a hand, and she sat back, lips compressing. Lew said, "Harry, what if I insist you go back there first thing tomorrow, and get that thing."

"Now, listen to me; all of you. Reference books were scattered all over three or four tables tonight. Dozens and dozens of them. Left lying there for the library staff to put back on the shelves tonight. I just folded the poster in half, and stuck it into the back pages of an open book lying on one of the tables. I didn't close the book or even look at the cover— deliberately. Because to make any sense, this has to be *real*, Lew; you know that. The danger has to be real, not something we can decide to call off, or something I can retrieve in the morning if you can't find it tonight. You're right: there's two, three thousand books there. And I haven't any idea—*I really haven't*—which one it's in. You have to go in and get it, Lew; you've got to. You *have* to find it. Tonight."

Lew sat blinking slowly, thinking about it, the women waiting, Jo's eyes narrowed and hard. "In the dark?"

Harry laughed, his belly trembling under the gray sweat shirt. "I don't know: have to leave something to your ingenuity, won't we, Lew?" And at that, the appeal, the absolute necessity of having to work out how to *do* this crazy thing flared up in Lew tangibly, he could feel it in his chest. Looking at Harry's big, tough grinning face, he had to grin in response: his heartbeat was up; he wanted to do it. Harry saw it in his face, reached down for his beer can, stood up, and stretched. Pleased with himself, he winked at the two women, and walked into the living room toward the kitchen area, can tipped over his mouth, finishing the beer.

Jo got up, came over to squat beside Lew's chair, and put a hand on his knee. "Lew," she said gently, reasonably, "you could get arrested. You *could*."

He had covered her hand with his, turning to smile down at her. "You're talking to Le Chat, famed cat burglar of the Riviera." But she wouldn't smile, and he closed his fingers to squeeze her hand. "Jo, I won't get caught: it's the *library*, not the Federal Reserve Bank. And it shouldn't be too hard to work out some way of doing this. To just sneak in, find that stupid poster"—Harry came strolling out onto the balcony carrying a new can of beer—"and show our juvenile friend here how easy it is."

"Right on." Harry lifted his can in salute, and sat down again.

"But there's no point in your going, Jo; it doesn't need two of us. I can—"

"Oh, I'd love to go!" Shirley cried. "I'd *love* it! Jo, if you don't want—"

"Oh, I'll *go*," Jo said quickly. "If you're really going to do it, Lew, then I want to help." She made herself smile, and stood up. "It might be fun."

Lew got up to go to the kitchen; it seemed to him that what was happening called for more than beer. In the doorway he turned. "One thing, Harry; I won't break in. No matter what. I like the library."

"Oh hell," Harry said easily, "you'll find some way to get in. They're understaffed; I don't think they check every last door and window each night."

"I'm not so sure."

Harry shrugged, lifting his beer. "You'll get in."

For a while then, it was fun; everyone chattering, even Jo, presently. Lew mixed drinks, handed them around, said, "To crime!" and they drank to that. Shirley made them synchronize their watches, then Lew got a yellow legal pad from his desk, laid it on the balcony railing, and drew a large rectangle with a felt pen: just the empty rectangle, nothing

else. Inside it he printed FLOOR PLAN, and held it up. "I want everyone
to memorize this!"

Harry said, "Jeez, boss, *all* of it?"

"Yeh: till you know it in your sleep."

They began talking movie-gangster talk, but in drawing even his joke
plan Lew had begun thinking about the library, picturing it: a low,
handsome concrete building less than ten years old, and built on the
edge of a large park of huge redwoods inside the town. One side of the
park and of the library fronted on a quiet residential street.

Lew sat down and, sipping his drink, visualized the building as though
standing across the street from it: a low tiled roof with huge skylights;
three enormous multiple-paned windows on the street side, eight or ten
feet tall, rising from floor to ceiling; the entrance of double glass doors.
In the daytime, light flooded the interior from these windows, doors,
and skylights, and from banks of fluorescent tubes, but at night . . . Lew
said, "Listen: there's not much of a moon tonight. And there are
redwoods all around the place. Damn big ones on all three park sides,
and in that little strip of dirt along the front. So the street lamp out there
won't help much. It'll be dark as hell inside! And we *can't* show a light
with all those windows. Even a match would show up like a bonfire."

Harry stood leaning back against the balcony railing facing the others.
"It'll be late at night: how many people go by there then?"

"I don't know, I'm not around there late at night. It's a quiet street
but that doesn't matter: one phone call to the cops about a light in the
library is all it would take."

Shirley said, "This is great: real problems!" In Chico Marx accent
she said, "So whatta we gonna do, boss?"

Jo said, "I don't remember any windows in the women's washroom.
We could carry books in there and turn on the light."

"Take forever," Lew said. "It's a long way from the reference section
to the washrooms. And we'd be carrying them back and forth in the
dark."

"Why take them back?" said Harry.

"No." Lew shook his head. "I'm not leaving the place messed up."

"What about a little pen flashlight?" Shirley said. "We've got one, if
the batteries are still—"

"Any light at all would show; those windows are *big*."

They discussed and discarded ideas, enjoying it, quietly excited.
Presently Lew made more drinks. Then Jo found the answer. They
worked her idea over, criticizing it, but it seemed to hold up, and Lew
said, "That's it, then; that's how we'll do it."

"Okay, what time?" said Harry. "Two-thirty?"

"Make it two; we may need every minute."

"Let's get some sleep, then." Harry glanced at his watch. "We'll go in my car; the getaway car, souped up to do a hundred and twenty-five in second. See you at two, Les Chats."

At a quarter after two, Harry driving slowly past the library from the north, they stared out at it as though they'd never before seen it—as they had not; not like this. In the front seat the Levys were dressed as they'd been earlier, except that Harry now wore his baseball cap; Lew wore his usual, the mask front of his cap rolled up; Jo a chocolate brown pants suit. In the darkness only the widely separated street lamps and the yellow parking lights of the slowly rolling Alfa showed. Beside the car just across the sidewalk, a ragged line of redwoods rose from a narrow strip of earth: behind the trees the long street facade of the library slid past. One by one the great floor-to-ceiling windows moved by, their panes shiny black, each reflecting light from the one dim street lamp ahead, and Lew thought he could sense the silent darkness on the other side of the wall. The busy, friendly, early-evening place this had always been for him had turned sinister now, drained of warmth and welcome; beside him Jo sat nibbling her lip.

No one spoke. A hundred yards beyond the dark building, and well past the street lamp, Harry stopped in a pool of darkness beside the redwoods of the rustic park. Across the street on the other side, the low white buildings of a grade school stretched for a short block, dark and still. Harry switched off lights and engine, and Shirley and Jo rolled down their windows a little. For a moment they heard only the small pings of the cooling engine, then became aware of the faint sough of moving air high in the redwoods. Except for the tree trunks and lower branches directly beside them across the walk, most of the park was a solid black wall; through the trees a single light bulb indicated the public toilets and a phone. Quietly Harry said, "All right," turning sideways to look back at Lew, his arm stretching along the seat back. "I'll keep watch every second. And if you two come a-running, I'll start the engine, ready to haul-ass out of here. Shirley will stand on the walk with the door open. You two pile in the back, and she'll—"

"Yeah, we know, we know," Lew said, suddenly irritable. He sat turned to look through the slanted rear window, studying the front and end walls of the building behind them. It looked tightly closed, locked up, and he wondered how and where they could possibly get in; he didn't feel quite sure, in this final moment, that he wanted to leave the safety of the car.

"You got the ground cloths?" Harry said, and Lew wished he'd shut up.

In a small, tight voice Jo said, "Yes. Ours and yours."

"Right." Harry turned front to search the motionless street as far ahead as he could see, to a sharp bend. Then he turned with difficulty, his body too big for the cramped space behind the wheel, to study the street to the rear. "All clear," he said, and grinned at Lew; Harry was happy, Lew realized, hugely enjoying this, and he smiled, too, suddenly excited again.

"Harry, let's go along!" Shirley said. "Instead of just *sitting* here!"

"We can't. We just can't; I've got a hunch they may need a getaway car; we have to stay here." He grinned at Lew and Jo. "Good luck. And good hunting."

Lew nodded. Shirley got out, and they slid past the front seat to the sidewalk, each carrying a folded ground cloth. On the walk, Shirley in the car again, Lew eased the door shut, and stood with Jo looking around them. Nothing stirred. Except for the school and the library this was a street of small, old Mill Valley houses, some built in the early years of the century. No light showed in any of them as far as he could see in both directions. Behind the library Mount Tamalpais filled the lower half of the sky, black on deep blue.

Lew touched Jo's arm, and they turned to walk back along the sidewalk toward the library. They had no plan for entering except to try doors and windows, hoping to find one unlocked. A few steps short of the library, Lew touched Jo's arm again, and they stopped on the walk, looking up at the dark bulk of the night-time building. "You really want to go in there?" he said gently. "You don't have to. There's no need at all."

"I don't know what I want." Still staring at the looming building, so close now, she said, "It gives me the creeps to think of feeling my way around in there. But to just go back and sit in the car waiting would be too drab to bear. What I really want, I suppose, is to have it over with. Do you want to? Really?"

He nodded. "Yeah. Now that we've started. Now that we're out here and really going in if we can. But I want to bring it off, not mess up, so let me think."

The front doors of the library, twenty yards ahead near the center of the long street facade, were a pair of heavy glass sheets opening out onto a wide, brick-paved veranda a few steps above sidewalk level. These doors especially were sure to be locked, Lew felt certain. In any case, he did not want to walk onto that open veranda and try them in full view of every darkened window across the street.

The library was built on a slope: only one story high on the street side, it was two at the rear. Along much of the rear face ran a wide wooden balcony overlooking the woods and the small stream that curled through the park, a fine, secluded place to sit and read on a sunny day. This balcony hung a story above the ground; underneath it ran a row of windows and doors opening into the basement which was divided into rooms for storage, exhibitions, board meetings. They could hope one of these doors or windows had been forgotten.

They stood directly beside the dirt path leading down the slope along the building's end wall, and Lew took Jo's hand, and turned onto it. Feeling their way with their feet through the almost complete darkness, they moved down the slope beside the end wall, and turned under the balcony. Here the darkness was absolute, and Lew reached to the back of his belt where he'd shoved a powerful four-cell flashlight he'd bought for a camping trip. They had to see; the building stood between them and the street, and he pulled the flash out, cupped his hand around the head to confine the beam, and pushed the stud. Aiming the hard white light, he found the first window, and in the light reflected from it gestured to Jo; she reached to the metal frame and pushed. It was locked, and they moved on to the first door. Jo gripped the knob, turning, but it barely moved.

The next window, next door, and the following window were locked. Lew found the knob after that, a dull weather-mottled bronze in the blob of light, tried it, and it turned, the door opening toward him, and Lew said, "I'll be damned."

"Lucky," Jo murmured, but her voice didn't sound as though she felt lucky.

They stepped inside, Lew pulled the door shut, pressing the stud that locked it, and they stood warily listening. Then he swept his beam across the room: it was the boardroom, a long, narrow table surrounded by a dozen neatly pushed-in chairs; at the room's other end stood the door to the inside corridor. He said, "This wasn't luck. Harry unlocked the god-damn door."

"How do you know?" She was whispering now.

"I know, that's all. They didn't forget to lock it: tonight at the library Harry just came down the stairs, into this room, and turned the knob, that's all you have to do to unlock the stud. When they closed, no one checked down here: why should they? They keep these doors locked all the time, you know they do." For a moment longer they stood hesitating, then Lew said, "Come on," and walked across to the inner door. He switched off the flash, slowly and soundlessly opened the door, and they stood, leaning forward in the opening, breaths held, listening. Nothing; no sound. Lew touched Jo's arm, and she stepped past him, out into the dead-black corridor. Behind her he eased the door closed, pulled down his face mask, and pressed the head of the flashlight to the underside of his chin. "Jo," he whispered, and as she turned he pushed the stud. The light flared up onto the Africanlike mask, weirdly illuminating it, and she punched at him, hitting his shoulder hard.

"Cut it *out!*" She began to snicker, through her nose, trying to repress it. "Damn it, if I wet my pants, I'm taking yours!"

The light still on, Lew shoved up his mask, grinning at her. "Well, we're in. Good old Harry; he wasn't taking any chances."

Their light on the carpeted stairs, they climbed quickly, feet making only faint muffled sounds. On the top landing Lew switched off the flash: they stood facing a pair of doors paneled with opaque glass, the shape of the panes barely visible against the dark of the other side. These doors opened into the great main room, and Lew slowly eased one open. Staring across the width of the room, they saw the dim silhouette of the big main desk against the lighter shape of the glass door which led onto the outside balcony. No sound, from inside or the street, and they stepped through, Lew noiselessly closing the door behind them. He led the way, half a dozen steps to the desk, a long waist-high counter at which books were checked in and out. Here they turned to face left, looking ahead into the main room of the library. Jo stood close, a shoulder lightly touching Lew's arm.

The great hushed room lay in deep shadow along the windowed side, and in almost complete darkness along its center and opposite side. But they knew the room, knew what lay where they could not see. The room occupied the entire width of the library and two thirds of its length; behind them lay the children's section. Far ahead, the distant back half of the huge room was stacks, shelf after shelf of books rising from floor to as high as could easily be reached. The stacks stood in a row across the width of the library like a dozen parallel walls. All they could see was the ends of the stacks, their lengths dissolving on into not-quite-darkness—a huge window of the distant end wall admitted a tinge of light from a street lamp.

Lew stood studying the front half of the room, lighter than the stacks because the dim illumination from the enormous side windows was uninterrupted. This front area was divided into sections by waist-high standing shelves; the section ahead and to their left was reference. Directly to their left stood the wide glass doors of the main entranceway, clearly defined against the street outside. With Jo close behind, Lew walked over to them.

His memory was correct: a hinged bar ran across each door at waist level, probably required by fire ordinance. Though the doors must surely be locked on the outside, he knew that if they had to, they could plunge through these doors at a run, the hinged bars unlocking them.

Taking Jo's hand, he turned back, leading her into the main room toward the left. Here vaguely defined parallelograms of yellowed light from the street lay distortedly across table tops, chairs, low divider shelves, and along the carpeting. Reaching the reference section, eyes now accustomed to the faint light from the windows, they moved quickly. The section was bounded by waist-high shelves, enclosing a small area of several tables and chairs. These shelves were packed with encyclopedias of various kinds, specialized dictionaries, Who's Whos of many varieties—references of all sorts, the largest local collection outside the university at Berkeley, larger even than the county's library. Standing at one of the tables, they set chairs aside, then unfolded and snapped together their two ground cloths to form one sheet. This they draped around the table on the three sides nearest the windows, making sure it touched the carpet all around. The cloth was heavy, rubberized, completely opaque; it came up onto the table top by only six inches, would slide off unless held. Jo stood, arms wide holding the cloth in place as Lew weighted it all around with a stack of books from the new-fiction shelf. He tested, tugging gently, and it held. Handing the flashlight to Jo, he whispered, "Crawl in, and wait till you hear me whistle. Then flick the light on for a second."

He walked to the street wall to stand beside a window, facing the draped table. Watching intently, he whistled softly, saw nothing. "Did you hear?" Her voice muffled by the heavy cloth, Jo called yes, and Lew walked to the first reference shelf.

From the top row, he took the first dozen books, and carried them balanced on his left forearm, right palm pressed to the top of the stack. At the open front of the little hut, he knelt carefully. "Turn on the flash." Jo pressed the stud, and the inside of the little enclosure lit up, the shadow of Jo's head and shoulders immense behind her. Lew set his books down, and crawled in. Sitting cross-legged beside Jo, he looked around him appreciatively, sniffing: the rubberized walls had the look and smell of a tent.

He positioned the light, balancing it on its end between them. The strong beam, striking the underside of the light-wood table, reflected downward, illuminating the floor before them, and when Lew took the first book from his stack, and riffled through it, it was well-enough lighted for their purpose.

Within minutes they had searched through two thirds of the stack, riffling through each book, then shaking it. As one of them finished with a book, Lew set it beside him on a new pile, carefully restacking them in the order he'd brought them in. Jo leaned toward him. "This is fun," she whispered. "Ridiculous but fun. It's so *cozy!*"

"Makes me think of camping out in Wisconsin when I was a kid. Listen: find the stupid poster quick, and there'll still be time for me to have carnal knowledge of you right here on the main floor of the library. A first, no doubt."

"First, nothing: you just haven't noticed some of the kids in here."

Leaving Jo to search the remaining few books, Lew crept out, carried those they had searched back to the shelf where he'd found them, and returned with a new load. For twenty minutes then, Lew returning searched books and bringing back others, they riffled through and shook out book after book; finding a canceled envelope addressed to V. Banheim at a Mill Valley address, and a claim check for The Clock Shop.

"How many have we done?" Jo said. They were no longer quite whispering.

"Oh . . . a hundred or so."

She thought for a moment, then her eyes widened. "Lew: they've got over three thousand reference books; I've heard them say it! We'll never finish!"

He frowned, then shrugged. "Probably won't have to; it could be in that one." He nodded at the book Jo had just taken from the pile.

But it wasn't, and presently Jo changed position, getting to her knees to lean forward over the book on the carpet before her. Again and again Lew crawled out with a load of searched books, and returned with a new load. Then, returning once more, careless now in the repeated action, he bumped hard against a corner of the table with his hip, and a side of the tarpaulin and a few inches along the back dropped loose, the light inside beaming across to and reflecting on the window behind them. Instantly Lew set down his books, plucked up the tarp, pulling it snugly around the table again, and blocked off the spill of light. Weighting it down again, he glanced over into the open front of the enclosure, and looked down onto Jo's bowed neck, her hair hanging forward over her face as she knelt riffling through the pages of the last book before her.

She hadn't even known that the tarp had slipped; but Lew knew that for two seconds a light clearly visible outside had shown from inside the library where no light should be. He set the new stack down before Jo, and took the others. These he replaced on their shelf, then walked on to the great window, and—invisible in the darkness—stood searching all he could see of the street through the intervening trees. Nothing moved that he could see. No light had come on in the windows he could glimpse across the street. He walked on to the next window for a view from a new angle, but saw no sign that their light had been seen.

A small rectangle hung in space before him at waist level an inch or two in from the window panes; he touched it, felt cold metal, and remembered what this was. In daylight he had read the block letters, invisible now, enameled across the face of this panel: PUSH TO OPEN AND SOUND ALARM. The panel was attached to a short rod which would unlock the lower hinged half of the big window, allowing it to swing outward as an escape from fire. Fingering it now, Lew smiled at the thought of pushing it: in his mind he could see Harry in the car somewhere ahead whirl in his seat as the gong ripped through the quiet of the street, could see Harry's face as he and Jo ran laughing down the walk toward him.

"Lew, what're you *doing?*" He turned to see the blur of Jo's face at the corner of the draped table.

"Just checking." He walked back, and saw that she had nearly finished with the new stack.

She knelt looking up at him. "Lew, we have to face it: we'll never finish at this rate."

"I know, I know." He frowned, squatting down to face her. "Each load I keep hoping we'll find it."

"I've been thinking: would Harry *really* put it in just any old book? That doesn't sound like him. He'd look at titles to find one he liked."

"You could be right"—Lew nodded. "I can see him; it would appeal to him. But what book?"

"Encyclopaedia Britannica?"

"Maybe; if there's a *Joliffe* listed."

"Where are they?"

"I don't know, but I think now we've got to take some chances. Turn off the flash, bring it along." He gathered up the books in the enclosure, and, Jo following, returned them to their shelf. "Turn sideways," he said. "With your back to the windows. Facing me. Press tight up against the shelves to shield the light." Jo did this, and the light snapped on, her hand cupped around the lens, narrowing the beam. She held it to the book spines on the top shelf where Lew had just replaced the last books, her body keeping all or most of the light from the windows behind her. As she walked slowly backward, Lew followed, scanning titles. They found the lineup of Britannica volumes, then the moving blot of light touched Jerez-Liberty, Vol. 13, and Lew pulled it down. Jo holding the light, Lew flipped pages, then looked up. "Nothing here. No Joliffe ever made it; typical." He replaced the book.

"Try Who's Who."

He thought he remembered where these were; on the other side of the section. They found them, and searched: first through the current Who's Who; then the volume for the past decade; finally through Who Was Who, which sounded promising to Lew, but found nothing; no Joliffes. "Is there one called Who Ain't Nobody?" he said, replacing the last book, then saw the title of the book beside it, and yanked it out. "This is it: I *know* it!"

"What?"

"Who's . . . Turn off the flash!" Her light vanishing instantly, they froze. He'd been waiting for this sound ever since they'd come in, knowing it could happen. Yet now he could hardly believe he had actually heard the small preliminary snick of key against lock plate at the front doors. But he had, and now distantly but distinctively they heard the small *whoosh* of air pushed inward by the opening front doors. Lew tugged Jo's arm, silently laid his book on top of the shelves, and they sank soundlessly to the floor in a squat, heads ducked below the level of the waist-high shelves surrounding the reference section.

Silence; not a sound; it was as it had been. But this was illusion now: someone had come in . . . was up there now at the main desk where they had stood, staring ahead into the gloom hoping to catch them unaware. They didn't move. Squatting low, Lew's hand gripping Jo's wrist, both aware of their heartbeats, they breathed shallowly through their mouths, listening for the listeners.

Two brilliant beams of solid white light shot the length of the library, crisscrossing it fast, searching for a body moving through the dark. "*All right, we see you!*"—it was a cop-voice, astonishingly loud in here. "Step out with your hands up, or we'll shoot!"

"They don't see us," Lew whispered, lips at Jo's ear. "Down on your knees now. Keep low. Crawl over toward the windows, then back into the stacks."

"Where the fuck is a light switch?" a voice up front said.

"I don't know," said a second voice. "The office maybe. How should I know?" Again the pair of lights swiftly swept the library wall to wall, crisscrossing over their heads. Moving fast and silently on hands and knees, Jo, with Lew following, crept along the side wall toward the blackness of the stacks. "Last chance! Stand up now, and you're okay; if you don't, we shoot on sight!"

Would they? Were their guns actually out? Maybe he should call to them: warn them he wasn't armed, and that he would stand up slowly. He could say he was alone, and let Jo hide. But she had reached the stacks, Lew right behind her, and now one of the cops betrayed his mind by using the past tense. "Hey, somebody *was* here! Look at this."

In the almost pitch-dark of the stacks, they crawled on, down a narrow aisle toward the far end.

"What the hell is it for? Some hippie sleepin' under that?"

"Nah, for crysake. Why would he sleep under something indoors?"

Silence. They reached the far back end of the stacks. The stacks paralleled the length of the big room, and very likely the cops would look down the length of each of them now, searching the aisles with their flashlights. But a back aisle ran across the width of the building here, along the ends of the stacks, and Lew rose to stand hidden behind the end of one stack; at the end of the next Jo stood facing him. Now a beam searching the lengths of the aisles wouldn't find them, and the cops might not—they just might not—come back here.

Standing very straight, Lew watched down the aisle along a ragged line of protruding book spines: at the ground-cloth-covered table the cops stood dimly visible behind the brilliance of their two beams held on the little hut. "Beats me," one of them said finally. "Kids maybe," and the pair of lights lifted to search the room again; but perfunctorily now, randomly. Lew watched a chair back become momentarily visible, then slide into darkness again as the hooded microfilm viewer appeared and vanished, then the arm of a chesterfield at the fireplace on the other wall. For an instant a flashlight beam slid across a blue-shirted chest, a silver star winking into visibility, and in that instant Lew saw the face above the star, under a peaked cap: it was the dull and hostile wedge-shaped face of Pearley, the cop they'd encountered at the Strawberry shopping center. Lew glanced at Jo, but her face only a white smudge in the semidarkness, he couldn't tell what she'd seen.

Suddenly he was scared. The possibility that even if they were caught nothing much would happen—that they might explain, and be let off with a warning since they'd caused no actual harm—that possibility was gone: the man out there was an enemy. He was mean, was probably scared, almost surely vindictive, and would certainly remember them—

with pleasure. And he was a cop, and a cop willing to use it had enormous power to hurt with impunity.

Lew felt certain now they'd be arrested if caught, and driven to the county jail a dozen miles north up 101; very possibly to be locked up for the night, if Floyd Pearley had anything to say about that. *What if he drove them up alone!* Lew stood suddenly remembering what had happened in Marin County, not to an unknown like Jo and himself but to an important, powerful man, a member of the State Public Utility Commission, and well known throughout the state. He'd come out of a Sausalito restaurant to the parking lot with friends, at night, had an argument with a cop there, been arrested, handcuffed, and driven to the county jail—alone in the car with the cop. On the way, he charged, the cop had alternately driven at high speed, then hit the brakes, over and again, causing him to fly helplessly off the rear seat smashing his face against the steel screen between him and the cop. He arrived battered and bleeding—caused by a fall in entering the car, the cop asserted. That kind of explanation, Lew knew, was always accepted; and remembering the anger last week of the man out there in the library now, Lew knew they mustn't be found. Yet they stood trapped in a cul-de-sac, no way out except past the cops who stood between them and the only exits.

The searching flashlights had steadied, oval splotches of light momentarily motionless on the carpet before the covered table. "Well? You think he's still here?" Pearley's voice said.

"Don't look like it. *Hey, you!* You still here?" A silence. "Don't answer; must be gone." The other voice laughed, the beams lingering indecisively on the carpet. "Well, what do you think?"

"Could be in them bookshelves."

A considering pause. "Okay, let's search them."

Sweeping up off the rug, the beams sliced ahead through the dark, bobbing gently as the cops walked toward the stacks: Lew stood holding his breath, then had to force himself to exhale and resume breathing. "Okay," said the other cop, and his beam swung to point off toward the park side of the room, "go walk up the first aisle with your flash. Walk around the far end, and come back down the second aisle. Keep on like that. Search every aisle, up and down. I'll stand out here, and see he don't try to come sneaking out."

Lew reached over, took Jo's wrist, and—there was nothing else left to do—led her around the end of the stack, and into the aisle along the street side of the library. Here they stood between building wall and the final stack. For the moment now, the entire row of stacks stood between them and the searching cop. The shelves were backless, and not solidly filled. Between books of one category and the next there was often empty shelf space, sometimes as much as several feet without books. Through these gaps, and across the tops of shelved books, they caught glimpses, looking through the dozen intervening stacks, of the searching cop's flashlight bobbing rhythmically up the first aisle across the room from where they stood watching.

The beam reached the end of the distant first aisle, then swung to shoot across the back aisle, searching it, touching and brightening the wall not a yard from where they stood. It swung away then, the cop started down the second aisle, and just as Lew thought of the possibility so did the cop on guard out front. "Hey, Floyd! Walk backwards coming out! So he can't sneak along the back aisle, and get past you!" Through the shelves Lew and Jo saw the light swing around to shine back along the aisle, lighting up the end wall. Then, the beam holding the end wall, it steadily lengthened as the man moved backward down the second aisle.

Steadily holding on the back wall, the flashlight reached the end of aisle two, and Lew stood staring through the stacks, fascinated. The cop out front was intelligent: he stood holding his flash down the same aisle, keeping the back wall lighted during the moment it took Pearley to side-step to aisle three—and now Lew knew there was no way at all to get past either cop.

The searching cop walked up the third aisle, his light bright on the back wall. The cop out front still stood at aisle two, his light on the back wall also. And now Lew made himself turn away, staring at the rug, trying to think. Within—what? Two minutes? Less?—Pearley would turn into this final aisle to find them standing here; there was no escape. If he'd been alone, Lew thought, he might have run for it; sneaked to the front end of this aisle, then run out into the library past the cop standing guard; ducking, dodging, trying to make it to the doors, out, and then down the street as fast as he could sprint to Harry's car. But the thought was time-wasting: Jo couldn't do that, and even if she could, he wouldn't risk the possibility of a shot. "Lew, I'm scared," she whispered, and Lew lifted his head: through the stacks he saw the cop begin to back down an aisle, the bobbing circle of his light remorselessly fixed on the end wall. "What if they have their *guns* out?" she whispered. "What if he turns into this aisle, and shoots when he sees us. It happens! You read about it."

"Take it easy," he whispered. But *would* Pearley have his gun out? Yes, he would: he couldn't know what he might walk into each time he turned into a new aisle; Lew knew the gun was in his hand right now. Would he shoot when he saw them? He damn well might; he'd be scared! Lew understood that he had to call out. Right now. Call to them, say where they were, and . . . what? That they were lying face down on the carpet, hands clasped at the backs of their heads, and *don't shoot, please don't shoot!* At the front end of an aisle, he saw across the book tops through the backless shelves, Pearley side-stepped and began to walk up the next, his light on the end wall, the other cop's light shining down the previous aisle. Hating it, hating to abjectly surrender to this man, Lew opened his mouth to call out.

Instead he continued to stand for a moment, motionless, mouth still open. Suddenly he squatted, sliced both hands into the books of the bottom shelf, and lifted out a length of them pressed between the flats of his hands. Very swiftly he rose, set them onto the vacant space of a shelf at eye level, and as fast as he could move squatted down again to seize a second length of books, and set them onto still another vacant space above.

Again squatted at the bottom shelf, making the least possible sound, he slid a third length of books as far as he could, to a vertical divider; and now he had cleared a space perhaps five feet long. He looked up at Jo but she had already understood, and she quickly lay down on the carpet before it. The cop reached another aisle—only two away now—and began backing down it; they could hear his rapid, muffled tread.

Lew turned to run silently half a dozen feet farther along the aisle, squatted, and began clearing another space along the bottom shelf. Watching Jo in side vision as he worked, he saw her lying on the carpet, her back to the emptied section of shelving just above the floor. Then she wriggled up onto it, facing out, and lay motionless. Her knees protruded slightly but so did books on either side of and above her, and now Lew no longer had time to look at Jo.

Hardly more than a yard of bottom shelving stood cleared, and he could find no other large gaps on the shelves above. Lew stood desperately hunting, the searching cop side-stepped to a new aisle—the next aisle but one, he saw—and there was not going to be enough time. He squatted, and seized between his flattened palms the greatest length of books he had yet tried to lift, more than two feet of them. Now he had cleared enough space, just barely, if somewhere he could find space for this stack. But as he straightened his knees and stood up, his arms began trembling; the books were big, their weight impossible to hold for more than another second or two, and there was simply no space for them anywhere.

The cop was well up the aisle, would turn next into the one just beside them—and the long stack of books Lew held at his chest like an accordion began to sag. His arms shaking with the impossible strain, there was no more holding them, and he thrust them straight out before him into the nearly solid wall of shelved books. They gave way—were shoved violently back on their enameled metal shelf onto the filled shelf in the next aisle behind them, tumbling the books there onto the floor, pages fluttering, spilling onto the carpet in a thudding cascade of noise Lew knew must be audible even out on the street. Feet instantly pounded, and Lew dropped to the floor careless of sound, and pushed himself back, up onto the five-foot length of empty space he had created, yanking down his face mask, knees drawing to chest.

Lights bobbing, feet thudding, the cops reached both ends of the aisle at his back. An instant's silence, lights frantically searching—"Keep your light outta my *face*, for crysake!" Then: "Not here! Next aisle!" Feet pounded again and lights glared from each end of the aisle in which Jo and Lew lay motionless on the shelves. "God damn, he made it out front!" One light vanished, the other hurtled down the aisle toward and past them, feet thumping as the cop from the back end raced down their aisle hard as he could go—watching through the eye-slits of his mask, Lew felt a terrible urge to reach out and grab a flying, white-socked skinny ankle.

Silence: peering past his knees Lew saw the two beams sweeping the main room, crisscrossing, touching ceiling, then floor, trying to search every inch of the great room in an instant. Then: "He's *gone*, god damn it! You shoulda stayed *out* here! What the hell you come inta the shelves for!"

"'Cause he was *in* there, that's why! Who the fuck you think dropped the books! He was in there with you, and you *missed* him, you asshole!"

"I didn't miss a god-damn—"

"All right, all *right!*" A pause. "Shit."

Again the two beams searched but slowly now, without hope. "Lousy hippies," Pearley's voice said then. "Stealin' books. They sell 'em to buy drugs, you know."

"I know, I know, for crysake."

"Wonder how he got in; the front door was locked."

"Came in downstairs," the other said shortly. "It's how he got out too."

Lew inched forward onto the carpet, and stood; Jo, too, getting to her feet in the dim light from the street lamps through the big windows beside them. Lew walked down to her, and she gripped his forearm hard, laughing silently. "We made marvelous bookends!" she whispered: her shoulders shook with suppressed laughter, and Lew put his arm around them, squeezing her to him, calming her as he led her to the front of the stacks. He felt exhilarated, wanting to *do* something, felt like yelling in sheer wild exuberance.

A flashlight emerged from the library office behind the big checkout desk up front, the other approaching from the children's section. The lights met, and with weary irritability one voice said, "All right, let's check downstairs." The lights bobbed across to the double doors of the interior staircase up which Lew and Jo had come, the doors swung open, closed, and again the library stood silent and dark.

Lew stepped forward, a hand clasping Jo's wrist, and they walked quickly along the street-side wall toward the outer doors, moving past the tall windows through the light patches from outside. Abruptly, Lew stopped, Jo bumping into him. Lying on top of one of the low standing shelves enclosing the reference section was the book Lew had put down when he'd heard the police arrive: he could make out the gold-leaf title: Who's Who in the Law. Without picking it up, he began riffling through it, certain that he would find and feeling no surprise when he immediately did, the crude photo-and-poster Harry had put there that evening. Lew held it up triumphantly, and Jo nodded rapidly, frowning, pushing at him to move on. Their tarps were still there, enclosing the table, and he stepped over, tugged them loose from the book weights, and walked on with Jo, bundling the tarps up under his arm, and looking down at the absurdly titled photograph of his naked grinning self between two anonymous women.

For this they had actually risked arrest and jail, maybe worse, and looking at it now, it didn't seem enough to Lew merely to have recovered it. Now what? Just toss it into a drawer at home? Lew murmured, "Wait here," and on pure neural impulse, without rational thought, he turned left, walking rapidly across the library along the main desk, away from the front doors. On the other side of the big room he stopped at the large bulletin board facing the main desk, felt for and found a thumbtack in its surface, and stuck the poster to the center of the board, overlaying the notices already there.

Just behind him, Jo fiercely whispered, "*No!*" and, reaching past his shoulder, yanked it from the board.

He didn't care. Walking back toward the front doors with Jo, an arm across her shoulders as she folded the paper, and gave it back to him, Lew was grinning: he felt wonderfully alive. Again it occurred to him that he'd like to yell, as loud and long as he could hold it, a Tarzan yell, and give the cops downstairs something to make their visit worthwhile. But he didn't. At the double glass doors he pushed one open for Jo; a

white-doored car labeled MILL VALLEY POLICE stood at the curb, its lights
out. As Jo stepped past him onto the brick veranda, Lew murmured,
"Meet you at the car, and don't waste time. Now do what I say: *run
down the walk! Fast!*" He pulled the door closed, leaving her outside
staring in at him through the glass, astonished. He gestured hard, waving
her on, and after a moment she turned away.

Swiftly now, Lew walked back along the street-side wall to the second
window: leaning to one side, he looked out toward Harry's car. It lay out
of sight somewhere ahead, but he saw Jo pass his window, not quite
running along the walk, walking rapidly toward the car. Then, behind
him, he heard the beginning murmur of voices coming up the inside
stairs. He waited, letting Jo move on, then shoved hard against the waist-
high, rectangular metal plate at the center of the window. As the lower
half of the big window swung outward, a frantic electric trill sounded
abruptly, directly beside him and astonishingly clamorous, an enormous
bung-bung-bung-bung-bung-bung that split the air of the motionless
street.

Lew stepped outside, edged between the trees of the narrow dirt strip
between library wall and sidewalk, then ran. Ahead, the door of Harry's
car stood open, Shirley standing on the walk beside it, waiting. He
reached it—laughing hard, the others staring in wonder—sidled into the
back seat beside Jo, and Shirley jumped in, and slammed the door.

In the moment of silence that followed, Lew realized that the engine
wasn't running. Behind them he heard the crash of the library doors
bursting open, and he swung around to the rear window: the two cops
came hurtling down the shallow brick steps to the sidewalk, actually
skidding on the soles of their shoes as they stopped, heads whirling,
searching. "Let's *go!*" Lew said, swinging to face front, still laughing.
But Harry sat motionless, head and shoulders thrust far out his window,
looking back. Still watching the cops, Harry's hand moved to the dash—
to start the engine, Lew thought. Instead, Harry pulled a knob, and their
lights came on.

"*There they are!*" a cop's voice shrieked over the clamor of the alarm,
and again Lew's head swung around: a cop was running hard around
the front of the police car, the other yanking open the door beside the
walk. They piled in, doors slamming . . . and still Harry sat staring back
at them, making no move to start.

"Harry, *start, start!*" Jo cried, but he didn't move, and now the cop's
headlights flashed on. Harry turned from his window to smile back at
Lew. "Here you are, Lew"—he brought up his hand, something
dangling from a finger—"a souvenir." Lew reached forward, and took

it, a ring of keys. "The cops' ignition keys," Harry said. "They ain't goin' nowhere." He turned to shove head and shoulders out his window. "Hey!" he yelled back. "You're too late! We got away with it: Tom Swift in the City of Gold, and you'll *never* get it back!"

Lew got out, pushing Shirley's seat, squeezing out to the sidewalk. The cops' doors opened, too, and they got out staring at Lew; the alarm clanging unendingly, lights coming on now in houses across from the library. Laughing, Lew yelled, "Hey, Slats! Your pants are too short!" He drew back his arm, and threw hard toward them. Their keys landed on the street, and before they'd stopped sliding along the pavement, Pearley was running for them.

Lew ducked head and shoulders to slip back into the car, then froze in astonishment: feet sliding to a stop, Pearley had yanked out his gun. Bringing it down to a point, he was yelling in rage: "You mother-fuckin' bastard, I'll shoot your fuckin' head—"

The other cop cut him off, voice loud but matter-of-fact. "You fire in town, the chief'll have your stupid ass." Pearley stood motionless, hesitating, and Lew shoved himself into the Alfa. The other cop yelled it now: "Get those *keys*, god damn it!" and Pearley holstered his gun, and ran for them.

Dropping to the seat beside Jo, Lew realized that it had simply never occurred to him—this had been a *joke!*—that the cop might shoot, and he felt his face flush, deeply, cheeks hot, because he knew that it should have. Harshly, angry with himself and Harry both, he said, "Okay, sonny: you better drive like hell now: you got maybe sixty seconds' start." Harry's starter was whirring before he had finished, the engine caught, and Lew looked back. The cop was snatching the keys from the pavement, then Lew was flung back in his seat as Harry shot forward, scorching rubber, the cop behind them racing for his car.

The two-block-long Mill Valley business district lay just around the curve ahead, and Harry swung into it at forty-five, accelerating. Street lamps on, curbs oddly empty of parked cars, the green twin of the Alfa Romeo flashed across dark store windows beside them as they reached fifty-five, touched sixty for an instant, then Harry braked, the squeal prolonged. They rounded the right angle onto Blithedale, fishtailing, then Harry's hand swept through the gears to fifth. A two-mile dogleg length of narrow city street lay ahead now, and Harry hung at sixty-five. Halfway, Lew watching behind, headlights swung into view at the second turn, and the glaring red eye flipped on. Shirley said quietly, "Harry, they could still decide to shoot."

Harry hesitated, and Lew said, "No, we haven't murdered the mayor."

Yet he wasn't quite sure. Watching at the slanted rear window, he first thought and then knew that the headlights behind them had enlarged, but he let Harry do the driving.

Ahead the traffic light flashed yellow, no other cars at the intersection. Reaching it, Harry downshifted to third—to cross with caution, Lew supposed—then Harry startled them by swinging left instead, and Lew understood. Even if Harry had wanted to drive all-out, and he probably did not, the police car would be faster still; they'd have been caught before they reached Strawberry. Instead he'd entered the old, two-lane county road to Corte Madera, an endless succession of short curves, left and right, left and right, over and over again for half a dozen winding miles. On this kind of road they could drive as fast as the other car would dare—and, in fact, Harry's shorter squatter car could swing through the short curves just a bit faster than the bigger one behind them.

This happened, Harry's fist sweeping unceasingly through the gears, accelerating hard up to each curve, then swaying around it, engine braking, and instantly accelerating again; hanging in their own lane, never crossing the line to risk a headon. The trees grew thick along the shoulders here, the houses set well back mostly—high up the slope at the left, well down the slope to the right. Lew sat watching across the curves through the trees, and for three minutes or more caught occasional glimpses of headlights and red eye across several bends. Then no more: they were gaining; a few feet, a yard, on each short swing. Lew said, "Harry, they've radioed. They'll have Corte Madera blocking the other end."

"I know." Harry said no more, head and shoulders ducked toward the windshield, a big hand gripping the wheel at eleven o'clock, other fist on the shift knob. He probably didn't know it, Lew thought, looking at Harry's profile, but Harry was smiling. Another long minute, possibly two, swinging left, then right, left, then right, the four of them leaning out on each curve, possibly helping to cut down the fishtailing. Then Harry moved closer to the windshield, ducking his head to watch for something on the left, never slowing. "Okay! Just ahead!" he said. "Hang on!"

Around the curve to the right, then Harry flicked off the lights and swung the wheel hard left. They shot across the road and up into a steep driveway, curving back toward the direction they'd come from. Harry's hand cut the ignition as he shoved in the clutch, and he toed the brakes. The driveway he'd remembered was a half-moon touching the road at each end. Its center, marked by a flight of wooden stairs leading still higher up the embankment to a house, stood perhaps eight feet above the surface of the road below and beside them. They waited, still rolling slowly forward, and almost immediately twin sharp white beams touched and swept along the dirt embankment beneath them, swinging back onto the road as the car and its red light appeared behind it. The car passed, and now, still slowly rolling, the Alfa dipped onto the downgrade, rolled faster, and re-entered the road in the opposite direction, Harry's fingers holding the ignition key, clutch shoved in. They rolled silently around the curve, then Harry's wrist turned, his leg rose from the clutch, and the motor quietly caught.

He drove fast as ever, pressing hard as he dared on each curve—the cops might have sensed what they'd done. But watching across the curves behind them, Lew saw nothing, and when they came to the Blithedale intersection again, Harry dropped to a moderate speed. On across the freeway overpass into Strawberry, down the service road past the great dark shopping center, then up and around the end of the ridge to home.

In his stall behind the buildings, Harry turned off the ignition, and Lew said, "That was damned fine driving, Harry; you've redeemed yourself, you stupid bastard."

Harry turned to grin at them. "Oh man," he said softly. "I've wanted to do that all my life; race them, and beat them. I tried it once in college, and got caught."

Shirley said, "I feel I ought to scream at you for twenty-five minutes. But it would be a lie, I feel so *good*."

"Well, I'd like to send him over Niagara in a barrel," Jo said. "With spikes in it. We could have been *shot*, we really could!" Then she smiled. "But it was more exciting than anything I've done for days. Weeks. Months. Ever."

Voice lazy and content, Harry said, "Yeah, you got to admit the old adrenaline sure flowed tonight."

"By the bucket," Lew said. "I could be a donor." He sat slouched in a corner of the back seat, hands clasped behind his head, grinning. He leaned forward, feeling in his pants pocket, then reached over the seat-back to drop the folded poster they'd rescued into Harry's lap. "Who's Who in the Law," he said contemptuously.

"You guessed, did you?" Harry turned to grin. "If you'd missed it, I'da gone in and got it first thing in the morning."

"That's not going to help you, Harry. I doubt if you'll survive whatever I work up for you next week. Better take out a big policy for Shirley."

"Yeah," said Shirley, "and I'll help Lew plan." Then her voice altered. "But no more cops! Okay? We keep *away* from them!"

Neither of the men replied, but they both nodded, getting out of the car. As Harry locked it, Jo said politely, "You want to come in? For tea, coffee, a nightcap?" She yawned unexpectedly.

"No," Harry said, then glanced at the sky. "Be strange," he murmured, "driving to work and respectability in just a few hours." He grinned at them. "G'night, Group: your fuehrer is proud of you."

• • •

CHAPTER EIGHT

• • •

Harry's trial over, the men resumed driving to and from work together. Jo finished a model Tuesday afternoon, the interior of a movie theater modified to show it divided in two; delivered it in the van; and brought home sketches for a new job, the "face-lifting" of a small apartment house. Shirley worked at the clinic. And the weather held, a typical Bay Area October, cool or even cold at night but the days more summery than the actual summer had been.

On Wednesday evening Lew and Jo had dinner on the balcony, Lew in jeans and long-sleeved plaid shirt, Jo in denim skirt and an old white blouse, the left sleeve streaked with black where she had wiped a drawing pen. Working together, they broiled hamburgers, then carried them out.

"You thought of anything for the Levys next week?" Jo said as she sat down.

His feet pressing the balcony railing, Lew tilted back in his chair; chewing, he held a finger up, meaning wait till he swallowed. "A couple possibilities," he said then, "I'm not sure. What do you think of some sort of treasure hunt? A few choice items they'd have to come back with."

"Like what?" Jo raised her feet to the railing, too, tipping back in her chair. Her skirt slid up, Lew eyed her, and she rolled her eyes.

"I don't know. Sneak that dumb cop's pants off when he wasn't looking—I don't really know. Can you think of anything?" He bit into his hamburger again.

She shook her head, and they sat silent for a time, eating. Then Jo said wistfully, "Lew, why can't we go back to the four of us doing something again. Just for fun the way we did."

"Well." He considered it. "Actually I don't know what more there *is* to do, just wandering around. We've about done all that. Anyway, I owe Harry something for that library stunt."

"What's your other possibility?"

"Well, I'm not too sure about this one; and it wouldn't include Shirley. Of course it doesn't have to this one time; Harry's the boy I'm after. It would be something he'd have to get. Like we did. Just one thing, it wouldn't really matter what. Because it's where he'd have to *go* that makes it interesting."

"Where's that?" A sparrow appeared on the railing, and Jo leaned forward to set a fragment of hamburger roll down, but the bird flashed off toward the eucalyptus trees across the street.

"Well." Lew hesitated. "To the top of a bridge tower."

"Bridge? What bridge?"

"Golden Gate."

She turned to stare at him. "Are you serious?"

"Well. Maybe. Why not? It could be done."

"*How*, for heaven sakes!"

"Walk up the cable."

She brought her feet and the chair legs down. "Lew, you're *crazy!* You're kidding, aren't you?"

"No." He shook his head. "Take a good look at the bridge cable next time you drive across. I've been looking them over, driving to work the last couple days, and those cables are thick. Immense. Maybe four feet across. And they come right down to bridge level at the center; walk along the sidewalk, and you can reach across the rail and lay your hand on the cable. On the ocean side, there's even some little metal stairs to make it easy; an old lady could get up onto the cable there."

No longer eating, her hamburger on its paper plate in her lap, Jo sat slowly shaking her head in rejection, and he said, "Jo, they're *made* to walk on. There are a couple wires strung all along each one for handholds. Bridge workers do it."

"*Bridge* workers, yes! But Harry's not a br—"

"Harry's done climbing; plenty of it. And rappelled *down*, which is more dangerous. We both have. Higher climbing, and more dangerous than walking up the cable."

"If it's so easy, what's the point!"

"It would be at night." Lew grinned. "The fog coming in, the wind sort of whistling through the wires. Walk up that damn cable with the ocean a million miles straight down under your feet. Have to walk up, and bring something back; that'll learn him!"

"Bring *what* back? How would it get there?" Her eyes widened. "Oh no!"

He began to laugh. "Yeah! That's the trouble! I'd have to put it there!"

"Lew, *no*. I mean it! *No!* It's ridiculous! Like boys playing chicken! I won't have you—"

"I didn't say we were going to: it's only an idea, is all. But it just wouldn't be that hard, Jo. It's been done. More than once. I don't mean bridge workers, I mean that every once in a while somebody has just hopped onto a cable, and walked on up to the top. Some go part way, and change their minds. In the daytime they're seen and arrested. But no telling how many have done it at night. It's no problem then; I've been thinking about it. Do it very late. Wait for a time when there isn't a car in sight. Then hop up onto the cable, grab the handrails, and walk up fast, don't stop to think. Any car comes along, freeze till it's g—"

"Lew, stop. Just listening to that gives me the chills. It's nightmarish! Even the bridge workers don't do that!"

"Yeah, well, I'll admit it's a sobering thought. Stand on the walk looking over the rail in daytime, and that water's a long way down. Be twice as far time you climbed to the top. But still . . . to finally stand up there, Jo. On the very top of the tower. At night, and look around. Across the Bay, and out over Marin. Walk around up there, and look out at the ocean—Jesus. It's why people climb, you know."

"Lew. Please think of something else. The treasure hunt. That sounds like fun, it really does, and I'll help you figure out things for them to get. But I don't even want to *talk* about you walking up that cable at night."

"Well, it was just a thought. Any dessert?"

"No; I could open some canned peaches."

"That's not dessert. Ice cream is dessert. Chocolate cake is dessert. Canned peaches are nothing. We doing anything tonight?"

"No, unless—*California Split* is on. In Tiburon. We've been waiting for it to come back."

"What time? The Levys want to go?"

"Eight twenty-five is the earliest we could make. No, they've seen it; I talked to Shirley at noon."

"Well, all right, let's see it. I like Elliot Gould, don't you?"

"So-so."

"You think I look like him? A little?"

"No."

"Okay, I thought you looked like Faye Dunaway, but now I don't."

On Thursday Jo finished a job, the facade of the face-lifted apartment house, and when Lew got home they went food shopping, driving down to the shopping center in Lew's VW. Daylight saving had ended, but it was still light, the sun near the horizon. Tonight the fog and chill were rolling in over the hills, and Jo wore her white knit sweater and cap, Lew a tan pullover sweater. Jo needed india ink, and they parked at the stationery store around at the side of the big center. Leaving the car there when she'd finished, they walked on, crossing one of the interior streets, to the big main building facing the freeway, and the Safeway store there. At the Safeway entrance they saw Harry and Shirley just leaving their car, up ahead by the bakery. They waved, and Shirley waved back, continuing on into the bakery; under a blue cardigan sweater she still wore her white work dress. Harry came walking toward them in tennis shorts and blue sweat shirt.

"Hi, where to?" he said, stopping. "Safeway?" Jo said yes, and to Lew Harry said, "Walk me to the camera shop." Jo went on into the big whitely lighted store, and the two men began walking along the store's long glass-fronted length.

As Harry began describing an incident of his recent courtroom experience, Lew casually noted a man standing up ahead at the other end of the store front: then he saw his face. Today he wore a short-sleeved sport shirt patterned in acid green, actually a blouse, hanging well down over the top of his pants, but only partially hiding the bulges of holster and folded handcuffs in the back. The pants were dark blue uniform trousers, too short, the ankles exposed; and above the blouse, the long, too thin and too bony face of the cop they'd encountered some ten nights before, almost at this very spot. Even in repose the face looked hostile.

It was too late to touch Harry's arm and turn back. The man would see it and recognize them, understanding that their turning back was an admission that they were who they were. Keeping his face calm, walking along listening to Harry, Lew turned his eyes from the man ahead. He might not recognize them; with luck they'd simply walk on by.

The man's head turned casually toward them, eyes uninterested. Then they narrowed. Lew glanced at him momentarily without apparent recognition, looking back at Harry again; listening, nodding. But it didn't work: abruptly the man stepped forward, directly into their path, blocking their way, brown eyes bright and belligerent. "Hold it; hold it right there!" They stopped, Harry looking at him in blank surprise, and Lew spoke first, hoping to somehow end this quickly.

"Yes?" he said in polite question, face unrecognizing, ready to bluff it out.

But Harry's voice overrode Lew's. "What do you mean, 'Hold it'? Who the hell are you!?"

The man hardly heard him; he stood staring at Lew. "Yeah," he said softly then, and nodded. "You was the guy at the liberry." Suddenly excited, he said, "I seen you!" poking a forefinger at Lew, jabbing the air at his chest. "You flang the keys!"

But there was a tinge of uncertainty in his voice. It had been dark, the street poorly lighted, the distance between them great, and Lew knew he should deny it—making his voice sincere, brows rising in innocence, persuading the man he was mistaken. But he couldn't: everything about this man had the quality of almost instantly antagonizing him; the nasal accent, the permanent look of know-nothing hostility, the aggressively short hair and blatant sideburns, even the skinny ankles. "Li-*brary?*" he said, stressing the pronunciation, brows lifting in a parody of pleasant exchange, helpless to stop himself. "Why, yes, I often visit the li-brary. To read Byron, Keats, Shelley. And others of my favorite poets."

"Your favorites, too, no doubt?" Harry added with leering politeness.

The man stood slowly nodding. "A wise-ass. A real wise-ass. The both of you. You was the other sumbitch at the liberry, wasn't you," he said to Harry. "They was two of you in there!" Again his eyes narrowed, studying them intently. "And you was the guys fuckin' around *here* that night!" His voice tried for the triumphant note, but again it had the sound of a question: they'd been wearing caps then, been dressed very differently. "*Wasn't* you!" he demanded. "With the wimmen!" He began looking rapidly around him, hunting for the women that would confirm his impression.

"You don't know what the fuck you're talking about," Harry said pleasantly.

"Don't talk to *me* like that, god damn you! I'm a cop!"

"So what?"

"Why, god damn you"—the man's voice had lowered in sudden rage—"you're *askin'* for it!" A woman passing by glanced at them, then looked quickly away, hurrying on. "And by God and by Jesus, I can give it to you! You hear? I'll make you wish you was *dead!*"

Almost conversationally Harry said, "Tell me something. If you will, *Officer.* If you please. *Sir.* You don't come from around here, do you." He waited. "Well? You ashamed to answer?"

"Hell, no, I'm not ashamed. I'm from Oklahoma, and proud of it."

"That figures. Been here what? Couple years, maybe?"

"Eighteen months: so what?"

"Well, I'll tell you so what. I've lived here in the Bay Area a hell of a lot longer than that. Since before you even heard of it. I *belong* here. Now I don't seem to have broken any law you know of or can prove. So how come, *tell me how come* some unemployed jerk from nowhere comes drifting up here and lands himself a job on the cops, how come he thinks he's been handed the power to make me wish I was dead? Because he doesn't like what I *said!* Where'd you *get* that kind of power! Who *gave* it to you!" A middle-aged man stopped on the walk to stand staring; Harry glanced at him, and he moved on.

"You'll find out, shitheel."

"Yeah, well, you'll find out something, too." Harry stooped, leaning forward to bring his face closer to the other's. "That's *not the reason you're on the cops*: that's not the job!" He stood erect again, and spoke quietly. "You catch me breaking the law, arrest me. But until then, cop or no cop, it's just man to man. You aren't God because they pinned a badge on you. You start tough-talking me, I'll tough-talk *you*." Harry turned to Lew. "*Look* at him!" he said incredulously. "A god-damn *king* couldn't be madder than this guy! It's like some dirty commoner spit on his robe!" Again Harry shoved his face forward. "You think a cop is some kind of king!? Nobody dares talk back to him? 'Yes, *sir*, Officer,' no matter what *you* say? Well, buddy, I won't *let* you shove me around. Try it, and you won't wish you were dead. You'll *be* dead, you stupid asshole."

The man stood speechless, eyes rapidly moving from one face to the other, then he nodded as at some finality. "Couple of mother-fuckers," he said in a low voice, still nodding. "Couple of real mother-fuckers, aren't you!"

"Yeah." Lew nodded, leaning forward to bring his face close. "*Your* mother," he said. The man's eyes widened, he stood stunned, and Harry stepped forward, brushing him aside.

They walked on, Harry without looking back, but Lew looked: the man behind them stood hunched, neck pulled to his shoulders, watching them from under his brows; his face had gone paper-white. His eyes met Lew's and he swung away.

Turning into a passageway that cut through the face of the long building, they walked through to the other side. There they entered the camera shop, and Harry stood waiting, his face serene, merely glancing once at Lew to smile. A clerk arrived, and Harry leaned forward on the counter on his big forearms, hands clasping, and began questioning him about several types of film. Presently he bought two rolls of different kinds. Standing erect, pulling out his wallet, he saw in the rack a new kind of film labeled "professional." He discussed it with the clerk, nodded, and bought a roll. He asked for mailer envelopes; the clerk hunted and found they were out of them. While he was waiting, Lew wandered the store, reading display signs, looking at photo blowups, trying to distract himself from what had happened outside. He didn't like the encounter now; neither the cop's part in it nor his own; his mind kept rerunning every word and move of it like a looped film, and he wanted to stop.

He strolled to the store windows, and stood looking out at the walkway, and the parking area, much smaller here on this side of the building. Faintly, he heard a woman's voice outside calling someone: *"Lew,"* he almost thought she had said, then he heard it more loudly: *"Lew! Harry!"* It was Jo's voice, and he turned, and shoved through the door.

She was running along the walkway toward him, people turning to stare. "Lew! Lew! *Harry!"* Behind Lew the store door knocked open violently. *"It's Shirley!"* Jo cried, eyes wild, and Lew felt his stomach knot: *She'd been hit by a car!* "She's been *arrested!"* Jo whirled to point toward the distant end of the long walkway ahead. "He's *handcuffing* her!"

Harry plunged past them full tilt, arms rising to pump hard; people yanked themselves out of his path. Then Lew and Jo were after him, sprinting on their toes, and Lew's mind began to work. "Listen. I don't know what's going to happen; Harry may go wild." Digging for his keys as they ran, he said, "Go move the car. Out in back. In the street by the cleaners so we'll know where to look. With the motor running." He shoved the keys at her, Jo snatched them, and angled off across the street.

Harry, and then Lew, hurtled out onto the parking lot at the end of the long building, heads twisting, searching: along the covered walkway across the end of the building a dozen people stood staring in open-mouthed uneasiness at something in a vacant parking slot. Between Lew and Harry and the empty slot stood a sun-faded old blue sedan, its rear fender an unmatching gray: they couldn't see but could hear on its other side feet shuffling on the asphalt, harsh, gasping breathing. Harry ran on, around the back of the old car, and Lew whirled to run around its front, pushing through the crowd on the walk.

The rear door of the old car stood open on torn, dirty upholstery. Directly beside it, arms handcuffed behind her, Shirley frantically fought with the man in the acid-green shirt. His arms clasping her bearlike, he stood struggling to shove her in through the open door of the old car, actually lifting her off her feet now, Shirley writhing wildly, kicking back at his shins, straining her head down to bite at his forearms, blocking the narrow entrance with her legs, tears of rage sliding down her face. *"Help* me, god damn you!" the man cried to the crowd. "She's under arrest! You're deputized!" But no one moved, and a man turned his head to one side and spat.

Harry's fist hit the side of the man's head with a loud popping sound like striking a melon, and the man's arms flew out to the side seeking balance or support as he staggered sideways toward the curb in a bent-kneed shuffle. He kept his feet, swinging to face Harry, a hand curving around to the rear hem of his shirt and Lew understood that Harry was about to be shot and stepped off the curb, knocking the man's groping arm up, and plucked pistol from holster as Harry rushed him. Harry hit him on the chin, sending him scuttling backward to the curb, the crowd parting as he struck curb with heels and went over, landing hard on his back with an audible thump.

Lew shot a glance toward the street: Jo was slowing at the curb, looking anxiously toward them. *"Harry!"* he cried, and as Harry looked toward him, he jabbed his finger in a moving point. Harry whirled, saw Jo and the car, grabbed Shirley. A hand gripping her under the armpit to support her, he ran her across the asphalt toward the wide driveway and street. Sprawled on his back, eyes closed, the man on the walk groaned, rolled to his knees, groaned again, and lay forward on his forearms, head between them in prayerlike attitude. His green shirt lay rucked up over his back, exposing paper-white skin above the top of his pants. Attached to a belt loop, a thick bunch of keys on a ring lay on the blue cloth of his pants, and Lew reached down, gripped them and yanked, tearing the belt loop open. Gun in hand, he turned, spectators stepping quickly aside, and ran for the car.

Harry and Shirley were in, and their door slammed. Jo drove the car slowly forward to the middle of the driveway, shortening Lew's run, and he ran straight on, down the driveway and past the end of the car; Jo's knit cap hung tautly stretched over the rear license plate. The front door stood open, and as Lew threw himself onto the seat beside Jo, she started instantly forward, his door slamming of itself.

A hundred yards ahead the road angled right: watching behind them as they approached the turn, they saw no one following. Then, in the moment of turning, a red Mustang bounced down onto the street from the shopping-center lot, and swung in behind them. Fifty yards, and Jo curved onto the Tiburon road, merging with the traffic, not speeding. Lew turned to pass the key ring to Harry, smiling at Shirley, hand dropping to squeeze her knee, and she smiled wanly, her breathing hiccuplike, just short of a sob. "You're okay now," Lew murmured.

"I know." She nodded rapidly, swallowing. "Oh, *God*, it was so good to see you guys! I'd have *gone*—I'd have got *in* if it had been a police car! And if he'd been in uniform! But that awful man in a *sport* shirt! That terrible *car!* It was like being *kid*naped!" She began to laugh, silently, shoulders shaking, tears welling. Harry had found the small key, and he turned Shirley away from him, fitted the key, and unlocked the cuffs. They had reached the next intersection, and, turn signal flashing, Jo swung off the highway back into Strawberry again. They watched, and a moment later the red Mustang flashed past the intersection behind them, the driver not even glancing their way. Jo drove on then, over and around the hills to their building, and parked in Lew's space behind the apartments. Quickly, they got out, doors slamming, hurrying to be gone from here before someone else drove in. Walking around the back of the car, Lew snatched Jo's cap off the back plate.

Inside his apartment, Lew bolted the door, and turned to Harry, intensely conscious of his hyperexcitement; but controlled, it seemed to him, his thinking lucid. "Well?" he said. "What do you think? The cops on their way here?"

Crossing the room toward the balcony doors, Harry said, "If someone down there knew us and identified us, then sure: they could be here in the next minute. If not, we may just be all right." Standing at the glass doors he searched the street: Jo sat with Shirley on the chesterfield, steadily patting her forearm. Turning from the doors, Harry said, "We're not surrounded at the moment anyway," then clapped his hands together in sudden exuberance, rubbing his palms. "Let's get in a fast drink while we're waiting to find out!"

Lew turned to the kitchen area, and began setting out glasses. He said, "They come here, we'll identify ourselves right away as lawyers: lawyers worry cops. You got a business card?" He was still interested in his own reaction: was he really thinking clearly or only sounding like it?

"In my wallet." Harry dropped into the upholstered chair across from the women on the chesterfield.

"And what do you think we claim illegal arrest?" Lew said; he stood pouring. "Because in that case you have every right to rescue your wife; he'd have no special standing. And I have a right to hel—oh, Jesus!" He clapped a hand to his back pocket, then brought out the pistol. "My god, Harry, what's the penalty for this—*life?*"

Harry rocked in his chair with sudden laughter, then drew the handcuffs from his back pocket. "If it is, so is this. We'll be cellmates!" He laughed again, Shirley and Jo smiling sadly, and Lew began passing drinks around. "Well, hell," Harry said then, still smiling, "if the arrest was illegal, everything's all right. If not, then nothing is. Shirley, that bastard read you your rights?"

She nodded. "While he was handcuffing me."

"He tell you the charge?" Lew said, handing her a drink.

"Yes: resisting arrest. The night we were all down there."

"Well, screw all that," Harry said. "It was an illegal arrest anyway, days after the fact." He took a swallow of his drink.

"That's our defense, at least." Lew sat down on an arm of the chesterfield. "But I'm afraid the arrest was legal; the son of a bitch *is* a cop, incredible as that sounds." He looked down at Shirley. "He identify himself?"

"Well, he stuck his wallet in my face; I didn't know what he was showing me or what was happening. Then he said he was a police officer, and that I was under—*oh!*"

"*What!?*" Harry sat forward abruptly, spilling a little of his drink.

"My cake! He took my cake, and set it on the hood of a car! It could still be down there!"

At this they roared, all of them now, longer and louder than her words justified, in sudden release from tension. Grinning, Shirley said, "Don't laugh, Harry: it was your favorite, a chocolate log! I ordered it special."

"Hell with them then: let's go down there and eat it!"

"I'll bring champagne!" Jo said. "We'll have another party!"

"And invite the cop!" said Lew.

They finished their drinks, and Lew gathered up their glasses. "Let's get in another while we can." Jo and Shirley began quietly talking, and Harry stood to follow Lew into the little kitchen area.

As Lew poured new drinks Harry said, "You know what gets me, Lew? We sit around worrying about legalities: was the arrest *legal*, for crysake. It had nothing to *do* with legality! That wasn't an arrest, it was an act of revenge! It had nothing to do with what happened ten days ago: it was to get even with *me*. The only crime committed is that I talked back. Didn't say, Yes, sir, Officer! And the punishment—handed out right on the spot! No trial!—is public humiliation for my wife."

Lew handed him a drink. "Yeah, well, *we* know that's true, but it won't be in a courtroom." He picked up the other drinks, and walked out with them. Standing before the women as they took theirs, he said, "Shirley, how you doing?"

"Very much better. You know, ever since I was about eleven I've wanted to be rescued from something by a good-looking stud. And now *two* of them! My cup runneth over. I want to give you about a fifteen-minute kiss."

"My fee is thirty." He sat down in the upholstered chair.

"I'll pay! Harry, I want to marry you all over again."

"Beg me. Again." He stood with his drink at the balcony doors, staring out at the street.

"Jo, you were spectacular," Shirley said. "That whole thing with the car was marvelous."

"Damn right," said Harry.

"Any time," Jo said. "That was something *I* always wanted to do."

Silence for a few moments: they sipped at their drinks. Then Lew said, "You know something? They're not coming."

"Could be." Harry leaned toward the glass doors to look both ways along the street. "Maybe nobody down there knew us. I didn't see anyone I knew."

"You never do down there," Jo said. "You hardly ever see the same face twice."

Grinning, Shirley said, "So we got away with it? Huck, is we free!?"

"Oh—oh," said Harry, and their heads swung toward him.

They stood watching at the glass doors: the sun down, dusk near, it was still gray daylight, and down on the street a black-and-white Mill Valley police car moved slowly along the curb toward them, the uniformed driver leaning out his window to look up at the buildings, searching the house numbers. "Oh, god *damn* it!" Harry said.

Shirley said, "Maybe this has nothing to do with us; it's not the same cop. Where's our cop?"

"Sitting in the chief's office," Harry said shortly, "explaining what happened to his gun." The car outside stopped, and Harry said, "Our building: it's us, all right. *Shit!* How did they know?"

Silently they watched as the cop set his brake, opened his door, got out: dark-haired, hatless but in uniform, about thirty. He slammed the door, turning to start across the street, and now in the hand nearest them as he turned, they saw something pink—a square cardboard box which he held by the white string wrapped around it. "Oh, *nooo!*" Shirley moaned.

"What!?" Harry swung around.

"It's my chocolate *log!* Oh, *Harry* . . . it was all ready, all wrapped. It's got our *name* on it . . . "

Lew and Harry turned simultaneously to walk quickly toward the bedroom. The women followed, and at the side window they stood watching the Levys' entrance.

The parking-area lights had come on, and the cop appeared, walking along the side of the building. "The only Levys in Strawberry," Harry muttered. "All they had to do was look in the phone book." The cop turned the back corner of the building, looked for and immediately found the Levys' door, labeled by Harry's business card inserted in the small brass frame under their bell. He pushed the bell, and stood waiting, pink cake box dangling from his hooked finger. Presently he pressed the bell again, and waited. Glancing at his watch, he turned away, with the cake.

Back at the balcony doors again, they watched him reappear, walking down the driveway, cross to his car, get in, and start it, glancing up at the

Levys' dark windows. He drove on, and Shirley said, "Oh, *Harry*; I'm so sorry."

"Not your fault." They all turned back into the room, faces solemn. "It's mine: I eat too much. My god: done in by a chocolate log." Harry suddenly set down his glass, and walked swiftly toward the door. "Got to get our stuff out of there!"

"I'll help," Lew said.

"No, no sense both of us getting busted."

"Harry, if they grab one of us, we're all in the soup. Come on: everybody. Many hands make busy work."

"Is that how it goes?" Shirley said, walking to the door.

"No," said Jo. "Many hands make—is it quick work? That doesn't sound right."

"Many hands . . . " Shirley said, and walking across the parking area they discussed it to the Levys'.

In less than ten minutes they emptied the apartment of everything the Levys owned, carrying their armloads to Jo's apartment, heaping the chairs, chesterfield, and Jo's work tables with tumbled armloads of clothing, sleeves dangling; a jumble of Harry's photographic and sporting equipment; a ragged tower of paperbacks; and Shirley's few cooking utensils. Then, in the camper, Lew and Jo drove to the shopping center, Lew hidden in the back, Jo at the wheel; she would be least vulnerable to recognition, they thought; Harry and Shirley should not be seen at all. Jo parked beside the Alfa Romeo, most of the stores closed now, plenty of room. She looked around as she turned off the motor; no one seemed to be watching. She got out, and walked along the covered walkway to the drugstore; it was nearly dark now. She stopped, looked in the lighted drugstore window for a few moments, then turned to walk back, bringing out Harry's ignition key. She got into the Alfa, started it, backed out, and drove away.

Half a minute later Lew moved from the back of the camper to the driver's seat, turned the ignition key Jo had left there, and backed out. He drove to Belvedere Drive, a quiet residential street a mile from the apartments. The Alfa sat parked at the curb, lights out, and he drew up beside it. Jo got out, stepped up into the driver's seat of the camper, and drove Lew home. She drove on then, parked half a mile away on Reed Boulevard, and walked home in the dark.

Supper was ready: Shirley had prepared it in Jo's little kitchen from canned goods Jo kept in supply for her lunches. Each of them with a plate wherever he could find room—Jo and Shirley on arms of the chesterfield, Lew sitting on the floor, Harry leaning back against the sink—they ate, talking about what had happened; joking, laughing, still excited. The Levys would take Lew's apartment tonight, they decided; Lew and Jo would use hers. Presently they grew quieter. Jo opened canned peaches for dessert. When Shirley walked to the kitchen to rinse out her dish, she said to Harry, standing beside her, "So okay: we're all right tonight. We hope. But what about tomorrow?"

"Tomorrow we move."

She smiled uncertainly. "We already have."

He shook his head, chewing, then swallowed. "First thing tomorrow we throw our stuff in the car, and head for the nearest state line."

"*What?*"

"Shirl, listen. This isn't some little hit-and-run fender-bender: *I took a prisoner away from a cop!* And for that every cop in the county—Mill Valley police, deputy sheriffs, even highway patrol—will be very happy to nab me. *And* Lew." He glanced at Lew, who nodded. "I beat up a cop, took his prisoner, we took his handcuffs, took his keys"—Harry grinned suddenly—"and Lew took his god-damned *gun!*" He tossed his hands into the air. "They'll hang us!" Both men laughed genuinely, the women staring at them.

"Everything but his pants," Lew said, and they laughed again.

Harry set his plate on the sink, and began wandering the living room. "I can't even go to the office again. Ever. My full business address right under our doorbell for the cop to read: address, phone number, extension, and zip code. Everything but my photograph, front view and profile. Oh boy." Passing Jo's big supply cabinet, he reached out to touch one of the lineup of models on its top.

"You think they'll go to your *office?*" Shirley said. She stood shaking liquid soap into the sink, preparing to wash dishes.

"Sure they will! Why not? They'll find out who Lew is at the office, too. We can't risk it anyway: I don't want to serve a god-damn jail term! Become a felon. Be disbarred. No kidding, that's what they're planning for us. Right now. They'll be back tonight." He stopped at the glass doors to nod at his apartment. "And the cop I hit will work twenty-four hours a day, he'll give up sleeping—oh, *man*, would he like to find us! They'll have warrants out: we won't dare risk being stopped for anything. They're going to break their collective *ass* to find us! We really could do six months in jail. Any of us. All of us. That's the handwriting on the wall, and what it says is—move. Fast and far. While we can."

After a moment Shirley said, "Well, we've talked about trying Seattle some day; now we can. Just throw everything in the camper—"

"Not that pile of scrap. It wouldn't make it over the next hill."

"Well, cram everything into the Alfa then, and leave the camper where it is." She began running water into the sink. "How about it, you guys? Anyone for Seattle?"

"Sometimes I've thought about Santa Fe," Lew said slowly. "I've heard that it's different there." They laughed, and so did he but insisted, "Really. I've heard it really is." He glanced uneasily at Jo. "If that suits you?"

She didn't reply to this but said, "Couldn't you guys beat the charges? You're lawyers."

"We might," Lew said. "Our defense would be the simple truth: bring out the cop's real motive, no true arrest, we were within our rights. But he'd lie about what really happened; you know it. And juries believe cops, God knows why, these days. And judges pretend to. Frankly, I wouldn't take my own case."

"What about notice at work?" Jo said.

"I'll phone Tom Thurber in the morning."

"And then we leave? Just like that?"

"Well, the rent's paid till the first, of course. On all three apartments. And the furniture. No lease, it's month to month, and they've got our cleaning deposits. All we have to do is leave a note for notice." The room was silent then, except for the little clinks and watery swishes of Shirley's dishwashing. Lew sat looking at the others, frowning, and when he spoke again his voice was startled. "You know, it's funny: it gets easier to move every time. I could leave in ten minutes from a standing start; pack most of what I own in my suitcase and backpack, and carry the rest under one arm. All our stuff will fit in the VW, with the skis on top. What about your tables though, Jo? And the supply cabinet?"

"Well," she said slowly, "I bought them used; I expect I could sell them back at the same place. Just take them over in the van."

"And sell the van when we sell the camper," Harry said: he stood at the glass doors to the balcony watching the street. "First used-car lot we come to in the city. Might get a buck and a half apiece."

"You'll want your models," Lew murmured uneasily. "The Town."

"Yes."

"Well, we can manage." He looked around at the others. "So? That's it? We leave in the morning?"

Harry nodded. "By way of the city, lost in the commute mob; our last battle with that, anyway."

Again, for some moments they were silent; Jo got up to begin drying the dishes. But it was an uneasy, dissatisfied silence, and presently Lew said, "Son-of-a-bitch," and they all looked at him, sitting on the living-room floor. "Less than three hours ago we were solid citizens. And now we're on the run. That little creep was right, wasn't he, Harry? We didn't say, Yes, sir, and snap to attention; now he's running us out of town." No one replied. Harry stood at the balcony doors, frowning. Lew stood up to take his plate to the kitchen, saying, "Well, all right, okay. We have to run; Harry's right. Pile our stuff in the cars, and *drive*." He turned back into the living room. "But not in the morning, not tomorrow; not me, anyway. Before I leave, god damn it, I want to say good-by."

"How do you mean?" Harry said, swinging around to look at Lew, voice sharp with interest, and Lew grinned.

"I want to fix that red-neck son-of-a-bitch first."

"Why, yes," Harry said softly, and grinned, too. "How!?" he demanded. At the sink the women stood motionless, listening.

Lew shook his head. "I don't know exactly." He shoved his hands into his back pockets, and walked to the balcony doors to stand beside Harry, staring out at the street; dark now, the street lamps on. "But, you know?—I've been sitting here feeling like some kind of invisible man. We'll all be *gone*, vanished. Wiped out without trace. Someone else in our apartments in a day or so; there's a waiting list. Our furniture scattered all over the Bay Area." He swung around, speaking to them all. "Yet we lived here, damn it! We *belonged* here, didn't we? As much as anyone else. I had a job, maybe even a career." He smiled. "Lew Joliffe, city councilman; state senator; governor; head of the firm, finally; known, loved, and respected by all." He shrugged, baffled. "Instead I'm being wiped away like chalk off a blackboard. Well, I don't give a shit about the city council, you all know that. I just don't like being erased. And before I am, I not only want to fix the guy who did it; I want the whole damn county and Bay Area to know Lew Joliffe was *here*."

"Right. *Right!*" Harry began walking the room, gesturing, hands flinging out angrily. "A creepy little shit of a nobody starts mouthing off at us. And we don't just stand there and take it. That's all that happened! That was our crime! And for that—he's a nobody, you wouldn't spit on him!—but he's got a job on the cops so he's free to punish *me* by humiliating my *wife*. Publicly! Handcuff her! Before a crowd! Manhandle her around a parking lot!" He was addressing Shirley directly now. "So what am I supposed to do? Stand there saying, 'So long, Shirl'? I take you away from him; I *have* to. And now I'm supposed to run like a fucking rabbit. Well, god damn it, Lew's right: first, we fix that guy, then we say good-by." He swung around to face Lew. "But *how*, Lew? You must have something in mind!"

"Well, yeah. Sort of. We'd have to work it out." He stood looking at

Harry appraisingly, then smiled suddenly. "You feel like some climbing? Some really weird climbing?"

"No!" Jo actually stamped her foot on the kitchen floor. "No, Lew: I know what you're talking about, and I won't have it! I won't! Oh, why can't we just *go*," she cried out. "Just leave in the morning, and forget the whole—"

"Because we wouldn't forget."

"*What, what?*" Harry demanded. "What's she talking about?"

"Well," Lew said, and he pushed aside a mound of clothing on the chesterfield, sat down, leaned back, and began to talk.

When he had finished, Harry, sitting on the floor at the balcony windows, began to laugh, silently, his big shoulders shaking. He said, "That's the worst thing I ever heard of. It's terrible, you know that: we'd be crazy." He shook his head, still laughing. "But it's too good to pass up."

They argued then, the women with the men: Lew sitting back on the chesterfield, hands clasped behind his neck, the others sitting on the floor. Then presently Shirley said, "Jo, look at them: look at their faces. They're going to *do* it. With or without us," and Jo nodded shortly, her lips compressed. Looking curiously from one to the other of the men, Shirley said, "Do you really have the nerve? Do you really?"

Lew smiled. "No. I haven't got the nerve at all. Except for one thing—the result. Oh, man, the *result* if we can bring this off! That's what will get me through it, I think. Like the carrot in front of the donkey."

Harry sat nodding, smiling, and Jo stood up abruptly. "All right, what the hell," she said. "It's late, the police haven't come back, and we're not going to Seattle or Santa Fe; not for a while, anyway. Let's get to bed."

• • •

CHAPTER NINE

• • •

At five-forty in the morning Shirley's eyes opened. She lay listening, hearing only Harry's slow breathing beside her. Yet something had awakened her, and she got up quietly, walked to the side windows, and in the gray dawn saw Floyd Pearley walking soundlessly up the driveway on the balls of his feet.

He wore uniform, including his cap. Behind him—hands busy under her chin knotting a green scarf over her gray hair—Mrs. Gunther, manager of the buildings, followed in slacks, red slippers over bare feet, a raincoat buttoned to the chin. Harry said, "What's going on?" and his blanket flew aside before Shirley could answer.

They stood watching, Shirley shivering a little in the morning chill. Pearley had pressed their bell, Mrs. Gunther turning casually to look carefully around her. Now he pressed again. A token wait of a second or two, then he nodded abruptly, and Mrs. Gunther brought out a key from her raincoat pocket, unlocked the door, and followed Pearley in. "Can they *do* that?" Shirley whispered. "Without a warrant?" and Harry shrugged.

In less than two minutes they reappeared, Pearley walking swiftly down the driveway as Mrs. Gunther pulled the apartment door shut; and Harry turned away. "Back to bed. If Stupid knew this was Lew's place he'd be pounding the door down."

Promptly at nine every morning Tom Thurber arrived at the office, the only partner to do so; and at nine-five Lew phoned him, tilting the earpiece so the others, standing close, could hear. "Lew! What the hell is going on!"

"Why, what's happened, Tom?"

"A cop was just here! Waiting at the doors when Freddie arrived to open up." The cop had asked about Harry, and then, Thurber was afraid, in reply to further questions Freddie, the office manager, had given him Lew's name and address as a friend of Harry's.

Lew covered the mouthpiece. "Start emptying my apartment!" As the others ran to the balcony doors, he said, "What'd the cop look like, Tom?"

Thurber described Pearley, then: "Now, what's this all about?"

Lew told him. For himself and Harry he apologized for their having to leave without notice, and Thurber said he understood. They were all packed, Lew went on, were leaving within minutes to drive out of the state today, and Thurber said quickly, "Don't tell me where!" He added that he was sorry, and that he wished them luck: Could he help? Lew said no, and as he replaced the phone Jo and Shirley hurried in from the balcony carrying armloads of clothing, Harry following with Lew's skis, his wet suit, his tennis equipment. From the clothes Jo dumped onto a bed, Lew took his tweed coat and, buttoning it as he ran, clattered down the outside stairs, and ran to the VW.

Standing at Mrs. Gunther's desk, the VW at the curb, engine running, Lew laid his apartment keys before her, smiling pleasantly. He had to give up his apartment immediately, he said; he'd been "transferred to Atlanta," to report on Monday. Since he had a long drive and wanted to get started right now, would she mind notifying furniture rental? She asked for a forwarding address, and Lew gave her one, slowly and carefully as she wrote it down on a printed form: 808 . . . South Crescent Drive . . . apartment 2B, the home of a friend in Atlanta with whom he'd be staying till he found a place of his own: no, he didn't know the zip. The Levys? Yes, he knew them slightly; had sometimes played tennis with them. No, he didn't know they'd moved, let alone where; was surprised to hear it. And the young lady next door? Miss Dunne? Was she staying? Lew shrugged, his face going coldly indifferent. "Far as I know." Then he smiled charmingly, offering his hand. "Good-by, Mrs. Gunther; I've enjoyed knowing you." She flushed slightly, and her eyes dropped.

Entering his car, Lew didn't glance back: what she had believed or thought, he didn't know. He drove on in the direction of the freeway. Making a three-mile loop, he returned to the apartment from the other direction, and parked behind the first of the buildings, four down from his own. With the pliers from his glove compartment he removed both his license plates, shoved them under a seat, and walked through the parking areas behind the buildings to Jo's van. He took off the front plate, returned, and attached it in the VW's rear plate-holder.

As Lew entered the apartment Jo, standing at the balcony doors, cried, "The cop's back!" and with the others Lew hurried over in time to see the Mill Valley black-and-white, Pearley at the wheel, swing into the driveway beside the building and disappear, accelerating.

They heard the brake squeal, the door-slam, then—all standing silent, the women's eyes widening—they listened to the faint peal of Lew's bell on the other side of the living-room wall. A moment's pause, then it rang four or five times in rapid, angry succession. Back at the balcony doors they watched the car bounce down into the street, shoot ahead to the manager's office and, brakes screeching, tires patching, park on the wrong side. The door flew open, and Pearley ran up the short walk to the manager's office.

On common impulse Lew and Harry stepped into movie pose, backs to the wall at each end of the double doors, hands on the butts of imaginary shoulder-holstered guns. "Shirl, *look* at them," Jo said. "They love this, they really do." Half a minute later Pearley reappeared, got into his car, and drove on.

In Jo's van all but Harry drove into Mill Valley—a chance they had to take—and emptied their bank and checking accounts. When they returned, Harry was kneeling before Jo's white table, set in the light beside the balcony doors. As they stood watching he sighted through his 35-mm camera mounted on its tripod; propped before the lens, against a stack of paperbacks, stood a small photograph. Harry unscrewed one of two closeup lenses he'd attached to the camera, refocused, made a short time exposure. He began arranging his next setup, a long yellow card, its blank spaces handwritten in ink, and the others began carrying Jo's long paste-up table out to the van.

In the van Lew and Jo drove to the city, Lew in back out of sight. As she entered the bridge, the empty Pacific sliding past her side vision far below beyond the red-painted railing, Jo sat conscious of the knot of dread which had appeared under her breastbone as soon as she'd awakened. It would stay there for the next three days, she knew, but she'd become aware that along with it during the morning there had come a sense of anticipation: now, she decided, she felt simultaneously frightened and intensely alive. She drove on beside the long loops of the great support cables, passing under the two great bridge towers, thinking how placid and almost entirely without risk her life had been; and at the toll plaza, dropping her coins into the collector's cupped hand, she smiled at him genuinely, thinking, "What would you say if you knew what I knew?"

It took five hours to draw a line through everything on their list. On Kearney Street, Jo dropped Lew off at Brooks Cameras, and drove on to Market where she sold her worktables and supply cabinet at the office-supply shop at which she'd bought them. She delivered her finished model at a California Street office building, enjoying the luxury of parking directly at the building entrance in the clearly marked NO PARKING ZONE. There she asked for and got her check immediately, and—no ticket on her windshield yet—walked a block to the bank it was drawn on, and cashed it. When she returned, a folded white ticket lay under her wiper; she slipped it out, tried to crumple and throw it into the gutter, and couldn't. She put it into the glove compartment and drove on to pick up Lew.

He stood waiting on the curb, straddling a cardboard carton, as she pulled into the yellow zone. He opened the back doors, and when he heaved the package up onto the floor, it shook the van.

At a Mission Street electronics store, Lew bought a good-quality transformer; at a hardware store, a hundred-foot coil of light cable, two one-hundred-yard rolls of nylon fishline, and a bolt cutter. At Sears, out on Geary Street, he bought four of their cheapest twenty-four-volt automobile batteries.

Just outside Sausalito on the way home, Jo stopped at Big-G market to buy food. This was the waterfront industrial area, and Lew walked across the road to the nearest sail loft and bought the cheapest and widest nylon sailcloth they sold. This turned out to come in 44-inch bolts at $2.42 a yard, and he took all they had, five hundred feet. At another loft nearby he bought two hundred feet more; at the building-supply store eight fourteen-foot lengths of threaded two-inch plastic pipe, and a sackful of couplings and caps. From their garden shop he bought a sack of gravel. They drove to San Anselmo, and at The Alpine Shop bought four hundred feet of eleven-millimeter perlon rope.

Shirley stood at the stove in Jo's purple terrycloth apron when they returned, potatoes boiling, frozen vegetables in their plastic sacks ready to heat; she took the wrapped package of steak from Jo. Harry sat on the chesterfield with a drink, his camera in its case on the mantel beside the folded tripod. "Get it all?"

"Yeah." Lew dropped two bundles of sailcloth, ninety pounds of it, onto the floor before the newly exposed fireplace. "But it's good you're sitting down; wait'll you hear what it cost."

"Who cares? It's a bargain."

Saturday morning Jo walked to the camper and brought it back, and Lew and Harry drove to San Rafael, Harry in the back. In the nearly empty living room, crawling on hands and knees, Jo and Shirley cut the sailcloth into fourteen fifty-foot lengths. Each took two of these strips and, sitting cross-legged on the floor, tailor fashion, began sewing them together in big, looping stitches along the sides. Beginning at ten-thirty they watched on the Levys' portable television set the morning cartoons, as they worked, and then whatever else came on, discussing it. They finished just before five, all the strips sewn together to form a fifty-foot square, a great white billow of cloth heaped along the side of the room.

In San Rafael Lew stopped first at a lumberyard, and bought several lengths of two-by-fours, some carriage bolts and washers. In the electrical-supply department he bought a short length of heavy insulated copper wire and some cutters. He drove to a tool-rental shop in the industrial area along the canal and rented a handsaw and drill. In an empty parking lot beside a closed-up cabinetmaker's—most of the small factories, supply, and service shops closed today—he and Harry cut and fitted inside the camper a solidly braced and bolted two-by-four frame, level with a side window. Harry connected the batteries and transformer, and lashed them together on the floor under the new framework.

On Sunday, breakfast over, they had very little to do. While Jo and Shirley washed dishes and made beds, Lew and Harry folded the giant square of sailcloth with great care and difficulty. One end of the wadded-up mass they dragged onto the balcony. From there they laid it, a huge puffed-up worm of white cloth, the length of the living room and on into the short hall. Even so, they had to curve the last dozen feet or so back on itself. Shifting it frequently as they worked, they folded this in accordion folds a yard wide. Then Lew knelt on the yard-wide fifty-foot length and, working his way backward, flattened and compressed the many-layered bulk with forearms and palms. Harry followed on his knees, rolling the long length into a coil, as tight as he could squeeze it. They wrapped it with a length of nylon cord, cinching it into a squat, fat roll which Harry lifted easily, though his arms wouldn't meet around it, and carried down to the van.

In the bedroom, Shirley and Jo packed Jo's Town, loosely wrapping each little building in tissue and fitting them into a small cardboard carton. Then, for most of the rest of the day they played a lazy, cheating game of Monopoly; each eating when he felt like it, searching the little kitchen area for whatever was to be found. In the afternoon they sipped white wine, not too much; Harry turned on the Raiders-Dallas game, and they watched it, continuing the Monopoly desultorily.

By four the Monopoly had dwindled into inaction; and when the Raider game ended at four-thirty, the men turned restless, glancing at their watches, walking to the balcony to glance out at the sky. At five Harry said, "I don't think a drink or two at this point could do anything but help," and Lew made them for everyone.

In the van after dark Jo drove north on the freeway in the slow lane at the steady fifty that was about all it could do; the men in back. Past San Rafael, she began, as always along this stretch, to watch for the break in the hills on the right that would suddenly reveal the great county Civic Center "in all its glory," she said to herself, meaning it.

It came: the van rolled on past a high bluff and then, no more than a quarter mile from the freeway, there it stood—exterior spotlighted, interior lighting on—the strange, beautiful building unlike any other she had ever seen; the last, she believed, ever designed by Frank Lloyd Wright. Slowing, glancing off at it as often as she could, Jo studied it again, thinking as always each time she saw it that some day she would make a model of it for herself. Long and narrow to give most of its rooms outside exposure, the building projected straight out from the side of a hill so steep that the end of the roof there nearly touched the ground. Jo had once stood beside it with Lew and, reaching up, had been astonished that her hand easily reached the eaves. Yet the other distant end of the long roof, extending out from the hillside far beyond its foot, stood several stories high. Now the roof lay in darkness, but Jo remembered it with pleasure, shooting ruler-straight out from the hillside, looking like a high-crowned road paved with tile of a rich, startling blue. The gold-ornamented eaves shone in the spotlighting from below, the beige walls exotically broken by enormous, scallop-topped windows. The black night-time hills began cutting the strange, lovely structure from view. Then it was gone, Jo smiling in the darkness of the cab, feeling that what she had seen was nothing so drab as a building of offices, courtrooms, a jail; it was more like Glinda's palace.

A mile past the Civic Center at a partly constructed building in a green-lawned industrial park beside the service road, Lew and Harry took two twenty-foot roof beams from a stack of them—heavy timbers half a foot thick, nearly a foot wide—and loaded them into the back of the van. Then Jo drove, fast, back along the narrow road—the obviously stolen beams projecting behind were a risk they had to take—and into the parking lot behind the Civic Center. Lights out, motor off, they waited. Nothing moved, the lot dark and silent, empty except for a lineup of orange-painted county road-maintenance trucks, and a single car. High on the hillside from which it projected, the great Civic Center loomed like a castle. Jo drove on, lights off, partly seeing and partly feeling her way up the dirt road at the back of the hill. Halfway up, she stopped at the padlocked gate in the high mesh fence. The men jumped down in back, dragged out the beams one at a time, and manhandled them over the fence. They climbed the fence, carried the beams on up to the Center, and dropped them in the weeds beside the road which ended here at a leveled area. Lew walked forward to the glass doors which, from up here on the hill, led directly into the top floor. He peered in: under the ceiling lighting the waxed floors shone; nothing moved. Turning away, he reached up as Jo had once done, and touched the roof edge, smiling. Back at the van, Lew tossed the bolt-cutter he had bought into the underbrush. Then they drove home.

From eleven o'clock on they tried to sleep, and presently did, lying partly dressed, women in the bedroom, the men lying on sleeping bags in the living room. Just before Lew drifted off, Harry said, "Lew?"

"Yeah."

"This gonna work?"

"Yeah."

"I hope so. I'd give a year of my life for a written guarantee from God."

At two o'clock when the alarm on the floor beside him rang, it took Lew some seconds to find it and shut it off; he could not understand what the persistent sound was, and didn't want to move and wake up. Then, heavily awake, thumb still on the stud he'd pressed, desperate to let his eyes close, he understood that he'd known what the ringing had meant, and that he was frightened.

It did not seem possible that they were actually going to do what it was time to do now. Propped on an elbow, blinking rapidly to hang onto wakefulness, he tried to find a way, a mental set, of accepting the truth; that there was almost nothing more between them and what they had said they would do. He felt unwell: was it possible he'd become sick while he slept? His stomach was an emptiness, and he was cold.

"Lew? How much you take to call off this whole fucking—"

"Don't say it! Or we will. We'll find reasons, and won't do it."

"Right: don't think, just get up." Lew heard Harry's movements, and he sat up, too. From the bedroom came the murmur of Jo's voice, and Shirley's muffled reply. Their light snapped on, slanting through the open door onto the nap of the beige hallway rug, and Lew was grateful that it didn't reach his eyes.

The drapes drawn, only a kitchen light on, they had coffee standing in the kitchen and living room. Lew wore his denims, blue zippered jacket, red mask-cap, and, tonight, a forest-green daypack. Harry was similarly dressed, his jacket dark green, his watch cap blue, his daypack red; and both men wore sneakers. Jo and Shirley wore pants suits, Jo's chocolate brown, Shirley's dark gray, and both wore berets. The coffee was too hot, Lew kept burning his lips, and he turned to the sink to cool it with water. Instead he took down the bottle of whiskey from the kitchen cupboard, and walked to the others, pouring a good slug of it into their cups and his own. It cooled his coffee and tasted good; burning his nose clear, warming him from throat to stomach in a palpable, glowing line, and what they were about to do once more became possible, just barely.

Lowering his cup, Harry said, "Bless you. Courage out of a bottle is a lot better than none at all." He swallowed down the rest, set his cup aside, and turned toward the outer door. "Well, c'mon, Sergeant; you want to live forever?"

• • •

CHAPTER TEN

• • •

At the wheel of the van, Shirley beside her, the men hidden in the back, Jo curved onto the freeway, greenly lighted, empty and quiet in the night; far ahead across the blackness of the Bay the lighted city shimmered remotely.

Presently, near stalling, the van crested Waldo, then picked up speed, rolling down toward the lighted tunnel. Inside the tunnel, framed in the dome-shaped opening of its other end, the great towers of Golden Gate Bridge appeared, rising black against the night sky, the beacons at their tops winking red, the orange-yellow lights of the great span arcing across the black water.

On the bridge she slowed; headlights had appeared in her big side rear-view. They grew, the mirror glaring, the car drew abreast and passed, its driver glancing over at her. Then once more there was nothing behind, and only the single pair of rapidly shrinking tail lights ahead.

Jo leaned toward the windshield to stare out; first, at the long, empty, lighted roadway; then, lifting her eyes reluctantly, up at the enormity of its soaring north tower straddling the roadway like a giant ladder—a leg on each side, four huge transverses like rungs between them. In the orange light of the bridge lamps the first thirty feet of the great twin tower legs showed rust-red; beyond reach of the lights they turned abruptly black, endlessly rising into the night sky. The tower was so *high*, she thought, terrifyingly so, higher than in daylight, the winking red beacons at its top remote as the lights of a plane.

The rivet-studded red base of the ocean-side tower leg grew in her windshield to the size of a small building; then they were beside it, Jo braking, checking her rear-view, still blank and empty. She stopped, and the van's rear doors flung open, banging the sides hard; then the body jounced as Lew and Harry jumped down onto the roadway.

Instantly Harry seized the rolled-up sailcloth, heaving it up onto his shoulder. Beside him Lew stood dragging out the taped-together bundle of long plastic pipes. Harry swung away, trotting to the low, dirt-splashed steel divider between roadway and sidewalk. He jumped up onto it, down onto the walk, and ran across it. Lew followed, the long pipes balanced on one shoulder, a swaying plastic sack dangling from each end. They ran around the great tower base onto the little railed and concrete-paved bay facing the ocean behind it. Here, completely hidden from the roadway by the tremendous steel wall of the tower base, they dropped their burdens to the walk.

Back they ran, hurdling the short barrier to the roadway, and hopped up into the van, pulling the doors closed; it had taken less than fifteen seconds. At the slam of the doors Jo started up, the roadway still empty as far ahead and behind as she could see. On each side of the bridge ahead lay blackness, but between the railings the long empty roadway seemed warm and enclosed under the orange lights, artificial in its motionlessness. Shirley, sitting beside Jo, murmured, "It's fake, a stage set. Wouldn't surprise me if the chorus of *West Side Story* came climbing up over the rails."

Jo smiled tightly, nodding: she was watching at the right, following the long, slow curve of the immense support cable; black high above where it thinned into invisibility against the night; turning orange-red where it curved, thickening, down into the light. Just ahead at the halfway point of the long empty bridge, the barrel-thick cable seemed almost to touch the railing beside it. Jo slowed, then braked to a stop directly beside this center point, the rear doors of the van banging open again. They slammed shut immediately, she watched the two men run across her right-view mirror to the walk, and far ahead the lights of an approaching car appeared.

Before it could see she was stopped she drove on toward it, nothing else to do; a truck, she realized, from the height of its headlights. It moved slowly, and Jo continued on toward the city. If the lights of still another car should appear, she would have to drive on through the line of booths, paying toll, to wait somewhere on the other side, then return.

Van and truck, an aluminum-sided U-Haul, she could see now, crawled toward each other. They passed, a young black man wearing an enormous lopsided knit cap, glancing at her impassively. Nothing else had appeared, and Jo slowed, watching the pattern of red and yellow rear lights dwindle in her mirror. Then she stopped the van completely to wait, eyes moving between rear-view and windshield, until the bridge should be completely clear.

Two minutes . . . three; then the distant lights in her mirror vanished, cut off by the curve of the approach at the other end of the bridge. Jo checked—nothing coming now from behind or ahead—drove forward, then swung the wheel hard for the U-turn, and Shirley said, "Whee!"

"You like that?"

"Love it. I'll bet it's the first U-turn on the Golden Gate Bridge in twenty-five years."

Glad of the distraction, Jo said, "Well, we aim to please!" and swung the wheel hard again, holding it this time and the van made a complete tight circle, pressing Shirley against her door. "How's that?" Jo straightened, and they rolled on, back toward Marin.

"Marvelous. The fine for that must be ten thousand dollars."

Driving on back across the bridge they became silent, and each leaned toward the windshield, eyes searching. Approaching the point where the cable dipped lowest, Jo slowed, but the little ladder and platform beside it stood empty. She slowed still further, eyes moving along the great main cable, then Shirley cried, "There they are!" and Jo saw them, and shoved in the brake pedal.

After a moment she said, "Oh, my god." Then they sat motionless, staring up through the glass. Above and beyond the bridge lighting, the two small figures moved—flickered—along the dark cable in tandem. That was all, two blurs of movement no longer recognizable as men. Hardly darker than the sky against which they were just visible, they moved upward along the black line that, high, high above, faded away in the sky. Shirley turned suddenly and crawled over the seat. Stooped under the skylight, she slid it aside and stood erect in the opening, head and neck protruding above the roof. Jo set the parking brake and joined her. From this foreshortened angle the moving shadows seemed to advance very slowly; but within a minute, the women's heads gradually tilting upward, the two vague blots had moved perceptibly higher, then seemed to stop.

"I can't watch any more"—Jo reached for the seat back. "I hate this." She crawled forward, Shirley following. Glancing at each other as Jo released the brake, each saw that the other's face had gone white.

They drove on, and up on the great ocean-side cable high in the darkness above them Lew clung to the handholds saying, "Jesus. Oh, *Jesus*," and could not move.

"Lew, for crysake," Harry said, "we don't have to *do* this stupid thing. We can just turn around—"

"No. No. I'm all right. I looked down, that's all; dumb thing to do. You okay?"

"As okay as you can be when you're scared shitless. I'll tell you something else not to do: don't look *up*. I nearly puked. I saw the red beacon, and oh, man, it's *way* up. You say the word, and I'll race you down."

"No, it's okay." Focusing all his will power into his right foot, Lew made it lift off the cable, and plant itself six inches ahead. Then the left, and—the handhold wires sliding slowly and roughly through his curled palms, a film of sweat breaking out all over his body—he walked on. They'd climbed higher than this, and more dangerously: up nearly vertical cliffs. But in daylight. No one belonged up here in the dead of night.

One foot, then the other: he made himself a mechanical man, achieving a kind of rigid calm. Then he said to himself that that wasn't enough. It wasn't why he was *here*, walking up the main cable of Golden Gate Bridge. *God damn it*, he said silently, *this is something to remember forever!*

The ascent was steepening, they were having to lean into it now. But Lew forced his head to turn left, and stare off into the void. *That's the ocean*, he said. Another few steps, and he deliberately looked straight down to the right. The lighted bridge was an aerial photograph of itself, its narrowness emphasized by the limitless blackness beyond its sides. Toes pressing, calves tensing, he climbed on, the terror still waiting but forced outside him and held off. As nearly as possible he began to enjoy what they were doing again, appreciating its strangeness; and, the fear postponed, his exhilaration gradually returned.

Off the bridge approach, Jo parked just beyond it, out of sight of the freeway around the first bend of the dirt road leading to a small ocean-side state park. She and Shirley walked back onto the bridge and to the north tower, then around it onto the little railed bay on its ocean side. Looking up the riveted red wall of the tower, they could see only the darkness into which it rose; and they sat down to wait on the rolled-up coil of sailcloth Harry had dropped here.

Five hundred feet directly above them the men climbed the final dozen yards, the cable slanting up at nearly sixty degrees here, their bodies tilted sharply back; each step up now took the strength of an arm tugging on the handhold to bring the torso along. Now the huge, winking red beacon stood incredibly close above them, the great two-foot lens reddening Lew's sneakers, turning the air itself a blinding pink, then mercifully blackening, over and again.

Three steps to go, Lew's arm trembling. Two steps, one, then his hand lifted from the handhold to close down on the rung of the small steel ladder leading from cable down to the great topmost transverse. He swung off onto the ladder, Harry followed, then they stood safe, safe, *safe* between the waist-high guard rails of the gloriously flat steel surface.

They stood on the topmost rung, wide as a road, of the tremendous, ladderlike north tower of Golden Gate Bridge, faces reddening and darkening, and they grinned at each other. Harry stuck out his hand, and said, "Hey, pardner, we climbed the god-damn bridge." They shook,

Lew saying, "Should have brought some wine, we could have drunk a toast," and Harry said, "Hey, yeah. How come you forgot?"

For perhaps two minutes they strolled the wide, high surface, feeling slightly stunned, tasting the joy of sanctuary attained. Gripping the railing then, they leaned forward to stare down at the strip, astonishingly narrow, that was the six-lane lighted roadway of the bridge. They watched a small dark rectangle push a pair of finger-length beams along it, till it passed directly under them and vanished. Harry said, "Yow." Then, loud as he could yell it, "*Yow, yow, yow, yow!*" HEY, down there! Look at *us!*"

Forearms on the railing, ankles crossed, they stared out across the Bay at the city lying darkly on its hills, its grid of streets picked out by dots of light. To the left stood the heaped shapes of its lighted downtown buildings shimmering distantly through the layers of night-time air; from them a dotted line across blackness, the lights of the Bay Bridge, led to the freckles of pale green light that meant Oakland.

They turned to the opposite rail to look out at the smoothly undulating Marin hill shapes against the sky, striped with the white winding of the freeway. Then they walked back toward the black nothingness of the ocean. Occasionally a remote dab of dingy white flickered on the blackness, an infinitely removed whitecap, and Lew said, "Harry, I was scared; I tell you I was *scared*. But this is worth it."

"Yeah, look at us. *Up* here."

And then, as they walked on, across the eighty-foot length of the huge topmost transverse of the tower, looking out over several counties spread across the night below, the prolonged moment of attaining it faded; and when they reached the ocean side of the tower again it was gone.

This was not their final goal but only a way-stop. It wasn't the topmost transverse but the middle one they had to reach, the second up from the roadway. They could not reach it from below—the great support cable led only up here. To reach the lower transverse they had first to climb to the top, then come down to the middle transverse; not down the cable— down the sheer wall of the tower leg, smooth and blank as the side of a windowless building fifty stories high. It was time to start, and Lew felt the tension re-forming: this was going to be worse.

The small ladder they had descended from cable to transverse led past a railed balcony. This balcony, made of thin steel rods and slats, was four-sided. It hung wrapped around the very top of the tower leg— higher than the transverse they stood on, lower than the great main cable. Lew climbed the ladder, Harry behind him, and halfway up it he stepped off onto the balcony. It was narrower than he could have wished,

his right shoulder lightly brushing the side of the tower as he walked to
the first corner. The steel rods on which he stepped were spaced more
widely than he would have preferred; some were loose, rattling as his
foot left them, the very soles of his feet conscious of the long black
distance beneath them.

Harry following, Lew turned the right-angled corner, and as they
walked on in the new direction toward the ocean, Lew saw themselves
again as from a distance; two matchstick figures moving across the south
face of the Marin tower at its very top; he wondered if Jo and Shirley
stood far below at just this moment, heads tipped back to watch them.
Passing under the great support cable, almost brushing his cap, Lew
reached up to slap its cold solidity and, hearing the echoless smack,
realized he'd become bored with being frightened. He knew what he
was about to do, knew how to do it, felt sure of himself, and the elation
of what they were doing tonight roared back.

Again they turned a corner, to move across the ocean-side face of the
tower. At midpoint they stopped, and from his daypack each brought
out a climbing harness of wide red webbing. They stepped into these
and buckled them at the waist. Then Lew took out a small flashlight;
Harry a rope coil, a fistful of webbing, and a rappelling ring: a two-inch
metal circle, a slim doughnut of steel. Squatting at the base of one of the
stanchions supporting the rails of the platform, Lew held the flashlight
for Harry, a hand cupped under it to shield it from view below. Harry
slipped an end of the webbing through the rappelling ring and knotted
both ends around the base of the stanchion. He stood up, and tested this
knot, gripping the rappelling ring in his hands and yanking till the
stanchion shook. "Hold a horse," he said, squatted again, and began
threading an end of the rope coil through the rappelling ring.

Lew stood clipping a carabiner to his harness; this is a metal loop with
an opening in one side, called a "beaner" by climbers. The opening
closed with a safety lock, and he closed it, tightening down the safety.
Then he stood waiting for Harry to finish, emptying his mind of
conscious thought, resisting a nagging urge to look over the side.

"All set," Harry said, and now Lew sat down on the balcony floor,
legs hanging over the side: the rule was, least experienced man goes
first. Beside him the loop of webbing hung from the base of the
stanchion; from the rappelling ring at the bottom of the loop hung the
doubled length of eleven-millimeter perlon climbing rope, dangling two
hundred feet down the ocean side of the tower. Lew reached for the
rope and brought it to his lap; to the rope Harry had attached a metal
device, the "descender," and now Lew opened his beaner, clipped in the

descender, refastened the beaner's safety lock. He was ready now, harness clipped to the sliding descender of the long rope. He gripped the doubled rope length in his left hand and glanced up at Harry to smile. "See you downstairs," he said, relieved to hear his voice come out calm.

"Right." Harry touched his shoulder. "Take it nice and easy, enjoy yourself."

Lew ducked head and shoulders under the middle railing, gripped the rope, squirmed forward, and slid off the edge of the balcony floor to hang suspended, legs dangling—swinging in a short, diminishing arc, twisting slowly toward the tower wall. He hadn't plunged, clawing at the air; everything had held. He had known it would, *known*, but still he felt the familiar, euphoric rush of relief.

Now he extended his legs to press both rubber soles against the riveted steel face of the tower wall, his back to the ocean, the sling and rope above him angling outward, the rest of the long doubled rope dangling below him into the darkness, a two-hundred-foot tail. His left hand gripped the rope, and now he slowly relaxed it, and the ropes began sliding through his fist, his body lowering. With the rope snubbed by the metal descender through which it was threaded and controlled by the pressure of his grip, Lew lowered himself at a steady speed, the steel balcony with Harry's face peering over it rising away like the underside of an ascending elevator.

In complete easy control of his descent, Lew watched the endless parallel rows of rivets just beyond his pumping knees rise into darkness: he could feel the small pressure of ocean air cool on his neck, and was conscious of the tendons steadily working inside the canvas of his sneakers. Walking backward down the ocean-side face of the great north tower of the bridge, he felt as happy, in the intensity of the moment, as he had ever been.

His heels bumping onto the steel-slatted floor, Lew backed down onto the next balcony below the top one; this balcony, identical with the one he had just descended from, hung wrapped around the tower leg just above the middle transverse. Unclipping his beaner from the descender, Lew turned to look down over the balcony railing. Three hundred feet below, the white blurs of two faces stared up from the walk at the base of the tower leg; and Lew thrust an arm over the railing to move his hand back and forth in a slow arc, hoping they'd see it.

Harry's swiftly walking legs appeared out of the darkness above. "Second floor," he called, "kitchenware, appliances, ladies' underwear." His body straightening, he dropped the final few feet, shaking the floor—

and now they had attained the level of the second transverse, where they wished to be. "The ladies here?" Harry turned to the railing, and Lew walked to the dangling, still swaying rope to pull it down from its loop high above them now, ducking as it came spilling onto their heads and shoulders. They would use the rope again, for their next descent, but before that happened they had work to do here; and Lew walked to the railing now, and began lowering an end of the rope over the balcony rail.

On the concrete walk of the little orange-lighted bay, Jo and Shirley stood waiting, faces upturned. When the rope end appeared, swaying down into the light, Jo jumped, missed, tried again, and brought it down. Shirley took it, knelt on the walk, and tied it to the rope enclosing the coil of sailcloth. She said, "Square knot, the one useful thing I learned in Girl Scouts. You in the Girl Scouts?"

"Oh sure."

"You like it?"

"I liked the camping."

"Me too." Shirley tugged the line, then they stood watching the fat white coil slide up the tower leg, bouncing outward occasionally. Shirley said softly, "Thank God they're down off the top," and Jo nodded, swallowing.

As he would roll a tire, Harry trundled the wheel-like coil along the balcony and around the corners to the ladder leading down to the transverse. He dropped it to the transverse, and climbed down after it. This transverse had no guard rails, and Harry unrolled the coil into a yard-wide, fifty-foot length of folded cloth, positioning it between the tower legs. As Harry worked, Lew stood on the ocean side of the balcony, hauling up the bundle of plastic pipes with its attached sacks of gravel and couplings.

On the transverse, the two men screwed pipe lengths together to form two fifty-six-foot-long pipes. One of them they filled with gravel, and capped the ends. The women had sewn sleeves across the top and bottom edges of the big sailcloth square; and Lew and Harry slid a pipe into each of these sleeves. They were nearly finished now.

The women stood waiting below, one on each side of the roadway; when the lights of an occasional car appeared, they stepped around out of sight behind the tower legs. Leaning back against the railing on the Bay side of the bridge, the green light flecks of Oakland twinkling behind her, Jo stood wondering once more whether or not she would ever again see the Levys when this was over. She felt she would not; that that was the way such things generally worked out. She shrugged a shoulder slightly, a corner of her mouth quirking; it would be an important loss.

Shirley stood across the roadway, ankles crossed, a shoulder against the riveted wall, looking over at Jo. She, too, was thinking of the coming separation of the two couples, but what she wondered, smiling, was whether or not Jo and Lew would marry. Harry thought not, but Shirley told herself that he didn't know; and, nodding unconsciously to confirm it, she decided that they would.

Up on the second transverse the two men had unrolled a coil of thin light cable across its length. Now each twisted an end around the base of a ladder leg at opposite sides of the transverse, and the cable lay flat along the steel floor, tautly stretched clear across it. To this cable they tied the unweighted pole in its sleeve, using several forty-foot lengths of nylon rope. Finally, each tied the end of a hundred-yard roll of new orange-colored fishline to the ends of the other weighted pole. Checking both directions to make sure no cars were in sight, they dropped the spools off the San Francisco edge of the transverse to fall, unrolling as they dropped, to the roadway below.

As Lew and Harry walked back to the ocean-side balcony, and their next-to-final descent, Jo and Shirley stood taping the ends of the orange fishline high on the walls of the twin tower legs, using strips of orange-colored Mystic tape. They dropped the empty spools over the bridge rails.

The men back—first Lew, then Harry, walking down out of the darkness to drop to the walk of the little bay behind the tower leg—they were finished with the bridge for tonight, their preparations complete. Chattering, hilarious with excitement, they walked back for the van; when a car passed on the bridge approach, another behind it, they waved wildly—one driver slowly lifting an arm to respond, puzzled, the other only staring in bewildered suspicion.

In the van, rolling down Waldo Grade, the men kneeling behind the front seat, Shirley said, "What if a bridge worker goes up there tomorrow?"

"He'll see it right away," Harry said, "and that'll be that. Just hope no one does, is all; they don't go up there every day, or anything like it."

Out of the tunnel, they rounded a long curve, and Richardson Bay bridge and the dark shoreline of Strawberry Point appeared far ahead and below like a map. Lew said, "Harry, it's been quite a night: we could call it quits right now, if you wanted. Tomorrow night is the big one."

Shirley said, "Yes! I vote yes. So does Jo. Democracy at work."

But Harry was shaking his head. "No. I want it all. Not just tomorrow night—I want to fix the cop, too. Okay?"

"Sure. I do, too. Just checking is all."

"It's after three," Jo said. "How do you know he hasn't been and gone? Or that he'll even show up tonight?"

"Well, we don't," Lew said. "We're just guessing that it's an every-night routine. But if he doesn't show, all we lose is a little more sleep."

At Strawberry, Jo curved off the freeway onto the service road, and slowed, leaning forward to study the driveways of the Texaco and Standard stations, the car wash beyond them, and McDonald's after that. But no black-and-white, lights off, stood parked in any of them. Across the freeway the lights and sound of a car shot by toward the city, but here on the service road nothing moved ahead or behind. Jo swung into the Standard station, switching her lights off, and she and Shirley sat watching, motor running. "Okay," she said then.

"Got the dimes?" Harry said, and from her pants pocket Shirley brought a small handful of dimes, and passed two of them back. From under the seat she pulled out a slim blue-and-silver package, a roll of aluminum foil, tore off a ragged scrap from each corner, and passed them back.

The rear doors opened, the men slid out, eased the doors shut, and Jo immediately drove on, down the driveway back onto the service road. Watching her rear-view, she saw Lew and Harry walk quickly across its face toward the pair of phone booths at the edge of the lot.

Each in a booth, doors left open, no light coming on, the men wrapped their foil fragments loosely around the dimes Shirley had given them. Then they stuffed them into the coin slots, forcing them down, the foil crumpling and packing the slots. Leaving his booth, Lew saw the van stopped in the car-wash driveway next door, Shirley inside the phone booth there. He and Harry walked quickly along the side of the white-painted station and turned the corner at the rear. Safely out of sight, they stood watching the van leave the car wash, then swing into McDonald's to stop beside the phone booth there.

Standing in the star-lit darkness behind the station, it seemed to Lew that these were the first moments of relative calm in many hours, though he knew it had been less than two. He began to stretch slowly, enjoying it, arms out at his sides, fingers clenching and splaying. Then he walked in a slow circle, stomping softly, working the last of the climb and descent from his muscles, it seemed, preparing for what might come next. Harry sat down, his back against the rear wall of the station, then Lew joined him, and they sat silent and listening, waiting.

He arrived twenty minutes later: they heard the motor, a tappet ticking, then the small bumper scrape on concrete as the car jounced up the driveway; heard the faint brake squeal, then the parking brake ratchet. Silently they stood up . . . heard leather on concrete out front, fading as he walked to the other side of the building. On rubber toes they ran to the other back corner, stopped just short of it . . . heard the slight key jangle, then the quiet distinct snick of key sliding into lock. From out front the hollow click of a loudspeaker coming to life; behind a slight fuzz of static, a woman's distant monotone spoke a few unintelligible words. Harry nudged Lew, eyes pleased, to whisper, "Roof speaker's on; means the engine's running." From around the corner, the chain-rattle of garage door rolling up . . . the snap of a light switch . . . footsteps receding across concrete . . . a moment's pause. Then a coin rattled down a slot, and they whirled and ran hard along the back, full speed on tiptoes, around the corner, and along the side to the front.

There it stood, the black-and-white, facing south away from them, exhaust purring quietly, clouding gray in the night air. On the driver's door, standing slightly ajar, MILL VALLEY POLICE, dim but readable in the starlight. Moving very fast they walked silently toward it, Lew first to yank open the driver's door, slide under the wheel and—lifting a uniform cap out of the way—across the seat. Right behind him, Harry slipped in under the wheel, slowly pulled the door closed till the latch clicked, then pressed down the lock knob, and rolled up the window to within an inch of the top. He found the parking-brake handle, very slowly released it, set his foot on the brake pedal, and pushed the shift lever to DRIVE. Then he turned to grin at Lew who grinned back, their eyes elated. Watching the yellow patch of light spilling from the side of the garage, they waited.

Overhead the roof speaker suddenly squawked, and they jumped. Harry irritatedly jerked his head at Lew to find the cutoff switch. Lew pushed a toggle and they heard the speaker-hum snip off. In the same moment, as though Lew had caused this too, the light at the side of the building snapped out, and the garage door clattered down.

For just a moment in the dim starlight, they couldn't quite be certain it was he: only the top of his black-haired head visible, eyes on the filled Styrofoam cup suspended from his spidered fingers, he appeared walking slowly around the corner in uniform. For a moment longer they watched, then grinned as they recognized him—and Harry blasted the horn.

The cup dropped, split, a black gout of steaming coffee dashed over the man's skinny ankles as his head shot up, and Pearley's wedge-shaped face stared at them, eyes bright with fright, feet suddenly dancing as the scalding coffee bit through the white cloth of his socks. Harry howled a wild banshee-shriek of laughter, and shot the car forward, black-streaking the concrete. They bounced down onto the road, swung into the freeway-entrance almost directly ahead, and as Harry straightened in the lane they saw the man—motionless, long jaw hanging open—suddenly whirl and run toward the phone booths, both of them yelled with glee.

Harry held to the outside lane at a steady sixty-five, ten miles over the limit but easily acceptable, they felt certain, in a police car on a nearly empty road. After half a mile Lew handed the blue uniform cap to Harry, who put it on and grinned; it was half a size too small, but he left it.

Four trucks passed on the other side, nothing on this, and in just under eight minutes by Lew's timing they had passed San Rafael, and were approaching the Civic Center. Then the lights of a car approached on the other side of the freeway; and in passing they saw the red dome light and green-and-white car of a deputy sheriff. Could he be hunting them, could Pearley possibly have reached a working phone so soon? They hadn't planned what they'd do if this happened. The driver glanced over at them, lifted a hand in greeting, and Harry responded equally casually. Another mile, and he slowed for the turnoff, then onto the road they'd ridden early in the evening with Jo. Back along the road then, winding a little, up and down the occasional slight hill.

At the entrance to the back parking lot of the Civic Center Harry switched off the headlights, drove forward, and stopped, waiting for his eyes to adjust. Without lights then, he drove forward in low gear, foot on the brake, half seeing, half feeling his way. He found the dark bulk of the van, parked in the same place it had been earlier, and he pulled in beside it on the driver's side, and turned off the motor. Lew rolled down his window, and two feet away at the wheel of the van Jo said softly, anxiously, "Any trouble?"

"No, he's probably still hunting for a phone that works."

Shirley got out, closed her door silently, and walked past the front of the van carrying Harry's folded tripod, camera and flash attachment mounted. Lew put out his arm to take it, but Shirley brushed past to the rear door, and Jo got out of the van. "Hey, what're you doing?" Lew said.

"Coming along. We want to watch."

"No," Harry said, but Lew said, "Harry, if they get one of us, they've got us all. Let 'em come," and the women climbed into the back.

Listening, watching, they waited through a dozen seconds more. Then Harry drove on, lights out, creeping along in the ruts, the car slowly jouncing on its shocks up the hill to stop at the wire mesh fence.

Lew got out, found the bolt cutters in the grass, and cut the lock chain. He threw the cutters down the hillside and opened the gate; Harry drove on through, Lew following on foot.

Harry stopped in the leveled area at the end of the long building which projected from the hillside here. Motor off, they got out, and the women watched as Lew and Harry carried the long beams they had left here to the narrow, slightly domed blue roof. One end of each foot-wide, six-inch-thick plank they set on the edge of the roof just above their heads, positioning them four feet apart, and stomped the other ends of the twenty-foot beams into the ground. Then, Lew squatting on the roof edge guiding him with the shielded flashlight, Harry slowly drove the police car up the ramp and onto the roof.

The roof ruler straight, wide as a road, and only slightly higher-crowned, he drove slowly on, keeping meticulously to the center: following on foot the others could hear the steady faint ripple of rubber on tile.

A dozen feet short of the end, Harry stopped, overlooking the asphalted entranceway five stories below. Parking brake pushed to its final rachet, gear lever in PARK, he got out, and they stood listening. Nothing moved, no shout sounded.

Harry set up his tripod at the front of the roof, facing the car and the open front door labeled MILL VALLEY POLICE. Twisting the lens to focus, he watched the others arrange themselves. Lew lounged at full length along the hood, his grinning head propped on an elbow before the windshield. The women stood each with a foot on the front bumper: Shirley with the shotgun from the front-seat rack held negligently in the crook of one arm, Jo with Pearley's pistol carelessly dangling from the trigger guard; both smiling sardonically at the camera in classic Bonnie and Clyde pose.

The camera set and buzzing, Harry ran toward them calling, "Ten seconds!" He dropped to a squat between the women, turning to grin at the camera. *Flash*—the car and their faces whitened, and Harry ran for the camera as Lew stood clicking Pearley's handcuffs through the two trigger guards and the ring of keys. The women already hurrying back along the roof, Harry trotted forward with his tripod, and Lew hung guns and keys from the base of the aerial, and the blue uniform cap from its top. Then they ran.

Four of them carrying the beams down the hill, stopping once for breath—listening, ready to drop them and run—they brought them back to the van: two minutes later they set them on the pile from which they had taken them.

Driving sedately home in the very first early widely scattered beginnings of what would swell to heavy commute traffic in the next hours, they twice watched police cars fly past at high speed, one in each direction, dome lights flashing; and they laughed softly and sleepily.

Five hours later at nine in the morning, Lew awakened, lying on Jo's chesterfield, closed his eyes again, then could not resist: he got up, turned on the portable television and, the volume low as he could tune it, he watched the news, including a black-and-white still photo apparently taken at first dawn showing the car and two uniformed men silhouetted on the Civic Center roof. It was a mystery, the announcer's almost inaudible voice murmured, the car first spotted at dawn from the freeway, and Lew smiled, turned it off, and returned to the chesterfield.

At noon they had lunch, watching the news, and saw a color film: the camera panning over a crowd down on the asphalt before the Civic Center, then up to others scattered over the hill beside the long beige building, finally lifting to the roof as a uniformed deputy sheriff, leaning out his open door, slowly backed the car along the blue road in the sky to the careful beckoning of a deputy behind him. The film continued till the car stopped at the back roof edge, then briefly returned to the faces of the watching crowd as it cheered mockingly. Latest word, said the announcer at his news desk, is that the car still stood at the roof edge awaiting a ramp workmen were preparing.

During the afternoon as the others desultorily played rummy, switching to casino later, Harry developed his films in the bathroom. Later, as he sat at the little white table mounting the pictures, the four of them watched the final descent of Pearley's car down an amply wide and well-braced ramp; this followed by a brief filmed interview with the Mill Valley police chief. With the good sense to know humor was his best refuge, he stood smiling on the walk before his police station, then responded affably to the interviewer's questions: Who put the car up there, and why? "That's easy," said the chief. "Officer Pearley was in hot pursuit. Of a stolen hang glider. Had him cornered up there on the roof. Unfortunately the thief managed to fly away in the darkness, and Officer Pearley didn't want to shoot for fear of hitting innocent planes. He has been commended, and will be transferred to our air force." The chief nodded pleasantly, and turned back toward the station, his smile fading quickly.

At three o'clock Jo walked to the camper, and brought it back to the building parking area. There she packed the VW and the Alfa, carefully cramming both trunks, filling the back seats and floors with their belongings, skis on the roof racks. She packed her own things into two suitcases.

At four-thirty, all dressed as they'd been the night before, the others stood waiting as Jo walked slowly through the apartment making sure it was empty of everything they were to take. For a moment or two then, she stood looking from Shirley to Harry, shaking her head. "I have the feeling that after tonight I'll never see you two again."

They protested. "We'll phone my folks the minute we find a place," Shirley said. "You phone them when you're settled, or we'll phone your folks—"

"Oh, sure, I know. And we will, of course. Then we'll all talk to each other. On the phone. And write. For a while. Send Christmas cards a while longer. But . . . you're going to Seattle. You think. And we're going to Santa Fe. Maybe." She shrugged, and no one replied.

Harry left first, not certain the camper could make it over Waldo Grade, and Shirley followed in the Alfa. As Jo checked the balcony doors, making sure they were locked before leaving, Lew said, "I'll miss those doors," and she smiled.

Down at the van Jo stood beside it looking up at the building. "Well, so long, 2E," she said. "And 2D. So long, rented dishes, white table, and Scotch-guarded furniture: will you remember us? When someone else is using you? Think of us now and then? Lew and Jo?" She shrugged. "No answer: let's go." She climbed up into the van.

In the slow lane, Lew hanging a few lengths behind in the VW, Jo's worn-out van slowly climbed Waldo. Watching its big wooden bumper projecting a good foot to the rear, Lew urged it on with a slight rocking motion, then reached out nervously to snap on his radio. Louis Armstrong faded in hoarsely with "Mack, the Knife," and as the van crept over the summit, and began picking up speed rolling down toward the tunnel, Lew burst into voice, singing along in fragmented snatches ("' . . . scarlet billows! . . . gleaming white! . . . '"). Coming out of the tunnel onto the long curving downgrade toward the bridge, he saw that Harry and Shirley were nowhere in sight, no sign of a stall up ahead on the bridge, and he grinned in relief. Behind his rolled-up windows he began to shout out the words he knew of the song.

Rolling across Golden Gate Bridge a car length behind Jo, Lew studied the traffic. The forty-year-old bridge was only six lanes wide, the lanes narrow for today's cars. Now, during the evening commute, they were separated into four northbound lanes toward Marin, nearly solid with cars; and two southbound lanes toward San Francisco, more lightly used. Separating these opposing traffic streams stood a row of yard-high sausagelike posts of spongy plastic dyed bright yellow and red.

Lew heard the rackety clatter of helicopter blades, and saw the tiny KGO traffic helicopter a hundred yards overhead curving toward the bridge from the Bay like an insect. From his radio came the brief identifying musical theme, then the familiar voice over the beat of the blades in the background. "Northbound traffic on Golden Gate Bridge is heavy, moving slowly but normally for five o'clock on a weekday; no stalls, no congestion. Up ahead toward the Waldo tunnel, it's moving freely."

To his right, in snatched glimpses through the bridge railings, Lew saw the enormous dull-orange disc of the sun edging into the horizon far out across the miniature whitecaps below. It was full daylight still but would begin fading within minutes, and at the thought of what was to be done when the sun had set, Lew felt the sweat pop at the roots of his hair. Traffic report finished, the little bug-shape hovering over the bridge suddenly curved gracefully away toward Oakland, beaters chopping the air. A commercial began, and in sudden anxious irritability Lew switched the radio off.

He followed the van through the toll booths, then both edged to the right, out of the traffic stream onto a curving descending road. This led down into a narrow tunnel passing under the bridge approach. Van and VW came out on the other side into a large parking area facing the Bay, a view place for tourists, crowded in the summer. But now in the dusk of a late fall day, only Harry's camper stood at one end, the Alfa a little distance away, two strange cars at the opposite end. Jo parked at the low stone wall facing the Bay, and Lew nearby.

They walked to the camper: the Levys sat in the front seat, Harry rolling down his window. "Made it," he said. "It didn't want to, but I cursed it over the Grade." The area they were in stood at the side of the bridge, well below the level of its roadway. From here they had a spectacular view of the bridge, a foreshortened profile of the entire arched span. They stared at it now. Before them, close and enormous, the south tower filled half the sky. From its top the long, beautiful curve of the twin cables swooped down to almost touch the road, it seemed. Then it rose again to dwindle to a thread where it finally reached the height of the distant north tower. "Can you believe it, Lew?" Harry said. "We walked up that son-of-a-bitch!"

"Fair makes me stomach churn."

"I almost *was* sick," Shirley murmured, looking out at them past

Harry, "when I saw those little *bumps* moving along the cable. Right, Jo?"

Jo nodded, then they all watched the sun visibly and rapidly sinking down into the water out beyond and under the bridge. First, half of it gone, then most of it, and finally the very edge of its upper rim flashed on the horizon line, and the great disc was gone. Its rays still filled the air, fanlike, at the horizon; and the daylight still seemed strong and clear, everything visible: the great rust-red bridge and its unending flow of cars high above them; the green-and-white Bay and its half dozen sails; the distant shorelines just beginning to speckle with light; the Bay islands.

Then suddenly, goldenly, the bridge lights came on all at once, and instantly the daylight diminished. The bridge's color vanished, and it stood stark and black against the luminous sky. Within seconds a few car lights flicked on, then very quickly all of them, the cars fading into darkness, and the commute traffic above became a stream of lights. "Jo, maybe you better start," Lew said, and she nodded. "You don't have to," he added quickly. "Really. Just say you've changed your mind, and we're all going to nod and agree, and feel damn relieved."

"That's right," said Harry.

"*You* say it," Jo answered. "Any of you. I've got the easiest job." She handed her keys to Lew, he gave her his, and she nodded at them all. "Well—good luck. See you." Abruptly she turned to walk swiftly to Lew's car, and he checked his watch.

The others watching, Jo drove up the narrow exit road to the bridge approach and stopped, the oncoming stream of traffic from the city flowing past her front bumper; it was nearly full dark now. At the first break, Jo wheeled swiftly into the lane, and they watched the VW's tail lights till they were lost in the Marin-bound traffic.

The two strange cars had left, and Lew walked to Jo's van, bringing out pliers, and removed her last license plate. Kneeling in the dark at the Alfa Romeo, he took off both its plates, and pushed them down into the Levys' heaped belongings on the rear floor.

Back at the camper he stood at Harry's door, and they waited: nervous now, wrapped in their thoughts, speaking very little. Harry sat frowning at the darkening Bay, his face set belligerently. Beside him, her face pale in the dark of the camper's cab, Shirley fidgeted: glancing out her window, at Harry's profile, and at Lew; yawning, checking her watch. Several times Lew turned away to pace slowly, returned, then walked away again. He looked up at the sky often, testing the quality of its deepening darkness.

Across the bridge on the Marin County side, Jo curved off into the view area there, which faced the similar area across the Gate in which the others waited. Only one other car stood parked here now, a man and a woman standing before it at the low guard rail, staring across the water at the lighted city. Getting out of the VW, Jo glanced at it, too, and stood for a moment, hand on the door. More lights appeared as she watched, the city taking on its shimmering night-time look, which always excited her. But she couldn't wait, slammed her door, and walked away toward the beginning of the sidewalk that led across the bridge.

Just short of the walk she turned onto a flight of concrete stairs, walked down its three shallow steps, and turned onto a narrow screened foot bridge which passed under the big bridge itself. She didn't like it here alone under the bridge, afraid of seeing someone turn onto it ahead and come walking toward her; and she hurried, half running. A few feet above her head the heavy bridge traffic rumbled steadily, and she didn't like this either.

No one else appeared, and Jo turned right on the other side to walk up a paved ramp to bridgeway level and turned right again onto the sidewalk leading across the ocean side of the bridge. Glancing brightly around, trying to appear as she imagined a tourist might look, she walked on, beside the double lane of traffic to the city. The sidewalk behind its low separating barrier stood several feet higher than the roadway beside it, and she could look over the roofs of passing cars. On the other side, the commute traffic toward Marin was a solid flow of headlights, the enameled bodies behind them winking yellowly under the bridge lights.

She reached the ocean-side leg of the south tower, and turned onto the little bay behind it where she had stood last night with Shirley. Hidden from the passing stream of cars on the other side of the enormous steel wall of the tower leg, she stood, hands on the railing, staring out at the night-time blackness of the ocean.

Across the bridge Lew looked at his watch. It had been fourteen minutes since Jo had left, time enough: she'd either be at her post or walking to it. But he waited the extra minute, then said, "Time."

"Okay"—Harry nodded from the open window of the camper. "What do you say, Lew?" he added quietly. "Still think this'll work?"

"Well, if somebody described it to me, I'd laugh. But it can work. Pretty easily. No reason it shouldn't, in fact. So logically, I say yeah, it'll work." He shrugged. "But emotionally, I won't even believe it when I see it."

"I wish we could stay and watch," Shirley said, climbing down to the pavement; she sounded eager, the waiting over. She walked to the Alfa, Lew walked to the van, and doors slammed. Lew started his engine, and

waited, watching Shirley back out, brake lights brightening the pavement
as she stopped to shift. Then, wheels turned hard, she drove forward,
and up the short narrow roadway Jo had taken. Lew turned to watch
Harry bring the camper up behind her, then he backed out the van, and
joined the waiting line.

Shirley waited, her front bumper at the edge of the traffic stream
moving sluggishly past it. Harry waited half a yard behind, Lew almost
as close behind Harry. A break appeared only two car-lengths long but
Shirley edged her bumper into it, the approaching car slowing to let her
in. She swung into the lane, Harry riding her bumper, Lew following
equally close, all crowding in together. Allowing no more than a few
feet of space between them, the three passed between the empty toll
booths, no toll being collected in this direction, and onto the bridge itself,
staying in the slow lane directly beside the walk.

Careful never to allow another car between him and Harry, Lew
watched the lane beside them in his outside rear-view. Here in the slow
lane they moved at under forty, often having to brake, the line beside
them moving a little faster.

He saw an empty space approaching in the rear-view, and flipped on
his turn signal. A brown Mustang moved past him, the empty space
behind it, and Lew slid smoothly over into it, his extended front bumper
passing only inches from the slanted rear end of the Mustang. He
touched his brakes, allowing the Mustang to move on, creating an empty
space before him, and Harry slid over into it.

In the curbside lane where she would remain, Shirley moved along
with the traffic. Harry, with Lew on his bumper, pulled abreast of Shirley,
then held even. Maintaining his close distance directly behind Harry,
Lew again began watching his rear-view, waiting now for an empty space
in the third lane. Seconds passed as they rolled on, moving under the
tower at the San Francisco end. Beside him, the slightly faster third-lane
traffic flowed past, but no empty space appeared. Lew felt his heartbeat
increase, and reminded himself that they had plenty of time, most of the
length of the bridge yet.

Seconds passed as they rolled on under the orange lights, the commute traffic at its peak now. Then Lew saw an empty space coming up
but before it reached him cars moved together, eliminating it, and again
he felt the sweat start at the roots of his hair. He was worried now, and
as they rolled on his eyes moved steadily between Harry's big wooden
bumper and the miniaturized string of cars moving toward him in the
rectangle of the van's mirror.

A break appeared in the mirrored lineup behind him, and Lew flipped on his turn signal. But as the empty space approached it began to contract. He could wait no longer, they were near the middle of the bridge, he had to move over *now*. Lew quickly rolled down his window, and shoved his arm straight out and pumping, pointing finger jabbing at the empty space as it came abreast. Now it was too short, obviously so, but Lew edged slowly toward it, his wheels crossing the lane-line, bumping along the warning nodules, the horn of the car behind blasting suddenly. Lew kept on, forcing, the rear of the van and the car's right front fender nearly touching; the man had to brake now or be hit. Lew pressed, edging fractionally closer, the horn stopped, the car slowing, and Lew slid into the line with no inch to spare. He waited for the renewed horn blast, but none came. A commuter, he thought, grinning, trained to resignation.

In the third lane now, Lew drew abreast with Harry and Shirley and they all held in a line. Then, passing the middle of the bridge where the cables dipped lowest, Harry began gradually slowing, dropping down through thirty-seven . . . thirty-four . . . thirty-two. Watching him intently, Shirley and Lew slowed with him, maintaining their lineup, and the cars in the three lanes ahead moved on, creating an empty space before them. The empty space grew to a car-length, then two, then three. At Lew's left the fourth lane moved steadily past him, drivers glancing curiously at the lineup of van, camper, and Alfa holding abreast and still slowing.

Again Lew watched his rear-view. Breaks in the fast fourth lane were more frequent, he saw one immediately, and as it came abreast he drifted left, wheels crossing the line, rumbling the markers. Simultaneously, Harry drifted over the line to edge into Lew's lane, and Shirley's left wheels slid over the line into Harry's. Each of them now straddling a lane-line, the three cars moving abreast blocked all four lanes behind them.

For eight or ten seconds no one protested: the bridge lanes were narrow, and cars did sometimes stray over the line. Then a horn tapped. Behind the three windshields, Lew smiled tensely; Harry grinned; Shirley frowned, glancing anxiously into her mirror. A long moment, then again a horn sounded, blasting this time, and immediately several more. An instant of silence again, as they rolled on down the orange-lighted roadway exactly abreast, straddling the lines, blocking all traffic behind them. Then almost simultaneously dozens of horns blared and continued, some held down steadily, others honk-honking. It sounded almost festive; Lew thought of a wedding party.

Again he and Shirley watched Harry. Leaning forward, Harry stared up at the north tower, rapidly growing in his windshield. Harry lifted a hand, brought it slowly down in signal, and they carefully slowed together: to thirty . . . twenty-five . . . twenty . . . and on down to seven or eight miles an hour, speedometers now wobbling erratically.

Behind them horns raged. Far ahead, tail lights shrank in the distance, the strange emptiness before them lengthening. Across the road in the San Francisco-bound lanes, drivers slowed, rapidly cranking down windows, to stare over in wonder. Up ahead, her eyes wide, Jo stood at her post beside the north tower watching them approach.

Staring up at the north tower, Harry again raised a hand, waiting until they were approximately a hundred yards from it, the length of a football field. Then, in signal, his hand flashed down like an ax.

Instantly Shirley slammed the shift lever forward, flooring the gas pedal, and the Alfa shot ahead, burning rubber. In the same instant Harry swung his wheel to nose into the space she had just vacated, nearly brushing her rear bumper. And in the moment Harry moved so did Lew, yanking his wheel in a sudden right turn, his big wooden front bumper swinging in an arc toward Harry's rear one. Then they hit their brakes, and stood motionless, almost sideways on the roadway, across all lane markers, blocking all four lanes.

Brakes squealing behind them, the nearly solid four-lane commute mass came to a halt: from far behind as the stop moved peristaltically back toward the toll booths, they heard a bumper crash, then another. Ahead and still accelerating, the Alfa flashed along the empty roadway, body winking under the overhead lights. Behind van and camper slewed sideways on the road, the horns had gone momentarily silent in astonishment.

Lew set his parking brake, turned off the engine, and flung open his door. He jumped to the road, slamming his door, yanked at the handle to be sure it had locked. Then, grinning, he drew his arm far back, and exuberantly threw the ignition keys curving over the bridge rail to the water below.

Inside the camper, kneeling on the front seat to face the rear, Harry reached to the squat metal box bolted to the wooden framework there; the box stood directly beside the camper's side window facing north toward Marin. From it, heavy insulated black wire led to the transformer and batteries on the floor. Harry's hand smacked down on a toggle switch, and a brilliant, hard-edged beam of blue-white light shot from the lens of the squat metal box and through the camper window, whitening the air far ahead.

Like a searchlight, this beam touched the curving green trunk of the speeding Alfa a hundred yards ahead in just the moment that Shirley pressed the brake pedal hard. In the white light, black smoke sprayed from the rear wheels, and the Alfa slid to a stop directly beside the great north tower of the bridge. Its door flew open, and Shirley sprang out to race for the sidewalk beside the car—across the roadway at the other tower leg Jo stood watching her.

Waiting for Harry to jump down out of the camper, Lew simply stood beside the van; grinning and facing the massed headlights filling the four lanes for a mile behind them. Elation flowed wild in him. A driver in the front line of stopped cars sat watching him, and when Lew's eyes met his, Lew winked at the man. From the camper window, Harry's beam of light began to rise up through the night like a probing finger, reaching for something high above.

Up ahead, Jo and Shirley now stood with their backs to this rising searching light, one on each side of the roadway and facing the north bridge tower. Their hands rose high, reaching, then each found the patch of orange tape she had smoothed onto the steel side of the tower last night. Each peeled loose her tape, and then in unison both women yanked hard on the two long lengths of orange fishline stretching invisibly up into the night—and the weighted plastic pole the men had left high on the bridge transverse over the roadway, dropped over the edge.

It fell fast, the accordion folds of white sailcloth popping open, and now there in the darkness high above the orange lights of the bridge, a great white square of cloth hung swaying over the roadway, suspended between the enormous tower legs.

In the camper swiveling the metal box, Harry moved the long finger of light, found the swaying square of sailcloth, and centered the beam upon it. Then his fingers twisted the stubby lens, and the intense blue-white beam illuminating the great cloth sheet changed from fuzzy indefinition to a gigantic hard-edged square of light. Far below in one of the stopped cars facing the great illuminated sheet, a woman in the front seat leaned intently toward the windshield, murmuring, "My God, it's a screen." Suddenly delighted, she swung around to the other carpool members—"We're going to have a *show!*"

Harry's palm smacked down on a push switch. A black drum on top of the powerful outdoor-theater projector revolved fractionally, and onto the giant screen hanging over Golden Gate Bridge flashed half a dozen carefully lettered words, enormously enlarged. In Harry's green, blue and red felt-pen lettering, they said, *Settle back, folks.* THIS . . . IS OUR LIFE! Harry jumped to the concrete, slamming and locking his door, and he and Lew began to run up the empty roadway toward the Alfa. Ahead and high above them, the huge screen went momentarily black, then lightened again, and Lew, running hard, began to laugh. A huge photograph now filled the screen—a face. Above it Harry's hand-lettered caption read, LEWIS O. JOLIFFE, PROMINENT S.F. ATTORNEY. Under the photo, in the careful, long ago white-ink script of Lew's mother: *Aged 3 months.* The photo itself, a sepia print, was a bonneted baby, the infant Lew Joliffe staring out as though astonished at the mile-long captive audience below—which stared back in equal astonishment at the huge round-eyed face in the night-time sky.

The Alfa was backing toward the two running men now, fast and erratically. Then it stopped, black-streaking the pavement, and Shirley flung open her door, then slid to the right. Lew piled in, squeezing into the back to sprawl across the piled-up belongings there; and Harry slid under the wheel. In the darkness off to the right of the bridge they heard the rackety clatter of a helicopter, and saw its running lights and dim dark bulk swinging down toward the bridge. Harry released the hand brake, slamming his door, and the screen high above them brightened once more.

They all leaned forward, staring up; an enormous black-and-white photograph filled the fifty-foot screen, a diapered baby on a lawn, an out-of-focus front porch in the background. JOSEPHINE DUNNE, said Harry's yard-high felt-tip lettering, WELL-KNOWN S.F. BEAUTY! Far behind the screen, down on the oceanside walkway, the real Jo Dunne hurried toward the end of the bridge.

Blades clacking the air, the helicopter swung low over the car roof, and Shirley cried, "Harry, *move, move!* Let's *go!*"

"Wait! I *gotta* see this next one!" Again the screen darkened, the helicopter hanging directly over the bridge now, slowly lowering to hang over the car-jammed roadway. Under the clattering blades its insect body turned to face north as another giant photo filled the opening between the great legs of the north tower. A naked infant lay on his stomach on a wide white towel staring with interest at the tiny helicopter before it. Across the picture's top, hugely: HARRY D. LEVY. Underneath it: FAMOUS SAN FRANCISCO BAREASSTER. Harry yelled with laughter, shot the car forward, and punched a dashboard button.

From the car radio as they raced toward the bridge end, a man's voice over the running-water sound of his copter motor said, "—king all lanes is *not* a jackknifed truck as we thought at first sight. It looks like— whoops, *here's another!* Another child, this one in color! A girl of about two, looks like, leaning over the handlebars of her tricycle and smiling right at me. Written above it is, 'Shirley Rosen,' and underneath, 'Harry's bride-to-be.' Folks, in fourteen years of commute-traffic broadcasting, I've never seen anything like this! We're heading for the toll plaza now to see what's happening back there." Harry slowed, then swung off the freeway into the view parking lot. Almost directly below his wheels Jo raced along the dark length of the footbridge.

"Here's another!" said the voice from the Alfa's radio. "A boy of about twelve. On the front porch of a house. Holding a diploma. Underneath in a woman's handwriting it says, 'He made it! Lew's graduation, Proviso High School, 1958.' I can't *believe* it!"—the radio voice broke into astounded laughter. Harry pulled in beside Lew's VW, turned off lights and engine, and they sat staring back at the foreshortened length of the bridge, its distant half brilliant with motionless headlights, the back of the huge white screen in the north tower going dark. "I've reported accidents, breakdowns, tieups of every kind," the radio voice shouted delightedly, "but never anything like this! Down on the bridge below me people are standing between their cars, they're up on both walks, they're sitting on car hoods. A group of young people are sitting cross-legged on the roof of their van, and they're *applauding*! There's a highway patrol car down there, its dome light revolving, but it can't move, it's locked in, can't move! Here at the toll plaza and beyond everything is bl—. There's a *report card* up on the screen! I mean it! A tremendous yellow report card forty feet high!"

Jo appeared beside the Alfa. "Did it work, did it work!?"

"Take a look." Pointing, Lew got out, sliding past Harry, and Jo turned to stare back at the bridge. The rear of the great screen hung in the black sky, yellowly tinted, and Lew said, "That's your report card, and now the whole world knows: C in arithmetic."

"But A-plus in art." The back of the screen went dim, and Jo said, "Listen . . . " Motionless, heads cocked, the four of them waited, hearing nothing, and Jo said, "The horns have stopped."

"Yeah!" Lew grabbed her, grinning. "They love it!"

"They'll want it every night now," Shirley cried. From the north, very faintly, a siren sounded, and the radio voice said, "It's a dog! A black-and-white mongrel with his head cocked looking out at us! Says, 'Lew's old dog, Jake: he could sit up, roll over, and play dead.' Oh, my god!"

Lew bent forward to lean in at Harry's window. "Well, kids. We all better take off. We'll be in touch."

"Right." Harry put out his hand, they shook. "Good show," he said quietly, smiling fondly at Lew, "in more ways than one."

Leaning across Harry, Shirley cried out, "You've got my folks' phone number, Jo, and I've got your dad's. You phone now! You hear?"

"I will, I will!"

Lew said, "So long, Shirl. Remember me whenever you lie down on the freeway," and she nodded, blinking rapidly, unable to reply. The siren sounded, closer now, and Harry said good-by to Jo, kissed his fingers at her, then the Alfa's lights came on, and he backed out.

Behind the Alfa, letting the distance between them grow, Lew drove north on 101, beginning the Waldo Grade climb. A highway patrol car, dome light flashing, siren growling, flashed by on the other side toward the bridge, and Lew leaned forward to turn on his radio, punching the button for KGO. "—monitoring our radio," said the helicopter-voice over the watery sound of its motor, "and the truck at this end can't get through. But the truck that parks up at the tunnel during commute time is on its way down, and will be—here's another: a color photo of a boy in scout uniform, a yarmulke, and the beginnings of a mustache—it's our old buddy, Harry Levy, again! Written underneath—it *must* have been his mother—is: 'Harry's bar mitzvah. Life Scout the same day!' Screen's black now . . . I *wish* I had a TV camera to *show* you these things! Here's another color photo: bald, middle-aged man in suntans, woman in a dress, girl in shorts. The caption—oh boy—the caption says, 'Our summer in Yellowstone. Dad, Mom and Shirley.' Oh, I tell you, there'll be a lot of late suppers tonight, but what an excuse!"

Driving through the night, the freeway strangely empty, Lew and Jo listened as the jubilant voice from the traffic helicopter described the scene on the bridge for late listeners, "There are a dozen or so men around the camper with the projector, but no one seems to be making any effort to break into it. They're just standing there, leaning against it, arms folded, enjoying the show. And so am I, so am I—forget traffic conditions on the Nimitz Freeway tonight! There's an enormous birthday cake filling the screen now high above San Francisco Bay: a woman's hands tilting the cake toward the camera. It has eleven lighted candles, and says, 'Happy Birthday, Jo!' "

They listened as the voice described Lew in Little League uniform . . . Harry's and Lew's law-school diplomas . . . Shirley in white uniform . . . Jo working on her Town . . . "And here's a great one—oh, this is great! Says, 'Harry and Shirley meet Lew and Jo.' A painted canvas; says 'Disneyland' in one corner. Shows four aerialists in costume: two men hanging from trapezes, arms out; one woman has just been caught by the wrists, the other is still flying through the air. And smiling out at us through cutout holes over the bodies are the four faces we've grown to

know and love tonight! Oh man, I tell you! Screen's going black again
. . ."

A huge tow truck, a Christmas tree of yellow, red, and white lights
raced by across the freeway, and Lew glanced at Jo to smile. The radio
voice described views of Lew, Jo, and the Levys skiing . . . playing tennis
. . . lying by the apartment pool. "Here's the tow truck," the voice cried
then, "racing along the bridge toward us! Up on the screen now there's
a car. Looks like it's up on a—*it's the car on the roof of the Civic Center
last night!* It is! The *police* car! Up on the *roof!* And Harry and Shirley,
Lew and Jo, are all over the car! With *guns!* The *cop's* guns! Oh, my
god, *they did it!* They put the cop's car up on the *roof!* Oh, *bless* you,
Harry and Shirley, Lew and Jo! . . . The tow truck is slowing . . .
stopping. Now it's swinging around on the bridge, getting into position
to back up to the camper. The screen goes dark, and . . . *oh, Jesus.*" The
voice suddenly choked. "Ladies and gentlemen, all I can do is report
the facts. And the fact is that up there on the screen is good old Harry,
Lew, Shirley and Jo . . . stark naked. They're standing before a fireplace,
looks like—*dancing.* Harry, modest Harry, is wearing a baseball cap and
cigar. But Lew and the girls—bless you, girls, bless you!—are wearing
only big wide smiles. Their thumbs are at their noses, all four of them,
fingers spread, and the caption across the top says, 'So long, Short Pants,'
and across the bottom, 'And so long, California.' One of the men from
the truck is down on the pavement now signaling the driver . . . truck's
backing toward the camper . . . up on the screen the slide is still there
. . . it doesn't go off. The truck's lowering its sling . . . slide is still there,
our four naked friends thumbing their noses down at the whole length
of Golden Gate Bridge at all of us . . . The front of the camper is lifting
now, and Lew and Jo, Harry and Shirley are slowly sliding off the
screen—and *listen* to those horns blast! *Pro*testing, I do believe! . . .
Screen's dark, the beam of the projector shining off toward the ocean—
and the show is over. Well, farewell to you, too, Lew and Jo, Harry and
Shirley. Never knew you, but we're gonna miss you now, believe me! I
know I will! The first of the stalled cars is edging around the camper . . .
Now here come the others, the tow truck leaving, the beam still shining
out the camper window. Traffic flow resuming on the Golden Gate
Bridge. Guess I better go report on the Nimitz now, but, oh man, it's
gonna be a letdown."

Lew reached out, turned off the radio, and they were silent for some
seconds. Off to the right and below, Strawberry Point appeared, and their
heads turned for a farewell look. They faced front, Jo sighing slightly,
and she said, "Well. That's that. Now on to Santa Fe, is that the idea?"

"Right." Lew nodded, then glanced at her. "But you almost didn't come this time."

"You knew that, did you?"

"Well, it occurred to me."

"Well, you were right. I was going to help through tonight: leave a note in the VW for you when I parked it, go help drag the screen down, then just walk on across the bridge to the city and a motel. I very nearly didn't come along when we moved from San Francisco."

"I know."

"You know a lot, don't you."

"Not too much."

"Well, I still might not! I might just get out at the next bus stop and go back to the city."

"Right. But you might not, too."

"Maybe."

"Jo, how come? How come you stick around? I want you to, but— why do you?"

After a moment she shrugged slightly. "Same old reason, I suppose; the reason I came with you in the first place."

"And what's that?"

"Who knows!" she said as though about to be angry. But then she looked at him, and smiled. "Maybe just to see what happens next."